THE ULTRAMARINES OMNIBUS

NIGHTBRINGER • WARRIORS OF ULTRAMAR
DEAD SKY, BLACK SUN

GRAHAM MCNEILL'S EPIC trilogy of Ultramarines novels is now collected together into a single, great-value omnibus edition. Containing the novels *Nightbringer*, *Warriors of Ultramar* and *Dead Sky, Black Sun*, plus the introductory short story *Chains of Command*, the series follows the adventures of Space Marine Captain Uriel Ventris and the Ultramarines as they battle to destroy the enemies of mankind. From their home world of Ultramar, into the dreaded Eye of Terror and beyond, Graham McNeill's prose rattles like gunfire and brings the Space Marines to life like never before.

A WARHAMMER 40,000 OMNIBUS

THE ULTRAMARINES OMNIBUS

Graham McNeill

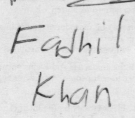

A Black Library Publication

Nightbringer copyright © 2002, Games Workshop Ltd.
Warriors of Ultramar copyright © 2003, Games Workshop Ltd.
Dead Sky, Black Sun copyright © 2004, Games Workshop Ltd.
Chains of Command first published in *Inferno!* magazine,
copyright © 2001, Games Workshop Ltd.

This omnibus edition published in Great Britain in 2006 by
BL Publishing,
Games Workshop Ltd.,
Willow Road, Nottingham,
NG7 2WS, UK.

10 9 8 7 6 5 4 3 2 1

Cover illustration by Karl Kopinski.

A CIP record for this book is available from the British Library.

ISBN13: 978 1 84416 403 5
ISBN10: 1 84416 403 9

Distributed in the US by Simon & Schuster
1230 Avenue of the Americas, New York, NY 10020, US.

Printed and bound in Great Britain by
Bookmarque, Surrey, UK.

See the Black Library on the Internet at
www.blacklibrary.com

Find out more about Games Workshop
and the world of Warhammer 40,000 at
www.games-workshop.com

IT IS THE 41st millennium. For more than a hundred centuries the Emperor has sat immobile on the Golden Throne of Earth. He is the master of mankind by the will of the gods, and master of a million worlds by the might of his inexhaustible armies. He is a rotting carcass writhing invisibly with power from the Dark Age of Technology. He is the Carrion Lord of the Imperium for whom a thousand souls are sacrificed every day, so that he may never truly die.

YET EVEN IN his deathless state, the Emperor continues his eternal vigilance. Mighty battlefleets cross the daemon-infested miasma of the warp, the only route between distant stars, their way lit by the Astronomican, the psychic manifestation of the Emperor's will. Vast armies give battle in his name on uncounted worlds. Greatest amongst His soldiers are the Adeptus Astartes, the Space Marines, bio-engineered super-warriors. Their comrades in arms are legion: the Imperial Guard and countless planetary defence forces, the ever-vigilant Inquisition and the tech-priests of the Adeptus Mechanicus to name only a few. But for all their multitudes, they are barely enough to hold off the ever-present threat from aliens, heretics, mutants – and worse.

TO BE A man in such times is to be one amongst untold billions. It is to live in the cruellest and most bloody regime imaginable. These are the tales of those times. Forget the power of technology and science, for so much has been forgotten, never to be re-learned. Forget the promise of progress and understanding, for in the grim dark future there is only war. There is no peace amongst the stars, only an eternity of carnage and slaughter, and the laughter of thirsting gods.

CONTENTS

INTRODUCTION

SPACE MARINES... IS there anything cooler in the Warhammer 40,000 universe? Sure, eldar are all kinds of debonair cool, the tyranids have their gribblyness and the Imperial Guard have got their hammer of the Emperor thang going on, but none of them hold a candle to Space Marines in my book. After all, what's not to like about a two-metre tall, genetically engineered killing machine? From the moment I read about the Legiones Astartes in *Rogue Trader*, I was hooked, their nobility coupled with their utter lethality struck a chord in me that's resonating to this day. So, of course, they were the first army I collected – though, confusingly, my Dark Angels were painted orange for reasons that escape me now – and Space Marines are the army I'm currently using in the Return to Vogen campaign we're playing in the Design Studio right now (4th Company Ultramarines, obviously...).

So what is it that makes Space Marines so popular? Is it their models, their art, their rules, their background? Actually, it's all of the above, but for me it was the background of these heroic warrior knights that hooked me in first. The fact that, unlike the faceless soldiers of the Imperial Guard (pre Dan Abnett's Gaunt's Ghosts), each individual warrior was a hero, with his own tale of valour and his own legends was just the coolest thing ever. The fact that such warrior brotherhoods willingly gave up any chance of a 'normal' life and dedicated the rest of their existence to the service of the Emperor and Mankind really ennobled them and made their sacrifices so much more heroic.

Working for Games Workshop allows me to write about Space Marines pretty regularly, which is nice, but my *real* chance to have fun with them came when I wrote a short story called 'Chains of Command', introducing a veteran sergeant by the name of Uriel Ventris. When I wrote that story, way back in the dim and distant time of February 2001, I had no real plan to take the story or character further, except maybe another short story if the Black Library liked it. So when I met the BL's Christian Dunn in Bugman's for a coffee one afternoon and he asked me whether I'd like to write a Space Marine novel, it took less than a nano-second for me to say yes. The one proviso was that it be a Codex Chapter, since Bill King's Space Wolf novels were already in print and very popular. Again, it was a matter of seconds before I said that it would be the Ultramarines. I decided I wanted to write about the XIII Legion because I think, at the time, they had a bit of a bad press about being boring simply because they didn't have uber-killy rules and weren't vampires or barbarians in space. I knew differently, and set about changing this deeply flawed perception.

Anyone that's read the background of the Ultramarines in 2nd edition Codex and the splendidly written Index Astartes article in White Dwarf should know that the Ultramarines have it all – a murdered father, civil war and a son's revenge. If that ain't classic then I don't know what is. So when I began to write about the Ultramarines in my first novel, *Nightbringer*, it was with this epic sweep of history behind them, which informed as much of the story as anything I came up with. As a first book, I wanted Uriel's journey to follow the same voyage of discovery I was on. He was learning to assume command of a Space Marine company and I was learning how to write a novel… neither of which is an easy task, I can tell you (though I've never tried leading a Space Marine company!). Originally, I only envisaged one main character, but once I saw the cover of *Nightbringer*, and the flamer-toting Space Marine, I knew he just had to be a character. Thus was born Veteran Sergeant Pasanius, who's rapidly becoming one of my favourite characters to write.

It's been said that you can't write for Space Marines, because they're not human and are faceless warrior automatons, but that's just not true. Yes, they have been psychologically modified, but this just makes it more of a challenge to do well, and what you need to remember is that the Space Marines are willing participants in all this. They are not being indoctrinated as this implies a surrendering of responsibility and I think it's much more heroic and interesting to portray the Astartes making deliberate, daily decisions to choose to undergo the rigours of being a Space Marine. This is an aspect of Space Marines I wanted to investigate in *Warriors of Ultramar*, where Uriel was placed side by side with soldiers that, had he not become an Ultramarine, he could have been just like. Shown the life he could have had, would Uriel regret the decision he made to become one of the Emperor's finest?

Some people then argue that it's hard to write Space Marines because they think that they don't experience the full gamut of human emotions. I disagree, and in *Dead Sky, Black Sun*, I explored this facet of Space Marines and threw Uriel and Pasanius into situations and meetings with other characters where it would be impossible for them not to have some emotional reaction. At the end of the day, Space Marines are human, albeit horrifically altered, and they can experience all normal human emotions including pride, anger, jealousy, desire, joy, hatred, affection and so on. They are however able to suppress their emotions using the conditioning and training they have received, but that doesn't mean they don't feel them.

So there you have it, a (slightly) rambling jaunt through Space Marines and why they're so damn cool! This volume contains the first three Ultramarines novels, but Uriel and Pasanius's story doesn't end with *Dead Sky, Black Sun*; I've still got more in store for them. Will it be fun and exciting? I hope so. Will it be darkly grim and packed with bullets and blood? You better believe it! I enjoy writing for villains (supposedly they have more fun) but you just can't beat writing for the noble defenders of humanity, and after all, everyone loves a hero.

See you in the 41st Millennium and enjoy the ride...

– Graham McNeill
January 2006

℧
CHAINS OF COMMAND

CONCEALED AT THE edge of the jungle, Veteran Sergeant Uriel Ventris stared through the pouring rain at the grey, rockcrete bunker at the end of the bridge and tallied off the number of sentries he could see. There were four rebel troopers in the open, but they were sloppy, unconcerned, and that was going to kill them. They sheltered in the lee of the bunker's armoured door, smoking and talking. It was unforgivable stupidity, but Uriel always gave thanks whenever his enemies displayed such foolishness. The hissing of the warm rain falling through the canopy of thick, drooping fronds and bouncing from the rocks muffled all sounds. The roaring of the mighty river in the gorge below only added to the noise.

Moisture glistened on his blue shoulder guards, dripping from the inlaid chapter insignia of the Ultramarines. He slipped from his hidden position and ghosted through the drizzle, the actuators in his powered armour hissing as the fibre-bundle muscles enhanced his every movement. Uriel slid clear his combat knife and tested its edge, even though he knew it was unnecessary. The gesture was force of habit, learned at the earliest age by the people of Calth. The long blade was triangular in section, its edges lethally sharp and designed to slip easily between a victim's ribs, breaking them as it penetrated.

It was a tool for killing, nothing more.

Thanks to the heavy rain, the visibility of the guards was cut to less than thirty metres. Uriel's eyesight was far superior to a normal human's, he could clearly see the outline of the men he was about to kill.

He felt no remorse at the thought. The enemies of the Emperor deserved no mercy. These men had made their choice and would now pay the price

11

for making the wrong one. Uriel slipped behind one of the bridge's adamantium stanchions, moving incredibly quietly for such a bulky figure. He was close enough to his victims for his enhanced hearing to pick out the individual sounds of their voices.

As was typical with soldiers, they were bemoaning their current assignment and superior officers. Uriel knew they would not complain for much longer. He was close enough for his superior senses to pick out the smell of their unwashed bodies and the foetid dampness of stale sweat ingrained into their flesh after weeks of fighting. His muscles tensed and relaxed, preparing for action. The rune on his visor display that represented Captain Idaeus flashed twice and with a whispered acknowledgement Uriel confirmed his readiness to strike. He waited until he heard the scraping footfall of his first target turning away and twisted around the stanchion, sprinting for the bunker.

The first guard died without a sound, Uriel's knife hammering through the base of his skull. He dropped and Uriel wrenched the blade clear, spinning low and driving it into the second guard's groin. Blood sprayed and the man shrieked in horrified agony. A lasgun was raised and Uriel lunged forwards, smashing his fist into his foe's face, the augmented muscles of his power armour smashing the man's head to shards. Uriel spun on his heel, dodging a thrusting bayonet, and thundered his elbow into the last guard's chin, taking the base of his skull off. Teeth and blood splattered the bunker door.

He dropped into a defensive crouch, dragging his knife clear of the corpse beside him and cleaning the blade on its overalls. The killing of the guards had taken less than three seconds. He glanced quickly around the corner of the bunker to the sandbagged gun positions further down the bridge. There were two, set in a staggered pattern to provide overlapping fields of fire. The dull glint of metal protruded from the glistening, tarpaulin covered positions and Uriel counted three heavy bolters in each emplacement. The rain and thundering river noise had covered his stealthy approach to the bunker, but there was nothing but open ground before the gun nests.

'Position secure,' he whispered into the vox-com, removing shaped, breaching charges from his grenade dispenser. He worked quickly and purposefully, fastening the explosive around the locking mechanism of the bunker's armoured door.

'Confirmed,' acknowledged Captain Idaeus. 'Good work, Uriel. Squads Lucius and Daedalus are in position. We go on your signal.'

Uriel grinned and crawled around to the front of the bunker, making sure to keep out of sight below the firing slit. He drew his bolt pistol and spun his knife, holding it in a reverse grip. He took a deep breath, readying himself for action, and detonated the charges on the door.

The bunker's door blasted inwards, ripped from the frame by the powerful explosion. Choking smoke billowed outwards and Uriel was in

motion even before the concussion of the detonation had faded. He heard
the crack of bolter fire from the jungle and knew that the remainder of the
Ultramarines detachment was attacking. By now the enemies of the
Emperor would be dying.

Uriel dived through the blackened doorway, rolling to a firing
crouch, his pistol sweeping left and right. He saw two heads silhouetted by the light at the firing slit and squeezed the trigger twice. Both
men jerked backwards, their heads exploding. Another soldier was
screaming on his knees, blood flooding from his ruined body. His
torso was almost severed at the waist, razor-edged metal from the
door's explosion protruding from his body. A las-blast impacted on
Uriel's armour, and he twisted, kicking backwards in the direction the
shot had come from. His booted foot hammered into a rebel guardsman's knee, the joint shattering. The man shrieked and fell, losing his
grip on his weapon and clutching his ruined knee. The remainder of
the bunker's complement crowded around Uriel, screaming and stabbing with bayonets.

Uriel spun and twisted, punching and kicking with lethal ferocity. Wherever he struck, bones crunched and men died. The stink of blood and
voided bowels filled his senses as the last soldier fell. Blood streaked his
shoulders and breastplate. His eyes scanned the dimness of the bunker,
but all was silent. Everyone was dead.

He heard sounds of fighting and gunfire from outside and moved to the
door, ducking back as heavy bolter shells raked the inside face of the doorway. He glanced round the edge of the bullet-pocked wall, watching with
pride as the Ultramarines assault squad now joined the fray, their jump
packs carrying them high over the bunker.

They dropped from above, like flaming angels of death, their
chainswords chopping heads and limbs from bodies with shimmering,
steel slashes. The first gun emplacement was in tatters, sandbags ripped
apart by bolter fire and tossed aside by the attacking Space Marines. The
poorly trained defence troopers broke in the face of such savagery, but the
Ultramarines were in amongst them and there was no escape. The assault
troopers hacked them down with giant, disembowelling strokes of their
swords. The battle became a slaughter.

The staccato chatter of massed bolter fire echoed from the sides of the
gorge, explosions of dirt rippling from the bullet-ridden sandbags of the
second gun emplacement. But even under the constant volley, Uriel could
see the gunners within were realigning their heavy bolters. Hurriedly, he
voxed a warning.

'Ventris to Idaeus. The second gun position has re-sited its weapons. You
will be under fire in a matter of moments!'

Idaeus's rune on Uriel's visor blinked twice as the captain acknowledged
the warning.

Uriel watched as the captain of Fourth Company barked a command and began sprinting towards the second gun position. Idaeus charged at the head of five blue-armoured warriors, and Uriel swore, leaping forwards himself. Without support, the assault troops would be prime targets! Tongues of fire blasted from the heavy bolters, reaching out towards the charging Ultramarines. Uriel saw the shells impact, bursting amongst the charging Space Marines, but not a single man fell, the blessed suits of powered armour withstanding the traitors' fire. Idaeus triggered his jump pack and the rest of his squad followed suit, streaking forward with giant powered leaps.

Las-blasts filled the air, but the Ultramarines were too quick. Idaeus smashed down through the timber roof of the gun nest, a fearsome war cry bursting from his lips. He swung his power sword, decapitating a rebel trooper, and backhanded his pistol into another's chest, smashing his ribcage to splinters. Uriel's long strides had carried him to the edge of the gun nest and he leapt, feet first, into the sandbagged position. He felt bone shatter under the impact and rolled to his feet, lashing out with his armoured gauntlet. Another rebel died screaming. The sound of gunshots was deafening. Uriel felt a shot impact on his shoulder, the bullet ricocheting skywards. He turned and fired a bolt into his attacker's face, destroying the man's head. He sensed movement and spun, pistol raised. Captain Idaeus stood before him, hands in the air and a broad grin on his face. Uriel exhaled slowly and lowered his weapon. Idaeus slapped his hands on Uriel's shoulder plates.

'Battle's over, sergeant,' he laughed.

Idaeus's grizzled face was lined with experience and his shaven skull ran with moisture and blood. Four gold studs glittered on his forehead, each one representing a half-century of service, but his piercing grey eyes had lost none of the sparkle of youth. Uriel nodded, scowling.

'It is, yes, but the Codex Astartes tells us you should have waited for support before charging that gun nest, captain,' he said.

'Perhaps,' agreed Idaeus, 'but I wanted this done quickly, before any of them could vox a warning.'

'We have heavy weapons with us, captain. We could have jammed their vox units and blasted them apart from the cover of the bunker. They sited these gun positions poorly and would not have been able to target us. The Codex Astartes says–'

'Uriel,' interrupted Idaeus, leading him from the charnel house of the gun nest. 'You know I respect you, and, despite what others say, I believe you will soon command your own company. But you must accept that sometimes it is necessary for us to do things a little differently. Yes, the Codex Astartes teaches us the way of war, but it does not teach the hearts of men. Look around you. See the faces of our warriors. Their blood sings with righteousness and their faith is strong because they have seen me walk through the fire with them, leading them in glorious battle. Is not a little risk to me worth such reward?'

'I think I would call charging through the fire of three heavy bolters more than a "little risk" though,' pointed out Uriel.

'Had you been where I was, would you have done it differently?' asked Idaeus.

'No,' admitted Uriel with a smile, 'but then I am a sergeant, it's my lot in life to get all the dirty jobs.'

Idaeus laughed. 'I'll make a captain out of you yet, Uriel. Come, we have work to do. This bridge is not going to blow up on its own.'

As the assault troopers secured the bridge, the remainder of Captain Idaeus's detachment advanced from the jungle to reinforce them. Two tactical squads occupied the bunkers at either end of the bridge while Uriel organised the third repairing the sandbagged gun nests. In accordance with the Codex Astartes, he ordered them re-sited in order to cover every approach to the crossing, rebuilding and strengthening their defences.

Uriel watched as Idaeus deployed their scouts into the hills on the far side of the ridge above the gorge. They wouldn't make the same mistake the rebels had made. If the traitors launched a counter-attack, the Ultramarines would know of it. He stepped over a dead guardsman, noting with professional pride the bullet hole in the centre of his forehead. Such was the price of defeat. The Ultramarines' victory here had been absurdly easy, barely even qualifying as a battle, and Uriel felt curiously little pleasure at their success.

Since the age of six, he had been trained to bring death to the Emperor's enemies and normally felt a surge of justifiable pride in his lethal skills. But against such poorly trained opposition, there was no satisfaction to be gained. These soldiers were not worthy of the name and would not have survived a single month in the Agiselus Barracks on Macragge where Uriel had trained so many years ago. He pushed aside such gloomy thoughts and reached up to remove his helmet, setting it on the wide parapet of the bridge. Thousands of metres below, a wide river thundered through the gorge, the dark water foaming white over the rocks. Uriel ran a hand over his skull, the hair close cropped and jet black. His eyes were the colour of storm clouds, dark and threatening, his face serious. Two gold studs were set into his brow above his left eye.

The bridges were the key to the whole campaign. The Emperor's warriors had driven the poorly armed and trained planetary defence troopers of Thracia back at every turn and now the rebel-held capital, Mercia, was within their grasp. Despite horrendous losses, they still had the advantage of numbers and, given time, they could pose a serious threat to the crusade. The right flank of the Imperial Guard's push towards Mercia was exposed to attack across a series of bridges, one of which Uriel now stood upon. It was imperative the bridges were destroyed, but the Imperial Navy had demanded days of planning for the missions to destroy the bridges, days the crusade could ill afford to waste. Therefore the task of destroying the bridges had fallen to the Ultramarines. Thunderhawk gunships had inserted the assault teams under cover of darkness, half a day's march from the bridges, and now awaited their signal to extract them after the crossings had been destroyed.

The rebellion on Thracia was insignificant but for one thing: reports had filtered back to the crusade's High Command that Traitor Space Marines of the Night Lords legion were present. So far, Uriel had seen nothing of these heretics and, privately, believed that they were phantoms conjured by the over-active imagination of guardsmen. Still, it never paid to be complacent and Uriel fervently hoped the reports would prove to be true. The chance to bring the wrath of the Emperor down on such abominable foes could not be passed up.

He watched a Techmarine wiring the bridge supports for destruction. Melta charges would blast the bridge to pieces, denying the traitors any way of moving their armoured units across the river and flanking the Imperial attack. Uriel knew that the same scene was being repeated up and down the enormous gorge as other Ultramarine detachments prepared to destroy their own targets. He scooped up his helmet and marched towards a mud-stained Techmarine hauling himself over the parapet and unwinding a long length of cable from his equipment pack. The man looked up as he heard Uriel approach and nodded respectfully.

'I suppose you're going to tell me to hurry up,' he grumbled, bending awkwardly to hook the cable into a battery pack.

'Not at all, Sevano. As though I would rush the work of a master craftsman like yourself.'

Sevano Tomasin glowered at Uriel, searching his face for any trace of sarcasm. Finding none, the Techmarine nodded as he continued wiring the explosives, moving with a lop-sided, mechanical gait as both his legs and right arm were heavier, bionic replacements.

The apothecaries had grafted these on after recovering his body from the interior of a wrecked Land Raider on Ichar IV after a rampaging carnifex had ripped it apart. The horrifying creature's bio-plasma had flooded the interior of the armoured fighting vehicle, detonating its ammo spectacularly. The carnifex was killed in the blast, but the explosion sheared Tomasin to the bone and, rather than lose his centuries of wisdom, the chapter's artisans had designed a completely new, artificial body around the bloody rags of his remains.

'How long until you and the servitors are finished?' asked Uriel.

Tomasin wiped the mud from his face and glanced up the length of the bridge. 'Another hour, Ventris. Possibly less if this damned rain would ease up and I didn't have to stop to talk to you.'

Uriel bit back a retort and turned away, leaving the Techmarine to his work and striding to the nearest gun nest. Captain Idaeus was sitting on the sandbags and speaking animatedly into the vox-com.

'Well make sure, damn you!' he snapped. 'I don't want to be left sitting here facing half the rebel army with only thirty men.'

Idaeus listened to the words that only he could hear through the comm-bead in his ear and cursed, snapping the vox unit back to his belt.

'Trouble?' asked Uriel.

'Maybe,' sighed Idaeus. 'Orbital surveyors on the *Vae Victus* say they think they detected something large moving through the jungle in our direction, but this damned weather's interfering with the auguries and they can't bring them on-line again. It's probably nothing.'

'You don't sound too convinced.'

'I'm not,' admitted Idaeus. 'If the Night Lords are on this world, then this is just the kind of thing they would try.'

'I have our scouts watching the approaches to the bridge. Nothing is going to get close without us knowing about it.'

'Good. How is Tomasin getting on?'

'There's a lot of bridge to blow, captain, but Tomasin thinks he'll have it done within the hour. I believe he will have it rigged sooner though.'

Idaeus nodded and rose to his feet, staring into the mist and rain shrouded hills on the enemy side of the bridge. His face creased in a frown and Uriel followed his gaze. Dusk was fast approaching and with luck they would be on their way to rejoin the main assault on Mercia before night-fall.

'Something wrong?'

'I'm not sure. Every time I look across the bridge I get a bad feeling.'

'A bad feeling?'

'Aye, like someone is watching us,' whispered Idaeus.

Uriel checked his vox-com. 'The scouts haven't reported anything.'

Idaeus shook his head. 'No, this is more like instinct. This whole place feels wrong somehow. I can't describe it.'

Uriel was puzzled. Idaeus was a man he trusted implicitly, they had fought and bled together for over fifty years, forming a bond of friendship that Uriel found all too rarely. Yet he could never claim to truly understand Idaeus. The captain relied on instinct and feelings more than the holy Codex Astartes, that great work of military thinking penned ten thousand years ago by their own Primarch, Roboute Guilliman. The Codex formed the basis of virtually every Space Marine chapter's tactical doctrine and laid the foundations for the military might of the entire Imperium. Its words were sanctified by the Emperor himself and the Ultramarines had not deviated from its teachings since it had been written following the dark days of the Horus Heresy.

But Idaeus tended to regard the wisdom of the Codex as advice rather than holy instruction and this was a constant source of amazement to

Uriel. He had been Idaeus's second-in-command for nearly thirty years and, despite the captain's successes, Uriel still found it hard to accept his methods.

'I want to go and check those hills,' said Idaeus suddenly.

Uriel sighed and pointed out, 'The scouts will inform us of anything that approaches.'

'I know, and I have every faith in them. I just need to see for myself. Come on, let's go and take a look.'

Uriel took out his vox unit, informing the scouts they would be approaching from the rear and followed Idaeus as he strode purposefully to the end of the bridge. They passed the far bunker, the one the rebels should have occupied, noting the glint of bolters from within. The two Space Marines marched up the wide road that led into the high hills either side of the gorge and for the next thirty minutes inspected the locations Uriel had deployed the scouts to watch from. The rain deadened sounds and kept visibility low and there was enough tree cover to almost completely obscure the jungle floor. There could be an army out there and they wouldn't see it until it was right on top of them.

'Satisfied?' asked Uriel.

Idaeus nodded, but did not reply and together they began the trek back to the far bunker where they could see Sevano Tomasin.

The warning came just as the first artillery shell screamed overhead.

Almost as soon as Uriel heard the incoming shell, the comm-net exploded with voices; reports of artillery flashes in the distance and multiple sightings of armoured personnel carriers and tanks. A blinding explosion in the centre of the bridge, followed by half a dozen more in quick succession, split the dusk apart. Uriel shouted as he saw the servitors and two Space Marines blasted from the bridge, tumbling downwards to the rocks below.

The two officers sprinted down towards the bridge.

Uriel dialled into the vox-net of the Scouts as he ran and yelled, 'Scout team Alpha! Where in the warp did they come from? Report!'

'Contacts at three kilometres and closing, sergeant! The rain held down the dust, we couldn't see them through the dead ground.'

'Understood,' snapped Uriel, cursing the weather. 'What can you see?'

'Can't get an accurate count, but it looks like a battalion-sized assault. Chimeras mainly, but there's a lot of heavy armour mixed in – Leman Russ, Griffons and Hellhounds.'

Uriel swore and exchanged glances with Idaeus. If the scouts were correct, they were facing in excess of a thousand men with artillery and armoured support. Both knew that this must be the contact the auguries on the *Vae Victus* had detected then lost. They had to get everyone back across the bridge and blow it right now.

'Stay as long as you can Alpha and keep reporting, then get back here!'

'Aye, sir,' responded the scout and signed off.

More shells dropped on the bridge, the echoes of their detonations deafening in the enclosed gorge. Each blast threw up chunks of the roadway and vast geysers of rainwater. Some were air-bursting above the bridge, showering the roadway with deadly fragments.

Uriel recognised the distinctive whine of Griffon mortar shells and gave thanks to Guilliman that the PDF obviously did not have access to the heavier artillery pieces of the Imperial Guard. Either that or they realised that to use such weapons would probably destroy the bridge.

Most of the Space Marines who had been caught in the open were in cover now and Uriel knew they were lucky not to have lost more men. He cursed as he saw the lumbering shape of Sevano Tomasin still fixing explosive charges and unwinding lengths of cable back towards the last bunker. The Techmarine's movements were painfully slow, but he was undaunted by the shelling. Uriel willed him to work faster.

'One and a half kilometres and closing. Closing rapidly! Dismounted enemy infantry visible!' shouted the scout sergeant in Uriel's comm-bead.

'Acknowledged,' shouted Uriel over the crash of falling mortar shells and explosions. 'Get back here now; there's nothing more you can do from there. Sword squad is waiting at the first bunker to give you covering fire. Ventris out.'

Uriel and Idaeus reached the bunker and splashed to a halt behind its reassuringly thick walls. Idaeus snatched up his vox-com and shouted, 'Guard command net, this is Captain Idaeus, Ultramarine Fourth company. Be advised that hostiles are attacking across Bridge Two-Four in division strength, possibly stronger. We are falling back and preparing to destroy the bridge. I say again, hostiles are attacking across Bridge Two-Four!'

As Idaeus voxed the warning to the Imperial Guard commanders, Uriel patched into the frequency of the Thunderhawk that had dropped them in position.

'Thunderhawk Six, this is Uriel Ventris. We are under attack and request immediate extraction. Mission order Omega-Seven-Four. Acknowledge please.'

For long seconds, all Uriel could hear was the hiss of static and he feared something terrible had happened to the gunship. Then a voice, heavily distorted said, 'Acknowledged, Sergeant Ventris. Mission order Omega-Seven-Four received. We'll be overhead in ten minutes. Signal your position with green smoke.'

'Affirmative,' replied Uriel. 'Be advised the landing zone will in all likelihood be extremely hot when you arrive.'

'Don't worry,' chuckled the pilot of the gunship. 'We're fully loaded. We'll keep their heads down while we extract you. Thunderhawk Six out.'

Uriel snapped the vox-unit to his belt and hammered on the bunker's door. He and Idaeus ducked inside as it slid open. The five Space Marines within were positioned at the bunker's firing step, bolters and a lascannon pointed at the hills above, ready to cover their brothers' retreat. Uriel stared through the anti-grenade netting, watching the scouts falling back in good order towards the bridge.

'As soon as the scouts are past you, fall back to the first gun nest and take up firing positions,' ordered Idaeus. 'The other squads are already in position and they'll cover you. Understood?'

The Space Marines nodded, but did not take their eyes from the ridge above the approaching scouts. Idaeus turned to Uriel and said, 'Get across and see how close Tomasin is to blowing this damned bridge. We'll join you as soon as we can.'

Uriel opened his mouth to protest, but Idaeus cut him off, 'Stow it, sergeant. Go! I'll join you as soon as Alpha Team are safe.'

Without another word, Uriel slipped from the bunker. Another series of thunderous detonations cascaded across the bridge and impacted on the sides of the gorge. Uriel waited until he detected a lull in the firing then began sprinting across the bridge, weaving around piles of rubble, debris and water filled craters left by the explosions. He could still see Sevano Tomasin behind the sandbagged gun nests, working on the detonators.

He heard gunfire behind him, the distinctive, dull crack of bolter fire and the snapping hiss of lasguns. He glanced over his shoulder as a terrible sense of premonition struck him.

Twin streaks of shrieking projectiles flashed overhead, one landing behind him and another before him with earth shaking detonations. The first shell exploded less than four metres above the men of Alpha team, shredding their bodies through the lighter scout armour leaving only a bloody mist and scraps of ripped flesh. The shockwave of the blast threw Uriel to the ground. He coughed mud and spat rainwater, rising in time to see Sevano Tomasin engulfed in blinding white phosporent fire.

The Techmarine collapsed, his metal limbs liquefying and the flesh searing from his bones. A second melta charge ignited in his equipment pack, also cooked off by the mortar shell's detonation. Tomasin vanished in a white-hot explosion, the rain forming a steam cloud around his molten remains.

Uriel pushed himself upright and charged towards the fallen Space Marine. Tomasin was dead, there could be no doubt about that. But Uriel needed to see if the detonator mechanism had gone up with him. If it had, they were in deep, deep trouble.

IDAEUS WATCHED THE first squadron of enemy vehicles crest the ridge above, hatred burning in his heart. Even in the fading light, he could clearly make out the silhouette of three Salamander scout vehicles and Idaeus vowed he would see them dead.

He could smell the acrid stench of scorched human flesh from the blasted remains of the scouts. They had died only ten metres from the safety of the bunker. Idaeus knew he should fall back to the prepared gun positions further along the bridge; if they stayed here much longer, they'd be trapped. But his thirst for retribution was a fire in his heart, and he was damned if he would yield a millimetre to these bastards without exacting some measure of vengeance for his fallen warriors.

'Nivaneus,' hissed Idaeus to the Space Marine carrying the lascannon. 'Do you have a target?'

'Aye, sir,' confirmed Nivaneus.

'Then fire at will. Take down those traitorous dogs!'

A blinding streak of las-fire punched from the massive weapon. A Salamander slewed from the road, its hull blazing and smoke boiling from its interior. The vehicles' supporting infantry squads fired their lasguns before the Space Marines' bolter fire blasted them apart with uncompromising accuracy. But Idaeus knew they were inconsequential. Killing the tanks was all that mattered.

Nivaneus calmly switched targets and another Salamander died, its crew tumbling from the escape hatches on fire. The last tank ground to a halt, stuttering blasts from its autocannon stitching across the bunker's face. Idaeus felt the vibrations of shell impacts. He smiled grimly as the Salamander's driver desperately attempted to reverse back uphill. Its tracks spun ineffectually, throwing up huge sprays of mud, unable to find purchase. Dust and an acrid, electric stench filled the air as Nivaneus lined up a shot on the struggling tank.

Before he could fire, a missile speared through the rain and smashed into the immobilised tank's turret. It exploded from within, wracked by secondary detonations as its ammo cooked off.

'Captain Idaeus!' shouted Uriel over the vox-net. 'Get out of there! There will be more tanks coming over that ridge any moment and you will be cut off if you do not leave now! We have you covered, now get back here!'

'I think he's got a point, men,' said Idaeus calmly. 'We've given them a bloody nose, but it's time we were going.'

The Ultramarines fired a last volley of shots before hefting their weapons and making for the door.

'Uriel!' called Idaeus. 'We are ready to go, now give me some fire.'

Seconds later a withering salvo of bolter fire and missiles swept the ridge top, wreathing it in smoke and flames. Idaeus shouted, 'Go, go, go!' to the Space Marines and followed as they sprinted through the rain. The mortar fire had ceased; probably due to the Griffon tanks being moved up into a direct firing position, thought Idaeus. Whatever the reason, he was grateful for it.

He heard a teeth-loosening rumble and a squeal of tracks, knowing without looking that heavy tanks had spread out across the ridge, moving into a firing position behind them. He saw two missile contrails flashing overhead and heard the ringing clang of their impact. A crashing detonation told him that at least one enemy tank was out of action, but only one.

'Incoming!' he yelled and dived over a pile of debris into a crater as the thunder of two battle cannons echoed across the gorge. He felt the awesome force of the impacts behind him, even through the ceramite of his power armour. His auto senses shut down momentarily to preserve his sight and hearing as the massive shell exploded, the pressure of the blast almost crushing him flat. Red runes winked into life on his visor as his armour was torn open in half a dozen places. He felt searing pain and cursed as he yanked a plate-sized piece of sizzling shrapnel from his leg. Almost instantly, he could feel the Larraman cells clotting his blood and forming a protective layer of scar tissue over the wound. He had suffered much worse and shut out the pain.

The two surviving Leman Russ tanks rumbled downhill, smashing the smoking remains of the Salamanders aside with giant dozer blades. Furious gunfire spat from their hull-mounted heavy bolters, sweeping across the bunker's face and the bridge, throwing up spouts of water and rock. None hit the Ultramarines and Idaeus shouted, 'Up! Come on, keep moving!'

The Space Marines rose and continued running towards the comparative safety of the far side of the bridge. More tanks and infantry spilled over the ridge, following in the wake of the Leman Russ battle tanks. Las-blasts fired at the Space Marines, but the range was too great.

Then, at the edge of his hearing, Idaeus heard the welcome boom of a Thunderhawk gunship's engines and saw the angular form of the aerial transport sweep from the above the jungle canopy. Rockets streaked from its wing pylons, rippling off in salvoes of three and the ridge vanished in a wall of flames. Heavy cannons mounted on the hull and wings fired thousands of shells into the rebels, obliterating tanks and men in a heartbeat.

Idaeus punched the air in triumph as the Thunderhawk swept over the ridge and circled around for another strafing run. He jogged leisurely into the sandbagged gun nest, the Space Marines who had followed him taking up firing positions.

'Uriel,' voxed Idaeus. 'Are you ready to get out of here?'

'More than ready,' replied Uriel from the bunker behind Idaeus. 'But we have a problem. Tomasin was killed in the shelling and he had the detonators. We can't blow the bridge.'

Idaeus slammed his fist into a sandbag. 'Damn it!' he swore, teeth bared. He paced the interior of the gun nest like a caged grox before saying, 'Then we're going to have to hold here for as long as possible and pray the Guard can realign their flank in time.'

'Agreed. The Emperor guide your aim, captain.'

'And yours. May He watch over you.'

URIEL SHUT OFF the vox-com and slid a fresh magazine into his bolt pistol, staring out at the flame wreathed hillside. The distant Thunderhawk had circled around, guns blazing at something Uriel could not see. Fresh explosions blossomed from behind the ridge as more traitors died.

Suddenly shells burst around the gunship and streams of fire, bright against the dark sky, licked up from the ground. Uriel swore as he realised the traitors were equipped with anti-aircraft weapons. The gunship jinked to avoid the incoming fire, but another stream of shells spat skyward and seconds later the gunners had the Thunderhawk bracketed. Thousands of shells ripped through the gunship's armour, tearing the port wing off. The engine exploded in a brilliant fireball. The pilot struggled to hold the aircraft aloft, banking to avoid the flak, but the gunship continued to lose altitude, spewing black smoke from its stricken frame.

Uriel watched with horror as the Thunderhawk spiralled lower and lower, its wobbling form growing larger by the second.

'By the Emperor, no!' whispered Uriel as the gunship smashed into the ground just before the bridge, skidding forwards and trailing a brilliant halo of sparks and flames. The wreckage crashed into the unoccupied bunker, demolishing it instantly and slewing across the bridge towards the Ultramarines with the sound of shrieking metal. The remaining wing sheared off, spinning the flaming gunship upside down and tearing up the roadway. The gunship ground onwards, finally coming to a halt less than two hundred metres from the gun nests.

Uriel let out the breath he had been holding. Movement caught his eye and he saw more enemy vehicles rumbling through the swirling black smoke towards the bridge.

'Targets sighted!' he shouted. 'Enemy tanks inbound. Mark your targets and fire when you have a clear shot!'

The lead rebel armoured column consisted of dozens of Chimeras, daubed in blasphemous runes. Uriel snarled as he recognised the winged skull motif of the Night Lords crudely copied onto the Chimeras' hulls. There could be no doubt now. The taint of Chaos had come to Thracia. Each vehicle mounted a powerful searchlight, sweeping blindingly back and forth in random patterns across the bridge as they charged. Missiles and lascannon blasts pierced the darkness, and the night was illuminated by scores of exploding tanks. No matter how many the Ultramarines killed, there were more to take their place. Soon the bridge was choked with burning wrecks. Hundreds of screaming soldiers dismounted from their transports, working their way forward through the tanks' graveyard.

Uriel fired shot after shot from his pistol. It was impossible to miss, there were so many. The darkness of the gorge echoed to the sounds of screams and gunfire. But Uriel was not fooled by the slaughter they were wreaking amongst the ranks of the traitors. Their ammunition was finite and soon the battle would degenerate into bloody close quarters fighting and, though they would kill many hundreds, they would eventually fall. It was simply a question of numbers.

He reloaded again and wished there was something else he could do, cursing Sevano Tomasin for dying and condemning them to this ignoble end. He pictured again the image of the Techmarine incinerated by the chain-reacting melta charge in his equipment pack.

Something clicked in Uriel's head and he stopped.

No, it was insane, utterly insane and suicidal. But it could work. He tried to remember a precedent in the Codex Astartes, but came up with nothing. Could it be done? A frag wouldn't do it and only the assault troops had been issued with kraks. He checked his grenade dispenser. He had one breaching charge left.

His mind made up, he grabbed a Space Marine from the firing step, shouting to be heard over the bolter fire.'I'm heading for the captain's position. Give me covering fire!'

The man nodded and passed on his order. Uriel ducked out the ragged doorway and crouched at the corner of the bunker. Streams of las-blasts and bolter rounds criss-crossed the darkness causing a weirdly stroboscopic effect.

Volleys of sustained bolter fire blasted from the bunker and Uriel leapt from cover, sprinting towards Idaeus's position. Instantly, lasgun fire erupted from amongst the burning tanks. Each shooter was silenced by a devastatingly accurate bolter shot. Uriel dived behind the gun nest and crawled inside on his belly.

Idaeus, bleeding from a score of gouges in his armour, directed disciplined bolter fire into the traitors' ranks. Two Space Marines lay dead, the backs of their helmets blasted clear and Uriel was suddenly very aware of how much less protection there was in the gun nest than the bunker.

Idaeus spared Uriel a glance, shouting, 'What are you doing here, Uriel?'

'I have an idea how we can blow the bridge!'

'How?'

'The assault troops have krak grenades. If we can attach some to one of the melta charges on the bridge supports it could set of a chain reaction with the others!'

Idaeus considered the idea for a second then shrugged. 'It's not much of a plan, but what choice do we have?'

'None,' said Uriel bluntly. Idaeus nodded and hunkered down in the sandbags, snatching out his battered vox. Hurriedly, he explained Uriel's plan to the sergeant of the assault troopers, receiving confirmation as to its feasibility of execution.

Idaeus raised his head and locked his gaze with Uriel. 'You picked a hell of a time to start thinking outside the Codex, sergeant.'

'Better late than never, captain.'

Idaeus smiled and nodded. 'We'll have about thirty seconds from the first detonation to get clear. If we're not off the bridge by then, we're dead. I've already called for another Thunderhawk, but it will not arrive before morning at the earliest.'

The captain opened a channel to the remaining Space Marines in his detachment and said, 'All squads, as soon as the assault troops move, I want enough firepower laid down on these bastards to blow apart a Titan. Understood?'

Shouted confirmations greeted Idaeus's order. He reloaded his pistol and motioned for Uriel to join him at the edge of the gun nest.

From the second gun nest, flaring jets of light erupted as the assault squad fired their jump packs.

'NOW!' yelled Idaeus and the Ultramarines fired everything they had. Volley after volley of bolter shells, missiles and lascannon shots decimated the rebel troopers. The swiftness of death was unbelievable. The Space Marines pumped shot after shot into their reeling mass.

It began with a single rebel turning his back and fleeing into the night. An officer shot him dead, but it was already too late. Others began turning and fleeing through the maze of wrecked tanks, their resolve broken in the face of the Emperor's finest.

And then it was over.

Uriel could not recall how long they had fought for, but it must have been many hours. He checked his visor chronometer and was surprised to find it had been less than two. He knelt and counted his ammo: six clips, not good. Risking a glance over the top level of sandbags, their outer surfaces vitrified to glass by the intense heat of repeated laser impacts, Uriel saw the bridge littered with hundreds of corpses.

The tension was palpable, every Space Marine ready to move the instant they heard the first detonation of a krak grenade. Long minutes passed with nothing but the hiss of the vox, the crackle of flames and moans of the dying outside. Everyone in the gun nest flinched as they heard the crack of rapid bolt pistol fire. The shooting continued for several minutes before dying away.

Uriel and Idaeus exchanged worried glances. Both sides were using bolt pistols.

Uriel shook his head sadly. 'They failed.'

'We don't know that,' snapped Idaeus, but Uriel could tell the captain did not believe his own words.

WEAK SUNLIGHT SHONE from the carcasses of the crashed Thunder-hawk and smashed tanks on the bridge, their black shells smouldering fitfully. The rain had continued throughout the night. Thankfully, the rebels' attacks had not. There was no detonation of krak grenades and Idaeus was forced to admit that the assault squad had been thwarted in their mission.

Uriel scanned the skies to their rear, watching for another Thunderhawk or perhaps Lightning strike craft of the Imperial Navy. Either would be a welcome sight just now, but the skies remained empty.

A sudden shout from one of the forward observers roused Uriel from his melancholy thoughts and he swiftly took his position next to Idaeus. He saw movement through the burnt out shell of the Thunderhawk, flashes of blue and gold and heard a throaty grinding noise. The sound of heavy vehicles crushing bone and armour beneath their iron tracks. Darting figures, also in blue and gold, slipped through the wrecks, their movements furtive.

With a roar of primal ferocity that spoke of millennia of hate, the Night Lords Chaos Space Marines finally revealed themselves. Battering through the wreckage came five ornately carved Rhino armoured personnel carriers, coruscating azure flames writhing within their flanks. Uriel was speechless.

They resembled Rhinos in name only. Bloody spikes festooned every surface and leering gargoyles thrashed across the undulating armour, gibbering eldritch incantations that made Uriel's skin crawl.

But the supreme horror was mounted on the tanks' frontal sections.

The still-living bodies of the Ultramarine assault squad were crucified on crude iron crosses bolted to the hulls. Their armour had been torn off, their ribcages sawn open then spread wide like obscene angels' wings. Glistening ropes of entrails hung from their opened bellies and they wept blood from blackened, empty eye sockets and tongueless mouths. That they could still be alive was impossible, yet Uriel could see their hearts still beat with life, could see the abject horror of pain in their contorted features.

The Rhinos continued forwards, closely followed by gigantic figures in midnight blue power armour. Their armour was edged in bronze and their helmets moulded into daemonic visages with blood streaked horns. Red winged skull icons pulsed with unnatural life on their shoulder plates.

Idaeus was the first to overcome his shock, lifting his bolter and pumping shots into the advancing Night Lords.

'Kill them!' he bellowed. 'Kill them all!'

Uriel shook his head, throwing off the spell of horror the spectacle of the mutilated Ultramarines had placed upon him and he levelled his pistol. Two missiles and a lascannon shot punched towards the Night Lords. Uriel prayed the tortured souls crucified on the Rhinos would forgive them, as two of the tanks exploded, veering off and crashing into the side of the bridge. The prisoners burned in the flames of their destruction and Uriel could feel his fury rising to a level where all he could feel was the urge to kill.

The Space Marine next to Uriel fell, a bolter shell detonating within his chest cavity. He collapsed without a sound, and Uriel swept up his bolt gun, emptying the magazine into the traitor legionnaires. A handful of Night Lords were dead, but the rest were closing the gap rapidly. Two more Rhinos died in fiery blasts. Disciplined volleys of bolter and lascannon fire from the Ultramarines in the bunker kept hammering the ranks of Night Lords as they attempted to overrun the gun nests. But few were falling and it was only a matter of time until the traitors reached them.

The Space Marines across the bridge from Uriel and Idaeus perished in a searing ball of white-hot fire as Night Lord warriors unloaded plasma guns through the firing slit of their gun nest. The backblast of the resultant explosion mushroomed into the dawn, incinerating the killers. Still they came on.

Uriel yelled in fury, killing and killing. An armoured gauntlet smashed into the gun nest.

Idaeus chopped with his power sword and blood sprayed.

Uriel yelled, 'Grenade!' as he saw what was clutched in the severed hand. He kicked the hand into the gun nest's grenade pit and rolled a dead Space Marine on top. The frag blew with a muffled thump, the corpse's ceramite back-plate absorbing the full force of the blast.

'Thank you, brother,' muttered Uriel in relief.

Another Night Lord kicked his way into the gun nest, a screaming axe gripped in one massive fist. His blue armour seemed to ripple with inner fires and the brass edging was dazzling in its brightness. The winged skull icon hissed blasphemous oaths and Uriel could feel the axe's obscene hunger for blood. Idaeus slashed his sword across his chest, but the blade slid clear. The warrior lunged, slashing his axe across Idaeus's shoulder and blood sprayed through the rent in his armour. Idaeus slammed his elbow into his foe's belly and spun inside his guard, hammering his sword through the Night Lord's neck.

He kicked him back outside as more enemies pushed themselves in. Uriel fired his pistol and rolled beneath a crackling power fist. He drove his combat knife into the gap between his enemy's breastplate and helmet, wrenching the blade upwards. Blood fountained and he yelled in sudden pain as the warrior fired his bolter at point blank range. The shell penetrated Uriel's armour and blasted a fist-sized chunk of his hip clear. He stabbed his opponent's neck again and again, stopping only when his struggles ceased completely.

Idaeus and the last Space Marine in the gun nest fought back to back, desperately fighting for their lives against four Night Lords. Uriel leapt into the combat, wrapping his powerful arms around one Chaos Space Marine's neck. He twisted hard, snapping his spine.

Everything was blood and violence. The Space Marine fighting alongside Idaeus fell, his body pulverised by a power fist. Uriel dragged his blade free from the Night Lord's helmet and beheaded the killer, blowing out another foe's helmet with a bolter shell. Idaeus drove his sword through the last Night Lord's belly, kicking the corpse from his blood-sheathed blade. The two Space Marines snatched up their bolters and began firing again. The gun nest stank of blood and smoke. The last Rhino was a blazing wreck, the prisoner on its hull cooking in the fires.

He tossed aside the bolter as its slide racked back empty and grabbed Idaeus by the shoulder.

'We need to get back to the bunker. We can't hold them here!'

'Agreed,' grimaced Idaeus. Grabbing what ammo they could carry, the two warriors ducked outside into the grey morning and ran back towards the bullet scarred bunker. The attack appeared to be over for now.

As they ran, Idaeus's vox crackled and a voice said, 'Captain Idaeus, do you copy? This is Thunderhawk Two. We are inbound on your position and will be overhead in less than a minute. Do you copy?'

Idaeus snatched up the vox and shouted, 'I copy, Thunderhawk Two, but do not over-fly our position! The enemy has at least two, but probably more, anti-aircraft tanks covering the bridge. We already lost Thunderhawk Six.'

'Understood. We will set down half a kilometre south of the bridge,' replied the pilot.

Uriel and Idaeus limped inside the bunker and dropped the bolter magazines on the floor.

'Load up. This is all we have left,' ordered Idaeus.

The Ultramarines began sharing out the magazines and Uriel offered another bolter to Idaeus, but the captain shook his head.

'I don't need it. Give me a pistol and a couple of clips. And that last breaching charge of yours, Uriel.'

Uriel quickly grasped the significance of Idaeus' words. 'No, let me do it, captain,' he pleaded.

Idaeus shook his head, 'Not this time, Uriel. This is my mission, I won't let it end like this. The seven of us can't hold the Night Lords if they attack again, so I'm ordering you to get the rest of the men back to that Thunderhawk.'

'Besides,' he said with a wry smile. 'You don't have a jump pack to get down there.'

Uriel could see there was no arguing with the captain. He dispensed the last breaching charge and reverently offered it to Idaeus. The captain took the charge and unbuckled his sword belt. He reversed the scabbard and handed the elaborately tooled sword to Uriel.

'Take this,' he said. 'I know it will serve you as well as it has served me. A weapon this fine should not end its days like this, and you will have more need of it than I.'

Uriel could not speak. Idaeus himself had forged the magnificent blade before the Corinthian Crusade and had carried it in battle ever since. The honour was overwhelming.

Idaeus gripped Uriel's wrist tightly in the warrior's grip and said, 'Go now, old friend. Make me proud.'

Uriel nodded. 'I will, captain,' he promised, and saluted. The five remaining Space Marines in the bunker followed Uriel's lead and came to attention, bolters held tightly across their chests.

Idaeus smiled. 'The Emperor watch over you all,' he said and slipped outside into the rain.

Uriel was gripped by a terrible sense of loss, but suppressed it viciously. He would ensure that Idaeus's last command was carried out.

He loaded a bolter and racked the slide.

'Come on, we have to go.'

IDAEUS WAITED UNTIL he saw Uriel lead the five Space Marines from the bunker towards the jungle's edge before moving. He had a chance to do this stealthily, but knew it wouldn't be long before the Night Lords realised the bridge was now undefended and the rebels drove their forces across. He would not allow that to happen.

He crawled through the mud and rubble, keeping out of sight of the enemy lines, eventually reaching the pitted face of the rockcrete sides of the bridge. He grabbed a handful of mud and ash, smearing it over the blue of his armour, then slithered onto the parapet. The river was thousands of metres below and Idaeus experienced a momentary surge of vertigo as he looked down. He scanned the bridge supports, searching for one of the box-like melta charges Tomasin had placed only the day before. He grinned as he spotted one fixed to the central span. Muttering a prayer to the Emperor and Guilliman, Idaeus pushed himself over the edge.

He dropped quickly, then fired the twin jets of his jump pack, angling for the central span. The noise of the rockets' burn seemed incredibly loud to Idaeus, but he could do nothing about it. It was all or nothing now.

He cursed as he saw his trajectory was too short. He landed on a wide beam, some twenty metres from the central span and crouched, waiting to see if he had been detected. He heard nothing and clambered through the multitude of stanchions, beams and tension bars towards the central column.

Suddenly, a shadow passed over the captain and he spun in time to see dark winged creatures in midnight black power armour swoop down alongside him. Their helmets were moulded in the form of screaming daemons and ululating howls shrieked from their vox units. They carried stubby pistols and serrated black swords that smoked as though fresh from the furnace. Idaeus knew the foul creatures as Raptors, and fired into their midst, blasting one of the abominable warriors from the sky. Another crashed into him, stabbing with a black bladed sword. Idaeus grunted as he felt the blade pierce one of his lungs, and broke the Raptor's neck with a blow from his free hand. He staggered back, the sword still embedded in his chest, taking refuge in the tangle of metal beneath the bridge to avoid the howling Raptors. Two landed between him and the melta charge as dozens more descended from the bridge. Three more swooped in behind him, their wings folding behind them and they landed on the girders. Idaeus snarled and raised his pistol as they charged.

Idaeus killed the first with his pistol. A second shot killed another, but he couldn't move quick enough to avoid the third. White heat exploded in his face, searing the flesh from the side of his skull as the Raptor fired its plasma pistol. He fell back, blind with pain, and didn't see the crackling sword blow that hacked his left arm from his body. He bellowed with rage as he watched his arm tumble down towards the river, Uriel's last breaching charge still clutched in the armoured fist.

The Raptor closed for the kill, but Idaeus was ready for it. He dragged the smoking sword from his chest and howled with battle fury as he hammered the sword through the Raptor's neck. He collapsed next to the headless corpse, releasing his grip on the sword hilt. Dizziness and pain swamped him. He tried to stand, but his strength was gone. He saw the Raptors standing between him and the melta charge, their daemon-carved helmets alight with the promise of victory.

He felt his lifeblood pumping from his body, the Larraman cells powerless to halt his demise and bitterness arose in his throat. He reached out with his arm, propping himself upright as weariness flooded his limbs. He felt a textured pistol grip beneath his hand and grasped the unfamiliar weapon tightly. If he was to die, it would be with a weapon in his hand.

More Raptors hovered in the air, screeching in triumph and Idaeus could feel a bone-rattling vibration as hundreds of armoured vehicles began crossing the bridge. He had failed. He looked down at the pistol in his hand and hope flared. The flying abominations raised their weapons, ready to blow him away.

Then the Raptors exploded in a series of massive detonations and Idaeus heard a thunderous boom echo back and forth from the sides of the gorge. He twisted his dying body around in time to see the beautiful form of Thunderhawk Two roaring through the gorge towards the bridge, its wing mounted guns blasting the Raptors to atoms.

He smiled through the pain, guessing the fight Uriel must have had with the pilot to get him to fly through the flak of the Hydras and down the gorge. He raised his head to the two Raptors who still stood between him and his goal. They drew their swords as Thunderhawk Two screamed below the bridge. Lascannon fire chased the gunship, but nothing could touch it.

Idaeus slumped against a black stanchion and turned his melted face back towards the two Raptors. Between them, he could see the melta charge. He smiled painfully.

He would only get one shot at this.

Idaeus raised the plasma pistol he had taken from the dead Raptor, relishing the look of terror on his enemy's faces as they realised what must happen next.

'Mission accomplished,' snarled Idaeus and pulled the trigger.

Uriel watched the unbearably bright streak of plasma flashing towards the central span of the bridge and explode like a miniature sun directly upon the melta charge. The searing white heat ignited the bomb with a thunderclap and it detonated in a gigantic, blinding fireball, spraying molten tendrils of liquid fire. The central support of the bridge was instantly vaporised in the nuclear heat, and Uriel had a fleeting glimpse of Idaeus before he too was engulfed in the expanding firestorm.

The echoes of the first blast still rang from the gorge sides as the remaining charges detonated in the intense heat. A heartbeat later, the bridge vanished as explosions blossomed along its length and blasted its supports to destruction. Thunderous, grinding cracks heralded its demise as giant sections of the bridge sagged, the shriek of tortured metal and cracking rockcrete filling Uriel's senses. Whole sections plummeted downwards, carrying hundreds of rebel tanks and soldiers to their deaths as the bridge tore itself apart under stresses it was never meant to endure.

Thick smoke and flames obscured the final death of Bridge Two-Four, its twisted remains crashing into the river below. Thunderhawk Two pulled out of the gorge, gaining altitude and banking round on a course for the Imperial lines. Even as the bridge shrank in the distance, Uriel could see there was almost nothing left of it.

The main supports were gone, the sections of roadway they had supported choking the river far below. There was now no way to cross the gorge for hundreds of miles in either direction.

He slid down the armoured interior of the Thunderhawk and wearily removed his helmet, cradling Idaeus's sword in his lap. He thought of Idaeus's sacrifice, wondering again that a warrior of the Ultramarines could command without immediate recourse to the Codex Astartes. It was a mystery to him, yet one he now felt able to explore.

He ran a gauntleted hand along the length of the masterfully inscribed scabbard, feeling the full weight of responsibility the weapon represented. Captain Idaeus of the Fourth Company was dead, but as long as Uriel Ventris wielded this blade, his memory would remain. He looked into the blood-stained faces of the Space Marines who had survived the mission and realised that the duty of command now fell to him.

Uriel vowed he would do it honour.

NIGHTBRINGER

PROLOGUE

60 million years ago...

THE STAR WAS being destroyed. It was a dwarf star of some one and a half million kilometres diameter and had burned for over six billion years. Had it not been for the immense, crescent-moon shaped starship orbiting the system's fourth planet and draining its massive energies, it would have probably continued to do so for perhaps another sixteen billion years.

The star generated energy at a colossal rate by burning hydrogen to helium in nuclear fusion reactions deep in its heart before radiating that energy into space. These reactions produced intense electro-magnetic fields in the star's core that rippled to the surface in seething magnetic waves.

A clutch of these surging fields erupted as a toroidal loop of magnetic flux some 200,000 kilometres in diameter, producing a dark, swelling sunspot within the star's photosphere.

This active region of magnetic flux expanded rapidly, suddenly exploding upwards from the star's surface in a gigantic flare, covering a billion square kilometres and becoming a bright curling spear of light in the star's corona. These powerful waves of electromagnetic energy and sprays of plasma formed into a rippling nimbus of coruscating light that spiralled a snaking route towards a rune-encrusted pyramid at the centre of the vast starship. Eldritch sigils carved into the ship's side blazed with the received energies and the hull pulsed as though the ship itself was swelling with barely contained power.

Every flaring beam of light ripped from the star that washed its power over the ship shortened the star's lifespan by a hundred thousand years, but the occupants of the starship cared not that its death would cause the extinction of every living thing in that system. Galaxies had lived and died by their masters' command, whole stellar realms had been extinguished for their pleasure and entire races brought into existence as their playthings. What mattered the fate of one insignificant star system to beings of such power?

Like some obscene mechanised leech, the ship continued to suck the vital forces from the star as it orbited the planet. An array of smaller pyramids and obelisks on the ship's base rippled as though in a heat haze, flickering in and out of perception as the massive ship shuddered with the colossal energies it was stripping from the star.

Abruptly the snaking beam of liquid light from the star faded and vanished from sight, the silver ship having had its fill for the moment. Ponderously it began to rotate and dropped slowly through the planet's atmosphere. Fiery coronas flared from the leading edges of the crescent wings as it descended towards a vast, iron-oxide desert in the northern hemisphere. The surface of the planet sped by below: rugged mountains, grinding tectonic plates and ash-spewing volcanoes. The ship began slowing as it neared its destination, a sandy dust bowl with a tiny spot of absolute darkness at its centre.

The ship's speed continued to drop as the shape resolved itself into a glassy black pyramid, its peak capped in gold. Its shimmering obsidian walls, smoky and reflective, were impervious to the howling winds that scoured the planet bare. Small, scuttling creatures that glittered in the burning sun crawled across its surface with a chittering mechanical gait. Runes identical to those on the orbiting starship hummed as powerful receptors activated.

The ship manoeuvred itself gracefully into position above the pyramid as the gold cap began to open like the petals of a flower. The humming rose to an ear-splitting shriek as the smaller pyramids and obelisks on the ship's underside exploded with energy, and a rippling column of pure electromagnetic force shot straight down the black pyramid's hungry maw.

Incandescent white light blazed from the pyramid, instantly incinerating the mechanical creatures that crawled across its surface. The desert it stood upon flared gold, streaks of power radiating outwards from the pyramid's base in snaking lines and vitrifying the sand in complex geometric patterns. The enormous vessel held its position until the last of its stolen energy had been transferred. Once the gold cap of the pyramid had sealed itself shut, the ship made the long trip back into orbit to repeat the process, its intention to continue ripping energy from the star until it was nothing more than a cooling ball of inert gasses.

The vessel settled into position before the star, the arcane device mounted upon its hull powering up once more.

An area of space behind the vessel twisted, shifting out of true and rip- ping asunder as the fragile veil of reality tore aside and a massive flotilla of bizarre alien vessels poured out from the maelstrom beyond.

No two ships were alike, each having its own unique geometries and form, but all had the same lethal purpose. As though commanded by a single will, the rag-tag fleet of ships closed rapidly on the crescent-shaped starship, weapons of all descriptions firing. A series of bright explosions blossomed across the mighty ship's hull, bolts of powerful energy smash- ing against the uppermost pyramid. The craft shuddered like a wounded beast.

But this starship could fight back.

Arcs of cobalt lightning whiplashed from its weapon batteries, smashing a dozen of its foes to destruction. Invisible beams of immense power stripped another group down to their component atoms. But no amount of losses could dissuade the alien fleet from its attack, and no matter how many were destroyed, it seemed there were always more to take their place. The faceless crew of the starship appeared to realise that unless they could escape, they were doomed. Slowly the ship began to rotate on its axis, a powerful, electric haze growing from its inertialess engines.

A multitude of alien weapons hammered the ship's flattened topside, tearing great gouges in its hull and blasting jagged chunks of metal from the vessel. Self-repair mechanisms attempted to stem the damage, but, like the ship itself, they were fighting a losing battle. Wreckage from the ship spun off into the darkness of space as its engines fired with retina-searing brightness. Time slowed and the image of the enormous ship stretched like elastic, the nearby gravity well of the star enacting its revenge on the vampire ship as it vainly attempted to escape.

With a tortured shriek that echoed through the warp, the crescent ship seemed to contract to a singular point of unbearable brightness. Its attack- ers were sucked into the screaming wake and together the foes were hurled into oblivion, perhaps never to return.

The star continued to burn and, far below, the glow emanating from the golden cap of the black pyramid faded until it was a dull lustreless bronze.

Soon, the sands obscured even that.

ONE

The 41st Millennium...

THE EIGHTEEN RIDERS made their way along the base of the frozen stream bed, their horses carefully picking their steps through the ice-slick rocky ground. Despite their caution, and the herd of nearly a hundred scaly-skinned grox they were driving through the snow, Gedrik knew they were making good time.

He twisted in the saddle, making sure the herd was still together.

Gedrik was lean and rangy, wrapped tightly in a battered, but well cared-for snow cape with leather riding trousers, padded on the inner thighs, and warm, fur lined boots. His head was protected by a thick colback of toughened leather and furs, his face wrapped in a woollen scarf to keep the worst of the vicious mountain winds at bay.

The green plaid so common on Caernus IV, Gedrik's home planet, was tied loosely across his chest, its frayed ends hanging over the wire-wound hilt of his sword. Hidden in his left boot, he also carried a slender bladed dagger. He had crafted both weapons himself from the Metal six years ago, and they were still as sharp and untarnished as the day he had forged them. Preacher Mallein had taught him how to use the sword, and they were lessons he had learned well; no one in the Four Valleys could fight as well as Gedrik.

To complete his arsenal he carried a simple bolt-action rifle slung across his wide shoulders. Gedrik knew they were almost home and he looked forward to a warm fire and the even warmer embrace of his wife, Maeren.

This last week on the mountains, gathering the herd for the slaughter, had been hard, as though the wind and snow had sought to scour the pitiful humans who dared their wrath from the rocky peaks.

But soon they would be home and Gedrik could almost taste the fine steak Maeren would cook for him once Gohbar had begun slaughtering the herd.

He turned as he heard a muffled curse behind him and grinned as his cousin, Faergus rode alongside him. Though Gedrik knew that 'rode' was a flattering term for Faergus's skill in the saddle.

Gedrik's cousin could only be described as a bear of a man, with huge shoulders and a thick, shapeless neck. His face was battered and lumpen, with a squashed nose broken in countless brawls and a thick, black beard.

His feet dangled almost to the snow and Gedrik could well understand his mount's desire to unseat him. He ignored his cousin's discomfort, content to simply enjoy the majestic beauty of the Gelroch Mountains as they travelled home.

The sun was an hour past its zenith when the snow-wreathed settlement of Morten's Reach came into view. Nestling in the loop of a sluggish river at the centre of a wide glen, the buildings of the community seemed to huddle together as though for shared warmth. Gedrik could see the inhabitants milling about the town square in front of the small stone-built temple to the Emperor, squatting on the slopes of the Hill of the Metal. Preacher Mallein must have just finished one of his sermons, and Gedrik smiled as he pictured his son, Rouari, telling him all about the winged angels and heroic deeds of the Emperor over supper. Mallein could spin a fine tale, that was for sure!

Smoke drifted from the forge and, on the near side of the village, Gedrik could see Gohbar the slaughterman preparing the iron-walled corral on the river bank for the grox.

Gedrik urged his mount on, fresh energy filling him at the thought of Maeren and a home cooked meal. Only the grox seemed reluctant to pick up the pace, but a few shouted oaths and well-placed blows from Faergus's shock-prod soon sorted that out.

Gedrik allowed his gaze to wander as he caught a flash of movement across the glen. He narrowed his eyes and raised a hand to shield his sight from the low, winter sun. Something had moved behind a thick copse of evergreens at the crest of the opposite rise, he could have sworn it. Automatically, he unslung his rifle and worked the bolt, chambering a bullet.

'Trouble?' asked Faergus, noting Gedrik's actions.

'I'm not sure. I thought I saw something,' said Gedrik, pointing to the dark tree-line.

Faergus squinted across the glen, drawing his own weapon, a stubby barrelled shotgun from its shoulder scabbard.

'I don't see–' began Faergus as a dozen, sleek prowed vehicles emerged from the trees. Wickedly angled with blades and curved barbs, the vehicles swept down the hillside towards the settlement, their open decks swarming with warriors. Black bolts spat from weapons mounted on the foredecks of the skimming craft, exploding with shocking violence amongst the buildings of Morten's Reach.

'Emperor's blood!' cursed Gedrik, raking back his spurs, all thought of the herd forgotten as he pushed his horse to the gallop. Without looking, he knew the rest of his men were behind him. Screams and the dull crack of gunfire echoed from below and hot fear gripped his heart at the thought of these terrible aliens in his home.

Heedless of the danger of such a mad gallop, Gedrik pushed his mount hard over the stony ground. Despite the horse's bouncing rush, he saw the alien vehicles begin to spread out, a group detaching from each flank to encircle the settlement while the remainder speared towards the heart of the township. Gedrik saw his people scatter, running for their homes or the sanctuary of the temple as the first skimmers blasted their way into the village, reducing building after building to rubble.

Closer now, the horse careering up to the outskirts of the village, he saw a woman clutching a child – Maeren and Rouari? – dash inside the church as Preacher Mallein was cut down by a flurry of lethal splinters fired from alien rifles. Whooping warriors in close-fitting armour of black and red somersaulted from the decks of their vehicles and sprinted through the township, firing long barrelled guns from the hip.

He shouted in horror as he saw the villagers gunned down where they stood, women and children running towards the church, their bodies jerking in the fusillade. Black smoke boiled skyward as more buildings burned and the screams of the dying cut Gedrik like a knife. Small arms fire blasted from a few windows, felling a number of the alien raiders and he knew the invaders would not take Morten's Reach without a fight.

His wild charge had carried him almost to the river, close enough to see old Gohbar run screaming towards a group of the alien warriors, a flensing halberd raised above his head. The aliens turned and laughingly despatched the slaughterman with a volley from their deadly rifles before disappearing into the smoke of the village's death throes.

Gedrik willed his horse ever faster as he thundered across the river bridge, beside the generator mill he had helped build with his own hands, and passed the convulsing Gohbar. The man's face was purple and distended, his tongue protruding from his mouth like a swollen black snake. The entire town was in flames, the heat and smoke intolerable.

Gedrik emerged into the settlement's square, stopping his horse violently. Two of the attackers' craft hovered before the temple, the alien warriors dragging screaming townspeople towards them. Their faces were exquisitely cruel and pale; humanoid, yet wholly alien. Gedrik stood forward in the stirrups and aimed his rifle at one of the red armoured invaders, placing its angled helm squarely between his sights.

He squeezed the trigger, punching the warrior from its feet, sending blood jetting from its neck. The others scattered and Gedrik yelled out, hammering his spurs into his mount's flanks. The horse leapt forwards and Gedrik fired twice more, pitching another two aliens to the ground before the rifle jammed.

The aliens turned their weapons on him, but the Emperor was with him and their whickering ammunition flew wide of the mark. Then he was amongst them and swung his rifle in a brutal arc, smashing an enemy's skull to shards. He dropped the gun and drew his sword. He caught a flash of red, before a bolt of dark light blasted his horse from under him.

Kicking his feet free of the stirrups, Gedrik jumped from the dying beast and landed lightly before a knot of the alien warriors and lashed out with his shimmering, broad bladed sword.

The first fell with its guts looping around its ankles and the second died with Gedrik's sword lodged deep in its chest. Their alien armour was no protection against the preternatural sharpness of Gedrik's sword, which cut through it with ease. The third thrust with a smoking blade on the end of its rifle and Gedrik dodged backwards, losing his grip on the sword. The alien advanced slowly, emotionless behind its smooth-faced helm.

Gedrik snarled and dived towards his foe. He rolled beneath the alien's weapon, dragging his dagger from his boot and hammering it through the warrior's calf. The alien fell, shrieking horribly, and Gedrik wrenched the knife free, plunging it repeatedly through the alien's chest.

He saw Faergus following him, blasting two of the aliens to bloody rags with a thunderous blast of his shotgun. Faergus wheeled his horse as Gedrik retrieved his sword and shouted to his cousin.

'Get everyone you can inside the temple. We'll try to hold them from there!'

Faergus nodded, but before he could move, a flaring wash of violet fire blasted from one of the alien vehicles and engulfed him. Faergus screamed as the horrifying energies burned the flesh from his frame in moments. Slowly his charred skeleton toppled from the shrieking horse and Gedrik felt his stomach lurch at his cousin's terrible death. The horse toppled, a bloody gouge burned through the beast's flank where the alien weapon had struck.

Gedrik bounded up the steps of the temple, hammering on the door, shouting out Maeren's name. Splinters were blasted from the building as more aliens converged on the centre of the village, firing wildly towards him. He dived from the steps and rolled to his feet. He saw the surviving inhabitants driven before the aliens to their deaths and, watching it all, a slender, white haired figure in jade green armour atop the lead vehicle.

The figure slashed his huge axe impatiently through the air and Gedrik screamed as his people were shot down where they stood. He wanted to plant his dagger in the alien leader's chest, but knew he would be dead before he got close.

He ducked back, knowing that the people inside the temple could not risk opening the doors now and sprinted around the side, hoping that they had not yet barred the vestry.

Gedrik heard the bark of commands being issued and a deep bass rumble of a powerful weapon. He prayed that someone had managed to send a warning to the nearby communities.

The vestry door was just ahead and he cried in relief as he saw it was still ajar. He skidded to a halt before it and gripped the iron handle.

Before he could pull the door open, the temple exploded, roiling orange flames mushrooming skyward and blasting Gedrik from his feet. Pain like nothing he had ever known engulfed him as the blast smashed him into the hillside behind the building. He flopped like a boneless creature, shocked to his very bones by the impact. His skin burned, patches of his anatomy exposed to the elements by the unnatural flames.

He sensed cool snow upon his body, but could feel no pain.

He knew that was bad. Pain meant life.

He rolled his eyes towards the smoking wreckage of the temple, timber columns poking upwards like blackened ribs. He couldn't make out any bodies, but knew that no one could have survived the explosion and grief swamped him.

Maeren, Rouari, Faergus, Mallein, Gohbar... all gone. Everyone was dead. Even him soon.

His breath rattled in his throat as he heard the low humming of the alien vehicles approaching and he tried to push himself upright, but his limbs would not obey him. Dimly he heard the aliens' sing-song voices, elegant but threatening, and tried to spit a defiant curse. But the voices passed him, climbing the Hill of the Metal. He watched as the green-armoured warrior pointed at the hillside and directed his warriors to spread out. He heard their voices chatter excitedly, but could not understand what they said. Was this the reason his community had been slaughtered?

For the Metal?

He heard the whoosh of flames and the hillside lit up, hissing as the snow flashed to steam. The aliens continued to work the flames of their weapons across the hillside, only stopping when a hooded figure wearing shimmering red robes climbed down from the nearest alien vehicle and raised its hand. The figure stepped forward to examine what had been revealed beneath the snow and a low gasp went up from the aliens as the steam dissipated.

Swirling like quicksilver, the exposed strata sparkled in the sunlight, its entire flank shining with a metallic sheen. Beneath the snow, a whole swathe of the hillside was formed from a smooth, silver metal. It rippled and twisted like a liquid where it had run molten under the heat of the flames, undulating like a living thing. Slowly it began reshaping itself, flowing with swirling currents into a smooth, glass-flat surface until it resembled a gigantic mirror. Gedrik watched as the hooded figure dropped to its knees before the metallic hillside and began chanting in rapture, the words rasping and artificial.

Moments passed before Gedrik realised that the figure's words were familiar to him. He did not truly understand them, but recognised the mantra from times he had spent working in the forge with Faergus.

It was a chant in praise of the Omnissiah. The Machine God.

The robed figure rose to face the aliens' leader and threw back his hood. Gedrik saw that most of the figure's face had been replaced by cybernetic implants. A brass-rimmed vox-unit nestled in the centre of his throat below his stitched lips, crackling with hissing white noise. Ribbed copper wiring curled from beneath his robes and plugged into his empty eye sockets, and meshed discs were sutured over the puckered skin where a normal man's ears would be. His flesh was pallid and grey, but despite all the deforming aspects of the figure's loathsome surgery, Gedrik could see that the man was clearly human, and the horror of such treachery made him want to cry with rage.

Cold agony began seeping into his body and he tried to scream, but unconsciousness swept over him and took the pain away.

TWO

THE AIR WAS chill as Captain Uriel Ventris of the Ultramarines made his way up the thousand steps to the chapter master's chambers. He carried his helm in the crook of his arm and his stride was sure, the servo muscles in his suit of power armour making light work of the climb despite the slight limp from the wound he had suffered on Thracia nearly six months ago. The steps wound their way upwards along the side of the valley of Laponis, site of the most magnificent structure on Macragge, the Fortress of Hera, bastion of the Ultramarines.

Constructed from great slabs of marble quarried from the valley sides, the vast body of the structure was a gigantic, columned masterpiece, its surfaces white and pristine. Graceful balconies, golden geodesic domes and slender glass walkways, supported by angled silver-steel buttresses, gave the impression of both great strength and light, airy weightlessness.

The fortress monastery of the Ultramarines was a wonder of engineering, designed by the Chapter's primarch Roboute Guilliman and constructed during the days of the Emperor's Great Crusade ten thousand years ago. Since that time, the warriors of the Ultramarines Chapter of Space Marines had dwelt here.

The fortress sat amidst the tallest peaks in the valley of Laponis, surrounded by highland fir and alongside the mighty Hera's Falls. Glacial water thundered over the falls to the rocks, hundreds of metres below, and glittering rainbows arced across the narrow width of the valley. Uriel stopped and cast his gaze towards the falls, remembering the first time he had seen them and the sense of humbling awe he had felt. A smile touched his lips as he realised he still felt it.

He placed his hand on the pommel of his sword, feeling the weight of responsibility it represented. As he took in the elaborate detailing along the masterfully carved scabbard, his mind returned to the carnage on the rebel world of Thracia where his company commander and trusted friend, Captain Idaeus, had presented him with the magnificent weapon before going to his death.

Tasked with destroying a bridge to prevent the traitorous soldiers of Thracia from flanking an Imperial army, Idaeus's detachment had become trapped in a desperate battle against a huge enemy contingent attempting to force the bridge. For a day and a night, the thirty Ultramarines had held nearly a thousand soldiers at bay until heretical warriors of the Night Lords entered the fray.

Uriel shivered as he remembered his horror at the sight of his comrades crucified upon the hulls of the Night Lords' transports, and knew he would carry their pain-filled faces to his grave. The Traitor Marines had come close to overrunning the Ultramarines' position, but thanks to a desperate gamble by Idaeus, one that had cost him his life, the bridge had been destroyed and the attack defeated.

The feeling of grief at Idaeus's passing rose once more in his chest, but he suppressed it quickly, continuing his journey upwards. It would not do to keep his lord and master waiting.

He climbed higher up the steps, their centres worn smooth by the passage of uncounted footsteps, and briefly wondered exactly how many had made this climb before him. Eventually, he reached the wide esplanade at the summit and turned to look back on the route his climb had taken him.

Snow-capped mountains stretched as far as the eye could see in all directions save one. To the west, the horizon shimmered a deep, azure blue where Uriel's genetically enhanced vision could make out the rocky coastline and the sea, far in the distance. The domed and marble roofed structures of the fortress stepped down before him, each step a citadel in its own right.

He turned on his heel and strode towards the mighty structure before him, passing beneath the many columned portico that led to the chambers of the chapter master of the Ultramarines, Marneus Calgar. Gleaming bronze doors swung open as he approached and two massive warriors of the First Company, clad in holy suits of Terminator armour and carrying long bladed polearms stepped through, their weapons held at the ready.

Even Uriel's armoured physique was dwarfed by the bulk of the Terminators and Uriel nodded respectfully to the veterans as he passed, emerging into the cool air of the vestibule. A servant of the chapter master, dressed in a plain blue tunic, appeared at his side and took his helm, pointing towards the central courtyard of the structure without speaking. Uriel offered his thanks and descended the steps into the sunken courtyard, his gaze sweeping around and taking in every detail. Gold-stitched battle honours hung from the courtyard's balconies above shadowed cloisters, and statues of Ultramarines heroes from ancient times ringed a gurgling fountain set in its marbled centre. Here was Ancient Galatan, a former bearer of the Banner of Macragge, and there was Captain Invictus, hero of the First Company who had died fighting the Great Devourer.

The fountain was carved in the form of a mighty warrior upon a massive steed, his lance raised to the heavens. Konor, the first Battle King of Macragge, his face artfully carved, fully capturing the man's fierce determination to do the best for his people. Another servant arrived, carrying a tray upon which sat an earthenware jug and two silver goblets. He deposited them on the stone bench that encircled the fountain and silently withdrew. Uriel nervously clasped the hilt of his sword, wishing that he felt worthy of its history.

'Konor was a giant amongst men,' said a voice laden with centuries of authority and power. 'He pacified the entire continent before his twenty-first year and set in motion events that enabled the Holy Guilliman to become the man he needed to be.'

Uriel turned to face the Lord of Macragge, Marneus Calgar.

'I remember well from my teachings at the Agiselus Barracks, my lord,' replied Uriel, bowing low.

'A fine institution. Guilliman himself trained there.'

Uriel smiled at Calgar's modesty, knowing full well that the chapter master had trained there also.

The lord of the Ultramarines was a giant of a man, even by the standards of the Space Marines. The lustre of his blue armour barely seemed able to contain his sheer dynamism and power, the bronze two-headed Imperial eagle on his right shoulder shining like polished gold. Black rings hung from the lobe of his right ear and his left eye had been replaced with a flat, gem-like bionic version, fine copper wiring trailing from its mechanics to the back of his skull. Calgar's venerable face appeared to be carved from oak, yet he had lost none of his cunning or insight. Over four hundred years old, his strength and vitality were the envy of warriors half his age.

'Well met, brother,' greeted Calgar, slapping both palms upon the shoulder guards of Uriel's armour. 'It is good to see you, Uriel. My pride and my admiration are yours. The victories on Thracia were honourable.'

Uriel bowed, accepting the compliment as Calgar bade him sit. The master of the Ultramarines lowered himself to the bench and poured two goblets of wine from the earthenware jug, offering one to Uriel. The goblet was absurdly tiny in Calgar's massive gauntlet.

'My thanks,' said Uriel, tasting the cool wine and lapsing into silence.

His aquiline countenance was serious and angular, his eyes the colour of storm clouds. He wore his black hair cropped close to his tanned skull and two gold studs were set into his brow above his left eye. Uriel was a warrior born, hailing from the underground, cavern world of Calth. His feats of bravery had earned him a fearsome reputation among the Ultramarines as a warrior of great strength and passion and his devotion to the Chapter was exemplary.

'Idaeus was a fine warrior and a true friend,' stated Calgar, guessing Uriel's thoughts.

'He was indeed,' agreed Uriel, placing his hand upon the tooled scabbard of the sword. 'He gave me this before he left to destroy the bridge on Thracia. He said it would serve me better than him, yet I do not know if I can do it the honour it demands or that I can replace him as captain of the Fourth Company.'

'He would not have wished you to merely replace him, Uriel. He would have desired you to be your own man, to make the Fourth Company your own.'

Calgar set down his goblet. 'I knew Idaeus well, Captain Ventris,' he began, acknowledging Uriel's new rank, 'and was aware of his more... unorthodox methods. He was a man of great gifts and true heart. You served with him for many years and know as well as I that Idaeus would not have bequeathed the sword he had crafted himself to an unworthy man.'

Calgar set his gaze in stone as he continued, 'Know this, son of Guilliman, the father of our Chapter watches over us always. He knows your soul, your strengths and, aye, even your fears. I share your pain at the loss of Brother-Captain Idaeus, but to dishonour his name with grief is wrong. He gave his life so that his battle-brothers would live and the enemies of the Emperor would be defeated. A warrior can ask for no better death than that. Captain Idaeus was the senior officer, and you were duty bound to follow his orders when they were given. The chain of command must not be broken or we are nothing. Discipline and order are everything on the battlefield and the army that lives by that credo will always triumph. Remember that.'

'I will,' affirmed Uriel.

'Do you understand all that I have said?'

'I do.'

'Then we will speak of Idaeus no more today, and instead speak of battles yet to come, for I have need of the Fourth Company.'

Uriel set down his goblet, anticipation surging through his body at the thought of serving the Emperor once more.

'We stand ready to fight, Lord Calgar,' stated Uriel proudly.

Calgar smiled, having fully expected Uriel's answer. 'I know you do, Uriel. There is a world some weeks distant from Ultramar that requires the force of your presence. It is named Pavonis and suffers the depredations of piratical activity from the accursed eldar.'

Uriel's expression hardened in contempt at the mention of the eldar, decadent aliens who refused to recognise the divine right of humanity to rule the galaxy. Uriel had fought the eldar before, yet knew little of their blasphemous alien ways. The indoctrinal sermons of the chaplains had taught him that they were arrogant beyond words and could not be trusted, which was enough for Uriel.

'We shall hunt them down and destroy them like the alien traitors they are, my lord.'

Calgar poured more wine and raised his goblet, saying, 'I drink to the battles and victories to come, Uriel, but there is yet another reason you must journey to Pavonis.'

'And that is?'

'The Administratum is much vexed with the planetary governor of Pavonis. They wish to take issue with her regarding her failure to deliver the right and proper tithes of an Imperial world. You are to transport an adept of the Administratum to Pavonis and ensure that he safely conveys their displeasure. I make his safety your personal responsibility, captain.'

Uriel nodded, unsure as to why this particular quill-pusher was to be accorded such protection, but dismissed the thought as irrelevant. That Lord Calgar had entrusted the man's safety to Uriel was enough of a reason to see that he came to no harm.

'Lord Admiral Tiberius has the *Vae Victus* ready for departure and your charge will be aboard on the morrow with more detailed information. I expect you and your men to be ready to depart before the next sunset.'

'It shall be so, Lord Calgar,' assured Uriel, truly honoured at the trust the master of the Ultramarines had bestowed upon him. He knew that he would die before he would allow that trust to be misplaced.

'Go then, Captain Ventris,' ordered Calgar, standing and saluting Uriel. 'Make your obeisance at the Shrine of the Primarch, then ready your men.'

Calgar offered his hand and Uriel stood, the two warriors sealing their oath of loyalty and courage to one another in the warrior's grip, wrist to wrist.

Uriel bowed deeply to Calgar and marched with renewed purpose from the courtyard. Calgar watched his newest captain pass through the bronze doors and into the evening sun, wishing he could have told him more. He picked up his goblet and drained its contents in a single gulp.

His enhanced hearing picked up the rustle of cloth behind him and he knew without turning who stood behind him in the shadow of the cloisters.

'That one carries a great responsibility now, Lord Calgar. There is much at stake here. Will he prevail?' asked the newcomer.

'Yes,' said Marneus Calgar softly, 'I believe he will.'

URIEL MARCHED ALONG the golden processional, between throngs of robed pilgrims, oblivious to the stares of wonder his presence garnered. Head and shoulders above those who had come to witness one of the most holy places in the Imperium, Uriel felt his heartbeats increase as he neared the centre of the Temple of Correction.

Like much of the Fortress of Hera, the temple was said to have been designed by Roboute Guilliman, its proportions defying the mind with the scale of its construction and the grandeur of its ornamentation. Multi-coloured radiance spilled from a massive archway ahead of him, light from the low evening sun shimmering through the stained-glass dome in gold, azure, ruby and emerald rays. The multitude of pilgrims parted before him, his status as one of the Emperor's chosen granting him hushed precedence over their desire to lay their eyes on the blessed Guilliman.

As always, his breath caught in his throat as he emerged into the awesome, humbling presence of the primarch and he cast his eyes downwards, unworthy of allowing his gaze to dwell upon his Chapter's founding father for too long.

The massively armoured form of Roboute Guilliman, primarch of the Ultramarines, sat upon his enormous marble throne, entombed these last ten thousand years within the luminous sepulchre of a stasis field. Gathered around the primarch's feet were his weapons and shield and, behind him, the first banner of Macragge, said to have been woven from the shorn hair of a thousand martyrs and touched by the Emperor's own hand. Uriel felt a fierce pride swell within his breast that his veins ran with the blood of this mightiest of heroes and warriors stretching back to the days of the Great Crusade. He dropped to one knee, overwhelmed by the honour his very existence brought him.

Even in death the primarch's features spoke of great courage and fortitude and were it not for the glistening wound upon his neck, Uriel would have sworn that the giant warrior could stand and march from the temple. He felt a cold, steel rage as his eyes fixed upon the scarlet wound. Beads of blood, like tiny, glittering rubies, were held immobile below the primarch's neck, suspended in mid air by the static time stream within. Guilliman's life had been cut short by the envenomed blade of the traitor primarch, Fulgrim of the Emperor's Children, his works undone, his legacy unfulfilled and in that lay the greatest tragedy of Guilliman's death.

Uriel knew that there were those who believed that the primarch's wounds were slowly healing and claimed he would one day arise from his throne. How such an impossibility could occur within the time-sealed bubble of a stasis field was a matter such prophets ascribed to the infallible will of the Emperor.

He could sense the presence of the silent masses behind him, aware of the holy esteem they held him in, and feeling unworthy of such reverence. He knew such thoughts marked him out from the majority of his brethren, but Idaeus had taught him the value of looking beyond the boundaries of conventional thinking.

The ordinary, faceless masses of humanity were the true heroes of the galaxy. The men and women of the Imperium who stood, naked and vulnerable, before the horrors of an infinite universe and refused to bow before its sheer incomprehensible vastness. It was for them that he existed. His purpose in life was to protect them so that they would go onto fulfil humankind's manifest destiny of ruling the galaxy in the name of the Emperor. Most would have travelled for many months or years across thousands of light years and sacrificed everything they owned to be here, but every one of them kept a respectful distance as one of the sons of Guilliman honoured his primarch.

Uriel dropped to one knee, and whispered, 'Forgive me, my lord, but I come before you to seek your blessing. I lead my men to war and ask that you might grant me the courage and wisdom to lead them through the fires of battle with honour.'

Uriel closed his eyes, allowing his surroundings to infuse him with its serenity and majesty. He took a deep breath, the scent of faded battle honours hung around the circumference of the high, domed ceiling filling his senses.

Sensations flooded through him as the neuroglottis situated at the back of his mouth assessed the chemical content of the air, redolent with the scent of alien worlds and crusades fought in ancient times. Memories came tumbling over themselves, one in particular reaching up from over a century ago. He had just turned fourteen, barely a month since he had first been brought to the Temple of Hera.

URIEL HAD BEEN racing uphill, his breath burning in his chest as his long stride carried him swiftly through the sprawling evergreen forests of the high mountain. Already his fitness was greater than most of the other recruits chosen by the Ultramarines and only Learchus was ahead of him now. Uriel was gaining on him though. Working the cavern farms of Calth and training at the Agiselus Barracks had kept his body lean and hard and he knew he had the stamina to catch Learchus before the top.

Only Cleander was close behind him, but Uriel could not spare a glance to see how near Learchus's friend was. Uriel was closing the gap on Learchus and only a few strides separated them now. He grinned as he slowly reeled in the larger youth, all his energy focussed on drawing past the race leader. Cleander's footfalls were close, but Uriel was too intent on catching Learchus.

Learchus threw a quick glance over his shoulder, worry plain on his exhausted features, and Uriel exulted. He could see the knowledge of defeat writ large on Learchus's features and pushed himself harder, arms pistoning at his sides as he drew level.

Uriel cut to the right to overtake Learchus, fighting through the burning pain in his thighs as he pushed himself to a sprint. Learchus glanced

round as he caught sight of Uriel in his peripheral vision and slashed back
with his elbow.

Blood sprayed from Uriel's nose and his eyes filled with water. Blinding
light sunburst before him and he stumbled forwards, hands flying to his
face. He felt hands seize his shoulders from behind and yelled as Cleander
pushed him from the track. He fell hard, cracking his broken nose on the
hard packed earth. He heard laughter and a terrible rage engulfed him.

Uriel groggily tried to push himself to his feet, wiping blood from his
nose and jaw, but dizziness swamped him and he collapsed. Through the
haze of pain he could make out other recruits passing him, loping after his
attackers to the top of the mountain.

A hand gripped his bare arm and hauled him to his feet. Uriel blinked
away tears of pain, seeing his squad mate Pasanius, and gripped his
friend's shoulders as he steadied himself.

'Let me guess,' said Pasanius breathlessly. 'Learchus?'

Uriel could only nod, glaring up the side of the mountain. Learchus was
far ahead now, nearly at the top.

'Are you fit to run?'

'Aye, I'll run,' snarled Uriel. 'Straight to the top and punch that cheating
animal's face in!'

He shrugged off Pasanius's hand and set off once more, each thud of his
bare feet against the ground lancing hot spikes of pain through his face.
Blood ran freely from his nose and he welcomed the bitter, metallic taste
in his mouth as his rage built. He passed runners, barely even noticing
them, his head filling with thoughts of vengeance.

Uriel crested the top of the peak and stumbled to the cairn at the centre
of the small, rocky plateau. He touched the column of boulders and
turned to where Learchus and Cleander sat. Jagged black mountains
stretched as far as the eye could see, but Uriel paid the spectacular view no
heed as he marched towards the lounging Learchus, who watched him
approach with a wary eye. Cleander stood to move between the pair as
Uriel approached, and he caught a flash of annoyance cross Learchus's
face. Cleander was younger than Uriel, but half a head taller, with great
slabs of muscle across his sweat-streaked chest.

Uriel stopped and met the larger boy's stare, then punched him hard in
the solar plexus with the heel of his palm.

Cleander sagged and Uriel followed with powerful uppercuts to his face
and neck, finishing with a thunderous right cross. The larger boy dropped
and Uriel stepped over his moaning form towards Learchus. The boy rose,
backing off and assuming a boxer's position, fists raised before him.

'You cheated,' accused Uriel, also raising his fists.

Learchus shrugged. 'I won the race,' he pointed out.

'And you think that is all that matters? The winning?'

'Of course,' sneered Learchus. 'You are a fool to believe anything else.'

The pair circled, feinting with jabs as the last of the recruits reached the mountaintop.

'Did you learn nothing at Agiselus, Learchus? A victory counts for nothing if you do not retain your honour.'

'Don't presume to lecture me, farm boy!' snapped Learchus. 'You should not even have been there. I at least earned my place. I was not granted one by virtue of my ancestry.'

'I also won my place fairly, Learchus,' replied Uriel darkly. 'Lucian had nothing to do with my choosing.'

'Horse dung! I know the truth of the matter,' hissed Learchus, darting in and hammering a blow to Uriel's temple. Uriel rolled with the punch, reaching up to wrap both hands around his opponent's wrist. He spun, pulling Learchus off balance and dropped to one knee, throwing him over his shoulder.

Learchus yelled as he flew through the air and grunted as the breath was driven from his lungs on impact with the ground. Uriel wrenched the boy's arm backwards and felt the wrist break, hearing the splintered ends of snapped bone grinding together over Learchus's scream of pain.

Uriel released his grip and walked back to the cairn. He slumped against it, his exhaustion and pain returning with a vengeance.

A group of boys moved to help the fallen recruits and Uriel was suddenly filled with shame. Learchus was well liked and Uriel would gain nothing from besting him.

But he could not take back the deed and must endure the consequences. A shadow fell across him and he saw Pasanius standing over him, his face reproachful.

His friend sat beside him and said, 'You should not have done that, Uriel.'

'I know. I wish it could be undone, I truly do.'

'Learchus will hate you for this.'

'You think I should apologise?'

'Yes, but not now. You have publicly shamed him and he will refuse such an apology just now. Speak to him when we return to the fortress and his wrist has been set by the apothecaries.'

'I will do as you say, my friend. It was foolish – I was blinded by my rage.'

'At least you realise it was foolish. Perhaps they did get something through that thick farmer's skull of yours at Agiselus after all,' smiled Pasanius.

'Careful,' warned Uriel, 'or I might have to knock you flat as well.'

'You could try, farm boy, but it will take more than you've got to put me down.'

Uriel laughed, knowing Pasanius was right. His friend was a giant of a lad. Though he had just entered his fifteenth summer, Pasanius was already taller than most fully-grown men. His muscles stood out like steel cables against his tanned skin and none of the other recruits had yet bested him in feats of strength.

'Come,' said Pasanius, pushing himself to his feet, 'we should get moving. You know Clausel seals the gate at sunset and I for one do not relish yet another night on the mountains.'

Uriel nodded and stood, groaning as his muscles protested at the sudden activity. He realised he had neglected to stretch them after completing the run and cursed himself for a fool once more.

The recruits set off with Pasanius at their head, taking it in turns to help the chalk-white Learchus when he stumbled with delayed shock and pain. The boy's wrist had swollen to twice its usual size, the flesh a grotesque purple, and several times during the journey down the mountain he almost fainted. Uriel offered to help once, but the scowls of his fellow recruits had dissuaded him from offering again.

When they had reached the Fortress of Hera, Learchus had told the apothecaries he had broken his wrist in a fall and in the days that followed Uriel found a gulf developing between him and the others. The realisation of its existence was not enough to prevent it widening, however, and only Pasanius remained a true friend to Uriel in the years that followed.

IN THE TEMPLE of Correction, Uriel opened his eyes, shaking off the last vestiges of the memory and rose to his full height. He rarely thought back to his days as a cadet and was surprised he had done so today. Perhaps it was an omen, a message gifted to him by the blessed primarch. He raised his eyes and looked into he face of Roboute Guilliman, searching for a sign of what it might mean, but the dead primarch remained immobile on his throne.

Uriel felt the weight of his command heavy on his shoulders and strode across the chamber to stand before a bronze-edged slab on the curved inner wall of the temple's inner sanctum. The inner circumference of the temple was lined with enormous sheets of smooth black marble, each veined with lines of jade. Carved into the slabs with gold lettering were the names of every Ultramarine who had fallen in battle during their ten millennia history. Thousands upon thousands of names surrounded the primarch and Uriel wondered how many more would be added to it before he returned to this holy place. Would his own be one of them?

His eyes scanned down the slab before him, dedicated to the hundred warriors of the First Company who had fought against the alien horror of the tyranids beneath Macragge's northern defence fortresses, some two hundred and fifty years ago.

Uriel's eyes came to rest at a single name, carved just below the dedication to the heroic Captain Invictus of the First Company.

Veteran Sergeant Lucian Ventris.

Uriel's finger traced the carved outline of his ancestor, proud to bear his name. His accidental relationship to a hero of the Chapter had granted Uriel the right to be trained at the prestigious Agiselus Barracks, but it had been his own skill and determination not to fail that had earned his selection by the Ultramarines.

Uriel bowed, honouring his ancestor, then saluted smartly before turning on his heel and marching from the temple.

He had a company to make ready for war.

℧
THREE

THE CLAMOUR OF hundreds of shouting voices was deafening. Judge Virgil Ortega of the Pavonis Adeptus Arbites smashed his shield into the face of a screaming man in heavy overalls and brought his shock maul round in a brutal arc. Bodies pressed all around him as he struck left and right. Hands grabbed at him as he and his squad pushed back the heaving crowd. A screaming man grasped at his black uniform and he brought his shock maul down hard, shattering the bone. Screams of pain and rage tore the air, but Ortega had only one priority, to prevent the rioters from reaching Governor Shonai. Already he could see that one of her party was down.

Enforcer Sharben fought beside him, ducking the clumsy swipe of a massive wrench and slamming her maul into her attacker's belly. Even amid the chaos of the riot, Ortega was impressed. For a rookie she was handling herself like a ten-year veteran. All around them, black-armoured judges clubbed screaming rioters back from the governor's podium.

This section of the plaza was a battlefield, as the angry workers of Brandon Gate lashed out. Against all reason and advice Governor Mykola Shonai and the senior cartel members had chosen to address a branch of the Workers' Collective in public, to reassure them that the so-called 'tithe tax' was a purely temporary measure.

Inevitably, tempers had flared and insults flew. Things quickly escalated as bottles and rocks were thrown. His men had taken most of this on their shields when, suddenly, a shot rang out, taking one of his squad in the leg.

Then everything seemed to happen at once. More shots were fired and Ortega saw one of the cartel men collapse, the back of his head blown off.

He had slumped forwards, carrying the governor to the ground. Ortega didn't know if she'd been hit or where the shots had come from and couldn't spare the time to find out. All that mattered was that some bastard out there with a firearm had upped the stakes. Well if that was the way these people wanted to play this game, then Virgil Ortega was only too willing.

The governor's personal guard were backing away from the epicentre of the riot, carrying her and the cartel members away from the violence, but Ortega saw they were heading in the wrong direction. They were falling back to the gates of the Imperial palace, but the damn fools couldn't see that more rioters blocked the way. Elements of the crowd had swept around their flanks to envelop the podium. The Adeptus Arbites were holding the crowd back, and the water cannons of the crowd control vehicles were helping, but their line was bending and it was only a matter of time until the press of bodies became too great to hold. The governor's guard were heading away from the protection of the Adeptus Arbites and, as far as Ortega could see, he and his men were all that would get the governor out of this mess alive.

'Sharben!' he shouted. 'Take one man and get a crowd suppression vehicle. Pick up the governor and get her to the palace. Hurry!'

Sharben nodded, her face invisible behind the mirrored visor of her helmet, and struck out in the direction of their vehicles, taking a member of his squad with her. The remaining judges in Ortega's line backed steadily away from the crowd, the closest rioters unwilling to approach too close for fear of the shock mauls.

This current disturbance was pretty bad, but Ortega had contained riots far worse than this and could see that the waves of violence hadn't spread out too far. Those in the centre of the mass of people had no one to vent their anger upon and simply pressed forwards. If Sharben could get to the governor quick enough then this situation could still be saved.

Ortega looked along the line for Sergeant Collix and waved him over.

'Collix, I want you to hold the line here. Sharben and I are going to try to get the governor out of here.'

'Aye, sir!' shouted Collix, returning to his position.

Ortega turned and withdrew from the line, hooking his shock maul to his belt. He was unsure of Collix, but he was the most senior judge left in the line. Ortega reached up pulled down his vox-bead and patched into the governor's security net.

'This is Judge Ortega to Security Detail Primus. Remain where you are. You are heading into more trouble. We will be with you shortly. I repeat, remain where you are.'

Ortega pushed the vox-bead back inside his helmet without waiting for an acknowledgement and set off towards the governor.

He heard Collix shouting orders behind him, but couldn't make out the words. He skidded to a halt as he heard the unmistakable sound of shotgun slides being racked and turned. Cold fear gripped him. The entire line of judges had their weapons aimed into the crowd. Emperor's Throne, they were going to fire on civilians!

Ortega shouted, 'Sling those damned weapons!' but he was too late and the judges fired, point blank, into the crowd. The line of rioters convulsed, dozens of people falling dead. Gunsmoke obscured the casualties, but Ortega swore as he heard the primal shout of anger from those who had survived the shootings. The crowd surged forward and the shotguns fired again. More people fell, but there were thousands more pushing behind them. Men and women were crushed underfoot as they tripped over the bodies of the fallen and were trampled into the cobbles. The screams of the crowd turned from anger to panic.

In unison, the judges took a step forward, shotguns carried at their hips. They fired another two volleys into the crowd before Ortega reached them and screamed, 'Hold your fire! Sling your weapons! That's an order dammit! Do it now!'

The judges brought their weapons back to shoulder guard as the smoke cleared before them. Hundreds of bodies littered the ground, their bodies mangled by close range shotgun blasts. Blood streaked the cobbles of the plaza and the moans of the dying were barely audible over the screams of the panicking crowd. The rioters had fallen back for now, but Ortega realised they would be out for blood any second.

'Fall back!' yelled Ortega. 'Everybody back to the Rhinos. We're leaving – now!'

Ortega began hauling his men back from the battle line, some of them only now appreciating the carnage their weapons had wreaked. The stink of cordite, blood and sweat filled the air and Ortega knew he only had moments before everything went to hell. The judges backed quickly towards the boxy black forms of the Rhino armoured personnel carriers, their powerful engines idling throatily. Several had been modified to mount a heavy-duty water cannon on the cupola and Ortega shouted at them to fire as a swelling roar of anger rose from the crowd.

The crowd lurched towards the judges, hungry for vengeance. The water cannon opened up, firing powerful jets into the crowd and knocking the nearest people to the ground.

But there were too many rioters and not enough cannons. The wrathful mob descended upon the judges, clubbing at them with fists and iron-shod boots. Disciplined shield drill and accurate strikes with shock mauls cleared the Arbites enough space and Ortega hauled open the armoured side door of the nearest Rhino APC, hustling his men inside. He jumped onto the running boards and ducked his head inside the armoured transport.

'We're clear! Get us the hell out of here!' he shouted to the driver. 'Find where Sharben is and link with her, she'll have the governor.'

The Rhinos began reversing, powering away from the surging crowd as the skilled drivers angled them towards the Arbites precinct. Ortega searched for Sharben and cursed as he saw the top of the crowd suppression vehicle she had commandeered in flames, not far from the armoured gate of the precinct house. The judge manning the water cannon lay sprawled over the weapon, his body ablaze. Ortega saw the left track hanging uselessly from the cogged wheel as rioters surrounded the vehicle, pressing in on its precious cargo. They rocked it from side to side in an attempt to tip it over.

Ortega slammed his shock maul on the roof of the Rhino and pointed towards Sharben's immobilised vehicle.

'Bring us alongside and stop beside it. Then get ready to go when I give you the word!'

The driver nodded his understanding and slewed the Rhino towards the stricken vehicle. Ortega hung on for dear life as the Rhino swung wildly from side to side.

'Sharben, come in,' called Ortega as they drew near the blazing tank.

'Sharben here, sir,' she replied over the vox, the strain evident in her voice. 'If you're anywhere near, we'd appreciate a ride out of here.'

'We're almost on top of you, Sharben. Hold on. Do you have the governor?'

'Affirmative.'

'Well done. Be ready for us.'

JUDGE JENNA SHARBEN felt the sweat run down her back inside her black leather armour. The heat inside the Rhino was becoming unbearable and it was only a matter of time until they baked to death. The vehicle was shaking violently and her civilian passengers were on the verge of hysteria. She muttered a quick thanks to the Emperor that Virgil Ortega was on his way. He might be a hard, humourless bastard, but he never left an officer behind.

'Judge!' snapped a man in a black suit whose name she didn't know. 'What are your plans? We must get to safety. I demand you facilitate our escape from this intolerable situation.'

She noticed a Vergen cartel pin on the man's lapel and bit back an angry retort. She took a deep breath and said, 'My superior officer is on his way with another vehicle and we will be underway soon.'

'I am sure we are quite safe, Leotas–' started Governor Mykola Shonai as the side of the vehicle tipped sickeningly upwards. Jenna realised the Rhino was finally going to tip onto its side.

'Brace yourselves!' she yelled, grabbing onto a stanchion and locking her legs around the crew bench. 'We're going over!'

The Rhino slammed onto its side with teeth-loosening force and an almighty crash. Jenna grabbed Governor Shonai's robes as she fell flailing towards the side of the vehicle and hauled her upright. She heard a muffled cheer from outside and repeated impacts on the hull. None were likely to penetrate, but the noise was deafening. The man the governor had referred to as Leotas lay unmoving, blood pouring from a deep laceration on the back of his head. The other occupants of the Rhino appeared almost as battered.

She released her grip on the stanchion and ripped a medi-pack from the crew locker, squatting beside the unmoving Leotas. She immediately saw she was wasting her time; the man's neck was broken and his skull fractured. The white gleam of bone was visible through his blood-matted hair.

'Will... will he be alright?' asked Governor Shonai, her voice quavering.

'No,' said Jenna bluntly. 'He's dead.'

Shonai's eyes widened and her hands flew to her mouth in shock.

Jenna dropped the medi-kit as she heard the rumble of a powerful engine and the crack of gunfire from outside. A powerful impact struck the immobilised Rhino and she steadied herself on the side of the interior as armoured boots thumped onto the wall that was now the roof above her.

The vox-bead in her ear crackled and she heard the clipped tones of Virgil Ortega.

'Sharben! Open the crew door, we're right next to you.'

Jenna clambered up the crew bench and spun the locking wheel, disengaging the door clamps. The door was wrenched open and weak sunlight filtered into the smoky crew compartment.

Ortega slung his maul and shouted, 'Give me the governor!'

Jenna grabbed a handful of Shonai's robes and dragged her to her feet. The governor cried out at Sharben's roughness, but allowed herself to be pushed towards the exit. Ortega took Shonai's outstretched hands and lifted her clear. He passed her onto another judge who waited at the crew door of his own Rhino, reaching back into Sharben's vehicle. The burst of fire from his Rhino's bolters had scattered the crowd from the damaged vehicle, but it was only a temporary respite.

'Come on!' he barked. 'Give me the rest. Hurry up, dammit!'

One by one, Jenna lifted the other passengers towards safety and Ortega transferred them to his own vehicle. Repeated bursts of bolter fire over the heads of the crowd kept them back as the rescue continued. When everyone was clear Jenna Sharben climbed out in time to see the Rhino carrying the governor rumbling through the gates of the Imperial palace.

'Time for us to go, Sharben,' observed Ortega as the mob closed in, howling as they realised they had been cheated of their quarry.

'Yes, sir,' agreed Sharben as they jumped to the ground and began sprinting towards the safety of the nearby Arbites precinct. Armoured pillboxes mounting more powerful water cannons hosed down their pursuers, breaking limbs with their force. More screams sounded behind the two judges, but they were clear of danger and pounded breathlessly into the defensive compound of their precinct.

The remainder of Ortega's Rhinos were waiting in the centre of the courtyard, surrounded by battered judges.

Jenna Sharben removed her dented helmet and ran a gloved hand through her short, black hair and over her sweat-streaked face as Ortega marched towards the sullen judges. She followed as Ortega dragged off his helmet and advanced towards Collix.

Virgil Ortega was a fireplug of a man, short and stocky, but who radiated power and authority. Sweat gleamed on his bald head and dripped from his trimmed beard.

'Sergeant! What the hell just happened out there? Did I give you an order to open fire?'

'No, sir,' replied Collix smoothly. 'But in the circumstances I felt that such an order would have been given had you been present in the battle line.'

'Then you show remarkably poor understanding of your superior officer, sergeant.'

'Perhaps,' admitted Collix.

'There's no perhaps about it, Collix. Our purpose is to enforce the laws of the Emperor, not massacre His subjects. Is that clear?'

'The crowd were in contravention of those laws, sir,'

'Don't play the innocent with me, Collix. I'll be keeping an eye on you'

Ortega glared at Collix for long seconds before stalking towards the precinct house. Without turning, he shouted, 'Good work out there, Judge Sharben.'

Jenna smiled at this rare praise and watched as Ortega vanished within the precinct.

She sat on the running boards of one of the Rhinos and laid her head back, letting the events of the morning drain from her. She felt pleased at her conduct today. She knew she had fought and behaved like a veteran member of the Adeptus Arbites, rather than the fresh-out-of-training, junior officer she actually was. Methodically, she reviewed her actions and could find no fault with her performance.

Yes, she had done well.

'YOU SHOULD ALLOW the palace surgeon to look at that cut, ma'am,' observed Almerz Chanda, pressing lightly at a swelling purple bruise on his own tonsured skull. He too had been pulled from the Arbites Rhino, but had only sustained a bump to the head. The gash on the governor's head was not deep and had been covered with synth-flesh by an Arbites corpsman, but this day had seen her nephew take a bullet for her and a close friend die in the chaos of the riot.

'Governor?' he said, when she did not reply.

'I'm fine,' she snapped, more brusquely than she had intended. She turned from the armoured glass of the window and smiled weakly at her chief advisor. 'I'm sorry, Almerz. I'm just...'

'No need to apologise ma'am, it has been a sad and terrible day for you.'

'Yes,' agreed Shonai. 'Poor Dumak and Leotas, they died before their time.'

Chanda nodded. 'We all feel their loss keenly, ma'am.'

'That bullet should have hit me,' said the governor. 'Dumak was only twenty. I planned to name him as my successor when he came of age next year.'

'He gave his life to save yours,' pointed out Chanda. 'He did his duty as a loyal member of the Shonai cartel. He will be remembered as a hero.'

'And Leotas, how will he be remembered?'

'As a dear friend who was taken from us by the Emperor for His own purpose.'

Governor Mykola Shonai smiled her thanks and said, 'You are a true friend, Almerz, but I wish to be alone for a moment.'

'As you wish, ma'am,' nodded Chanda, closing the door behind him as he left the governor of Pavonis to her thoughts.

Mykola Shonai turned back to the window as she felt her iron composure slipping. Her friend and ally, Leotas Vergen, was dead. Gone. Just like that. Only this morning he had been talking animatedly of his daughter's forthcoming marriage to the Taloun's son, and the dawn of a new age of co-operation between the cartels, but now he was dead and the Vergen cartel without a leader. Much as she hated to admit it, she realised his dream of co-operation would probably die with him.

No doubt the Taloun would be pleased, plotting even now to move the marriage forward in order to establish his son as de-facto head of the Vergen cartel. Of course the Vergen cartel would now do everything possible to block the union, but Vergen's daughter was known for her headstrong nature and the Emperor alone knew the ramifications of Leotas's untimely death. Shonai felt sorry that the young couple's relationship was now a political weapon, but that was politics on Pavonis, she reflected sourly.

She dismissed the couple's doomed relationship from her thoughts and looked out over Liberation Square.

By the Emperor, it was a mess. Rain had begun to fall, washing the pools of blood and detritus of battle into the sewers, but Shonai knew that her troubles would not be so easily banished. Bodies lay strewn across the cobbles, weeping groups of people gathered around fallen friends and loved ones. How could a day that had started with such noble intentions have gone so horrifyingly wrong?

Pavonis had been a peaceful planet a few years ago, largely untroubled by the strife that afflicted the rest of the galaxy. The tithes had been paid on time and periodically the young men of Pavonis would gather for the mustering of the Emperor's armies. In all respects Pavonis had been a model Imperial world. The people worked hard and were honoured for their labours. Riots were things that happened on other worlds.

But oh, how times had changed.

Crumpled parchments littered her desk, each one telling of similar scenes across the globe. In Altemaxa the workers had stormed the Office of Imperial Outlays and gutted the building with fire. Rioters at Praxedes had prevented the crew of an off-world trader from manning their vessel and looted the man's cargo. A petition from the trader for compensation was on its way to her office even now.

There had been yet another fire-bombing by the Church of Ancient Ways, killing thirty people and irreparably damaging the production facil- ities of two of the Vergen's manufactorum. A member of the Abrogas cartel had been stabbed in one of the Jotusburg ghettos and was lucky to have survived, though what he had been doing there in the first place wasn't clear. And near Caernus IV, yet another supply ship had been ambushed by the eldar pirates that had been plaguing Pavonis for the last six years. It had been carrying material and goods that were supposed to go some way to reducing the huge debt Pavonis owed to the Imperium in late tithes.

She felt the burden of each failure crushing her with their vast weight and wondered what she could have done differently. She had tried her best to meet the tithes required by the Administratum, but there was simply nothing more she could squeeze from Pavonis.

Her production facilities were stretched to the limit and few of those goods they could produce were actually getting through. Her 'tithe tax' had been an attempt to make up the deficit until the crisis could be resolved, but it had the people rioting in almost every major city. She had tried to explain the situation to her people, to show them that the hardships they were enduring were for the ultimate good of Pavonis, but no matter which way she turned, there seemed to be no escape from the inevitable down- ward spiral of events.

And here, in her own capital, she had been shot at. She still couldn't quite believe it. When the first shot had echoed shockingly around the plaza, Dumak had rushed to her side and tried to pull her to safety. She closed her eyes, trying to will the image of his exploding face from her mind. He'd fallen and carried her to the floor of the podium, his blood and brains leaking over her as he spasmed in death.

Mykola Shonai had cleaned her hair and sent her robes of office to have his death washed from them. She had changed into fresh clothes of plain blue, but imagined she could still feel the stickiness of her nephew's blood on her skin. Her heart ached for her younger sister, remembering that she had been so proud when Mykola had confided in her that Dumak would one day take over the Shonai cartel from her.

She saw priests and local apothecaries moving through the crowd, tending to the wounded or administering the Emperor's Absolution to the dead. She offered a prayer for the souls of the departed and took a deep breath. She was a planetary governor of the Imperium and she had to keep control. But it was so difficult when everything kept slipping from her grasp, no matter how hard she tried to hold on.

She slumped in the green leather upholstered chair behind her desk, scanning the dozens of reports of violence and unrest. She gathered them together and placed them in a pile to one side. She would deal with them later. She had more pressing business to take care of: her political survival.

She smoothed down her damp grey hair and rubbed the corners of her pale green eyes dry. Her face was careworn and lined and Mykola Shonai felt every one of her sixty-two years bearing down heavily upon her. It did not matter that she had suffered loss today. She was the governor of an Imperial world and that duty did not pause for bereavement.

She pulled a long, velvet rope that hung beside her desk and stared at the sculpted bust of her great, great grandfather, Forlanus Shonai, that sat next to the fireplace. Forlanus had set up the Shonai cartel three centuries ago, building it from a single, small manufactorum to one of the most powerful industrial cartels on Pavonis. How would old Forlanus have dealt with this, she wondered?

She was spared thinking of an answer by a polite knock at the door and the arrival of four men in black suits, each with a Shonai cartel pin in their lapels. Almerz Chanda was at their head and he bowed to the governor as they filed in. Their expressions were dark and gloomy and Shonai could well understand their unhappiness.

'Well, gentlemen,' began Shonai, before they could offer her any banal platitudes regarding her loss. 'How bad is it?'

The men appeared uncomfortable with the question, none of them willing to volunteer an answer.

Governor Shonai snapped, 'When I ask a question I expect an answer.'

'This riot certainly wasn't the worst yet, ma'am,' said the newest member of her advisory staff. His name was Morten Bauer and his thin face was earnest and full of youthful exuberance. Shonai felt a stab of maternal protectiveness towards the young man and wondered if he even realised that he had joined a staff on the brink of collapse.

'Give me numbers, Morten. How many dead?' asked Shonai.

Bauer consulted his data slate. 'It's too early for firm numbers, ma'am, but it looks like over three hundred dead and perhaps twice that wounded. I'm just getting some figures in from the Arbites and it seems that two judges were killed as well.'

'That's not as bad as at Altemaxa,' pointed out an older man whose body had patently seen better days. 'The judges there lost an entire squad trying to hold the rioters.'

The speaker's name was Miklas Iacovone and he managed the governor's public relations. It had been his idea to address the Workers' Collective, and he was desperately attempting to put a favourable spin on today's events. Even as the words left his thick lips, he knew they were a mistake.

'Miklas, you are a fool if you think that we can come out of this smelling of roses by criticising another city's law enforcement officers,' snapped Almerz Chanda. 'We don't do negative campaigning.'

'I'm only trying to emphasise the upside,' protested Iacovone.

'There is no "upside" to this, Miklas. Get used to it,' said Chanda.

Governor Shonai laced her fingers together and sat back in her chair. Personally she felt Iacovone's idea had merit, though did not wish to contradict her chief advisor in public. She addressed the fourth man in her advisory staff, Leland Corteo.

'Leland, how badly will this affect us in the senate? Truthfully?'

The governor's political analyst let out a sigh and pulled at his long, grey beard. He removed a tobacco pipe from his embroidered waistcoat and raised his bushy eyebrows. Shonai nodded and Corteo lit the pipe with a pewter lighter before answering.

'Well, governor, the way I perceive it,' he began, taking a long, thoughtful draw on his pipe. 'If events continue in this way, it is only a matter of time until the other cartels call for a vote of no confidence.'

'They wouldn't dare,' said Morten Bauer. 'Who would propose such a motion?'

'Don't be foolish, dear boy. Take your pick: Taloun, de Valtos, Honan. Any one of them has a large enough base of support to survive a backlash even if the motion fails.'

'We're barely hanging on as it is,' agreed Miklas Iacovone. 'Our majority is only held together with promises of co-operation and trade agreements we've made to the smaller cartels. But we have to assume the big guns are lobbying them to renege on their agreements.'

'Spineless cowards!' spat Bauer.

'Opportunists, more like,' said Corteo. 'Who can blame them after all? We did the same thing ten years ago when we aligned ourselves with the Vergen and ousted the Taloun.'

'That was completely different,' said Bauer defensively.

'Oh come on now, boy. It's exactly the same. It's politics; the names may change, but the game remains the same.'

'Game?' spluttered Bauer.

'Gentlemen,' interrupted Chanda, before the smirking Corteo could reply. 'These petty arguments are getting us nowhere. The governor needs solutions.'

Suitably chastened, her advisors lapsed into an embarrassed silence.

Governor Shonai leaned forward, resting her elbows on the desk and steepling her fingers before her.

'So what can we do? I can't buy any more support from the smaller cartels. Most of them are already in the pocket of de Valtos or Taloun, and Honan will simply follow their lead. Our coffers are almost dry just keeping the wolves at bay.'

Corteo blew a blue cloud of smoke from his pipe and said, 'Then I fear we have to acknowledge that our time in office may soon be at a premature end.'

'I'm not prepared to accept that, Leland,' said Shonai.

'With all due respect, ma'am, your acceptance or otherwise is irrelevant,' pointed out Corteo. 'You pay me to tell you the truth. I did the same for your father and if you wish me to pretty up the facts like fat Miklas here, I can do that, but I do not believe that is why you have kept me around all these years.'

Shonai smiled, waving the outraged Iacovone to silence, and said, 'You're correct of course, Leland, but I still don't accept that there's nothing we can do.'

She pushed the chair back and rose to her feet. She did her best thinking while she was pacing and began a slow circuit of the room, pausing by the bust of old Forlanus. She patted the marble head affectionately before facing her advisors.

'Very well, Leland. If we accept that a vote of "no confidence" is inevitable, how long do we realistically have until such a motion is tabled? And is there any way we can delay it?'

Corteo considered the question for a moment before replying.

'It does not matter if we delay such a motion,' he said finally. 'There is nothing we can do to prevent it, so we must be ready to face it on our terms.'

'Yes, but how long do we have until then?' pressed Shonai.

'A month at best, but probably less,' estimated Corteo. 'But what we should be asking is what can we do to ensure we survive it when it comes.'

'Suggestions, gentlemen?' invited Almerz Chanda.

'We need to be seen to be restoring order,' suggested Morten Bauer.

'Yes,' agreed Iacovone enthusiastically, relieved to have been thrown a morsel he could sink his teeth into. 'We have to show that we are doing our best to catch these terrorist scum, this Church of Ancient Ways. I hear they bombed another forge hangar in Praxedes and killed a dozen workers. A terrible business.'

'We can promise to put a stop to the pirate activity of the alien raiders as well,' added Bauer.

Leland Corteo nodded thoughtfully. 'Yes, yes, well done, dear boy. That would allow us to potentially split our opposition. We could seek de Valtos's support on this issue. He has more reason to hate the eldar scum than anyone.'

Shonai paced around the room, her brain whirling with possibilities. Kasimir de Valtos probably would support any action that would see him revenged on the aliens who had captured and tortured him many years ago, but could he be trusted? His organisation was a serious contender for the position of Cartel Prime and Shonai knew that de Valtos had even used his war injury kudos to foster popular support amongst the workers.

She followed the logic of Bauer's proposal. The Taloun would no doubt see any overtures made to de Valtos as an attempt to divide her political opponents. He would probably try to sway de Valtos with similar promises, offering his own ships to hunt down the eldar.

If the Taloun's ships succeeded in wiping out the eldar pirates, well that was fine too. Their elimination would allow the tithe shipments to get through to the Administratum, allowing her to ease the pressure on her people and thus weather the coming months.

Shonai returned to her desk and sat down again. She turned to Chanda and said, 'It might be opportune to arrange a meeting with de Valtos. I'm sure he will be happy to hear of our determination to destroy the foul eldar pirates.'

Almerz Chanda bowed and said, 'I shall despatch an emissary immediately.'

Chanda withdrew from the room as the governor addressed her advisors.

'We need to stay on top of this situation, my friends. Today's unfortunate events have proven that we need to be more careful in how we are perceived,' said Mykola Shonai, pointedly staring at Miklas Iacovone. 'We lost face today, but not so much that we can't repair the damage. We can always shift the blame to heavy handed crowd control if need be.'

'I'll get right on it, ma'am,' promised Iacovone, eager to earn back his favour.

'Very well, Miklas. Let today be a lesson learned.'

Leland Corteo coughed, shaking his head as he removed fresh tobacco from a pouch at his waist.

'You disagree, Leland?' asked Shonai.

'Frankly, yes, ma'am. Loath as I am to agree with such a hidebound bureaucrat, I am afraid I concur with Mister Chanda regarding criticism of our law enforcement officials,' said Leland Corteo, filling his pipe with fresh tobacco. 'I believe shifting blame to the Adeptus Arbites would be a mistake. They will not take such allegations lightly.'

Further discussion on the matter was prevented by the return of Almerz Chanda, who marched straight to the governor's desk clutching a data slate. He offered it to Mykola Shonai, his face pale and drawn.

'This just came in from the Chamber of Voices,' whispered Chanda.

'What is it?' asked Shonai, reading the worry in Chanda's voice. The Chamber of Voices was the name given to the psychically attuned chamber where the palace astrotelepaths sent and received messages from off-world. In an empire of galactic scale, telepathy was the only feasible method of communication and, normally, such messages were relatively mundane.

Chanda's manner told Shonai that this was far from mundane.

'I don't know, it was encrypted by the quill servitors and requires your personal gene-key to unlock. It has an omicron level Administratum seal.'

Shonai took the slate and warily held her thumb over the identifier notch. Whatever this slate contained could not be good. She was savvy enough to realise that when the Administratum took an interest in a world as troubled as hers, it meant trouble for those responsible. And on Pavonis, that meant her.

She slid her thumb into the slate, wincing as the sample needle stabbed out and drew her blood. A collection of lights flashed on the side of the slate as the spirit within the machinery checked her genetic code against that stored in its cogitator.

The slate clicked and hummed, chattering as it printed a flimsy sheet of parchment from the scriptum at its base. Shonai ripped the message off and placed the slate on her desk.

She slipped on a delicate set of eyeglasses and read the message. As her eyes travelled further down the message, her face felt hot and her chest tightened. She reached the end of the message, feeling a heavy, queasy sensation settle in her stomach.

She handed the parchment to Chanda who swiftly scanned the message before placing it carefully back before the governor.

'Perhaps it will not be as bad as you fear, ma'am,' said Chanda hopefully.

'You know better than that, Almerz.'

Corteo leaned forward, his pipe jammed between his lips. 'Might I enquire as to the content of this message?' he asked.

Mykola Shonai nodded and said, 'Of course, Leland. It seems we are soon to receive an envoy – an adept from the Admin-istratum who will be reviewing our failure to meet Imperial tithes and maintain the Emperor's peace. We may not need to try and keep the cartels from impeaching us before our time. The Administratum will do it for them.'

She could tell from the worried faces around the room that they all realised the significance of this adept's imminent arrival.

'That wretch Ballion must have sent word to the Imperium,' hissed Iacovone.

'No doubt at the behest of the Taloun,' cursed Leland Corteo.

Governor Shonai sighed. She had asked for more time from the Admin-istratum's representative on Pavonis, but couldn't really blame the man, even if the Taloun had pressured him into it.

'Can this adept simply remove you from office without due process?' asked Morten Bauer.

'He comes with the highest authority,' answered Chanda solemnly.

Governor Shonai picked up the parchment once again and reread the last few lines.

'But more importantly, Almerz, he comes with the Angels of Death. He comes with the Space Marines.'

FOUR

THE ULTRAMARINES STRIKE cruiser *Vae Victus* slipped rapidly through the darkness of space, wan starlight reflecting from her battle scarred hull. She was an elongated, gothic space-borne leviathan with protruding warp vanes. The antenna atop the arched cathedral spire of the command deck rose from her centre and grew towards the powerful plasma drives at her rear.

To either side of the angular prow and bombardment cannon lay the crenellated entrances to her launch bays from where Thunderhawk gunships and boarding torpedoes could sally forth. Her entire length bristled with gargoyle-wreathed weapon batteries and conventional torpedo launch bays.

The *Vae Victus* was old. Constructed in the shipyards of Calth almost three millennia ago, she displayed the trademark design flourishes of the Calthian shipbuilders in the ornamented gothic arches surrounding her launch bays and the flying buttresses of her engine housings.

In her long life, the strike cruiser had crossed the galaxy several times over and had fought unnumbered battles against foes both human and alien. She had grappled with the tyranids at the Battle of Macragge, destroyed the command barge of the renegade flag-captain Ghenas Malkorgh, delivered the killing blow to the ork hulk, *Captor of Vice* and, more recently, destroyed the orbital defences of Thracia in the Appolyon Crusade.

Her hull proudly bore the scars of each encounter. The artificers of the Ultramarines had reverently repaired every wound, rendering the honour of her victories unto the vast spirit that dwelt within the beating mechanical heart of the starship.

* * *

THE COMMAND BRIDGE of the *Vae Victus* was a wide, candlelit chamber with a vaulted ceiling some fifteen metres high. Humming banks of glowing holo displays and ancient, runic screens lined the cloisters either side of the raised command nave, a shaven headed half-human, cyborg-servitor hard wired into each of the ship's regulatory systems. A broad observation bay dominated the front of the chamber, currently displaying a view of empty space before the ship. Smaller screens in the corners of the bay displayed the current course and speed of the ship along with all local objects picked up by the ship's surveyors.

The wide nave was bisected at its rear by an arched transept with ordnance and surveyor stations located to either side. Space Marine deck officers wearing plain hessian robes over their armour also monitored each station.

The recycled air was heavy with the fragrance of burning incense from censers swung by hooded priests and a barely audible choral chant drifted through the bridge from the raised sacristy and navigator's dome behind the captain's pulpit.

The commander of the *Vae Victus* stood atop his pulpit and fixed his hoary eyes on the lectern beside him. Tactical plots for the *Vae Victus* and Pavonis were displayed next to the chrono-display showing their projected course.

Lord Admiral Lazlo Tiberius cast his heavy lidded eyes around the bridge, searching for anything out of place, but satisfied that all was as it should be.

Tiberius was a giant, dark skinned Space Marine of nearly four hundred years who had fought in space almost his entire life. His fearsomely scarred face was the result of a close encounter with a tyranid bio-ship that had smashed into the *Vae Victus*'s command bridge during the early stages of the Battle of Circe. His skull was hairless and his skin the texture of worn leather. The moulded breastplate of his blue armour was adorned with bronze clusters of badges of honour, the gold sunburst of a Hero of Macragge at its centre.

Lord Admiral Tiberius stood with his hands clasped behind his back and studied the tactical plot with a critical eye, calculating how long it would take the *Vae Victus* to achieve orbit around Pavonis. He glanced at the corner of the screen and was satisfied to note that his estimate almost perfectly matched up with the logic engine's prediction.

He felt his estimate was the more realistic of the two, however.

Before him, robed crewmen worked over their extensive sensor runes, sweeping space before them with all manner of surveyors and augury devices. Tiberius knew that the captain of a starship was only as good as the crew he commanded. All the tactical acumen in the galaxy would count for nothing if he were given inaccurate information or his orders were not obeyed quickly and without question below decks.

And Tiberius knew he had one of the best crews in the Ultramar fleet. Proved time and again in the heat of battle, they had always performed exactly as commanded. The *Vae Victus* had been through some desperate battles, but her crew had always acquitted themselves with honour. This was in part due to Tiberius demanding that the highest possible standards be constantly maintained by every crewman upon his ship, from the lowliest deck hand to himself and his command staff. But it was also a reflection of the dedication and loyalty amongst the servants of the Ultramarines who provided the majority of the vessel's crew.

Once again they were entering harm's way and Tiberius felt the familiar exultation that they would soon be bringing the Emperor's fiery sword of retribution to His enemies. It had been a long time since the *Vae Victus* had tasted battle against the eldar and though he hated their alien ways with a zealot's passion, he was forced to admit that he had a grudging respect for their mastery of hit-and-run tactics.

Tiberius knew the devious eldar would rarely engage in a ship-to-ship fight under any but the most favourable terms since their ships were absurdly fragile and did not have the divine protection of void shields. They relied on stealth and cunning to close with their target, then blasphemous alien magicks to confound the targeting cogitators of their foes' weapons. Tiberius knew that often the first warning of such an attack was the impact of prow lances that disabled a ship's manoeuvring thrusters. After that it was academic who had the biggest guns; the eldar ship would run rings around its more ponderous opponent, taking it apart piece by piece.

Tiberius vowed that such a fate would not befall his ship.

IN THE DARKNESS of space, six hours ahead of the Vae Victus, an elegantly deadly craft slipped from the shadows of its asteroid base. Its segmented prow tapered to a needle point and jagged, scimitar-like solar sails gracefully unfurled, soaring from the cunningly wrought engines at its rear. Joining the engines and prow was a slender, domed command section, and it was from here that the captain of this lethal craft ruled his ship.

That captain of the graceful vessel, the *Stormrider*, now stared with undisguised relish at the return signal on the display before him. At last, a foe worthy of his talents. A ship of the Adeptus Astartes! Archon Kesharq of the Kabal of the Sundered Blade had grown tired of ambushing lumbering merchantmen, outwitting system defence ships and raiding primitive mon-keigh settlements. Kesharq cared not for the spoils of these raids, and even torturing the screaming souls aboard the captured vessels beyond the known limits of pain had grown stale to his dulled senses.

Such poor sport had not even begun to stretch the limit of his abilities.

A thin line of blood dribbled from the corners of his mouth and Kesharq tipped his head back, pulling the lifeless skin of his face taut over his skull and hooking the ragged edges over the sutures at the back of his neck. He had grander dreams than this and had begun to fear that his pact with the *kyerzak* was a mistake.

But now came worthy meat indeed.

THREE DECKS BELOW the command bridge of the *Vae Victus*, the chapel of Fourth Company echoed softly to the sounds of Space Marines at their prayers. The chamber was wide and high ceilinged, easily capable of holding the assembled battle brethren of the company. A polished, stone-flagged nave led towards a glassy black altar and wooden lectern at the far end of the chapel.

Stained glass windows of wondrous colour and majesty dominated the upper reaches of the chapel. Each window sat within a leaf shaped archway, electro-flambeaux set behind them casting ghostly illumination upon the assembled warriors. Each window depicted a portion of the Imperium's long history: the Age of Strife, the Age of Apostasy, the Emperor Deified and the Emperor Victorious. Battle honours the company had won in a dozen crusades hung below the windows, each testament to a tradition of bravery and courage that stretched back ten thousand years.

The company stood at parade rest in the flickering light of the flambeaux, eyes cast down at the smooth floor of the chapel. Each chanted a litany of thanks to Him on Earth, contemplating their holy duty to the God-Emperor.

Silence descended on the chapel as the iron bound door at the far end of the nave opened and two figures entered. The Space Marines snapped to attention as one.

The captain of Fourth Company, Uriel Ventris, marched down the wide nave, his ceremonial cape flaring. A pale, grim-faced warrior led him with a milky white cloak trawling behind.

Fourth Company's chaplain, Judd Clausel, wore midnight black power armour embossed with fanged skulls. Brass and gold trims on his cuirass and greaves winked in the dim light. His grinning, skull faced helmet was hooked to his hip belt alongside a voluminous tome, bound in faded green ork hide.

In his left arm he swung a smoking censer, aromatic herbs and sacred oils filling the chapel with the wild, intoxicating scent of the highlands of Macragge. His right fist gripped the crozius arcanum, his weapon and the symbol of office of a chaplain. The crozius arcanum was a carved adamantium rod surmounted with a glittering golden eagle, its spread wings razor edged. A grinning skull topped the crozius, its eyes jewelled and blood red.

Power palpably radiated from the man. Clausel did not just deserve respect, he demanded it. His build was enormous, bigger even than that of Uriel, and his stern, unflinching gaze missed nothing. One flinty grey eye searched every face for weakness, while his remaining eye regarded his surroundings through the soulless mechanics of a crudely grafted blinking red orb.

His skull was a shaven dome save for a gleaming silver topknot that trailed from the crown of his head to his shoulders. A thick face, heavily scarred and twisted into a grotesque parody of a smile, surveyed the Space Marines before him.

'Kneel!' he commanded. The order was instantly obeyed, the sound of armoured knees reverberating around the chamber as they slammed down in unison. Uriel stepped forwards to receive the smoking censer and the crozius. He moved behind the massive chaplain, his head bowed.

'Today is a day of joy!' Clausel bellowed. 'For today we are offered the chance to take the Emperor's light into the darkness and to destroy those who would stand in the way of His servants. We are not yet a full company again, my brothers. Many of our comrades met their deaths on Thracia, but we know that they did not die in vain. They will take their place at the side of the Emperor and tell the tales of their bravery and honour until the final days.'

Clausel extended his gauntleted fist then slammed it into his breastplate twice in rapid succession.

'De mortuis nil nisi bonum!' intoned the chaplain, reclaiming the censer from Uriel.

Chaplain Clausel strode from the altar towards the kneeling Marines, dipping his hands into the smoking umber ash. As he passed each warrior, he drew protective hexes and ritual symbols of battle on the armour of each man, chanting the Litany of Purity as he went. As he anointed the last man, he turned back to the altar and said, 'The Rites of Battle are complete, my captain.'

'We are honoured by your words, Chaplain Clausel. Perhaps now you will lead us in prayer?'

'That I will, captain,' replied Clausel.

Striding to the fore, he mounted the steps, knelt and kissed the basalt surface of the altar, mouthing the Catechism of Affirmation.

Rising to his feet, he began to chant as the Ultramarines bowed their heads.

'Divine Master of Mankind. We, your humble servants offer our thanks to you for this new day. As we steer our might to honourable battle, we rejoice in the opportunity you offer us to use our skills and strengths in your name. The world of Pavonis is plagued by degenerate aliens and riven with strife. With your grace and blessing, Imperial wisdom shall soon prevail in your name once more. For this we give thanks and ask for nothing, save the chance to serve. This we pray in your name. Guilliman, praise it!'

'Guilliman, praise it!' echoed the Space Marines.

Clausel lowered his arms and stood aside, arms folded across his chest as Captain Uriel Ventris stood before his men. He was nervous at addressing his company for the first time and he mentally chided himself for his lack of focus. He had faced the enemies of mankind for over a century and now he fretted over speaking to a company of Space Marines?

Uriel let his gaze wander over the assembled battle-brothers of his company, these greatest of men, and nodded in recognition towards the giant, bear-like Sergeant Pasanius. His friend from youth had continued to grow during their training and was, far and away, the strongest Space Marine in the Chapter. His massive form dwarfed most of his battle-brothers and, early in his training, the Tech-marines had been forced to craft a unique suit of armour for his giant frame composed of parts cannibalised from an irreparably damaged suit of Terminator armour.

Pasanius gave Uriel a tiny nod and he felt his confidence soar. The veteran sergeant had been a rock for Uriel to anchor himself to in his rise through the ranks and he was proud to call him a true friend. Behind Pasanius, he saw the regal, sculpted features of Sergeant Learchus and his compatriot, Cleander.

They had all grown far beyond any childish rivalry and had saved each other's lives on more than one occasion, but they had never become friends nor formed the bond of brotherhood that permeated the rest of the Chapter.

It irked Uriel that he still found such difficulty in connecting to his men in the way that truly great officers did. Idaeus had been a natural leader, who had frequently relied on his own solutions to fight his battles rather than turning to the holy Codex Astartes, the tome of war penned by the great Roboute Guilliman himself. He had led his men with an instinctive ease that Uriel found difficult to match. He drew himself up to his full height as he resolved he would take Idaeus's advice and be his own man. Fourth Company was his now and he would make sure they knew it.

'At ease!' he called and his warriors relaxed a fraction. 'You all know me. I have fought beside most of you for over a century. And it is with this wisdom that I say, be thankful for this chance to display our devotion to our primarch and the Emperor.'

Uriel deliberately placed his fist on the pommel of Idaeus's sword, reinforcing the fact that the company's former captain had passed it to him.

'I know that I have not been your leader long and I also know that some of you would prefer it if I was not your captain,' continued Uriel.

Uriel paused, gauging his next words carefully. 'Captain Idaeus was a great man, and the hardest thing I have ever done was to watch him die. No one grieves for him more than I, but he is dead and I am here now. I have taken the Emperor's light to every corner of this galaxy. I have fought the tyranids in burning hive ships, I have killed the dread warriors of Chaos on worlds of unspeakable horrors and I have defeated orks on barren deserts of ice. I have fought alongside some of the greatest warriors of the Imperium, so know this:

'I am captain of this Company. I am Uriel Ventris of the Ultramarines and I will die before I dishonour the Chapter. I am honoured to be part of this brotherhood and had I the choice of any warrior by my side, I could choose no better men than those of Fourth Company. Every man here and every one of our honoured dead acquitted themselves in a manner our kin would be proud of. I salute you all!'

At this, Uriel drew Idaeus's power sword from his side with a flourish and raised it high above his head.

Sapphire coils of energy coruscated along the length of the master-crafted sword, catching the light thrown by the electro-flambeaux.

The Marines rose to their feet and slammed their clenched fists to their breastplates, a deafening boom that echoed round the chapel.

'We are Ultramarines,' called Uriel. 'And no foe can stand against us while we keep faith with the Emperor.'

Uriel crossed to stand behind the wooden lectern and consulted the data slate cunningly fashioned into its surface. He did not need to read from the slate; he had memorised the details of their mission in the week spent travelling through warp space, but to have the details near was reassuring.

'We travel to a world named Pavonis and have been entrusted with the task of bringing it back within the fold of the Imperium. Pavonis has failed in its duty to the Emperor. It does not provide Him that which is His due. To rectify this situation, we have been entrusted with the protection of an adept of the Administratum who will instruct the rulers of Pavonis in the proper execution of their duty. The rulers of Pavonis appear to think they are exempt from the Emperor's laws. Together we will show them that they are not. Blessed be the primarch.'

'Blessed be the primarch,' repeated the Space Marines.

Uriel paused before continuing, wishing he knew more about this adept they were supposed to guard. He had not even met the man he had been entrusted with protecting by Marneus Calgar. Thus far, the adept had spent the entire voyage in his chambers, attended only by his entourage of scribes, clerics and valets.

Well, he would have to come out soon; the *Vae Victus* was only a day's travel from her destination.

Uriel lowered his voice as he moved onto the next point of his briefing.

'Perhaps as a result of Pavonis's leaders' failure to properly enforce the Emperor's rule, a group calling themselves the Church of Ancient Ways has been allowed to emerge. These heretics have embarked upon a campaign of terror bombings, seeking a return to the times before the coming of the glorious Imperium.'

A murmur of disbelief rippled through the ranks.

'To date, they have killed three hundred and fifty-nine servants of the Emperor and caused untold damage. They bomb His manufactorum. They kill His priests and they burn His temples. Together we will stop them. Blessed be the primarch.'

'Blessed be the primarch.'

'But, brothers, not only does the world of Pavonis suffer the evil of heretics within. No, the heretical scourge of the alien is upon Pavonis. For years now, the eldar, a race so arrogant they believe they can plunder our space and steal the chattels that are rightfully the Emperor's with impunity, have plagued this region of space. Together we will show them that they cannot. Blessed be the primarch.'

'Blessed be the primarch.'

Uriel moved away from the lectern.

'Return to your cells, my brothers. Honour your battle gear that it may protect you in the days of war to come. The Emperor be with you all.'

'And with you, captain,' said Pasanius, stepping from the ranks and bowing to Uriel.

Hesitantly at first, but witnessing Pasanius's acceptance of Uriel, the company took a step forward and bowed to their new captain before filing from the chapel.

Pasanius was the last to leave and turned to face him.

Uriel nodded his thanks to his oldest friend.

ARCHON KESHARQ NODDED to his second-in-command.

'Bring main power up slowly and be ready to activate the mimic engines on my order,' he commanded, his voice wetly rasping and ugly.

'Yes, dread archon.'

Kesharq dabbed at his weeping neck with a scented cloth, coughing a froth of bloody matter into a goblet beside him. Even speech was becoming difficult for him now and he swallowed hard, once more cursing the Life of a Thousand Pains upon the name of Asdrubael Vect.

The suppurating wounds on his neck would never seal. Vect's haemonculus had seen to that in the torture chambers beneath the palace of his kabal. Kesharq's bid for command of the kabal had been planned in minute detail, but Vect had known of his treachery and the coup had failed before it had begun.

Months of torture had followed. He had begged for oblivion, but the haemonculus had kept him always just at the brink of the death before dragging him back to their hell of infinite pain.

He had expected to die there, but Vect had ordered him released and his suit of skin sutured back to the wreckage of his musculature. He remembered Vect's beautifully cruel face smiling down upon him as he lay in a rare moment of sanity and coherence. He tried to close his eyes, to shut out Vect's gloating smile, but his eyelids had been neatly sliced off a week ago.

'You think you will die here?' enquired the supreme lord of the Kabal of the Black Heart. Without waiting for an answer, the dark eldar lord shook his head slowly and continued.

'You shall not. I will not allow you that luxury,' promised Vect, tracing his perfectly manicured nails along the exposed bone of Kesharq's ribs. 'You were a vain fool, Kesharq, boasting of your plans for my death when you must have known my spies would tell me everything you uttered before the words were even cold.'

Vect had sighed then, as though he were more disappointed than angry. 'Treachery and deceit I can understand, even forgive. But stupidity and incompetence merely irritate me. Your colossal vanity and rampant ego were your undoing and I think it only fitting that they be your constant companions in failure. I shall exile you from Commorragh, send you from our dark city and cast you into the wilderness with the prey species.'

Kesharq had not believed Vect, thinking that this was some elaborate ruse to raise his hopes that he might yet live, only to have them dashed before him.

But Vect had not lied. Less than a week later, he and the surviving members of his splinter kabal had limped from Commorragh in humiliation and disgrace. Kesharq had sworn vengeance on the house of Asdrubael Vect, but his former lord had merely laughed and the sounds of his mirth were whips of fire on his soul.

Vect would not be laughing soon as Kesharq thought once more of the prize that awaited him once he had outwitted the foolish *kyerzak*. But first he must take care of this newly arrived threat to the carefully orchestrated scheme.

The kill was so close that Kesharq could almost taste the blood of the Space Marines on his nerveless lips. He rose from his command chair and strode to the main screen, his movements as lithe as a dancer's despite the looseness of his skin and the wide bladed axe slung across his back. His segmented green armour shone like polished jade, highlighting the pallid dead skin mask of his face. Lifeless white hair, streaked with violet, spilled around his shoulders, held in place by a crimson circlet at his brow. He moistened his lidless eyes with a fine spray from a tiny atomiser and studied the view before him.

Slithering at his heels came a snapping pack of grotesque creatures, each constructed from scraps of random flesh sewn together to form a heaving mass of razor claws and fangs. These were the excrents, Kesharq's pets, shat into existence by a whim of his chief haemonculus. They swarmed around their master's legs, hissing mindless malevolence with their yellowed, venomous fangs at anything and anyone that dared come near.

The meat was almost in the killing zone and Kesharq's excitement began to mount. Blood pounded through his veins at the thought of inflicting pain on the corpse god's warriors. The corners of his mouth twitched in anticipation and his fingers tingled at the thought. Kesharq decided he would keep one alive as a pet, mewling in constant agony as he watched his comrades slowly dismembered to provide new flesh for his excrents.

'Dread archon, the prey vessel has entered weapons range,' hissed his second-in-command.

'Excellent,' smiled Kesharq beneath his skin. 'Power up the weapons and align the mimic engines.'

The enemy ship was still too far away to see through the viewscreen, but Kesharq fancied he could sense its nearness. He returned to his command chair and slipped his axe from its scabbard. He liked to tease the onyx blade of the weapon as he made each kill and keep its soul hungry for blood.

'Bring us in on his starboard forequarter with the sun at our backs,' ordered Kesharq.

He stroked the fractal edge of his axe.

'PERMISSION TO COME aboard the bridge, lord admiral?'

Tiberius turned from the lectern to see two robed men standing at the entrance to the command bridge and fought to mask his annoyance. Civilians on his bridge were something he tried to avoid, but this adept carried with him the highest seal of the Administratum and it would be impolitic to refuse his request.

Tiberius nodded his approval and descended from his pulpit as the robed duo shuffled their way up the cloister steps to the command nave. One of the pair was a venerable ancient in thick robes who walked with an ivory cane while the other was a man perhaps in his forties with an unremarkable face and bland features. Tiberius reflected that the man looked like every other faceless adept of the Administratum he had ever met.

The older man looked unimpressed by his surroundings, but the bland faced man positively radiated enthusiasm.

'Many thanks, lord admiral. Most kind of you to allow us onto the bridge, your sanctum, your crow's nest if you will. Most kind.'

'Is there something I can do for you, Adept Barzano?' asked Tiberius, already weary of Barzano's incessant barrage of words.

'Oh please, lord admiral, call me Ario,' replied Barzano happily. 'My personal scribe Lortuen Perjed and I merely wished to see the bridge of your mighty starship before we arrived at Pavonis. What with being so busy so far, we haven't had much of a chance to admire our surroundings.'

Barzano marched down the nave towards the viewing bay, which at present displayed the diminutive disc of Pavonis and the flaring ball of her sun.

Barzano examined several of the servitor-manned stations as he passed. He turned back and indicated that Tiberius and Lortuen Perjed should follow him.

The scribe shrugged and set off after his master, who was bent over a monitor station, waving his hand before the blank, expressionless face of a servitor. The lobotomised creature ignored the adept, its cybernetically altered brain incapable of even registering his presence.

'Fascinating, absolutely fascinating,' he observed, as Tiberius joined him. 'What does this one do?'

Controlling his impatience, Tiberius said, 'This station monitors the temperature variance in the plasma engine core.'

'And that one?'

'It regulates the oxygen recycling units on the gun decks.'

But Barzano had already moved on towards the surveyor stations through the arched transept, where Space Marine officers worked alongside the motionless servitors.

A few faces turned towards him as he entered, but Barzano shook his head, saying, 'Don't mind me. Pretend I'm not here.' He stood over a stone-rimmed plotting table in the centre of the chamber and rested his elbows on the side, studying the wealth of tactical information displayed on the embedded slate.

'This is truly fascinating, lord admiral, truly fascinating,' repeated Barzano.

'I thank you for your interest Adept Barzano, but–'

'Ario, please.'

'Adept Barzano,' continued Tiberius. 'This is a vessel of war, it is not–'

'Lord admiral,' interrupted Philotas, Tiberius's deck officer.

Tiberius hurried over to the bewilderingly complex array of runic display slates that the deck officer operated from.

'You have something?'

'New contact, lord admiral. Sixty thousand kilometres in front of us,' said Philotas, adjusting the runes before him and squinting at the readout before him, 'I have just detected a plasma energy spike on the mid-range auguries.'

'What is it?' asked Tiberius quickly. 'A ship?'

'I believe so, lord admiral. Bearing zero-three-nine.'

'Identify it. Class and type. And find out how it managed to get so damned close without us detecting it before now!'

Philotas nodded and bent to his controls once more. Ario Barzano studied the tactical plot on the central table and pointed to the blip that represented the unknown contact. Rows of numbers scrolled down the slate beside it, an exhaustive array of information regarding the unknown vessel.

'This is the contact?' he asked.

'Yes, Adept Barzano, it is,' snapped Tiberius. 'But I do not have time to instruct you in the finer points of starship operations just now.'

'Lord admiral?' called Philotas.

'Yes?'

'I have identified the unknown contact's engine signature, Lord Admiral,' confirmed the deck officer. 'It is the *Gallant*, a system defence ship out of Pavonis.'

'TARGET APPROACHING LANCE range, dread archon.'

Kesharq ran his tongue across his teeth, tasting the stale blood congealed there and shivered with barely controlled excitement. Yes, the fools were taking the bait, believing the *Stormrider* to be one of their own.

'Divert main power to the lance batteries and hold it in reserve. I wish to deliver a killing blow with one strike.'

'Yes, dread archon.'

TIBERIUS STRODE BACK to his captain's pulpit and said, 'Communications, contact the *Gallant* and pass my compliments to her captain.'

'Yes, lord admiral.'

The captain of the *Vae Victus* stared at the viewing bay, hoping to see the outline of the system defence ship, but the flaring corona from the star at the system's centre prevented him from seeing much of anything. He turned back to surveyor control and felt his temper fraying as he watched Barzano standing over the data entry booth of one of his ship's logic banks.

'Adept Barzano?' asked Tiberius.

The adept waved a dismissive hand, too intent on the slate before him and Tiberius decided he had had enough of Adept Ario Barzano. Adept of the highest clearance or not, nobody showed the commander of a starship that kind of disrespect. Tiberius descended from his pulpit – as Barzano suddenly hurried from surveyor control to meet him.

'Lord admiral, raise the shields and power up the weapons!' ordered Barzano, his voice infused with sudden authority.

Tiberius folded his arms across his massive chest and looked down into the adept's tense face.

'And why should I do that, Adept Barzano?'

'Because,' hissed Barzano urgently, 'according to the Ultima Segmentum fleet records, the governor of Pavonis reported the *Gallant* destroyed with all hands five years ago, lord admiral.'

Tiberius felt the blood drain from his face as he realised the implication and the scale of the danger his ship and crew were in.

'Hard to starboard!' he shouted. 'Raise void shields and build power in forward liner accelerators!'

'FIRE!' SHOUTED ARCHON Kesharq as he saw the massive prow of the Space Marine vessel begin swinging to face them. The ship shuddered as the forward lance batteries hurled deadly pulses of dark energy towards its prey.

In a heartbeat they had closed the gap. The viewscreen flashed as colossal amounts of energy smashed into the strike cruiser and exploded with unbelievable force.

A bright halo exploded around the *Vae Victus* as the first impacts overloaded the vessel's void shields. The following bolts detonated on the armoured prow of the ship, sending plumes of fire and oxygen flaring from her stricken hull.

To see so much destructive power unleashed at such close range was truly exhilarating and Kesharq roared in triumph.

Even at this range, he could see that the damage the pulse lances had inflicted was horrendous. Metre-thick sheets of adamantium had been peeled back from the starship's structure like tin foil and jagged tendons of steel hung limp from the shattered section of the prow where they had struck.

Jets of freezing oxygen crystallised as they spewed from the ruptured hull, blast doors struggling to contain the breach. Kesharq knew that hundreds must have died in the initial blast and many more would soon have followed them screaming into hell as their compartments suddenly vented into space.

Kesharq laughed.

'Bring us about and move around to their rear quarter. Disable their engines.'

THE BRIDGE OF the *Vae Victus* heeled sideways, flooring the entire command crew as the massive explosion rippled its force along the ship's structure. Secondary blasts followed quickly behind, the detonations sounding like hollow thumps from the bridge.

Warning bells tolled and the command bridge was bathed in red as the strike cruiser went to battle stations. Emergency teams battled fires and tended to the wounded as steam, smoke and flames burst from shattered conduits and monitor stations. Dozens of servitors slumped lifeless from their chairs.

Tiberius picked himself up from the deck, a deep gash in his cheek. The blood had already clotted and he shouted, 'Damage report! Now!'

He ran to the ordnance station, wrenching the targeting servitor from the panel. It was dead, the ashen flesh burned and black and its controls shattered. The logic engines struggled to determine the extent of their hurt, but Tiberius already knew they had been grievously wounded. Not a fatal wound yet, but still a serious one.

'Void shields overloaded and we have hull breaches on decks seven through to nine,' shouted the deck officer. 'Prow bombardment cannon are temporarily offline and main launch bay took a hit. We were lucky. The last few blasts only grazed us, lord admiral. Your turn into the fire saved us.'

Tiberius grunted, feeling unworthy of such a compliment and returned to his command pulpit. Barzano's warning had come not a moment too soon and it was that which had saved the ship. Barely had the shields come up before the *Vae Victus* shuddered as the enemy struck.

Tiberius glared at the viewing bay, angry with himself for being caught out, watching as a fluid black shape, its graceful mainsail rippling in the solar wind, slid from the concealing flare of the sun and slipped out of sight around their starboard flank.

'Eldar!' cursed Tiberius. Where in the nine hells had that ship come from? How in the name of Guilliman had it fooled their surveyors and auguries?

'Surveyor control! Give me a full amplification sweep of the local area. Tell me what in the name of holy Terra is out there! Starboard broadside batteries fire at will!'

Philotas nodded, hurriedly relaying the lord admiral's orders.

'And someone stop that damned bell ringing!'

The bridge was suddenly quiet as the sacristy bell fell silent. The hiss of damaged machinery, the crackling of sparks and the insensate moans of wounded servitors were the only sounds. He felt the vibrations of the starboard batteries opening fire, but without proper ordnance control, doubted they would hit anything.

Tiberius mopped the congealed blood from his forehead as Ario Barzano staggered towards the captain's pulpit, supporting the slumped form of his scribe. Perjed was bleeding from a cut to the head, but it was not deep and once Barzano had deposited the venerable scribe on the cloister stairs, he ran back to surveyor control.

Tiberius shouted over to the adept, 'My thanks, Adept Barzano, for your timely warning.' He then called up the tactical plot onto his lectern, but the display was cluttered with anomalous readings and the close range surveyors were picking up dozens of return signals. Cursed alien magicks! Any one of them could be the eldar raider.

He had to save his ship, but what could he do with such confused information? But a bad decision was better than no decision.

'Helm control, hard to starboard and fire all batteries. Get us some distance from this bastard! We need space to manoeuvre.'

'No, lord admiral!' yelled Barzano from the tactical plot table. 'I believe we face a ship of the eldar's dark kin. I have read of such vessels and we must not move away from him.'

Tiberius hesitated, unused to being contradicted on his own bridge, but the adept had been proven correct so far and seemed to know more about the capabilities of the enemy ship.

'Very well, Adept Barzano. Time is short, what would you have me do?'

'We must close with the enemy, barrage him with firepower and hope to strike a lucky hit through his holofields.'

'Do it!' snapped Tiberius to his helm officer. 'Fire port manoeuvring thrusters and come to new heading zero-nine-zero!'

KESHARQ WATCHED THE damaged ship turn about its axis on the viewscreen before him. The ruptured prow was swinging around rapidly and, he suddenly noticed, was getting closer. He cursed as he realised that someone on board that vessel must be aware of his ship's capabilities.

He pointed to the viewscreen and shouted, 'Keep us behind it, curse your souls!'

The bridge shook as the explosions of heavy battery fire burst around the ship. The enemy gunners could not pinpoint their location, but with such weight of fire, it would only be a matter of time until they were hit. And the *Stormrider* was not built to take that kind of punishment.

The *Vae Victus* was struggling to match their turn, but such a contest could have only one winner.

'Prow torpedo bays ready to fire, dread archon!'

'Full spread,' screamed Kesharq. 'Fire!'

'INCOMING TORPEDOES, LORD admiral!' warned Philotas.

'Emperor damn them to hell! Hard to port! Defensive turrets open fire!'

'Broadside batteries lock onto the torpedoes' origination point and fire!' shouted Barzano.

'Weapons control, do as he says!' confirmed Tiberius.

The bridge swayed violently and Tiberius gripped the edge of the pulpit as the *Vae Victus* reversed her turn.

SIX TORPEDOES STREAKED towards the *Vae Victus*, alien targeter scrambling systems pumping out a distortion field that made it extremely difficult for their prey to intercept them. At such close range, and flying through such heavy fire, it was inevitable that some of the torpedoes would not get through and two exploded as the broadside gunners found their mark. Another was deceived by the radiation flaring from the damaged prow and flashed harmlessly below the *Vae Victus*. The last three closed unerringly on the strike cruiser and into range of the ship's close defences.

'THREE TORPEDOES DOWN!' yelled Philotas hoarsely.

'That's still three left,' said Tiberius. 'Take them out!'

'Close-in defensive turrets targeting now!'

The giant viewing bay showed the dark of space, painted with bright smears of explosions and the icy contrails of the incoming torpedoes. The entire bridge crew could see the weapons hurtling towards them and every man felt that the warheads were pointed right between his eyes.

The crew held their breath or muttered prayers to the Emperor as the *Vae Victus*'s last line of defence opened fire.

EACH CLOSE-IN TURRET was manned by a servitor equipped with its own auguries which allowed it to independently track the torpedoes as they neared. The torpedoes were programmed with evasive manoeuvres, but it was in their final stage that they were most vulnerable. As they began to slow for final target point acquisition, their speed bled off to a level where they could not evade effectively and one of the torpedoes disintegrated in a spray of high-velocity cannon fire.

A single shell from the defensive turrets clipped another torpedo. The grazing impact was not solid enough to destroy the torpedo, but knocked its internal gyroscope off track. Its guidance system now believed the *Vae Victus* was directly above it and altered course to roar upwards for nearly three hundred kilometres before exploding.

The last torpedo completed its final manoeuvre and closed for the kill.

Every gun brought their fire to bear on the projectile and, at a range of less than two hundred metres, they brought it down.

Hundreds of shells ripped into the torpedo, which detonated in a huge ball of fire and shrapnel. However, the wreckage was still moving at incredible speed and burning shards of the torpedo slammed into the hull, destroying a close-in defence turret, shredding a surveyor antenna and collapsing a number of external statuaries.

The torpedo attack was over.

TIBERIUS SAGGED AGAINST the pulpit as he watched the last torpedo die and knew he had never seen a sweeter sight. A ragged cheer of relief burst from the throats of the bridge staff along with fervent prayers of thanks.

'Well done, lord admiral. We did it,' sighed Barzano, limp with relief and drenched in sweat.

'This time, Ario,' cautioned Tiberius. 'We were lucky, but let's not break out the victory wine just yet.'

He shouted over to his deck officer. 'What of our return fire?'

'Engaging now,' said Philotas.

'Good,' said Tiberius with a vicious grin. 'Time to show that we still have teeth.'

KESHARQ COULD NOT believe the evidence of his own eyes. The torpedo spread had been defeated! The odds against such a thing was unthinkable. As he contemplated the sheer unfairness of it all, the bridge lurched sickeningly, pitching him to the ground. The massive vibrations of nearby explosions caused the ship to shudder violently. Lights flashed and smoke billowed from smashed machinery.

'Dread archon, we have been hit!' shouted his second in command.

'Yes, thank you for that perceptive insight,' sneered Kesharq. 'And if I am killed, be so good as to point it out. How badly have we been damaged?'

The dark eldar lord picked himself up. A flap of his skin hung from his throat, exposing his wetly glistening anatomy beneath. Impatiently, he pushed it back around his neck as his underlings ran to obey his orders.

Information came at him in a barrage, each morsel more serious than the last.

'We have lost power to the holofields.'

'The mainsail has been damaged and some of the cable stays have been severed.'

'Hull integrity lost on the tormentor deck. The prisoners awaiting torture are all dead.'

Kesharq knew that this battle was over for now. Stripped of the protection of her holofields, the *Stormrider* was too exposed and would be an easy target for its enemy's gunners. The prey had proved worthy indeed and he would not make the mistake of underestimating this foe again.

'Disengage!' he ordered. 'We will return to our lair and effect repairs to the ship. This meat will wait for another day.'

'ELDAR VESSEL IS retreating!' shouted Philotas, and Tiberius released a pent-up sigh of relief.

'Very well,' said Tiberius. 'Set course for Pavonis and when we are in range of secure communication, inform fleet control of the eldar's ability to masquerade as Imperial vessels.'

'Yes, lord admiral.'

Tiberius rubbed a calloused hand across his skull. They had been caught off-guard by the eldar and had been taught a painful lesson in humility. He tapped at his lectern and assigned himself thirty nights of penitent fasting and tactical study for his failure to anticipate the attack before climbing down to the buckled command nave.

Ario Barzano squatted by the base of the pulpit, wiping blood clear of Perjed's brow and smiled as Tiberius knelt beside him.

'Well done, lord admiral. Your quick manoeuvring saved us.'

'Let us not mince words, Adept Barzano–'

'Ario.'

'Very well... Ario. Had it not been for your warning we would all now be dead.'

'Possibly,' admitted Barzano. 'But I'm sure you'd have guessed what they were up to soon enough.'

Tiberius raised a sceptical eyebrow and said, 'How is it a man of the Administratum knows so much of alien vessels?'

Barzano grinned impishly. 'I have been many places, Lazlo, met many interesting people and I am a good listener. I pick up things from everything I see and everyone I meet.'

He shrugged and said, 'In my position, a great deal of esoteric things come my way and I make sure that I digest them all. But come, lord admiral, the real question is not how I know anything, but how did our enemies know where to find us? I am assuming you brought us in away from the normal shipping lanes.'

'Of course.'

Barzano raised his eyebrows. 'Then how did they know we would be here? My signal went only to the governor of Pavonis.'

'Do you suspect her of being in league with the eldar?'

'My dear lord admiral, I am a bureaucrat. I suspect everyone,' laughed Barzano before becoming serious. 'But you are right, the allegiance of the governor is one of many concerns I have.'

Before Tiberius could ask any further questions, Lortuen Perjed groaned and raised a liver spotted hand to his forehead. Barzano helped the scribe to his feet and bowed briefly to Tiberius.

'Lord admiral, if you will excuse me, I should take Lortuen to see my personal physician. Anyway, it was most educational to visit your bridge. We must do this again some time, yes?'

Tiberius nodded, unsure of this glib tongued adept. And the more he thought about it, the more he suspected that Barzano had expected the attack on the *Vae Victus*. Why else would he have come to the bridge at this point, for a tour? And when things had suddenly exploded into deadly action, Barzano had certainly known his way about the bridge of a starship.

Sourly, he wondered what other surprises were in store for him on this voyage.

℧
FIVE

THE OCTAGONAL SURGICAL chamber was cold, the breath of its occupants misted before them. The two figures in charge of the procedure moved with a silky elegant poise through the shadowed chamber. The light was kept low, as the Surgeon's eyes were unaccustomed to brightness and it was widely reckoned that he did his best work in near-darkness anyway.

A channelled metal slab was bolted to the floor in the centre of the chamber, surrounded by arcane devices festooned with scalpel blades, long needles and bonesaws. The chamber's third occupant, a naked human male, lay unmoving atop its cold surface. There were no restraints holding him there. The Surgeon needed total freedom of movement of the body in order to work and the drugs would keep the subject from moving.

The Surgeon had administered the precise amount to achieve such an effect, yet not so much as to prevent him from feeling something of the procedure.

Where was the art if the Honoured could feel nothing?

The Surgeon wore an anonymous red smock and pulled on thick, elbow length rubberised gloves, the fingers of which ended in delicate scalpels and clicking surgical instruments. His assistant watched his fastidious preparations from the shadows with a mixture of languid boredom and reverence.

She had seen the Surgeon's skill with his instruments many times before, and though the things he could do were wondrous, she was more interested in her own pleasures. The Surgeon nodded to her and she span, naked, towards the slab on her tiptoes, a wicked leer splitting her full red lips.

She gripped the edges of the table and pushed herself upwards and forwards, lifting her legs slowly until she was completely vertical. She walked astride the prone human on her hands then propelled herself into the air, twisting on the descent to land astride the figure.

She could see the fear of the procedure in his eyes and smiled to herself. It was always the fear that aroused her. Aroused her and repulsed her. That this human ape could think that she, who had learned the one thousand and nine Pleasures of the Dark, could actually enjoy this. Part of her was filled with self-loathing as she realised once again that she did, and it took an effort of will not to plunge her envenomed talons through his pleading eyes and into his broken mind. She shuddered, the man mistaking it for her pleasure, and leaned forwards, trailing her tongue along his exposed chest and feeling the skin pucker beneath her. She worked up to his neck and gently bit on the skin, her sharpened teeth penetrating his skin and tasting the bitter flavour of his bad blood.

He moaned as her teeth moved up his face, feathering razor kisses along the line of his jaw. Her long, blood red nails trailed up his ribs, leaving smoking, poisonous tracks in their wake. Her thighs tightened over his hips and she knew he was ready. The blood was singing in his rotten veins.

She looked over her shoulder and nodded to the Surgeon. Even though the human could not move, she sensed the terror rise up in him. The woman vaulted gracefully over his head, landing with a gymnast's grace behind the slab, spitting the blood that coated her teeth onto the floor. The Surgeon pressed the first of his bladed digits against the man's belly. Expertly, he opened him up, paring back the skin and muscle like the layers of an onion.

The Surgeon worked for another three hours, dextrously unravelling every centimetre of the man to the bone, laying his flesh and organs open in gory ribbons of meat. How easy it would be to just continue with the opening and take it on to his skull, leaving him a screaming, fleshless skeleton. The temptation was great, but he resisted it, knowing that Archon Kesharq would visit a thousand times such misery on his own frame were he to let the kyerzak die too soon.

Humming alien machinery of rubber tubing, hissing bellows and gurgling bottles of blood surrounded the procedure, gently feeding the still-living cadaver with life preserving fluids. A loathsome metallic construction, like a serrated gallows, swung upwards and over the table, supporting a glossy, beetle-like organism that pulsed with rasping breath. Fine, chitinous black needles stretched from its distended belly and worked at each flensed slab of flesh. Moving too quickly to be seen by the naked eye, they stripped diseased, stringy matter from each organ and hunk of meat, weaving new translucent strands of organic matter in their place.

As the throbbing, eyeless thing finished with each segment of flesh the Surgeon would gently lift it back onto the body and meticulously rework it onto the subject's frame until he was once again whole.

Only the head remained unopened, his mouth moving in a soundless scream of pain and revulsion. The razor gallows lowered the glistening creature onto the man's face, its fleshy underside undulating warmly over his skin. The black needles extended once more from its body, slithering across his cheeks and working their way into his skull through the nose, ears, mouth and eyes. Threads of agony wormed through his brain as each nerve, capillary and blood vessel was stripped out and renewed.

Finally it was done. The grossly swollen organism was lifted from the subject's head and deposited on a wide metal tray at the end of the slab. The Surgeon lifted a narrow bonesaw as the creature began convulsing, its colour fading from lustrous black to a necrotic brown. Before it rotted away to nothing, the Surgeon split it across the thorax with the saw and removed a dripping yellow egg sac. It would be needed to grow another organism for the next time.

The Surgeon nodded to the naked woman who sashayed back to the slab and raised the man into a sitting position. His movements were slow and awkward, but she knew that his discomfort would soon pass. He gathered his clothing and sullenly pulled a short, blue velvet pelisse with silver stitching around his shoulders. He picked up a bronze tipped ebony cane and painfully shuffled towards the chamber's door.

Without turning, he snapped, 'Well? Are you coming?'

She cocked her head to one side, her venomously beautiful features twisting into a sneer of contempt. He turned to face her, as though sensing her loathing of him.

His eyes locked on hers with a mixture of hatred and arousal and she could see from his beseeching eyes that he had suffered greatly. She was glad, and guessed that it would take at least six of the one thousand and nine Pleasures of the Dark to placate him this time.

It was such a shame that human understanding of such things was so limited.

SIX

URIEL RESTED HIS head against the thrumming internal wall of the gunship, his hands clasped in prayer before him as they began the final approach to Brandon Gate, the capital of Pavonis.

Every man under Uriel's command sat in reverent silence, his thoughts directed to the glory that was the Emperor. At the far end of the crew compartment, Adept Ario Barzano sat with his small army of followers and Uriel shook his head slowly. How many servants did one man need?

All his years of training at the Agiselus barracks had hammered discipline and self-reliance into Uriel, and it was strange to see a man with someone to perform his every menial task for him. From the earliest age, children of Ultramar were taught to live a life of discipline, self-denial and simplicity.

Barzano was listening intently to the man he had introduced as Lortuen Perjed, nodding vigorously at whatever the old man was telling him. Adept Perjed was wagging his finger under Barzano's nose as though he were giving him a stern lecture and for a second Uriel wondered exactly who was in charge.

He dismissed the adept from his thoughts and stared out of the thick viewing block set in the side of the gunship as the last filmy clouds vanished from sight and the primary continental mass of Pavonis was laid out before him like a map.

Uriel's first impression of Pavonis was one of contrasts.

Amid the vast green and open landscape, dozens of sprawling manufactorum covered scores of square kilometres in all directions, complete with material bays, warehousing and transportation nodes to link them together. Vast cranes and yellow lifting machinery crawled through these industrial hubs, passed by lumbering rolling stock laden with fuel and supplies for the ever hungry forges. Smoke-belching cooling towers filled the air with clouds of vapour and a yellowish smog clung to the ground, coating the buildings in a filthy ochre residue.

But ahead of them, further out from the manufactorum and set amid a swathe of forest at the foot of some high mountains, Uriel could see a well-designed estate of white stone buildings and guessed that this must belong to the one of the ruling cartels that oversaw production on Pavonis. The Thunderhawk passed over the estate, startling a herd of lithe, horned beasts and passing close enough for Uriel to make out the marble columned entrance of the largest building.

The estate was soon lost to sight as the gunship roared along the line of a fast flowing river and, as the gunship rounded a rocky bluff, Uriel could see the marble city of Brandon Gate on the horizon. The gunship gained altitude and gave the city a slow circuit, allowing Uriel to look down into the star-shaped city below him. Clustered round its defensive, arrowhead bastions, black and smoking manufactorum towns sweltered and bustled in the day's heat while the interior of the city lay indolent and relaxed within, the polished white marble of the buildings radiant in the midday sunshine.

The architecture of the city was comprised of a mixture of old and new: ancient, millennia old structures abutting steel and glass domes and crystal towers. The streets were cobbled, lined with statuary and tall trees.

At the centre of the conglomeration of marble and glass lay the Imperial palace of the governor of Pavonis. A wide cobbled square stretched before the palace gates, its circumference marked by yet more statuary. The palace itself rose high above the streets below, its white towers and crenellated battlements designed in the High Gothic styling popular several thousand years ago. Bronze flying buttresses supported a massive fluted bell tower embellished with a conical roof of beaten gold and studded with precious stones.

Uriel could see from the bell's great, rocking motion that it was tolling, but could not hear it over the roaring of the Thunderhawk's engines.

The many buildings that made up the palace complex stretched over a huge area, encompassing a leafy park, athletics pavilion and a small lake. It was clear that the rulers of Pavonis liked to live well. How much, Uriel wondered, would they be willing to sacrifice in order to keep such a state of affairs? How much might they have already sacrificed?

In addition to the aesthetics of the palace, Uriel's practiced eye took in the many gun emplacements worked cunningly into the building's structure and the entrances to underground launch bays. The palace, and indeed the entire central city, would be a formidable bastion to hold in the event of an insurrection or war.

The gunship began slowing and descending towards the blinking lights of a landing platform set within a ring of tall trees just outside the palace walls. A small observation building and fuel tank, protected by raised blast shielding, sat at its edge.

Uriel snapped his fist against the release mechanism of his restraint harness as their altitude dropped to ten metres, the rest of the Space Marines following suit, and snatched his boltgun from its housing.

Pasanius and Learchus stalked the length of the crew compartment as the green disembarkation lamp began flashing.

'Everybody up! Be ready to debark, secure the perimeter.'

While the sergeants prepared the men for landing, Uriel knelt before the small shrine set in the alcove next to his captain's chair and bowed his head, speaking the Prayer of Battle and Catechism of the Warrior. He gripped the hilt of his bequeathed power sword and rose to stand at the head of the armoured crew ramp at the front of the gunship.

With a decompressive hiss and squeal of hydraulics, the ramp quickly lowered, slamming onto the landing platform. Even before it was fully down, the two squads of Ultramarines swept out from the gunship and moved to perimeter defence positions. Their bolters were held at the ready as their helmeted heads scanned left and right for possible threats.

'My goodness, they're keen aren't they?' clapped Barzano over the shrieking of the Thunderhawk's engines as they powered down.

Pasanius hefted his massive flamer as Uriel rolled his eyes and marched down the crew ramp after Barzano.

As the blast shields at the platform's edge lowered, a plump, red-faced man dressed in the plain black robes of an adept and carrying a geno-key-pad emerged from the observation building.

An entire squad of bolters turned on the man, who squealed and threw his hands up before him.

'Wait! Don't shoot!' he pleaded. 'I'm here to meet Adept Barzano!'

Barzano, Lortuen and Uriel stepped onto the platform as two Ultramarines moved to flank the man and escort him towards their captain. The man was sweating profusely, dwarfed by the armoured giants either side of him.

Barzano stepped forward to greet the florid-faced man, extending one hand and placing the other on his fellow adept's shoulder.

'You must be Adept Ballion Varle. Good morning to you, sir. You already know me, Ario Barzano, we don't need to go over that, but these fine fellows are from the Ultramarines.'

Barzano guided Varle towards Uriel and waved a hand towards Uriel in a comradely gesture. 'This is Captain Uriel Ventris and he's in charge of them. They've come to make sure that everything here goes swimmingly and hopefully put the kibosh on some of the troubles you've been having here, yes?'

Adept Ballion Varle nodded, still looking up in wonder at the expressionless faces of the Space Marines' helmets, and Uriel doubted he was taking in more than one word in three that Barzano was saying.

Barzano slipped his arm over Ballion's shoulder and pressed his thumb onto the geno-keypad the trembling adept carried. The machine clicked and chattered, finally chiming with a soft jingle. Varle managed to tear his eyes from the giant warriors and glanced at the keypad.

'Well, at least you know that I'm no impostor,' smiled Barzano. 'You received my message then?'

'Ah, yes, adept. I did, though to be honest, its contents were rather confusing.'

'Not to worry though, eh? Everything will sort itself out, no need to fret.'

'Yes, but if the governor finds out I knew you would be arriving early and didn't tell her... she'll...' trailed off Varle.

'She'll-?' prompted Barzano.

'Well, she won't be pleased.'

'Excellent, then we're off to a good start.'

'I'm sorry, I don't understand, Adept Barzano,' protested Varle.

'No need to apologise, no reason you should understand. Games within games, my dear chap.'

Lortuen Perjed coughed pointedly, tapping his cane on the metal crew ramp and stared at Barzano, who waved his hand dismissively. 'Pay no mind to me, my dear fellow, I'm rambling. Do that a lot whenever I meet someone new. Now, to business. I think we'll pay a visit to the Imperial palace first, what do you think?'

'I think that the governor won't be expecting you so soon.'

'Then again...' mused Barzano, pointing to a gap in the trees where a cobbled road led towards the city walls. Uriel watched as an open-topped carriage drawn by a quartet of trotting horses made its way along the road towards the edge of the landing platform.

The carriage was borne aloft on anti-grav technology similar to that used by the Chapter's land speeders and its lacquered sides bore a heraldic device depicting a garlanded artillery shell.

Uriel knew that such technology did not come cheaply and that this conveyance must have cost a small fortune.

The horses, surely an affectation of tradition, came to a halt in a cloud of dust and a tall, rakishly handsome man clad in a black suit and blue velvet pelisse with an elaborate feathered bicorn hat clambered down from the carriage and hurried over towards the Thunderhawk, his full features smiling in greeting.

Lortuen Perjed moved to stand beside Barzano and Uriel, his emaciated frame appearing skeletal beside the armoured bulk of the Space Marine captain.

'Vendare Taloun,' whispered Perjed. 'His family cartel produces artillery shells for the Imperial Guard. Governor Shonai ousted him ten years ago and now he leads the opposition to her in the Pavonis senate. Rumour has it that he engineered the death of his brother after they were deposed in order to become family patriarch.'

'Is there any real proof?' whispered Barzano before Taloun reached them.

'No, not as yet.'

Barzano nodded his thanks without turning and stepped forward to greet the new arrival. Uriel noticed a frightened look cross Ballion Varle's face and stood beside Barzano, his hand straying to his sword hilt.

Vendare Taloun bowed elaborately to Barzano and Uriel, doffing his hat and sweeping it behind him. As he stood erect once more Barzano gripped his hand and pumped it vigorously up and down.

'A pleasure Lord Taloun, an absolute pleasure. The name's Ario Barzano, but of course you know that. Come, let us take your magnificent coach into the city, eh?'

Taloun was taken aback by Barzano's manner, but recovered well.

'Certainly, adept,' smiled Taloun, indicating his hovering carriage. 'Would any of your companions care to join us? I believe we can accommodate another one or two.'

'Uriel and Lortuen will join us I think. Adept Ballion, be a good chap and have some food and drink brought to the fellows here will you? Very good!'

As Barzano and Vendare Taloun strode towards the carriage, Lortuen Perjed whispered up to Uriel, 'Well at least we know not to trust Ballion.'

'What do you mean?' asked Uriel as he watched the rounded adept make his way dejectedly back to the observation building where he emerged with a long cape and longer frown.

'How else do you think the Taloun knew to come and greet us?'

Uriel considered the question. 'You suspected you could not trust him and still told him our time of arrival?'

'Adept Barzano felt it was likely that the local adept was in the pocket of one of the local highborn. At least this way we know whose.'

Seeing Uriel's surprise at his candour, Perjed smiled indulgently. 'It's common enough on worlds like these out here in the eastern fringes where a planet might go for decades without official contact from the Administratum.'

'Not in Ultramar,' declared Uriel fiercely.

'Perhaps not,' agreed Perjed. 'But we're not in Ultramar anymore.'

JENNA SHARBEN SMASHED her shield into the man's yellow-stained face and pushed him back into the crowd. The holding cells in the back of their Rhinos were already full. More were on their way from the precinct, but for now all the two lines of judges could do was lock shields and keep the crowd back from the roadway that led to the palace gates.

Nearly five hundred people had gathered since the palace bell had begun ringing but the great, dolorous peals were sure to bring more. She cursed whoever had thought to ring the damned thing. It had been used in the early days of Pavonis's history to gather the members of its senate, but now it was only rung out of tradition.

A damn stupid one at that, reflected Jenna as she pushed the crowd back with her shield. She knew full well that the cartel senators were all contacted directly when required for an assembly. All the bell summoned now were lots of disenfranchised workers who were angry at the very people who would soon be passing this way towards the palace.

'Keep those people back!' shouted Sergeant Collix from behind the line of judges.

What did he think they were doing, wondered Jenna? Enjoying a quiet discussion with scores of furious workers? She had heard the talk around the precinct about the massacre he'd caused in Liberation Square and how he had apparently only stopped the shooting when Virgil Ortega had ordered the judges to cease fire and fall back. What other mistakes might he make and how many people would pay for it?

She realised that this line of thinking was dangerous and tried to push it away as another man reached to grab the top of her shield. She smacked its top edge sharply across his nose and he dropped screaming to the ground.

The pitch of the crowds yelling changed and she risked a glance over her shoulder, seeing a horse-drawn hover carriage approaching the gates. The crowd pushed forward and she grunted as its weight bent the judges' line back.

She dug in her heels and pushed back.

SOLANA VERGEN RECLINED in the padded leather couch of the skimming carriage and examined her moist eyes in a small compact, pondering if they looked suitably grief-stricken. Satisfied that she presented the perfect image of a grieving daughter, beautiful but also teasingly vulnerable, she ran an ivory and silver brush through her long, honey blonde hair as she peered through the velvet-draped window onto the brightness of Liberation Square.

She gave a yawn, seeing more of the tiresome workers lining the road, yelling at her carriage as she passed towards the palace gates. Really, what did they hope to achieve? Then she noticed that many of them were wearing the green and yellow overalls of the Vergen cartel. Why weren't they at work in the manufactorum? Didn't they realise that they were working for her now?

Just because her father had foolishly got himself killed last week did not mean that people could just swan off work whenever they felt like it. She made a mental note to contact the local overseer and have him gather names of all those who had been absent today. To teach them all a lesson she would dismiss them and the overseer for allowing such indiscipline amongst the workforce.

They would all soon see that she was not the soft touch her father had been.

Remembering her father, she pouted as she thought of the condescending crocodile tears Taloun had shed with her after the riot that had seen her father die. Did the man really think that her marriage to his idiot son was anything more than one of convenience? No doubt he thought to install his son as puppet head of the Vergen cartel, but he had reckoned without Solana Vergen.

She already had contacts in the other cartels who would be only too pleased to listen to some of the things her fiancé had sobbed to her as they lay in the darkness after satisfying his baser urges.

Her father's advisors had been horrified at the idea of her taking over the reins of production, but for the life of her she could not imagine why. The head of the Shonai cartel was a woman and governor of the entire planet, for goodness sake! She pulled her pelisse tighter and rested a silk-gloved hand on the edge of her carriage as she pondered the future.

Yes, the Vergen cartel was definitely going to see some changes.

TARYN HONAN TAPPED his fat, beringed fingers in a nervous tattoo on the window of the carriage, feeling the uncomfortable vibration of his carriage's wheels with the cobbles on his ample backside.

He cursed again that he had not been allowed to spend his own cartel's money to invest in an anti-grav carriage. And it was an investment, couldn't the committee see that? It was so humiliating to arrive at the palace on a clattering wagon rather than on a smooth, prestigious conveyance like the ones used by Taloun and de Valtos.

One day he hoped to be as successful as them and have the respect and admiration of the lower cartels. He resolved to watch them closely at this gathering of the senate. Whichever way Taloun and de Valtos went, so too would he. They would be sure to recognise him as an equal if he continued to support their politics. Wouldn't they? Or would they think him spineless, following their lead simply to curry favour? Taryn Honan chewed his bottom lip and wondered what the committee would do.

But his thoughts turned petulant as he pictured them behind the long, oaken desk shaking their humdrum heads as they turned down yet another exciting business venture he had brought before them.

It was so unfair that he alone of the cartel leaders had to answer to a committee. He knew the others all laughed at him because of it, even the tiny, one-manufactorum cartels who could barely afford a seat on the senate.

So he had made a few mistakes. Who in business had not?

Yes, a few trade deals had not gone nearly as well as he might have hoped, and, yes, there had been the unfortunate business of the boy-courtesan who had accessed his credit slate and run up a mammoth debt before fleeing Pavonis on one of the many off-world freighters. But was that any reason for the committee to strip him of executive power and install themselves as omnipotent masters of his finances?

Honan fervently hoped the boy had been aboard one of the ships raided by the eldar and tortured in all manner of sordid ways. That brought a smile to his fleshy face and he licked his rouged lips at the thought, picturing the boy's debasement at the hands of eldar slavers.

He gripped his ebony cane tighter.

KASIMIR DE VALTOS yawned, wincing as his lungs burned with the bitter smog in the air and closed his eyes as his anti-grav carriage smoothly carried him towards the palace. Briefly he wondered what the Shonai bitch could want now, but dismissed the thought as irrelevant. Who really cared what she wanted any more? He smiled as he wondered if it was perhaps to announce her absurd proposal to hunt down the eldar raiders. Did she really think that his cartel could be bought so easily or that the Taloun would not see through her transparent ploy in a heartbeat?

If she thought they were going to play so easily into her hands, then she was even more stupid than de Valtos had given her credit for.

Mykola Shonai may have been a worthy political adversary once, but now she was just a tired old woman. She was barely hanging onto power by her fingertips, not realising that there was a queue of people waiting to stamp on them.

And Kasimir de Valtos was first in line.

He withdrew a silver tobacco tin from beneath his pelisse, pulling out and lighting a thin cheroot. He knew they were bad for his lungs and laughed bitterly at the irony.

After the eldar had finished with him on their infernal ship all those years ago, a breath of fog could sometimes cause his lungs to seize up, but he was damned if he was going to let that stop him from doing exactly what he pleased.

He always had done and always would do, and damn anyone who tried to stop him.

VENDARE TALOUN SMILED, exposing a row of perfect teeth, and Uriel was reminded of the fanged grins of the hissing hormagaunts he'd killed on Ichar IV. Uriel had only met the man ten minutes ago, but already did not like him.

'So, Adept Barzano, Ballion Varle tells me that your ship was attacked during your journey. A bad business indeed. The governor must do more to prevent such atrocities.'

Uriel noticed Taloun was cleverly not trying to hide the fact that Varle had told him of their early arrival, guessing that Barzano must have already known. He wondered if Taloun thought that Barzano could be bought as easily.

'Yes, my dear Taloun, a bad business,' agreed Barzano. 'We were indeed attacked, but saw the rogues off sharpish.'

'That is good to know,' nodded Taloun. 'We have heard such tales about these despicable aliens.'

The man smiled at Uriel, patting his armoured knee. 'But now the brave warriors of the Ultramarines are here, we have nothing to fear, yes?'

Uriel inclined his head, unimpressed by the man's over-familiarity.

'I thank you for your vote of confidence, Guilder Taloun,' replied Uriel, using the local form of address for one of the cartel chiefs. 'By the Emperor's grace we shall rid you of these blasphemous aliens and return peace to Pavonis.'

'Ah, would that it were that simple, my dear Captain Ventris,' sighed Taloun, 'but I fear that Governor Shonai has led us down too ruinous a path for the simple elimination of some bothersome raiders to save our beloved world's economy. Her tithe tax hurts us all, and none more so than myself. Why, only two days ago I was forced to dismiss a thousand people from my employ in order to lower costs and improve margins, but does the governor think of people like me? Of course not.'

Uriel masked his contempt for the man's selfishness and allowed his words to wash over him.

'And what of the extra manpower she promised us to protect the manu-factorum from the Church of Ancient Ways? I have lost over seven thousand man-hours of production to their bombs!' continued Taloun, warming to his theme.

Uriel wondered how many actual men he had lost or if he even cared.

'Perhaps, Guider Taloun,' suggested Uriel with steel in his voice, 'we might leave all this talk of politics for the senate chambers and just enjoy the journey?'

Taloun nodded in acquiescence, but Uriel could see annoyance briefly flare behind his eyes. Taloun was obviously a man unused to being put down by those he perceived as his political inferiors.

Uriel ignored the man and studied the landscape as it sped past them. The city walls were high and sloped inwards towards an overhanging rampart. He could see grenade dumpers worked into the machicolations and power field generators studded along its length. From his readings on Pavonis, Uriel knew that virtually everything would have been produced locally by one or other of the family cartels. The cities of Ultramar did not need such technological trinkets to defend themselves. No, they had stronger defences. Courage, honour and a people that embodied the best examples of all human nobility.

Trained from birth and educated in the ways of the Blessed Primarch, they would never break, never surrender and never submit to such unnecessary luxuries.

Uriel was startled from his bombastic reverie by a pointed cough from Perjed as they moved through the bronze gates of the city.

When seen from ground level the buildings on the inside edge of the walls were much less impressive, functionally constructed, with little or no ornamentation. The buildings of Macragge, while simple, were cunningly constructed to provide a solid, dependable structure as well as presenting something of aesthetic value. He realised that the boxy constructions of Pavonis were designed to be as cost effective as possible and lamented the fact that those who held the purse strings so often hamstrung the architect's art. Here and there, Uriel saw men and women cleaning the building walls of a filmy, ochre residue, the inevitable fallout of living so close to heavy industry. He noticed that all the cleaners wore white overalls so as to be less visible.

The carriage sped effortlessly along the cobbled streets, passing smartly dressed inhabitants in black who doffed their feathered hats as the coach passed. The peals of the palace bell echoed through the affluent streets.

Taloun waved to the passers by and Uriel was struck by his confident, easy manner.

'You are well known in these parts?' asked Barzano.

'Yes, indeed. I have many friends within the city.'

'I take it that the majority of these friends are cartel members?'

'Of course. The common people generally do not venture within the walls of the city. It's the tolls, you see. Most of them cannot afford to come inside. Especially now, what with the governor's tithe tax squeezing every last coin from them.'

'People have to pay to enter this part of the city?'

'Why, yes,' replied Taloun, as though any thought of any other possibility was ridiculous.

'And how much is this toll?'

Taloun shrugged. 'Not sure exactly. Cartel members are exempt from its payment of course, but I contribute a small amount from the yearly profits towards my comings and goings.'

Barzano leaned forwards and waved his hand over the edge of the carriage. 'How then are the city's parks maintained? The buildings cleaned? Who pays for that? The Imperium?'

'No, no, no!' explained Taloun hurriedly. 'I believe a portion of general taxes go towards their upkeep,'

'So in other words,' mused Barzano slowly, 'the populace all contribute towards this lovely place, but cannot enjoy it unless they pay for the privilege once more?'

'I suppose that's one way of looking at it,' replied Taloun haughtily. 'But no one complains.'

'Oh, I don't know,' pointed out Uriel, nodding towards the angry mob gathered before the black gates of the Imperial palace. '*They* don't look too happy about it.'

JENNA WATCHED THE latest carriage approach the palace gates and rolled her eyes as she saw that this one was open-topped. Didn't these fools realise what was happening on the city streets? Those carriages that had already passed had been pelted with bottles and cobbles torn up from the square and only by the Emperor's grace had no one been injured.

'How can you do this?' screamed a soot-smeared man in Jenna's face. 'Don't you know you're helping prop up a corrupt regime of thieves and liars?'

Sergeant Collix was suddenly at her side and slammed his shock maul into the man's face. The man collapsed, blood spurting from his shattered jaw and Collix dragged him over the line of judges. The sergeant hauled the insensible man's bleeding body towards the Rhinos.

True, the man's words had been illegally subversive, but she realised that there was the very real possibility he was right.

Barely five years out of the Schola Progenium and her Adeptus Arbites training only completed six months ago, such concerns were far above Jenna's head. Her superiors would decide if the rulers of Pavonis had become criminally incompetent and remove them from office should that prove to be the case.

She tensed her leg muscles, ready to push the crowd again, but suddenly realised there was no need as the people before her took a collective step backward, staring in wonder at something behind her. Making sure there was nobody threatening nearby, she spared a hurried glance over her shoulder.

A splendid hover carriage swept by, but it was the blue armoured giant sitting along with the Taloun and two men she didn't recognise that claimed Jenna Sharben's attention.

She had never seen a Space Marine in the flesh before, but had seen the devotional placards and posters on her homeworld of Verdan III. Never had she imagined that the outlandish proportions they ascribed to Space Marines could actually be real. She recognised the alabaster white emblem on his shoulder guard as belonging to the Ultramarines and felt a flutter of unreasoning fear as the enormous warrior glanced over at her.

The carriage raced through the palace gates and the Ultramarines warrior was lost to sight. She shook herself free of her awe at the Space Marine's size and turned back to the crowd, ready for more trouble.

But such a physical reminder of the Imperium's power had robbed the crowd of any further desire for troublemaking and slowly it began to break up. First in ones and twos, then in greater numbers as word of the enormous champion of the Emperor's arrival spread to those at the rear of the crowd who hadn't seen him. A few die-hard demagogues tried to keep the crowd together with attempts at fiery rhetoric, but they were soon clubbed to the ground and dragged towards the holding cells of the Rhinos.

'Did you see the size of him?' declared the judge next to her. 'The Space Marines are here!'

Yes, thought Jenna Sharben, the Space Marines are here.

But did that mean things had just got better or worse?

THE DOME OF the Pavonis Senate Chambers of Righteous Commerce was cast from solid bronze, its inner face lined with a rich patina of age and smoke. Beneath the dome, the circular chamber was tiered and filled with shouting members of the Pavonis cartels. The tier nearest the red and gold chequered floor was reserved for the heads of the twenty-four cartels, though the burgundy leather seats were rarely fully occupied except at the beginning of the financial year.

Sixteen of the positions were currently occupied. The heads of the six most profitable cartels – the Shonai, the Vergen, the de Valtos, the Taloun, the Honan and the Abrogas – were all in attendance, making ostentatious displays of friendship.

Behind them sat the members of their families or those who could claim some relation by marriage or adoption.

Finally, in the highest tier, at the rear of the chamber, sat the equally vocal members of each cartel who could not claim a blood tie to its owners, but nevertheless had signed exclusive contracts of loyalty to its charter. This was by far the largest tier in the chamber and its segregated members shouted venomously at one another despite the repeated calls for order by the bewigged Moderator of Transactions. These were the hangers-on and opportunists who sought social advancement through their association with the cartel of their choice. Uriel noticed Adept Ballion Varle sitting shiftily in the section reserved for supporters of the Taloun.

Guests and those without formal written remit to be part of the chamber's activities were permitted to sit in the bare wooden benches of this tier and it was from here that Ario Barzano, Lortuen Perjed and Uriel Ventris watched the dealings below.

Uriel could feel the eyes of many of the upper tier spectators upon him and forced himself to ignore them as he listened to proceedings on the floor below.

'Can't see or hear a damned thing from here,' grumbled Barzano, straining over the brass rail of the tier.

'I believe that is the idea,' observed Perjed acidly. 'Many worlds in the galactic east are notoriously reluctant to allow observers to participate in their government. Even observers as… ah, influential as you.'

'Is that so?' snapped Barzano. 'Well, we'll see about that.'

Uriel could understand Barzano's frustration about being placed here, but thanks to his genetic enhancements, he could hear and see perfectly well from their lofty position.

'Now who's that big fellow in black?' asked Barzano pointing to a corpulent man in the centre of the chamber banging a long polearm topped with a bronze sphere.

'That is the Moderator of Transactions,' answered Lortuen Perjed. 'He acts as the chairman of senate meetings, approves the agenda and decrees who may or may not speak.'

'Doesn't look like he's doing a very good job of it. What in blazes is he saying anyway?'

'He is appealing for quiet,' said Uriel.

Barzano and Perjed stared at him for a second before remembering his enhanced senses.

'Still, it won't do, Uriel,' snapped Barzano. 'It won't do at all. You might be able to hear, but I don't want to find out what's happening secondhand. No offence to you of course, my dear fellow.'

'None taken,' assured Uriel. 'First-hand battle information is always more reliable.'

'Exactly so. Now come on, let's get out of this perch and a bit closer to the action.'

Barzano led the way down the stone steps towards the lower tiers. A few muscular bailiffs in fur lined robes and bicorn hats with golden chains of office around their necks tried to bar their way with black staffs tipped with bronze. Uriel could see that they carried the cudgels like they knew how to use them and guessed that some senate meetings required breaking up when the 'discussions' became overly heated. One look at the massive Ultramarines captain soon convinced them that discretion was the better part of valour, however, and within minutes, Barzano, Perjed and Uriel were ensconced in the padded leather seating behind the heads of the cartels.

The Moderator of Transactions tapped his cane on the tiled floor and stared pointedly at the three interlopers in his senate chambers. The bailiffs behind them shrugged. Heads were turning to face them and a pregnant hush fell over the crowded hall as they waited what steps the Moderator of Transactions would take.

Uriel folded his massive arms and stared back at the sweating man. The tension was broken when Vendare Taloun stood and waved his cane in the direction of the Moderator.

'Moderator, might I be permitted to address our guests?'

The man scowled, but nodded. 'The floor recognises the Honourable Vendare Taloun.'

'Thank you. Friends, fellow cartel members and traders! It is with great pleasure that I welcome Adepts Barzano and Perjed and Captain Uriel

Ventris of the Ultramarines as our guests here today. These honoured visitors from the Emperor have come to our troubled world to see what can be done to remedy the terrible hardships we have been forced to endure these last few, painful years. I feel it is only good manners to welcome them to this, our humble assemblage and extend every courtesy during their stay on Pavonis.'

Applause and jeers greeted Taloun's words in equal measure as Perjed leaned over to whisper to Barzano and Uriel. 'Very clever. He infers that it was his influence that brought us here and thus he is seen as a statesman with a greater perspective than the governor while at the same time avoiding criticising her directly.'

'Yes,' agreed Barzano, his eyes narrowing. 'Very clever.'

As the jeering, clapping and calls for other potential speakers continued, Uriel studied the other members of the cartels sitting in the front tier. The bench nearest the moderator bore the governor of Pavonis and her advisors. A thin, acerbic faced man stood behind the governor and sitting beside her was an older man with an enormous grey beard, smoking a pipe. Both men were whispering urgently to her.

Uriel liked the look of Mykola Shonai. Despite the chaos of the senate chambers, she comported herself with dignity and he could see she had great strength in her.

As Taloun sat down, Uriel noticed a white haired man seated near him whose scarred, burned face had the unhealthy pallor of synth-flesh. This man seemed uninterested in speaking and stared with undisguised hatred at governor Shonai.

'That's Kasimir de Valtos,' whispered Perjed, noticing the direction of Uriel's stare. 'Poor chap's ship was attacked by the eldar pirates. Apparently they did all manner of horrible things to him before he escaped.'

'What sort of things?'

'I don't know. "Horrible" is all my records mention.'

'What does his cartel produce?'

'Engines and hulls for Leman Russ battle tanks and heavy artillery pieces mainly, though I think that much of that is overseen by his subordinates.'

'Why do you say that, Lortuen?' asked Barzano.

'Administratum records for this world have listed Guilder de Valtos as applying for no less than seven Imperial permits to lead archaeological expeditions throughout the system. Many of the finest pieces in the Pavonis Paymaster's Gallery have come from his own private collection. He is quite the patron of the arts and has a passion for antiquities.'

'Really? It seems we share an interest then,' chuckled Barzano.

Uriel wondered exactly what that meant as Perjed threw his master a sharp look, and also pondered why Barzano himself did not know these facts. He nodded towards a bearded man with a ponytail who sat slumped on the bench close to de Valtos and Taloun. He could see that the man's eyes were glazed and even over the bodily odours of the hundreds of individuals in the hall, Uriel could detect the faint aroma of a soporific emanating from the man, possibly obscura.

'What about him, who is he?'

Perjed squinted along his nose and sighed in disappointment. 'That, Captain Ventris, is Beauchamp Abrogas, and a more sorry specimen of humanity you will be hard pressed to find this side of the Ophelian Pilgrim trail. He is a waster who could barely spell his own name if you handed him the quill and wrote half the letters for him.'

The bile in Lortuen Perjed's voice surprised Uriel and the old man seemed to realise this. He smiled weakly and explained, 'My apologies, but I find the squandering of an individual's Emperor-given talents such as this wasteful. And if there is one thing the Administratum hates, it is waste, my dear captain.'

Uriel turned his attention back to the floor of the chamber where a modicum of order had been restored. The moderator was pointing his sphere-topped staff at a fat man in a powdered white wig that cascaded across his shoulders as a shrill voiced woman with long blonde hair yelled at the moderator.

Uriel raised a questioning eyebrow to Perjed, who shrugged. 'She sits in the seat normally reserved for the Vergen, so I can only assume she is his daughter. I know nothing about her,' admitted the adept.

The woman would have been attractive, thought Uriel, had her face not been set in a permanent sneer of self-righteous indignation. She gripped the rail before her and tried to make herself heard over the shouts of the other members.

'I demand senate chambers recognise my authority to speak in the name of the Vergen cartel!' she spat. 'As the daughter of Leotas Vergen I demand the right to be heard.'

The moderator of transactions blatantly ignored the woman as two bailiffs moved to stand before her. The moderator turned away and said, 'The floor recognises the... Honourable Taryn Honan.'

A few bawdy laughs greeted this last comment from the high tiers along with balled up agenda sheets. The man appeared flustered at the reaction and puffed out his considerable chest before loudly clearing his throat and speaking in a high pitched, nasal voice.

'I think I speak for all of us when I join with Guilder Taloun in welcoming our honoured guests to Pavonis, and I for one wish to extend to them the full hospitality of my country estates.'

'Has the committee approved that, Honan?' shouted a voice from the opposite side of the hall. Applause and laughter greeted the joker's comment and Uriel noticed Guilder Taloun rubbing the bridge of his nose in exasperation, as though embarrassed by the support of Honan.

Guilder Honan sat back in his seat and rested his hands on his belly, bewildered and shamed by the laughter at his expense. The shrill voiced woman again began yelling at the moderator as he stamped the staff onto the tiles and shouted, 'If you are quite finished, gentlemen, today's first order of business is an Extraordinary Motion tabled by the honourable Guilder Taloun.'

Across the chamber, the governor of Pavonis surged to her feet.

'Moderator, this is intolerable! Will you allow Guilder Taloun to hijack proceedings like this? I called this assembly of the senate and the right of first voice is mine.'

'An Extraordinary Motion takes precedence over the right of first voice,' explained Taloun patiently.

'I know the conventions of procedure!' barked Shonai.

'Then can I assume you will allow me to continue, governor?'

'I know what you're doing here, Vendare. So just get on with it, damn you.'

'As you wish, Governor Shonai,' replied Taloun courteously. Vendare Taloun pushed himself to his feet and spread wide his hands, making his way to the centre of the chequered floor and taking hold of the staff offered to him by the Moderator of Transactions.

Once divested of the staff, the Moderator of Transactions consulted a data slate and said, 'Guilder Taloun, I notice that your submitted motion does not bear a title. Under article six of the conventions of procedure, you are required to fill subject form three-two-four dash nine, in triplicate. Can I assume that you will do so now?'

'My profound apologies for the absence of a title, but I felt that to announce the topic of my motion would be to cause unnecessary bias had its subject matter become common knowledge before my raising it. Rest assured I shall complete the said form immediately following this assembly.'

The moderator nodded in acceptance and yielded the floor to Vendare Taloun.

He rapped the staff sharply on the floor.

'Friends, we live in troubled times,' he began, to sycophantic applause.

Taloun smiled, accepting the applause graciously and raised his hands for silence before continuing.

'Seldom in our proud commercial history have we faced such threats as we do today. Vile alien raiders plague our shipping, the Church of Ancient Ways bomb our manufactorum and kill our workers. The business of trade has instead become the business of survival as costs rise, taxes bite harder and margins shrink.'

Obsequious nods and shouts echoed around the hall as Taloun began to pace the floor, jabbing with the staff to accentuate his words, and Uriel recognised a powerful orator in Vendare Taloun.

'And what does our vaunted governor do about this crisis?' demanded Taloun.

Heated shouts of 'nothing' and other, less savoury comments roared from the assembly as Taloun continued. 'There is not one amongst us that does not suffer under her financially oppressive regime. My own cartel groans under the weight of Governor Shonai's tithe tax as I know others do too. Brother de Valtos, you yourself were attacked by these despicable alien raiders who plague us so, and tortured most horribly. And yet the governor does nothing!

'Sister Vergen, your own dearly beloved father was murdered a stone's throw from where we sit. And yet the governor does nothing! Brother Abrogas, your own blood relative was nearly murdered on the streets of his hometown. And yet the governor does nothing!'

Solana Vergen was too startled by Taloun's acknowledgement of her loss to respond in a suitably grief-stricken manner, while Beauchamp Abrogas did not even register that he had been named.

'Our world is under siege, my friends. The vultures gather to pick our carcass clean. And yet the governor does nothing!'

Thunderous applause greeted Taloun's words and Uriel could see the governor's two advisors practically holding her down as Taloun turned to address the moderator of transactions directly. The chamber suddenly fell deathly silent as the assembly waited for what Taloun would say next.

'Moderator,' he announced formally, 'I table a motion that the senate cast a vote of no confidence in Governor Shonai and remove her from office!'

℧
SEVEN

MAGOS DAL KOLURST, tech-priest of the Tembra Ridge deep-bore mine, checked the map on his data slate for the third time to make sure he was in the right place. The glow of the display threw his face into stark relief and cast a flickering green halo around him in the darkness of the mine. He glanced above him, checking that the line of glow-globes and electrical cable was intact and connected to the power transformer. He leaned closer to the transformer, hearing the reassuring hum that told him it was operational.

Yes, everything seemed to be in order. The proper obeisance had been made to the Omnissiah and he had checked that all the correct cabling was connected.

So why was he standing alone in the sweltering darkness of the mine, with only the glow of a data slate and his shoulder lamp to illuminate his surroundings?

He checked the map one more time, just to make sure he was in the right place. Shaft secundus, tunnel seventy-two, junction thirty-six. Kolurst knew he was in the right place, and couldn't understand why there was no light here, when everything told him this part of the mine workings should be lit up as bright as day.

He sighed as he realised he would have to request another generator, knowing that Overseer Lasko wasn't going to like that, what with times being so hard and the cartel clamping down on costs. It was the third generator they'd gone through in as many weeks and Kolurst just couldn't understand what was going wrong with them. He and his fellow tech-priests had hooked up each one correctly, blessing them with the Prayer to the Omnissiah and striking the rune of activation upon their surface. Each generator would be fine for a few days, maybe a week until the same thing kept happening.

One by one the transformers would stop feeding power to the glow-globes and from the depths upwards, the mine would slowly revert to darkness. Kolurst had checked each transformer again and again and found the same thing. They were supplying power, but none of it was being routed where it was required. The power was there, but where was it going?

Kolurst jumped as he heard a soft, rustling noise behind him.

He spun, directing his lamp where the sound had come from.

There was nothing there, just a soft susurration of sand hissing from a crack in the wall. Kolurst released the breath he'd been holding and wiped the sweat from his brow. He turned back to the transformer and shook his head. He began to–

There it was again. Kolurst shone his lamp into the darkness. He panned the beam back and forth, jerking it quickly as he caught a flash of movement at the edge of the light.

Something gleaming skittered out of sight round a bend in the tunnel.

'Hello?' he called, fighting to keep the tremor from his voice. 'Is someone there?'

There was no answer, but he hadn't really expected one.

Slowly, he edged towards the turn, craning his lamp further and further into the darkness. He heard a soft tapping, as of thin metal rods clicking together.

He jumped as his data slate crackled, and he closed his eyes, fighting for calm. He was letting the foolish stories the mineworkers were telling get to him. Their stupid superstitions had spooked him and he tried to dismiss them as the delusions of overactive imaginations.

That was all very well on the surface, but here, ten thousand metres below ground, it was a very different matter indeed. Sweat trickled from his brow and dripped from his nose. It was nothing, just some…

Some what?

He glanced at the slate and gave it a perturbed tap as the display began to fade. Soon the display was dead and he cursed the ill-fate that had seen him assigned to this wretched place rather than one of the cartels' manufactorum.

The sound came again and he shivered, despite the dry heat of the deep mine. He slowly backed away in the direction of the elevator shaft as the skittering noise began growing in volume.

He swallowed hard. His heart was beating a desperate tattoo on his ribs.

The shoulder lamp flickered, its weak glow fading.

Suddenly, Kolurst could see movement at the edge of its beam, dozens of tiny, glittering reflections carpeting the floor of the mine. He took another step backwards.

And the movement followed him.

Abruptly, the light from his lamp failed completely, plunging him into utter darkness.

Magos Dal Kolurst whimpered in terror and turned to run.

But they had him before he managed more than two paces.

♈

EIGHT

THE SENATE CHAMBER erupted. Many had expected Taloun's words, but to hear them said so baldly was still a shock. A hundred voices all shouted at once and Uriel noticed that the governor sat calm and immobile, as though a long-feared event had finally transpired.

Taloun stood silently in the centre of the floor, the speaker's staff held before him like a weapon. The moderator shouted for calm as bailiffs moved through the crowd, quieting the more vocal members of the upper tiers with sharp blows from their cudgels.

Taloun raised his hands in a mute appeal for quiet and slowly the shouts of approval and denial died away, to be replaced by an excited buzz. He tapped the staff on the floor and asked, 'Who amongst the heads of the families will second my motion?'

Kasimir de Valtos rose from his seat with a feral grin of vindication and rested his pale hands on the railing. Uriel noticed that these too were the mottled white of artificial skin and he saluted the man's courage at having escaped his alien torturers.

'I, Kasimir de Valtos, will second the honourable Taloun's motion.'

Taloun bowed deeply. 'My thanks, Guilder de Valtos.'

Jeers and boos came from the tiers behind the governor.

The moderator retrieved his staff and waved it above his head as Taloun made his way back to his seat. He rapped his staff sharply on the floor.

'A motion of no confidence has been tabled and seconded by two members. To decide whether such a vote shall indeed be cast, I ask the heads of the cartels to indicate their support or otherwise for this motion.'

The moderator moved to his chair of office and pulled on a long velvet rope, exposing a large display slate behind a wide curtain on the rear wall of the chamber.

'This should be interesting,' whispered Barzano. 'Now we'll see who's in bed with who.'

Slowly at first, the icons of the family cartels began appearing on the slate.

Barzano nudged Perjed, who began copying the votes onto his own slate. De Valtos and Taloun's icons were, unsurprisingly, the first to appear in favour of the vote with Shonai's vote against the motion following closely. The Honan icon appeared next to Taloun's to mocking laughter from the upper tiers.

A gasp of surprise echoed around the chamber as the Vergen icon flashed up in favour of the vote. As the icon appeared, the men behind Solana Vergen desperately began waving towards their cartel's scion and shouting at her to listen to reason.

'My, my,' breathed Perjed. 'Now there's an upset.'

'In what way?' asked Barzano.

'Well, the Vergen have been allies of the Shonai for nearly ten years ever since they allied to win the election from the Taloun. Leotas Vergen and Governor Shonai were rumoured to be very good friends indeed, if you take my meaning. It seems that Leotas Vergen's daughter does not intend that friendship to continue.'

Governor Shonai stared with undisguised anger at the smug, smiling face of Solana Vergen, her fury clear for all to see.

A wadded up agenda smacked the top of Beauchamp Abrogas's head and he sat up suddenly, pressing a button at random on his voting panel. The Abrogas icon appeared beside the governor's and its members let out a collective sigh of exasperation in the foolishness of their leader.

With the votes of the major players cast, the smaller cartel heads began allocating their votes, having seen which way the political wind was blowing. Eventually all the votes were cast and the result was clear. The Shonai cartel had lost.

Lortuen Perjed nodded as he entered the last cartel's vote into his slate.

'The governor has lost this round and the matter will now be thrown open to a full vote of the entire senate, though this will largely be a formality since I doubt any of the cartel members will vote against their commercial masters.'

'So the planetary governor has been overthrown. Just like that?' asked Uriel.

'Not quite,' grinned Barzano, rising from his seat.

'What are you doing?' demanded Lortuen Perjed.

'I'm going to stretch my legalistic muscles. Uriel, come with me.'

Perjed gripped Barzano's robe and hissed, 'This is hardly fitting behaviour for an adept of the Administratum.'

'Exactly,' smiled Barzano with the glint of mischief in his eyes.

URIEL FOLLOWED ADEPT Barzano down the last few steps to the chequered chamber floor, easily lifting aside a startled bailiff who blocked their way. Barzano pushed open the wooden swing gate and strode into the centre of the chamber. An astonished hush descended on the chamber at his audacity and the sheer physical presence of an Imperial Space Marine. The Moderator of Transactions stood incredulous below the voting slate, his face red with fury.

His annoyance at having the normal order of business disrupted overcame his common sense and he advanced on Barzano, spluttering in indignation.

'This is completely out of order, sir! You cannot flout the regulations that govern our lawful assemblage in this manner.'

'Oh, I think I can,' smiled Barzano, pulling the red seal of the Administratum from his robes and holding it above his head for the chamber to see. Uriel kept a wary eye on the senate bailiffs, though none appeared willing to rise to the defence of the senate's regulations.

Barzano placed the seal back in his robes and addressed the assembly of Pavonis.

'Good day to you all. My name is Ario Barzano and I come here in the name of the Divine Emperor of Mankind. It is my task to set this world back on the path of righteousness, to stamp out the corruption and troubles that plague your world. I come with the highest authority and the strength to enforce the Administratum's will.'

Uriel could not help but notice worried glances passing between several of the cartel heads as the word 'corruption' was mentioned. Barzano swept his arms wide in a gesture that encompassed the entire senate chamber.

'Consider this vote on hold, gentlemen. And ladies,' added Barzano with a nod to Solana Vergen, who fluttered her eyelashes at the adept. Angry voices were raised, but died away as Barzano stood beside Uriel's armoured bulk.

'Now if you will excuse me, my learned friends, the governor of Pavonis and I have a great many things to discuss. Good day to you all.'

Barzano bowed deeply and indicated that Lortuen Perjed should join him on the floor. The old man shuffled out to meet Barzano and Uriel, his face a deep red. As he reached them, he gripped Barzano's arm and whispered, 'That was entirely inappropriate.'

'I know,' answered Barzano, pulling free of Perjed's grasp and marching over to the governor's seats.

Mykola Shonai sat dumbfounded at this unexpected development and numbly rose to her feet as Barzano approached.

'You have my thanks, Adept Barzano. I had not expected you until later this evening.'

Barzano winked and leaned in close to the governor, 'I like to make an entrance, Governor Shonai, but don't thank me yet, this is not a reprieve. It is merely a stay of what may still inevitably happen.'

Governor Shonai nodded, understanding the distinction, but grateful for the lifeline nonetheless.

'I thank you anyway.'

'Now, before your Moderator of Transactions has an apoplectic fit, I suggest we all retire to somewhere a little less public?'

'Agreed.'

ARIO BARZANO AND Lortuen Perjed sat in the governor's chambers while Uriel stood at ease behind them. Governor Shonai sat behind her desk with Almerz Chanda and Leland Corteo either side of her. Smoke from Corteo's pipe layered below the ceiling, circulated by a leisurely spinning fan.

'I have to say, adept,' began Mykola Shonai, 'that I had not expected you to allow me to remain in office.'

'I still may not, Governor Shonai, 'that decision remains to be taken.'

'Then why did you not just allow me to fall to Taloun's vote?'

Almerz Chanda leaned forwards. 'Surely, governor, it is enough for now that the adept did not?'

'No, Almerz, it is not. Well, adept? Why?'

'I liked the look of you, and I could tell Uriel did too,' explained Barzano. Uriel had not thought he had been so obvious in his appraisal of the governor and his respect for Barzano's powers of perception raised a notch.

'Besides, my dear lady, from what I could see of the other potential candidates, you appeared to be the least, how shall I say...?'

'Slimy, deceitful and untrustworthy?' she suggested.

Barzano laughed. 'Yes, something like that. But on a more serious note, we dislike upsetting the stability of a world too much if we can at all avoid it. Replacing you at this juncture would have achieved little of value.'

'So in other words, this may only be a temporary arrangement?'

'Exactly. I will be blunt, governor. You have failed in your duties as an Imperial commander. The tithes that are the right and proper duty of the Emperor have not been forthcoming and your inability to maintain the peace on this world has resulted in my despatch to rectify the situation.'

'It is certainly true that we have been having our fair share of problems, but past circumstances have–'

'Past circumstances do not interest me, Governor Shonai,' snapped Barzano and Uriel was surprised at the vicious tone that edged his words. Perjed appeared concerned also and leaned forward in his seat as Barzano continued.

'What does interest me, however, is your lack of progress in eliminating this Church of Ancient Ways, an organisation that sounds dangerously like a cult to my way of thinking. What also interests me is the inability of your system defence ships to hunt down the eldar raiders that attacked our ship and caused the deaths of a great many servants of the Emperor. But what concerns me most of all is the fact that you did not feel it necessary to report any of this to the Imperium. An explanation of these circumstances would be most edifying.'

'What would you have me tell you, adept? The Adeptus Arbites and our own local security forces have tried to stamp out the Church of Ancient Ways, but they are like shadows and we can find no clue as to how they are being supplied with their weaponry,' snarled Shonai. 'As to the eldar raiders, our ships are ready to be mothballed; there is not one amongst them less than two thousand years old. How would you have us fight them?'

Barzano smiled as the governor finished her tirade and sat back in his chair, apparently satisfied with her answer.

Mykola Shonai placed her hands, palm down, on her desk. 'I admit it was… unwise not to have come forward sooner regarding our troubles, but I believed we could deal with them internally. If I am guilty of anything, it is that I placed too much faith in my own abilities to manage this crisis.'

'Yes,' agreed Barzano. 'But I do not believe your administration is quite beyond redemption. I propose that we put aside past mistakes for now and work to resolve the current situation as quickly as possible. You agree?'

'Of course,' said the governor quickly. 'What can I do to help?'

'The first stage in any operation is information gathering and to facilitate my researches, I shall need complete access to the data files you have in the palace logic engines and cogitators. And of course that includes all your own private files.'

'Outrageous!' stormed Almerz Chanda. 'You overstep your mark, sir!'

'Really? You have things in the files you would rather I not see, Mister Chanda? Records of bribes placed, illegal dealings with xenos and the like?' joked Barzano, though Uriel wondered how much of the question was in jest.

'Certainly not,' blustered Chanda. 'But it is a huge breach of protocol to have the governor's personal files rummaged through as though she were a common criminal.'

Mykola Shonai reached up and placed a soothing hand on Chanda's arm.

'It's alright, Almerz, I have nothing to hide. Adept, you shall have all that you require. What else do you need?'

'Since I do not particularly wish to be seen to be choosing sides amongst the cartels by accepting any offers of accommodation which I am sure will soon be forthcoming, I will require a suite of rooms in the palace for myself and my entourage. At present they are waiting at a landing platform on the edge of the city. I would appreciate it if you could send word to them along with adequate transport to convey them and my effects to the palace.'

'It shall be done at once,' assured the governor, nodding to Chanda. He bristled at such a menial task, but bowed and left the room. 'Anything else?'

'Yes. As I will no doubt be dealing with the local security forces during my investigations I shall be requiring a liaison with the Adeptus Arbites. Contact them and have them assign me an officer.'

'They won't like that much,' noted Leland Corteo.

'I don't much care whether they like it or not, just make sure it happens.'

Leland Corteo flinched at Barzano's tone, but nodded and scratched an entry in his notebook.

'Right, that should take care of matters on the domestic front. Turning our attention to the question of the eldar raiders, I propose that the *Vae Victus* commence patrol operations in the local area as soon as possible. Uriel? I think it best if you appraise the governor of any assistance you will be requiring.'

Uriel snapped to attention and stepped forward. 'To be fully effective, we shall require complete annotated dossiers on every settlement raided and ship attacked, complete with crew manifests and payload records. Also, a system map recording the exact time and location of each attack. From this it will be possible to obtain a central locus of attacks and devise an efficient patrol circuit.'

'I shall see to it personally, Captain Ventris.'

Uriel nodded and stepped back.

'When can you begin patrol operations, Uriel?'

'The Tech-marines are ministering to the ship as we speak and as soon as the requested information is transferred to the *Vae Victus* we can begin.'

Barzano rubbed his chin thoughtfully. 'Excellent. I want you to return to the ship and hunt down these deviants. I cannot stress enough the importance I attach to this task, captain.'

'Return to the ship? Adept, I was entrusted with your personal safety and I gave my word to Lord Calgar that you would come to no harm.'

'And I shall not, for you shall leave me Sergeant Learchus's squad as a bodyguard. Unless you have any reservations regarding his ability to protect me?'

'Of course I have not, Learchus is a proven veteran of many campaigns. I trust him absolutely.'

'Then I share your trust also.'

Suddenly Uriel realised how cunningly Barzano had manoeuvred him. Learchus was a great warrior and would die before allowing the adept to come to any harm, and to relieve him of this duty would be to insult his honour. Uriel had sworn to Marneus Calgar that he would protect Barzano, but to remain with the adept would mean that his men would go into battle without their captain. Reluctantly, Uriel realised that as captain of the Fourth Company he had to be able to trust the officers appointed beneath him.

He bowed to Barzano. 'You have a fine bodyguard in Sergeant Learchus and his warriors. He comes from a family of honour and will not fail you.'

'And nor will you, I'm sure, Uriel.'

'Not while my body draws breath,' the Space Marine assured the adept.

ARIO BARZANO RUBBED his eyes and leaned back in his chair as he felt the onset of a splitting headache. His researches had been fruitful, but he was growing weary of the catalogue of betrayals, double crosses and plain, human unpleasantness he had unearthed in the last two days. He pushed himself away from the desk and poured himself a strong measure of uskavar, the local drink of choice on Pavonis.

The chambers the governor had allocated his entourage were dim, the candles having nearly burned down to rippled puddles of wax. He lit another batch as he sipped the strong liquor and pondered exactly how he was going to combat the Church of Ancient Ways. Mykola Shonai had not lied when she had said that they were like shadows. In fact clutching a shadow would be easy compared to learning the whereabouts of this group.

The sect had first appeared seven years ago when a massive explosion destroyed one of the Honan's manufactorum, the resulting fire ripping through the nearby supply depots and causing untold damage. It had been put down to poor safety controls until a coded communiqué had arrived at the governor's office denouncing the financial greed of Pavonis's rulers and vowing the continuance of the bombings.

Soon, every cartel had suffered at the hands of the terrorists and the security forces had been powerless to prevent the atrocities from continuing. Nearly four hundred people had died thus far and, while on a galactic scale, such numbers were inconsequential, Barzano knew that each life was a link in a chain that would one day unravel if he and his ilk could not prevent such acts.

The local security forces on Pavonis had had little success in apprehending the terrorists, and Barzano was not surprised. He had quickly realised that their organisation was a farce. Funded by the cartels, they were no more than private security groups who protected their paymasters' interests and maintained a policy of brutal discipline on the workers, but nothing else. The few, small Adeptus Arbites garrisons scattered across the planet could do little other than enforce the Emperor's laws in the heart of the cities. In the shantytowns and worker districts that surrounded the manufactorum, the only law was that decreed by the cartels.

And they were little better than criminals themselves from what Barzano could tell. A more devious nest of scheming vipers he had scarce encountered – outside his own organisation, he reflected with a wry grin. Each of the cartels had, at one point or another, allied with one other in return for short-term goals and profits, before reneging on their contracts and supporting yet another cartel. It appeared that this was a quite normal state of affairs and it depressed Barzano immensely to think that, as the forty-first millennium drew to a close, humanity still could not put aside its differences when virtually every alien race in the galaxy was bent on its destruction.

Across almost every system in the galaxy, orks slaughtered and pillaged their way at random, and he viciously suppressed his memories of the wartorn world of Armageddon. And this close to the eastern fringes, he knew it was only a matter of time until the expanding borders of the Tau Empire reached Pavonis.

Yes, the galaxy was a hostile place, and only united through stability could the Imperium of Man hope to survive. Any other course of action was folly of the worst kind and he had sworn an oath to ensure that its stability was preserved. What had the rulers of Pavonis done to preserve the sanctity of the Emperor's realm?

He returned to his chair and activated the display terminal. The corner of the display blinked with yet another message, but he ignored it, knowing it would be another invitation to sample the hospitality of one of the cartels. Invitations to dine, to hunt, to drink and partake in other, less savoury, pastimes had come in from the every one of the commercial houses. He had politely declined them all.

He scrolled down the information he had collated over the last two days.

Of the smaller cartels, he had found nothing more than the usual round of alliances, counter alliances and pact breaking. The leaders of the larger cartels were a much more interesting cast of rogues, however.

Beauchamp Abrogas spent his time destroying his central nervous system with illegal drugs and squandering his family's fortune.

Taryn Honan was a fat fool, who spent fabulous sums on courtesans and would have a hard time managing a room full of lobotomised servitors.

He didn't know much about Solana Vergen, but had sensed the falseness of her grief over the death of her father. And changing her cartel's vote so spectacularly in the senate chamber did not bode well for the stability of her personality.

De Valtos spent most of his time locked away at his estates or chasing after antiques scattered throughout the system. Even a blind man could see the hatred and bitterness he harboured towards the governor, though Barzano could find no direct cause for that rancour. That definitely warranted further investigation. There was also the tangible link between de

Valtos and the dark eldar, but Barzano understood it was not the sort of link that would engender co-operation. He had been tortured almost unto death aboard the alien vessel and, despite all the odds against such an occurrence, survived.

Barzano had discounted Mykola Shonai at the start of his investigations. He had felt no deceit from her upon their meeting and, in any case, her second, six-year term as planetary governor was almost at an end and the constitution of Pavonis forbade her to serve a consecutive third. She had nothing to gain and everything to lose by prolonging the current state of affairs. Ario Barzano knew that this fact alone could not discount her from his suspicions; he had exposed traitors with far less motive than Shonai. But affairs such as these had been his daily bread for too many years now and he fancied that he had a talent for spotting a liar, and Mykola Shonai did not seem like one to him.

Truth be told, he admired the woman. She had tried her best for her world. But he knew that simply trying one's best was not good enough on its own. Effort had to be coupled with results and the results on Pavonis spoke for themselves.

But the Taloun…

That was a different story. Defeated twice in the elections by the combined power of the Shonai and Vergen cartels over the last ten years, Vendare Taloun had everything to gain. Whenever he approached problems such as these, he always began by asking the same question. Who has the most to gain? In the chaos of terrorist activities, alien pirates and political upheaval, Taloun's cartel stood out amongst all the others.

It had suffered less than the others in the bombings with the possible exception of the Shonai, and Barzano had long ago accepted the truth that there was no such thing as coincidence in this existence. The synchronicity of timing in the arrival of the eldar raiders and the emergence of the Church of Ancient Ways spoke of an orchestrating hand to him. Taloun had already displayed his cunning and Barzano knew that the serpentine paths of his mind were easily capable of devising such a scheme.

He pushed himself away from the terminal and finished his glass. He had an early start tomorrow and wondered what else he might uncover. He had told his Adeptus Arbites liaison to dress in civilian clothes and suddenly wondered if she actually owned such things. She looked like the kind of person who lived for her calling and he smiled, realising that they were very much alike then.

Barzano heard the low voices of his Ultramarine bodyguards outside his chambers and spared a thought for Uriel Ventris. It was unfortunate that he could not tell Uriel the truth, but Barzano knew that if he had done so, he might very well have had a problem with the Space Marine captain.

He looked over to the secure safe in the wall, hidden behind the portrait of a man called Forlanus Shonai, where he had secreted the box.

He fought the urge to open it and examine the thing it contained. For the sake of the Pavonis he prayed that he would not need to.

URIEL COULD SEE that it irked Lord Admiral Tiberius to have a system pilot aboard his vessel, but knew the admiral was canny enough to accept its necessity. The quickest route Uriel and Tiberius had plotted towards Caernus IV, site of the most recent eldar attack, took them directly through a wide asteroid belt and, without local knowledge of the safe routes through, they would surely come to grief.

Six tense hours had passed with the pilot expertly guiding them through the maze of enormous asteroids and Uriel prayed to the Emperor, Guilliman and all the saints that they would be through soon.

The system map provided by Governor Shonai had proved to be extremely useful, marking the location of every attack of the eldar raiders. Uriel had not appreciated the scale of the raids until he had seen the map; just over a hundred attacks in just six years. Almost every attack had seen a settlement utterly destroyed or a vessel crippled and its crew slaughtered. Uriel's admiration for Kasimir de Valtos had grown as he contemplated the courage and determination it must have taken for him to engineer his escape from these despicable aliens.

'Helm control, come right to heading zero-two-five, thirty degrees down angle,' called the system pilot. 'Come on, my beauty, we can fit you through there.'

Uriel glanced up from the plotting table in surveyor control towards the viewing bay and blanched as he saw the gap in the gently spinning asteroids the pilot was aiming for. He held his breath, watching as the two giant rocks, each bigger than the *Vae Victus* by several million tonnes, slid past the ship. Uriel saw Tiberius gripping the edge of the captain's pulpit tightly, his knuckles white and his face lined with worry. He had only reluctantly allowed a pilot with local knowledge to direct his ship, but had drawn the line at allowing him to do so from his pulpit.

'Do you have to fly so close to these damned rocks?' snapped Tiberius, his patience with the pilot finally fraying. 'If you even graze one of them, we'll all be sucking vacuum.'

The pilot, a native of the Altemaxa forges by the name of Krivorn grinned, exposing yellowed stumps of teeth.

'This?' he scoffed. 'Ha! I'm takin' it easy on you boys. This is the easy route. I coulda taken you along Derelicts' Alley. Then you would've seen some flying.'

'Derelicts' Alley?' quizzed Uriel. 'That's not marked on this chart of yours.'

'Nah,' agreed Krivorn. 'It's just a name I came up with after I nearly lost a ship there once.'

'You nearly lost a ship!' exploded Tiberius.

'Yeah, weren't my fault though,' protested Krivorn. 'We was flyin' along, happy as an ork in fungus, when all of a sudden this damn great hulk appears outa nowhere! I swear, one minute it weren't there, the next, we're losing power and hauling hard to starboard on full reverse.'

'I expect you made a navigational error, pilot.'

'Me? No, my lord, I checked the surveyors not a second before and it weren't there. Helm control come to new heading three-two-four, ten degrees up angle.'

'So what was it?' asked Uriel, unnerved by Krivorn's lackadaisical helm directions.

'Never did find out, but I reckon it was one of them space hulks you always hear about,' replied Krivorn. 'And I ain't the first to have seen it, neither. Lot of space-farers say they seen it around the Pavonis system. They calls it the half-moon ship on account of its shape. Helm control come to new heading zero-zero-zero, all ahead level.'

Uriel knew of such derelict vessels, wrecks lost in the warp, destined to become ghost ships, forever plying the icy depths of space.

No one could predict their movements and their appearances were completely at random, as capricious fate vomited them from the immaterium. The thought that there might be such a ship in the vicinity filled Uriel with nothing but loathing.

'Look, enough of this damn nonsense,' said Tiberius. 'How long until we are through this asteroid belt and reach Caernus IV?'

Krivorn smiled his gap toothed grin and bowed deeply to Tiberius. 'We just came through the belt, my lord. At current speed and heading, we'll be in orbit around the planet in roughly an hour. And you're welcome.'

KASIMIR DE VALTOS felt his guts contract again and vomited a froth of viscous, blood-flecked matter into the bowl of the commode. Sweat beaded his brow and painful cramps locked his belly in their powerful grip. His vision blurred as another surge of black vomit burned along his throat and into the pan.

Those damned aliens. Every day his body rebelled against the foul toxins with which they had poisoned him. Only daily infusions of intense purgatives kept the most debilitating effects at bay and even then it was only marginally less painful.

He hauled himself up from the floor of his ablutions cubicle and pulled his bathrobe tightly about his slender frame. He splashed water onto his face as the last of the wracking spasms faded. De Valtos swilled ice-cold water around his mouth in a futile attempt to clear away the acidic taste and dried himself with a silk towel. He ran an ivory comb through his albino white hair.

He stared into the mirror and wondered how his life had taken such a turn. The answer came easily enough. It had begun the day his expedition had discovered the caverns beneath the ruined city on Cthelmax and the inscriptions of the heretic abbot, Corteswain. If only he had not translated the inscription there. If only he had not followed their dire words of prophecy.

If only he had not encountered the eldar.

But follow them he had, and this was what it had led him to. He raised a pallid, blotched hand to his face and prodded the nerveless synth-flesh that covered his skull, knowing that he touched his face only by the reflection before him. Once, he had been considered handsome and had courted the finest beauties of Pavonis, but no longer. The white-hot blade of an alien torturer had seen to that.

He had considered suicide many times after his encounter with the eldar, but had lacked even the courage for that. The lure of Corteswain's words had too firm a hold on his soul and de Valtos realised that hope was indeed the greatest curse of humankind.

Why else would he continue down this path if not for hope?

De Valtos tossed aside the towel and stepped into his private bedchamber. The room was mirrorless and spartanly decorated, with none of the finery many would have associated with the leader of such a wealthy cartel. He removed his robe and strolled naked into his walk-in dresser, selecting his favourite midnight blue suit, the one with the narrow lapels and high collar. He donned the suit, the scar tissue the eldar torturer had gifted him pulling painfully tight across his chest and arms. His guest would be arriving soon and he did not want to be late.

No matter that he despised him and every petty small-minded thing he believed in.

No matter that scant years ago he had believed those same things himself.

Times had changed since then and his responsibilities had grown far beyond profit and loss, production and labour. He selected the black, carnodon-skin shoes to wear with his suit and sat on the end of his blood-stained bed as he slipped them on his feet and straightened his suit coat.

He heard the chime from the vestibule and knew that his guest had arrived. Right on time as usual. Fully dressed, de Valtos moved to the head of his bed and gathered up the bloody knives that lay scattered about the mutilated human carcass on the mattress, careful to avoid the sticky pools of blood that had collected.

He placed his items of torture in a black, leather case and slid them under the bed, feeling the familiar sense of disappointment as he stared at the corpse. This one had not even come close to satisfying his urges and he knew he would soon need to procure another fleshy canvas on which to exorcise his demons.

He pictured Solana Vergen on the bed and his heart raced with eagerness.

De Valtos turned on his heel and exited his chambers, descending the wide marble staircase to the vestibule and his guest.

He saw him below, nervously shuffling from foot to foot.

Almerz Chanda looked up at the sound of de Valtos's footsteps.

Kasimir de Valtos smiled.

JENNA SHARBEN FELT acutely uncomfortable out of her judge's uniform and wished for the hundredth time that Virgil Ortega had not assigned her to baby-sit this infernal adept. She wore a functional, close-fitting blue tunic with loose sleeves and an internal holster, where an autopistol nestled under her left armpit. She stood at parade rest in the adept's chambers and examined his quarters.

She prided herself that she could tell a lot about a person by the way they lived: their tastes, their likes and dislikes, whether they were a stickler for order or whether they liked to live in a constant state of disarray.

Her brow creased at what the varied signals the man's quarters were telling her. A dozen books stacked on the desk were arranged in alphabetical order though they had clearly not been part of the room's furniture, yet a pile of clothing lay untidily pooled on top of the bedcovers. A gunmetal grey footlocker had been placed at the bed's foot, securely locked by a geno-keyslot, while on the desk was an open journal with all the adept's hand-written notes. A half drunk decanter of uskavar sat next to the journal, alongside a crystal glass containing last night's dregs.

What kind of man was this adept?

'Seen enough?' asked a voice from the far end of the room and she started, her hand involuntarily reaching for her gun. A man in stained overalls, in the red of the Taloun cartel, slouched against the wall, chewing on a piece of tobacco. He was unshaven and rough looking, with three days' worth of growth on his round chin.

Jenna opened her mouth to ask the man his business here when she suddenly realised that it was the adept she had introduced herself to the previous evening. The change was quite remarkable.

'I have now,' she said, as the adept ambled towards her.

Barzano smiled. 'Today I am going to be Gulyan Korda, technician secundus, Smeltery three-six-two of the Taloun. What do you think?'

Jenna was speechless. Had she not known differently, she would have sworn the adept was a native of Pavonis. He had the accent, the clothes and the same apathetic slouch the manufactorum workers effected. His hair had been slicked back and she could see that his cheeks were now fuller.

As though reading her mind, Barzano withdrew two wads of cheek padding and winked before replacing them in his mouth.

'You think I'd pass for a local?'

'Without a doubt,' assured Jenna. 'Though why would you want to?'

'Well, I hardly think that given the local climate of unrest and the unpopularity of the current administration, anyone is going to open up to an off-worlder, let alone one from the Administratum. Do you?'

Jenna could see he had a point, then suddenly his insistence on her wearing civilian clothes made sense to her. He wanted to go outside and mingle with the workers. And she was to be, what – a bodyguard, a guide? Both?

'Just what are you planning, Adept Barzano?'

'Oh, just a little jaunt into the worker areas outside the city walls. Nothing too strenuous, I promise.'

Barzano indicated the books and data terminal. 'It's all very well getting information from these, but I always think that you get the best raw data from the ground up. Don't you? Yes, today Gulyan Korda, recently dismissed from the service of the Taloun, will be mingling with similarly minded malcontents and discussing the terrible state of affairs the governor has led us to.'

'And what will be my purpose there?'

'You, my dear, are my bodyguard,' whispered Barzano, obviously enjoying this new role immensely. 'You see when Gulyan left the employ of the Taloun, he took some rather incriminating records with him.'

'He did?'

'I think so. Yes, in fact I'm almost certain he did.'

'And what would that incriminating information concern?'

'Haven't a clue,' chuckled Barzano. 'Something juicy though, I'm sure.'

'What about the Space Marines outside? You're not going to be able to pass unnoticed with two armoured giants following you about everywhere.'

'Oh I know that, but they're not coming.'

'And how are you going to get out of the palace without them?'

'Simple, they won't see me,' promised Barzano. 'They'll see you and a rather disreputable looking fellow in overalls heading outside and believe that the slugabed adept is still within. Believe me, it's easier than you think.'

Jenna Sharben shook her head.

'I really don't think that this is such a good idea,' she said.

NINE

Uriel stared at the scorched human wreckage lying on the small cot bed and wondered how, in the name of all that was holy, this man could still be alive. The instant he had laid eyes upon the poor, tormented soul, he had called for the company apothecary to minister to the young man. The physician of this settlement had done what he could, but his skills were no match for the horrendous damage done to his body.

Apothecary Selenus gently lifted the man's leg, unwrapping bandages soiled with seeping blood and pus, and applied soothing balms to the scraps of seared flesh that still clung to his wasted frame. The apothecary worked by the light of a dozen sputtering candles and the sickening stench of atrophied, burned meat filled the room with choking pungency.

Caernus IV was the site of the most recent attack by the eldar raiders and information provided by the governor had indicated that one person had survived the butchery.

Looking at the man, whom the town's alderman had called Gedrik, Uriel felt nothing but pity at his survival.

They had come to this world to glean information from a living eyewitness, and Uriel had a strange sense that it was vitally important he talk to Gedrik.

Sergeant Pasanius leaned close to Uriel and whispered, 'Will he live much longer, do you think?'

Uriel shook his head. 'Selenus says not, but this one is a fighter. By rights he should be dead already. Something has kept him alive.'

'Like what?'

'I do not know, Pasanius, but the town's alderman tells me that he would not allow their physician to grant him the Emperor's Peace. He kept saying that he was waiting for the angels. That he had a gift for them.'

'What does that mean?' scoffed Pasanius. 'The pain must have made him delusional.'

'No,' whispered Uriel. 'I believe he was waiting for us.'

'For us? How could he know we would be coming?'

Uriel shrugged. 'It is said that those who feel death's touch yet live are sometimes granted visions and wondrous powers by the Emperor. His survival is a miracle and perhaps that is reason enough to believe it.'

Pasanius looked unconvinced. 'I always said living underground on Calth all these years couldn't be good for you, captain. You really think that just because this poor wretch is not dead means that he was touched by the Emperor himself?'

'Perhaps, I don't know. They say the blessed Saint Capilene lived for three days after the bullet that killed her entered her heart, that the Emperor would not allow her to fall until she had led the troops to victory against the Chaos-scum on the shrine world that now bears her name. I can't give you a sound explanation, my friend, but my gut tells me that something has kept him alive for a reason. I can't explain it, I just have a feeling.'

'Now you are starting to sound like Idaeus,' grumbled Pasanius. 'I always knew that when he had "one of his feelings" it meant we were heading for some real trouble.'

Apothecary Selenus rose from the bed and bowed to Uriel. 'Brother-captain, there is no more to be done for him. I have applied unguents that will prevent evil vapours from infecting the wound and dressed them as best I can, but it is wasted effort. He will die soon. Nothing now can prevent that.'

'You have done all that you can, brother,' said Uriel. As Selenus moved past Uriel, he placed his hand upon the apothecary's shoulder guard and said, 'Remember, Selenus, helping those in need is never wasted effort. Rejoin the men; I would speak with the boy now. I believe he has waited for us and that he has a message for me.'

Selenus nodded. 'As you wish, brother-captain.'

The apothecary ducked his head below the lintel and left the stinking room. Uriel and Pasanius approached the bed and knelt by the Gedrik's head.

Uriel removed his helmet, setting it on the tiled floor, and ran a hand across his scalp. He leaned in close to Gedrik, trying not to breathe in the awful scent of cooked human meat.

The young man's eyes fluttered as he felt Uriel's nearness and his chest heaved, drawing in a great sucking breath.

Gedrik's head lolled towards Uriel. His cracked and swollen lips leaked a clear fluid as he formed his words.

'I knew you would come,' he hissed, the words barely audible.

'Yes, we came. I am Uriel Ventris of the Ultramarines.'

Gedrik nodded, a weeping smile creasing his lips. 'Yes. I saw you when I stared into the night yet to come.'

'You saw me?' asked Uriel, throwing a puzzled glance towards Pasanius. The practical-minded sergeant merely shrugged, his disbelief plain.

'Yes – you and the Death of Worlds. Light and Dark, two avatars of the same angel.'

Uriel struggled to make sense of the man's words. Death of Worlds, Light and Dark?

Was Pasanius right? Had the boy been driven insane by the things he had seen and the pain he had endured?

'Do you know why you were attacked?' pressed Uriel. 'Can you tell me anything about who did this to you?'

'They came for the metal... The machine man ripped out its heart and now it dies.'

Uriel was mystified. Caernus IV was an agri-world. According to the Segmentum records, there were no metal deposits worth mining here. Certainly none worth slaughtering an entire community for.

'I don't understand, Gedrik. What machine man? A cyborg? A servitor? What metal?'

'The metal that flows. It dies now. My sword... I forged it myself. Now it dies.'

Pasanius lifted a leather scabbard from beside the bed and gripped the wire-wound hilt of the weapon. He pulled a rusted sword from the scabbard and held it close to the candlelight.

Uriel and Pasanius shared an amazed look as they beheld the blade of the sword. Its outline exuded a faint bluish radiance, dimly illuminating the room's interior. Only the very edges of the blade remained silver, for a throbbing vein of leprous brown buried in the heart of the sword pulsed with a loathsome necrotic life. Worm-like tendrils of blackness infested the translucent metal and Uriel could see them slowly spreading throughout the weapon. He ran his gauntlet across the flat of the blade and flakes of dead metal fluttered to the floor.

'Gedrik, what is happening to the sword?'

'It dies. The white-hair and the machine man came and killed the Hill of the Metal, and now it all dies. They killed Maeren and Rouari,' wept Gedrik. 'I don't know why – we would have shared it.'

'The white-hair? Did he come with the machine man?'

'Yes. The machine man, the priest of machines.'

Uriel and Pasanius reached the same conclusion together. A priest of machines could mean only one thing. But an adept of the Machine God, a tech-priest of the Adeptus Mechanicus working with aliens? The very thought was preposterous.

'He can't mean–' began Pasanius.

'No, surely not,' agreed Uriel. 'Gedrik, I think you may have been mistaken.'

'No!' hissed Gedrik, shaking his head feebly on the stained pillow. 'The angel you serve bade me pass on these words. The Death of Worlds and the Bringer of Darkness await to be born into this galaxy. One will arise or neither, the choice is in your hands.'

'What does that mean? Did the... angel tell you what it means? Please, Gedrik.'

Gedrik sighed and his breath rasped in his throat like a dead thing. His head rolled back on limp tendons.

He whispered, 'Please, bring a priest. I want to make confession...'

Uriel nodded and said, 'Sergeant Pasanius. Fetch Chaplain Clausel, a servant of the Emperor awaits his ministrations.'

The sergeant bowed and left the death room as Uriel sat with the dying man. His mind was reeling with the possibility of a priest of the Machine God working alongside the eldar. Who could have imagined such a thing? And the Death of Worlds, the Bringer of Darkness. What were they?

Uriel heard the massive footfalls of Chaplain Clausel and turned to face the scarred warrior-priest.

'He has served the Emperor well, brother-chaplain. Hear his confession and, if he so desires, administer the Finis Rerum. I shall await you outside.'

'It shall be done, my captain.'

Uriel gazed into the death mask of bandages that was all that remained of the young man's face and snapped to attention, slamming his fist into his breastplate.

'Gedrik of Morten's Reach, I salute your bravery. The Emperor be with you.'

Uriel about turned, ducked through the doorway and left the building.

Pasanius and thirty warriors of the Ultramarines awaited him in the centre of the settlement. Beyond the edge of the settlement, Uriel could see the boxy form of their Thunderhawk gunship. Clusters of frightened townspeople watched from the township's edge.

Pasanius had collected his flamer, its bulk slung across his back, and now marched towards him.

'We're ready to move out, captain. Just give the word.'

'Very good, sergeant.'

'Can I ask you something, captain?'

'Of course, Pasanius.'

'Did you believe him? About the angel, I mean?'

Uriel did not answer Pasanius immediately. He stared into the mountains surrounding the settlement. They soared into the clouds; the achievements of mankind insignificant beside their majesty. It was said that a man's life was a spark in the darkness, and that by the time he was noticed, he had vanished, replaced by brighter and more numerous sparks.

Uriel did not accept that. There were men and women who stood against the darkness, bright spots of light that stood in defiance of the inconceivable vastness of the universe. That they would ultimately die was irrelevant.

It was that they stood at all which mattered.

'Did I believe him?' repeated Uriel. 'Yes, I did. I don't know why, but I did.'

'Another feeling?' groaned Pasanius.

'Aye.'

'What do you think he meant? The Death of Worlds and Bringer of Darkness? I do not like such concepts. They cannot bode well for the days to come.'

'Who knows? Perhaps Adept Barzano can shed more light on the subject when we return to Pavonis.'

'Perhaps,' grunted Pasanius.

'You do not like him?'

'It is not for me to criticise an adept of the Administratum,' replied Pasanius stiffly. 'But he is not like any quill-pusher I have ever met.'

The black-armoured form of Chaplain Clausel emerged from the town's small infirmary and rejoined the captain of Fourth Company.

'It is done, my captain. His soul is with the Emperor now.'

'My thanks, chaplain.'

Clausel bowed and moved to stand beside the rest of the men.

'What are your orders, captain?' asked Pasanius.

Uriel looked back at the infirmary and said, 'Fetch the boy, sergeant. We leave for Morten's Reach and will bury him with honour in his home.'

'I STILL CAN'T believe it, Kasimir. She should be out on her ear and I should be sitting in the palace,' fumed Vendare Taloun. 'All those years of negotiation with the smaller cartels wasted. Wasted!'

Kasimir de Valtos handed his fellow cartel head a crystal glass of uskavar and sat across from him in the wood-panelled drawing room of his estate house in the Owsen Hills. Taloun took the glass without looking up and continued to stare into the roaring fire in the marble hearth.

'She'll be gone soon enough, Vendare. She cannot hold on forever.'

'The bitch should be gone *now!*' roared Taloun hurling his glass into the fire, where it exploded into shards. 'Emperor damn her soul. We were so close. What does it take to get rid of her? We had every one of the smaller cartels in our pocket and even allowing for that buffoon Abrogas we still had a clear majority.'

'Well, if she won't fall, she can be pushed,' offered de Valtos.

'What are you talking about? We got a vote against her, but that damn Barzano pulled the rug from under our feet. Damn him, but I thought him to be a foppish numskull.'

'The adept is not a problem.'

'Really?'

'Indeed. Should he prove troublesome, we can dispose of him at our leisure.'

'Don't be foolish, Kasimir. You can't just kill an adept of the Imperium.'

'Why not?'

'Are you serious?'

'Deadly serious,' assured de Valtos. 'And in any case, who will miss him? He is merely one of millions of feather-licking scribes.'

'That Ultramarines captain might have something to say about his vanishing.'

'Do not concern yourself with him, my dear Taloun.'

'I am still not sure about this, Kasimir.'

'Is it any worse than what we plan for the Shonai cartel? Your tanks as well as my guns await in the mountains, Vendare.'

'That's completely different, Kasimir. We do that for the good of Pavonis.'

De Valtos laughed, a hollow, rasping sound, utterly devoid of humour. 'Don't play the innocent with me, Vendare Taloun. I know too much of your dealings. Your idiotic son has a loose tongue and his future wife has one even worse. She wags it in all the wrong places to all the wrong people.'

Taloun flushed and rose from his chair to pour himself a fresh glass of uskavar. His hands shook and the glass clinked as he poured a generous measure of the amber spirit from the decanter.

'Whatever you think you know is a lie,' he said finally.

'I believe you, Vendare,' soothed de Valtos, smiling at Taloun's back. 'But there are many people who would enjoy seeing the Taloun cartel, and especially you, fall. And you know how allegations can stick to a man's reputation, even though they may later be proved false. Just look at what happened when you allowed word to leak out about the Honan and his... liaisons.'

'But that was all true.'

'Admittedly, but my point is no less valid. It would be a shame if certain allegations regarding your brother's death were to enter the public domain. It would mean the termination of our arrangement as I could not be seen to be allying with a man guilty of fratricide.'

'Alright, dammit, Kasimir. You've made your point. So what do you intend?' asked Taloun, returning to his seat.

'Simple,' explained de Valtos. 'We proceed as planned.'

RAIN FELL IN an ever-increasing deluge as the mud-caked Thunderhawk passed low over the roofs of the destroyed township of Morten's Reach. The screaming engines threw up huge sprays of muddy water as the aerial transport touched down in the central square of the settlement, steam hissing from the hot exhausts.

Barely had the landing skids touched down before the engines rumbled throatily and the armoured doors slid back on oiled runners. Three squads of Ultramarines efficiently debarked and fanned out through the town. Two sprinted to the settlement's perimeter as the third, led by Uriel, moved towards the burnt out shell of a building that had obviously once been a temple.

Uriel swept his boltgun left and right. The rain cut visibility dramatically and even his power armour's auto-senses were having a hard time penetrating the greyness.

He could discern no movement or signs of life in the settlement and the evidence of his own sense told him that there had been nothing living in this place for many weeks.

'Sector Prime, clear!' came a shout over the vox-net.

'Sector Secundus, clear!'

'Sector Tertiarus, clear!'

Uriel lowered his weapon and slid it into the restraining clip on his thigh.

'All squad sergeants converge on me. Keep perimeters secure,' he ordered.

Seconds later, Uriel's sergeants, Venasus, Dardino and Pasanius, his flamer sputtering in the falling rain, gathered at the foot of the temple stairs.

'I want this place searched from end to end, house-to-house. Assume all locations are hostile and report in the moment you find anything.'

'What are we looking for, captain? Survivors or victims?' asked Venasus.

'Anything out of the ordinary. There may be some clue as to what the eldar are doing in this system. If there is, I want it found.'

Uriel indicated the weapon impacts on the blackened walls of the temple behind him. 'Servants of the Emperor died here and I want to know why.'

URIEL REMOVED HIS helmet and tipped his head back, allowing the rain to flow across his face, then spat a mouthful of water into the mud. He slicked his short, black hair back as examined the splintered remains of the temple doors, running his free hand across the burnt timber and impacts of small arms fire.

He slid out his combat knife and dug the point of the weapon into a small impact crater and worked the tip back and forth.

Something dropped from the wood into his hand and he lifted it closer to his face. His cupped palm swam with rainwater, but Uriel could clearly see a long splinter of jagged violet crystal. There were scores of these embedded in the wall and, from their grouping, Uriel could tell they had come from one shot.

The tactical briefings he had digested on the eldar had told that they favoured weaponry that fired a hail of monomolecular, razor-edged discs of metal. But there had been other weapons, described as belonging to a darker sub-sect of these aliens, which fired just this kind of ammunition.

Some texts codified this sub-sect as a divergent split of the eldar race, but to Uriel they were all the same: vile aliens that required cleansing in the holy fire of his bolter.

He levered aside the doors and entered the temple, fighting down his rising fury at such desecration. The stench of scorched human fat still clung to the burnt timbers and Uriel pushed his way through to the front of the church where a blackened statue of the divine Master of Mankind lay half buried under a smashed pew. He pulled the statue clear and, though it was heavy, lifted it from the rubble.

At the open rear of the temple he saw a muddy hillside with a number of simple grave markers hammered into the ground at its base. He splashed down from the temple, still carrying the statue, sinking calf deep in the mud. Uriel was saddened at the sheer number of graves. The people who had discovered and cared for Gedrik must have dug them for the people of Morten's Reach.

'Pasanius,' called Uriel over the vox-net. 'I am behind the temple. Bring me the boy's body from the gunship. He should be buried here with his people.'

'Acknowledged,' hissed the voice of the veteran sergeant.

Uriel rested the rescued statue before him and awaited Pasanius's arrival silently in the rain.

Sergeant Pasanius marched slowly around the temple carrying the bandage-swathed body of Gedrik, the green plaid of Caernus IV wrapped around his waist and his sword laid across his chest. An honour guard of Ultramarines followed the massive sergeant as he approached the mass grave.

Uriel nodded to his friend and turned to the warriors who stood behind him.

'Find a grave marked with the name Maeren. We will bury him with his woman.'

The Ultramarines fanned out through the rain, scanning the names on the wooden cross pieces on the grave markers and, after a few minutes' searching, found the grave of Gedrik's wife and child. An honour guard dug in the muddy earth until the body of the young man was finally laid to rest in the soil of his home.

Uriel marched through the graves to where the ground began to rise, intending to plant the statue of the Emperor into the soft earth to watch over His departed flock. He lifted the statue high above his head and rammed it down into the earth, where there was a dull, mud-deadened clang of stone on metal.

Uriel pulled the statue clear, laying it to one side as he dropped to his knees and scraped away the mud at his feet.

Perhaps half a metre down, the ground changed from soft, sucking mud to a wet, flaked metal. He cleared more of the mud away, revealing a rust pocked plate of metal.

'Sergeant!' he shouted. 'Get over here and bring your squad with you. I think we may have found the Hill of the Metal the boy spoke of.'

HALF AN HOUR later, the Ultramarines had cleared a vast swathe of the hillside of mud, and Uriel was amazed at the scale of what lay beneath. A strata of rusted metal lay beneath the hillside, its translucent depths awash with the same evil brown tendrils that had infested Gedrik's sword.

'Guilliman's blood!' swore Dardino when the hillside was revealed. 'What is it?'

'I have no idea,' answered Uriel. 'But whatever it is, the eldar obviously thought it was worth dying for.'

Uriel and Pasanius clambered up the slope towards a triangular depression in the centre of the otherwise flat surface of the metal. Metal crumbled beneath their armoured boots and each footfall was accompanied by squealing groans. The corrosion was converging upon the central point and Uriel knew that soon there would be nothing left. He and Pasanius squatted by the depression in the metal's surface.

The interior of the depression was lined with sockets and hanging wires that trailed into the depths of the metal.

The exact purpose of the niche was a mystery, but it had obviously contained something roughly cylindrical, which had been removed. Was this what had caused the metal to die? Ancient script surrounded the niche and Uriel traced the outline of the strange alien letters with his finger.

'Can you read it?' asked Pasanius.

'No, nor would I want to. These sigils are obviously alien in origin and their blasphemous meaning is best left undisclosed. But we should record them for those whose purpose is to delve into such mysteries.'

Uriel wiped the rusted metal and mud from his armour. 'Get a sample of this and we'll take it back to the *Vae Victus* with us. Perhaps the techs will be able to identify this substance and decipher this script.'

Uriel scooped a handful of mud and metal up in his hands, letting the ooze drip slowly from his fingers. 'I don't like it, Pasanius. Whenever xenos start acting out of character it worries me.'

'What do you mean? Out of character?'

'Well, look at this place. Every body is in its grave, perhaps two hundred people, enough to populate a settlement of this size, agreed?'

'Agreed.'

'And you checked the remains of the dwellings, was anything taken?'

'Hard to tell, but no, I don't think so. It looks like everything was burned to the ground rather than plundered.'

'Exactly my point. Why didn't they take prisoners? Have you ever known eldar raiders leave people behind when they could be taken for torture and slavery? No, these aliens came to this place for one thing only – whatever was in that metal.'

'And what do you think that was? A weapon of some kind? Maybe something of holy significance to them?'

'That's what worries me, old friend. I don't know and I can't even begin to guess either. I'm beginning to think that we may have more to deal with than a simple case of alien pirates.'

They returned to the foot of the hill and marched to the centre of the destroyed township. Rain fell in drenching sheets and Uriel welcomed it, allowing its cold bite to cleanse his skin of the evil sensation he had felt while standing at the hillside.

A piece of a puzzle lay before him, yet he could not fathom its meaning. The eldar obviously had good reason to risk Imperial retribution by attacking one of the Emperor's worlds, and he knew that these aliens would never undertake such action without good reason.

Before he could ponder the matter further, he was interrupted by a burst of static from the vox-net connection to the *Vae Victus*, and Uriel heard the excited tones of Lord Admiral Tiberius.

'Captain Ventris, return to the ship immediately. Repeat, return to the ship immediately.'

'Lord admiral, what is the matter? Has something happened?'

'Indeed it has. I have just received word that system defence ships encountered a vessel with an anomalous engine signature around the eighth planet some two hours ago and fired on it.'

'Somebody obviously listened to our warning then. Did they destroy the alien vessel?'

'No, I do not believe they actually hit her, but they have driven it in our direction. We are almost directly in its flight path, captain. The alien vessel cannot know we are here. We can spring our own ambush on these bastards.'

Uriel smiled, hearing the admiral's anticipation even over the distortion of a ship-to-shore vox-caster.

'How long before you can get back here, Uriel?'

'We can be ready to depart in less than a minute, Lord Admiral. Transmit the surveyor data to the Thunderhawk's avionics logister.'

'Hurry, Uriel. They are moving fast and we might not get another shot at this.'

'We shall be seeing you shortly. Ventris out.'

Uriel replaced his helmet and faced his warriors.

'The foe we have come to fight approach our position and we have a chance to avenge those who fell to their traitorous attack. Honour demands that we accept this challenge.'

Uriel drew his power sword and shouted, 'Are you ready for battle?'

As one, the warriors of Fourth Company roared their affirmation.

ARIO BARZANO RECLINED on his bed, sipping a glass of uskavar and scanning through a sheaf of papers delivered to his chambers by a grim-faced Sergeant Learchus. Barzano had endured the full wrath of the sergeant when he and Jenna Sharben had returned to the palace chambers after their excursion into the manufactorum districts of the city.

The pair had hit a few beerhalls and alehouses, but had learned nothing much more than the fact that there was whispered talk of a mass demonstration planned. Most of the talk had been aimed simply at deriding the planetary rulers and the general miserable lot of the workers. After three fruitless hours, they had decided to cut their losses and return to the palace.

The situation on Pavonis was in many ways more serious than he had imagined. There was more going on here than simple piracy and population unrest.

He put down the papers and swung his legs out onto the floor, rubbing the bridge of his nose and sighing deeply. He pushed himself to his feet and shuffled towards the table where a system map had been spread out over the detritus of his evening meal. Dimly he could hear the persistent scratching of quills and the low prayers of his retinue of scribes. Lortuen Perjed was with them, directing their researches and collating their scrivenings, and Barzano felt a smile touch his lips at the thought of the old man. He had been stalwart support these last few weeks and Barzano doubted he could have come this far without his help.

He returned his attention to the map and set his glass down on a curling corner.

A line of blue ink recorded the course of the *Vae Victus* and Barzano wondered if this one ship would be enough. He quickly dismissed the thought. If they could not prevent the Bringer of Darkness from returning then the entire Ultima Segmentum battlefleet would not make a difference.

The prospect depressed him and he refilled his glass.

'Shouldn't you go easy on that?' asked Lortuen Perjed, appearing from the shadows. 'It's quite strong, you know.'

'I know, but it is rather good,' replied Barzano, pouring another glass.

Perjed accepted the drink and sat on the edge of the bed. He sipped the drink, his eyes widening at its potency.

'Yes, quite strong,' he confirmed, taking another swallow. Barzano slumped into the chair before his display terminal and retrieved his glass from the map.

'So what are you still doing up anyway, Lortuen?'

The old adept shrugged. 'Not much else to do at the moment.'

'True,' agreed Barzano. 'I dislike playing a waiting game.'

'You used to enjoy it. Waiting until your prey made a mistake and played right into your hands.'

'Did I? I don't remember.'

'Yes, in the old days you were quite the patient hunter.'

'The old days,' snorted Barzano. 'How long ago were they?'

'Oh, a good few decades ago.'

'A lot's changed since then, Lortuen. I'm hardly the same man any more.'

'My, you are in a sour mood tonight, Ario. Was it not Saint Josmane who said that any service of the Emperor should be rejoiced in?'

'Yes, but I'll bet he never had to do the things we've had to.'

'No,' admitted Perjed, 'but then he was a martyr and got himself killed, Emperor rest his holy soul.'

'True,' laughed Barzano, 'a fate I'd be happy to avoid if I can.'

'That goes for me too,' agreed Perjed, raising his glass.

Barzano rubbed the heel of his palm against his temple and squeezed his eyes shut.

He reached over the desk and picked up a small glass jar of white capsules.

'Are the headaches bad?'

Barzano nodded without replying, swallowing two of the capsules with a mouthful of uskavar. He shook his head and stuck out his tongue at their vile taste.

'It is worse than before. I have felt it ever since we landed, something vast and older than time, pressing in on my skull.'

'Then perhaps you should go easy on the uskavar. It can't help.'

'On the contrary, my dear old friend, it is the only thing that helps. To blot everything out in a haze of alcohol is one of the few pleasures I have left to me.'

'No, that's not the Ario Barzano I have served for thirty years speaking.'

'And just who is that anyway? For I no longer know. The adept, the hive ganger, the courtier, the rogue trader? Who is the Ario Barzano you have served for all those years?'

'The servant of the Emperor who has never once faltered in his duty. Maybe you no longer remember who you are, but I do, and it pains me to see you do this to yourself.'

Barzano nodded and put down his glass with exaggerated care.

'I am sorry, my friend. You are correct of course. The sooner we are done here the better.'

'There is no need to apologise, Ario. I have served many masters in my time and almost all were harder work than you. But to change the subject, has there been any more contact with the *Vae Victus* and Captain Ventris?'

'Not since they arrived at Caernus IV, no.'

'Do you expect them to be able to stop the eldar?'

'I think if anyone can, it will be Uriel. I do not believe he is a man who gives up easily. He was a protégé of Captain Idaeus, you know?'

'Yes, I remember reading the report from Thracia. Was that why you picked him?'

'Partly, but he has something to prove and that's the kind of man I want on my side when it all comes down to the final scrap.'

'And you are hoping that some of Idaeus's unconventional thinking may have rubbed off on Uriel?'

'Hoping?' laughed Barzano. 'My dear Lortuen. I am counting on it.'

URIEL WATCHED THE blips indicating the incoming eldar ship and the Vae Victus on the Thunderhawk's augury panel and the ghostly green lines that connected their approach vectors. It was going to be close; the alien vessel was approaching at high speed and they had still to return to the Vae Victus to refuel. The question was: did they have time?

He pointed towards the glowing panel and said, 'How long until we can rendezvous with the *Victus*?'

The pilot checked the augury panel. 'Twenty-six minutes, captain.'

Twenty-six minutes. Add another fifteen to refuel, eight if they refuelled hot, with the engines still turning over in the launch bay. The Codex Astartes strictly forbade such a dangerous practice, but time was of the essence here and he could not afford to waste it. But then the *Victus* only had this one operable Thunderhawk and if it blew up in the launch bay...

'Can we reach the eldar ship without refuelling?'

'No, sir.'

Uriel swore. They were unlikely to get a better shot at the eldar than this, but they were hamstrung by distance and logistical necessity.

If only the eldar could be made to turn towards them.

'Quickly, patch me through to the lord admiral!'

The co-pilot opened a channel to the *Vae Victus*.

'Admiral, this is Captain Ventris, I do not believe we have time to reach you and refuel before the eldar will be beyond our reach.'

'What are you talking about?' stormed the voice of Lord Admiral Tiberius from the command bridge. 'You have to refuel, you don't have enough to reach the eldar if you don't.'

'I know that, Admiral, but if we return to the *Vae Victus* we will miss our chance to take the fight to them on their own ship. You can retrieve us when we're done.'

The vox link crackled as Tiberius considered Uriel's proposal. The admiral's tone was cautious when he finally answered.

'I do not consider this wise, Captain Ventris. You may be correct, but it goes against everything in the Codex Astartes regarding ship operations.'

'I know that, but it is the best chance we have to cripple them. If we can get on the bridge we can do some serious damage. If you can drive them towards us with some well aimed battery fire, we can manoeuvre more effectively to get a better breaching position.'

'Very well, Captain Ventris, but I shall be noting in my log that I disapprove of your flagrant disregard for the words of the Blessed Primarch.'

'That is your right and privilege, admiral, but we can discuss this at a later date. The enemy approaches.'

ARCHON KESHARQ CRADLED his axe, its blade sticky with the blood of the deck officer responsible for the maintenance of the holofields and ground his teeth in anticipation. The raid on the last site indicated by the kyerzak had been absurdly easy. The stupid mon-keigh had thrown themselves on his mercy, not realising that he had none to give. He had ripped their souls screaming from their bodies and stolen that which they had removed from the asteroid.

It was unfortunate that some of the lumbering ships of the mon-keigh had been so close, but Kesharq had not been worried. They were no match for the *Stormrider* and he had arrogantly steered a course through them, trusting to his holofields to confound their primitive weapons. And so they had until damage suffered during their engagement with the Astartes vessel had caused the holofields to fail. He knew he could stay and fight. The *Stormrider* could easily defeat these vessels, but they carried the final piece of the key now and its worth was far greater than a few moments of hollow glory. The crewman responsible for the failure of the holofields had been executed and his replacement was working to repair them even now.

Thinking of the prize that lay in his hold, Kesharq pictured the form of Asdrubael Vect, weeping and begging for his life before he destroyed him.

He could taste his vengeance on Vect in the blood that coated his teeth and knew that this was the most critical time. The *kyerzak* would try and rob him of his prize, but his continued existence was only due to Kesharq allowing the Surgeon to practise his art upon his flesh. Kesharq knew that this alone would not be enough of a threat to prevent him from trying. He already knew that the *kyerzak*'s electro-priest they carried had made several attempts to distil an antidote to the toxin that daily ravaged his master's body.

Kesharq knew he would not be successful. Before his disgrace by association, the Surgeon had been known as one of the finest Venomists of the Kabal and the threat of his lethal creations was the bane of every Archon's food table.

No, the *kyerzak* would not be successful and soon he would allow the Surgeon to torture the pitiful figure to death over the course of the coming months.

He glanced up at the viewing screen, calculating how long it would take to reach Pavonis.

Not long. Not long at all.

'Do you HAVE him, Philotas?' whispered Lord Admiral Tiberius, as though shouting would somehow alert the alien vessel that sat in the centre of his viewscreen.

'Yes, lord admiral, the alien ship appears to be without its disruption shields. Broadside batteries are establishing a firing solution now.'

'Excellent.'

Tiberius drummed his fingers on the wood panelling of his pulpit and chewed his bottom lip. He did not like Uriel's method of war. Despite the sense of it, it railed against everything he had learned after centuries of combat in space. Everything the Blessed Guilliman had set down in the holy tome, the Codex Astartes, avowed that ships should go into battle with their full complement of craft and no ship should launch boarding actions without first having disabled close-in batteries.

He did not like it, but he could see that Uriel was right. To return to the *Vae Victus* would mean their best chance at destroying the alien vessel would slip away. To launch an assault against an enemy's bridge was the dream of every boarding party and, if successful, would usually mean the capture or death of the enemy captain.

He did not like it, but he would go along with it.

'Broadside battery commanders report they have a firing solution. Target vessel has entered weapons' range.'

Firing at a vessel at this range would be unlikely to inflict many hits, but then that was not the plan. Were he to wait much longer, the alien craft would in all likelihood detect them and evade. All he had to do was spook the alien captain and drive him towards Uriel's approaching Thunderhawk, its engine emissions masked by the close proximity of the planet's atmosphere.

'On my command, order battery gunners to open fire. Then engage engines in full reverse and fire starboard manoeuvring thrusters. I want him driven over the polar-regions and into Captain Ventris's path.'

'Yes, lord admiral.'

URIEL SQUINTED THROUGH the pilot's canopy, but could see little other than the flaring discharges of the planet's atmosphere washing over the Thunderhawk's hull. The feed from the Vae Victus gave them the position of the eldar vessel and if it would just move a little closer they would have him.

Tech-marine Harkus intoned the Chant of Dissolution upon the Thunderhawk's boarding umbilical and the shaped breaching charges that would blast their way through the alien vessel's hull. Chaplain Clausel led the Ultramarines in prayer, blessing each warrior's gun and blade. Uriel had ordered chainswords issued to everyone, knowing that the fighting was sure to get close and bloody. Uriel rejoined his men and drew his power sword, bowing to receive the chaplain's blessing.

'DREAD ARCHON! I am detecting an energy build-up three hundred thousand kilometres directly in front of us!'

Kesharq hurried over to the warrior who had spoken and stared at the sensor returns in horror.

There was no mistaking the energy signature. An enemy ship was building power in its weapon batteries and preparing to fire.

'Hard to port, take us low over the planet. Lose him in the atmosphere!'

'BROADSIDE BATTERIES OPEN fire!' ordered Tiberius. 'Engage a reverse port turn!'

The enormous vessel shuddered as the entire port broadside unleashed a hail of fire upon the eldar vessel. Tiberius gripped the edge of the pulpit as the mighty war vessel began turning to face its foe and bring its prow bombardment cannon to bear.

They might not be doing this by the book, but by the Emperor, they were going to do it with their biggest guns.

EACH BROADSIDE BATTERY hurled explosive, building-sized projectiles towards their target. But at such extreme range, most flew wide of the mark, detonating hundreds of kilometres from the Stormrider. Some shells exploded close, but caused no real damage save peppering the hull and mainsail with spinning fragments.

The ship nimbly altered course, its needle-nosed prow sweeping left and diving hard towards the planet's atmosphere. More shots were fired and a vast explosion blossomed above the ship's position as the strike cruiser's bombardment cannon entered the fray.

The *Stormrider* was an obsidian dart, knifing through the atmosphere of Caernus IV, its superior speed and manoeuvrability carrying it from the guns of its enemy.

The *Vae Victus* tried to match the turn and follow the *Stormrider*, but she was nowhere near as nimble as her prey.

The eldar vessel slowed as it angled away from Caernus IV. At this point, a ship was effectively blind as its sensors realigned from the fiery journey through the upper atmosphere.

As the *Stormrider* cleared the atmosphere, a streak of blue flashed upwards and settled in behind the tall sails of the graceful ship. The Thunderhawk's powerful cannons stitched a path of fire across the rear quarter of the vessel, blasting off bladed fins and barbed hooks.

Before the eldar ship could react, the Thunderhawk swooped in across its curved topside. Drill clamps fired from the gunship's belly, burrowing into the wraithbone hull of the *Stormrider*, and dragging the lighter assault craft down hard onto the eldar ship.

TECH-MARINE HARKUS TRIGGERED the firing mechanism of the boarding umbilical and shouted, 'Fire in the hole!' as he detonated the shaped breaching charges at its end. Even through the armoured deck plates of the Thunderhawk, Uriel could feel the tremendous blast. He spun the locking handle and wrenched open the circular hatch that led through the umbilical towards the breach in the eldar vessel's hull.

Speed was essential now. Hit hard and hit fast.

'Ultramarines! With me!' he bellowed and dropped through the boarding umbilical.

URIEL HIT THE deck of the alien vessel and rolled aside as the next Ultramarine warrior slammed down behind him. He sprang to his feet and drew his power sword and bolt pistol in one fluid motion. He swept his pistol around the room as he took in his surroundings, a low-ceilinged room stacked with round containers.

He thumbed the activation rune on the hilt of his sword and the blade leapt with eldritch fire just as a pair of crimson-armoured warriors charged through an oval shaped doorway. Their armour was smooth and gleaming, adorned with glittering blades, and they carried long rifles with jagged bayonets.

'Courage and honour!' screamed Uriel, launching himself at the eldar warriors.

He smashed his power sword down on the first alien's collarbone, shearing him from neck to groin. The other alien stabbed with its bladed rifle and Uriel spun inside its guard. He hammered his elbow into his attacker's face, pulverising its helmet visor and breaking its neck.

He spared a glance behind him as more of the Ultramarines dropped through the hull breach. Pasanius was there, the blue-hot burner of his flamer roaring and ready to incinerate the enemies of the Emperor.

Uriel raised his power sword and yelled, 'The bridge!'

He sprinted through the doorway, finding himself in a narrow, shadowed corridor, with smooth walls that tapered to a point above his head.

A strange, truly alien aroma filled his senses, but he could not identify it. Two curving passages radiated forwards, their ends disappearing from sight.

Uriel picked the left hand corridor, and charged down its length.

He shouted, 'Pasanius with me! Dardino and Venasus take the right.'

Uriel heard the beat of footsteps from up ahead and saw dozens of the armoured warriors charging to intercept him. They carried the same bladed rifles and Uriel could see a number of larger, more dangerous weapons amongst their ranks.

Raising his flamer, Pasanius shouted, 'Get down!'

Uriel dropped and felt the whoosh of superheated promethium as it washed over him down the corridor. Alien screams echoed from the glassy walls as the liquid flames cooked their bodies within their armour and seared the flesh from their bones.

Uriel pushed himself to his feet and charged forwards, hurdling the burning corpses and leaping amongst the eldar. His sword slashed left and right and where he struck, aliens died. With a wild roar, the Ultramarines followed their captain, swords hacking and cutting amongst the aliens. Screaming, chainsaw-edged blades ripped through the flexible armour plates and flesh of the aliens with ease.

Chaplain Clausel bellowed the Canticles of Faith as he smote the aliens with his deadly crozius arcanum.

Uriel felt a close range blast of splinter fire impact on his arm. He ignored it, his armour absorbed the blast. Another blast slammed into his helmet and he snarled, spinning and beheading his attacker.

The last of the eldar died; the corridor had become a stinking charnel house.

None of the Ultramarines had fallen, though several bled from minor wounds. Pasanius fired short bursts of flame along a bend further down the corridor, deterring any counterattack.

Uriel opened a vox-channel to his other squads.

'Dardino, Venasus. What's your status?'

Venasus answered first, his voice steady and controlled despite the sounds of fierce battle raging around him. 'Strong resistance, captain. We have encountered what looks like a major defence point. Dardino is attempting to flank the aliens. I estimate six minutes until we overwhelm them.'

'Make it four! Ventris out.'

Gunfire spat towards the Ultramarines, ricocheting from the walls and filling the air with whickering splinters. The same type of splinters Uriel had dug from the church wall on Caernus IV.

Pasanius was on the ground, a dark, smoking hole punched in his shoulder guard. Uriel could hear the sergeant's cursing over the vox-net as the big man dragged himself away from the bend in the tunnel, never once releasing his grip on his flamer. Uriel could hear the sounds of more aliens moving to intercept them and thumbed a pair of frag grenades from his belt dispenser.

The weight of fire began to intensify and Uriel knew they had to keep pushing on lest the assault be halted in its tracks before it had even begun.

He rolled around the corner and fired two shots from his bolt pistol. The heavy crack-thump of bolter ammunition was reassuringly loud compared to the aliens' weaponry. A pair of aliens fell, their chests blown open by the mass-reactive shells as Uriel flipped both frags down the corridor. He fired twice more before diving back into cover as the grenades detonated simultaneously, hurling bodies through the air in the fiery blast.

Uriel leapt to his feet and dragged Pasanius upright.

'You ready for this, old friend?'

'More than ever, captain,' assured Pasanius hefting the flamer.

Uriel nodded and spun around the corridor, bolt pistol extended before him.

'For the Emperor!'

The Ultramarines followed Uriel as he pounded towards a crimson door, embossed with intricate designs of curving spikes and blades. Even from here he saw it was heavily armoured.

Cross-corridors bisected this one and Uriel could hear the sounds of battle from elsewhere in the ship. Red armoured figures dashed along parallel corridors and he shouted to watch the rear. With so many cross-corridors, there was a very real possibility of being outflanked and surrounded.

He slammed into the door and smashed it from its frame.

Uriel charged through the door, battle-hungry Ultramarines hard on his heels. They entered a vast, high-roofed dome and Uriel grinned with feral anticipation as he realised they must be on the command bridge at last. An ornate viewscreen dominated the far wall, with wide, hangar-like gates to either side. Iron tables with black leather restraint harnesses stood in a line, alongside racks of horrendous, multi-bladed weapons.

In the centre of the chamber, standing atop a raised command dais, was a tall, slender alien wearing an elaborately tooled suit of armour, similar to that of his warriors, but coloured a deep jade. He wore no helmet and his violet-streaked white hair spilled around his shoulders like snow. His skin was a lifeless mask, devoid of expression, and a thin line of blood ran from his lips. He carried a gigantic war axe, its blade stained red.

Dozens of aliens filled the room, heavily armoured warriors, hefting long, halberd-like weapons that pulsed with unnatural energy.

The room reeked of death and terror. How many souls had met their end in this desolate place, wondered Uriel?

He had no time to ponder the question as the wide doors to either side of the viewscreen slid open. A horde of near naked warriors, both male and female, riding bizarre skimming blades and carrying long glaives, swept from each door.

Bolter shots felled half a dozen, but then they were amongst the Ultramarines, slashing and killing with their weapons. Uriel saw Brother Gaius fall, severed at the waist by the bladed wing of one of the flyers. His killer looped overhead as Gaius's body collapsed in a flood of gore.

Uriel put a bolt round through the whooping alien's head, watching with grim satisfaction as his limp body plummeted to the ground. The shrieking blade-skimmers spun high in the air, coming around for another pass.

Bolter rounds exploded amongst them as Dardino and Venasus led their squads into battle. Uriel shot dead another flyer as Venasus moved to stand beside him, his armour slick with alien blood.

'My apologies, captain. It took us five minutes.'

Uriel grinned fiercely beneath his helmet. 'I know you'll do better next time, sergeant.'

A skimmer exploded as Pasanius's flamer gouted a vast stream of liquid fire over its rider and fresh gunshots echoed through the dome. The vox in Uriel's helmet crackled to life as the Thunderhawk pilot patched into his personal link.

'Captain Ventris, we will have to pull back soon. The alien vessel is increasing in speed and we will not be able to maintain the umbilical for much longer. I suggest you begin falling back, before I am forced to disengage the docking clamps.'

Uriel cursed. He had no time to acknowledge the pilot's communication as he smashed a leather-harnessed warrior from his sky-board and rammed his sword through his belly. He saw the jade-armoured, albino warrior cutting a path towards him and wrenched his sword clear.

Some shapeless mass writhed around the warrior's legs, but Uriel could not discern its nature in the gloom. A trio of the skimming warriors swooped in towards Uriel. He blasted two from their boards with well-placed bolter fire and beheaded the third. The jade warrior cut down two Ultramarine battle-brothers with contemptuous ease as they tried to intercept him.

Uriel shouted at his warriors to stand fast.

'This one is mine!'

From the icons on his helmet visor, Uriel could see that seven of his men were dead, their runic identifiers cold and black. His breathing was heavy, but his stamina was undiminished.

A space cleared around the two warriors as battle continued to rage throughout the bridge. The shapeless forms around the alien's legs resolved into clarity and Uriel was horrified as he clearly saw the heaving mass of creatures that hissed and spat beside the alien leader. A repulsive, horrifying and piteous agglomeration of thrashing, deformed flesh, sewn together in a riot of anatomies, writhed at the alien's feet. Each one was unique in its nauseating form, but all hissed with the same lunatic malevolence, baring yellowed fangs and jagged talons.

Uriel extended his sword, pointing the tip at the alien leader's chest.

'I am Uriel Ventris of the Ultramarines and I have come to kill you.'

The alien leader cocked his head to one side before speaking. His voice rasped, unused to forming human words.

'You are nothing but a mon-keigh, an animal, and I shall feed you to the excrents.'

Uriel brought his sword back to the guard position as the boiling mass of loathsome creatures surged forwards, their shrieks both terrifying and pitiful. He slashed his sword through the first beast, stinking pus jetting from its soft body as the blade easily sliced through its flesh. He stabbed another, but there were simply too many to kill.

Fangs snapped shut on his calf and Uriel grunted as he felt hot pain lance through him as venom pumped into his bloodstream. His sword hacked the beast's fanged appendage from the mass of its form, splattering him with its internal fluids.

Kesharq stepped forward and swung his axe in a crushing arc, hammering the wide blade into Uriel's chest.

Uriel had seen the blow coming and hurled himself back, robbing the impact of much of its force. He rolled, slashing wide, a terrible screeching from another excrent his reward. He kept rolling as Kesharq's axe hammered into the deck.

He leapt upright parrying another blow from the axe. The impact rang up Uriel's arm, but he could tell that there was little strength behind the blow. This alien was relying on the weight of the axe to do his killing. He thundered his fist into the onyx shaft of the axe and barrelled into the slender alien.

The warrior dodged Uriel's shoulder charge, slipping around the Space Marine's side and hammering the weapon into his shoulder.

The blade tore a great gouge from Uriel's armour, skidding upwards and clipping the edge of his helmet. Uriel staggered, dizzy from the impact, but raised his sword in time to parry a lighting reverse cut to his head.

Another of the excrents fastened its jaw upon Uriel's leg. He stamped his armoured boot down on its head, pulping the skull in a mash of bone and brain. Flames licked around him and a shrill screeching and stench of scorched meat filled the air as Pasanius turned his flamer upon the horrific creatures. The pilot's icon on his visor flashed urgently.

Kesharq spun his axe in a dizzying series of loops and twists, the blade a glittering web of silver. He slowly advanced on Uriel, his dead face remaining utterly immobile.

'I was wrong to think of you as worthy meat,' rasped Kesharq. 'The *kyerzak* was a fool to fear you.'

Uriel feinted with his sword, then reversed the direction of his cut, but Kesharq had anticipated the blow and parried with the shaft of his axe. The blade reversed and hammered into Uriel's side, biting deep into his armour. Hot agony flooded him and he could feel blood streaming from his body.

Bloody froth gathered at the side of Kesharq's mouth. Uriel roared and dropped his sword, gripping the axe blade lodged in his side as Kesharq attempted to pull it clear.

Uriel snatched his bolt pistol from his side and swung it to bear on Kesharq's head.

The alien moved with preternatural speed, but even he was not fast enough to completely dodge a bullet.

The bolt tore into the side of Kesharq's cheek, gouging a chunk of his pallid flesh from his skull, but the range was too close for the bolt to fully arm itself and it detonated well past the alien's head.

Kesharq howled in pain and fell back, releasing his grip on the axe. Uriel dropped to his knees as Kesharq stumbled back to his armoured warriors.

Uriel felt hands grasp at his shoulder guards. He weakly raised his pistol, but lowered it when he saw that it was Pasanius. The massive sergeant gripped the alien axe lodged in his side and pulled it clear in a welter of blood, before dragging his captain to his feet.

'We have to get out of here now!' hissed Uriel.

Pasanius nodded and began shouting orders to his squad. Uriel bent to retrieve Idaeus's sword and joined the rest of his warriors as they began to withdraw towards the Thunderhawk. The bodies of the fallen were carried with them.

Uriel knew they must not leave the honoured dead in this blasphemous place. Apothecary Selenus would remove the progenoid glands that would allow their precious gene-seed to be returned to the Chapter.

None of the alien warriors seemed willing to give chase, however, and Uriel had a fleeting glimpse of the alien leader staring at him with undisguised hatred before he was lost to sight.

THE ULTRAMARINES FELL back in good order to the Thunderhawk and disengaged from the hull of the eldar vessel. The pilot deftly swung the gunship about on its axis and feathered the thrusters until the fuel tanks eventually ran dry. The eldar ship soon vanished in the darkness, its engines rapidly carrying it away from the battle.

The gunship drifted powerless for another hour before being recovered by the *Vae Victus*.

By then, Selenus had tended to the wounded and Chaplain Clausel had intoned the Litany of the Fallen upon the dead.

The *Vae Victus* picked up the engine trail of the eldar ship. Though fast, the Ultramarines strike cruiser could not hope to match the speed of the alien craft, but as the carto-servitors plotted its course, it seemed they would not need to.

The alien vessel was on a direct course for Pavonis.

TEN

GUNNER HARLEN MORGAN ran his hand along the flank of the vast, sixty-tonne tank and smiled as he pictured himself one day riding at the head of an armoured column of such mighty war machines. The tank was a Conqueror pattern Leman Russ, though he reluctantly conceded that the armour and technical specification of this locally produced model was inferior to those fabricated on the Conqueror's original production forge world of Gryphonne IV.

His commander, Major Webb, was lounging high on the cupola of the tank, smoking a stinking cigar, while the tank's loader, Mappin, fixed a pot of caffeine for the crew. The driver, Park, lay half-concealed by the track assembly as he attempted to fix a leaking fuel line.

Slatted sunlight filtered through the camo-netting overhead and, despite their altitude this high in the mountains, the air was still warm. He handed a ration pack up to the major who nodded his thanks and tore the foil container open, grimacing with distaste at its contents.

Morgan sat down, cross-legged, and leaned back against the earthen berm the tank was concealed in, dropping another couple of ration packs beside Mappin and Park.

'You took your bloody time,' grumbled Mappin.

'You can go and get the food next time,' he replied and began to eat.

The meal consisted of some bread, cheese and an ambiguous-looking meat product. Morgan sniffed it and was still none the wiser.

The others began eating, tearing into their food as Trooper Park finally pulled himself out from under the tank and picked up his own ration pack. He stared at it suspiciously and tossed it aside.

'By all that's holy, I'll be damn glad to get on the move and get some real food in my belly,' groused Park, unscrewing the cap from a battered hip flask he produced from within his oil-stained overalls.

'Do you ever stop complaining?' asked Mappin between mouthfuls of bread and the gluey, brown meat from the ration pack. Park took a slug from his flask and offered it to Mappin, who shook his head, but picked up Park's ration pack.

'No. Do you ever stop eating, you fat bastard?' countered Park. 'This uskavar's all I need to get me through the day.'

'Yeah, we know,' laughed Morgan, 'we've seen you drive.'

Trooper Park made an obscene gesture with both hands and said, 'Up yours, boy. Food's for lightweights anyway.'

Morgan shut out the bickering banter of his crewmates, it was a familiar ritual come mealtimes, and turned his attention to the rest of the concealed bunker complex in the Owsen Hills. From here the camouflage the tanks were concealed in looked flimsy and unconvincing, but he guessed that from the air or down on the dusty plains far below, it must look pretty good. Well, no one had discovered them yet, had they?

Their tank's berm overlooked the country estate of their heroic leader far below. A collection of marble-faced buildings, it represented more wealth than he could possibly imagine. Herds of horned stag ran wild in the grounds and a great deal of activity seemed to go on in the dark of night. He'd borrowed Park's infra-goggles and watched whole troops of men dispersing throughout the countryside.

Sensibly, he'd not mentioned this to the major.

Soldiers with shoulder-launched missiles and bipod mounted autoguns were placed around the eastern perimeter of the complex, standing ready to defend them from attack, though the major had assured them that such an attack was pretty unlikely.

But they'd all had a scare when that boxy blue gunship had roared past them last week. Everyone had run scared like panicked kids and it had been a wake up call to the men stationed here that they must be vigilant at all times.

Scores of troopers wandered about the plateau beneath the camo-net: gunners, loaders, drivers and mechanics, all the kinds of men you'd need to keep a force like this ready for action. When that action might come, Morgan didn't know, but the major had assured them it would be soon.

Altogether Morgan knew there were three hundred and twenty-seven armoured vehicles concealed on the plateau and within the mountainside. Basilisks, Griffons, Leman Russ, Hellhounds and various other patterns. He'd counted them once, when his crew had pulled patrol duty. The numbers and types sounded impressive, but Morgan had studied enough about armoured vehicles to know that these were inferior copies of Imperial forge world constructions.

That didn't matter though.

United, they were stronger than adamantium. Faith in the justice of their cause would be their armour and belief in their destiny would be their weapon.

Morgan smiled, remembering the words of Colonel Pontelus of the Pavonis Defence Force (Brandon Gate), which had brought him here. The colonel had spoken passionately about the treachery of the Shonai cartel, how it had traitorously allied itself with like minded individuals within other cartels to squeeze every last shred of money and dignity from the working man. Why, her tithe tax was nothing more than an attempt to line her own pockets before she was removed from office.

Morgan had been unsure at first, seeing the Taloun cartel pin on his commander's uniform jacket. He knew that the Taloun and Shonai were political enemies, but Pontelus's words had struck a nerve in the young tank officer. Together they would fight for their freedom from the oppressive regime of the Shonai.

Morgan understood that freedom had to be paid for and that the price was patriot's blood. He was a patriot and was more than ready to stand up and be counted. The Shonai were dragging Pavonis down and the governor's policies had become unacceptable.

Governance without freedom was tyranny by another name and he was unwilling to live one more day under the governor's yoke.

No more would the sons of Pavonis be forced to work as slaves in the sweltering manufactorum of corrupt cartels. Progressive thinkers like the Taloun and de Valtos knew that men of courage and honour needed to stand up for what they believed in, and Morgan's heart swelled.

He knew he was such a man.

☡
ELEVEN

THE SUN ROSE further in the sky above Brandon Gate, baking the streets with its relentless heat. Despite the lateness of the year, the temperature remained high and the city below sweltered in unseasonal warmth. The towering cooling stacks of the manufactorum were bare of their gaseous halos and the hammering machineries sat idle in their hangars.

A bustling sense of purpose held sway over the city below, as thousands of people filled the streets of the outer manufactorum districts, slowly con verging on the white walls of the financial and administrative heart of the city.

Vast columns of men, women and children gathered ready to march. Almost every local manufactorum and business had shut down, either by choice or simply because its workers were now on their way to Liberation Square. The transport networks had shut down and the only rail routes still functioning were those ferrying more workers in from the outlying regions to join the demonstration.

There had been fears amongst the demonstration's organisers that the news of the Space Marines' arrival would dissuade people from attending, but, perversely, the reverse seemed to be true. There was a festive mood to the crowd. Families walked, hand in hand and, scattered throughout the swelling crowd, musicians played stirring, patriotic songs to lift the hearts of the people. Colourful flags and banners flapped in the light breeze, displaying the heraldry of various branches of the Workers' Collective and proclamations of unity.

Here and there, bands of self-appointed route-marshals distributed placards bearing uplifting slogans and helped direct the motion of the crowd.

Tens of thousands of people choked the streets, forming a steadily moving mass of humanity united in a common cause.

Security personnel displaying lapel badges of various cartels lined the frontages of buildings owned by their masters, but did nothing more to interfere with the demonstration's progress. Unsurprisingly, there were none from the Shonai cartel on the streets. Every now and then, laughing members of the crowd walked up to them, exhorting them to join the march. Sometimes it worked, sometimes it didn't, but there was no hostility evident either way.

As the crowd continued to grow, its organisers began to realise that the demonstration march was taking on a whole new aspect. It had changed from a show of united strength to a tremendously dangerous enterprise. Such a mass of people on the city streets, despite their peaceful nature, made this day's events perilously close to what might be considered outright rebellion. It would take only the slightest provocation for the planetary officials to regard it as such and use lethal force to break it up.

They had already proved that they were willing to take such measures. The newly sanctified Hall of Martyrs bore the names of those who had found that out the hard way and the march organisers cast nervous glances around them for the forbidding black-armoured forms of the Adeptus Arbites.

But there was no obvious signs of the judges yet, for they were marshalled beside their precinct house, deployed around the wrought iron gates of the governor's palace and at the approach streets to Liberation Square.

The march picked up speed as the streets widened on the approaches to the marble inner walls, converging upon the heart of the city from every compass point. The wide toll gates on the walls were abandoned, the gates open, their keepers unwilling to face this marching leviathan.

Ranks of Brandon Gate's ordinary citizens followed the workers, some in organised bands, some merely individuals wanting to show their support. Helmeted labourers, men in dirty overalls and plain working clothes mingled with those in bicorned hats and fine black suits that would have cost most workers a year's salary.

The march passed through the city gates, slowing slightly as the people funnelled through the gates and along wide, tree-lined boulevards. Pride shone from every face, along with a passionate determination that their voice would at last be heard. There was little anger, those more agitated members of the crowd having been calmed by the marshal teams.

All in all, the Workers' Collective demonstration was off to a good start.

GOVERNOR SHONAI WATCHED the numberless mass of people as it trod the cobbled streets of her capital and felt a shiver of apprehension, wrapping her arms tightly about herself. She had tried to guess the numbers of the crowd, but had long since given up. The numbers pouring into the city were endless. Already, thousands had spilled into Bellahon Park on the inner face of the walls, trampling delicately cultivated topiary and splashing in the shallow lake where priceless varieties of fish were bred by the palace biologis.

All the predictions regarding the threatened demonstration had told her that it could not occur. There was no organising power behind the people. Each branch of the Workers' Collective was too busy squabbling amongst themselves to organise much of anything, let alone a demonstration of any magnitude.

Well, this looked like a demonstration to her. Looking over the thousands of people thronging her city, she vowed never to listen to the predictions of her analysts again.

Was this the end, she wondered? Had the collective mass of the population simply decided that they had had enough? No, she decided. If she was to be removed it would be by the ballot or the bullet.

This was simply another entry in her list of events she would have to endure.

Her meeting with Barzano had given her some hope that she could see out the remainder of her term in office with a little dignity and perhaps set a more peaceful course for her successor, but it seemed as though even that was to be denied her.

She had not seen the Administratum's representative since he had first arrived with the Ultramarines, though the palace had been turned upside down by Sergeant Learchus when Barzano had gone missing. It turned out he and his Arbites liaison had made an excursion into the manufactorum districts, but Shonai was at a loss to understand why. There was nothing there except shabby worker bars and smoke stained hab units. She could not imagine an adept having any business in such places.

Shonai wondered if the adept had had any contact with Captain Ventris as she had since heard that the eldar raiders had attacked another outpost, this time an archaeological site. Apparently system defence ships had fired on the alien craft, and at least three captains were claiming they had hit it. She knew that was unlikely, but it was concrete proof that her administration was now taking a pro-active stance against the raiders.

The plan to enlist de Valtos's support in her aggressive policy towards the eldar and split him from the Taloun had come to naught. Her envoy to the de Valtos cartel had returned with a polite thanks from Kasimir de Valtos, but nothing concrete in offers of aid.

After the events in the Chamber of Righteous Commerce, she wasn't surprised.

To compound matters, her morning briefing had included a report from the judges that had made her groan in frustration.

Last night, the Adeptus Arbites had arrested Beauchamp Abrogas, running half-naked through the seedier end of the northeastern manufactorum district. Screaming nonsensical babble, he had been brandishing a loaded gun and taking pot shots at passers-by. Apparently he had wounded several people, and when the Arbites finally apprehended him, they discovered him raving and out of his mind on opiatix, a highly addictive and proscribed narcotic.

At present Beauchamp was languishing in a cell beneath the Arbites precinct house and would remain there until his family arranged to have him released. Shonai guessed they would let him sweat in the cells for a few days before coming for him.

There was a polite knock at her chamber door.

She shouted to her visitor to come in and glanced round to see Almerz Chanda enter, his hands clasped behind his back. She returned her attention to the scenes beyond the window. People were still entering the city.

'So many, Almerz,' whispered Shonai.

'Yes,' agreed Chanda.

'I want no trouble today, is that understood? It will take only the slightest provocation for these people to degenerate into a mob and tear the city apart.'

'I am assured that the judges are taking a hands-off approach, ma'am.'

'Good.'

'After last week's events, I am sure they are aware of today's sensitive nature.'

Governor Shonai nodded, watching as the square before the palace gates began filling.

By the Emperor, they'd better be.

YET MORE EYES watched the crowd from the upper storey of a marble building set within a low-walled garden with entirely different sentiments. Nine men worked with the quiet hustle of professional soldiers, stripping from plain grey uniforms and changing into black leathers and carapace breastplates. They carefully removed jangling dog-tags as well as any other identifying items and placed them in a canvas pouch.

Their command post was set up in a plain summer-house belonging to the Honan cartel. Dustsheets covered the furniture and the place reeked of abandonment. It was perfect.

No one spoke as another two men entered the room, the first talking softly on a portable vox-caster carried by the second.

The leader of this group, a man named Amel Vedden, handed his subordinate the vox handset and observed the thousands of people streaming into the city. He remained unimpressed. In this situation numbers meant nothing; he had sufficient force to break this demonstration into pieces.

Any idiot could break up a crowd. The key was to strike quickly and with maximum violence, so that the survivors were left stunned and unable to respond in any meaningful way.

But he did not want to break up this demonstration, he wanted it transformed from the sleeping giant into a rampaging monster, and that was even easier.

Vedden was a professional and disliked leaving anything to chance. To that effect, he had stationed another ten men downstairs with flame units and assault weapons, and the roof had been cleared, ready for their extraction by ornithopter.

His vox operator gathered up the canvas bag of dog-tags as Vedden turned to his men, now all clad in the threatening black carapace armour of Adeptus Arbites judges. Most carried automatic combat shotguns, but two carried bulkier, drum-fed grenade launchers. The slow-moving crowd was now almost in the noose of Liberation Square and he knew it was time for action.

He picked up his own shotgun and the ten 'judges' turned on their heels to leave the room.

FROM THE SAFETY of one of the gold-roofed palace towers Jenna Sharben, Ario Barzano and Sergeant Learchus also watched the gathering crowd. Learchus could see that the Arbites woman was unhappy about being here; she wanted to be down on Liberation Square with her comrades and he could understand that.

At first, he had been resentful of being left behind on Pavonis, but when Captain Ventris had explained the oath he had sworn to Lord Macragge, Learchus understood the honour and trust the captain had placed in him.

That did not make it any easier to know that he was denied the honour of battle. Still, as the Blessed Primarch was fond of saying, 'What the Emperor wills, be sure it will seek you out.'

From here they had a prime spot from which to observe the people of Pavonis voice their discontent. The animated singing and music were a muted, tinny sound through the armoured glass.

It did not sit well with Learchus that a populace behaved in this way. Where was their discipline and pride in working for the betterment of society? This kind of mass demonstration would never have occurred in Ultramar, there would have been no need for it.

On Macragge, you had discipline thrashed into you at an early age at the academies and woe betide the boy who forgot the lessons of youth.

The Arbites woman fidgeted constantly, straining against the glass to better observe the deployment and movement of her fellows, who were sensibly keeping a low profile at the palace gates and approach roads.

Heavy handed tactics would only incite the crowd to violence and Learchus just hoped that a cool head commanded the judges this day.

* * *

VIRGIL ORTEGA WAS sweating inside his carapace armour and, though he told himself it was the heat, he wasn't sure he sounded convincing. The sheer scale of the demonstration was unbelievable. Every report indicated that such an undertaking was far beyond the capabilities of the Workers' Collective, yet here it was in front of him.

His line of judges was solid. Every one of them had their shotguns slung and their suppression shields held in the guard position. Parked behind them, a line of Rhinos, most armed with powerful water cannon, were idling, ready to haul them out of trouble.

The mood of the crowd did not seem overtly hostile, but you could never tell with these kind of things. One second all would be well, and a heartbeat later, the smallest provocation would cause an eruption of violence. He would do all in his power to make sure that did not happen today and hoped that whoever had organised this felt the same way.

Ortega had expressly ordered his troops not to fire unless he ordered it. He glanced over at Collix. He couldn't see his face beneath the protective visor of his helmet, but had made especially sure that the sergeant had understood his orders. Ortega was keeping Collix close nonetheless.

The demonstrators had halted some fifteen paces from their line and, sensibly, were making no further move towards them.

Ortega could see that half a dozen people had climbed the statue of the Emperor in the centre of Liberation Square and were using its wide plinth as a podium from which to address the crowd. They carried bullhorns, shouting to their audience, punctuating each remark with a sweeping gesture, punch at the sky or pointed finger.

Ortega could not make out many of the words from this distance, but he could hear enough to know that there were no cries demanding the crowd rise up.

Cheers and claps greeted each statement from the orators and Ortega sighed in relief.

It seemed the people of Pavonis had nothing more troublesome on their minds.

VEDDEN'S TEN MAN squad emerged from the Honan's summer house and into one of the approach streets that led to Liberation Square. The street was jammed with people and they roughly pushed their way through with their shields. Shouted oaths followed in their wake, but the march organisers had been insistent: there must be no violence.

This was to be a peaceful show of unity before the planetary rulers, and thus the judges passed unmolested through the crowd.

They emerged onto Liberation Square, less than five hundred metres from the palace gates and the line of genuine Adeptus Arbites. Directly ahead of them, Vedden could see the statue of the Emperor and six people shouting at the crowd through bullhorns.

Vedden did not listen to the words.

'Wedge formation,' he hissed, and his men formed into an arrowhead shape, three either side of him with their shields facing outwards, and three men in the centre with their shotguns cocked and loaded.

'Let's go.'

They moved off, pushing a path towards the statue.

VIRGIL ORTEGA SCANNED the crowd, eyes alert for trouble, despite the avowed intentions of the speakers on the Emperor's statue. He'd just received check-ins from each of his squads and thus far, all was well.

A flash of movement and a ripple of shouting through the crowd caught his attention as he saw a group of judges emerge from the approach street ahead and to his left. He frowned in puzzlement.

Whose squad was that and what the hell were they doing out of position?

Ortega cycled through his vox frequencies, checking every squad's location and coming up with everyone in their proper place. Had the chief put more squads on the ground?

Instantly, he discounted that possibility. The chief was not so idiotic as to put uniformed troops in the square and not tell him.

A shiver passed down his spine, despite the day's heat, as he watched the unknown judges form a wedge and begin pushing their way through the crowd.

His eyes traced where their route would take them.

'Hell and damnation, no!'

'Sir,' inquired Collix.

Virgil Ortega dropped his shield and ran back to where the Rhinos rumbled throatily. He jumped on the front bull-bars of the nearest and lifted his helmet visor, scrambling up onto its roof.

The judge inside popped the top hatch and poked his head out.

'Sir?'

'Give me the damn loud-hailer. Now!'

The judge retreated into the Rhino, emerging seconds later with the loud-hailer handset which Ortega snatched from his outstretched hand.

He flicked the talk button and shouted, 'Attention. Attention. This is Judge Virgil Ortega, you people on the statue, get down now!'

The Rhino's loud-hailer was easily able to carry across the square, but his plea was ignored. Scattered shouts and jeers greeted his words and a few inaudible replies were hollered from the statue's plinth.

Damn them! Didn't these fools realise he was trying to save their lives?

He tossed the handset back and jumped from the Rhino's roof. Running back to the judges' line, he grabbed Collix and a handful of judges.

'Judges, form wedge on me. We have to get to that statue quickly. Come on.'

With practiced precision, the judges formed a wedge around Ortega, the twin of the one already within the crowd. Ortega knew he had to get to the statue first.

But even as they set off, he could see they would be too late.

THE SHOUTS SURROUNDING their advance through the crowd were getting louder, but Vedden ignored them. The statue of the Emperor was their objective and anyone who wasn't quick enough to get out of their way was brutally clubbed aside. A few kicks and punches were aimed at them, but their solid shields made fearsome bludgeoning weapons and soon most people were getting out of their way rather than defy them.

Vedden heard a rough voice ordering the speakers to get down from the statue, and saw a judge commander standing on the back of a Rhino shouting and waving his arms frantically.

But the cretins on the podium ignored him. They were making it too easy.

Like a pebble thrown in a pond, angry ripples of their advance were spreading outwards, as more people began stumbling back, bruised and bloody. A threatening rumbling spread as news of the judges' aggressive tactics began filtering through the crowd. The people on the statue now saw Vedden and his men approaching, and turned their attention to them.

Cries of abuse and self-righteousness were hurled at them, as the speakers denounced the criminal violence employed by the lackeys of a morally bankrupt administration.

The mood of the crowd had turned ugly, but it didn't matter, they were almost there.

A ring of heavy-set men surrounded the statue's base and there was no mistaking their threat. Vedden stopped as a wiry man with a long beard addressed him directly from the podium.

'Brother! We are doing no harm, we have assembled peacefully. Let us continue and I guarantee there will be no trouble.'

Vedden did not answer him.

He unlimbered his shotgun.

He racked the slide.

And in full view of thousands of demonstrators, shot the man dead.

ORTEGA SAW THE leader of the unknown judges unsheath his shotgun and pull the trigger as though in slow motion.

The sluggish echo of the weapon's discharge washed over him as he saw the man on the podium hurled languidly backwards against the alabaster effigy of the Emperor of Mankind. His blood splashed up the statue's thigh as he toppled over a carven foot and tumbled to the ground. His skull burst open with a sickening, wet crack on the cobbles of Liberation Square and, as his brains emptied from his cranium, time snapped back into focus.

The judges in the killer's shield wall crouched, bracing their shields on their thighs as the ones in the centre of the wedge took aim at the stunned survivors on the statue's podium. A volley of automatic shotgun fire blasted the remaining speakers from the Emperor's feet and Virgil knew that they would be lucky to live through this.

MYKOLA SHONAI SQUEEZED her eyes shut as she heard the echo of the shotgun blast and saw the man fall. That was it, she knew. There would be no coming back from this.

A final line had just been crossed and nothing would ever be the same again.

JENNA SHARBEN SURGED to her feet as the man toppled from the statue's plinth, a shout of denial on her lips. She faced Barzano, her face full of mute appeal, dumbfounded at what had just occurred. Barzano chewed his bottom lip, his fists curled.

She made to move past him, but he grabbed her arm with a strength that surprised her and his previously bland features took on a steely hardness. He shook his head.

He dragged his eyes from hers and scanned the crowd, taking in the tactical situation in Liberation Square in an instant. He turned to Sergeant Learchus.

'Sergeant, I need you down there.'

Gone was Barzano's jocular tone and in its place was a full, rich voice, obviously used to giving orders and having them obeyed.

Learchus had seen all that Barzano had, and understood the situation as well as he.

'What would you have me do?' asked the massive Space Marine.

'Whatever you can.'

VEDDEN FIRED ANOTHER volley of shotgun blasts into the crowd, relishing the screams of pain and terror he was causing. Those nearest to him frantically pushed away from the slaughter, but the press of bodies in the square was preventing them from getting out of the way quick enough.

Too bad for them, thought Vedden, pulling the trigger again.

Damn, but it felt good to be killing something, even if it was just dumb civilians. He'd wanted to have a crack at the judges themselves, but his orders were specific; only civilians. Kill as many as you can, capture one of their leaders and get back.

It made sense to capture one of the leaders. The Workers' Collective would demand that leader's release from the Arbites precinct house and the judges would truthfully claim that they were not holding anyone. Of course they would not be believed and it would be taken as another sign of the corruption rife within the planetary administration. It was perfect.

Vedden rushed forwards, stepping over the twitching bodies of the speaker's bodyguards and picked up a weeping girl, no older than twenty and roughly shucked her over his shoulder. She screamed in pain and he slammed his fist into her face to shut her up.

His men formed a rough circle and he stepped into their midst.

'We've got what we came for; now let's get out of here.'

HIS ARMOUR WAS dented in a dozen places and blood ran freely from his temple as he pushed another screaming man from his path. Ortega tasted blood and its coppery stink reeked of failure. He had failed to stop the senseless murders of the demonstration's speakers, failed to keep the Emperor's peace and now all hell was breaking loose.

He heard the hollow boom of more shotgun blasts from the far edges of the square and despaired. He hoped that none of his troops had fired these shots, but if things were going to hell elsewhere as badly as they were here, then he could not discount the possibility.

Bodies pressed in all around him and he angrily shouldered them away. This could not last much longer, it was only a matter of time until they were overwhelmed and killed. He slammed another man aside as he heard a series of cough-thumps and suddenly white smoke was clouding up in billowing geysers.

Grenade canisters of choke gas fired from the line of judges at the palace gates landed amongst the crowd, spewing caustic fumes outwards in obscuring banks of white. The canisters were landing just in front and beside his group and Ortega made a mental note to thank whoever had given the order to fire them. He slammed down his visor, engaging his rebreather.

Through a gap in the choking smoke, Ortega espied the retreating squad of murderers.

Knots of stunned demonstrators stumbled aimlessly through the clouds of smoke, eyes streaming and chests heaving. Many vomited on the cobbles or curled up in foetal balls.

The noise was incredible, like a great beast had awoken and roared. Ortega knew they were in the belly of that beast. He sprinted after the architects of this carnage, weaving round stumbling workers and leaping the dead bodies left in the killer's wake.

Collix and the six judges he had hastily pulled from the line charged after him, similarly eager for revenge. He shoulder charged a man wildly swinging a huge wrench, his eyes bloody where he'd torn at them.

Then they were at the mouth of the approach street and he could clearly see the backs of the killers as they made their way towards a plain white building.

He yelled an oath and levelled his shotgun. The range was not good and he couldn't get a good bead with his visor down.

Virgil squeezed the trigger and one of the killers fell, clutching his shoulder. Collix also fired and scored a hit, but neither of their shots were lethal and the wounded men were dragged along by their comrades.

'Come on,' he shouted. 'Before they get into cover!'

Their prey skidded to a halt and formed a disciplined firing line. Ortega was surprised, but not so surprised that he didn't drop to his knees and brace his shield before him as their enemy's shotguns fired controlled volleys down the street. The shield rocked under a terrible impact, and a fist-sized dent appeared in the metal next to Ortega's head. But it held and screams ripped the air as demonstrators who had chased them down the street were hit.

He sprang from behind his shield, and was punched from his feet as a second, unexpected volley hammered into the breastplate of his armour.

Ortega grunted, more in surprise than pain as he hit the ground. Collix rolled over to him.

'Sir? Are you hurt?'

Ortega groaned, and pushed himself upright and winced as he felt a sharp pain stab into his chest. The breastplate had absorbed the majority of the shot's impact, but it was holed, and blood streamed down its front. He was surprised at Collix's concern, but shook his head.

'Maybe a rib broken I think. Nothing serious.'

Collix hauled him to his feet and they continued down the street. Both men swore as they saw their prey dart through a thick, timber gate in a high wall that led into the grounds of a large town house.

Virgil Ortega jogged a few steps before he was forced to pull up short as the stabbing pain in his chest intensified. His vision blurred and he had to steady himself against the street wall. Collix turned.

'Come on, sir!'

'Go! I'll catch up,' he wheezed. Perhaps his wound was more serious than he had imagined. His breath heaved, a great sucking rasp.

He staggered after his men, casting a quick glance over his shoulder. There was no one else following them down the street, which surprised him, but he was thankful for small mercies. He took another step and closed his eyes as a wave of dizziness and nausea threatened to overcome him. His throat felt constricted and every breath felt like broken glass in his chest. He forced back the pain, biting his lip hard enough to draw blood and willed himself onwards.

His men had reached the gate the killers had gone through and Collix professionally directed them in breaching it. Two judges blasted its hinges as a third slammed an iron-shod boot into the lock, thundering the gate from its frame.

The roar of assault weapon fire blasted from the gateway, snatching the first judge from his feet. Collix and the others dodged back as another blast of gunfire raked through.

He lurched drunkenly up to his men, fighting for each breath and slammed his back into the wall. Collix risked firing his shotgun blind through the gateway and another hail of automatic fire sawed through in reply.

He dared a quick glance around the doorway, catching sight of at least four or five men with heavy stubbers, autoguns and a flame unit sheltering behind a sandbagged emplacement. Ortega swore. Anyone who showed their face in that doorway for more than a fleeting second was a dead man. A burst of gunfire fragmented the plasterwork around the gateway and he ducked back.

Collix and the others risked occasional shots through the doorway, but shotguns were no match for assault weapons and men who knew how to use them. A gout of fire spurted through the gate and the judges leapt back as the smashed edges of the frame were set alight, wreathing the entrance in flames.

Smoke and shadows danced around the street as cloudy tendrils of gas from Liberation Square oozed down the tributary street they occupied. Ortega thought he saw bulky shapes moving towards them, but his vision was blurring with pain and blood loss and he couldn't be sure.

They were at an impasse. To go forward was to die, but he wasn't willing to let these murdering swine get away. Another tongue of flame licked through the door, briefly illuminating the smoky street.

A shadow fell across Virgil Ortega as a massive form moved from behind him to stand in the entrance to the town house.

And the sandbagged emplacement disintegrated in a hail of thunderous gunfire. Flames whooshed through the gateway, wreathing an enormous armoured giant in a flickering orange glow.

Standing impervious in the flames, like some war-god of legend, a gigantic warrior in brilliant blue armour clutched a massive weapon that sprayed bolts through the gateway at a fearsome rate. Ortega's mouth fell open as he saw that there was not just one of these behemoths, but eight.

The giant turned its armoured visor to face him and he felt himself shrink under his gaze.

'We will take it from here, judge,' said the warrior, his voice distorted by his helmet vox.

Virgil Ortega nodded, unable to reply and waved his hand in the direction of the townhouse.

'Be my guest,' he wheezed.

SERGEANT LEARCHUS NODDED in acknowledgement towards the wounded judge and charged through the burning doorway, his bolter spitting explosive shells ahead of him. Cleander was beside him and the other Ultramarines fanned out behind him, firing from the hip. The immediate threat was neutralised, the men behind the sandbags torn apart by massed bolter shells, but there was more assault weapon fire spraying from the upper windows of the building.

From the sharp crack of the report, Learchus knew it was autogun fire, nothing that should trouble his holy suit of power armour. Flames still flickered over his chest where the promethium had gathered. He felt shots ricochet from his shoulder guard and returned fire. A scream sounded.

He hurdled the bloody ruin of the gun emplacement and slammed his armoured bulk against the door to the building. The heavy door exploded into splinters and the Space Marines were inside. He knew they had to hurry, his enhanced hearing had caught the distinctive whine of ornithopter engines approaching and that could only mean one thing.

Learchus rolled as gunfire sawed a path towards him, tearing up the floor tiles in terracotta chunks. He rose and fired his bolter one-handed, blasting a man in a judge's uniform on a set of wide stairs to rags and waved his men inside.

'The traitors will be on the roof awaiting pick-up. They must not leave this building,' ordered Learchus. The Ultramarines nodded and followed their sergeant as he took the steps upwards five at a time.

Learchus emerged into another long, tiled room, stacked with furniture covered in white sheets. Another, narrower flight of steps led up to an oblong of sunlight and he could hear the sound of ornithopter engines even louder now.

As he ran towards the opening to the roof a man rose up from behind one of the sheets, but before he could fire, Cleander put a bolt through his head. Learchus leapt up the steps and emerged onto the flat roof of the building.

AMEL VEDDEN WATCHED as the twin dots of the ornithopters drew closer, sourly reflecting that one would now be enough as he cast his eyes over the seven men who'd survived. He'd lost a lot of soldiers on this mission, but he couldn't bring himself to feel sorry for them.

But what a mission!

Who could have expected the Space Marines to get involved?

He'd be sure to ask for a damn sight more money for dealing with that unexpected threat. He still held the unconscious girl in his arms, knowing that he'd enjoy killing her as soon as they were safe.

He glanced back to the opening in the roof as he heard barks of gunfire from below.

Couldn't these bloody ornithopters hurry up? This was getting too close.

The insect-like shapes buzzed in on wide nacelles, bulbous gunpods like stingers slung under their noses, eerily tracking with the pilot's head movements as they circled the building.

Why didn't they land?

Vedden spun as he heard the thud of armoured footfalls and dragged out a pistol, pressing it hard into the girl's temple.

Five Space Marines stood with their unfeasibly large boltguns pointing at him and his men. His own men levelled their shotguns, but nobody moved.

The air seemed to stagnate, as though unwilling to pass through this unfolding drama. Even the sounds of the circling ornithopters and the baying crowd as they tore the city apart seemed strangely muted. His mouth was dry as he faced these mighty warriors and he felt a tremor begin in his arm.

These were Space Marines; what the hell was he doing? He dug deep within himself, searching for some untapped reserve of bravery and licked his lips.

Amel Vedden never got the chance to find out whether he had the courage to face down a Space Marine as it was at that point the guns of the ornithopters opened fire.

Heavy autocannon fire sprayed the roof of the building, churning up its pebbled surface and shredding human flesh. The men who had been awaiting rescue in the flyers were the first to die, ripped apart in seconds by the heavy calibre, armour piercing shells. Vedden screamed as an auto-cannon shell clipped him, instantly shearing his leg from his body in mid-thigh. He collapsed, dragging the girl to the ground with him.

The Ultramarines scattered, firing at the ornithopters, but their bolter rounds were ineffective against the armoured undersides of the gunships.

Learchus sprinted forward, diving to the ground to gather the girl in his arms and rolling on top of her as the ornithopter's shells ripped towards her. He supported his weight on his elbows so as not to crush the girl and felt the powerful impacts hammer into his back plate. He offered a short prayer of thanks to his armour for standing firm against the traitorous fire.

Abruptly, the weapons ceased fire and the ornithopters gained altitude, spinning away from the town house, their murderous mission complete. Bolter fire chased them, but they were soon out of range and vanished amid the hazy smog surrounding the manufactorum.

Learchus rose to his knees and pulled the girl out from under him. She was covered in blood, but how much of it was hers, Learchus was unsure. From a cursory inspection, he believed she would live.

He stood and lifted her into his arms. The man who had abducted her stared with glassy eyes at the sky, hyperventilating and clutching at the stump of his leg. He scrabbled weakly at the churned roof, whimpering for help. Cleander gave him emergency first aid, and put a tourniquet on his leg, hoping that the man would prove a good source of information if he lived.

The sounds of battle still raged from Liberation Square and Learchus could see orange flames and smoke spreading throughout the city as the people of Pavonis reacted to the day's events in the only way they knew how.

THE DESTRUCTION RAGED throughout the day, with the mob rampaging through the marble city with murder on their minds. Statuary on the main thoroughfares was toppled, beautifully maintained gardens and parks put to the torch and homes ransacked as the baser elements of the crowd sought to take advantage of the rioting.

Fires spread unchecked and whole districts were razed to the ground with no organised fire-fighters willing to risk their lives on the city streets. People huddled terrified, in their homes as screaming workers broke down doors and stole anything of value. Some of the wealthier inhabitants fought back, gunning down those who broke into their homes, but against the mob they had no chance and were torn apart, their priceless heirlooms and treasures smashed.

Saner heads in the crowd appealed for calm, walking through the streets with their arms upraised, but against the chaos of the riot, their voices went unheard.

Knowing that to venture into the city was to invite certain death, the judges had pulled back within the palace grounds, protected behind its armoured walls and defence turrets. A few rioters had attempted to storm the gates, but roaring blasts of gunfire from the bastions had cut them down mercilessly.

The judge squads stationed at the approach roads had quickly realised that they were cut off from the precinct house and had taken refuge in the nearest shelter they could find. They fought desperate sieges for hours until flyers from the palace were dispatched to carry them and the dwellings' owners to safety.

Protected by the Ultramarines, Virgil Ortega's ad hoc squad of judges had little to do but await a pick up from one of the palace's ornithopters. Slipping in and out of consciousness, Ortega experienced a momentary surge of panic as the propwash of the ornithopter roared over him, thinking that its guns were about to open fire.

Ortega and the wounded prisoner were carried away along with his judges. The aircraft could not carry the weight of eight fully armoured Space Marines, but the pilot assured Learchus that he would be back directly.

The sergeant assured the pilot that he and his men could make their own way back to the palace quite safely, and ordered him to pick up any remaining judge units holed up in the city.

Darkness drew in and the rioters had still not exhausted themselves. Red flames licked at the sky, smoke boiling from each blaze. Whole districts were shrouded in darkness, their frightened residents unwilling to advertise their presence with illumination. It would later be learned that over four thousand people had died this day, killed in the fighting, murdered in their homes or burned to death as fires raged, unchecked, throughout the city. It would be a day long mourned by Pavonis.

Slowly at first, then with greater speed as the chill of night took hold, many of the workers of Pavonis filed from the city. But a great many remained to vent their frustration on those they felt deserved it. Some felt shame at what was occurring, while others felt nothing but a sense of triumphant vindication.

ARIO BARZANO WATCHED, expressionless, as the palace physician worked on the wounded man, lifting bloody swabs and clamps from the ragged stump where his leg had once been. Barzano had seen enough combat trauma wounds to know that the man would not die.

Not from that wound anyway.

He was unconscious just now, pumped full of sedatives and pain suppressants. His limbs were held immobile by the bed's restraints as the physician worked to clamp the spurting artery. Brother Cleander's observance of battlefield triage had probably saved his life. It was a situation the prisoner would later come to regret, thought Barzano.

Judge Ortega lay on the pallet bed next to the traitor, his barrel chest swathed in bandages. Two of his ribs had been broken by the shotgun blast, one of the splintered ends puncturing his left lung. He was lucky to be alive and from the shouts and curses he'd made as the physician had tended to his wound, Barzano wondered if it was his sheer stubbornness that had kept him alive.

Jenna Sharben sat beside him, quietly describing the day's events he had missed while unconscious and the list of those judges who had lost their lives. His face remained set in stone, but Barzano could tell he was hurting.

The third patient was the girl these murdering scum had kidnapped from the Emperor's statue. Despite the vast quantities of blood on her clothes, she had come through her experience relatively unscathed. The physician had dug out a number of shotgun pellets embedded in her flesh and treated her for concussion, but other than that she was unharmed. At present she was sleeping off the last effects of a sedative.

Behind Barzano, Sergeant Learchus, Governor Shonai and Almerz Chanda waited in tense silence for the physician to finish his work. Barzano turned and strode towards them.

Barzano thanked Learchus for his courageous efforts during the chaos of the day. The Space Marine's armour was dented and blackened in places, yet he was unharmed. Then he turned his attention to the governor of Pavonis.

She had aged since he had last seen her. Her grey hair hung loosely about her shoulders and her face seemed to have acquired a whole new set of lines. Only Chanda seemed unmoved by the day's bloodletting.

'A bloody day,' offered Barzano, placing a hand on Mykola Shonai's shoulder.

She nodded, too choked to answer. Chanda had just provided her with a slate with the estimated death toll from today's violence and its scale had numbed her.

Barzano opened his arms to her and she accepted his embrace. He enfolded her shuddering body as she wept for the dead. Barzano looked Chanda in the eye.

'Get out,' he said simply.

Chanda looked ready to protest, but caught the iron resolve in Barzano's stare and departed through the infirmary door with a curt bow.

Ario Barzano and Mykola Shonai stood locked together for several minutes as the governor of Pavonis allowed the years of failure and frustration to wash through her in great, wracking sobs. Barzano held her, understanding her need to let out her burden that had been dammed for too long.

When she had finished, her eyes were puffed and red, but a fire that had been smothered there for so long had now been relit. She wiped her face on a handkerchief offered by Barzano and took a deep, cleansing breath. She smiled weakly at Barzano and straightened her shoulders, pulling her hair back into its tight ponytail.

She looked over to the bed containing the man whose leg had been blown off. Until now, her enemies had been faceless entities, robbing her of a means of striking back, but here, she had one of those enemies before her and she smiled in grim satisfaction. The man was unconscious and according to the physician would probably remain that way for several days.

But soon he would wake and the governor of Pavonis would show him no mercy.

LATER, ARIO BARZANO, Jenna Sharben, Mykola Shonai, Sergeant Learchus, Almerz Chanda and Leland Corteo gathered in the governor's chambers, a large pot of caffeine steaming on the table. Barzano poured a mug for everyone, except Learchus, who politely declined. Everyone looked haggard and weary, with the exception of Mykola Shonai, who bustled around the room with pent-up energy. She stopped by the bust of old Forlanus and smiled, patting his carved shoulder.

Corteo reflected that it was a smile of the hunter.

Shonai returned to her desk, taking a drink from her mug and leaned forwards, her fingers laced before her.

'Right, to business, people. We have one of our enemies below. What do we know about him?'

Jenna Sharben dumped a canvas bag on the governor's desk and tipped out its contents. A pile of silver dog-tags and assorted personal effects tumbled out: a lighter, a small clasp knife and other soldiers' knick-knacks.

'One of the stiffs we pulled from the house, a vox operator by the looks of things, was carrying this. We think he was left in the house while the others carried out their mission and then called for the ornithopter extraction when they got back. I guess they didn't count on their ride opening fire on them.'

'Do we know whose gunships they were or where they went?' enquired Shonai.

'I'm afraid not,' said Almerz Chanda. 'Our aerial surveillance systems were offline for scheduled maintenance at the time.'

'So we don't know where the gunships went,' cursed Shonai, 'but I take it those dog-tags tell us who the men that attacked the crowd were?'

Jenna Sharben answered. 'Yes, looks like they were all lifers in the Planetary Defence Forces. The highest rank we found was a captain and I'm betting that's the prisoner we have below.'

'Does he have a name?' asked Barzano.

Sharben nodded towards the adept. 'If he is the captain, he's called Amel Vedden, an officer in the Kharon barracks.'

'That's one of the regiments sponsored by the Taloun,' pointed out Chanda.

'Does he have a record?' asked Barzano.

'No, it's been expunged. Recently too.'

Barzano turned to Shonai. 'Who could expunge a military record like that? Only a commanding officer of a regiment has the power to do that.'

Shonai was quick to grasp the implication of Barzano's deduction.

'So now the loyalty of an entire regiment of PDF troopers is in question?' She swore. 'That's nearly five thousand men.'

Governor Shonai pondered the situation in silence before coming to a decision.

'Very well, I'll authorise the mobilisation of more regiments to contain their base until we can be sure where their loyalties lie.'

'How long will that take?' inquired Barzano, looking over at Leland Corteo.

The old man sighed deeply and took a great draw on his pipe. 'It's hard to say, it's been decades since we needed to mobilise the PDF. The last time was in the governor's father's time.'

'Yes, but how long?' pressed Barzano.

'Perhaps two or three days. That's if enough of the soldiers answer the muster. There's a good chance a great many of them were in Liberation Square today.'

'The *Vae Victus* and Captain Ventris will return in less than three days,' added Sergeant Learchus. 'Then you will have a company of Ultramarines at your disposal, Governor Shonai.'

'Thank you, sergeant. I am most grateful for the aid provided by the Ultramarines. You do your Chapter honour.'

Learchus bowed his head, saying, 'We serve the Emperor.'

Shonai took another sip of her caffeine and said, 'So what else do we have to go on? Do we know who the town house belongs to yet?'

'We do indeed,' chimed Almerz Chanda with great relish. He produced a sheaf of papers, deeds of purchase and city records. 'It is a summer house belonging to Taryn Honan.'

'Honan?' exclaimed Corteo, almost choking on his pipe smoke. 'I don't believe it! That fat fool? Surely not?'

'It's all here in black and white,' gestured Chanda to the records.

'These are irrelevant,' put in Barzano. 'Whoever was behind this planned it carefully. They had no intention of picking up the soldiers after they had completed their mission. I hardly think that if Honan had been behind this, he would have been stupid enough to launch his attack from one of his own houses. Though it wouldn't hurt to bring him in to answer some questions.'

'So where does that leave us?' said Jenna Sharben.

'It leaves us,' continued Barzano, 'with a lot of work to do.'

KASIMIR DE VALTOS stabbed his fork through a succulent cutlet of meat and forced himself to swallow, despite the taste of sour bile in his throat.

The meat tasted of rancid maggots and he washed it down with a drink from a crystal goblet of wine. He was reliably informed that this particular vintage was amongst the most sought after in the sector, but to him it was as tasteless as vinegar.

Yet another legacy of his torture.

But that would soon be a thing of the past. Lasko had informed him that his men would soon breach the final chamber and it had taken all of his considerable willpower not to rush off and see for himself. He felt his grip on the fork tightening convulsively and hid it from sight beneath the table.

His guest said something trivial and banal. He smiled politely and mouthed something equally meaningless in reply. He couldn't hear the words; a roaring sounded in his ears and a hot dryness formed in his mouth. He took another drink of wine.

Beneath the table his fist beat a rhythmic tattoo on his thigh, the fork pricking his flesh deep enough to draw blood through his trousers. He couldn't feel it and it was only when he raised the fork to his plate once more, that he noticed the blood.

His breath caught in his throat at the sight of the sticky red liquid and his tongue flicked out to catch the ruby droplets as they ran from his hand.

His guest said something else, but the words were lost to him as he tasted his blood.

He could not feel the pain in his leg. He could feel no pain at all.

De Valtos felt his gaze being drawn towards the dining hall's ceiling, picturing the black leather case sitting beneath his bed, but he forced himself to look away.

It was too soon.

It was always that much sweeter when savoured. He forced his mind clear of blades, saws, pliers and barbed hooks, attempting to focus his attention on his guest. But it was impossible to concentrate on the mindless babble that spewed from its rouged lips. Sweat poured down his face as he forced another lump of meat down his throat.

He didn't think he could wait much longer to kill it.

He realised he no longer thought of his guest as human, and that was a bad sign. The hunger was growing in him and he pictured it naked. It was just meat, flesh to be carved, a cathartic release for the pain he could no longer feel.

To feel that pain again, he would inflict suffering and misery on its body, feeling his own pain echo its cries.

Blood dribbled down his chin and he realised he had bitten down hard on his lip. He wiped his chin as his guest pushed back its chair and walked down the length of the table towards him, false concern written across its bovine features.

It put its hand on his shoulder and he recoiled in horror at its touch.

'Are you feeling alright, Kasimir? You look awfully pale,' asked Solana Vergen.

Kasimir de Valtos swallowed, holding back his disgust and fury.

'Yes,' he managed, thinking of the black case. 'I will be.'

♆
TWELVE

IT WAS INCREDIBLE, thought Mine Overseer Jakob Lasko. No matter how much juice they put through this damn cutter, it never, ever, got above half power. They were burning out generators at the rate of five or six a day and though the cost implications still rankled, he knew he had no choice but to replace each one as it failed. They had to breach this last barrier soon.

The chamber throbbed with the whine of the cutter and he was thankful for the ear protectors he wore. Not only did they make the shriek of the cutter bearable, but it also shut out the weird noise he'd been hearing recently. In his more fanciful moments – which weren't many – he could almost swear he could make out babbling voices amongst the noise, subtly layered and overlapping.

Damn, but he had been down in this bizarre place too long!

He cast his professional eye around the chamber. It was absolutely square, its proportions perfect to the last micron, or so his cartographers had told him. The walls were covered in a tight, angular script, etched into the smooth surface in triangular groups. What it said or meant was a mystery to him.

The only breaks in the script were four featureless alcoves, two on the east wall, two on the west. Each contained a giant, well-proportioned alabaster figure gripping a strange copper staff, edged with a patina of green oxide. What they were or who they were supposed to represent was yet another mystery he left to others.

All that concerned Jakob Lasko was breaching the door at the far end of the chamber.

So far the smooth black slab had resisted diamond-tipped drills and breaching charges. Only the lascutter had any effect, and this was making headway at the slowest pace.

Two tech-priests prayed and swung incense censers over the cutter alongside six miners armed with picks and shovels who looked like they'd rather be any place but here. Things had got so bad recently that none of the men were willing to go anywhere on their own. He couldn't blame them; the darkness and spook stories that had been spreading over the last few years about this place would give anyone second thoughts. But that was no excuse for the kind of worker turnover he was seeing here. The money was a lot better than a man would get any place else, so he figured that if a man signed on, he'd damn well better do his job properly.

Sure, there had been a few disappearances over the years, most recently that damn fool Dal Kolurst. Stupid idiot probably fell down a shaft in the dark. They may know about machines, these tech-priests, but they know damn all about real work. So far, they hadn't found Kolurst's body, but it was just a matter of time before someone tripped over his broken corpse.

He looked up as the lights flickered again and snapped an angry glance over at the chanting priests. The light was bad enough in here as it was without being plunged into total darkness.

The gem-smooth eyes of the statues in the alcoves glittered in the flickering light, and Lasko shivered despite himself. Yes, he decided, the money was good, but he'd be lying to himself if he claimed he wouldn't be damn glad when this job was over and he could get back to proper mining.

This archaeology might pay better money, but it didn't sit right on his worker's soul to put in so much work without seeing something tangible for your efforts. What had they hauled out of this place so far? Nothing but a few skeletal figures made of some weird, greenish metal.

The tech-priests had got all excited about them, but none of them had been able to tell him what they were or what kind of metal it was. Some experts they were.

Well, looking at the work at the door, he could see that the cutter had penetrated perhaps a metre. According to the tech-priests, there couldn't be too much more to go through, but Lasko would wait until they were through before breaking out the fifty year old uskavar. As rich as the boss was, Lasko didn't think he'd be willing to shell out for too many more generators and cutters. This operation must have cost a fortune already.

The lights flickered again, plunging them all into darkness for long seconds until, with a dull hum, the light swelled from the glow-globes once more.

Lasko was more relieved than he cared to admit and licked his dry lips. What the hell could be behind this door that was so damned important? He just hoped he got to find out soon.

♉ THIRTEEN

TARYN HONAN STEPPED into the vestibule of Kasimir de Valtos's home and glanced through the open door that led to the dining hall. Broken crockery and fine crystal littered the floor at one end of the table. Such a shame to see such fine workmanship so thoughtlessly destroyed.

He tore his attention away from the dining hall as he noticed a lady's pelisse hung on a hook beside the front door. He licked his rouged lips and lifted the edge of the garment to his face, inhaling its sweet-scented aroma. Ah yes, he recognised this perfume as belonging to the lovely Solana. Was she here also, he wondered? Strange, he hadn't seen her carriage when he arrived.

A cough sounded from the stairs and he spun, dropping the pelisse, blushing in guilty surprise.

Kasimir de Valtos and Vendare Taloun stood on the landing watching him. Honan shuffled into the middle of the vestibule and cleared his throat as the two cartel leaders descended to meet him. He noticed that Kasimir looked flushed and in good sorts, whereas Vendare was chalk-white, as though he'd just had a profound shock.

'What are you doing here?' demanded Kasimir and Taryn flinched at the hostility in his voice.

'I told you not to come, remember?'

'Y-y-yes,' stammered Taryn, 'but I had to see you. I was summoned to the palace this morning, by the governor. The questions they asked me! I mean it was quite beyond the pale. All sorts of things. They–'

'Taryn, slow down,' ordered Kasimir, putting his arm around Taryn's ample shoulders. 'Come, let us have a seat in the drawing room before the fire and discuss this like civilised men, yes?'

Taryn nodded gratefully and allowed himself to be guided through the door opposite the dining hall.

As promised, a large fire was blazing and Taryn settled himself into a high backed leather chair as de Valtos poured three generous measures of uskavar from a bottle on an expansive drinks tray. Taloun walked quickly towards Kasimir and downed his drink in a single swallow. The two cartel leaders exchanged a hurried conversation in whispers then Kasimir sat down opposite Taryn, handing him a crystal class of amber spirit. Vendare remained standing by the drinks tray, pouring himself another drink.

'Now, Taryn. You were saying?'

He sipped his drink before beginning, to calm himself.

'Yes, it's a bad business when an influential cartel leader like myself is treated like a common criminal by a member of the Administratum. That new adept, Barzano, hounded me with all sorts of questions about my town house, you know, the one I loaned you for a time?'

Kasimir nodded, chewing on his bottom lip and Taryn noticed he seemed to be suffering from the heat of the fire, beads of sweat breaking out on his forehead.

'Are you alright, Kasimir?' asked Taryn.

'Far from it,' snorted Vendare, pouring himself another drink.

Kasimir shot him a vicious glance and nodded, saying, 'Please continue, Taryn. Do not concern yourself with Barzano, he will not be a problem for much longer. But what did he want to know?'

'Well, he claimed that the Church of Ancient Ways had used my town house to launch another of their despicable attacks. Can you imagine? From my house? Ridiculous, isn't it?'

'Not really, Taryn,' brayed Kasimir with an edge of hysteria to his humourless laugh. 'You see it's true. All of it. You're just too stupid to understand.'

Taryn opened his mouth to protest, but Kasimir cut him off. 'You have no idea what's happening on this planet, do you? Events are moving in a manner decided by me. Me! I have invested too much, lost too much, to have things messed up by a globulous waste of space like you, Taryn.'

Tears swelled in Taryn Honan's eyes at this unwarranted attack.

'Come, Kasimir, surely there's no need to say such things? We are friends after all. Aren't we?'

'Friends?' mocked Kasimir de Valtos. 'No, Taryn, we are not friends. You are just a pathetic piece of filth I stepped on on my route to immortality. And now it's time I discarded you.'

Taryn heard the sound of a door opening behind him. Kasimir raised his eyes to smile at the newcomer, but there was no warmth in the expression. Taryn desperately looked over to Vendare Taloun for support. Surely his dear friend Vendare would not allow Kasimir to talk to him in this way, would he?

But Vendare Taloun was staring open-mouthed in horror at the person who had entered the room. Taryn heard the sound of soft footfalls approaching the back of his chair, and a pale, delicately veined hand slipped onto his shoulder.

The nails of the long, thin fingers were sharp and painted black. A strong smell of disinfectant wafted from the hand.

Taryn swallowed in fear.

'Kasimir? What's going on?' he whimpered.

He twisted his bulk around in the chair to see a tall, slender figure dressed in a plain red smock and surgical mask. Only his eyes were visible above the mask and they were the deepest shade of violet. The figure's other hand slipped onto his neck, stretching his skin taut and despite his fear, Taryn felt his skin goosebump under the soft touch.

Kasimir de Valtos sat back in his chair and sipped his drink.

Taryn was about to speak when he felt a sharp stabbing pain in his throat as a massive needle slid into his neck. He winced, but instantly the pain was gone, replaced by a warm, floating sensation that infused his body, and his eyes drooped, suddenly feeling absurdly heavy. Kasimir was speaking and he had to concentrate to make out the words.

'Taryn, this is my surgeon. I think you and he should get to know one another better, don't you?'

Taryn Honan smiled and nodded dreamily as the fast-acting soporific raced through his metabolism.

The glass of uskavar slipped from his fingers and shattered on the floor.

BARZANO LEFT THE interrogation chamber, where Ortega and Sharben were interrogating the girl Learchus had rescued from the murderous judges. Governor Mykola Shonai, Almerz Chanda and Leland Corteo stood before the window to the interrogation chamber, watching the judges work. Shonai's face was granite hard, but Chanda and Corteo looked distinctly queasy at the violence they were seeing.

'Does she know anything?' asked Shonai.

'I don't think so. Nothing useful anyway. She'll give us some names and we can round them up, but she's too small a fish to know anything of real value.'

'So why all this... unpleasantness?' enquired Chanda, waving his hand at the dejected figure through the glass.

'Because you never know under which rock you'll find the pieces of the puzzle, my dear Almerz.'

Chanda frowned at Barzano's over familiarity and looked away.

'She was on the statue,' said Mykola Shonai. 'She's one of the ringleaders. She must know something.'

'Possibly,' admitted Barzano. 'She's hard-core militant. She won't break easily.'

'Do what you have to do to break her,' ordered Shonai. 'I don't care how, just find out who was behind this so I can make them pay.'

'Oh we'll find out who did this, I guarantee it,' promised Barzano. 'I believe that one of your rivals has been very clever and very subtle, using cut-outs and cells of activists to make sure that we can't just unravel their treachery with one arrest. I know how these things work. Nothing will have been written down, no record will have been made, but everyone in the loop knows about it. I should imagine that once a few events were put in motion, the demonstration took on a life of its own and required very little in the way of orchestration to get it started.'

Shonai nodded. 'All it needed was a spark to light it,' she said.

'Just so. Ably provided by Captain Vedden, curse his soul.'

'Is he conscious yet? Can we question him?'

'Not yet, no, but your physician believes we will be able to later today, though he wasn't at all happy about letting us talk to him so soon.'

'Damn him and his concerns, I want that bastard broken in half. We're close, Ario, I can feel it.'

'Come on,' he suggested, 'I could use a drink. Any takers?'

Shonai shot Barzano a hard look, but her grim expression softened and she nodded.

'Yes, why not?'

Corteo chuckled. 'Well, I've always said that it is bad luck to let a man drink on his own, so yes, I'll join you.'

'Almerz?' asked the governor.

The governor's chief advisor shook his head. 'Thank you for the offer, governor, but I shall stay here, just in case the judges learn something of value that needs to come to your immediate attention.'

As she turned to leave with Barzano and Corteo, Governor Shonai placed her hand on Chanda's shoulder with a weary smile. 'You are a good man, Almerz. Thank you.'

Almerz Chanda bowed and returned to watching the girl's questioning.

'So you've had experience in these matters before, Adept Barzano?' asked Leland Corteo, filling his pipe once more. Barzano sat cross-legged upon his bed and nodded, sipping his uskavar. An informal mood had descended upon the trio almost as soon as they had entered his chambers.

'Yes, Mister Corteo, I have. I have travelled to lots of different places and dealt with many people who believed that they were exempt from the Emperor's laws.'

'And you showed them that they were not?' put in Mykola Shonai.

'I did indeed,' smiled Barzano.

'And what will you do here once you have what you want?'

The question was casually asked, but Barzano could sense the seriousness behind the words. Briefly he considered lying to her, but realised that she deserved to know the truth.

'In all likelihood you will be removed from control of this world. Failure to maintain one of the Emperor's worlds is a crime, and your regime here can hardly be qualified as a success, can it?'

Corteo's face reddened in anger at Barzano's forthright answer and slammed his glass down on the adept's table. 'Now see here, damn you! You may be some fancy trouble-shooter from Terra, but you have no right to speak to an Imperial Commander like that.'

'No, Leland, he has every right,' whispered Shonai. 'He is correct, after all. I did fail, I let the small things mount up and tried to hide what was going on for too long. Perhaps we do deserve to be replaced.'

Barzano leaned forward, setting his drink down beside him and resting his elbows on his knees. 'Perhaps you do, but I haven't decided yet. After all, who would I put in your place? Ballion Varle? Vendare Taloun? Taryn Honan? I hardly think so, my dear governor. No, let us leave talk of dismissals for the moment and concentrate on the problem at hand.'

'Which is?' snapped Corteo, still angry at Barzano's rudeness.

'I think it is possible that persons on this planet are working with the eldar, using their piratical raids to cover up other activities while fermenting discord on Pavonis to divert attention from what their true purpose may be,' explained Barzano, leaning back against the wall. Both the governor and Corteo were speechless. The idea that their planet's troubles had been set in motion deliberately was appalling, and neither knew how to respond.

'I do not believe that the events which have occurred here could have done so without some guiding influence. There are too many coincidences, and I do not believe in coincidences.'

'But who?' finally managed Shonai.

Barzano shrugged. 'I don't know yet. That's what I'm hoping we can find out soon, for I fear events are approaching critical mass.'

'And what does that mean?'

'It means, my dear governor, that things are about to explode.'

IN A SECLUDED corridor of the Imperial palace, a shimmering point of light fluttered in the air, bobbing like a tiny balloon caught in a gentle updraught. Slowly the point of light began to expand, swirling in a lazy spiral with a violet glow. The fabric of the air seemed to stretch like a painting with an invisible weight placed at its centre, pulled insistently towards the glow.

The illuminators on the ceiling suddenly imploded as a soft moaning issued from the light, a gurgling, chittering sound that reeked of obscene lusts and eternal hunger. Four points of darkness began forming within the light, twisting and swelling like fluid cancers in its heart. The liquid shapes followed the spiral of the twisting nimbus of dirty light, their jelly-like forms gradually coalescing into more solid matter and pushing clear of the glowing mass.

Enveloped in membranous, amniotic skins, the rapidly solidifying things pushed through the light, creaking and twisting the air out of shape with the pain of their dark birth.

With a tortured shriek, the fabric of reality ripped and the four pur-ple-red forms dropped to the stone floor as their glowing womb spiralled back on itself, vanishing with incredible speed, leaving the corridor in semi-darkness once more.

The four glistening forms lay shuddering for a few seconds only, before unfolding long, sinuous legs, envenomed spines, rippling mus-cle-ridged arms and fang filled maws.

Sloughing their dripping birth sacs, the creatures sniffed the air in unison, their entire existence enslaved to the one imperative their mis-tress had seeded them with.

To kill the prey.

TROOPERS KORNER AND Tarnin crept down the darkened corridor, las-guns held before them. There was something down here, that was for sure. Korner had heard some damn strange noises and had voxed the guard station that they were investigating.

Tarnin took the lead, noticing the shattered glow-globes and hearing glass crunch underfoot.

A slithering, dripping sound was coming from up ahead.

Without turning, he hissed, 'Korner, gimme your illuminator,' and reached behind to receive the portable light source.

He flicked on the illuminator and trained it down the corridor. He never really saw the creature that killed him.

A fluid shape launched itself from the darkness and disembowelled him with one stroke of its massive claws. Twenty centimetre talons tore him in two, and his skull was crushed with one snap of massive jaws.

Korner caught a glimpse of roaring fangs and talons, spraying blood and heard Tarnin's hideous scream abruptly cut short. He turned to run.

Something heavy hammered into his back, smashing him to the ground. His lasgun spun away. Furnace-hot breath burned his skin and he felt his uniform and flesh dissolving under the beast's paws. Korner opened his mouth to scream.

The warp-spawned beast tore his head off in a welter of gore and swallowed it whole in a single bite. It buried its bloody fangs in the trooper's back, swallowing great chunks of meat and crunching his bones as it began to feed.

A second beast snapped its lethal maw, a threatening growling emanating from its wide chest. Chastened, the bloody hound abandoned its feast and followed the leader as the four beasts padded unerringly through the palace corridors.

The prey was close.

Barzano's head snapped up. He unfolded his legs, standing with a smooth grace and glanced hurriedly at Governor Shonai, worry plain on his features. He dashed to the door of his chambers, wrenching it open and stepping into the corridor.

The two Ultramarines guards snapped to attention as the adept emerged, bolters held across their breastplates. Brother Cleander turned and looked down at the adept.

'Brother Barzano, is something amiss?'

Barzano nodded hurriedly. 'Oh, yes, very much amiss, I believe. Where are the rest of your squad?'

'At the cardinal entry points to this wing of the palace. Nothing will approach without coming past one of my battle-brothers.'

'Or through him,' muttered Barzano.

'I beg your pardon?'

'Nothing. Brother Cleander, I need you to vox everyone on duty and tell them that something extremely dangerous has penetrated the security of the palace. We are all in grave danger.'

Cleander indicated that his fellow sentry should carry out the adept's wishes and racked the slide on his bolter.

'What is happening, adept?'

'I don't have time to explain right now. Just tell all the guards to be ready for anything and shoot anyone or anything they don't recognise. Do it!'

Brother Cleander's face was hidden within his helmet, but Barzano could feel his anger at being ordered about by a lowly scribe.

'Your tone is disrespectful–,' he began.

'Damn my tone, Cleander. Just do it!' snapped Barzano as the heavy crack of boltgun fire sounded from somewhere close by. More shots followed and a ululating howl echoed through the palace corridors.

'Too late,' said Barzano.

The three beasts raced along the corridors at a terrifying rate, speeding around corridors and evading cries of pursuit in their wake. The body of the fourth lay behind them, dissolving into a foetid pile of indigo ooze atop the armoured corpses of two Ultramarines.

The net was closing on them, but they had no thought for their own survival.

The prey was all that mattered.

* * *

BARZANO RUSHED BACK into his room and skidded onto his knees before the long footlocker at the end of his bed. He slid his finger into the geno-key as Shonai and Corteo rose to their feet. Both were panicked by his behaviour, and he couldn't blame them.

'What the hell is going on?' demanded Shonai.

The lid of the footlocker slid open and Barzano reached inside, saying, 'Remember that burning fuse you talked about earlier?'

'Yes, of course.'

'Well, it turns out it's a lot shorter than we thought. Our enemies have just raised the stakes. Here,' said Barzano, tossing each of them a pistol. 'You know how to use these?'

'Not really, no,' admitted Corteo.

'Governor?'

'No. I've never fired a weapon before.'

'Hell and damnation. Oh well, no time like the present to learn.'

Quickly he demonstrated cocking the weapons and how to reload them. 'When you fire, aim low, because they'll kick like a grox in heat.'

'But what are we supposed to be shooting at?' protested the governor. 'What's going on?'

Barzano returned to the footlocker and pulled out a slender bladed sword with an ornate tracery pattern etched along the length of the blade. He rose to his feet, a large pistol with ribbed coils around its flattened muzzle held in his other hand. Gone was his garrulous manner and in its place was a deadly earnestness.

'Our enemies have sent creatures from the depths of hell to hunt us and they will not stop until we kill them or they kill us.'

Barzano thumbed a rune on the pommel of his sword and Shonai and Corteo jumped as the weapon leapt to life, amber fire wreathing the blade in spiralling coils of energy.

'A power sword!' exclaimed Corteo in surprise. 'What manner of adept are you?'

Barzano grinned, but there was no humour evident.

'The worst kind,' he assured Corteo.

BROTHER CLEANDER COULD hear gunfire, the heavy crack of bolters and the snap of lasfire echoing from the walls as whatever was out there moved closer.

The echoes and twisting passages made it impossible to tell from which direction the foe was approaching, so Cleander covered one route while Brother Dambren covered the other. Cleander dearly wished he could charge to the assistance of the hunters, but this was his duty, defending the adept's quarters. Cleander was a citizen of Macragge and he would die before deserting his post.

The percussive blast of Brother Dambren's bolter was the first indication that their foes were upon them. Cleander spun to see three monstrous creatures charging towards them. He added his own fire to Dambren's, tearing the leading beast to shreds as the hail of mass-reactive bolts blew it apart from within.

But the beasts' speed was phenomenal and barely had the first died than the remaining two pounced. Cleander dropped as a beast leapt at him, rolling and firing as it sailed over him. His bolts missed, blasting great chunks of masonry from the roof.

He glanced around to see the second beast bite through Dambren's arm, ripping the limb clear in a flood of crimson. He had no time to go to his brother's aid as the beast before him charged once more.

Cleander fired, a single bolt punching through the creature's belly. It howled in fury, but kept coming, thundering into Cleander's chest. The pair hammered backwards into the doorway, smashing it to splinters and tumbling into the adept's chambers.

SHONAI SCREAMED AS the door exploded inwards and one of the Ultramarines guards tumbled inside, a beast spawned from her nightmares frenziedly clawing at his helmet. Its long body rippled with iridescent light, a loathsome reddish purple with bony spikes running the length of its spine. Its massive head was horned and its fangs dripped blood. Each heavily muscled limb ended in vicious, barbed claws and its eyes were jet black, dead and unfeeling.

Barzano leapt forward, swinging his blazing sword at the hell beast before him.

Its speed was incredible for such a large creature and the sinuous head ducked below the crackling blade, leaping clear of the Space Marine it squatted upon. It lashed out with a taloned paw, narrowly missing Barzano, but tearing a splintered chunk of timber from the heavy desk.

Cleander rolled towards the beast, wrapping his powerful arms around the creature's neck. It snapped at the Space Marine, its blackened claws easily tearing through his breastplate. Blood poured from the gouges and Cleander snarled in pain as his flesh burned at the beast's touch.

'Get out the way!' yelled Barzano, aiming his plasma pistol.

Cleander ignored the adept, tightly gripping the thrashing monster, roaring his own battle cry as its fangs and claws tore his armour open. The second beast appeared at the doorway, its bestial jaws dripping with blood, and Barzano shifted his aim.

The white-hot plasma bolt punched through the creature's flank, hurling it backward. Foul ichor spurted from the wound and it slumped to the ground, its fabric swiftly un-knitting.

Cleander wrestled for his life against the last creature, vainly trying to hold its claws at bay, but he knew it was a fight he could not win. The beast was stronger than him. The hound slammed its jaw into Cleander's face, snapping his head back against the stone floor. His helmet cracked under the impact and his grip on the beast's neck loosened a fraction.

It was the only opening the creature needed. Its talons rose and fell, punching through Cleander's breastplate and tearing his ribcage apart.

Corteo and Shonai fired their pistols at the wounded beast, but neither was trained in firearms and their shots went wild.

Barzano pushed them back as Cleander's killer wrenched its talons clear of the body and lurched towards him. Its movements were slowed, but it was still capable of killing them all. His plasma pistol hummed, its energy cells still recharging and Barzano knew it was no use to him yet.

The beast reared up on its reverse jointed legs and charged.

Ario Barzano dived forwards, beneath its lethal talons.

He rolled to his knees, swinging his power sword in a low, sweeping arc.

The energised blade hacked the beast's legs out from under it and it crashed to the ground, thrashing the cauterised stumps of its thighs in fury.

Barzano sprang to his feet and stood beside Governor Shonai and Leland Corteo as the beast clawed its way towards them across the floor, its substance unravelling in smoky trails of darkness even as it neared.

Only its rapidly dissolving torso and head remained as Barzano stepped in, reversing his grip on his sword, and drove the blade down through its head.

Barzano slumped next to its fading remains, pulling the blade from the floor as Sergeant Learchus and his squad arrived.

Learchus dropped to his knees beside Cleander's corpse and bunched his fist in anger. Barzano left him to his grief, turning to face the ashen-faced Mykola Shonai and Leland Corteo. He tossed the pistol onto the bed and deactivated his sword, laying it upon the sagging remains of the shattered desk.

'You killed it,' gasped Shonai. 'How did you do that?'

'Better I show you,' replied Barzano, pulling aside the painting of Forlanus Shonai and exposing the secure safe in the wall.

He punched in a ten digit code and pulled the door open.

Inside was the box, which he removed and placed on the floor beside him.

Barzano reached back inside the safe and removed a smaller item which he handed to Shonai, who took it with an expression of fear and surprise.

She held a rectangular block of sapphire crystal, no larger than fifteen centimetres by eight and less than five centimetres deep. It was an inconsequential thing but for the symbol it encased.

A grinning skull embossed with a stylised capital 'I'.

Governor Shonai looked up into the face of a man she no longer knew.

'I am Ario Barzano,' he said, 'of the Holy Orders of the Emperor's Inquisition.'

☡
FOURTEEN

AT PRECISELY 07:00 hours on the morning following the Workers' Collective demonstration in Liberation Square, tanks from the Kharon planetary defence barracks rolled through the gates of their base along Highway 236 towards Brandon Gate. Within twenty-five minutes, the column of forty tanks, locally produced Leman Russ Conquerors bearing the artillery shell motif of the Taloun, had reached the outskirts of the city, rumbling towards its centre and the Imperial palace.

A constantly repeating message blared from speakers mounted on each tank's hull, proclaiming that this manoeuvre was intended only to keep the peace and that people should not panic. The populace of Brandon Gate risked hurried glances through their windows as the tank column rumbled past, fearful of what this latest development might herald. The tanks passed the main population and manufactorum centres, halting only when they reached the marble walls of the inner city.

Within an hour of the Taloun's tanks taking to the streets, armoured vehicles rolled out from other PDF barracks sponsored by those cartels allied to the Taloun. Tanks bearing the crest of the de Valtos cartel mobilised from their base at Tarmegan Ridge and infantry carriers from six other cartel sponsored bases mounted up and made for Brandon Gate.

By midday, one hundred and nineteen tanks and over seven thousand infantry were stationed outside the city limits. The hull speakers fell silent and a repeating vox signal cut across every frequency, announcing the PDF's intention to keep the peace that the governor obviously could not. However, in deference to her position, none of the tanks would enter her city until such time as their armoured might would be required. Nervous heads within the city pondered exactly what that might mean.

Despite repeated demands from Mykola Shonai, none of the mobilised PDF units withdrew from the city limits and to all intents and purposes, Brandon Gate became a city under silent siege.

As HE LIMPED through the shattered doorway to Ario Barzano's chambers, Uriel was shocked at the devastation the hell beasts had wreaked. The Thunderhawk had landed less than an hour ago and his mood was sombre as he remembered the downcast face of Learchus as he had informed him of the death of Cleander and three other battle-brothers.

Pasanius entered the room behind him, both men ducking their heads below the lintel. The massive sergeant carried a stasis vessel containing the metallic fragments from the hill on Caernus IV.

Despite the ministrations of Apothecary Selenus, Uriel's movements were still painful from the wounds inflicted by the eldar leader's axe, and the bites of his abominable pets. He would live, but his heart hungered for revenge on the dead faced warrior.

Barzano stood with his back to Uriel, resting his hands on an ancient looking box, which sat upon a splintered and sagging desk. He spoke in a low voice to Governor Shonai and Leland Corteo. Lortuen Perjed sat on the edge of the bed, while Jenna Sharben and Sergeant Learchus stood immobile at the back of the room. The sergeant had his bolter drawn and chainsword at the ready.

Barzano turned at the sound of Uriel's footfalls and the captain of Fourth Company was shocked at the change that had come over the man. Learchus had already informed Uriel of Barzano's true identity, and, at first, he had scoffed at the idea of the adept really being an inquisitor.

But to see the man now, he had no trouble in accepting the fact. Barzano no longer stood in the stooped, slightly subservient pose of a typical Administratum adept. Dressed in a loose fitting tunic and knee high boots with a sword and pistol belted at his side, his pose was proud and erect. He stepped forwards, gripping Uriel's hand and placing the other on his elbow, single-minded determination shining in his eyes.

'Captain Ventris, my prayers are with your honoured dead. They died well.'

Uriel nodded in acknowledgement as Mykola Shonai moved to stand beside the inquisitor.

'It is good to see you again, captain,' she said. 'I also offer my prayers for your fallen brothers, and hope that no more shall fall defending our planet.'

'As the Emperor wills it,' replied Uriel, waving Pasanius forward. The sergeant placed the stasis vessel next to the box.

'So what have you brought me, Uriel? Something from the eldar ship?'

'No, it comes from one of the worlds attacked by the raiders.'

'What is it?' asked Barzano deactivating the stasis seal and lifting the lid.

'We were hoping you could tell us. It came from a hillside almost entirely composed of metal. According to the local populace and a survivor of the raid, this metal once ran like liquid and their smiths used it to fashion blades and ploughs. Though this practice had been going on for generations, the metal would somehow regenerate each shorn piece.'

Barzano's face paled visibly as he reached into the vessel and removed the fragment of faintly glowing metal. His eyes were wide as he traced his fingertips around the angular script carved in the metal.

Even as Uriel watched, the last of the glowing silver threads at the centre of the metal turned into the ruddy colour of rust and its lustre faded completely. Carefully, almost reverently, Barzano placed the metal on the desk and lifted his gaze to meet Uriel's. 'You said there was a survivor? I take it they are aboard the *Vae Victus* awaiting debriefing?'

'No. He was mortally wounded. I had Chaplain Clausel administer the Finis Rerum and we buried him in his home.'

Barzano struggled to contain his outrage at this valuable source of information being so casually squandered and simply nodded.

'Very well,' he managed finally, glancing at the locked strongbox his palm rested upon.

'Well?' prompted Uriel, pointing to the dead metal. 'What is it?'

Barzano drew himself up to his full height and said, 'This, my dear captain, is a fragment of wreckage from a starship more than one hundred million years old. It is also the reason we are here on Pavonis.'

'One hundred million years,' mused Leland Corteo. 'Surely that's impossible. Mankind only reached the stars less than fifty thousand years ago.'

'I did not say it was a human ship,' snapped Barzano.

'This has something to do with the troubles on Pavonis?' asked Mykola Shonai.

'I'm afraid so. Remember the deeper purpose I believed was behind your troubles? This is it. Someone on this planet is attempting to discover the whereabouts of the rest of this ship.'

'What could anyone hope to gain by its recovery?' asked Uriel.

'Power,' stated Barzano simply.

'Then if you know where it is, tell me the location and *Vae Victus* shall destroy it.'

'Ah, Uriel. If only it were that simple. It does not exist in this reality as we understand it. It drifts between time, forever flitting between this world and the immaterium. Would that it remain so for all eternity.'

'Why do you fear it so?'

Barzano lifted his hand from the locked strongbox, placing his thumb on the geno-key and crouched before the lock, allowing the box's guardian spirit to confirm his identity.

Finally, he punched in the thirteen-digit password into its lid and spoke the word of opening. The lid swung open and the inquisitor removed a heavy, iron-bound book with thirteen small golden padlocks securing its pages shut. The locks looked fragile, but each had been imbued with hexagrammic sigils of great power.

Barzano touched each lock in turn, whispering as though persuading the locks to grant access to the precious tome. One by one, the locks snicked open and Barzano straightened as the creaking cover of the book slowly opened without help from any human hand.

Uriel hissed and the others stepped back in alarm. Barzano took a deep breath and closed his eyes and Uriel felt a tinny, electric sensation pass through him. The book heaved, mirroring the inquisitor's breath and Uriel felt his hand involuntarily reach for his pistol. Sorcery!

Barzano extended his palm towards Uriel and shook his head.

'No, captain. I am entreating the spirit within the book to impart a measure of its knowledge to us.'

'Spirit within the book?' hissed Uriel.

'Yes. You have heard the expression that knowledge is power, yes? Did you think those were just empty words? Knowledge is indeed power, and knowledge has power.'

Seeing the book pulse like a beating heart, Uriel muttered a protective prayer. Suddenly he realised that there could only be one way that Barzano was, as he put it, entreating the book's spirit.

'You are a psyker?'

'Of sorts,' admitted Barzano, his brow knitted with the effort of speaking. 'I am an empath. I can sense strong emotions and feelings.'

The book suddenly seemed to swell and its pages fanned forwards as though in a strong wind, faster than the eye could follow. Abruptly, the book settled, its yellowed pages sighing and settling into immobility.

Barzano relaxed, opening his eyes and Uriel noticed beads of sweat on his brow. A trickle of blood ran from his nose, but he wiped it clear and leaned over the pages the book had revealed to him.

Hesitantly, Uriel, Pasanius, Shonai and Corteo approached the table.

At first Uriel could not understand what he was looking at. The pages had been scrawled by a crazed hand, hundreds of words overlapping and spinning in lunatic circles or viciously crossed out.

'What is it?' asked Shonai.

'These are some of the writings of the heretic tech-abbot, Corteswain.'

'And who was he?'

'Corteswain belonged to the Adeptus Mechanicus. He travelled the galaxy searching ancient archaeological sites for working STC systems. Instead he found madness.'

Uriel knew of the Adeptus Mechanicus's ceaseless quest for Standard Template Construct systems, techno-arcana priceless beyond imagining. Every single piece of Imperial technology was derived from the few, precious fragments of STC systems that remained in the hands of the Adeptus Mechanicus. Even the flimsiest rumour of an STC's existence prompted whole fleets of Explorators to set off in search of this most valuable treasure.

Barzano continued his story. 'Corteswain was the only survivor of an expedition to a dead world, whose name has long since been lost, in search of STC arcana. Something attacked his expedition and he claimed to have been taken to a world beyond this galaxy by a being of unimaginable power he called a god.'

'A god?' whispered Shonai

'Yes, a god. He claimed to have seen the true face of the Omnissiah, the Machine God. Needless to say, this didn't make him particularly popular within some factions of the Adeptus Mechanicus, who accused him of blasphemy. It caused a schism in their ranks that exists even today and within a year Corteswain disappeared from the omniastery on Selethoth where he had begun preaching his dogma.'

'What happened to him?' asked Uriel.

Barzano shrugged. 'I don't know. His rivals probably had him abducted and killed. But some of his writings survived, carried from the omniastery by his acolytes.'

'What does it mean? I can hardly make anything out,' said Shonai, slipping on her glasses.

'This particular passage talks of a vessel Corteswain claims he saw,' said Barzano, pointing out a barely legible scrawl in the corner of one page.

His fingers traced the outline of a badly sketched crescent with a pyramid shape sitting atop its middle.

Uriel squinted as he tried to read the words scratched into the parchment below the sketch. The same words were written again and again, at every angle, overlapping and curling back on themselves.

His eyes followed the least obscured portion of the spidery writing and he silently mouthed the words as he slowly pieced them together.

He finally grasped what the words said and the hairs on the back of his neck rose as he realised he had heard them before – from the burned lips of a man on the brink of death.

Bringer of Darkness.

Barzano glanced sharply at him and Uriel was reminded that the inquisitor could sense his emotions.

'Uriel,' said Barzano slowly. 'Do those words mean anything to you?'

Uriel nodded. 'Yes. The survivor on Caernus IV, a man named Gedrik, spoke them to me just before he died.'

'What did he say? Quickly!' hissed Barzano.

'He said that the Death of Worlds and the Bringer of Darkness awaited to be born into the galaxy and that it would be in my hands to decide which. Do you know what he meant by that?'

'No,' said Barzano, a little too quickly. 'I don't. What else did he say?'

'Nothing. He died soon afterwards,' replied Uriel, pointing to the crescent shaped sketch on the book. 'So the Bringer of Darkness is an alien starship. What can it do?'

'It can unmake the stars themselves, bleed them dry of energy and leave nothing alive in a star system. And it can do this in a matter of days. Now do you see?'

Uriel nodded. 'Then we must find it before the eldar.'

'Agreed. We must also discover who they are working with here on Pavonis,' said Barzano, pacing the room, hands laced behind his back.

'The eldar leader spoke a name as we fought, perhaps it was his accomplice.'

Barzano stopped pacing and spun to face Uriel, a look of disbelief on his face.

'He mentioned a name?' hissed Barzano. 'What? Quickly man!'

'I'm not sure it was a name. It was one of their foul words, it sounded like... *karsag*, or something like that.'

Barzano's brow knitted and he cast a glance at Shonai. 'Does that name have any meaning to you? It isn't one of the cartels here?'

'No, I don't recognise it.'

'Captain Ventris,' said Lortuen Perjed. 'Could the word you heard have been *kyerzak* perhaps?'

Uriel closed his eyes, picturing the corpse-faced warrior, recalling the sounds that rasped from his expressionless mouth. He nodded.

'Yes, Adept Perjed. I believe that it could very well have been that.'

Barzano rushed to his aide and knelt before the old man, gripping his shoulders tightly. His face was alight with excitement. 'Lortuen, do you know what that word means? Is it a name?'

Perjed shook his head. 'No, it is not a name, rather it is a term of address. Its roots are indeed eldar in origin and it is used to denote one who is to be honoured.'

Barzano released his grip on Perjed's shoulders and stood, perplexed. 'Helpful though that is, it gets us no nearer to who the eldar are working with.'

'On the contrary, Ario, it tells us exactly who we are looking for.'

'It does?' replied Barzano, 'Explain yourself, Lortuen. We don't have time to indulge your sense for the dramatic.'

'The word *kyerzak* means an honoured one, but in the writings of Lasko Pyre, he talks of how the torturers of the dark kin, beings he called the haemonculi, would tell him that he should appreciate the honour they did him, inflicting the most sublime pain they could imagine upon his flesh.'

Uriel and Barzano made the connection as Perjed continued.

'You see, the dark kin have corrupted the word, debasing its meaning to refer to one who has been honoured with their most painful artistry.'

Shonai clenched her fists and hissed the architect of her troubles' name.

'Kasimir de Valtos.'

CONSTRUCTED IN A hardened bunker in the eastern wing of the palace, orbital defence control was responsible for the monitoring of aerial and spatial traffic in the local area around Pavonis. It was heavily fortified and fully self-contained, with its own energy grid and reserve power supplies that would allow it to defend Pavonis for up to a year without primary power.

Second Technician Lutricia Vijeon sat at her control panel, sweeping the space around Pavonis for any unauthorised traffic.

Her commanding officer, Danil Vorens, sat with his back to her at the command console staring at a holo display projected from the plot before him.

Lutricia noticed a faint return on her surveyor scope and began noting the time of its appearance on her log. It had to be a ship, it was too large to be anything else. She checked the flight plans pinned beside her station to check if anything was expected in her sector of responsibility. There was nothing logged and she adjusted the runes before her to sharpen the image on her display.

It didn't look like anything she'd seen before, with its long, tapered prow and what appeared to be long sails rising from its engine section. What the hell was it?

The image swam hazily on the display, its image blurring as she tried to lock down its form. The image snapped into focus as a thick hand dropped onto her shoulder, squeezing it tightly. She started and looked up into the grim face of Danil Vorens.

'Sir, I've got this signal on the–' she began.

'I know about it, Vijeon. Everything has been properly logged. I have authorised it personally,' said Vorens, shutting off her surveyor scope.

'Oh, I see. But shouldn't we log it in the daily report?'

'No, Vijeon,' whispered Vorens, leaning close to her ear and squeezing her shoulder even tighter. 'This ship was not here and you did not pick it up on your surveyors. Understood?'

Vijeon didn't, but wasn't going to tell Vorens that.

Still, what did it matter to her?

She nodded and switched her scope to another sector of space.

Obviously Vorens had been expecting this ship.

THE ULTRAMARINES' THUNDERHAWK gunship landed in the country estates of Kasimir de Valtos in the foot of the Owsen Hills, nearly seventy-five kilometres west of Brandon Gate.

'Everyone out!' yelled Uriel, charging from the belly of the gunship, bolter at the ready.

He emerged into the late afternoon sun, seeing the splendour of de Valtos's country estates spreading before him. A large, multi-winged house sprawled in front of them, two black coaches sitting before the main entrance. The Ultramarines fanned out, forming a defensive perimeter as the gunship howled skyward on a pillar of fiery smoke.

Uriel waved Dardino's squad left and Venasus's right, leading Pasanius's towards the main doors.

The main door was already open and Uriel sprinted through into the chequered entrance hall. Ultramarines barged through the door and Uriel directed them with sharp jabs of his fist. He indicated that Pasanius and two other Space Marines should follow him and charged up the staircase, his bolter constantly searching for targets.

The upper landing was empty, a long carpeted passageway stretching left and right.

To the right, the passageway curved out of sight, while on the left it ended at a large oaken door. Something told Uriel that this house had been abandoned, but his soldier's instinct was too well honed not to treat this place as an anything less than hostile.

Uriel and Pasanius made their way cautiously down the passageway, bolters trained on the door. His auto senses could detect no noise from the room beyond, though he could smell a faint, but disturbing odour.

Uriel smashed the door from its frame, going in low and fast, Pasanius behind him, bolter sweeping left and right. Given the confines of the dwelling, he had opted for his bolter rather than his preferred flamer. Behind him, Uriel could hear the sounds of Ultramarines, kicking down doors and searching room-to-room.

The stench hit him before he realised what he was looking at on the bed.

It had once been a human being, but almost every vestige of humanity had been stripped from the corpse's frame by blades, saws, needles and flame. A golden halo of hair framed the body's head, its leering skull-face stripped of skin below the eyes, both of which had been gouged from their sockets with the bloodstained shards of a broken mirror that crunched underfoot.

Uriel's gorge rose at the sight. 'Guilliman's oath!'

Pasanius lowered his bolter, taking in the full horror of the dead woman.

'By the Emperor, who could do such a thing?'

Uriel had no answer.

Despite the horrific mutilation, Uriel recognised the features of Solana Vergen and he added her name to those for whom he would seek vengeance upon Kasimir de Valtos.

SERGEANT VENASUS LED his squad carefully through the lower reaches of the traitor's dwelling place. It was colder here, his suit of power armour registering a drop of fourteen degrees.

So far they had found nothing, and Venasus dearly hoped to find some of their enemies soon. Three of his men had died on the alien ship and there was a blood price to be paid for their deaths.

The bare stone passage led along to an iron door, padlocked shut and Venasus wasted no time smashing it from its frame with a well-placed kick. The sergeant powered through the doorway, his men following close behind. The room was in darkness, but his armour's auto senses kicked in.

He saw the gleam of metal to his left. A grinning skull face leapt from the darkness of the room. Venasus swung his bolter up and opened fire at the deathly apparition.

URIEL HEARD THE burst of gunfire from the top landing and sprinted downwards, following the stairs to the lower levels of the house. His blood pounded in his veins, hoping that there would be enemies to slay, his heart hungry for vengeance.

As he reached the source of the gunfire, he could see that he was to be denied such vengeance for now. The corridor was cold, its walls glistening with moisture.

Sergeant Venasus stood at the buckled doorway to a dimly lit room.

'Report,' ordered Uriel.

'False alarm, captain. I was first through the door and acquired what I thought was a target. I opened fire, but I was mistaken.'

'Assign yourself ten days of fasting and prayer to atone for your lax targeting rituals.'

'Yes, captain.'

'So what was it you fired upon, sergeant?'

Venasus paused before answering. 'I am not sure, some kind of metallic skeleton. I do not know exactly what it is.'

The sergeant moved aside to allow Uriel and Pasanius to enter the room. A single glow-globe cast a fitful illumination around the small room, which looked like some insane mechanic's workshop. All manner of tools lay strewn upon chipped and blackened benches, their exact use incomprehensible. In one corner of the room lay the shattered remains of Sergeant Venasus's target. As the sergeant had described, it resembled a metallic skeleton, its once gleaming surface stained with a patina of green and its limbs twisted at unnatural angles.

Another skeleton of stained metal lay propped up on an angled bench, bundles of wires running from its open chest to rows of yellow battery packs with red lettering stencilled on their sides. Panels on its chest and skull had been prised open and Uriel peered into the darkness within its grotesque anatomy. It resembled a skull in that it had eye sockets and a skeletal grin but there was something horrendously alien about this construction, as though its maker had set out to mock humanity's perfection.

The metallic form repulsed Uriel, though he could not say exactly why. Perhaps it was the loathsome malevolence that radiated from its expressionless features. Perhaps it was the metal's resemblance to the substance they had removed from beneath the hillside on Caernus IV.

'What in the name of all that's holy is this?' asked Pasanius.

Uriel shook his head. 'I have no idea, my friend. Perhaps they were the crew of the ship Barzano spoke of.'

Pasanius pointed at the machine on the bench. 'You think it is dead?'

Uriel walked over to it and wrenched the wires from the metal skeleton's chest and skull.

'It is now,' he said.

URIEL WATCHED THE temperature reading on his visor creep slowly downwards as he approached the last door. Steam hissed from the power unit on the back of his armour and he could feel a strange sense of foreboding as he neared the rusted portal.

The door wasn't shut, a sliver of darkness and stuttering light edging the frame. Wisps of condensing air soughed through from behind it.

He glanced behind him. Pasanius, Venasus and six Ultramarines stood ready to storm the room on his order. The remainder of his command were tearing the house apart from top to bottom, searching for a clue to de Valtos's current whereabouts. He nodded to Pasanius and hammered his boot against the metal of the door.

It slammed inwards, Pasanius charging through with Venasus hot on his heels. Uriel spun into the room, covering the danger zone on their blindside as the remainder of the men charged in.

Uriel heard the clink of chains and soft moans emanating from the centre of the room. His auto-senses had trouble adjusting to the flickering light and he disengaged them, activating his armour lights. The other Ultramarines followed his example and slowly the horrendous centrepiece of the octagonal room became visible.

Atop a stinking, gore-smeared slab lay a large human skeleton, the bones bloody, its former wrapping suspended above it.

Chunks of excised flesh hung from the ceiling on scores of butchers' hooks, each one set at precisely the correct height to shape the outline of the body they once enclosed. As though frozen a millisecond after his body had suffered some internal explosion, the flesh and organs of Taryn Honan hung suspended above his skeleton, each fatty slice of his body ribboned together with dripping sinew and pulsing cords of vein.

'By the Emperor's soul,' whispered Uriel, horrified beyond belief. Honan's head was a segmented, interconnected jigsaw of individual lumps of flesh, the wobbling jowls and severed chins circling his steaming brain, each still juddering in an imitation of life.

Uriel saw that his eyes still rolled in their sockets, as though the corpse continued to relive its last agonising moments and Uriel commended his tortured soul to the Emperor.

The slab of fatty flesh that contained the mouth worked soundlessly up and down like a macabre marionette controlled by some unseen master. The gently spinning meat containing the lidless eyes fluttered and Uriel watched, horrified, as they focussed on him and a low moaning again spilled from Taryn Honan's lips.

Fat tears rolled down Honan's pallid flesh as his mouth impossibly gave voice a low, anguished moan that tore at the hearts of the Ultramarines. Uriel wanted to go to the man's aid, but knew that it was beyond his, or any other man's power to save Honan. There was a terrible pleading desperation in Honan's eyes and his mouth kept flapping in a heroic effort to speak.

Uriel moved closer to the man's exploded anatomy, masking his horror at the mutilation.

'What are you trying to say?' he whispered, unsure whether the fleshy jigsaw could hear him, let alone understand him.

Honan's lips formed a pair of words and Uriel knew what the man desired.

Kill me...

He nodded and raised his bolter to point at Honan's head. The grotesque form of Honan's mouth formed more words before his eyes closed for the last time.

Uriel whispered the Prayer for the Martyr and pulled the trigger. A hail of bolts shredded the suspended chunks of flesh, tearing them from the hooks and granting oblivion to the mutilated cartel man.

Uriel let his fury flood through him in the cathartic fire of his bolter. His squad joined him, emptying their magazines in a storm of gunfire that tore the octagonal room to shreds, blasting great holes in the walls, smashing metal tray racks and utterly destroying any trace of the crime against nature, visited upon this latest victim of Kasimir de Valtos's insane schemes.

As the smoke of their gunfire dissipated, Uriel felt his breathing return to normal and lowered his weapon. Honan's soundless valediction echoed within his skull.

Thank you.

Their prey had flown.

No matter. They would hunt him down.

'Inform Inquisitor Barzano what has happened here and tell him that we are returning to the palace,' snapped Uriel. He turned on his heel and marched from the devastated room.

KASIMIR DE VALTOS reclined on the leather seats of his ground car. The vehicle was of a less traditional design than was usual on Pavonis, but since this was a time of change, it was not inappropriate, he thought.

He once again pictured the helpless face of Solana Vergen as he showed her the contents of his black leather case. He had savoured every scream and every pleading whimper as she begged for her life, not realising that she had signed her own death sentence the moment she had accepted his dinner invitation. He was only sorry that he had not had the opportunity to watch the Surgeon work on fat Honan, but his own needs and desires had taken priority.

Yes, Solana Vergen had been exquisite. Her death would keep the demons from assailing his every thought with blood and pain for a time. But he knew they would be back soon enough and that he would have to wash them away in the blood of another.

Kasimir looked up from his reverie at the other passengers in his vehicle, experiencing an uncharacteristic desire to share his good spirits.

The Surgeon sat opposite him, hands clasped in his lap and his eyes drifting over Kasimir's body, as though pondering the best method of dissecting him. He remembered all too well the pain of the last procedure to purge his ravaged internal organs and renew his polluted circulatory system.

Two could play at that game, vowed de Valtos, remembering the screams of over a hundred different victims he had practiced his own art upon. Soon there would be a reversal of roles when he was in possession of the Nightbringer. Its sleeping master would grant him the immortality he so craved and these upstart aliens would understand that they were the servants, not he.

The Surgeon's female accomplice reclined next to him, her long, ivory legs stretched languidly across the floor of the vehicle. Her eyes glittered playfully, arousing and repulsive at the same time. She blew him a kiss and he flinched as though she had threatened to touch him with her loathsome, yet sensual flesh.

Despite her proud words, her warp-spawned beasts had failed their mission, but he did not feel disappointed. He would, after all, get the chance to see Shonai's face as she realised he was the person behind all her years of misery.

He could feel his good mood evaporating as the tap, tap, tapping of the vehicle's last occupant intruded on his thoughts. Vendare Taloun studiously avoided looking at his fellow passengers, rapping his ring finger on the one-way glass of the window. He wanted to pity Vendare, but that emotion had died within him the moment the haemonculi's blades had peeled the skin from his muscles.

If anything he felt contempt for the man. His petty, small-mindedness had led him into this pact with de Valtos. How else did he think they were going to wrest control of this world from Shonai? With words and democratic process? He wanted to laugh and had to stifle the urge to erupt in hysterical laughter.

He forced himself to get a grip on his wildly fluctuating emotions, knowing that with the end in sight, he must not lose control. Control was everything.

As the car rounded a corner in the road, he caught a glimpse of the city of Brandon Gate ahead. He lifted his hand and squinted through a gap he formed with his forefinger and thumb. He could fit the image of the distant city between his digits and smiled as he pressed them closer together, imagining that the shortening distance separating them was the lifespan of Governor Shonai. He rolled his arm, noting the time on his wrist chrono patch as the Surgeon removed a long, curved device from the inside of his robes and peered intently at it. De Valtos was struck again by the delicate structure and dexterity of his finger movements.

The alien's lips were pursed together in displeasure. He replaced the device in his robes and said, 'The flesh sculpture has expired. There are enemies within the vivisectoria.'

De Valtos was surprised, but hid his reaction. If someone had discovered Honan, they must already know a measure of his plans.

No matter. Events were already in motion and nothing now could prevent their ordained path. They were almost at the shuttle platform where he would board the craft that would carry him to his destiny in the palace.

He thought of Beauchamp Abrogas in the cells of the Arbites precinct and almost laughed.

He spoke to the hateful alien woman, 'You gave the Abrogas boy the inhaler?'

She nodded, not even deigning to speak to him.

So strange that it would be a fool like Beauchamp who heralded the beginning of Pavonis's new age.

But that was in the future. There were matters afoot now that demanded his attention.

'So it has begun then?' asked Mykola Shonai.

'It certainly looks like it. De Valtos wouldn't abandon his home unless his plans were moving into their final stages.' answered Inquisitor Barzano snapping off the vox-caster and drawing his pistol and sword. He was possibly overreacting, but after the attack of the warp beasts, he was taking no chances.

His mood was foul, as he had just learned that Amel Vedden, the traitor Learchus had captured following the riot in Liberation Square, was dead.

Despite being kept in restraints the man had somehow managed to dislodge one of his intravenous lines and blow an air bolus into his bloodstream, resulting in a massive embolism and heart attack. It was a painful way to die and, though Vedden had escaped justice in this world, Barzano knew that all the daemons of hell were now rending his soul.

Scores of armed guards ringed the governor's private wing of the palace and Learchus had pulled the Ultramarines back to the inner chambers. Mykola Shonai and Ario Barzano were about as well protected as they could be.

'So what do we do now, inquisitor?' said Leland Corteo, obviously trying to hide the nervousness he felt. Barzano turned to the ageing advisor and placed a reassuring hand on his shoulders.

'Our first priority must be to ready all the loyal armed forces. Vox a warning to the Arbites and place the palace guard on full alert. Also, tell the defence commander to have each of his weapon emplacements acquire one of the tanks waiting outside the city walls. Hopefully it won't be required, but if de Valtos tries anything, I want us to be ready for him. You understand?'

'Of course, I'll see to it personally. I know the commander, Danil Vorens, and I shall ensure that your wishes are carried out.'

Corteo sped from the room, leaving Barzano, Jenna Sharben, Almerz Chanda and Mykola Shonai staring through the armoured glass of the governor's chambers over the smouldering city.

The exhaust fumes of dozens of tanks rose from beyond the walls, and Barzano knew it was just a matter of time until their guns were turned upon the walls of the palace.

'Judge Sharben?'

'What?' she asked, turning to face him.

'I want you to escort the governor to her personal shuttle. Then you are to travel with her to the *Vae Victus*.'

Mykola Shonai's face hardened, and she folded her arms across her chest.

'Inquisitor Barzano, this is a time of crisis for my planet and you wish me to flee? My duty is here, leading my people through this.'

'I know, Mykola,' explained Barzano, 'and normally I would agree with you, but our enemies have shown that they can reach into your most protected sanctum and strike at you. I am moving you to the *Vae Victus* for your own safety until I can be sure that the palace is secure. If this is the opening move in a full-scale rebellion, then logic dictates that there will be another attempt on your life.'

'But surely we are well protected here? Sergeant Learchus assures me that I am quite safe.'

'I do not doubt the sergeant's capabilities, but I will not be argued with. You are bound for the *Vae Victus*, and that is the end of the matter.'

'No, it is not,' stated Mykola Shonai. 'I am not leaving Pavonis, running like a scared child. I will not let my people down again. I will not run, I will stay, and if that puts my life in danger, then so be it.'

Barzano took a deep breath and scratched his forehead. Determination shone in Shonai's features and he saw that if he wanted her on the shuttle he was going to have to order Learchus to drag her there.

'Very well,' he relented, 'but I want your word that if things deteriorate further and it becomes too dangerous to remain here, then you will allow us to move you to the *Vae Victus*.'

For a moment, he thought she would refuse, but at last she nodded. 'Very well, if the situation here becomes too dangerous, I will accede to your request.'

'Thank you, that's all I ask,' said Barzano.

WHEN THE DOOR to his cell had opened and the surly gaoler told him that a member of his family had come to pay his fine, it was the best news Beauchamp Abrogas could remember hearing in a long time.

His head pounded with a splitting headache. He squinted as he was led along a long corridor, bright and featureless save for the bare iron doors to the cells that studded its length.

Already he felt superior to those poor unfortunates locked inside. Not for them the speedy payment of a fine, paid from bulging ancestral coffers.

His thoughts felt clearer now than they had for many months and Beauchamp vowed to go easy on the opiatix, perhaps even give it up for good.

Beauchamp was marched along some depressingly drab corridors, filed through several offices, and made to sign various forms, none of which he read, before finally being allowed to depart the detention level.

His spirits soared as he entered the elevator, carrying a bundle of his own clothes. They were absolutely filthy and he doubted whether even his faithful servants could get the stains from them.

He licked his lips as the elevator doors opened and he was again marched through a series of featureless corridors towards his freedom. Eventually, he was led to a plain room containing a chipped table and chairs bolted to the floor. A judge pushed him into one of the seats and said, 'Wait.'

Beauchamp nodded and crossed his arms, propping his feet up on the table as his former arrogance and poise began returning. Long minutes passed and he began to get restless, pacing the small room as his impatience mounted. Tired of pacing, he returned to the chair as he heard the locks on the door disengage.

A new judge entered, leading a heavyset man in long robes with a short, neatly trimmed beard. The new arrival carried a metal box and wore an Abrogas cartel pin in his lapel, but Beauchamp didn't recognise him.

The judge left the room as the Abrogas man sat opposite Beauchamp and slid the box forward across the table.

'I am Tynen Heras, my lord. I have come to take you home.'

'Well it's about time,' snapped Beauchamp irritably. He was damned if he'd show any gratitude to a servant. He pointed at the box and said, 'What's that?'

'I took the liberty of signing for your personal effects, my lord,' replied Heras, opening the box. Inside was a pile of cash, some jewellery, a deck of cards and–

Beauchamp's eyes widened at the sight of the plain black opiatix inhaler the raven-haired woman from the Flesh Bar had slipped into his pocket, just before his arrest. He smiled slyly, slipping the inhaler into his palm as he pocketed his effects. He decided he could be magnanimous after all, and nodded towards Heras.

'My thanks, Guilder Heras. You have done your leader a great service today.'

'My lord,' acknowledged Heras, lifting the empty box and rising from his chair. He circled Abrogas and rapped on the door.

'I shall return this to the officers and then we shall be on our way, my lord.'

'Yes, you do that, I am anxious to return home.'

The door opened and the man hurriedly left.

Left alone again, Beauchamp could feel the weight of the inhaler pressing into his sweaty palm and ran his hand over his stubbled chin, feeling the need grow within him.

No, he couldn't. Not here. Not in the Arbites precinct. There would be pict-recorders hidden in here.

But it was too late; the idea had taken hold.

It would be his own tiny bit of revenge on the Adeptus Arbites, to break the law within their own stronghold. The idea was too delicious to resist and he giggled suddenly, feeling an overwhelming urge to take the entire inhaler's worth of opiatix in one huge hit.

But that would be stupid; he'd be tossed back in the cells. Especially if it was as strong as the first batch that had gotten him arrested in the first place.

No, just a small draught then.

Well, perhaps a little more.

No more than half.

Beauchamp lifted his hand to his mouth, as though preparing to yawn and placed the nozzle of the inhaler against his lips. He tasted the plastic of the mouthpiece, felt the familiar anticipatory surge of pleasure just before he pressed the dispenser button and heaved in a breath.

Hot grains of opiatix surged down his throat and into his lungs.

Immediately, Beauchamp knew something was wrong.

By the Emperor, what the hell was in this?

But by then it was too late for Beauchamp Abrogas.

Blazing heat raced around his body, his nerves were on fire and shrieking agony knifed up his spinal cord. His legs convulsed spastically and his hands clawed at the table, ripping the nails from his fingers and leaving bloody trails in its surface. He screamed in agony and heaved his body from the chair, crashing into the concrete floor.

His entire body felt as though it was on fire.

Alien chemicals distilled from ingredients so lethal they were thought to be mythical now mixed with those the Surgeon's aide had given him at the Flesh Bar.

His brain felt like it was boiling within his skull. He clawed at his head, tearing out great clumps of hair. Beauchamp rolled to his knees, screeching like a banshee, every movement sending hot bolts of pain through his body. Molten lava filled his bones as he somehow managed to haul himself to his feet, slamming his body against the door.

He could form no words, but beat his body bloody, insane with the agony ravaging his nervous system.

The door opened and Beauchamp barrelled into an Arbites judge, knocking him from his feet. He ran blindly.

Shouts followed his mad dash, but Beauchamp was deaf to them as he shambled in a random direction, not knowing where he was going, but unable to stop moving.

He dropped to his knees, alien fire searing his body from within.

Shouting voices surrounded him.

When the chemical reactions churning in his bloodstream had absorbed enough of his body's fuel to reach critical mass, they achieved their final state of existence.

Pure energy.

And with the force of a dozen demolition charges, Beauchamp Abrogas exploded.

FIFTEEN

THE SHOCKWAVE OF Beauchamp Abrogas's explosive death ripped the front of the Arbites precinct house off, collapsing it in a billowing cloud of dust and smoke, and blew out the windows of every building within a kilometre of the blast.

Barely seconds had passed before the engines of the tanks idling before the walls of the marble city roared into life and surged towards the city gates. Two Leman Russ Conquerors from the Kharon barracks opened fire on the bronze gates, the heavy shells blasting them and a sizeable portion of the walls inwards. When the smoke cleared, a twenty-metre breach was visible and the armoured vehicles ground over the rubble and into the city.

Swiftly, two dozen tanks roared along the cobbled streets towards the Imperial palace while others spread out towards peripheral landing platforms, and troop carriers moved to secure strategic cross-roads and junctions that led to the centre of the city. Rebel PDF soldiers debarked from their carriers and sprinted through the manufactorum districts, seizing control of key factories and munitions stores.

There was resistance to the take-overs, and vicious battles erupted in the streets between the PDF troops and groups of workers loyal to the Shonai cartel. More fires were sparked as stray shots hit chemical containers and more than one raging inferno was ignited as the battle spread further into the manufactorum district.

Within the marble city, the lead tanks sped across Liberation Square, fanning out to avoid the gunfire from the palace turrets. Macro-cannons blasted huge craters in the square and several tanks erupted in geysers of flame as the huge projectiles smashed through their armour and detonated their ammo stores.

But as more tanks poured into the city, the servitor gunners were swamped with targets and simply could not take out enough tanks to prevent them from reaching the walls of the palace and the smoking Adeptus Arbites precinct house.

Dozens of burning wrecks littered the square, but too many tanks were penetrating the palace's defensive cover. For some reason, its energy shield had not yet activated and battle cannon shells began dropping within the walls of the planetary governor's fastness.

The defence turrets were the first targets, each tank trading shots with the palace gunners. Each defensive turret was swiftly bracketed and destroyed, crashing from the walls in bright flames.

Explosions rained down indiscriminately on the palace, buttresses and columned arcades that had stood for thousands of years blasted to rubble by the high explosive rounds, the ornate frescoes and galleries within destroyed in a heartbeat. Dark explosions mushroomed all across the gleaming structure, toppling gilded archways and blowing out stained glass windows of ancient wonder and priceless beauty.

The great bell tower cracked, twin detonations blowing out its midsection. The tower sagged and, with ponderous majesty, toppled into the palace grounds, the bell that had been brought to Pavonis by her first human colonists tolling one last time as it impacted on the cobbled esplanade and exploded into great brass shards.

Other tanks began shelling the walls of the Arbites precinct, but here they met fiercer resistance. The power fields incorporated into the precinct's walls were, thus far, holding the worst of the damage at bay, crackling and flashing with energy discharges. A few tanks attempted to lob shells over the walls and into the precinct, but their guns were incapable of elevating high enough or firing at a low enough velocity to land their shells within the judges' compound, and every shot was long, detonating within the hab units further east.

But as more shells slammed into the energy fields protecting the walls, it became clear that it was simply a matter of time until they failed and the wall would be reduced to rubble.

Both the palace and the Arbites precinct house were living on borrowed time.

ARIO BARZANO STRUGGLED out from under a pile a timber and plaster, wiping a trail of blood from the side of his cheek where splinters had cut him. He scrambled to his knees as yet more blasts thundered against the palace walls and crawled towards Mykola Shonai.

He dragged the governor's limp body from beneath shattered remains of her desk and pressed his fingers against her neck. He pulled her away from the wall, keeping low and out of sight from the smashed window. Swiftly he examined her, checking for any serious wounds, but finding only bruised flesh and lacerations from the flying glass.

Satisfied that Mykola Shonai was alright, Barzano crawled across the debris-strewn floor of the office to check on the room's other occupants. Jenna Sharben didn't seem too badly hurt, though she cradled her left arm close to her chest. She gave him a curt nod of acknowledgement and jerked her head towards the prone form of Almerz Chanda, who lay beneath a buckled section of wood panelling. The governor's aide groaned as Barzano threw off the wreckage.

'What happened?' he slurred.

'It seems the tanks in Liberation Square decided to try and remove the governor by more direct means,' answered Barzano, helping the bruised man against the wall. 'Are you hurt?'

'I don't think so. A few cuts perhaps.'

'Good, don't move,' advised Barzano, casting wary glances at the wide cracks in the ceiling as more rumbling explosions shook the room. He crawled to the remains of the wall where the window had once been and furtively poked his head around the ragged stonework.

Scores of Leman Russ tanks filled the square, some of them burning wrecks, but many more grinding towards the palace, their guns elevated to fire on the upper levels. The room shook, and plaster dust floated from the groaning ceiling as timber split and cracked. The lower reaches of the palace were in flames, the vaulted entrance now nothing more than a pile of fire-blackened stonework.

In the wake of the tanks came scores of Chimera armoured fighting vehicles, all heading in the direction of the palace and Arbites precinct.

He rolled back to where he'd left Mykola Shonai. She was starting to come round and he wiped blood and dust from her face.

She coughed, opening her eyes, and Barzano was pleased to note the absence of fear. Shonai pushed herself upright and surveyed the devastation wreaked in her personal chambers.

'Bastards!' she snapped, attempting to stand. Barzano kept her down as another volley of shells struck the palace a series of hammer blows.

He looked over at Jenna Sharben who knelt beside Almerz Chanda and nodded.

'We have to get out of here, Mykola. I don't think there's any doubt that things have deteriorated, is there?'

Despite the destruction around her, Shonai grinned weakly and shook her head. 'I suppose not.'

She pressed her hand to her temple and winced, 'All I remember is a terrific explosion and next thing I was lying on the floor.'

Shrugging off Barzano's helping hand, Shonai rose unsteadily to her feet and brushed her robes of office clear of dust as the door to her chambers was wrenched from its frame by a battered looking Sergeant Learchus. The giant warrior ducked into the room, followed by the two warriors Uriel had ordered remain with the inquisitor.

'Is everyone alright?' demanded Learchus.

'We'll live, sergeant,' assured Mykola Shonai, striding past Learchus and into the undamaged outer chambers, 'but we must act with haste now. Our enemy is at the gates and we have little time.'

Learchus picked up the stumbling Chanda in one arm as Jenna Sharben and Ario Barzano followed the governor's retreating back. Dozens of palace guards and soldiers ringed her, as though seeking to make up for their failure to protect her from the shelling. Suddenly Shonai stopped, her head cocked to one side and spun to face them.

'Why isn't the energy shield up?'

Barzano paused for a moment. 'That's a damn good question actually,' he said at last.

He opened a channel to his quarters and Lortuen Perjed.

'Lortuen, old friend. Is everyone there alright?'

After a long silence, Perjed finally answered, 'Yes, we're all fine, Ario. What about you?'

'We're alive, which is something, but we're getting out of here and heading for the *Vae Victus*. I want you to gather everybody and make your way to the landing platforms on the east wing roof. We'll meet you there.'

He shut off the communication and turned to Learchus, saying, 'Sergeant, I need you and your men to get to the aerial defence control room and find out why the shield isn't up. Do whatever needs to be done to raise it.'

Learchus looked ready to mount another protest, but Barzano cut him off, waving at the dozen palace soldiers. 'Don't worry about my safety, sergeant. We have enough protection here, I'm sure.'

The sergeant didn't look convinced, but nodded and handed the swaying Chanda to a pair of grey uniformed soldiers.

'I'll show you the way,' offered a young defence trooper.

Learchus grunted his thanks and the four set off at a jog towards the control room.

THE ONCE GRIM and imposing façade of the Arbites precinct house looked as though a siege titan had taken its gigantic wrecking ball to it. The entire west face had caved in, exposing plascrete floor slabs and twisted tendons of reinforcement. Huge metre wide cracks stretched from ground to roof and giant holes gaped in the building's fabric.

Casualties were high and the compound was choked with rubble and dust. Blood-covered judges pulled wounded comrades from the wreckage and dug for survivors while medics desperately tried to seal wounds and breathe life into crushed bodies.

Virgil Ortega pushed his way through the shell-shocked throng, trying to make some kind of sense of the events of the last few minutes. The precinct house was in ruins, and he tried to fathom how such a disaster could have occurred. It wasn't a shell impact; that much was certain, since the blast had exploded from within. There was no way anyone could have smuggled a bomb inside, but how else could it have happened?

Explanations and retribution could come later. If there was a later, he reflected, listening to the deafening thunder of shellfire as the traitor tanks attempted to batter their way in. Hastily he mentally reprimanded himself for that tiny heresy. He was a warrior of the Emperor, and while there was life in his body, there would be no surrender.

He grabbed every man that was fit to fight, shouting his orders to them. This was the first strike in armed rebellion, and when the walls failed, they were sure to be hit hard.

His breath came in short, painful bursts and his head pounded viciously. He'd only just discharged himself from the precinct infirmary and his splintered ribs still ached fiercely, but he'd be damned if he'd sit this fight out.

He would have preferred to mount his defence from within the precinct, but its structure was far too unstable and looked ready to collapse at any moment. Gun batteries on the crenellated battlements added some heavy punch to the defence, but many of these had been damaged in the explosion and subsequent collapse.

Satisfied that he was making all possible precautions for the defence, he returned to the huge gates of the precinct house where he'd left Collix with the vox-caster. Collix was blood soaked, his carapace armour dented and dust covered. Virgil had been pleasantly surprised at how the young officer had changed in the last few days. He had matured into a fine officer and Ortega was glad he had survived the explosion.

'Any luck?' asked Ortega.

'Nothing yet, sir. All the other precincts are off the net. We're being jammed.'

'Damn it!' swore Virgil. This was much worse than he'd feared.

'Try the PDF net,' he suggested.

'I've tried that already. It's jammed solid.'

'Well keep trying and call me if you get anything,' ordered Virgil.

Collix nodded and returned to the communications gear.

Ortega stared out over the rubble-strewn ground before him. The defensive perimeter of the precinct house extended three hundred metres from the front of the building's structure with angled walls, tank traps and concealed ditches providing a layered defence that his hastily prepared fire teams were even now rushing to occupy. But what should have been a clear field of fire was now littered with giant slabs of rock and steel. When the enemy breached the walls, they would have plenty of cover.

He glanced over to the buckled roller doors that protected the precinct's vehicle hangar. Inside, he could hear the three Leman Russ tanks the judges had available, their engines idling. Hopefully they could yet surprise their enemy.

A massive explosion from the walls and a whipcrack of blazing energy announced the failure of the walls' protective power fields, the machine spirits within them overwhelmed by the weight of fire. Seconds later a portion of the wall blasted inwards and a whole section collapsed.

This was it, the attack was coming and Virgil knew that with the limited time and resources available, he'd done as much as he could.

Now he would see if it had been enough.

DANIL VORENS LOWERED his smoking laspistol and returned his attention to the viewscreen before him. A stunned silence filled the defence control room, the technicians agog at what had just happened.

Lutricia Vijeon stared in open-mouthed horror at the corpse lying in the centre of the room with a ragged hole where its face had been. The old man had come in waving his pipe and screaming at them to raise the energy shield, cursing them all to hell for allowing traitors to defile the palace walls.

She had been surprised that Vorens hadn't already raised the shield, and was about to voice her concerns when the old man had burst in. She didn't know who he was, but understood that his clearance must be extremely high to allow him access to this command centre.

He'd raged at Vorens, who had calmly drawn his pistol and shot him in the face.

Vorens had holstered his pistol and turned his gaze upon the control centre technicians.

'Anyone else have any objections to my not raising the shield?' he asked mildly.

No one said anything, and Lutricia felt a deep shame burn in her heart. This was murder and treason. Safe within this reinforced structure, they could feel only the barest hint of the artillery bombardment that was pulverising the rest of the palace, and she muttered a brief prayer to the Emperor for His forgiveness.

DESPITE THE PRESENCE of a dozen palace defence troops, Ario Barzano still felt acutely vulnerable. The corridors shook as more tanks advanced into Liberation Square and added their guns to those shelling the palace. He could hear shouts and screams throughout the palace as its inhabitants ran to the shelters in the basement and the shuttle platforms. Mixed in with those shouts were those of invading soldiers.

He'd seen troops pouring into the palace and knew that the men here could not hope to hold them for long. Cut off from reinforcements and stunned at the horrendous casualties they had suffered so far, it would not be long until the palace was overrun.

It was imperative for him to get Mykola Shonai out of here. With her as a symbol for loyalist troops to rally around, they might yet hold this planet together before de Valtos's plan came to fruition.

Mykola Shonai held onto his arm and, behind him, Jenna Sharben helped Almerz Chanda. The governor's aide was slowing them down, his injuries apparently more serious than they had appeared.

'How much further is it to the shuttle bays?' asked Barzano, sure the shouts of attacking troops were closer than before.

'We're close. We should be there in a few minutes,' replied Shonai breathlessly.

The passageway rocked as fresh shells rained down and Barzano pulled up short as a section of the roof crashed down in front of them, burying the first six men in their group and filling the air with choking dust and flying debris.

Barzano picked himself up from the floor, cursing like a navy rating as he saw the passageway ahead was completely blocked with rubble. He hauled a gasping trooper to his feet, yelling, 'Is there another way to the landing platforms? Quickly man!'

The young soldier coughed, his face covered in a film of dust, and nodded.

'Yes, sir, back the way we came. It'll take longer, but we can still make it.'

Screams and the noise of small arms fire sounded dangerously close.

'Damn, this looks bad,' hissed Barzano.

JUDGE ORTEGA DIDN'T see the first shot to hit the precinct until it blew one of the gun batteries from the walls. He watched as the flaming wreckage tumbled majestically from the battlements and crashed to the ground, crushing a dozen members of his right flank's fire team.

The remaining batteries opened fire on the first tanks through the breach in the wall. The lead vehicle blew apart, its turret spinning high into the air. No sooner had the smoke cleared than a trio of Conquerors smashed their destroyed comrade aside and fired a volley of shells at the precinct, blasting huge chunks from the face of the building. The already unstable structure finally gave way.

Judges scattered as huge chunks of plascrete and steel smashed downwards in a deadly rain, burying the wounded personnel below utterly. Huge, rolling clouds of choking dust blinded Virgil, but he could clearly hear the roar of engines and he shouted over the continuing rumble.

'Stand to! No surrender!'

His voice was lost in the sharp bark of cannon fire as the precinct guns duelled with the enemy tanks. It was an unequal struggle, as the

Conquerors would fire then swiftly displace to another position before the precinct batteries could acquire them. Despite this, all three Conquerors were blown apart before following rebel troops carrying missile launchers and mortars swiftly destroyed the judges' guns with concentrated volleys of fire.

Through the smoke and dust, Virgil could make out the shadowy forms of armoured vehicles and dived for cover as heavy lasfire from the turret of an approaching Chimera raked towards him.

He rolled upright behind one of the reinforced defensive walls and shouted to the nearest fire team, 'Chimera! Eleven o'clock!'

The two-man fire team heard his cry and swung their missile launcher to bear on the tank.

The shell slashed from the recoilless launcher, slamming into the Chimera's frontal section and exploded, severing the tracks but not penetrating its hull. The vehicle skidded and crashed into a torn slab of concrete, slewing round as the other track continued to roll. The rear ramp dropped and its crew began to disembark before the transport became their coffin.

Virgil swore as he saw the attackers clearly for the first time.

Pavonis PDF!

He'd known it must be the PDF, but to see them openly attacking his men was still a shock. His fury built within him until it threatened to burst from him in an uncontrolled frenzy, but he suppressed his rage, knowing that a cool head was required here.

Another missile sailed through the open crew door of the Chimera. The tank exploded, its fuel and ammunition cooking off and blasting from its rear like an immense flame-thrower. Burning PDF soldiers scattered, screaming from the wreck as a cheer went up from the Arbites line.

The cheer died as the unmistakable, metallic cough of massed mortar fire sounded.

'Incoming!' yelled Virgil, dropping to the ground and burying his head in his hands.

The mortar rounds landed in a string of thudding detonations and screams that rocked the compound. Most of the Arbites had managed to reach safety before the rounds landed, but those that did not were torn apart in a storm of shrapnel fragments.

Virgil burrowed further into his shelter as volley after volley impacted around them.

So long as they kept their heads down behind the walls, Virgil knew that the casualties from the mortar fire would be minimal. But equally, he knew that every second they sheltered, the PDF would be closing. Virgil risked a look over the wall, cursing as he saw four Chimeras nearing his position.

The sudden quiet as the mortar fire ceased was a blessed relief and Virgil rose to his feet, shotgun at the ready.

The six PDF troopers facing him across the wall were just as surprised as he to be facing one another.

Virgil blasted a volley of scatter shot into their midst.

At such close range, the blast felled two of the soldiers immediately and dropped a third, screaming, to the ground.

He vaulted the wall and swung his legs round, smashing his feet into the face of the nearest trooper and sending him sprawling into the remaining two. He racked the pump of the shotgun as he landed.

Before they could recover themselves, he blew each away with a blast to the chest.

A shot punched into the wall beside him. He dodged back as the wounded trooper fired his pistol again.

Virgil leapt forwards and brought the butt of his shotgun down hard on the man's head. Quickly, he made his way back behind the wall.

He looked along the length of the battling Arbites line. The situation was bad, but not beyond saving. The rebel PDF had more men and light artillery support, but Virgil had some of the most feared soldiers in the Imperium fighting for him. And the superior training, weaponry and discipline of the Arbites was now proving its worth as Virgil could see that the PDF attack had lost its momentum.

Instead of advancing, their attackers were sheltering behind their transports, sporadically firing their lasguns. He knew that to break them, they had to hit back with a strong counterpunch.

'Collix!' he shouted, 'Get over here!'

Sergeant Collix ran in a crouch towards Virgil, firing his shotgun from the hip.

'Captain?' said Collix, his breath and pulse racing with the beat of adrenaline.

'Get onto Veritas squadron, tell them we need them now! I need them to engage the enemy's right flank. If they can hit them hard enough and quickly enough we can roll up the rebel line and force them back!'

As Collix spoke hurriedly into the vox-caster, Virgil thumbed more shells into the shotgun's breech and racked the pump.

'Captain! Squadron Leader Wallas reports that only the Righteous Justice has been properly consecrated. Divine Authority and Holy Law will not be blessed and ready for some minutes yet.'

Ortega snarled and snatched the vox-caster from Collix and shouted into the handset.

'Wallas, get those bloody tanks out here right now or I'll come in there and rip your Emperor-damned heart out and feed it to you! Do you understand me?'

He didn't wait for a reply and tossed the handset back to Collix.

Seconds later, the armoured door to the vehicle hangar juddered upwards and the Righteous Justice, a venerable Leman Russ battle tank, rolled out with its guns blasting huge holes in the PDF ranks.

Two Chimera exploded in quick succession as the Arbites gunners found their marks. Small arms fire rattled from its thick armour as the Righteous Justice hosed its attackers in heavy bolter fire, dropping men by the dozen.

Virgil grinned to himself. By the Emperor, they could do it!

The PDF were scattering before the Righteous Justice's charge, unable to dent its hide. His breath caught in his throat as he saw a missile contrail spear towards the tank. The missile impacted on the vehicle's flank, obscuring it in smoke.

The tank sped clear of the explosion and Virgil could see that the hull mounted lascannon had been blown clear, but no further damage had been inflicted.

Virgil sighed in relief.

He shouted, 'Men of the Emperor, now is our time! Charge!' and again leapt the defensive wall.

The Arbites rose up and charged madly across the shattered, body-littered compound, firing as they went. Their blood was afire and the sight of the Righteous Justice smiting their foes gave them the punch to crush the traitors beneath their boot heels. The soldiers of the PDF fell back, overwhelmed by the twin blows of Righteous Justice and the screaming judges.

Virgil shot a trooper in the back and another in the chest as he caught sight of a trio of Conqueror tanks crashing over the breach in the walls. The heavy bolters mounted on their hulls sprayed the battlefield before them, the commanders' firing cupola mounted weapons and screaming at the judges.

The gunfire was indiscriminate and the bloodshed prodigious as bullets and lasers felled PDF soldiers alongside the judges.

The Righteous Justice's brief charge was brought to an abrupt close as a missile and the bright lance of a lascannon shot impacted simultaneously on its turret, igniting the battle cannon shells and blowing the tank high into the air.

The demise of Righteous Justice coincided with the arrival of Divine Authority and Holy Law. Bursting into the compound like a thunderstrike, their heavy bolter fire raked across the exposed PDF troops and their battle cannon blasted huge craters in the ground.

Virgil shouted a warning as he saw a group of PDF officers charge towards the Divine Authority. He could see one of the enemy officers was equipped with a power fist, its massive form wreathed in destructive energies that could easily tear through the armour of a tank.

The officer leapt forward, power fist raised to smash down. The lascannon mounted on the frontal section of Divine Authority fired, vaporising one of his companions, but the rest kept coming.

The driver of Divine Authority realised his danger and attempted to turn away from the charging officers, but it was too late. The first officer smashed his power fist through the vehicle's side, tearing the armoured hull wide open and peeling the adamantium skin back. The tank slewed round, smashing into a concrete wall and flattening it along with four cowering PDF troopers.

The other officers emptied the magazine of their weapons through the huge tear in the tank's side, slaughtering the crew in a hail of bullets.

Grenades burst around them as Arbites men rushed to avenge their fallen comrades, but the officers fled into the smoke of battle and escaped retribution. Virgil saw yet more Chimeras pour into the compound. Hundreds of troopers followed in their wake and shellfire from the three Conquerors blasted more judges to oblivion.

The Arbites counterattack, a fragile thing at best, faltered in the face of such horrendous bloodshed. As the death toll mounted, the Arbites' line suddenly broke, unable to withstand the terrible losses inflicted by the Conquerors.

At first Virgil was able to hold them together, but as more explosions and gunshots mowed down the withdrawing judges, the retreat became a rout.

Holy Law skidded round the smoking remains of Divine Authority and fired at will, attempting to buy the judges time to fall back. The PDF scattered before the tank as it rumbled towards the supporting Chimeras. Its lascannon fired, punching through the rear armour of one of the vehicles and destroying the engine in a gout of yellow flame, the huge blast somersaulting the Chimera into the air.

The burning wreck smashed down at an angle on a second vehicle, crushing its left track unit. The impact snapped the main drive shaft and pistoned it explosively downwards. Its engine revving madly, the Chimera was catapulted upwards. Spinning crazily, it crashed to the ground, exploding in a bright orange fireball and incinerating a score of PDF troopers.

Despite their loss, the Conquerors and the PDF were tearing the beating heart from the defence. Most of the judges had been cut down as they fled and Virgil knew the precinct house was lost.

He saw the same enemy officer who had ripped open the Divine Authority charge the Holy Law, his power fist crackling with lethal energies. Virgil fired his shotgun at the man, desperate to aid the last of his tanks, but the range was too great.

Holy Law gunned its engines. The driver had seen his brother tank torn to pieces by power fists and was in no mood to suffer a similar fate. Realising that speed was his only hope of survival, he turned towards the officer, hoping to crush the man beneath his armoured treads.

The traitor leapt forwards and slashed his power fist down at the speeding vehicle, the links of the tracks snapping beneath his grip.

The toothed, track cogs spun wildly.

Orange sparks flared and the track unit snarled as the power fist became caught in its grip.

The entire vehicle shuddered, the thrashing drive-unit dragging the struggling officer into its depths. The officer shrieked as he was jerked down. His arm ripped from its socket in a welter of blood and bone as the remains of the shattered tracks brutally pulled him under the tank's mass.

He was able to scream once more before the huge vehicle rolled over his body and crushed him utterly.

Virgil sprinted towards the remains of the precinct house, bleeding from a score of wounds. The battle was lost and now all that mattered was to try and get as many of his men to safety as was possible.

He knew that their chances were slim to say the least, but Virgil Ortega was not the kind of man to give up without a fight. Anything he could do to obstruct and hamper these traitorous scum was definitely worth doing.

But first he had to try and get out of here with some kind of fighting force at his command. They had themselves a respite for now. The surviving PDF troopers had paused in their attack, stunned at the horrific death of their commander and the bizarre destruction of the two Chimera transports. The reprieve didn't last as a fresh burst of lascannon fire destroyed the Holy Law before any of the crew could escape the disabled tank.

Virgil rounded up all the able-bodied judges he could find and shoved them towards the ruins of the precinct. If enough of the lower levels had escaped the blast, they could move through the tunnels below the precinct and make their way to the palace. He saw that Collix was amongst the survivors.

Good, they may yet have need of the vox-gear.

Virgil knew that escape was their only chance now and if they could lay their hands on the heavy weapons held in the armoury below the palace, their chances of holding out would be increased immeasurably.

He vowed they would make these damn rebels rue the day they had crossed Virgil Ortega.

LUTRICIA VIJEON'S THOUGHTS tumbled like an uncontrolled rail car as she tried to make some kind of sense out of what was happening here. Vorens had killed a man in front of everyone here, and was allowing the palace to be shelled.

Lutricia was a loyal servant of the Emperor and she knew that someone had to do something, but who? Her?

Her entire body shook with fear as she realised that she was no match for Vorens and that her superior officer would undoubtedly kill her. She was a technician, for the Emperor's sake! She wasn't trained for this sort of thing. How could she be expected to fight a man armed with a laspistol?

Sweat dripped into her eyes in a steady flow.

Everyone jumped as a dull thud echoed around the control room, sounding like a massive hammer blow on the main doors. Even Vorens looked concerned and she spun to look at the external pict-display. Her heart leapt as she saw three massive warriors clad in the armour of Space Marines. Yes! These holy warriors would end this nightmare and she felt a huge weight lifted from her shoulders at this answer to her prayers.

But the more she watched the pict-display, the more her hopes fell. The entrance to the command centre had been built to withstand the heaviest assault, and not even the power of three Space Marines could smash through the metre-thick layer of plate steel.

A flickering motion caught her eye and she watched as her display indicated an incoming aircraft. Telemetry flashed across the display as the logic engines flashed up identifying runes telling her course, speed and altitude of the new contact.

It was a Thunderhawk gunship.

She stole a furtive look at Vorens, who was grinning at the sight of the three Space Marine vainly attempting to break into the command centre. Lutricia realised she only had a few moments to seize this opportunity; Vorens was sure to notice the approaching craft soon. She struggled to think how she could turn the situation to her advantage.

A frightening calm replaced her fear as she realised what she had to do.

Like the trained professional she was, her fingers danced over the runes of her station, transmitting exact positional data of the command centre's location to the Thunderhawk. It might not be much, but it was all she could do.

She saw Vorens catch sight of the Thunderhawk on the main display and just hoped her own small contribution would be enough as he raced to activate the servitor defence routines.

BARZANO'S SMALL GROUP emerged into the sunlight of the landing platform and the inquisitor had never been more relieved to see the sky as he was now. They staggered towards a black shuttle, its engines shrieking as the pilot kept the power ready for immediate take off. Through the open side hatch, he could see Lortuen Perjed and his group of scribes.

He smiled as the welcome sight of the Ultramarines Thunderhawk gunship roared overhead.

Jenna Sharben led, dragging Mykola Shonai towards the shuttle and safety. The last palace guard helped the struggling Almerz Chanda. The governor's aide stumbled and fell to his knees as Barzano passed him. He kept going, catching up to Jenna Sharben and helping her with the governor.

A lasbolt fired, shockingly loud, even over the screaming engines of the shuttle. Barzano spun, wondering how the rebels could have caught up so soon. He unslung his rifle and dropped to his knees, trying to make sense of the scene before him.

Almerz Chanda stood over the body of the palace guard, expertly holding a smoking lasgun. He snapped off a shot at Barzano, taking the inquisitor high in the shoulder and slamming him back against the shuttle's hull.

Barzano yelled in pain and dropped his weapon. Jenna Sharben turned and was punched from her feet by an equally well-placed shot. Governor Shonai stood at the shuttle, staring in horror at Chanda as he strode across towards her.

He raised his rifle and aimed through the pilot's canopy, making a chopping motion with one hand across his throat. The whine of the engines died as the pilot powered down the engines and unstrapped himself from his bucket seat.

Chanda shot him through the canopy.

Barzano struggled to push himself upright as grey uniformed PDF troopers swarmed onto the landing platform from the palace and Mykola Shonai stood before Chanda, her face a granite mask of fury.

'Why?' she asked simply.

'You are the past,' replied Chanda. 'Weak, pathetic, clinging to your outdated loyalty to a withered corpse on a planet you have never even seen.'

'You disgust me, Almerz. To think I once called you a friend.'

She slapped Chanda hard and spat in his face.

Chanda slammed the butt of his rifle into the governor's head, dropping her to the ground with blood spurting from her broken nose. But, still she stared at him with defiance and anger.

Barzano tried to ignore the pain of the laser burn on his shoulder. He knew they had failed, but he was determined to take this piece of blasphemous filth with him on the road to hell. He tried to raise his hand, to aim his digital needler, but Chanda knelt beside him and gripped his hair.

'I've wanted to do this for a long time,' whispered Chanda, slamming Barzano's head against the shuttle's hull.

'Get on with it and go,' snapped Barzano, nauseous from the impact.

'Oh, I'm not going to kill you, Ario. No, there is a... specialist in the service of my employer who I believe you have an appointment with. A surgeon of wondrous skill.'

Barzano coughed blood. 'Why can't you say his name? Does the stench of your betrayal stick in your throat? Can your tiny mind comprehend the scale of the mistake you have just made?'

Chanda laughed as PDF troopers surrounded the shuttle.

'Mistake?' hissed Chanda so that only Barzano could hear. 'I think not. You made the mistake of coming here. Soon I will be part of an immortal band of warriors, fighting alongside a reawakened god!'

Now it was Barzano's turn to laugh, though the act sent jolts of pain across his chest and pounding through his skull.

'Did de Valtos tell you that?' he smirked. 'Then you are a bigger fool than I took you for. I can sense your fear of him. If de Valtos succeeds, you will die. Your life energy will be stripped away to feed the hunger of this creature he calls a god.'

Chanda stood, his face angry, turning away and speaking hurriedly into a hand-held vox-caster he removed from his pocket. Barzano strained to hear the words over the heavy thump of laser fire and shelling, but couldn't make them out.

He looked up, hoping to see the Thunderhawk gunship hammering down on the platform and disgorging charging Ultramarines, but the aircraft was speeding into the clouds, chased by a fearsome amount of anti-aircraft fire. That explained why the energy shield hadn't been activated at least. Somehow de Valtos had managed to get one of his people into the defence control staff and prevent it from being raised. He wondered what had become of Learchus and the two Space Marines he had sent to the control centre.

Another shuttle swooped low overhead, setting down in a cloud of exhaust fumes on the far edge of the platform. The shuttle's door slid back and a small group emerged. Clutching a leather case tightly to his chest, the gloating figure of Kasimir de Valtos stepped down onto the platform. Vendare Taloun followed him, and Barzano saw he had the desperate look of a man trapped by circumstances beyond his control. Behind the cartel men came two slim and graceful figures, and Barzano felt a flutter of apprehension as he recognised the sinuous gait of the eldar.

These two aliens were from the darker sects that lived beyond the normal realms of the galaxy and he knew in an instant that it might have been better for them all if they had been killed. The female moved with the grace of a dancer, her every gesture suggesting sensual lethality, while the male walked stiffly, hunched over, as though unused to the daylight. Both had cruel violet eyes and skin as pale as polished ivory.

The woman barely spared him a glance, but the other gave him a look of such emptiness that it chilled even Barzano's hardened soul.

Almerz Chanda handed his rifle to a nervous looking PDF trooper and Barzano could sense their unease at the sight of the eldar. None of them had expected this.

Kasimir de Valtos stood over the prone governor and smiled, savouring the moment of his triumph.

'This has been a long time coming, Shonai,' he said at last.

Barzano struggled to remain conscious, as Chanda stood before his true master.

'I have delivered them to you as I promised I would, my lord.'

Kasimir de Valtos turned to face Chanda and nodded.

'Indeed you have, Almerz. You have proved your treachery is complete.'

Barzano could sense Chanda's confusion and unease even above that of the PDF troops on the platform.

'I have done all that you asked of me, my lord.'

De Valtos inclined his head briefly in the direction of the eldar woman.

Her hand flashed to her leather belt in a blur of motion and suddenly there was a black dart embedded in Chanda's throat.

The man dropped to his knees, the skin around the dart swelling at a horrifying rate.

'My dear Almerz,' crooned de Valtos. 'You betrayed one master, why should I trust you not to betray me also? No, better it ends like this.'

Chanda scrabbled at his throat, fighting for breath. Within seconds his gurgling cries were silent as he slipped into unconsciousness, and collapsed on the ground. De Valtos addressed the eldar male, saying, 'Do with them as you see fit.'

He tapped his boot against Chanda's slumped body. 'But make sure you honour this one first.'

Barzano felt no satisfaction at Chanda's fate, merely a sickening sense of impending disaster. For if Kasimir de Valtos was truly as insane as he appeared to be, then he was about to unleash a force that not even Barzano knew how to defeat.

De Valtos turned his gaze upon Barzano and the inquisitor felt his empathic senses recoil from the pits of the man's madness.

'I know what you are doing, de Valtos,' croaked Barzano. 'And so does Captain Ventris. He knows everything I do and I promise you he will not let you succeed. Even now he will be calling for more ships and men to defeat you.'

Kasimir de Valtos shook his head.

'If you truly understand what I intend, then you know as well as I that more men and ships will achieve nothing.'

Barzano wanted to respond, but the words died in his throat.

Because he knew that Kasimir de Valtos was right.

♡
SIXTEEN

Barzano listened to the screams of Almerz Chanda echoing through the prison level, hoping that the torture was as painful as it sounded. It did not matter to him that an alien was torturing a human being. By betraying his oaths of loyalty to the Emperor, Chanda had given up any right for pity.

The inquisitor had no clear idea of how long they had been incarcerated, having earlier passed out with the pain from his wound. He had awoken in this cell to find himself stripped of his weapons, even the digital one secreted within the ring on his right forefinger, and the lasburn on his shoulder cleaned and bound with surgical dressing. Mykola Shonai's broken nose had been set as well. Apparently the alien surgeon did not wish to work on damaged subjects.

The prison level they were held in had been incorporated into the groined foundations of the palace, steel bars cemented into each stone archway. Each cell was furnished with a simple bed and ablutions unit bolted to the floor. As far as jails went, it was better than many he'd thrown traitors into.

Lortuen Perjed and his scribes languished in the cell opposite, and Barzano was pleased to see that none of them had been hurt in the coup.

Sharing Barzano's cell, Mykola Shonai sat in the corner, her face a mask of fury, and Jenna Sharben lay on the bed, her wound untreated. The judge had taken a lasbolt to the belly and though the heat of the shot had cauterised the wound, Barzano suspected she might be bleeding internally. She had not recovered consciousness since Chanda's treachery at the landing platform, and Barzano knew that without medical attention she would die in a few hours. It seemed she was not worth the attention of the surgeon's scalpel.

When the governor had come round, she had raged at the cell door, kicking and screaming oaths that would have made a stevedore blush.

Barzano had pulled her away, calming her with promises of rescue and retribution. He was unsure how he was going to fulfil these promises, but knew they still had options open to them.

He returned to the bed and mopped Jenna Sharben's brow with his sleeve. She was cold to the touch and her skin was grey, already the colour of a corpse.

'I promise you won't die, Judge Sharben,' whispered Barzano.

'Another promise you're not sure you can keep?' asked Shonai.

'Not at all, Mykola. I never make promises I can't keep,' assured Barzano. He placed a hand across his heart. 'I promise.'

Despite herself, Mykola Shonai smiled, 'Do you really think we can get out of here? I mean, there are at least three regiments' worth of soldiers in the city, probably over two hundred on this level alone, and the Emperor alone knows how many prowling the palace.'

Barzano winked, 'Do not forget the three Space Marines.'

'I haven't, but surely Sergeant Learchus and his men must be dead?'

'I seriously doubt that, my dear Mykola. I'm sure de Valtos would have enjoyed parading them past us by now if they were. No, I do not believe Sergeant Learchus will be an easy man to kill, and he will have found a way to communicate with the *Vae Victus*.'

'And you think Captain Ventris will attempt to rescue us?'

'I am sure that even the daemons of the warp would not prevent him.'

'It would be a virtual suicide mission to break us out.'

'Possibly,' agreed Barzano, 'but can you see that stopping Uriel?'

'No, I suppose not,' said Mykola, leaning her head back against the stonework of the cell. She closed her eyes and Barzano thought she had fallen asleep. But without opening her eyes, she said, 'This ship you think de Valtos is after – can he really get it?'

'I'm not sure. My ordo know that one of an ancient race of beings we know as the C'tan went into a form of stasis somewhere in this sector, but not exactly where. We think that the *Nightbringer* was once his, for want of a better word, flagship. There are ancient writings and hints about the ship and its master scattered throughout history, but we still know next to nothing about it. It is of a time before the ascendancy of man and little is known for sure.'

'This... C'tan, what was it like?'

'No one can say for certain. It has probably been dormant for millions of years and records are unclear to say the least. I've read every fragment I could lay my hands on concerning the Bringer of Darkness, but I still know almost nothing about it, save one thing.'

'And that is?' asked Mykola hesitantly.

'The Nightbringer is death incarnate. Its dreams are the stuff of every race's nightmares, becoming the very image of their doom. Every thought you have ever had regarding the horror of death and mortality comes from this creature. When it walked between the stars in aeons past, it left that legacy in the collective racial psyche of almost every species in the galaxy.'

'Can we defeat such a creature?'

'Do you want the truth?'

'Of course.'

Barzano waited until the echoes of a fresh clutch of screams torn from Almerz Chanda's throat had died away before answering. 'No,' he said softly, 'I do not think we can.'

THE MAJESTIC FORM of the *Vae Victus* slowly angled its massive bulk towards the surface of Pavonis, powerful energies building in her forward linear accelerators. Few men knew the awesome power of destruction the captain of a starship possessed; the power to level cities and crack continents. For all that the captains of the Imperial Navy might strut and boast of the capabilities of their ponderous warships, there was nothing that could compete with the sheer destructive speed and efficiency of a Space Marine strike cruiser.

Defence lasers periodically stabbed upwards from armoured silos far below on the planet's surface. None of the mighty guns could match the speed of the strike cruiser and though their powerful beams pierced the sky with their colossal energies, there was a desperation to the fire. So long as the *Vae Victus* remained in high orbit, the guns below were impotent.

Closer in, however, the smaller, aerial defence batteries were a different matter. Scores of such silos were scattered around Brandon Gate and incorporated into the planet's surface. Though these were incapable of harming a starship, even one in low orbit, they could shred any aircraft that came within fifteen kilometres of the city. All were crewed by lobotomised servitors, hard-wired into their weapons, and controlled from the defence control bunker secreted somewhere within the palace grounds.

While the guns cast their protective cover over the city, any airborne assault was doomed to failure.

KASIMIR DE VALTOS rubbed the bridge of his nose, growling at the image on the vox-holo before him.

'Lasko, if you don't give me a straight answer then I will have you buried in one of your precious mines. Now tell me, in words of two syllables or less, have you breached the door yet? I do not have time to waste.'

The flickering image of his mine overseer, Jakob Lasko, appeared furtive even through the heavy distortion of the encrypted signal from Tembra Ridge nearly one hundred kilometres from the palace.

'Well, the last cutter made it through the door, but we're having trouble moving it.'

'And why is that?' pressed de Valtos, leaning forward, his features predatory.

'We're not sure, my lord. The tech-priests say that the density of the door far exceeds what should be possible for something of its dimensions. We've had to disassemble one of our heaviest rigs and transport it down the main shaft in pieces. The techs are putting the last parts together now, and once they've blessed it, we'll be ready to go.'

'When?' hissed de Valtos, incessantly rubbing at his forehead.

'Later today, I expect.'

'It had better be,' said de Valtos snapping off the link and reclining in the ex-governor's sagging leather chair. He massaged his temples and took a gulping breath before hawking a froth of black phlegm onto the floor. The pain was getting worse and the Surgeon's specialised facilities and equipment had been destroyed by the Ultramarines. There would be no more stripp-ing his body down to its bare bones and reassembling it in its temporarily healthy form again. He had to succeed, and soon. If that damn fool Lasko could not break into the underground tomb complex soon, then he was a dead man.

But once within, he would know the twin joys of revenge and immortality.

He remembered the day he had first learned of the C'tan from the scrolls of Corteswain. Most of his fortune had since been ploughed into the search for its resting place, but the final irony was that it had been below him all this time. Surely the hand of fate was at work that it should turn out to be below the mountains of Pavonis.

It had been a revelation the day he had finally discovered the forgotten tomb, buried beneath the world when it was nothing but an uninhabited ball of lifeless rock.

De Valtos chuckled mirthlessly as he realised soon it would be that way again.

Soon he would walk in the halls of a god! Not the pitiful, dust filled corridors of Terra that was home to a rotting corpse masquerading as a god, but a living, breathing creature with the power of creation and eternal life at its fingertips.

When had the Emperor last walked among his people? Ten thousand years ago! Where was the Emperor when the Apostate Cardinal Bucharis plunged whole sectors into war in His name? Where was the Emperor when the tyranids devoured world after world?

Where was the Emperor when the eldar boarded his ship and tortured him to the brink of death? Where was He then?

De Valtos felt his fury growing and struggled to control his rage as blood dripped from where his artificial fingernails had dug into the meat of his palms. He wiped the blood clear and ran a hand through his sweat-streaked hair, fighting down his rapid breathing.

He rose and paced the shattered remains of the room, stepping over the splintered desk, broken chairs and heaped piles of plaster. His foot hit something solid and he looked down.

He smiled, bending down to pick up a cracked bust of white marble, cradling it gently in his scarred hands. He stroked his hand across the stern face of Forlanus Shonai, blood smearing the old man's patrician features, and strode to the devastated wall of the governor's private chambers.

The city below was wreathed in a pall of black smoke and dull, coughing detonations from pockets of resistance still fighting the inevitable. His tanks and troops lined every street and, though he knew it was regrettable that these men would all die, it was a small price to pay for his impending godhood.

He patted the head of Forlanus Shonai and smiled, before hurling the bust as far as he could from his vantage point. He watched it spin down through the air, finally shattering into fragments as it impacted on the cobbled esplanade below.

LORD ADMIRAL LAZLO Tiberius followed the blip representing Uriel's Thunderhawk on the surveyor plot table as it drew near the capital city of Pavonis. An air of tense expectation hung over the bridge and even the astropathic choir had fallen silent. The feeling gripping Tiberius was the same as that of going into battle, which he supposed was correct, even though they themselves were in no danger.

Captain Uriel Ventris was the one flying into harm's way along with his warriors. The astropaths on the *Vae Victus* had reported powerful sigils and hexagrammic wards incorporated into the walls of the cells and this, combined with the energy shield that now enveloped the palace, ruled out a teleported assault.

With time against them, they were going to have to do this the old fashioned way.

'How long?' he asked tersely.

'A few moments yet,' answered Philotas.

'The co-ordinates are dialled into the attack logister?'

'Yes, lord admiral, everything is prepared. The firing solution has been confirmed.'

Tiberius caught the hint of restrained impatience in his officer's voice and smiled, grimly. He already knew everything was prepared, but couldn't help wanting to make double and triple sure. Almost time, thought Tiberius, praying that the anonymous transmission Uriel had received as he had flown towards Brandon Gate earlier that day had been genuine.

The Emperor help him if it was not.

Forcing himself to return to his captain's pulpit, Tiberius gripped the edge of his lectern and addressed his crew.

'Brothers, we come now to this gravest hour and it is to realise that there is only one way that we can triumph, and that is together as one. We have only determination, and single-minded desire. Not one amongst us has proven willing to give up or accept defeat and for that I commend you.'

Tiberius bowed his head as Philotas reported, 'They are at the edge of the defence guns' lethal envelope, lord admiral.'

The lord admiral nodded. 'Gunnery officer,' he ordered. 'Fire prow bombardment cannon.'

LUTRICIA VIJEON'S HEART sank as she watched the incoming Thunderhawk gunship on her scope. The aircraft was flying nap-of-the-earth and the pilot was good, skilfully hugging the contours of the landscape.

But it was wasted effort. The command centre had been tracking them since they had entered the atmosphere and Vorens grinned with predatory glee as he paced the room, eagerly awaiting the gunship. She had seen his momentary fear as the three Space Marines appeared at the entrance to the command centre, but his mask of vicious arrogance had reasserted itself when they had vanished. Where had they gone, wondered Lutricia?

Most of the control centre staff prayed silently at their stations, only the servitors carrying on with their allotted tasks in the face of Vorens' treachery. She made to wipe a tear from the corner of her eye, blinking as she saw something detach from the icon representing the Space Marines' strike cruiser.

A second gunship?

No, the signal was too small and, as she looked closer, she saw that it was moving too fast for a gunship. Suddenly she realised what it was and where its trajectory would cause it to land.

A warning klaxon sounded as the aged defence cogitators came to the same conclusion, sounding the alert as a flurry of other blips fired from the cruiser.

Danil Vorens gripped the edge of his chair, rising to his feet with a look of pure terror creasing his features.

'No,' he hissed, watching as the salvo of magma bombs launched from the *Vae Victus* hurtled towards them, homing in on the precise co-ordinates provided by Lutricia Vijeon.

His knees sagged and Vorens collapsed back in the commander's seat.

Lutricia watched the bombs speed their way towards them, slashing down through the atmosphere of Pavonis at incredible speed. They would impact soon, wiping this facility from the face of the planet, and not even the energy field would protect them.

Suddenly calm, she rose from her station and strode to the centre of the chamber.

Danil Vorens watched her. He wept openly at the prospect of death, but made no move to stop her as she picked up the laspistol beside him. Though she had never handled a weapon in her life, she knew exactly what to do.

Lutricia Vijeon shot Danil Vorens in the heart, letting the pistol fall from her fingers as the proximity alarms of the command centre began screaming.

She turned to the main viewscreen and sank to her knees.

Lutricia smiled, an enormous sense of satisfaction flooding her. She knew she had done the right thing and offered her thanks that she had been granted this chance to serve Him.

She extended her hands and said, 'Come, brothers and sisters. Let us pray.'

The remainder of the control centre staff joined her in a small circle, weeping and joining hands as they prayed to the Emperor for the last time.

THE MAGMA BOMBS impacted within seconds of one another.

The first clutch hammered into the energy shield, overloading the field generators protecting this portion of the palace, and punching a hole. Subsequent bombs blasted through the wing the control centre was buried beneath, obliterating it in a thunderous detonation and hurling tank-sized blocks of stone high into the air. The next penetrated ten metres of reinforced rockcrete, blasting a crater almost a hundred metres in diameter.

Two bombs malfunctioned, the first corkscrewing wildly as it hit the upper atmosphere and landing at the edge of the Gresha Forest, immolating a sizeable portion of the Abrogas cartel's country holdings. The second hit over nine hundred kilometres from its intended target, splashing down harmlessly in the ocean.

But the rest slashed into the crater and punched deep into the command centre, their delayed fuses ensuring they exploded in its heart. Firestorms flared, incinerating every living thing within and collapsing what little remained standing. A vast black pillar of smoke, pierced with volcanic flames rose from the destroyed command centre, the shockwave of its demise rippling outwards for kilometres as though an angry god had just smote the earth.

The aerial approach to Brandon Gate was suddenly wide open as servitor controlled batteries sat idle, awaiting targeting instructions that would never arrive.

URIEL LET OUT the breath he had been holding as he heard the pilot's voice over the vox.

'Guilliman's oath! Look at that!'

He'd seen the flash of the magma bombs' impact through the vision blocks, knowing that nothing could stand before the righteous fire of a starship sanctified by the Emperor himself.

'No incoming ground fire,' confirmed the co-pilot. 'Commencing our attack run now.'

The message had been genuine then, and Uriel closed his eyes, offering a prayer of thanks and blessing upon the courageous servant of the Emperor who had managed to get the co-ordinates of the defence control centre to them, thus sealing its fate.

Lord Admiral Tiberius had wanted to level the entire palace with orbital bombardment, but Uriel had resisted such a plan, knowing that the vast forces the *Vae Victus* could unleash would level everything within fifty kilometres of the palace. The greatly reduced yield on the magma bombs had struck with precisely the correct force, and though there was certain to be some collateral casualties, Uriel hoped that that they had been kept to a minimum.

They were here to save these people, not destroy them. Leave such simple-minded butchery for the likes of the Blood Angels or Marines Malevolent. The Ultramarines were not indiscriminate killers, they were the divine instrument of the Emperor's wrath. The protection of his subjects was their reason for existing.

Too many of those who fought to protect the Imperium forgot that it was a living thing, made up of the billions of people that inhabited the Emperor's worlds. Without them, the Imperium was nothing. With the Emperor to bind them, they were the glue that held His realm together and Uriel would have no part in their deliberate murder.

A chill passed through him as he remembered Gedrik's words on Caernus IV.

The Death of Worlds and the Bringer of Darkness await to be born into this galaxy...

He now understood their significance and did not relish the prospect of what they presaged.

The Thunderhawk swayed wildly as the pilot circled the palace, swooping in low through the gap in the energy shield the magma bombs had blasted. Gunfire spat from the towers, a few shots even striking the speeding gunship, but its armour was untroubled by such pinpricks.

The gunship's crew chief glanced out of the door and shouted, 'Get ready brothers! Debarkation in ten seconds!'

Uriel tensed, tapping his breastplate and bolt pistol in honour of their war spirits. Bracing himself against the side of the gunship, he drew his power sword and watched the ground hurtle towards them.

The Thunderhawk slammed into the cobbled esplanade before the palace.

Uriel shouted, 'Courage and honour!' and leapt from the gunship.

The Ultramarines echoed his war-cry and charged after their captain.

BARZANO AND SHONAI stared fearfully at the roof of their cell as the massive shockwave of the magma bombs' detonation rocked the prison level with the violence of an earthquake. Cracks snaked across the vaulted ceilings and dozens of archways collapsed, burying the cells' screaming occupants beneath tonnes of rubble.

Stone split with the crack of a gunshot and steel groaned as millions of tonnes of rock spread its load over the blasted foundations. Barzano scrambled to his feet. The bars to their cell squealed in protest, bowing outwards under the compression as the archway sagged.

'About time,' he muttered.

'What's happening?' shouted Mykola Shonai over the rumble of collapsing stonework.

'Well, to me that sounds like the opening strike in an orbital bombardment,' replied Barzano coolly, reaching into his mouth and tugging. Shonai watched him, bemused, as the juddering tremors of the bombardment continued.

'What are you doing?'

'Getting us out of here,' replied Barzano, finally pulling out a tooth with a grunt of pain. Blood dripped from the corner of his mouth and the ivory coloured tooth he held before him.

He hurried to the cell door working the 'tooth' deep within the lock and checking for any guards. Shouts echoed up and down the prison, inmates screaming to be let out of their cells and guards yelling at them to shut up.

Barzano moved quickly from the door and grabbed Shonai, the pair of them hauling the bed with Jenna Sharben towards the rear of the cell. Barzano knelt, protecting their bodies with his own.

'Mykola, close your eyes, cover your ears and open your mouth so the blast pressure won't burst your eardrums,' advised Barzano, pressing his face into Jenna Sharben's shoulder

The governor ducked down as the compact explosive that had been secreted inside Barzano's false tooth erupted, blasting the lock-plate of the cell door across the corridor. The door itself didn't move, pressed tightly into its frame by the lowering ceiling. Before the roar of the blast had even dissipated, Barzano rose to his feet and kicked his booted foot against the cell door.

It opened a handbreadth, but another kick slammed it wide and Barzano was through.

Holding his wounded shoulder, he turned back to Shonai, saying, 'Stay here and look after Sharben. I'll be back soon.'

'Be careful!' ordered Mykola Shonai.

'Always,' grinned Barzano, scooping up a fist-sized rock that had fallen from the ceiling and jogging cautiously down the corridor, keeping close to the walls. He reached a bend in the corridor, hearing panicked voices of the guards from around the corner. He could sense they were strung out, nervous and not thinking straight.

Hefting the rock, he affected his strongest Pavonian accent and shouted, 'Quick! The prisoners are escaping from their cells!'

Seconds later three men sprinted around the corner.

Barzano hammered the rock into the first guard's face, crushing his skull and dropping him to the floor. He leapt at the second man, cracking the rock against his helmet. The inquisitor threw himself flat as a lasbolt slashed the air above him, and rolled to his knees, driving his elbow up into the third guard's groin. Barzano caught the man's lasgun as he fell and cracked the rifle butt hard against his temple. The second guard tried to rise, but Barzano shot him in the face and he collapsed.

The inquisitor raised the rifle to his uninjured shoulder and scanned for fresh targets. His wound throbbed painfully and the dressing was leaking blood, but he didn't have time to spare to redress it.

He heard fresh shouts behind him and dropped to his knees as a flurry of blasts vaporised the rock walls beside him. He spun, firing a wild volley of shots, and two guards dropped screaming to the floor. Over half a dozen remained though, and Barzano rolled around the corner his first victims had come from.

Swiftly rising to his feet, he sprinted down the corridor, the shouts of the prison guards hard on his heels. Ahead, the corridor split into two passageways and Barzano ducked into the left one as another shot plucked his sleeve, leaving a painful, burning weal across his arm. The corridor was chill and dark, the glow-globes dim and barely illuminating this section.

Cell doors punctuated the corridor's length and at its end was a featureless door of rusted metal. Barzano's empathic senses felt an overwhelming aura of despair emanating from beyond this door and the magnitude of it made him stumble.

He fought through the palpable horror and pushed on, knowing he had seconds to reach cover before being shot by his pursuers. He sprinted down the corridor and launched himself feet first at the door.

It slammed open and he rolled through onto his back, grunting as the wound on his shoulder reopened. He fired back into the corridor, hearing another scream and kicked the door shut, slamming the locking bar into place.

He rose to his feet and swung the rifle to bear on the room's occupants.

The Surgeon stood beside a blood-soaked slab, working a buzzing saw into Almerz Chanda's bones.

Barzano's knees sagged and the rifle barrel dropped as he saw how the Surgeon had honoured Almerz Chanda's flesh.

* * *

URIEL DIVED INTO the cover of some rubble and sprayed the rebels' trench line with bolter fire. Explosions of red blossomed where his shots struck flesh and the screams of the wounded added to the din of battle. Despite the ministrations of Apothecary Selenus, the wound inflicted by the eldar leader pulled painfully tight with his every movement.

The entrance to the palace's prison level lay at the far end of this wide area of open ground strewn with rubble and small fires. Two bunkers of rockcrete flanked the entrance, covering every possible approach, and a slit trench ran in a troop-filled line before them, protected by recently laid coils of razorwire. Roaring blasts of gunfire sprayed from the defensive position: bright stabs of lasguns and the crack of heavy bolters.

Ultramarines poured fire over their own makeshift barricades, peppering the thick walls of the bunkers with bolts. A pair of missiles lanced out, slamming into the bunkers' thick walls, but they had been designed to withstand all but a direct artillery impact.

Concentrated bursts of heavy gunfire raked the Ultramarines' position and Uriel knew that they were running out of time; the enemy were sure to bring up heavy armour and counterattack. As formidable as the warriors of the Adeptus Astartes were, they would have no option but to fall back in the face of such firepower.

He called over his sergeants and hurriedly outlined the situation.

'Options?' he asked.

Pasanius scabbarded his bolter and hefted his flamer. 'Call in a limited strike from the *Vae Victus*, blow a hole in their line and fight through the gap.'

Uriel considered the possibility of an orbital strike. It was tempting, but unrealistic.

'No. If the targeting surveyors are even a fraction out, we could find ourselves the target or if the yield is too high, the entire prison complex might be buried beneath hundreds of tonnes of rubble.'

'Then I suppose we have to do this the hard way,' said Sergeant Venasus grimly.

Uriel nodded. Venasus was not noted for his subtlety of command, but as he considered the options, Uriel knew that the sergeant was right. They would have to throw tactical finesse out the window. Superior training and faith in the Emperor was vital, but in any war there would always come a time when the battle would have to be won by taking the fight to the enemy through the fire and meeting him blade to blade, strength to strength. That time was now.

Another burst of heavy fire blasted along their line, the PDF gunners working their guns methodically left and right, turning the area before the Ultramarines into a murderous killing ground.

'Very well,' said Uriel at last, 'Here's how we are going to do this.'

* * *

BARZANO BROUGHT THE rifle up in time to block the upward sweep of the Surgeon's bonesaw, the alien device hacking through the barrel in a shower of purple sparks. He ducked another sweep of the saw, barrelling into his slender opponent. The pair collapsed in a pile of thrashing limbs and Barzano screamed as he felt the whirring saw-blade slice across his hip, the screaming teeth scraping across his pelvis before sliding clear.

He slammed his forehead into the Surgeon's face. Blood sprayed as his nose cracked and the alien screeched in pain. Barzano rolled as the saw blade swung again, scoring a deep gouge in the stone floor. He bent to retrieve what remained of his lasgun. The weapon would never fire again, but its heavy wooden stock would serve as a bludgeon.

He backed against the door, bracing his weight against it as he felt the repeated lasblasts impact upon it. It wouldn't hold for long.

The Surgeon advanced towards him, the bonesaw spraying blood from its whining edge. The alien's face was a mask of crimson and his violet eyes were filled with hate.

Behind him, the shattered body of Almerz Chanda groaned on the slab, his bloody and raw flesh shuddering as the soporific effects of the Surgeon's muscle relaxants began to dissipate.

URIEL BRACED HIMSELF on the rubble and whispered a brief prayer to the blessed Primarch that this attack would succeed. All along the line of Space Marines, men awaited his orders. Chaplain Clausel intoned the Litany of Battle, his stern, unwavering voice a fine example to the warriors of Fourth Company. Uriel knew that he had to provide a similar example, by leading this charge himself.

The PDF gunners were firing blind now. Dozens of smoke and blind grenades had gone over the top, and billowing clouds of concealing smoke were spewing from the grenade canisters.

When he judged that the smoke had spread enough, Uriel yelled, 'Now! For the glory of Terra!' and surged from behind the cover of rubble and debris.

As one, the Ultramarines roared and followed their captain into the smoke, bullets and lasers tearing amongst them in a deadly volley. Deadly to anyone not clad in suits of holy power armour, blessed by the Techmarines and imbued with the spirits of battle.

Immediately the Space Marines fanned out, so a concentrated burst of fire wouldn't hit them all. This was a gauntlet every man would run alone. Uriel sprinted through the clouds of white, lit by the eerie glow of flickering flames. He ran across burned bodies, patches of scorched ground, and piles of discarded battlegear. The whine of bullets and lasers surrounded him, the smoke whipped by their passing. His every sense was alert as he led the charge.

His auto-senses fought to pierce the obscuring fog of the blind grenades, the bright flashes up ahead the only clue to the distance left to cover.

One hundred and fifty paces.

Throughout the smoke he could make out the blurred shapes of his warriors, weapons spitting fire towards the rebel line.

One hundred paces.

Roars of pain sounded. Cold fury gripped him as he closed the gap.

Then the ground exploded around him, spraying him with stone fragments and flaming metal as heavy bolter fire hammered around him. A shell clipped his shoulder guard and helmet, spinning him from his feet. Another impacted on his power sword, the shell blasting the blade from the hilt in a shower of sparks.

Uriel fell, rolling into cover as his vision was obscured by red, flashing runes on his visor. Blood ran into his eyes and he wrenched the helmet clear, wiping the already clotted substance from his face. His rage built as he saw the damage done to the sword.

The hilt bore only a short, broken length of blade, the intricate traceries that contained the war-spirit within shattered and broken. His legacy from Idaeus had been destroyed, the one tangible link to his former captain's approval of his authority was no more.

Uriel angrily sheathed what remained of the blade and rose to his feet.

The smoke was thinning and he could see he were less than a hundred metres from the bunkers. He was almost there, but this close, the fire from the slit trench was telling and their charge had lost its momentum. The weight of fire was simply too heavy to advance through and live.

A sense of utter conviction gripped Uriel and he walked calmly through the hail of gunfire and knelt beside the body of a fallen battle brother, prising the chainsword from his fingers. Bullets stitched the ground beside him, but Uriel did not flinch or even acknowledge that he was under fire.

'Captain! Get down!' shouted Pasanius.

Uriel turned to the sheltering Ultramarines and shouted, 'Follow me!'

A lasbolt struck him square in the chest.

Uriel staggered, but did not fall, the eagle at the centre of his breastplate running molten. Chaplain Clausel rose to his feet, crozius arcanum held above his head.

'See, brothers! The Emperor protects!' he bellowed, his voice carrying over the entire battlefield. The massive Chaplain shouted, 'Up, brothers! Up! For the Emperor! Forward!'

Uriel pressed the activation rune of the chainsword, the blade roaring into life.

He turned back to the enemy line.

They would make it. There would be no mercy.

He began sprinting through the fire towards the foe.

BARZANO SWAYED ASIDE as the Surgeon thrust the bonesaw at his belly. He gripped his weapon arm and spun inside his guard, powering his elbow into the alien's side. He rolled forward, avoiding the reverse stroke of the bonesaw, crashing into the table of surgical instruments beside the slab and dropping all manner of scalpels and drills to the floor beside him. He could hear Almerz Chanda groaning in pain above him and snatched up a long, hook-bladed scalpel as the Surgeon came at him again.

Barzano's strength was failing and he knew that he could not last much longer. He pushed himself to his feet, the scalpel gripped tightly in his fist. The Surgeon swung the bonesaw at Barzano's head.

The inquisitor blocked the blow with his forearm, screaming as the tearing teeth of the bonesaw sheared into the meat of his arm, shrieking along the bone towards his elbow. The whining edge of the saw juddered to a halt, the teeth caught in the bone of the inquisitor's arm. Barzano swung his injured limb, complete with the embedded saw, away from his body and stepped in close, hammering the scalpel into the Surgeon's temple.

The alien staggered. Blood burst from his mouth as his knees gave way, a full fifteen centimetres of steel rammed into his brain. He gave a last sigh before toppling forward, the rattling bonesaw pulling clear of Barzano's arm.

Barzano slumped against the slab, fighting to stay conscious through the screaming agony of his shredded arm. A thick layer of skin and muscle flapped from his elbow and he forced himself not to look at the damage.

Fresh impacts slammed against the door and he bent to snatch a pistol of strange appearance from the Surgeon's belt, his every movement causing supernovas of agony to explode in his skull.

He felt, rather than saw, movement beside him and he swayed, bringing the pistol to bear.

Almerz Chanda pushed himself into a sitting position, his ruined body making one last surge before death claimed him.

His features spoke of the most hideous pain imaginable and Barzano could sense the madness the Surgeon's art had pushed the man into. But he also sensed his desperate need for atonement behind the pits of insanity.

As Barzano fought to remain upright, the door to the Surgeon's chambers finally crashed open.

URIEL HAMMERED HIS fist through a guardsman's visor, the man's face disintegrating under the blow. A lasbolt scored his breastplate, but the armour held firm and Uriel killed the shooter with a well placed bolter round. He swung his chainsword in a brutal arc, beheading another trooper and disembowelling a second. He fired his pistol into the face of a third and roared with the savage joy of combat.

The trench was a killing ground.

The wrath of the Ultramarines knew no bounds as they tore the men of the PDF to pieces, overrunning the trench with the fury of their charge. Bolt pistols fired, chainswords flashed red in the sunlight and gouts of liquid fire roasted men alive. There was no quarter given and within seconds the trench was nothing more than an open grave for the men of the PDF.

Before the impetus of the charge could be lost, Uriel yelled at his men to follow him, scrambling from the trench and sprinting onwards to the bunkers. Heavy calibre shells ripped a path towards him, but he jinked to one side, avoiding the hail of bullets. Firing as he ran, his charge carried him to within ten metres of the bunker. He could see Pasanius firing a long stream of liquid fire through the firing slit of the second bunker, the orange flames licking all around the giant warrior as he filled the enemy strongpoint with searing death.

Uriel dived and rolled to the foot of the bunker, narrowly avoiding being cut in two by a point blank burst of gunfire. His back slammed into its front wall. The bunker was a squat slab of rockcrete, protruding a metre above ground level with narrow gun slits in every side. Grenades would be useless. The bunker was sure to have a grenade sump, a protected chamber where the troops inside could dump grenades in order to negate their force.

More shots spewed from the bunker and Uriel waited until he heard the distinctive sound of a heavy bolter slide racking back empty. He held his breath, straining to hear the double click of a new belt feed of shells being shucked into a hot breech.

Uriel roared and rose up in front of the bunker, driving his chainsword through the firing slit and into the gunner's face. A bubbling scream and crack of bone sounded, and Uriel reached inside, dragging the heavy weapon through the slit.

He quickly spun the weapon and pushed the muzzle into the bunker, squeezing the trigger and working the bucking gun left and right, filling the bunker with explosive shells. The screaming from inside was short lived, but Uriel waited until the last of the shells from the belt feed had been expended and the firing hammer clicked down empty.

Uriel dropped the weapon, sweat and blood coating his features.

The bunkers were theirs and the prison complex lay open before him.

THE PRISON GUARDS burst into the torture chamber to be confronted by an apparition from their worst nightmares. Almerz Chanda threw himself forward with the last vestige of his strength, carrying the first men through the door to the ground.

Thrashing and screaming, the dying Chanda wailed in agony, the sound tearing at the nerves of everyone within earshot. Instinctively, the attackers fired. Lasbolts blasted Chanda's ravaged body, punching through him into the men beneath.

Chanda's death scream was one of release rather than pain.

The following troops tore their eyes from the horrifically mutilated man to the chamber's sole remaining living occupant. Barzano swayed, one side of his body completely drenched in blood. Chanda's death had bought him precious seconds he did not intend to waste. He aimed the Surgeon's pistol at the guards and pulled the trigger.

A hail of dark needles fired in an expanding cone, shredding the closest guards and killing them instantly. The guards behind were not so fortunate and the venom-tipped needles flooded their bloodstreams with lethal alien toxins.

Barzano staggered to the door as the guards fell back, some spasming in their death throes as the poison did its evil work, others retreating as they saw the fate of those in front. The inquisitor pushed shut the door, sliding to the floor as his strength poured from him in the wash of blood from his ruined arm.

More screams sounded from outside, gunfire and explosions. He felt something push against the door and weakly tried to hold it shut, but he could not prevent it from opening. He slumped to the floor, his vision blurring and attempted to raise the alien pistol.

Sergeant Learchus plucked the pistol from the inquisitor's hand and hurled it aside as he and two of his battle brothers entered the torture chamber along with Mykola Shonai, Lortuen Perjed and half a dozen petrified scribes. One of the Space Marines carried Jenna Sharben and gently deposited the wounded judge on the Surgeon's slab.

'See to him,' ordered Learchus, pointing at the unconscious Barzano.

Learchus activated his vox. 'Captain Ventris, we have Inquisitor Barzano. He is alive, but badly wounded. We will need to get him aboard the *Vae Victus* soon if we are to save his life.'

URIEL CHARGED THROUGH the smoking remains of the prison complex gateway, firing as he ran. The blast had killed most of the defenders on the inside; over the ringing echoes of the gate's destruction, only the moans of the dying could be heard.

His spirits had soared when Learchus had informed him of the inquisitor's safety, knowing that he had made the right decision to have the sergeant remain within the palace and break into the prison complex from above.

Learchus had Barzano, but there were several hundred men below ground. They still had to reach their brethren and pull them to safety. Pasanius poured another sheet of fire down the rough-hewn stairs that led into the darkness of the prison.

Screams boiled up from below, and Uriel once more led the charge of the Ultramarines.

* * *

LEARCHUS FIRED ANOTHER blast of bolter fire through the door, felling two guards and wounding a third. Thus far they had held off three attacks, but ammunition was low and they were running out of time. There were another two entrances to this chamber and each of the Space Marines fought desperately to hold off the waves of attackers with bolter and chainsword.

Mykola Shonai and Lortuen Perjed desperately battled to halt the flow of blood from Barzano's arm, but it was a fight they were losing. The Surgeon's blade had cut him to the bone from wrist to elbow and this place had only instruments for the taking of life, not its preservation. Barzano's flesh was ashen, his pulse weak and thready.

More and more guards hurled themselves through the doors, each time to be cut down by deadly bolts or hacked apart by shrieking chainswords. The stink of death filled the chamber.

Learchus dropped his bolter as his last magazine finally exhausted itself and charged the door as more enemies tried to force their way inside. His sword hacked the first men to death, before lasbolts hurled the sergeant from his feet. Status runes flashed red on his visor. He rolled and chopped the legs out from one man, thundering his fist into the groin of another. Bayonets stabbed at him, most sliding clear across his armoured might.

He stabbed and chopped, kicking and punching in all directions, feeling bones break with every motion of his body. Gunfire boomed as he pushed himself clear of his attackers, roaring with battle fury, a living engine of killing frenzy.

They were holding, but they could not continue to do so for long.

A BACKHANDED BLOW sent another enemy screaming into hell as Uriel and Pasanius pushed deeper into the prison complex. Uriel's helmet lay abandoned on the battlefield above them, so he followed Pasanius, the locator augers within the sergeant's helmet directing them towards Learchus.

He could hear the screams of dying men and furious battle from up ahead and sprinted round a corner to see scores of men pushing themselves forward through a wide door. Pasanius did not even wait for the order, simply engulfing the men in fire from his lethal flamer. Screams and the stench of scorched flesh filled the cramped corridor as the Ultramarines fell upon the prison guards from behind.

It was a massacre. The soldiers had nowhere to run to. Caught between the fury of Sergeant Learchus and this new assault, the survivors threw themselves at the mercy of Uriel. But there was none to be had and every soldier perished.

Uriel pushed himself into the Surgeon's torture chamber, breathing heavily and wiping blood from his face. Bodies littered the chamber and the stink of blood was overpowering. The silence was a sudden contrast from the screaming combat of moments ago and Learchus blinked, lowering his blood-sheathed chainsword.

Uriel marched to meet Learchus and gripped his hand.

'Well met, brother,' whispered Uriel.

Learchus nodded. 'Aye, well met, captain.'

THE THUNDERHAWK ROARED upwards, chased by a few hastily converted shuttle-gunships and ornithopters. Designed to strafe slow moving ground targets, they were out of their element against the Space Marine craft and, after losing seven of their number, pulled back.

The rescue of Inquisitor Barzano had cost the lives of three Ultramarines and two of Barzano's scribes who had been killed in the crossfire raging throughout the torture chamber. Lortuen Perjed was adamant that they receive full honours upon their burial.

Before attending to the wounded, Apothecary Selenus had removed the vital progenoid glands from the bodies of the fallen Space Marines. The recovery of the precious gene-seed took precedence over normal battlefield triage.

He stabilised the inquisitor and set up a live transfusion of blood from a scribe with a matching blood type. The man expressed his willingness to be bled dry in order to save the inquisitor's life, but Selenus assured him that such drastic measures would not be necessary.

He had treated Jenna Sharben's wound and though she would be incapacitated for many days yet, she would live and suffer no long-term damage from her injury. Of the surviving Ultramarines, the majority of their wounds were largely superficial.

The battered Thunderhawk pulled into high orbit, finally making rendezvous with the *Vae Victus* and bringing her warriors home.

THE SENIOR OFFICERS of the Pavonis expedition gathered in the captain's briefing room, assembled around a circular table hewn from the slow growing mountain firs that surrounded the Fortress of Hera on Macragge.

Lord Admiral Tiberius sat with his back to the wall, below a magnificent silken banner listing the victories of his vessel and her previous captains stretching back to a time centuries before his birth. To one side of Tiberius sat the battle-weary Ultramarines, fresh from their battles on Pavonis: Uriel, Learchus, Pasanius, Venasus and Dardino. On the opposite side of the table sat Mykola Shonai and Lortuen Perjed.

Between them was an unoccupied chair and as Mykola Shonai took a sip of water, the last member of the council of war arrived, cradling his left arm in a synthflesh bandage and walking with a pronounced limp.

Uriel watched Barzano hobble into the briefing room, noting the telltale gleam in his eyes that indicated heavy stimm use. The inquisitor was obviously using medical stimulants to block the pain from his wounded arm and shoulder. He sat opposite Uriel, his face ashen.

'Very well,' began Barzano, 'I think it's fair to say that the situation is grim. Kasimir de Valtos has control on Pavonis, and at any moment could have his hands on an ancient alien weapon capable of unleashing destruction on a system-wide scale. Would everyone agree that is a fair assessment of our situation?'

No one disagreed with the inquisitor.

'What do you suggest then, Inquisitor Barzano?' asked Tiberius.

'What I would suggest is that you send a coded communication to Macragge and have a battle-barge armed with cyclonic torpedoes despatched to Pavonis.'

Uriel slammed his fist down on the table.

'No!' he stated forcefully, 'I will not have it. We came here to save these people, not to destroy them.'

Tiberius placed a calming hand on Uriel's arm. Mykola Shonai looked from Uriel to Barzano, a confused look upon her features.

'Perhaps I am missing something,' she said. 'What are cyclonic torpedoes?'

'Planet killers,' answered Uriel. 'They will burn the atmosphere of Pavonis away in a storm of fire, scouring the surface bare until there is nothing left alive. The seas will boil to vapour and your world will become a barren rock, wreathed in the ashes of your people.'

Shonai turned a horrified stare upon Barzano. 'You would destroy my world?' she asked incredulously.

Slowly, Barzano nodded. 'If it means preventing a madman getting his hands on the Bringer of Darkness, then yes, I would. Better to sacrifice one world than lose Emperor knows how many others because we shirked from doing our duty.'

'It is not our duty to kill innocent people,' pointed out Uriel.

'Our duty is to save as many lives as we can,' countered Barzano. 'If we do nothing and de Valtos succeeds in retrieving the alien ship, many more worlds will die. I do not make this decision lightly, Uriel, but I must rely on cold logic and the Emperor to guide me.'

'I cannot believe this is the Emperor's will.'

'Who are you to judge what the Emperor wants?' snapped Barzano. 'You are a warrior who can see his enemies on the battlefield and smite them with sword and bolter. My enemies are heresy, deviancy and ambition. More insidious foes than you could ever imagine and the weapons I must use are consequently of greater magnitude.'

'You can't do this, Barzano,' said Uriel. 'My men have fought and bled for this world, I will not give up on it.'

'It is not a question of giving up, Uriel,' explained Barzano. 'It is a question of prevention. We do not know where de Valtos is or how he intends to find the ship and without that information we can do nothing. If we hesitate and are too late to prevent him gaining possession of the *Nightbringer*, how many more lives will be lost? Ten billion? A thousand billion? More?'

'Surely there is something we can try to stop de Valtos?' asked Shonai. 'There are millions of people on Pavonis. I will not just stand by and hear the fate of my world discussed as though its destruction were a matter of no import.'

Barzano turned to face Shonai and said, 'Believe me, Mykola, I am not some heartless monster and I do not believe the death of even a single world to be of no import. Were there another way, I would gladly choose it. I have never been forced to destroy a world before, and if I could stop de Valtos any other way, I would.'

As Barzano spoke, the words of Gedrik echoed in his head once more.

The Death of Worlds and the Bringer of Darkness await to be born into this galaxy. One will arise or neither, it is in your hands to choose which.

'Do you really mean that, Inquisitor Barzano?' he asked.

'Mean what?' asked Barzano, his tone wary.

'About choosing another way if you could.'

'Yes, I do.'

'Then I believe there is another way,' said Uriel.

Barzano raised a sceptical eyebrow and leaned forwards, resting his arms on the tabletop, careful to avoid jarring his wounded arm. 'And what would that be, Uriel?'

Uriel sensed the criticality of this moment and mustered his thoughts before speaking.

'When I was in the home of de Valtos, and we found the two skeleton warriors in the depths of his house, I noticed the battery packs they were hooked up to had identification markings on them.'

'So?'

'They were marked with the words "Tembra Ridge" – perhaps the governor can shed some light on that,' answered Uriel.

'Tembra Ridge? It's a range of mountains roughly a hundred kilometres north of Brandon Gate. They stretch from the western ocean to the Gresha forest in the east, nearly a thousand kilometres of rocky uplands and scrub forests. It's a mining region: there are hundreds of deep bore mines along its length. Most of the cartels own title to land along Tembra Ridge. The de Valtos cartel have several.'

'If those things were unearthed from one of the mines along Tembra Ridge, is it not likely that the *Nightbringer* itself lies beneath the ground there too?' pointed out Uriel.

Barzano nodded with a smile. 'Very good, Uriel. Now if we could only pinpoint which one they came from we would truly have something to celebrate.'

Barzano's tone was mildly sarcastic, but Uriel could see he was at least considering the idea that the extermination of Pavonis might not be inevitable. The inquisitor turned to Mykola Shonai.

'How deep do these bore mines go?' he asked,

'It varies,' replied Shonai, 'but the deepest are perhaps ten thousand metres, while others are around three or four thousand. It depends on the seam that is being mined and how deep it's economically viable to continue drilling.'

'Then we find out which of the mines are owned by the de Valtos cartel and bombard them all into oblivion from orbit,' growled Uriel.

'Lortuen?' said Barzano, turning to his aide, who nodded thoughtfully and closed his eyes. His breathing slowed, his eyelids fluttering as he culled facts, figures and statistics from the wealth of information he and his scribes had gathered during their researches.

Uriel watched as the old man's eyes flickered rapidly from side to side as though reading information flashing past on the inside of his eyelids, noticing for the first time the tiny glint of metal behind his ear. The old man had been fitted with cybernetic implants, presumably something similar to those of a lexmechanic or savant servitor.

Without opening his eyes, Perjed spoke in a flat monotone, 'There are four mines along Tembra Ridge owned by the de Valtos cartel. All produce mineral ore to be refined into processed steel for tank chassis and gun barrels, but the northernmost's production level is by far the lowest. I suspect that its shortfall is being covered by over-production in the other facilities, which would account for the higher number of worker accidents reported at the other mines.'

Perjed's head bowed, his breathing slowly returning to normal, and Uriel stared triumphantly at Barzano.

'There,' he said, 'We have the location and can attack without resorting to genocide.'

'I'm afraid that this changes nothing, Captain Ventris,' said Tiberius softly.

'Why not?'

'Even at full yield on our bombardment cannon, the magma bombs will not be able to penetrate that far into the planet's crust.'

'Then we take the fight to the surface once more,' shouted Uriel. 'The Techmarines tell me that we now have two Thunderhawks operational. I say we launch as soon as we can rearm and break de Valtos out from beneath the planet's surface by hand if need be.'

Uriel stared defiantly at Barzano, waiting to shout down any objections the inquisitor might have.

But Barzano merely nodded.

'Very well, Uriel. We'll try it your way, but if you fail, Pavonis will die. By my hand or that of de Valtos.'

'We will not fail,' assured Uriel. 'We are the Ultramarines.'

♄ SEVENTEEN

VIRGIL ORTEGA DUCKED as another rattling blast of gunfire peppered the wall behind him, showering him with stony fragments. He slid behind the angled rockcrete barricade and ejected the spent drum magazine from the heavy stubber, slotting another one home and racking the slide.

Ortega swung the ponderous weapon back up onto the barricade as another rush of troops came at them, bracing the heavy stock hard into his shoulder and pulling the trigger. A metre long tongue of flame blasted from the perforated barrel and a deafening roaring ripped the air as hundreds of high velocity bullets churned the first wave of attackers to shredded corpses. The vibration of the gun's fire was almost too much for Ortega, his muscles straining to keep the gun steady. With such firepower, it wasn't so much a question of accuracy, but of ammunition capacity; the stubber could empty its magazine in a matter of seconds.

Of the twenty-seven judges he'd pulled from the disaster at the precinct house, eighteen were still alive. Emerging from hidden tunnels beneath the palace that not even the governor knew about, the judges had seized the armoury after a brief but fierce firefight. Surprise had been total and the Imperial armoury, designed to indefinitely withstand attack from the outside, had fallen within an hour.

It took less than that for the rebel forces to muster a counterattack and attempt to force the judges from their new refuge. Buried beneath the palace, the armoury was inaccessible to anything but infantry and, with a vast selection of powerful guns at his disposal, Virgil Ortega was proving to be a particularly troublesome thorn in the rebels' side. Without the enormous stockpiles of heavy weaponry stored in the armoury, this rebellion would be seriously deprived of firepower when the wrath of Imperial retaliation descended upon it.

He'd despatched Collix and six judges to rig as many explosives as they could find and prepare the armoury for destruction. With a bit of luck they could set some charges, make their escape and blow this place to the warp.

The corridor before him was littered with enemy dead, the mounds of corpses forming makeshift banks of cover for their attackers. Ortega worked the fire from the stubber mercilessly back and forth, firing bursts into any sign of movement. The judges on the line with him fired a mix of shotguns, bolters and stubbers, filling the air before them with death.

He could hear muffled curses and spared a glance behind him to see Collix dragging a wheeled gurney with a linked pair of autocannons fitted to a circular pintel mount. Ortega grinned. The weapon was designed to be mounted on a vehicle of some kind, possibly a Sentinel, and was far too heavy to be carried by a man.

Stuttering blasts of gunfire ricocheted from the walls, and Ortega pulled a judge down from the barricade as he slumped over, half his head blown away.

'Get a move on, Collix!' he shouted.

'Coming, sir!'

'How long until we can get the hell out of here?'

'I'm not sure we'll be able to, sir.'

'What are you talking about?'

'The detonators for the explosives are not stored here,' explained Collix. 'I should imagine in order to prevent an enemy from doing what we are attempting to do.'

Ortega swore and set down the heavy stubber, scrambling away from the barricade, careful to keep his head down as he made his way to help Collix with the massive guns.

'Then we have to find another way to set them off,' snarled Ortega.

'It could be done manually,' suggested Collix.

Ortega locked eyes with Collix, aware of what his sergeant was suggesting.

'Let's hope it does not come to that, sergeant.'

'Yes,' nodded Collix, grimly.

'Set them up here,' ordered Ortega, siting the guns to cover the barricade.

Collix halted the gurney and hauled on the brake lever, locking the wheels into position and extending the stabiliser legs. The recoil of the autocannons was sure to be enormous and Ortega wasn't sure the makeshift gun bed was up to the task.

Screams and desperate shouts sounded behind him and he cursed, seeing grey uniformed men struggling with his judges. Blood and smoke filled the passage as every man and woman fought with desperate savagery.

The judges were amongst the most disciplined, dedicated troops the Emperor could call upon, but the PDF fought with the frenzy of soldiers who had come through the fire of battle and survived long enough to exact their vengeance on their would-be killers.

Ortega snatched the shock maul from his belt and surged into the swirling melee, savagely clubbing his enemies. Collix swung a massive power glaive, effortlessly slicing a PDF trooper in two. There were many exotic weapons to choose from – power swords and great energy axes amongst them – but Ortega trusted the solid feel of his trusty maul.

He crushed a man's skull with a backhanded swing. He had depleted seven energy charges in his maul so far, but there was no shortage of ammo in this place. And even on the occasions he had been forced to use it without its shock field, half a metre of solid metal was a powerful weapon in the hands of a man who knew how to wield it.

Ortega fought back to back with Collix, cutting a swathe through the bloodied PDF troopers, crushing bones and breaking faces with their clubs and fists.

'The Emperor's justice is upon you, sinners!' shouted Collix, kicking a trooper in the groin then beheading him with a lethal swipe of his glaive. Ortega jabbed his maul into another soldier's belly, driving his knee into the man's face as he folded. Blood sprayed and he lashed out again, knowing that they had to hold off their attackers just a little longer.

A space cleared around him and he dropped his shock maul, sweeping up the heavy stubber once more. He braced himself and squeezed the trigger, his entire body quaking with the powerful recoil. His ribs screamed painfully with each blast, and he was sure he'd rebroken them.

Heavy calibre shells ripped through the ranks of the PDF and a dozen men dropped, their thin flak vests unable to stop such powerful bullets. Ortega roared, an inchoate yell of released anger and pain.

'Death to those who defile the Emperor's laws!'

Blood gathered at the corners of his mouth and he could feel a hollow ache in his chest.

Yes, now he was sure he'd rebroken at least one rib.

Suddenly it was over.

The last of the attackers fell or turned tail and ran, broken by the ferocity of the judges' defence. Ortega showed no mercy, gunning the fleeing soldiers down as they ran.

A scant handful of soldiers made it to safety, firing back as they ran.

A lasbolt clipped Ortega's chest, spinning him around and the floor rushed up to meet him, the cold concrete slamming into his face. He felt hands upon him, dragging him back, but could see that his judges had held the barricade.

Another six of his men were down, but they had held.
For now.

URIEL AND PASANIUS sprinted uphill towards the collection of iron sided
buildings on the mountain plateau. The heat in the mountains was fierce
and the glare from the white stone of this region dazzling.

Behind him, the Ultramarines advanced uphill through the rocky, scrub-
covered slopes of the Tembra Ridge mountains towards the deep bore
mine Lortuen Perjed had named TR-701. It did not sound like a place worthy of heroic death and Uriel hoped that he was right in demanding this
one last chance to stop de Valtos.

Ario Barzano waited six kilometres west of the mine in one of the Ultramarines' Thunderhawks, anxiously waiting for Uriel's signal that this was
the place they sought.

The six squads of Ultramarines made their way uphill with no more difficulty than marching across a parade ground. Fire and movement teams
covered the advance, as they were sure to have been spotted; the blue of
their armour was too stark a contrast to the pale mountain stone for them
not to have been.

Scalding jets of flammable gasses spewed from exhaust ports scattered
across the flank of the mountain, venting for the fumes released by drilling
at such depths, and Uriel was reminded of the restless volcanoes in the
southern oceans of Macragge.

Squad Dardino advanced on the left flank, the slope of which was
steeper, but these warriors had been equipped with jump packs, making
light of the journey up the scree covered mountain. Squads Venasus, Pasanius, Elerna, Nivaneus and Daedalus marched on a wide, staggered front,
each squad overwatching the other.

The mine complex shone in the sun, its silvered sides reflecting the light
in dazzling beams. It was impossible to tell whether there were any enemy
forces inside or not. Plumes of exhaust fumes rose from behind the
perimeter buildings, but whether they were from armoured vehicles or the
daily work of a mine was unclear.

They were now within three hundred metres of the plateau.

KASIMIR DE VALTOS followed his mine overseer, Jakob Lasko, beneath the
flickering line of glow-globes. Lasko mopped his brow repeatedly, but de
Valtos appeared too excited to care about the relentless heat this deep in
the earth.

In their wake came a cadre of heavily armoured eldar warriors, their features invisible behind ornate crimson helmets. Between them, they carried
a large silvered metal container, its lid sealed tight.

At their centre was the dread leader of the Kabal of the Sundered Blade,
Archon Kesharq. Like his warriors, his face was concealed behind a visored

helm, its jade surface smooth and featureless. He carried a huge war axe, and at his side sashayed the beautiful, raven-haired wych who had, until now, been the inseparable shadow of Kasimir de Valtos.

Snapping at his heels came the excrents, shambling after their master by whatever method of locomotion the Surgeon had gifted them with. They hissed and spat, uncomfortable in the hot, dark environment. Perhaps some latent, instinctual sense of their former lives spoke to them of the evil that this place contained.

Following the eldar warriors, a full company of PDF troopers brought up the rear. In their midst walked Vendare Taloun, his shoulders slumped dejectedly, wearily mopping his sodden skin with the edge of his robe.

The air was thick with dust and fumes and at regular intervals along the rocky walls, rebreather masks hung from corroded hooks alongside signs cautioning against the risk of toxic gases and explosion.

The procession made its way deeper into the mine, their environs changing from the bare rock of Pavonis to smooth walled passageways, their sloping sides tapering to a point some four metres above their heads.

Kasimir de Valtos paused in the square chamber that had contained the huge door that had barred his entry to this place for so long. Excitement pounded along his veins and he nodded respectfully to the room's four inanimate guardians in their shadowed alcoves. Their eyes glittered, but if they harboured any resentment towards the intruders they gave no sign of it.

Thick rusted flakes marked where the door had been, and de Valtos could sense the vast presence inside. His limbs began to shiver and he fought to control his sense of impending destiny. Within this place lay a sleeping god and he could feel the whisper of ages past in the musty wind that sighed from the tomb's interior.

Archon Kesharq strode up to de Valtos. 'Why do we wait, human? The prize is within, is it not?' snarled Kesharq. The alien's voice bubbled, his stilted High Gothic rendered almost unintelligible by the damage caused by Uriel's bolt round.

'Indeed it is, Archon Kesharq.'

'Then why do we wait?'

'Don't you feel it?' said de Valtos. 'The sense that we stand on the brink of greatness? The sense that once we enter this place nothing will ever be the same again?'

'All I know is that we are wasting time. The Astartes have the one called Barzano back and we should not spend any more time here than we have to. If the prize is inside we should take it and leave.'

'You have no soul, Kesharq,' whispered de Valtos.

He brushed past the alien and entered the resting place of a creature older than time.

THE FIRST ROCKET streaked towards the Ultramarines and exploded amongst the warriors of Squad Nivaneus, scything white-hot fragments in all directions. Two warriors fell, but picked themselves up seconds later.

As the echo of the explosion faded, a rippling roar of gunfire sprayed from the mining compound. Uriel sprinted into the cover of one of the wide exhaust vents and tried to estimate the numbers opposing them. Judging by the number of muzzle flashes he could see, he guessed there were around two hundred guns firing on them.

They were well positioned, covering every approach to the mine complex. Uriel smiled grimly, vindicated in his decision to attack the mine.

But now he and his men were faced with the prospect of attacking a well dug in enemy of superior numbers, uphill and over relatively open terrain. It was the stuff of Chapter legends, wonderful to hear, but a different matter entirely when you had to face such odds yourself.

His men were now in cover and returning fire. The Codex Astartes laid out precise tactics for dealing with such situations, but he had neither the numbers, equipment or time to follow such strict doctrine.

A geyser of fumes belched through the grille of the exhaust vent beside Uriel, enveloping him with acrid fumes and hot ash. He coughed and spat a mouthful of the mine's foul excreta, the neuroglottis situated at the back of his throat assessing its chemical content even as he wiped his face clear.

A burning mix of various sulphurous gasses, fatal to a normal human, but simply irritating to a Space Marine. He slid across the face of the grilled vent and gripped the hot, ash-encrusted metal. Parts gave way beneath his grip and he wrenched it clear, tossing it aside and staring inside.

A hot, mustardy stench wafted out. Uriel's enhanced vision could only pierce a hundred metres of the steaming darkness within, but he could see the passage sloped downwards at a shallow angle. He opened a vox-channel to Sergeant Dardino as a plan began to form in his mind.

'DAMN!' SWORE MAJOR HELIOS Bextor of the 33rd Tarmegan PDF regiment as he watched the blue armoured warriors of the Ultramarines go to ground in the rocks below his position.

He'd given the order to open fire too soon, and cursed his impatience. But who could blame him? The thought of facing the might of the Space Marines was enough to scare even the most courageous of men, and Major Bextor was not fool enough to think that he was such a man.

Though he knew he was not a man of great bravery, he was a reasonably competent military thinker and he felt the defences were as secure as he'd been able to make them. Two full companies defended the mine head alongside a mortar platoon equipped with incendiary rounds. Briefly he wondered what was so important about this place that it required defending, there had not been any open trade wars for centuries, but quickly discarded such thoughts. Guilder de Valtos had entrusted him with the safety of this place and that was enough for him.

He watched the rocks for a few minutes more, but there was no further movement from the slopes.

Major Bextor keyed in the vox frequency of his mortar platoons and said, 'Overwatch teams, commence volley fire. Targets at two hundred metres plus. Fire for effect!'

SECONDS LATER, URIEL heard the thump of mortar fire and saw the darts of shells as they rose on a ballistic trajectory. In the time it took them to reach the apex of their climb, he saw they would land short.

'Incoming!' he yelled.

The mountain itself seemed to shake with the concussive detonations. A second salvo launched before the echoes of the first had died. Whickering fragments and tendrils of phosphorescent light burst from each shell as they landed with bone-jarring force, sending storms of rock splinters flying through the air alongside the shrapnel.

Shells landed in a string of roaring booms, marching in disciplined volleys towards the Ultramarines. Uriel kept his head down as the ground convulsed with each burst of strikes.

They had no choice but to wait for Dardino's signal and take the punishment the enemy commander was dishing out. To advance forward through concentrated mortar fire into the teeth of enemy guns was tantamount to suicide and Uriel had no desire to see his command end in such a way.

Sheets of flame rose from each impact, craters blasted into the soil of the mountain spewing thick smoke from the flames. Uriel caught the stink of promethium on the air and frowned in puzzlement. Incendiaries? Was the enemy commander mad? Against lightly armoured troops, incendiaries would sow havoc and panic, but against warriors clad in power armour they were almost useless. Then he realised that the enemy commander was PDF and almost certainly had no prior experience fighting Space Marines.

Huge banks of black smoke rose from burning streams of fuel, drifting and spreading slowly in the mountain breeze and obscuring the combatants from one another. The Ultramarines had just been given the cover they sorely desired.

SERGEANT DARDINO PUNCHED his fist through the steel of the vent tube and peeled it back with powerful sweeps of his arms. Daylight flooded the rifled metal vent and he leaned out, training his bolt pistol upwards lest anyone was keeping a watchful eye on this portion of the mineshaft.

Before him, he saw a mass of cables descending into darkness and deep adamantium girders spanning the huge width of the mine, supporting lifting gear and dozens of thick-girthed vent tubes like the one he now pushed himself clear of.

He dropped onto the huge adamantium beam the vent pipe was bolted to and motioned for the rest of his squad to join him. One by one, the warriors of his assault squad clambered out onto the beam. Their armour was scorched and blackened from the mine's exhaust fumes. The status runes on Dardino's visor told him that his rebreather units were badly clogged.

They were deep within the cylindrical shaft of the mine, the sky a bright disc some five hundred metres above them. Too far for jump packs.

He edged out along the beam, trying not to look down into the impenetrable darkness of the mine, knowing that it dropped over nine kilometres. He holstered his pistol and turned to the nine men of his squad.

'There's only one way up. Follow me!' he ordered and leapt into the centre of the mine, grabbing onto the cables hanging from the lip of the crater nearly half a kilometre above them.

Hand over hand, Sergeant Dardino and his men began climbing back to the surface.

URIEL ROSE FROM cover and shouted, 'Men of the Emperor, forwards!'

He sprinted uphill, the augmented muscles of his power armour carrying him forwards at a terrifying rate. With a roar of defiance, the Ultramarines followed their captain into the smoke from the incendiary shells, leaping over burning pools of superheated fuel.

Mortar rounds continued to drop, most falling behind them, the artillerymen unable to correctly shift their fire.

Uriel could hear the snap of lasgun fire and crack of heavier weapons, but it was uncoordinated and sporadic. A shot grazed the top of his shoulder guard, but most of the fire was too high, further proof that they were up against poor opposition. Firing downhill, most soldiers tended to shoot high.

Uriel burst from the clouds of smoke, blinking in the sudden brightness. Gunfire leapt out to meet them, plucking at their armour and a handful of warriors fell, but all picked themselves up and charged onwards.

A missile lanced out and struck Sergeant Nivaneus, a veteran of the Thracian campaign, disintegrating his upper body in a burst of crimson. Autocannon fire sprayed a group of Space Marines from Sergeant Elerna's squad. Four went down; only two got back up.

One of the survivors had lost his right arm, but continued upwards, picking up his pistol with his remaining hand and firing as he ran.

'Spread out, don't bunch up!' yelled Uriel as the autocannon fired again.

MAJOR BEXTOR PUNCHED the air as the autocannon cut a swathe through the Ultramarines' ranks. He fired over the parapet into the charging warriors.

This was his first battle and he'd begun to enjoy himself immensely. They were holding off the Space Marines, though the analytical part of his brain told him that there were less coming at his position than had begun the assault.

He attributed this to his initial awe at the size and apparent power of the Space Marines, but now he had their measure and they did not seem nearly so fearsome. He would be a hero! The man who had beaten the Ultramarines. The men would tell tales of this battle in the regimental mess hall for decades to come.

Bextor reached for another energy cell, smiling at the trooper next to him.

'Soon see these buggers off, eh, son?' he joked.

The boy's head exploded, showering Bextor with blood and brains and he fell back, repulsed beyond words at the horrid death of the trooper. He lost his balance and fell from the firing step, thudding painfully into the hard-packed ground. He turned in the direction the shot had come from in time to see hulking figures clamber over the lip of the mine shaft and begin the systematic butchery of his soldiers.

Blackened giants with hideously grinning masks of fury, they struck his line like a thunderbolt, hacking men in two with great sweeps of shrieking swords or pumping explosive rounds into their bodies from roaring pistols.

He rolled onto his side, feeling blood run from a gash in his forehead, weeping in terror at these dark nightmares that had emerged from the bowels of the planet. Chattering gunfire ripped his men to pieces and swords surely forged in the heart of Chaos chopped and chopped, severing limbs and ending lives.

All around him, his men were screaming and dying. Weakly he pushed himself to his feet and picked up his fallen lasgun. Death surrounded him, but he vowed he would take one of these devils screaming into hell with him.

He heard a crashing impact behind him and spun. A black shape emerged from the smoke with a grinning skull mask, raising a golden weapon high. Bextor felt his knees sag in terror and his gaze fixed upon the winged eagle atop the golden staff the black armoured figure held.

Its red eyes seemed to shine the colour of blood as its energy-wreathed edge clove him in two.

VIRGIL ORTEGA FOUGHT through the pain of his shattered ribs as he fired around the door at the PDF troopers. The corridor outside the armoury was thick with dead bodies and smoke, both sides firing blindly into the stinking blue cordite fog in the hope of hitting something.

The twin linked autocannons had not proved as useful as they had hoped, the furious recoil tearing the guns loose from their mount and demolishing most of the barricade in a hail of explosive rounds. It had brought a brief respite in the fighting, however, as the PDF proved reluctant to advance into the jaws of such a weapon. It had taken them several minutes to realise that it was no longer a threat.

In the intervening time, Collix and Ortega pulled the last two surviving judges back into the armoury itself. With the barricade mostly gone there was no realistic way to hold the corridor.

Ortega hurled a pair of grenades around the door, ducking back as the explosion filled the passageway outside with shrapnel and screams.

Collix skidded next to him, handing him a canvas satchel filled with shotgun shells and clips of bolter ammunition for his pistol.

'At least there's no shortage of ammo,' grunted Ortega.

Collix nodded, 'Or traitorous curs to fire it at.'

Ortega grinned and pushed himself to his feet as he heard muffled shouts from beyond the armoury doors.

'There is no escaping the Emperor's justice, even in death!' he shouted to their attackers, wincing as his cracked ribs flared painfully.

They jogged back to a hastily constructed barricade of emptied ammo crates and tipped-over racking, taking up position as they waited for the inevitable next attack. A wealth of weaponry lay clustered behind the barricade along with a box of each weapon's ammunition. Lasguns, bolters, autoguns, two missile launchers, a grenade launcher, a lascannon and six heavy bolters.

It was an impressive array of guns, but with only four of them left alive, most of the weapons would remain unfired. Thirty metres behind them, their surviving compatriots worked furiously to rig the armoury for destruction. Without detonators much of the explosive stored here was useless, but the time that had been bought with Arbites' lives had not been wasted.

At key points throughout the cavern, they'd stacked opened crates of ammo and ordnance in large piles, placing a cluster of grenades in the centre of each stockpile, the pins pulled and arming mechanisms wired to the vox-caster's battery unit.

Within minutes, they should have a crude but effective method of setting off a chain reaction that would cook off every shred of ammo in the cavern.

THE CHAMBER OF the god was far smaller than Kasimir de Valtos had imagined, but the sense of power it contained was enormous. Its walls sloped inwards to a golden point above the chamber's exact centre, where a rectangular oblong of smooth black obsidian rested, magnificent in its solitude. The base of each wall was lined with rectangular alcoves, each containing a skeletal figure, identical to those his workers had pulled from the outer chamber of the tomb complex some months ago.

Even the eldar and Vendare Taloun looked impressed with the chamber, staring in wonder at this alien structure that had been buried beneath the surface of Pavonis for sixty million years.

'It's magnificent,' de Valtos breathed, moving to stand before one of the alcoves. The skeletal warrior within was as lifeless as the ones back at his house, its sheen dulled with a verdigris stain. Unlike the ones in his possession, these carried bizarre looking rifles, their barrels coated in dust. It was quite fascinating and he looked forward to learning more of these strange creatures when he was free of the shackles of mortality.

Enthralled by the rows of warriors as he was, he could not deny the diabolical attraction of the central sarcophagus and marched across the echoing chamber towards it.

It was enormous, fully five metres on its long edge, and as he drew nearer he saw that its surface was not smooth at all, but inscribed with runic symbols and pitted with precisely shaped indentations. His heart pounded as he recognised them as the same as the ones he had read beneath the ruins of Cthelmax.

The same runes he had been scouring the sector for since that day.

Channels cut in the floor radiated from the sarcophagus, each twisting in precise geometric patterns towards the wall alcoves.

Kesharq stood alongside him and raised the visor of his helmet. Despite the immobile nature of his face and the crudely stitched bullet wound on his cheek, de Valtos could see the hunger in the alien's eyes.

'You feel it too, don't you?' he whispered.

Kesharq sneered, quickly masking his emotions and shook his head. 'I merely wish to secure the device and be away.'

'You're lying,' giggled de Valtos. 'I can see it in your eyes. You want this as much as I.'

'Does it matter? Let us be about our business.'

De Valtos wagged his finger below the eldar warrior's nose and jerked his head in the direction of the silver case carried by his warriors.

'Very well. Give me the pieces you secured for me and I shall unlock the key to the weapon.'

Kesharq held de Valtos's stare before nodding curtly. The alien carried the silver box forward, depositing it before his leader. Kesharq opened the box without taking his eyes from de Valtos and said, 'How do I know I can trust you?'

'You can trust me as much as I trust you, my dear Kesharq.'

He could see the alien visibly strain to hold his hand away from his pistol, but knew that it would not dare shoot him until he had summoned the *Nightbringer* from the shadowy realm it now occupied.

Anchored to Pavonis by ancient science, it had remained a ghost ship in this sector since the day it had been lost.

De Valtos knew that today would see it reborn, and the galaxy would mourn its second coming.

COLLIX WAS DYING. Scything grenade fragments had blown out a chunk of his belly and his guts were leaking from his armour across the floor of the armoury. The sergeant propped himself against the barricade, firing a heavy bolter, though the recoil caused him to grunt in pain with each shot. Ortega's left arm hung uselessly at his side, a lasbolt having all but severed it at the elbow.

He fired and racked his shotgun one handed, shouting the Litanies of Justice at the rebel troopers as they broke themselves against their stubborn defence.

The explosives were rigged and now all that remained was to detonate them. There was no choice any more. Virgil had hoped that they could defend the place long enough for loyalist forces to relieve them, but that didn't seem likely any more.

He and Collix were all that was left. The other judges were dead, killed in the last attack, and now it was down to them.

Ortega had always wondered how death would come, and now that it was here, he found that it was not something to be feared, but to be embraced. It would bring the righteous wrath of the Emperor upon those who thought they could transgress His laws.

He could hear rebel officers gathering their men for another charge. Collix painfully dragged a fresh belt of bolter ammunition from the ammo crate into the weapon's smoking breech, his face ashen and twisted in pain. The shells kept slipping in his bloody hands and Ortega reached over to help his sergeant.

'Thanks, sir,' nodded Collix, closing the breech. 'Couldn't quite get it.'

'You've done well, sergeant,' said Virgil.

Collix heard the finality in Ortega's words and glanced over at the battery pack detonator they'd rigged.

'It's time then?'

'Yes, I think it is.'

The sergeant nodded, cocking the heavy bolter and drawing himself upright as much as his wounded body would allow. He saluted weakly and said, 'It has been an honour to serve with you, sir.'

Virgil returned the salute and took Collix's outstretched hand, gripping it firmly. He nodded over the barricade.

He smiled imperceptibly. 'You would have made a fine officer I think, Judge Collix.'

'I know,' replied Collix, 'Judge Captain within four years I thought. That was my plan anyway.'

'Four years? Six maybe. I think Sharben would have given you a run for your money in the promotion stakes.'

Collix nodded. 'Maybe, but think how my courageous actions here will help my chances for promotion.'

'Good point,' conceded Ortega. 'Remind me to mention it to the chief when we get out of here.'

'I'll hold you to that, sir.'

Both men turned serious and Ortega said, 'Just give me enough time to blow this place.'

Collix nodded, pulling the gun's stock hard against his shoulder and sighting on the wide doors to the armoury.

Virgil stumbled towards the vox-caster. The sharp crack of bolter fire and lasbolts heralded the next attack, but he did not dare look back.

Flashes of lasgun fire snapped around him, a round clipping his thigh. He yelled in pain as another bolt took him high in the back, sending him crashing to the floor. His wounded arm hit hard and he rolled, fighting to remain conscious over the agony that engulfed him.

He heard Collix shouting in anger over the storm of gunfire and willed the sergeant to give him just a little more time. He crawled towards the vox-caster, trailing a lake of blood from his ruptured body.

A massive explosion showered him with splintered wood, metal and chunks of rock. The PDF had finally managed to bring up some heavy weaponry and all that was left of the barricade was a smoking heap of mangled metal and bodies.

Troops began pouring into the armoury, galvanised by the destruction of their foe.

Ortega snarled and pulled himself forwards.

Another lasbolt struck him in the back.

He wrapped his arms around the vox-caster as a flurry of lasgun shots blasted through his armour and ripped him apart.

The last thing Virgil Ortega managed before death claimed him was to thumb the activation rune on the vox-caster, sending a jolt of power along the insulated wire towards the detonators of sixty grenades.

VIRGIL ORTEGA WAS dead before the first shockwave of the armoury's detonation even reached his body, but the results were more spectacular than he could ever have hoped.

Within seconds of his activating the vox-caster, the grenades he and his men had planted detonated the vast swathe of weapons and ammunition stored beneath the palace.

Even before the initial blasts had faded, a lethal chain reaction had begun.

Heat and vibration sensors registered the explosions and initiated containment procedures, but so rapid was the escalation of destruction that they could not even begin to cope with the vast forces Virgil had unleashed.

At first the inhabitants of Brandon Gate thought they were being bombarded again by the *Vae Victus* and waited in fear for the next salvo of magma bombs to rain down from the heavens.

The massive shockwave swept outwards through the ground with the force of an earthquake, shaking the entire city with the violence of the underground blast. Geysers of flame roared upwards from cracks ripped in the streets and entire districts vanished as the force of the explosion spread, incinerating buildings, people and tanks in seconds.

Shells streaked skyward, falling amid the city like deadly fireworks, adding to the panic and destruction. A number of cartel force commanders believed themselves to be under attack, either from newly arrived loyalist forces or treacherous rival cartels, and vicious tank battles erupted as decades of mistrust and political infighting was fought out on the streets of Brandon Gate.

Tanks from the Vergen cartel fought those of the Abrogas, who fought the de Valtos, who fought the Honan, who fought anyone who came in range. In the confusion, it took the commanders more than an hour to restore command and control, by which time over fifty tanks had been destroyed or taken out of action.

The unstable structure of the Arbites precinct house rumbled deafeningly, huge chunks of loosened rockcrete tumbling from its face as the esplanade cracked and whole sections were swallowed. PDF tanks revved their engines madly, vainly trying to escape the destruction, but too slow to avoid the tipping ground and collapsing building.

The statues in Liberation Square rocked on their pedestals, all but the effigy of the Emperor in its centre crashing into the square.

The Imperial palace shook to its foundations as forces it was never meant to endure slammed into it, disintegrating yet more of its already weakened structure. Whole wings collapsed in roiling clouds of dust, burying entire companies of PDF troopers beneath tonnes of smashed marble.

A vast crater yawned between the Arbites precinct house and the palace, a section of the defensive wall slumping downwards into the flaming hell of the destroyed armoury. Enormous flames licked skyward amid a gigantic pillar of smoke. Within seconds Brandon Gate looked as though it had been under siege for weeks.

In a single stroke, Virgil Ortega's sacrifice had denied the rebels the largest cache of weapons and military supplies on Pavonis.

URIEL STARED INTO the darkness of the mineshaft, a hundred metre wide wound on the face of the planet as the two Thunderhawks towards them. The circumference of the shaft was lined with massive cranes and cantilevered elevator gear to transport workers and materials both to and from the mine galleries below.

Huge funicular elevator cars secured to massive rails descended into the depths of the planet, each one capable of holding over a hundred men.

A winch wheel and control room, supported on a central pair of beams, hung over the pit, clusters of cables dropping into the darkness of the mineshaft.

When Dardino's infiltrators had torn into the defences from behind, the soldiers were doomed. Caught between the hammer and anvil of the Ultramarines attack they had had no chance.

He recalled the pride that had filled him as he watched his men follow him across the walls, cutting down the foe with righteous fury and holy purpose. They had followed him unquestioningly into battle and the zeal they had displayed was the equal of anything he had ever witnessed. Uriel felt humbled by the honour these men had brought to the company this day.

The lead Thunderhawk touched down in a howling cloud of dust and exhaust fumes, its front ramp dropping almost as soon as its engines began powering down.

Ario Barzano and a number of the thralls from the *Vae Victus* strode out to meet Uriel. The inquisitor's face was alight with anticipation. He had requisitioned a plasma pistol and power knife from the strike cruiser's armoury.

'Well done, Uriel, well done!' he beamed, glancing over at the mineshaft and the elevators.

'Thank you, inquisitor, but we're not done yet.'

'No, of course not, Uriel. But soon, eh?'

Uriel nodded, catching the inquisitor's confidence. He shouted over to his warriors. 'Get the rappelling gear disengaged from the gunships. Hurry!'

'Rappelling gear?' repeated Barzano. 'You can't be serious, Uriel, that shaft's nearly ten kilometres deep. It's far too deep to use ropes.' He pointed to the hulking form of the workers' elevator. 'What about that? We can use that surely?'

Uriel shook his head. 'No, the rebels are sure to have men stationed at the base of the mine. Anyone who goes down in that will either be stranded half way or gunned down the moment they hit the bottom.'

'So how do you intend to get down?'

Uriel turned the inquisitor around, marching him back to the Thunderhawk, where the Ultramarines were stripping blackened metallic cylinders from each rappelling rope.

'We shall use these,' said Uriel snapping one of the units from a rope. It resembled a plain cylinder of metal with a textured hand grip on its outside surface and a wide, toothed groove cut vertically along its length.

The device fitted snugly into Uriel's palm and as he clenched his fist the 'teeth' in the central groove snapped back inside the cylinder. As he released his grip, they clamped back into the groove.

'We use these for high-speed drops where we cannot use jump packs. We shall attach them to the lifting gear cables and drop along their length into the mine, achieving surprise on any defenders below.'

'You'll drop, one-handed, for ten thousand metres?'

Uriel nodded with a wry grin.

'And how, dear boy, do you intend that I get down?'

'You intend to come too?'

'Of course, you don't think after all that's happened I'm going to miss the chance to see you take down de Valtos do you?'

'Very well,' answered Uriel, walking the inquisitor towards the worker elevator. 'Then you will join us after we have dropped. I calculate it will take us almost five minutes to drop the ten kilometres to the bottom of the mine. Wait for that long until beginning your descent. After all, we will need a means of getting back to the surface.'

Barzano clearly did not like the idea of travelling down in the elevator car, but could see that there was no other way for him to reach the bottom of the mine. He certainly could not descend in the same manner as the Ultramarines. Reluctantly, he nodded.

'Very well, Uriel,' said Barzano, unsnapping the catch on his pistol holster, 'shall we?'

'Aye,' snarled the Ultramarine. 'Let's finish this.'

THE ULTRAMARINES WOULD descend in four waves, each following five seconds after the one before it. Uriel sat on the central beam, the massive winch wheel beside his right shoulder and his armoured legs dangling into the infinite darkness before him.

He and the first wave of warriors clambered down the beam, sliding the rappelling clamps over the elevator cables and clenching their fists around them, locking them in place, ready for the drop.

Uriel licked his suddenly dry lips as a sudden sense of vertigo seized him. He looked over his shoulder towards Ario Barzano in the worker elevator and sketched the Inquisitor a salute.

Barzano returned the salute.

Uriel checked left and right, to make sure the first wave was ready.

Taking a deep breath, he shouted, 'Now!' and dropped into the depths of the world.

THE METAL FELT warm to the touch, soft and yielding despite the fact that Kasimir de Valtos knew it was stronger than adamantium. Reverently, he lifted the first piece from the box and turned it in his hands, inspecting every centimetre of its shimmering surface. He had spent years of his life in search of these pieces and to see them now before him took his breath away.

Reluctantly, he tore his eyes from the object and turned to the sarcophagus, sensing the power that lay within and the attraction the metal had for it. He felt the object twitching in his hands and watched, amazed as its surface began to flow like mercury, reshaping itself into some new, altered form. Holding the glimmering metal before him like an offering, he took a hesitant step towards the sarcophagus, unsure as to whether he or the metal was more anxious.

The metal's malleable form settled into that of a flat, circular disc, like a cogwheel, yet with a subtle wrongness to its angles.

De Valtos could see the mirror of its form on the side of the sarcophagus facing him and knelt beside the dark oblong, pressing the metal into its surface. It flowed from his fingers, slipping easily into the perfectly sized niche. The metal liquefied once more, running and spreading in glittering silver trails across the surface of the sarcophagus, trickling along the patterns carved there.

Abruptly the glistening trails stopped, straining as though at the end of their elasticity, and de Valtos knew what he had to do next. He dragged the silver box over to the sarcophagus, hearing the metal fragments within clattering together, as though excited about the prospect of returning to the bosom of their maker.

As he lifted each piece, its structure rebelled from its original form, transforming into something new, shaping itself into the form required to fit into yet another niche on the sarcophagus's side. Working as fast as he could, de Valtos placed each piece of the living metal into its matching niche. As each piece was added, the quicksilver lines reached further around the basalt obelisk, an interconnecting web of angular lines and complex geometries.

Finally, he lifted the last piece from the box, a slender cruciform shape with a flattened, hooped top, and circled the sarcophagus, searching for its place. This final piece alone retained its initial form and he could find no similarly shaped niche in which to place it. Then de Valtos smiled, standing on tiptoe to find the metal's exact shape carved on the thick slab that formed the lid of the sarcophagus. He reached over and dropped it into place, stepping back to admire the beauty of the rippling silver structure before him. The sarcophagus lay wrapped in a glittering web, lines of the living metal interwoven across its surface and glowing with their own internal light.

'Now what?' whispered Kesharq.

'Now we wait,' answered de Valtos.

'For what?'

'For the rebirth of a creature older than time.'

'And the *Nightbringer*? What of it?'

De Valtos smiled, humourlessly. 'Do not worry, my dear Archon. Everything is unfolding as I have planned. The ship will soon be ours. And then we–'

His voice trailed away as a deep, bass thrumming suddenly tolled from the very air, like the beating of an incomprehensibly vast heart. Nervous PDF troopers raised their rifles as the pulsing rumble sounded again, louder.

'What's happening?' snapped Kesharq.

De Valtos didn't answer, too intent on the silver lines draining from the sarcophagus and running in eager streams through the channels on the floor. Liquid rivulets of silver flowed from the centre of the chamber towards the alcoves that surrounded them, four running from the chamber towards the antechamber outside.

The streams ran up the walls, spilling into each alcove.

Vendare Taloun dropped to his knees, a prayer to the Emperor spilling from his lips.

'Stand firm!' shouted a PDF sergeant, as several troopers began backing towards the door. The rumbling heartbeat pounded the air and de Valtos could feel a power of ages past seeping into the chamber as the gold cap at the apex of the ceiling began to glow with a ghostly luminescence.

Archon Kesharq gripped his axe tightly, scanning the room for the source of the booming vibrations. Kasimir de Valtos moved to stand beside the sarcophagus, placing his hands on its warm, throbbing side.

A cry of terror sounded.

He looked up to see the skeletal guardians of the tomb take a single, perfect step down from their alcoves, each warrior acting in absolute concert with its silent brethren. Were these the advance guard of the creature he had awoken?

A gleam of movement and light at the entrance to the chamber caught his eye and he watched as the four silent guardians from the antechamber entered the tomb, their movements smooth and unhurried. Each figure's androgynous features remained expressionless, but they carried their strange copper staffs threateningly before them.

A spectral light glittered within each of the tomb's guardians, pulsing in time with the booming heartbeat, yet none moved, content just to watch the intruders within their sanctuary.

With a noise like thunder, a great crack tore down the middle of the slab on top of the tomb. Questing tendrils of dark smoke seeped from within and de Valtos staggered back, falling to his knees as his mind blazed with unbidden thoughts of death and destruction. He reeled under the sensory overload of pain and suffering radiating from the sarcophagus.

Slowly, the sarcophagus began to unravel into wisps of smoky darkness.

ʊ
EIGHTEEN

DEEPER AND DEEPER into the surface of Pavonis they fell, dropping past nine thousand metres and still going. Uriel saw a point of light below him and ordered the Ultramarines to begin slowing their descent.

He loosened the grip on his rappelling clamp, orange sparks flaring as the teeth dug into the thick wire cables. The speed of his depth counter's revolutions began to slow and Uriel watched as the collection of lights below him resolved into glow-globes and a lighted portion of tunnel. There were men there, looking up in confusion at the strange sight of sputtering sparks above them. Uriel didn't give them time to realise what they were seeing and released his grip on the rappelling clamp, dropping the last ten metres in free fall.

His armoured weight smashed down onto the first trooper, killing him before he knew what had happened. Uriel rolled, firing his pistol in quick bursts.

More Ultramarines dropped around him, quickly fanning out from the base of the mineshaft, pistols blasting and chainswords roaring.

There were forty troopers stationed at the bottom of the shaft, weapons trained at the elevator car from behind sandbagged gun nests. Gunfire blasted out to meet the attacking Ultramarines, bullets and las-bolts filling the air. Smoke billowed and blistering gouts of steam and exhaust gasses belched from shattered vents and the air grew dense with fumes.

Three powerful strides and Uriel was over the defences into the first gun nest, chopping left and right with his chainsword. A trooper brought his lasgun up.

Uriel hacked through the barrel, his reverse stroke chopping the man's head from his shoulders. In a bloodthirsty frenzy, he killed every enemy around him, savage joy flooding through him. He shot and cut his way through ten men before finally there were no more foes in reach. The fury and surprise of the Space Marine assault could not be resisted and within minutes the defenders were dead, their position now their tomb.

Uriel rejoiced in the bloodshed and his senses flooded with the urge to kill and destroy. He roared with primal rage, picturing the slaughter of hundreds, thousands of enemies, seeing their split-open corpses, flies and carrion feasting on their butchered flesh. Prisoners butchered and their blood drunk as a fine wine was his only desire and–

Uriel fell suddenly to his knees, dropping his pistol and sword as the horrific images continued to pour into his mind. He roared in anger, fighting against the torrent of filth that washed over him with all the mental discipline his training had granted him.

Gradually, he forced the images of death and murder from his mind, straining to keep the walls around his thoughts impenetrable. He could see his men fighting the same mental battle and shouted, 'Courage and honour! You are Ultramarines! Stand firm! These things you see are not your own. They belong to the creature we have come to slay! Fight them!'

One by one, the Ultramarines picked themselves up, dazed and repulsed by the horrifying visions that assailed them.

He voxed a swift acknowledgement to Barzano on the surface and watched the controls for the lift wink to life as the elevator began its rapid descent.

Pasanius's and Dardino's warriors moved to secure the perimeter while Squad Venasus checked the bodies of the fallen to ensure there were no survivors, though Uriel could see that this was unnecessary. The fury of their attack had been fuelled by unnatural alien desires and the men they had killed were little more than chunks of bloody meat. Uriel felt shame at the mindless violence they had unleashed, and not even the knowledge that their actions had been swayed by an alien power made it easier to bear the knowledge that the capacity for such wanton slaughter existed deep within them all.

He shook his head, whispering a mantra of steadfastness.

Now that he had time to determine the properties of their position, Uriel's enhanced senses could detect the rising levels of combustible fumes. Gunfire and explosions had shattered the venting mechanism here and the build-up of fumes, while non-lethal to a Space Marine, would eventually reach dangerous levels for ordinary humans.

Four passages radiated in the direction of the compass points. Palpable waves of horror emanated from the entrance to the eastern tunnel. Uriel could taste it on the air and within his bones, but kept the feeling at bay.

His thoughts still echoed with images of violence and death, torture and mutilation. Even if Barzano had not told him about the being that slept below these mountains, Uriel would have known immediately that this was the route they must take.

Uriel stood in the tunnel mouth, forcing the images of burned bodies, severed limbs and destroyed civilisations from his mind. They were not his thoughts. The taint of them in his head sickened him, but they steeled him to face the foe that lay ahead.

Uriel turned to face his men, pride burning through the hateful images in his head.

'Warriors of Ultramar, you have proven yourselves men of valour and strength, and we will soon face an enemy the likes of which has not been seen for uncounted years in the Emperor's realm. You can feel its presence clawing at your mind even now. But you must be strong: resist the impulses it creates within you. Remember that you are Space Marines, holy warriors of the Emperor, and that it is our duty to Him and our primarch that gives us our strength, courage and faith. This fight is not yet won. We must steel ourselves for the final test, where each of us must look within and discover the true limit of courage. Never forget that every man is important; every man can make a difference.'

Uriel raised his sword, its blooded edge reflecting the light of the glow-globes. 'Are you ready to be those men?' The Ultramarines roared in affirmation.

The high-speed elevator whined to halt at the base of the mineshaft and Uriel lowered his sword as Barzano stepped out. The inquisitor stumbled, raising his hands to his forehead. Uriel could scarce imagine what a terrible place this must be for the empathic inquisitor.

Barzano walked stiffly towards Uriel, his face lined with the strain of holding the horrific visions at bay.

'By the Emperor, can you feel its power?' whispered Barzano.

Uriel nodded. 'I feel it. The quicker we can be gone from this place the better.'

'My sentiments exactly, my friend,' replied Barzano, staring in revulsion down the eastern tunnel. He pressed the activation stud of the power knife and drew his pistol.

'Time to finish this, eh, Uriel?'

'Yes. Time indeed.'

Fighting the sickening power that pressed against their minds, the Ultramarines set off towards the tomb of the Nightbringer.

BLACKENED FINGERS SLID over the edge of the sarcophagus, long, dirt encrusted nails and shroud wrapped arms following as the Nightbringer arose from its tomb. Kasimir de Valtos climbed to his feet, smiling as the thoughts within his head shrieked with horrors he had not dreamed existed. Blood, death, suffering, mutilation and torment unknown for millions of years filled his skull; it felt so good.

The PDF soldiers fell to the ground scrabbling at their eyes, their pitiful screams rending the air as they sought to pluck out the horrific things in their heads. Vendare Taloun fainted dead away and even the loathsome eldar appeared to be in awe of the magnificent creature that was slowly revealing itself.

Kesharq gripped Kasimir's arm, his alien face enraptured.

'It's wondrous,' he breathed.

Kasimir nodded as the Nightbringer gripped the side of the sarcophagus and pulled itself upwards. Slowly its massive head cleared the edge of its tomb and Kasimir de Valtos stared into the face of death.

URIEL FOUGHT AGAINST the pulsing waves of violence that crashed against his mind, gripping his chainsword tight. From up ahead he could hear the screaming of the damned and he steeled himself for the coming confrontation. Barzano ran beside him, pale and drawn.

The tunnel dipped downwards, the rock giving way to sloping walls of smooth black obsidian. The wailing screams from ahead tore at Uriel's mind, feeding the evil that pounded relentlessly on his thoughts.

He entered a square room with two empty alcoves on either side. He could feel that the chamber beyond was the source of the evil in his head and a miasma of gritty darkness filled the air within.

There was nothing to be gained by stealth at this point; fast, lethal force was what was needed now.

Uriel charged into the pyramid-chamber of the Nightbringer, to find a scene of utter bedlam.

PDF troopers convulsed on the chamber's floor, faces bloody where nails and fingers had ripped eyes from heads. Those men still conscious beat themselves bloody with broken fists, mewling in terror at nightmares only they could see.

A ring of metallic skeletal beings advanced implacably towards a central block of dissolving black stone where a group of heavily armed eldar surrounded a jade-armoured warrior, the same one he had fought on the eldar space ship over Caernus IV. Kasimir de Valtos and a dark haired alien female sheltered in their midst.

He spared this scene but a cursory glance as he saw the huge creature pulling itself free of its stone prison. Swathed in rotted robes, it rose up from its tomb, the solid stone unravelling atom by atom and reshaping itself in a swirling black shroud.

More and more of the black stone disintegrated to form the concealing darkness of the creature. Soon all that was left was the slab of the tomb with the final piece of the metal burning brightly in its surface.

Uriel had a barely perceived vision of a gaunt, mouldering face with twin pits of yellow glowing weakly from within. There was insanity and a raging, unquenchable thirst for suffering in those eyes. A cloak of ghostly darkness hid its true form, a pair of rotted, bandage-swathed arms reaching from its nebulous outline. One limb ended in long, grave-dirt encrusted talons, the other in what appeared to be a huge blade of unnatural darkness, angled like a vast scythe.

As the creature rose to its full height, Uriel saw that it towered above the mortals beneath it; swirling eddies of darkness at its base snaking around the bodies of those not quick enough to escape its grasp.

The cloak of darkness swept two of the alien warriors up. The scythe arm flashed, passing through their armour and bodies with ease, and their withered corpses dropped, no more than shrivelled sacks of bone.

The aliens scattered as another of their number was engulfed by the vast alien. The alabaster figures with the copper staffs took their place at their master's side, their perfect faces devoid of life and animation.

'De Valtos!' yelled Barzano. 'By the Emperor's soul, do you know what you've done?'

Kasimir de Valtos screamed in triumph as the Nightbringer bloated the chamber with dark energies, filling his mind with the most wondrous things imaginable. The eldar warriors fell back towards the Ultramarines, ready to fight their way clear of this nightmare they found themselves within.

But the Nightbringer was hungry for soul morsels, the darkness around its form swelling and billowing as though plucked by invisible winds. A deep throbbing beat filled the chamber as the metallic skeleton warriors turned their attention to the interlopers within their master's chambers.

Uriel shuddered in revulsion as the skeletal creatures marched towards him, raising their strange weapons in perfect unison. He dived out of the way, rolling and lashing out at the nearest warrior, the chainsword hacking through its legs and toppling it. He sprang to his feet as the metallic warriors opened fire.

Uriel watched with horror as Sergeant Venasus shuddered under an invisible impact, the fabric of his armour peeling away in flayed layers, his flesh following with horrifying rapidity. The sergeant dropped to his knees as his musculature was revealed then stripped away until nothing but his crouching skeleton remained.

Another Ultramarine died in agony as his body was stripped, layer by layer, by the skull-faced warriors' weapons. Clawed hands grasped at Uriel, tearing at his armour, and he spun to face the metal skeleton he had just felled, the metal of its body re-knitting even as he watched.

He lashed out with his sword and put a bolt round through its ribcage. The warrior fell once more, but Uriel pounded the machine to fragments beneath his boot lest it somehow manage to regenerate once more. All around him was chaos.

Space Marines grappled with the metallic skeletons and were, for the most part winning, smashing them to the ground and blasting them apart with bolter fire. Sergeant Learchus tore one apart with his bare hands, smashing its skull to destruction against the floor.

But many of the deathly creatures simply picked themselves up once more, untroubled by wounds that would have killed a man twice over. Barzano fought beside Uriel, his glowing knife cutting a swathe through the enemy. His face was ashen and his movements slowing as the agony of his wounds began overcoming the pain balms.

The eldar fought alongside them and as Uriel kicked out at another foe, he kept a close eye on the aliens, ready to turn on them the second the machine warriors had been despatched. Their jade-armoured leader fought and killed with a deadly grace, his axe lashing out in a dizzying spiral of death. Wherever he struck a machine collapsed and each blow struck brought a screeching cry from the swirling darkness at the chamber's centre. But to Uriel it sounded more like a sound of amusement rather than displeasure.

The excrents snapped and bit, bearing their master's foes to the ground by sheer weight of numbers. The hideous alien weapons stripped great swathes of flesh from their deformed frames, but they fought on, oblivious to the ruin of their anatomy, until there was little left save scraps of torn, convulsing body parts.

Uriel fought like he had never fought before, cutting, shooting and killing with a skill he had not known he possessed. His reflexes were honed to perfection. He dodged killing thrusts and lethal blows with preternatural speed, deflecting clawed hands and shattering metal skulls with dazzling skill.

The last of the metal warriors were smashed to ruins, their gleaming limbs and bodies scattered in pieces across the chamber's floor. Uriel heaved a painful breath, his side burning where an alien rifle had stripped away a portion of his armour and flesh. Clotted blood caked his head and armour where grasping hands had ripped into him.

A strange calm settled as Space Marines and eldar faced one another across the chamber. The Nightbringer stood unmoving beside the slab of what had been the top of its tomb, the cruciform shaped piece of metal still glowing with eldritch fire.

Barzano joined Uriel, his breathing ragged and uneven. Uriel saw the wound on his arm had reopened, blood leaking through the synthflesh bandage.

Kasimir de Valtos stood in the undulating shadow of the Nightbringer, his features twisted in savage glee.

He raised a finger to point at the Ultramarines and screamed, 'Destroy them! I command you!'

Whether the words were aimed at the eldar or the vast alien and its bodyguards, Uriel did not know, but it was the eldar who leapt forwards. Their leader made straight for him, his war-axe raised high.

The Ultramarines roared and charged to meet them, the chamber ringing with the clash of arms as battle was joined once more.

Uriel blocked a cut and stepped in to hammer his fist into the side of the alien's helmet. His foe ducked, slamming the barbed haft of his axe into Uriel's belly, ripping a long gash in his armour.

Uriel gasped in pain, powering the hilt of his sword into Kesharq's back, slamming the alien to the floor. He reversed the grip on his sword and spun, hammering the roaring chain blade downwards.

His opponent was no longer there, but somersaulting to his feet and spinning his axe at Uriel's head. A burst of flaring light exploded as Barzano's knife intercepted the blow and Uriel took advantage of the alien's momentary distraction to smash his sword into his head.

Kesharq saw it coming and twisted his neck, robbing the blow of much of its power. The whirring teeth ripped off his helmet, the dented metal catching on the loose skin of his face and tearing it free in a wash of blood.

Kesharq screamed in pain, his fleshless face hideously revealed. He staggered back, regaining his balance and blocked Barzano's reverse cut, deflecting the blade away from him and hammering his axe into the inquisitor's chest.

Bones shattered as the axe clove downwards through Barzano's ribcage, exiting in a bloody spray above his hip. Barzano fell, the power knife dropping from his hand.

Uriel screamed a denial, slashing at the alien leader's back. Kesharq spun away from the blow, trapping Uriel's sword in the jagged barbs of the axe blade and snapping it with a flick of his wrist. Before he could reverse the stroke, Uriel dived forwards, over Barzano's body, and swept up the fallen inquisitor's blade in time to deflect a sweep meant to remove his head.

Kesharq came at him again. The axe swept round and Uriel blocked it with the glowing weapon he had taken from Barzano.

Kesharq advanced more cautiously now, the red mask of his bloody features a truly repulsive sight, the twitching of glistening facial muscles clearly visible. He spat a mouthful of blood and charged, axe raised to smash down.

Rather than step back, Uriel ducked low and caught the haft of the axe on his forearm, feeling the force of impact crack his armour open. He roared, spinning inside the eldar's guard and gripped his arms, slamming his body into the alien and pulling.

The momentum of Kesharq's charge carried him sailing over Uriel's shoulder and he smashed into the ground on his back. Uriel spun the power knife and drove it with all his strength through Kesharq's breastplate and into his heart. The alien leader spasmed, dark blood bursting from his throat as Uriel twisted the knife in the wound and plunged it home again and again.

Yells and war-cries echoed around him, but all Uriel could see was the ecstatic form of Kasimir de Valtos at the chamber's centre.

He wrenched the knife clear of Kesharq's corpse and stumbled towards the man who had set these events in motion.

KASIMIR DE VALTOS watched the furious battle raging around him with unabashed pleasure. To see so much blood spilt was pleasing to him, and the terrible things swarming through his head were a revelation. So much slaughter filled his mind! His entire being felt elevated as he savoured the thought that the things he was seeing and feeling were but the tiniest morsel of the bloodshed the Nightbringer could unleash.

It was still weak, its substance not yet fully formed, but incredibly powerful. Whether it was simply his nearness to the creature that empowered him with such knowledge or some deeper link he did not know. Perhaps it recognised in him a kindred spirit. Certainly it displayed none of the lethal hostility to him that it had to the eldar in its first moments of awakening.

The alien woman of Kesharq's stood behind him. He could feel the fear radiating from her in waves and it felt wonderful to drink in that emotion. She collapsed to her knees, her skin blistering and cracking as every shred of her life force was leeched from her body. She was able to scream once before the last vestiges of her existence was swallowed by the Nightbringer. Was this the beginning of his transformation into an immortal, wondered de Valtos? Was this the first of the new powers he was soon to manifest?

The violence around him felt truly intoxicating. He could feel the combined hatred and aggression of the enemies flaring bright and succulent, filling him, making him stronger. So pleasing to have such things to feast upon rather than the cold, tasteless energies that had sustained its form these millions of years.

Kasimir de Valtos blinked in puzzlement. Millions of years? Where had that thought come from? Suddenly he realised that the sensations flooding through him, the fear, the anger, the terror were not his own, but borrowed from the alien creature before him. Anger filled him as he realised he had been nothing more than a conduit for emotions that this being had forgotten over the passage of aeons it had spent locked away from the sight of man.

As though sensing his thoughts the Nightbringer slowly turned to face him, the yellow pits of its eyes burning his soul, boring into the core of what made him human.

But Kasimir de Valtos had set himself to becoming an immortal god and utter single-mindedness filled his thoughts as a creature from the dawn of time swept its darkness around him.

'Make me like you! I freed you. I demand immortality – it is my right!' shrieked de Valtos as the Nightbringer lowered its gaze to his.

He felt himself sucked into the creature's eyes, the emptiness of its stare more terrifying than anything he could comprehend. He saw the dawn of the alien's race, the things they had done, the misery and suffering they had inflicted upon the galaxy and the blink of an eye that was the race of man.

He dropped to his knees as the sheer insignificance of his existence trembled before the unutterable vastness of the alien's consciousness. The fragile threads that were the twisted remains of Kasimir de Valtos's sanity shattered under such awful self-knowledge. This being had tamed stars and wiped entire civilisations from existence before the human race had even crawled from the soup of creation. What need had it of him?

'Please...' he begged, 'I want to live forever!'

The Nightbringer closed its clawed hand over de Valtos's head, the blackened fist completely enclosing his skull. Kasimir shrieked in terror at its touch, his flesh sloughing from his bones as it fed on his life energies.

The dark scythe slashed towards his neck.

He had a brief moment of perfect horror as he felt his own death flow through him, feeling his own terror and pain as the flimsiest morsel, barely worth feeding on, yet inflicted for the sake of the death it caused.

His head parted from his body.

The Nightbringer released its grip on de Valtos, letting his ravaged body topple to the ground. Slowly, deliberately, it turned its attention to the glowing metal fixed in the centre of its former tomb, passing its gnarled fingers over the shape.

And in space, a crescent shaped starship began to slowly drag itself from the shadowy realm it had occupied for the last sixty million years, called back into existence by its master.

URIEL WATCHED DISPASSIONATELY as the alien creature killed de Valtos. He felt nothing at his foe's death; the stakes were now far higher than personal revenge. He must somehow destroy this creature, or banish it; at least, stand against it.

The alabaster guardians stepped to intercept him, but Uriel was not to be denied. Pasanius, Learchus and Dardino joined him in his dash for the alien creature. Crackling emerald energies fired from the staff of the first two warriors. Uriel blocked the first bolt with the power knife and dodged the second. Pasanius raked one of the perfect figures with bolter fire, blasting porcelain-like chunks from its body, as Learchus drove his chainsword through its belly. A sweep of its staff smashed both sergeants from their feet, wreathing their bodies in green balefire.

Dardino hacked the warrior's legs from under it with a sweep of his power sword and Uriel leapt feet first at the second. His boots hammered home, but it was like striking a solid wall. The white figure rocked slightly, but did not fall, stabbing at Uriel with its copper staff. Uriel barely raised the knife in time, the power behind the blow sending hot jolts of agony up his arm. He rolled to his feet, punching the power knife through the figure's groin, slashing upwards and outwards. The alien warrior toppled, its leg severed at the hip, and Uriel ducked below the sweeping slash of yet another of the emotionless warriors' weapons.

Pasanius rose to his feet, firing at the remaining figures and punching another from its feet in a hail of white splinters. The final figure took a step back, Learchus's sword slashing at its head. Its master's clawed hand swept out and felled Learchus with a single blow. The sergeant groaned and struggled to rise.

Uriel, Pasanius and Dardino faced the awesome form of the Nightbringer, weapons drawn, feeling waves of horror breaking against them, but standing firm in the face of the enemy.

Uriel had nothing but contempt for the massive alien creature before him. The darkness of its spectral cloak billowed around its form and twin pools of sickly yellow pulsed within the darkness where its head might be.

The howling darkness of its scythe-arm lashed out, faster than the eye could follow. Sergeant Dardino grunted, more in surprise than pain as his torso toppled from his body and his legs crumpled in a flood of gore.

Pasanius opened fire, his bolts stitching a path across the swirling night of the alien's form. Hollow, echoing laughter pealed from the walls as each bolt flickered harmlessly through the enveloping darkness. The scythe licked out again and Pasanius's bolter was sheared in two perfect halves. The return stroke removed his right arm below the elbow.

Uriel used the distraction to close with the alien, slashing the power knife into the darkness. He screamed as the glacial chill of the being's substance enfolded his arm.

The creature's awful talons swung in a low arc, punching through Uriel's chest, tearing through a lung and rupturing his primary heart. He hurtled backwards, landing awkwardly across the remaining slab of the tomb, the glowing metal burning its image into the back of his armour. Pain ripped through him, deep in his chest, along his arm and within every nerve of his body. He groaned, fighting to push himself to his feet as he watched the Nightbringer begin the slaughter of his men.

INQUISITOR BARZANO WATCHED with pride as Uriel and his comrades stood before the power of the Nightbringer, despite the utter impossibility of victory. He pulled himself towards the slab even as life ebbed from his body. He could feel the flow of powerful energies flooding through the chamber, nightmarish visions the proximity of the Nightbringer was generating, and something else...

A soundless shriek, dazzling in its purity of purpose, called into the depths of space, calling the lost ship home. The living metal that shaped its form could not resist, pulled back from the realm it had been stranded in all these years.

So powerful was the summons that he could practically see the rippling waves of power radiating from where the C'tan's tomb had once stood. Or, more precisely, the glowing metal talisman buried in the slab.

His strength was all but gone, but still he tried to pull himself across the floor. He moaned as he watched Pasanius fall and Uriel thrown across the chamber, the Nightbringer's long, claws punching effortlessly through his armour.

Barzano felt the last of his strength drain from his body, but desperately held onto life. Where there was life, there was hope. He saw Uriel fight to pick himself up from the temple floor and realised he had one chance left.

URIEL ROARED WITH rage as the Nightbringer effortlessly butchered his men. Knowing that there was no chance to defeat this impossible creature, still they faced it, refusing to give in. Pasanius fought one-handed, slashing wildly at the creature as it darted about the chamber, cutting and slicing. A dazed Learchus bellowed at the Ultramarines to stand firm.

Horrid roars, like breakers against a cliff, echoed throughout the tomb and with a start Uriel realised that the alien creature was laughing at them, taking them apart slowly, painfully and sadistically.

Hot anger poured fuel on the fire of his endurance and he rose to his feet, a snarl of anger and pain bursting from his lips. He gathered up his fallen knife and hobbled forward, pulling up short as a sudden powerful imperative seized him. For a second he thought that the Nightbringer's infernal presence had breached his mind once more.

But there was a familiarity in these thoughts, a recognition.

Uriel turned to see Inquisitor Barzano staring at him, sweat pouring in runnels from his face, veins like hawsers on his neck.

The metal, Uriel, the metal! The metal...

The thought faded almost as soon as it formed within his head, but Uriel knew that the inquisitor had given his all to make sure he had heard it and he would not allow that effort to have been in vain.

He dropped to his knees at the edge of the slab, the glare of the glowing metal blinding to look at. He could feel its heat through the rents in his armour. What was he to do? Shoot it, stab it? Shouts of pain and rage from his men decided the issue.

Uriel hammered the power knife into the edge of the metal, wedging it between the stone of the slab and the glowing icon. He sensed a shift in the tortured energies filling the chamber and looked up to see the vast shape of the alien towering above the Ultramarines, two battle brothers held impaled on its claws.

He pushed down on the inlaid handle, feeling the blade bend as the metal's substance resisted him. He did not have the strength to force it from the slab.

The Nightbringer hurled the Space Marines aside, spinning with a ferocious sweep of its dark matter. Uriel felt its fury, its outrage that this upstart prey creature dared meddle in its affairs.

The alien's mind touched his with an anger that had seen stars snuffed out and Uriel let it in, feeling its monstrous rage flood through his body, feeling that rage empower him.

His own hatred for this being merged with its fury and he used the power, turning it outwards, ripping the metal from the slab with the sheer force of his anger-fuelled strength.

The metal clattered onto the floor of the tomb, the Nightbringer roaring in bestial rage as the connection to its star-killing vessel was severed, stranding it once more in the haunted depths of the immaterium. Uriel gripped the blazing metal and scrambled backwards. He snatched at his grenade dispenser as Pasanius leapt towards the creature.

A casual flick of its midnight talons sent him sprawling, but the veteran sergeant's attack had given Uriel the chance he needed. As the Nightbringer swept towards him, he held up the glowing metal, showing the hideous alien what he had fixed to its surface.

Uriel doubted the Nightbringer had any concept of what a melta bomb was, but somehow he knew that it would understand what it could do.

The creature drew itself up to its full height, spreading wide its taloned fists, the burning yellow of its eyes fixing Uriel with its deathly gaze.

Uriel laughed in its face, feeling the alien's terrible power pressing in on his skull. Visions of death tore at Uriel's mind, but held no terror for a warrior of the Emperor. He could feel the creature's consternation at his resistance.

The darkness began to swell around the creature's form, but Uriel moved his free hand to hover over the detonation rune. He smiled, despite the pain and tormented visions in his head.

'You're fast,' whispered Uriel, 'but not that fast.'

The Nightbringer hovered before him, flexing its claws in time with the boom of its alien heart. Uriel could feel its power and anger as a physical thing pressing in around him, but he could also sense something else.

Unease? Doubt?

The connection made between them by the Nightbringer granted Uriel the barest insight into the manifestation of this utterly alien being and suddenly he knew that despite the carnage it had wreaked, it was but a fraction of its true power. It was still so very weak and needed to feed. Uriel knew that every second that passed granted the Nightbringer fresh power as it fed on the strong life energies blazing in this place.

This was as close a chance as he was going to get to defeat the alien. Keeping his voice steady he said, 'This place is filling with explosive fumes and if I detonate this device, you will be buried beneath ten kilometres of rock. I don't know what you are or where you come from, but I know this. You're not strong enough yet to survive that. Can you imagine another sixty million years trapped below the surface of this world, with nothing to sustain you? You will be extinguished. Is that what you want? If you can reach into the minds of men, know this. I will destroy us all before I allow you to have that vessel.'

The pressure on his mind intensified and Uriel weakened his mental barrier, allowing the alien to see his unshakeable resolve. Its claws rose and fell, the darkness swirling around its nebulous form as its rage shook the chamber. Cracks split the walls and the red soil of Pavonis spilled through.

Uriel watched as the veil of darkness spiralled around the Nightbringer's form, sweeping up and over it like a dark tornado, gathering up the shattered remains of its guardian creatures within its furious orbit.

Uriel had a last glimpse of the Nightbringer as its yellow orbs were swallowed up by the encroaching darkness of its ghostly shroud. An alien hiss filled the chamber as the black storm shot upwards, impacting on the gold cap of the ceiling, shattering it into a thousand of pieces.

Then it was gone.

URIEL LOWERED HIS arm, his mind feeling as clear as a summer's day as the oppressive weight of the Nightbringer's horrific thoughts departed. He smiled, unable to prevent a huge grin splitting his face. He felt no desire to smile, but the sheer clarity of his own thoughts, freed from visions of murder and torture allowed no other reaction.

He put down the metal, its surface now cold and lifeless, and crawled towards Ario Barzano, who lay unmoving in a vast pool of blood. Uriel knelt beside the inquisitor, searching for a pulse, almost laughing in relief as he felt a weak beat.

'Get Apothecary Selenus!'

Barzano's eyes fluttered open and he smiled, his empathic senses also free of the Nightbringer's visions.

'It's gone?' he coughed.

Uriel nodded. 'Yes, it's gone. You held it at bay for just long enough.'

'No, Uriel, I only pointed the way. You held it off yourself.'

Barzano shuddered, his lifeblood flooding from him.

'You did well, I am proud of you all. You–' Barzano's words were cut off as a coughing fit overtook him and his body spasmed, fresh blood frothing from his chest wound.

'Apothecary!' shouted Uriel again.

'The governor...' gasped Barzano, through clenched teeth, 'Look after her, she trusts you. She'll listen to you... others will too... she will need your counsel and support. Do this for me, Uriel?'

'You know I will, Ario.'

Inquisitor Ario Barzano nodded, slowly shut his eyes and died in Uriel's arms.

HAVING GATHERED THEIR dead, the Ultramarines left the chamber of the Nightbringer. The only other survivor of the carnage was Vendare Taloun, whose unconsciousness had prevented the Nightbringer's visions from driving him insane. Uriel personally marched the man back to the elevator car at gunpoint. There was little need for force; Taloun was a broken man. It irked the Space Marine to have to hand his prisoner a rebreather mask for fear he would succumb to the fumes and escape just punishment for his treachery.

Along with their honoured dead, Uriel took the piece of metal he had removed from the alien's tomb, its glimmering surface still unblemished despite the none too tender ministrations of his power knife. It would go back to Macragge, to be sealed forever within the deepest vault in the mountains.

When his men had returned to the worker elevator that had brought Barzano to the bottom of the mine, Uriel handed Taloun over to a white-faced Pasanius and said, 'Wait.'

He returned the way he had come, picturing the faces of all the men he had lost on this mission, but knowing that their sacrifice had not been in vain.

Standing alone in the alien's tomb, he watched the earth of Pavonis pouring into the chamber, knowing that soon it would be buried once more. But Uriel needed more.

He knelt and placed a cluster of melta bombs on the slab the metal had come from and set the timers.

As he had promised the Nightbringer this blasphemous place would be buried forever under ten kilometres of rock.

Uriel turned and marched wearily from the chamber.

℧

NINETEEN

Three months later...

VENDARE TALOUN WAS executed three months to the day after the battle at Tembra Ridge. During a very public trial, he confessed to his alliance with Kasimir de Valtos, the murder of his brother and a number of other appalling acts in his time as head of the Taloun cartel. He had been led, weeping and soiled, to the wreckage of Liberation Square, where he was hanged from the outstretched arm of the Emperor's statue.

Several more battles were fought before Imperial rule was restored to Pavonis, most between the squabbling PDF units whose cartel affiliations overcame any sense of loyalty to the cause they had supposedly been fighting for. Deprived of leadership, the cartel followers had soon reverted to their natural prejudices and suspicions.

When the deaths of Solana Vergen, Taryn Honan, Kasimir de Valtos and Beauchamp Abrogas became public knowledge, the cartels were thrown into disarray, paralysed by inaction as the scions and heirs fought for political and financial control.

The battalion commanders who had managed to retain a semblance of order amongst their units pulled back to their barracks to await whatever retribution might come their way. The tanks and soldiers of the Shonai cartel fought several actions to bring those men who had betrayed their oaths of loyalty to justice.

But when the *Vae Victus* lent her support to an attack on the de Valtos-sponsored barracks with devastating orbital barrages, the flags of surrender were raised as soon as the Shonai tanks came in sight of every other enemy stronghold. The Space Marine vessel had also hunted down the damaged eldar starship and, much to Lord Admiral Tiberius's delight, blasted it to atoms as it attempted to escape the Pavonis system.

When Mykola Shonai returned to Pavonis it was alongside Lortuen Perjed and at the head of the Ultramarines, their armour repaired and wounds dressed (though the Chapter's artificers would never be able to remove the cruciform shape burned into the back of Uriel's armour).

As she took her seat in the Chamber of Righteous Commerce after Vendare Taloun's execution there were shouts of approval and support from every section of the chamber.

URIEL SAT ON a marble bench, its surface cracked and pitted. This was the only portion of the palace gardens to have escaped the devastation of the shelling and the annihilation of the underground arsenal. Pasanius waited by the far entrance to the gardens, his bolter gripped tightly in his new bionic arm.

The grass was freshly cut, the scent of its fragrance reminding Uriel of the mountains back on Macragge. A simple headstone marked the final resting place of Inquisitor Ario Barzano. Beneath his name, a short inscription was engraved in a flowing script:

Each man is a spark in the darkness.

Would that we all burn as bright.

Uriel had carved it himself; he hoped that Barzano would have approved.

He rose to his feet as Mykola Shonai entered the garden. The wounds he had suffered fighting in the deep of the world were healing, but it would be some weeks yet before he would be fully fit.

Shonai's hair spilled around her shoulders and she clutched a small garland of flowers in her hands.

Three guards accompanied her, but kept a respectful distance as she approached the headstone.

She nodded to Uriel and knelt beside grave, placing the flowers gently beside the stone. She straightened, brushing the folds from her long dress and turned to face him.

'Captain Ventris, it is good to see you,' she smiled, sitting on the marble bench. 'Please, sit with me awhile.'

Uriel joined the governor on the bench and they sat in a companionable silence together for several minutes, neither willing to spoil this moment of peace. Eventually Shonai inclined her head towards Uriel.

'So you are leaving today?'

'Yes. Our work here is done and there are more than enough Imperial forces to maintain order.'

'Yes, there are,' agreed Mykola Shonai sadly. Imperial Guard transports had landed four days ago, the soldiers and tanks of the 44th Lavrentian

Hussars turning the city into an armed camp. Ships of the Adeptus Administratum and Adeptus Ministorum had also arrived, their purpose to restore a measure of political and spiritual stability to Pavonis.

Preachers and confessors filled the streets with their words, taking renewed pledges of piety and devotion from the populace.

At the recommendation of Lortuen Perjed, the Administr-atum had permitted Shonai to remain as governor of Pavonis, on condition that at the end of her contract of service, she never again stand for political office. Lortuen Perjed was appointed permanent Administratum observer to Pavonis, replacing the criminally negligent Ballion Varle, who Jenna Sharben, the last surviving judge in Brandon Gate, had arrested and shot.

The rebel PDF troopers rounded up by the Shonai cartel were even now being transported onto a freshly arrived penal barge, bound for warzones in the Segmentum Obscurus.

The future of Pavonis had been assured, but it would no longer be under the autonomous regime of the cartels. The governmental system of Pavonis had been found lacking and would now fall under the watchful gaze of the Administratum.

Uriel could understand Shonai's frustration. She had come through the worst ordeal of her life and now, when they had won the final victory, everything was being taken from her.

'I did mean to come here before now,' explained Shonai, staring at the grave, 'but I was never sure quite what I would feel if I did.'

'In what way?'

'I owe my world's survival to you and Ario, but had things been different, he would have destroyed Pavonis and killed everything I hold dear.'

'Yes, but he did not. He gave his life in defence of you and your world. Remember him for that.'

'I do. That is why I came here today. I honour his memory and I will ensure that he will be forever known as a Hero of Pavonis.'

'I think he'd enjoy that,' chuckled Uriel. 'It would appeal to his colossal vanity.'

Shonai smiled and leaned up to kiss Uriel's cheek. 'Thank you, Uriel, for all that you have done for Pavonis. And for me.'

Uriel nodded, pleased with the governor's sentiment. Noticing her serious expression he asked, 'What will you do when your time as governor is at an end?'

'I'm not sure, Uriel. Something quiet,' she laughed, rising to her feet and offering her hand to Uriel. He stood and accepted the proffered hand, his grip swallowing Shonai's delicate fingers.

'Goodbye, Uriel. I wish you well.'

'Thank you, Governor Shonai. May the Emperor walk with you.'

Mykola Shonai smiled and walked away, vanishing back into the shattered edifice of the palace.

Uriel stood alone before Barzano's grave and snapped smartly to attention.

He saluted the inquisitor's spirit and hammered his fist twice into his breastplate in the warrior's honour to the fallen.

Uriel marched to the edge of the garden where Pasanius awaited his captain, flexing the unfamiliar tendons of his new, mechanical arm. The massive sergeant looked up as his commander approached.

'Still doesn't feel right,' he complained.

'You'll get used to it, my friend.'

'I suppose so,' grumbled Pasanius.

'Are the men ready to depart?' asked Uriel, changing the subject.

'Aye, your warriors are ready to go home.'

Uriel smiled at Pasanius's unconscious use of the phrase 'your warriors'. He rested his hand on the pommel of Idaeus's power sword and clenched his fist over its golden skull.

With the rebellion over, he had scoured the battlefield outside the prison complex, at last finding the broken blade. He had intended to repair the weapon, but for some reason he had not. Until now he had not realised why.

The weapon was a symbol, a physical sign of his previous captain's approval for the men of Fourth Company to follow. But now, in the crucible of combat, Uriel had proved his mettle and he no longer needed such a symbol. It had been Idaeus's last gift to Uriel and he knew that it would find a place of honour in the Chapter's reliquary.

He would forge his own sword, just as he had forged his own company in battle.

It was his company now. He was no longer filling the shadow of Idaeus or his illustrious ancestor, he was walking his own path.

Captain Uriel Ventris of the Ultramarines turned on his heel and together he and Pasanius marched towards the city walls where a Thunderhawk gunship awaited to take them aboard the *Vae Victus*.

'Come, my friend. Let's go home,' said Uriel.

ʊ
EPILOGUE

Seventy thousand light years away, the star known to Imperial stellar cartographers as Cyclo entered the final stages of its existence. It was a red giant of some ninety million kilometres diameter and had burned for over eight hundred million years. Had it not been for the billowing black shape floating impossibly in the star's photosphere and draining the last of its massive energies, it would probably have continued to do so for perhaps another two thousand.

Normally, it generated energy at a colossal rate by burning hydrogen to helium in nuclear fusion reactions deep in its heart, but its core was no longer able to sustain the massive forces that burned within.

Powerful waves of electromagnetic energy and sprays of plasma formed into a rippling nimbus of coruscating light that washed from the star in pulsing waves.

The Nightbringer fed and grew strong again in the depths of the dying star.

WARRIORS OF ULTRAMAR

PHASE I – DETECTION

♈ PROLOGUE

Low clouds scudded across the clear blue sky of Tarsis Ultra, drifting in the light breeze that bent the fat stalks of corn stretching in all directions as far as the eye could see. The air was warm, scented with the pungent aroma of crops ready for harvest.

A tall, high-sided vehicle lumbered through the gently waving fields on a road of hard-packed earth, flashing blades on extended tilt arms efficiently scything the crops on either side into a huge hopper on its back. The sun had yet to reach its zenith, but the hopper was almost full, the harvester having set off from the farming collective of Prandium before dawn's first light had broken.

Smoke from the harvester's engine vented through a series of filters and was released in a toxin-free cloud above the small cab mounted on its frontal section.

The harvester lurched as it veered to one side before one of the cab's two occupants pulled the control levers away from its more reckless driver.

'Corin, I swear you drive this thing like a blind man,' snapped Joachim.

'Well I'm never going to get any better if you keep taking the controls from me,' said Corin, throwing his hands up in disgust. He ran a gloved hand through his unruly mop of hair and stared in annoyance at his companion.

Joachim felt his friend's glare and said, 'You almost had us in the irrigation ditch.'

'Maybe,' admitted Corin. 'But I didn't, did I?'

'Only because I took over.'

Corin shrugged, unwilling to concede the point, and allowed Joachim to continue driving the harvester in relative peace. He removed his thin gloves and flexed his fingers, attempting to work out the stiffness in his joints. Holding onto the juddering control columns of a harvester and trying to guide it around the huge fields was punishing work.

'These gloves are useless,' he complained. 'They don't help at all.'

Joachim grinned and said, 'So you haven't padded them out yet?'

'No,' replied Corin. 'I was hoping your Elleiza would do it for me.'

'I wouldn't hold your breath, she already runs after you like she was your wife.'

'Aye!' chucked Corin, 'She's a good lass. She looks after me well, so she does.'

'Too well,' pointed out Joachim. 'It's time you got your own woman to look after you. What about Bronagh, the medicae in Espandor? I heard that she was sweet on you.'

'Bronagh. Ah, yes, she's a girl of rare taste,' laughed Corin.

Joachim arched an eyebrow and was on the point of replying when the world exploded around them. A thunderous impact struck the side of the harvester and both men were hurled against the cab's interior as the giant vehicle lurched sideways. Joachim felt blood on his scalp and reached for the controls as the harvester began to tip.

He pulled back on the column, but it was too late, the left track slid from the road into the ditch and the entire vehicle rolled over.

'Hold on!' yelled Joachim as the harvester toppled onto its side with a crash of twisted metal. Broken glass showered them and Joachim felt a jagged edge slice open his temple. The harvester slammed down into the field, hurling giant clouds of corn and dust into the air as it toppled onto the dry earth. Its enormous tracks ground onwards, churning air as the engine continued to turn over.

Almost a minute passed before the side door of the cab swung open and a pair of booted feet emerged. Gingerly, Joachim lowered himself out of the cab and splashed down into the knee-high water of the irrigation ditch that ran between the road and the field. He landed awkwardly and cursed, clutching his bruised and gashed head. Corin groggily followed him into the ditch, cradling his arm close to his chest.

Wordlessly, the two men surveyed the damage done to the harvester.

The hopper was a twisted mass of buckled metal, smoking fragments and the stinking residue of burned corn all that remained of its centre section, where it appeared that something immensely powerful had struck.

'Guilliman's oath, what happened?' asked Corin, breathlessly. 'Did someone shoot at us?'

'I don't think so,' replied Joachim, pointing to a pillar of white smoke billowing skyward some hundred metres further into the field. 'But whatever it was, I bet it's got something to do with that.'

Corin followed Joachim's pointing hand and said, 'What the hell is it?'

'I don't know, but if it's a fire, we've got to get it out before the whole crop goes up.'

Corin nodded and clambered painfully back into the harvester's cab, unclipping a pair of fire extinguishers from its rear wall and dropping them down to Joachim. With some difficulty they climbed the sloping rockcrete wall of the ditch, Joachim turning to pull Corin up as he reached the top.

Hurriedly, they made their way through the field, their passage made easier by virtue of the long, dark scar gouged in the earth that led towards the column of smoke.

'By Maccrage, I've never seen anything like this,' wheezed Corin. 'Is it a meteor?'

Joachim nodded, then wished he hadn't as hot stabs of pain thundered in his head. 'I think so.'

They reached the lip of the crater and pulled up in astonishment at what lay within.

If it was a meteor, then it didn't look anything like either man imagined it might. Roughly spherical and composed of a leprous brown material, it resembled a giant gemstone rippling in a heat haze. Its surface was smooth and glassy looking, presumably from its journey through the atmosphere. Now that they could see it clearly, the two men saw that it wasn't smoke that billowed from the object in stinking waves, but steam. Geysers of the foul smelling vapour vented from cracks in its surface like leaks in a compressor pipe. Even from the edge of the crater they could feel the intense heat radiating from the object.

'Well it's not on fire, but it's still damned hot,' said Joachim. 'We need to cool it down or it could still set light to the crop.'

Corin shook his head and made the sign of the aquila over his heart. 'No way. I ain't going down there.'

'What? Why not?'

'I don't like the look of that thing, Joachim. It's bad news, I can feel it.'

'Don't be simple all your life, Corin. It's just a big rock, now come on.'

Corin shook his head vehemently and thrust the fire extinguisher he carried towards Joachim. 'Here. You want to go down there, then go, but I'm going back to the harvester. I'm going to vox Prandium and get someone to come out and pick us up.'

Joachim could see there was no arguing with Corin, and nodded.

'I'm going to take a closer look,' said Joachim. 'I'll be right back.'

Slinging an extinguisher over each shoulder, he picked his way carefully down into the crater.

Corin watched him until he reached its base and turned back the way they had come. He touched his wounded arm, wincing as pain flared just above his elbow: it felt broken. He glanced over his shoulder, hearing a loud hissing, like water being poured on a hot skillet, but continued walking.

The hissing continued, followed by an almighty crack.

Then the screaming started.

Corin jumped, spinning around as he heard Joachim shriek in agony. His friend's scream was abruptly silenced, and a keening screech cut the air, utterly alien and utterly terrifying. Corin turned and sprinted back towards the harvester, fear lending his limbs extra speed.

There was an autogun in the cab, and he desperately wished he'd brought it with him.

He stumbled along the gouge torn in the earth, tripping on a buried root and falling to his knees. The thump of heavy footfalls sounded behind him. Something large and inhumanly quick was speeding through the corn. He could hear snapping stalks as it came nearer and nearer; Corin was in no doubt that it was hunting him.

He moaned in fear, stumbling to his feet and running onwards. He risked a glance over his shoulder, seeing a blurred form ghost from sight into the swaying corn.

The tread of something large seemed to come from all around him.

'What are you?' he screamed as he ran.

He ran blindly, bursting from the corn and yelling as he fell headlong into the irrigation ditch. He landed hard, cracking his elbow against the rockcrete, swallowing a mouthful of brackish water as he screamed in pain. He scrambled backwards, spitting water and shaking his head clear.

He looked up as a dark shape blotted out the sky above him.

Corin blinked away the water in his eyes and saw his pursuer clearly.

He drew breath to scream.

But it was on him in a flurry of scything blows that tore him apart before he could give voice to it.

A lake of blood spread from the dismembered corpse. Corin's killer paused for the briefest second, as though scenting the air.

It scrambled easily up the slope of the ditch and set off in the direction of Prandium.

PHASE II – APPROACH

ONE

THE BASILICA MORTIS was home to the Mortifactors.

The ancestral home of the Mortifactors Chapter of Space Marines rotated slowly in the wan light of Posul and her faraway sun, its surfaces craggy and mountainous.

For nearly ten thousand years, since the Chapter's founder, Sasebo Tezuka, had been led here by the Emperor's tarot, the Mortifactors had stood sentinel over the night world of Posul, and since that time, these holy knights of the Imperium had trained members of their warrior order within the walls of their orbiting fortress monastery.

In appearance, it resembled some vast mountain range cast adrift in the void of space. The Imperium's finest tech-priests and adepts had come together to create this orbiting fortress; the Basilica was a marvel of arcane technical engineering that had long since been forgotten.

For millennia, the Mortifactors had sent warriors from the Basilica Mortis to fight alongside the armies of the Imperium in the service of the divine Emperor of Man. Companies, squads, crusaders and – three times – the entire Chapter had been called to war, most recently to fight the orks on the blasted wastes of Armageddon. The honours the Chapter had won rivalled even those of such legendary Chapters as the Space Wolves, Imperial Fists or Blood Angels.

At full occupation, the monastery was home to the thousand battle-brothers of the Chapter and their officers, with a supporting staff of servitors, scribes, technomats and functionaries that numbered seven and a half thousand souls.

Vast docks jutted from the prow of the adamantium mountain, spearing into space with slender silver docking rings rising from the jib. Two heavily armed Space Marine strike cruisers were berthed in the docks, with smaller, Gladius frigates and Hunter destroyers either returning or departing on patrol throughout the Mortifactors' domain. Battle barges, devastating warships of phenomenal power, were housed in armoured bays deep in the bowels of the monastery, terrible weapons of planetary destruction held in their silent hulls.

A beacon, flaring in the darkness upon the furthest jib of the docks, reflected the light from the hull of an approaching strike cruiser. The ship slipped gracefully towards the darkened fortress monastery, escorted by six rapid strike vessels of the Mortifactors. Ancient codes and tortuous greetings in High Gothic had been exchanged between the ship's captain and the monastery's Master of the Marches, but still the Mortifactors were taking no chances with security. The ship, the *Vae Victus*, drifted slowly, powered only by attitude thrusters that controlled her approach to the docks.

The *Vae Victus* was a strike cruiser of the Ultramarines, the pride and joy of the Chapter's Commander of the Fleet, and normally travelled with a full panoply of escort craft in her wake. But the ships of the Arx Praetora squadron lay at anchor near the system's jump point, forbidden to approach the ancient sepulchre of the Mortifactors.

The ship's structure was long, scarred by thousands of years of war against the foes of humanity. A cathedral-like spire, braced by ornamented flying buttresses, towered over her rear quarter and, in deference to the Mortifactors, her guns and launch bays were shuttered behind their protective blast shields. The portside of the vessel's prow gleamed where the shipwrights of Calth had repaired the horrendous damage done to her by an eldar ship, and the insignia of the Ultramarines shone with renewed pride from her frontal armour.

As the *Vae Victus* drew near the Basilica, her prow swung slowly around until her starboard was broadside to the mountainous fortress monastery. Here, she hung silently in space until a flurry of small pilot ships emerged from the Basilica Mortis and swiftly took up position on her far side.

Other ships, bearing vast mooring cables, each thicker than an orbital torpedo, flew out to meet the *Vae Victus* and attached them to secure anchor points as the pilot ships gently approached the portside hull of the Ultramarines vessel. Little more than powerful engines with a tiny servitor compartment bolted to its topside, the pilot ships were used to manoeuvre larger vessels into a position where they could dock. A dozen of them gently nuzzled the *Vae Victus*, like tiny, parasitic fish feeding on a vast sea creature, and flared their engines in controlled bursts. At last, their combined force overcame the inertia of the larger ship and, slowly, the *Vae Victus* eased towards the Basilica Mortis, the thick cables reeling her in and guiding her towards the enormous, claw-like docking clamps that would moor her safely to the fortress monastery.

Deep within the starship, armoured footsteps and the distant sound of the pilot ships on the hull were the only things to break the calm, meditative silence of her corridors. Well lit by numerous electro-candles, the marble-white walls seemed to swallow sounds before they had a chance to echo.

The gently arched walls were smooth and spartanly ornamented. Here and there along their length, tiny niches, lit by a delicate, diffuse light, held stasis-sealed vessels containing some of the Chapter's holy relics: the thigh bone of Ancient Galatan, an alien skull taken on the fields of Ichar IV, a fragment of stained glass from a long ago destroyed shrine or an alabaster statue of the Emperor himself.

Four Space Marines marched towards the starboard docking bays where they would at last be able to set foot on the Basilica Mortis. Leading the delegation was a bald giant, his skin dark and tough as leather, with a network of scars criss crossing the left side of his face. His features were drawn in a scowl of displeasure, his eyes darting to the corridor's roof at every groan of metal that came from the hull, imagining the damage the pilot ships were inflicting upon his vessel.

Lord Admiral Lazlo Tiberius wore his ceremonial cloak of office. The stiff foxbat fur ruff surrounding his shoulders chafed his neck and the silver cluster securing it to his blue armour scratched his throat. He wore a wreath of laurels around his forehead and the many battle honours he had won glittered on his breast, the golden sunburst of a Hero of Macragge shining like a miniature sun.

'Damned pilot ships,' muttered Tiberius. 'She's only just out of the yards at Calth and now they'll be buckling Emperor knows how many panels and arches.'

'I'm sure it won't be as bad as you think, lord admiral. And she will see worse before we are done with Tarsis Ultra,' said the warrior immediately behind Tiberius, the captain of the Fourth company, Uriel Ventris, his emerald-green dress cloak billowing behind him.

Tiberius grunted. 'As soon as we get back to Tarsis Ultra I want to put into dock at Chordelis and check. I'll not take her into battle without making sure she is at her best.'

As captain of the Fourth company, one of Uriel's titles was Master of the Fleet, but in recognition of Tiberius's greater knowledge of space combat, he had deferred the position to the lord admiral, who had taken on the role with gusto. There was no dishonour in this, as the warriors of the Ultramarines followed the teachings of their primarch's holy tome, the Codex Astartes, which stressed the importance of every position being held by those most suited to it, regardless of station. Tiberius and the *Vae Victus* had fought together for nearly three centuries and Uriel knew that the venerable lord admiral would make a better Master of the Fleet than he.

In the month since the destruction of the space hulk, *Death of Virtue*, the ship's artificers had done their best to repair the damage Uriel's armour had suffered, replacing his shoulder guard and filling and repainting the deep grooves cut by alien claws. But without the forges of Macragge, it was impossible to completely heal the damage.

Pinned to his green cloak was a small brooch with an embossed white rose, marking Uriel as a Hero of Pavonis, and below this a number of bronze stars were affixed to his breastplate.

His face was angular, the features classically sculpted, but serious and drawn. His storm-cloud eyes were narrow and heavy-lidded, the two gold long-service studs on his left temple shining brightly below the darkness of his cropped scalp.

Uriel's senior sergeants marched in step behind him, Pasanius to his left and Learchus on his right. Pasanius easily dwarfed the others; his armour barely able to contain his bulk, despite the fact that much of it had come from an ancient suit of irreparably damaged Terminator armour. Both he and Learchus wore the green cloak of the Fourth company, and like their captain, sported brooches bearing the white rose of Pavonis.

Pasanius wore his blond hair tight into his skull and though his face was serious, it was also capable of great warmth and humour. His right arm gleamed silver below the elbow where the tech-priests of Pavonis had replaced it following the confrontation with the ancient star god known as the Nightbringer in the depths of that world. Its monstrous scythe had sliced through his armour and bone, and despite the attentions of Apothecary Selenus, the tissue touched by its glacial chill was beyond saving.

Learchus was a true Ultramarine. His heritage was flawless and of the finest stock, his every stride that of a warrior born. During their training, he and Uriel had been bitter rivals, but their shared service to the Chapter and the Emperor had long since overcome any such rancour.

Lord Admiral Tiberius tugged at the fur ruff around his neck and adjusted the laurel wreath at his temples as they rounded a bend in the corridor and approached the docking bay. A ringing clang that sounded throughout the ship told Tiberius that the docking clamps of the Basilica had them secured.

He shook his head, saying, 'I'll be glad when this is over.'

Uriel could not bring himself to agree with Tiberius. He was eager to meet these brothers of his blood, and the threat they were soon to face on Tarsis Ultra made him doubly glad the *Vae Victus* had come here.

Split from the Ultramarines during the Second Founding, nearly ten thousand years ago, the Mortifactors were descended from the same lineage of heroes as Uriel himself.

Ancient tales told of how Roboute Guilliman, primarch of the Ultramarines, had held the Emperor's realm together after its near destruction at the hands of the treacherous Warmaster Horus, and how his tome, the Codex Astartes, had laid the foundations of the fledgling Imperium. Central to those foundations was the decree that the tens of thousands strong Space Marine Legions be broken up into smaller fighting units known to this day as Chapters, so that never again would any one man be able to wield the fearsome power of an entire Space Marine Legion. Each of the original Legions kept their colours and title, while the newly formed Chapters took another name and set out to fight the enemies of the Emperor throughout the galaxy.

An Ultramarines captain named Sasebo Tezuka had been given command of the newly created Mortifactors and led them to the world of Posul, where he established his fortress monastery and earned many honours in the name of the Emperor before his death.

Despite their shared descent from the blood of Guilliman, there had been no contact between the Ultramarines and the Mortifactors for thousands of years, and Uriel was looking forward to meeting these warriors and seeing what had become of them, what battles they had fought and hearing their tales of valour.

An honour guard of Ultramarines lined the columned approach to the starboard docking hatches and the four warriors passed between them. A thick, golden door with a locking wheel and Imperial eagle motif beneath an elaborately carved pediment lay at the end of the honour guard. A brass-rimmed light above the door flashed green to indicate that the passage ahead was safe and as the Ultramarines approached, a cybernetically altered servitor on tracks rolled forward to turn the wheel. It turned smoothly, steam hissing from the vacuum-sealed edges.

The door lifted from the hatch with a decompressive hiss, and slid aside on oiled runners, revealing a long, dark tunnel of black iron that led towards a dripping portal ringed with black skulls.

Icicle fangs hung from the jaws of the skulls and moisture gathered on the stone flagged floor of the docking umbilical. Tiberius shared an uneasy look with Uriel, who moved to stand alongside the lord admiral.

'Doesn't look particularly inviting, does it?' observed Tiberius.

'Not especially,' agreed Uriel.

'Well, let's get this over with. The sooner we are on our way back to Tarsis Ultra the happier I will be.'

Uriel nodded and led the way along the docking tunnel. He reached the door at its end, which was formed from the same dark iron as the rest of the tunnel. Behind them, the pressure door slammed shut, sealing with a booming clang. A rain of melting ice pattered from Uriel's shoulder guards, running in rivulets along the scores in his breastplate and soaking the top of his cloak. He raised his fist and hammered twice on the door, deep echoes ringing hollowly from the walls. There was no answer and he raised his fist to strike the door again when it swung inwards with a tortured squeal of metal.

Dry, dead air, like the last breath of a corpse, soughed from inside the Basilica Mortis, and Uriel caught the musty scent of bone and cerements. Inside was darkness, lit only by flickering candles, and the chill of the internal air matched that of the docking tunnel.

Uriel stepped through the skull-wreathed portal and set foot in the sanctum of the Mortifactors. Tiberius, Learchus and Pasanius followed him, casting wary glances around them as they took in their surroundings.

They stood in a long chamber, seated statues running along its length and its ceiling shrouded in darkness. Faded, mouldy banners hung from the walls. Water pooled behind them as it splashed in from the docking tunnel. Ahead, a softly lit doorway set in a leaf-shaped archway provided the chamber's only other visible exit.

'Where are the Mortifactors?' hissed Pasanius.

'I don't know,' said Uriel, gripping the hilt of his sword and staring at the statues either side of him. He approached the nearest and leaned in close, sweeping its face clear of dust and cobwebs.

'Guilliman's oath!' he swore, recoiling in disgust as he realised that these were not statues, but preserved human corpses.

'Battle Brother Olfric, may his name and strength be remembered,' said a deep voice behind Uriel. 'He fell in combat with the hrud at the Battle of Ortecha IX. This was seven hundred and thirty years ago. But he was avenged and his battle brothers ate the hearts of his killer. Thus was his soul able to go on to the feast table of the Ultimate Warrior.'

Uriel spun to see a robed and hooded figure standing in the doorway, his hands hidden within the sleeves of his robes. From his bulk, it was plain that the speaker was a fellow Space Marine. A pair of brass-plated servo-skulls hovered above the man, a thin copper wire running between them and dangling metallic callipers twitching as they floated into the chamber. One carried a long, vellum scroll, a feathered quill darting across its surface, while the other drifted towards the Ultramarines, a red light glowing from a cylindrical device slung beneath its perpetually grinning jaw.

It hovered before Uriel, the red light sweeping across and over his head, and he had to fight the superstitious urge to smash the skull from the air. The skull moved on from Uriel to Pasanius and then to Learchus, bathing each of their heads in the same eerie red light. As it reached Tiberius, the lord admiral reached up angrily and swatted it away.

'Damn thing!' snapped Tiberius. 'What is the meaning of this?'

The skull squealed and darted back, rising into the air and hovering just out of reach. Its twin followed it, pulled up by the copper cable that connected them.

'Do not be alarmed, lord admiral' said the figure in the doorway. 'The devices are merely mapping and recording a three-dimensional image of your skull.'

Seeing Tiberius's confusion, the robed Space Marine said, 'So that upon your death, it may be placed in the position that most suits its dimensions.'

Tiberius stared open-mouthed at the figure, who pulled back his hood and stepped forward into the light.

His skin was the colour of ebony, his dark hair pulled back in long braids and woven with coloured crystals. Four golden studs glittered on his brow, his full features and dark eyes sombre as he addressed the startled Ultramarines.

'I am Brother-Chaplain Astador of the Mortifactors, and I bid thee welcome, brothers.'

THIS WAS NOT what Uriel had expected of the Mortifactors. After announcing himself, Astador had turned and marched from the chamber of corpses without another word, leaving the astonished Ultramarines to follow. The two servo-skulls floated alongside their master, bobbing just above his head and Uriel wondered what other technological artefacts the Mortifactors utilised. The Ultramarines shunned the use of servo-skulls, preferring that the mortal remains of fallen Imperial servants be interred whole that they might sit at the right hand of the Emperor complete.

The halls of the Mortifactors were gloomy and silent as a tomb. Every portal and chamber they passed through bore more skulls and only now, as he looked closer, did Uriel realise that none were carved or fashioned by human hand. All were real, bleached and dusty with age. Though they saw no inhabitants of the fortress monastery in their long journey, the silence was broken by occasional snatches of hymnal dirges and sombre chants of remembrance.

Uriel's sense of bewilderment rose the further they penetrated this dismal sepulchre. How could warriors of the same blood as his dwell in such a morbid place? How could these sons of Guilliman have deviated so far from the teachings of the primarch? He increased his pace until he was level with Astador.

'Brother Astador,' began Uriel. 'I do not wish to cause offence, but has your Chapter suffered a great loss in its recent history?'

Astador shook his head in puzzlement. 'No. We have returned from the world of Armageddon with much honour and the bones of our fallen. Why do you ask?'

Uriel searched for the right expression. They needed the help of the Mortifactors and the wrong words could dash any hopes of aid. 'The halls of your monastery suggest your Chapter is in mourning.'

'It is not like this on Macragge?'

'No, the Fortress of Hera is a place of celebration, of joy in the service of the Emperor. It echoes with tales of courage and honour.'

Astador was silent for a moment before replying. 'You are a native of Macragge?'

'No, I was born on Calth, though I trained at the Agiselus Barracks on Macragge since I was six years old.'

'And would you say that you were shaped by your homeworld?'

Uriel considered Astador's question. 'Yes, I would. I worked on an underground farm from the day I was able to walk. They breed them tough on Calth, and you either buckled down and worked hard or you felt the birch across your back.'

'Did you enjoy your life there?' asked Astador.

'I suppose so, though I barely remember it now. It was hard work, but I came from a family who loved me and cared for me. I remember being happy there.'

'And yet you gave it all up to become an Ultramarine.'

'Yes, in Ultramar everyone trains to be a soldier. I discovered I had a natural talent for war, and I swore that I would be the best warrior Macragge had ever seen.'

Astador nodded. 'You are who you are because of where you come from, Captain Ventris, so do not presume to judge me by your own standards. The world below us was my home, and until I was chosen to become one of the Emperor's warriors, I knew neither sunlight nor joy. These things do not exist on Posul, only a brutal life of darkness and bloodshed. I took three hundred skulls in battle before I was chosen to become a Space Marine and since that day I have killed the enemies of the Emperor. I have since seen the sun, yet still I know no joy.'

'A Space Marine needs not joy, nor glory,' said Learchus. 'Service to the Emperor shall be his wine and sustenance, and his soul shall be content.'

Astador stopped and turned to face the veteran sergeant.

'You quote from the Codex Astartes, sergeant. We have grown beyond the need for such dogma and forge our own path from the wisdom of our Chaplains. To be bound by words set down an age ago is not our way.'

The Ultramarines halted in their tracks, horrified by Astador's casual blasphemy. To have the holy writings of Roboute Guilliman dismissed so lightly was something they never expected to hear from the mouth of a fellow Space Marine.

Tiberius was the first to recover his wits and said, 'Forgive us, Brother Chaplain. But it is surprising for us to hear one whose lineage can be traced back to the blessed primarch speaking in such a manner of the Codex Astartes.'

Astador bowed in respect to Tiberius.

'I apologise if my words caused offence, lord admiral. We venerate the primarch, just as you do. He is our Chapter's father and all our oaths of allegiance are sworn to him and the Emperor.'

'Yet you scorn his greatest work?' snapped Learchus, clenching his fists.

'No, my brother, far from it,' said Astador, moving to stand before Learchus. 'We look upon its words as the foundation of our way of life, but to follow its teachings without consideration for what we have learned and that we see around us is not wisdom, it is merely repetition. Repetition leads to stagnation. And stagnation dooms us.'

Uriel placed a hand on Astador's shoulder and said, 'Brother Astador, perhaps we should continue? We have come to speak with your Chapter Master and do not have time for theological debate. The world of Tarsis Ultra is under threat from the most deadly enemy and we would petition your master for his aid in the coming conflict.'

Astador nodded without turning, then spun on his heel and marched off into the darkness once more. Uriel released the breath he had been holding and unclenched his jaw.

'Damn it, Learchus,' he whispered. 'We are here for their help, not to antagonise them.'

'But you heard what he said about the codex!' protested Learchus.

'Uriel is correct, Learchus,' said Tiberius. 'We are all warriors of the Emperor and that is the most important factor. You know there are other Chapters that do not follow the words of the primarch as closely as we do. The sons of Russ follow their own path, and we count them as allies do we not?'

Learchus nodded, though Uriel could see he was not convinced.

Uriel's gaze followed Astador as he continued onwards through the darkness of his fortress monastery. The skulls of fallen Mortifactors stared back at him from the walls. Uriel sighed. Certainly time and distance could change a Chapter a great deal, no matter how similar their ancestry was.

Astador turned and beckoned them onwards.

'Come, Lord Magyar awaits.'

THE GALLERY OF Bone was aptly named, thought Uriel as he stood awaiting the audience with Lord Magyar, Chapter Master of the Mortifactors. A carven cloister of bone surrounded a stone flagged floor paved with hundreds of tombstones. Niches set within the columns of the cloister contained skeletal warriors clutching swords and the entire, domed ceiling was formed from interlocked skulls, their eyeless sockets glaring down at those who stood within their domain. The four Ultramarines stood in the centre of the wide space enclosed by the cloister, Uriel and Tiberius to the fore, Learchus and Pasanius standing at parade rest behind them.

Mortuary statues of angels flanked a vast throne composed of the bones of long-dead Space Marines. Uriel could pick out individual femurs, spines and many other bones as well as grinning skulls leering from the armrests and above the tapered top of the throne.

A bone-legged table stood beside the throne with a flattened bowl of dark enamel atop it. Everywhere Uriel looked, death was venerated and exalted above all things.

Astador stood close to the throne, the hood of his black robe cowling his face once more.

A deep gong sounded, and hidden doors behind the throne swung silently open. The first of a long procession entered the Gallery of Bone. Dozens of hooded figures shuffled into the chamber, some swinging smoking censers, others chanting a sombre lament, but all with their heads cast down. One by one they took up positions around the chamber until each skeleton-filled niche had a living twin standing before it. Two Terminators in dark armour decorated with bone trim marched into the chamber, each carrying a long, wide-bladed scythe. Their helmets were carved to resemble screaming skulls and Uriel could well imagine the terror that these warriors must evoke in their enemies. The Terminators took up position either side of the throne as a winged skeleton, no larger than a child, flapped into the gallery on fragile-looking wings with thin, membranous remnants of tattered vestments fluttering between each of its wing bones. It settled upon the top of the throne and squatted there, silently regarding the shocked Ultramarines. Brass wire glittered at its joints and Uriel could see a tiny suspensor generator attached to the spine between its wings.

Uriel's lip curled in distaste at the sight of the winged familiar as a tall figure, clad in armour of bone entered the gallery. His movements were slow and unhurried, every step considered and solemn. His breastplate was formed from long ribs, bent and fashioned into shape, the Imperial eagle at its centre as skeletal as the winged familiar that watched the proceedings below. Every piece of this warrior's armour, from the greaves to the vambrace, cuissart and gorget was formed from bone. He carried a gigantic scythe, its blade silvered and sharp, the haft gleaming ebony.

Lord Magyar, for it could surely be none other, stood before his throne and bowed to the Ultramarines. His long, silver hair was tied in numerous crystal-wrapped braids reaching to the small of his back and his coal-dark skin resembled a lunar landscape, cratered and ridged with numberless wrinkles. A long, forked white beard fell to his waist, waxed into sharp points.

His eyes were dark pinholes and though it was impossible to guess the age of the Chapter Master, Uriel was certain he must have been at least seven hundred years old.

Lord Magyar sat upon his throne and said, 'You are welcome, brothers of the blood.'

Uriel was shocked at the strength and powerful authority in the ancient warrior's voice, but hid his surprise as he stepped forward and bowed.

'Lord Magyar, we thank you for your welcome and bring greetings from your brothers of Ultramar. Lord Calgar himself bade me convey his regards to you.'

Lord Magyar nodded slowly, accepting Uriel's greeting.

'You come with dark tidings, Captain Ventris. Our Chaplains have seen grave portents and they have seen you.'

'Seen me?' asked Uriel.

'Seen you drenched in blood. Seen you triumphant. Seen you dead,' proclaimed Magyar.

'I do not understand, my lord.'

'Long have we known of your coming to us, Uriel Ventris,' nodded Magyar, 'but not why. Tell me why you have come to my monastery, brother of the blood?'

Pleased to be on a topic he could understand, Uriel bowed again to Lord Magyar.

'We come before you in hopes that you will honour the Warrior's Debt and join us in battle against a terrible enemy.'

'You speak of the oath Guilliman swore on Tarsis Ultra during the Great Crusade.'

'I do, Lord Magyar.'

'Such an oath binds your Chapter still?' asked Magyar.

'Yes, my lord. As has been our way since the blessed primarch swore his oath of brotherhood with the soldier who saved his life, we are sworn to defend the people of Tarsis Ultra should their world ever be threatened,' said Uriel.

'Is it so threatened?' asked Magyar formally.

'It is, my lord.'

'You are sure?'

'Yes, my lord. A tendril of the Great Devourer is moving towards it and will attack soon. My warriors and I recently boarded and destroyed a hulk codified as the *Death of Virtue* that was bound for Tarsis Ultra. The accursed vessel was filled with genestealers and we fought them with courage. Upon returning to our ship, our astropaths detected the psychic disturbance known as the Shadow in the Warp moving towards us. The tyranids are coming, my lord. Of this I am sure.'

'And what do you wish of me?'

'My Chapter is honour bound to defend these realms and I call upon the blood that flows between us for your aid. The tyranids are a monstrous foe and we will be sorely pressed to defeat them. With your valiant warriors by our side, we would stand a much greater chance of victory.'

Lord Magyar grinned, exposing brilliant white teeth. 'Do not think to appeal to my warrior's vanity, Captain Ventris. I know of this debt and the bond that exists between us full well.'

'Then your warriors will fight beside us?'

'That remains to be seen,' said Magyar, beckoning to Astador.

Astador stood beside his lord and master, awaiting his command.

'You will perform a vision-quest, Brother Chaplain Astador?'

'Yes, my lord. As you command,' said Astador opening his robe and allowing it to fall to the tombstone floor. His armour was the colour of spilt blood, dark and threatening, the trims formed in gold. Obsidian skulls adorned each shoulder guard. He carried a golden-winged crozius arcanum, his weapon and a Chaplain's symbol of authority.

He leaned down and removed one of Lord Magyar's gauntlets, placing it next to the bowl on the table. Next, he raised the razor edge of his crozius and slashed it across his master's palm, allowing the blood to spatter into the bowl. Lord Magyar clenched and unclenched his fist repeatedly to prevent the blood from clotting until the bowl was full.

Astador lifted the bowl and offered it to Lord Magyar who accepted it with a respectful nod. The Chapter Master supped his blood and handed the bowl back to Astador.

The Chaplain lifted it to his lips and poured the blood over his face in a red rain. He drank deeply of his master's blood and Uriel grimaced in distaste. What manner of barbaric ritual was this that required the blood of fellow Space Marines to enact? Had the Mortifactors become so debased that they had fallen into rituals more commonly associated with the Ruinous Powers? He glanced over at Tiberius.

The lord admiral's face was unreadable, but Uriel could see the muscles bunched at his jaw and took his cue from him. Astador groaned and reached out a hand to steady himself. The bony familiar perched atop Magyar's throne took to the air and flapped noisily towards the swaying Chaplain, catching the bowl as it fell from his slack fingers.

Uriel could contain himself no longer and shouted, 'What is he doing? This reeks of impure sorceries!'

'Be silent!' roared Magyar. 'He seeks guidance from our revered ancestors. Their wisdom comes from beyond the veil of death, unfettered by the concerns of the living. He seeks their counsel on whether we should join you in this fight.'

Uriel was about to answer when he felt an iron grip on his arm. Lord Admiral Tiberius shook his head slowly.

'The Devourer comes from beyond the galaxy, and even by naming it, men betray their ignorance,' groaned Astador. 'The immortal hive mind controls its every thought. So many beings... A billion times a billion monsters form the overmind and there is none here who can comprehend its scale. It comes this way and seeks only to feed. It cannot be negotiated with, it cannot be reasoned with, it can only be fought. It *must* be fought.'

Astador dropped to his knees and vomited a gout of glistening blood, but the winged familiar was there and caught the vital fluid in the bowl. It flapped towards Magyar and handed him the blood-filled bowl before resuming its perch above the Chapter Master.

Lord Magyar locked eyes with Uriel and smiled, before drinking a measure of his returned blood.

Uriel heard Learchus retch behind him, but forced himself to conceal his revulsion.

The Chapter Master of the Mortifactors wiped a rivulet of blood from his beard and said, 'The omens are not good, Uriel Ventris of the Ultramarines.'

Uriel's heart sank, but Lord Magyar was not yet done. He rose from his throne and crossed the floor of the dead to stand before Uriel. The Chapter Master of the Mortifactors leaned over Uriel and offered him the bowl. Saliva-frothed blood swirled in its bottom.

'Will you seal the pact of our brotherhood, Captain Ventris?'

Uriel stared into the bowl. The blood was bright scarlet.

He felt his gorge rise, but took the proffered bowl from Lord Magyar.

He raised it to his lips. Blood-stink filled his nostrils.

Amusement glittered in Lord Magyar's eyes and Uriel felt anger flare.

He tipped the bowl, feeling the hot blood fill his mouth, and swallowed.

It slipped down his throat, and Uriel could taste a measure of Lord Magyar's vitality and strength fill him. The blood carried the weight of ages in its hot, metallic flavour and Uriel gagged as a powerful vision of slaughter suddenly filled his senses, redolent with an eternity of death. He saw a pair of alien, yellow eyes and once again he felt the touch of the Nightbringer stab into his mind.

Lord Magyar took the bowl from Uriel's nerveless fingers and turned to face Astador, who nodded.

'We will honour the Warrior's Debt, Captain Ventris. I shall give you a company of my warriors and Chaplain Astador to lead them. You shall fight beside one another as equals. The blood has spoken and you have renewed our bond of brotherhood.'

Uriel barely heard him, but nodded anyway, sick to the pit of his stomach.

But whether it was the blood or the memory of the Nightbringer, he could not say.

TWO

THE VAST CITY of Erebus shone like a bright jewel in the flanks of the Cullin Mountains. It was built in a great wound in the rock, as though a giant had taken a shovel and cut a gigantic oval scoop into the south-western flank of the tallest peak. Set within a steep sided, rocky valley, fully nine kilometres wide at its opening, the city cut deep into the mountains for nearly forty kilometres. Bisected by the River Nevas, and home to some ten million people, Erebus was a crawling anthill and the most populous city of Tarsis Ultra.

Hab-units, factories, hydroponics domes, pleasure boulevards and other structures vied for space on the steep sides of the valley. Huge, teetering metal structures of glass and steel rose like metal flowers from the valley's side, and almost every square metre of rock was built upon or bolted to. From the valley floor to the soaring majesty of the luxury habs and exotic spices of the flesh bars, every available sliver of rock was festooned with girders, beams, angles and unfeasibly slender columns, supporting an architecturally eclectic mix of styles that clashed jarringly with the simple, marble elegance of the ancient structures built by the Ultramarines ten millennia ago.

When Erebus City, as it had been known then, was constructed, it was a model of the perfect city, but a lot had changed since those heady days. Where once the city had served as an example of all that was good about human society, ten thousand years of continued expansion had taken its toll on its utopian ideal, bringing it closer to the grim reality of hives on worlds such as Armageddon or Necromunda.

Zooming sculptures of steel rose steeply above the sides of the mountains, each wrapped in hab-units. As each structure climbed higher and higher, accidents became more and more common. Lattices of steel would give out under the horrendous loads imposed upon them, tearing free of the valley's side, to slide majestically down the rock face, pulling walkways, bridges and people with it until they crashed spectacularly to the valley floor in a jagged jumble of twisted metal, rockcrete and bodies.

Yet even here at the bottom, amidst this constant turmoil of debris, people thrived.

The brooding underbelly of the city – the Stank – held twisting baroque corridors and chambers of anarchic splendour that gave sanctuary to the skum gangs – the outcasts and the lawless. The Adeptus Arbites, known locally as the Bronzes, had declared some of the wilder zones of the Stank as no-go areas and even the toughest members of the Arbites Execution squads took care to travel in groups, combat shotguns locked and loaded. Feral gangs roamed the depths of the Stank, scavenging what they could from the ruins of collapsed habs, production towers and each other.

Violent skirmishes would often break out as rival gangs battled for control of newly collapsed structures, eager to plunder their resources.

Or sometimes they fought simply for the hell of it.

SNOWDOG VAULTED OVER the counter of the Flesh Bar. Bullets ripped towards him, blasting the wooden front to splinters as he rolled across it. He racked the slide of his shotgun and dropped behind the bar as bottles shattered and the mirror behind him exploded into reflective daggers. The barman screamed and collapsed next to him, clutching a bloody wound on his shoulder. Glass had cut his face open and red lines streaked his features.

Snowdog winked at the weeping man. 'I guess this really isn't your lucky day.'

The pounding music almost drowned the roar of gunfire. Six Wylderns carrying some heavy-duty weaponry had just walked in and hosed the bar, killing its patrons indiscriminately with bursts from automatic weapons. Who'd have seen that coming? Snowdog took a deep breath and crawled to the end of the bar. He shouldered his combat shotgun. Its blue-steel surface glinted like new, and now more than ever was he glad he'd killed the Bronze who'd carried it.

Screams and panicked yells filled the bar as people sought to make themselves scarce, desperate to avoid getting caught up in another of the gang wars that were becoming an all too common occurrence in Erebus hive.

Heavy blasts of gunfire echoed through the bar and more screams sounded. The music died as the speakers blew out in an explosion of sparks. People dropped, craters blasted in chests and bodies torn in two by heavy calibre shells.

Snowdog risked a glance around the side of the bar. Tigerlily was pinned down behind an overturned table, a throwing knife in each hand, and Silver had found shelter behind a thick steel column. He couldn't see Jonny Stomp or Lex, but figured that one was too smart and the other too lucky to have been caught in the initial salvo of autogun fire.

Damned Wylderns! Life for a fledgling gang leader was hard enough without these crazies making it even more precarious. It was bad enough that the Bronzes came down like an iron hammer on anyone who broke the law – which meant just about everyone in this part of the hive – from their grim and imposing fortress precinct on the edge of the Stank, the worst of the city's badzones. Not even the Bronzes would come in here without some serious hardware. But the Wylderns...

He couldn't figure them out. He robbed and killed for money, and to be the top dog of the Stank, but these psychos just killed. There was no telling where or when they'd strike, bursting in with powerful weapons and blazing away until everyone was dead. Killing for profit he could understand, but he could see no reason for these massacres and that bugged the hell out of Snowdog.

'Come out, come out wherever you are,' shouted a Wyldern in a singsong voice.

Snowdog heard the snap of more ammunition being loaded and nodded to Tigerlily. Like a coiled spring, the young redhead rose and hurled a throwing knife with unerring accuracy. The thin blade plunged into the eye of the nearest Wyldern and he crumpled wordlessly.

Tigerlily ducked back as gunfire blasted sparking chunks from the metal table she sheltered behind. Her black catsuit had been torn by a spinning shard of the table and Snowdog could see she was really mad now. As soon as the Wylderns were distracted, Snowdog rose from behind the bar and yelled, 'You picked the wrong bar to patronise, boys!'

He put another Wyldern down with his first shot and winged a second before they reacted and sprayed the bar with fire. Snowdog leapt aside, hundreds of bullets turning the bar to matchwood as he rolled.

Silver burst from hiding, a pistol in each hand. Her long, white hair was pulled in a severe ponytail and her ice-blue eyes were cold and unforgiving. She calmly double tapped another two Wylderns before spinning back behind the pillar, her long black coat billowing around her.

'And then there were two,' he muttered, seeing the sudden fear and confusion of the remaining two Wylderns. He stood and walked from behind the bar, sauntering into the middle of the blood-soaked killing ground. Bodies littered the place and it reeked of gunsmoke.

'Didn't expect this kinda welcome, did you?' asked Snowdog. 'We're the Nightcrawlers, and you interrupted our business here.'

'We'll kill you all!' shrieked one of the Wylderns, but there was no conviction in his voice.

'I don't think so, man,' said Snowdog, catching sight of Jonny Stomp and Lex on the upper balcony of the Flesh Bar, circling behind the Wylderns. He shook his head. Where else would Jonny and Lex be but with the girls and sex drugs, sampling the wares before doing the job?

'What do you say to you guys putting your guns away and letting us get on with this, huh?' said Snowdog.

He could see their hesitation and knew he had to appeal to their sense of self-preservation before their stupidity or bravado could resurface. He said, 'Look, no one else has to die here, okay?'

His voice was soothing and he slowly lowered his shotgun, taking in their high-priced clothing and coloured hair. Their faces were pierced with metal spikes and their full features spoke of healthy eating. Expensive looking electoos writhed up their arms and around their necks, throbbing in time with their racing heartbeats. These were rich kids on some narcotic high; he could see it in their eyes.

And suddenly it all made sense. They were thrill killers. Rich kids who killed because they were bored and because they could. But now that the tables had turned, the killing frenzy had gone out of them.

He continued to slowly walk towards the Wylderns and set his shotgun down on the bar. 'You just want out of here in one piece.'

The Wylderns nodded and Snowdog spread his arms.

'I can understand that,' he said, 'but it ain't going to happen.'

His eyes darted up towards the balcony.

'Now, Jonny,' said Snowdog mildly.

The Wylderns registered puzzlement for the briefest second before all one hundred kilogrammes of Jonny Stomp landed on them, smashing them to the ground. Jonny swiftly rose to his feet and dragged the first Wyldern to his feet, snapping his neck with a dry crack and rounding on the other as he tried to scramble away.

'No, please!' he begged. 'My family's rich, they'll give you any–'

'Not interested,' said Jonny and thundered his fist into the young Wyldern's face.

Blood and teeth flew as Jonny beat the young man to death with his bare hands.

Snowdog turned and lifted his shotgun from the bar, resting its barrel on his shoulder. He took a deep breath now that the fight was over, running a hand through his bleached and spiked hair as he leaned on the splintered bar.

Flickering neon bathed his rugged features in an unhealthy glow and glass tinkled as it fell from shattered frames.

He rapped his knuckles on the bar. The dazed barman rose to his feet, hands clasped on top of his bloody head.

'Okay, man. Now where were we before all this unpleasantness?' said Snowdog.

He grinned ferally. 'Oh yeah, now I remember. This is a raid, hand over all your money.'

'GOOD TAKINGS?' ASKED Lex, eyeing the pile of cash on the upturned crate.

Snowdog eyed Lex suspiciously. 'Good enough, Lex.'

He pushed the money back into his small backpack and rose to his feet, flipping open a carton of bac-sticks and dragging one out. He pulled a brass lighter from his pocket and lit the aromatic stick, drawing in a lungful of smoke. He lifted the backpack by the straps and dumped it on his iron bedframe.

Snowdog sat on the bed and watched as Lex shrugged and sloped off to join Jonny Stomp in the front room of their current hideout. Night had well and truly fallen and the glittering lights of the valley sides shone in through the holed roof and windowless frames. There was a sharp chill and Snowdog could feel a harsh winter coming on the air.

Lex was a problem. Snowdog knew it would only be a matter of time before Lex got himself killed. Normally, Snowdog would have cut him loose and moved on, but no one knew explosives like Lex. The things he could cook up with everyday items were beyond belief and many of the Bronzes had cause to regret an over-eager pursuit of the Nightcrawlers when they'd run into one of Lex's booby traps.

Lex didn't say much about where he came from, but Snowdog had seen a cog-toothed tattoo on his upper arm and guessed he'd once been apprenticed to the tech-guilds that worked the factory hangars and forge temples further down the valley. He'd come to them nearly six months ago and it didn't take a genius to figure out why he'd been kicked out of the guild. Lex was an addict, probably had been for years, permanently strung out on kalma or spur and was too dumb to realise that routine chem-screens would pick them up.

He banished Lex from his thoughts and rested a hand on the score from the bar. There was enough here to pay for some real big guns, then they could really carve themselves some turf. And he knew just the guy to get those weapons from.

Yeah, it had been a good heist, but the Wylderns had stolen the show and that bugged him. How was he supposed to build the Nightcrawlers into the most feared and respected gang in the Stank with practically no one left alive to spread the word? Perhaps they should have let the last Wyldern live, but Snowdog quickly dismissed that thought. Trying to stop Jonny Stomp from killing someone when his blood was up wasn't a healthy option if you wanted to stay alive yourself. The big man was a stone-cold killer, pure and simple, but he was useful and trusted Snowdog utterly.

Which just went to show that Jonny wasn't the sharpest tool in the box, but Snowdog would take what muscle he could get. He took a last draw on the bac-stick then dropped it on the floor, crushing it out beneath his boot. He stretched and lay down on the bed.

Snowdog was of average height, but was blessed with a wiry musculature that belied his whipcord-thin body. He wore tiger-striped combat fatigues, tucked into a heavy pair of boots he'd pulled from a dead Bronze and a white t-shirt with a faded holo patch of a mushroom cloud that expanded and contracted as he moved.

The score at the Flesh Bar would keep the wolves from the door, but he'd need to think of another pretty soon if he was to keep his crew together. They would follow him for as long as they thought he was good news. But he needed a regular gig that would keep the cash flowing with the minimum amount of effort.

He looked up as he heard a tap on the doorframe and smiled as Silver strolled up to the edge of his bed and sat beside him.

'Some day, huh?' she said.

'Some day,' agreed Snowdog. 'Where's Tigerlily?'

'She went off to a pound club with Trask,' answered Silver sleepily. 'Kominsky's, I think.'

'Maybe I'm getting old, but this pound music is something I just don't understand. Loud music I get, but it's like a sonic assault on the senses.'

'A lot of people like it,' pointed out Silver. 'Hell, even I don't mind it.'

'So why didn't you go with her?'

'I couldn't be bothered with Trask. You know what he's like with stimms.'

'Tigerlily obviously doesn't mind.'

'That's cause she's too young and dumb to realise what a loser he is.'

'You're cynical tonight.'

Silver smiled and Snowdog felt himself loosen up as she bent down to kiss him.

'I'm tired,' she said. 'And besides, what can Trask do for me that I can't get better from you?'

Snowdog chuckled, remembering the last time Trask had gotten overly amorous towards Silver after a heavy night on the stimms. The poor bastard hadn't walked straight for a week afterwards. He decided to change the subject. 'How're the rest of the troops?'

Silver shrugged, 'Okay, I guess. Lex is getting antsy and Jonny wants to head out to bust some heads. He keeps talking about taking on the High Hive gangs.'

Snowdog chuckled. 'They're gonna find Jonny face down in the sump if he thinks he can take on the High Hive gangs. Tell him he'd better stick to busting up Jackboy parties if he knows what's good for him. We ain't ready for that kind of action yet.'

Silver yawned and slid off her long coat, pulling her albino-white hair free of its ponytail and allowing it to spill around her shoulders. She climbed over Snowdog to lie with her back to the wall, laying her arm across his waist and resting her head on his chest. Snowdog kissed her forehead and put his arm around her shoulders.

'Did you notice that there weren't any citizens' militia units around the Flesh Bar?' asked Silver, pushing her hand beneath his t-shirt and running her fingers through the hair on his stomach.

'Yeah, I did. That was kinda weird, wasn't it?'

'I wonder where they were? Normally you can't move in the upper valley without seeing at least a few of them.'

Snowdog nodded slowly. 'I don't know, but now you mention it, the whole city has been pretty wired recently, on edge. I seen a lot of Bronzes, but it's been pretty quiet in the way of soldiers. I wonder why? And those Wylderns. Normally they'd never dare hit a bar that close to the High Hive.'

'What do you think is going on?'

'Damned if I know, hon, but if it keeps the militia and the Bronzes off our backs, then I'm all for it.'

Snowdog could not have been more wrong.

℧
THREE

URIEL WATCHED THE landscape speed past the Thunderhawk, circling round white-capped mountains of soaring majesty. A hard winter was coming to this part of the world and the beauty below was breathtaking. Frozen mountaintop lakes glittered in the thin light and the rugged splendour reminded him wistfully of the landscape surrounding the Fortress of Hera.

The Thunderhawk banked, following the line of the mountains, and Uriel caught a glimpse of the black gunships of the Mortifactors as they turned in formation with those of the Ultramarines. His expression turned sour as the memory and taste of Lord Magyar's blood surged strong and vivid through his senses.

The Chapter Master of the Mortifactors had laughed, calling him brother, and slapped his palms on Uriel's shoulder guards, leaving bloody handprints. How any Chapter descended from the blessed Roboute Guilliman could have fallen so far from his vision of a sacred band of warriors was utterly beyond him. He also had the feeling that it had been his drinking of Magyar's blood that had convinced the Chapter Master to send his warriors rather than any bond of shared brotherhood. How could such a Chapter operate, let alone thrive, without recourse to the Codex Astartes?

Upon returning to the *Vae Victus*, Uriel had immersed himself in prayer and rituals of cleansing, but the lingering vision that ripped through his mind could not be purged. He could not deny the feeling of power he had experienced drinking the blood and he knew that part of him, Emperor forgive him, longed for that power again.

In the month it had taken them to return to the Tarsis Ultra system, there had been precious little contact with the Mortifactors, a situation the

299

Ultramarines were more than happy with. It had been a shock to everyone to know that a Chapter founded from their honourable legacy had changed so much.

They would fight alongside the Mortifactors, but Uriel knew there would be no renewal of brotherhood and no pledges of loyalty sworn anew between the Chapters.

They would face the common threat and that would be the end of it.

He realised he was clenching his fists and slowly released a deep breath.

The Thunderhawk began descending as they cleared the mountains and Uriel tried to shake his angry thoughts, returning his gaze to the world below.

They flew over ordered farming collectives, their sprawling fields a striking green amid the patchy white frosts of oncoming winter. Gleaming train tracks and hydroways snaked across the landscape, efficiently connecting the scattered communities and, every now and then, Uriel caught a glimpse of a silvered land train speeding between them.

The view was eerily reminiscent of the surface of Iax, sometimes called the Garden of Ultramar, one of the most productive worlds of the Imperium. Uriel briefly wondered if the inhabitants had also built their own version of Iax's fortress city of First Landing.

So far as he could tell from the air, Tarsis Ultra looked to be a model world that would not have been out of place in Ultramar itself. But Uriel knew it had not always been this way.

Ten thousand years ago, it had been enslaved by the lies of heretics for decades, before its liberation by Roboute Guilliman and the Ultramarines during the Great Crusade. Its grateful populace had incorporated their liberators into their world's name, that they might always remember and honour them. When the Ultramarines Legion moved on to fresh campaigns, Roboute Guilliman left the foundations of an ordered world, established on ideals of justice, honour and discipline, instead of the blasted wastelands many of his brother primarchs' victories left. Guilliman left teachers, artisans and people skilled in the ways of engineering and architecture to help with the rebuilding of Tarsis Ultra.

Its civilization was remade in the image of Ultramar, its society ordered and just, its people content and productive. Once more, Tarsis Ultra became a functioning world of the Emperor. Its output was prodigious, but unlike many other industrial worlds, whose unthinking plundering of their natural resources led to them becoming polluted, toxic deserts, sustainability and a careful husbanding of resources assured that Tarsis Ultra remained a verdant and pleasant world.

After the grim revelations regarding the Mortifactors, Uriel was looking forward to setting foot on a world touched by the primarch. What he had seen on the Basilica Mortis had shaken him to the core, and it would do him good to see a physical reminder of Roboute Guilliman's legacy.

And what he had seen thus far of Tarsis Ultra and its defences had impressed him greatly. Hulking star forts hung in geo-stationary orbit above the primary continental mass and already a sizeable fleet had been assembled in the months since their warning of the approaching tyranids had been given.

The *Argus*, a Victory class battlecruiser, and veteran of the First Tyrannic War, headed a detachment of fearsome vessels of war, including the *Sword of Retribution*, an Overlord battleship, three Dauntless cruisers and a host of escort ships. Flotillas of planetary skiffs, laden with the men and women of the Imperial Guard, were constantly shuttling back and forth from the planet's surface and four vast transport ships hanging in orbit. Within days, the entirety of two vast regiments, the 10th Logres and the 933rd Death Korp of Kreig, would be deployed to Tarsis Ultra.

More ships were being diverted to the system by segmentum command at Bakka and fresh regiments raised from nearby systems and sub-sectors, but they would not arrive for several months. For now they were on their own.

Lord Admiral Tiberius was even now planning the strategy for the combined naval forces with Captain Gaiseric of the Mortifactors strike cruiser *Mortis Probati*, and the commander of the fleet, Admiral de Corte, a student of Lord Admiral Zaccarius Rath himself.

'Two minutes,' came the pilot's voice over the speakers.

Uriel shook himself from his reverie and watched as Learchus paced the length of the Thunderhawk, his normally stoic features alive with anticipation. It seemed as though Learchus was more anxious than anyone to set foot on Tarsis Ultra.

Pasanius sat opposite Uriel, looking relaxed and unconcerned that they were about to see a world touched by their primarch. His heavy flamer was stowed above him and he nodded to Uriel as the Thunderhawk came about for its final approach. 'This should be interesting,' he said.

'Interesting?' laughed Learchus. 'It will be wonderful. To see the handiwork of the blessed Guilliman halfway across the galaxy is proof that our way of life is the way forward for humanity.'

'It is?' asked Pasanius.

'Of course,' said Learchus, surprised that Pasanius had even queried his statement. 'If the way of life we have followed for millennia thrives here, it can thrive elsewhere.'

'Is it thriving here?'

'Obviously.'

'How do you know? You haven't seen it yet.'

'I don't need to see it, I have faith in the primarch.'

Uriel let his sergeants argue the finer points of Guilliman's vision as he caught his first glimpse of Erebus city, a dark scar on the snow-covered flank of a vast mountain filled with silver towers. A huge reservoir glittered on the adjacent plateau, high above the kilometres-wide valley mouth, its rocky slopes crowned with white marble buildings and elegant, columned structures. A wide, statue-lined road rose through the centre of the valley, towards the first of the city's defensive walls, throngs of buildings crowding in on all sides. The interior of the city was a glittering spiderweb of silver and white.

Save for the buildings at the very edge of the valley, Uriel could see no discernable pattern to the city's construction. Here and there he recognised flourishes of Macraggian architecture, but where there should have been space and light, he saw newer, brasher constructions, towering carbuncles overshadowing the elegance of the oldest buildings.

The Thunderhawk gained altitude and altered course so that it was flying parallel to the valley. Uriel could see that the valley floor rose the further into the mountain it penetrated until it reached a long, defensive wall, a foaming waterfall at its centre, that in turn rose towards another, shorter wall as the valley narrowed. The stepped structure of the city's defences continued towards the valley's end and now that he could look down into the city, he saw ruined areas, collapsed structures that looked as though they had been shelled. Hundreds of jumbled structures squatted here in the frigid shadows of the high towers of the deep valley, thin plumes of white smoke rising from a multitude of cooking fires.

The sense of disappointment in what had become of Guilliman's legacy was a physical pain in Uriel's chest. He sat back in his captain's chair and felt his fists clenching again.

He looked over as he heard a shocked intake of breath from Learchus.

'What is this?' he breathed. 'Are we too late, has the war begun?'

'No,' said Uriel sadly. 'It has not.'

THE GUNSHIPS OF the Space Marines touched down on the upper landing platforms of Erebus city, the screaming of their engines drowning out the pomp and ceremony of the hundred-strong band that played rousing tunes of welcome. Uriel marched down the ramp of the gunship, feeling the sharp bite of the cold air as he moved away from the heat of the engines.

'Now this is a welcome,' said Pasanius, raising his voice to be heard.

Uriel nodded in agreement. The platforms were awash with men, thousands upon thousands of soldiers drawn up in ordered ranks before the Space Marine gunships. Vast banners flapped from standard poles thirty metres high, supported by a dozen men with suspensors and guy ropes. Gold braid fluttered and the blue and white of the Ultramarines Chapter symbol rippled hugely on their fabric. The company banners of all ten of the Ultramarine companies were present as well as those of individual heroes from Chapter legend. At the forefront of the banners, Uriel could see the heraldry of Captain Invictus, and next to that, the banner of the

Fourth company. He did a double take as he saw that a battle honour in the shape of the white rose of Pavonis had been added to the design.

Chaplain Astador joined him from the ramp of his own Thunderhawk.

'It seems your fame precedes you, Captain Ventris,' he said.

Uriel nodded, staring at this full ceremonial reception. He had expected to be met, but this was insane. How much time and effort had been put into this welcome that could have been better spent strengthening the city's defences or training? Did these people not realise that they would soon be at war?

An honour guard of perhaps two hundred armoured troopers formed up in ordered ranks either side of the Thunderhawks, dressed in ridiculously impractical blue armour. Fashioned to resemble power armour, the soldiers looked absurd next to the bulk of the Ultramarines.

A cold wind whipped across the landing platforms as another column of men strode towards them between the honour guards. The soldiers marched in perfect step, their drill flawless and uniforms spotless. In front of them came another group, headed by three men who, judging by the elaboration of the leader's dress, commanded this gathering.

The lead officer wore the same ceremonial blue armour as the honour guard, with a silver trim and gold braid looping around his shoulders and trousers. He wore a dazzling silver helmet with a long, horsehair plume that reached down to his waist, and he carried a golden, basket-hilted sword before his face. His chest was awash with gold and silver insignia and his boots were an immaculately polished black leather. His companions obviously eschewed such frivolous adornment, preferring the simple dress uniforms of their Imperial Guard regiments.

Uriel recognised the heavy greatcoat and fur colback of the Krieg regiment and, from the silver laurel and pips on his collar, deduced that this was that regiment's colonel. The final member of the group was a thickly-waisted older man, with a neatly trimmed beard, wearing simple, well-pressed fatigues and a thickly padded jacket with a fur collar. Like the colonel of the Krieg regiment, he wore a fur-lined colback and, also like his fellow colonel, seemed deeply uncomfortable at this ostentatious welcome.

'Captain,' said Pasanius, pointing towards the edges of the landing fields.

Further down the valley, huge crowds gathered beyond the high fencing that surrounded the platforms. Expressions of worship and awe stared back at the Ultramarines and Uriel could see people praying and weeping tears of joy.

The delegation of officers came to a halt before them, their over-dressed leader slashing his sword through the air in an elaborate gesture of salute. He sheathed the sword and stepped forward, bowing his head and dropping to one knee before Uriel.

'Honoured lords, I am thine humble servant, Sebastien Montante, Fabricator Marshal of the world of Tarsis Ultra, and in the name of the Divine Master of Mankind I bid thee welcome,' said the man in tortured High Gothic. 'May your beneficence shine over our world at the glory of your return. A thousand times a thousand prayers of thanks shall be offered up in praise of your names. Many are the salute–'

'I thank you for your welcome, sir,' interrupted Uriel brusquely. 'I am Uriel Ventris, captain of the Fourth company.'

Montante looked up, startled and more than a little crestfallen to have had his speech halted in its tracks. Uriel saw he was about to continue, and hurriedly said, 'These are my senior sergeants, Pasanius and Learchus. And this is Chaplain Astador of the Mortifactors.'

Realising that he wouldn't be able to finish his speech, Montante rose to his feet and brushed his trousers flat. He bowed nervously to Astador and said, 'Chaplain Astador, we have heard of your illustrious Chapter and bid you welcome also.'

Astador nodded and returned the bow. 'Your display of welcome is overwhelming, Fabricator Montante and we thank you for it.'

Montante smiled crookedly and nodded, turning to face the two colonels who had accompanied him.

'Allow me to introduce the senior officers of our brave defenders,' said Montante, recovering well.

The leader of the Krieg regiment stepped forward and snapped a curt salute to the Space Marines, saying, 'Colonel Trymon Stagler, regimental commander of the 933rd Death Korp of Krieg and overall theatre commander. I apologise for this waste of time, but Fabricator Montante kept it from us until an hour ago.'

Stagler ignored Montante's frown of indignation as the second man stepped forwards and offered his hand to Uriel. 'Colonel Octavius Rabelaq, commander in chief of the 10th Logres regiment. Pleasure to meet you, Uriel. Heard a lot about you from Sebastien. Looking forward to fighting with you. Well, not fighting with you, but you understand, eh?'

Uriel took the proffered hand and Rabelaq enthusiastically pumped his hand up and down, gripping Uriel's elbow with his other hand as he did so. Eventually, he released Uriel and stepped back with a brisk salute as Montante nodded briskly in the direction of the honour guard.

'Yes, yes, well, now that we all know each other, we should get on with the formal inspection, yes? Then onto the feast of welcome, eh? Don't want to let all that delicious food and amasec go to waste,' smiled Montante, again indicating that the Space Marines should follow him towards the honour guard.

'Fabricator Montante,' said Uriel. 'We do not have time to tarry here and should begin preparations for the coming battles. The tyranid fleet is probably less than a month from your system at best and you would have us indulge in frivolity?'

Montante's mouth flapped as he considered this breach of formal welcoming etiquette and looked towards the Guard colonels for support.

'Captain Ventris is correct' said Colonel Stagler. 'We must begin planning. The enemy is at the gates.'

Uriel thought he could detect just a hint of anticipation in the colonel's voice.

'Indeed it is,' said a figure emerging from the honour guard behind Montante.

Uriel saw a hooded adept with a retinue of scribes, lexmechanics and green robed astropaths limp painfully towards them using a claw-topped silver cane.

'The enemy is indeed at the gates,' repeated the hooded adept. 'My astropaths tell me that the first vanguard droneships are even now entering the outer reaches of the system. The rest of the hive fleet cannot be far behind.'

'And who are you, sir?' asked Uriel.

The man pulled back his hood, revealing an ancient, weathered face, with a tonsured crown of silver hair. His features had the pallid, waxy texture of frequent juvenat treatments, but his eyes had lost none of the fire that Uriel remembered from the numerous images of him in the Chapel of Heroes on Macragge.

'I am Lord Inquisitor Kryptman of the Ordo Xenos, and we do not have much time.'

SIXTY THOUSAND POUNDS of thrust roared from the twin engines of each Fury attack craft as they howled along the internal flight deck of the *Kharloss Vincennes*, a Dictator class cruiser, and shot from the launch bays of their cruiser's flank like bullets from a gun.

Two squadrons, each of three fighters, lifted off and circled back around, ready to begin their intercept. An anomalous contact had registered on the powerful surveyor systems of Listening Station Trajen, a lightly manned orbital anchored at the edge of the Tarsis Ultra system. Their job would be to investigate the contact and, if circumstances were favourable, engage and destroy it. Should that not be possible, they would provide exact positional data and allow the heavier guns of the *Kharloss Vincennes* to obliterate it.

The Furies were aerodynamic fighters with swept-forwards wings and twin tails with a rack of high-explosive missiles slung under each wing. Designed to shoot down incoming torpedoes, intercept attacking bombers and destroy other fighters, Furies were the workhorses of the Imperial Navy.

Each Fury carried extra fuel in a centreline tank, which would enable them to remain on patrol for longer periods of time without having to return to their carrier.

The Fury could carry up to four crew, but for scouting missions, a pilot and a gunnery officer were all that was required.

'Angel squadrons, sound off,' came the voice of the ordnance officer from the *Kharloss Vincennes*.

'Angel squadron nine-zero-one, clear,' acknowledged Captain Owen Morten, commander of the *Kharloss Vincennes'* fighter squadrons, thumbing the vox-toggle on his control column as he checked left and right for his two wingmen. He waited for Lieutenant Erin Harlen, lead pilot of the second squadron of Furies to call in as Kiell Pelaur, his gunnery officer, fired up the surveyor link to the *Kharloss Vincennes*.

'Ditto. Angel squadron nine-zero-two. We are clear, and that's official,' came the drawling voice of Erin Harlen over the vox-net.

'Cut the chatter nine-zero-two. Combat readiness is in force. Do you understand that at all, Lieutenant Harlen?' replied the ordnance officer in a voice that suggested he had been through this routine many times.

'Yes, sir! That order has been understood, sir!' shouted Harlen.

'Harlen, keep it down for a second will you?' said Pelaur over the internal vox-net. 'Let's find out where we're supposed to patrol before you start driving us all mad, huh?'

'Understood, Lieutenant. We were beginning to wonder that ourselves,' replied Harlen's gunnery officer, Caleb Martoq.

The Furies circled the *Kharloss Vincennes* as they awaited navigational data to be transferred into their own attack logisters.

The voice of the ordnance officer came again. 'Angel squadrons, confirm patrol circuit.'

Kiell Pelaur checked the pict-slate before him as the tactical plot of their squadron appeared and thumbed the vox. 'Confirmed. Circuit is acquired.'

'Confirmed. Angel squadrons one and two are weapons-free and cleared to engage. Good hunting.'

'You bet we'll have good hunting. We don't take prisoners,' said Harlen. He glanced through the toughened canopy to where his squadron commander and the rest of his squadron were flying on station with him.

'Ready, Captain Morten?' he said, the anticipation in his voice unmistakable even over the vox-net. Morten smiled beneath his helmet and said, 'Angel squadron nine-zero-one has the lead. Harlen, take our lower quadrant and stay close.'

'Understood, Captain. Nine-zero-one has the lead.'

Captain Morten turned his control column to the required heading, took a deep breath and opened up the Fury's throttle.

It felt as though he had suddenly been kicked in the back as the giant engines thundered and hurled the craft forwards. The suspensor wired pressure suit expanded to prevent his blood from pooling, counteracting the horrendous forces exerted on his body by such rapid acceleration.

Super-oxygenated blood pumped directly into his body via spinal connections and the contoured helmets both he and his gunnery officer wore exerted outward pressure on the surrounding air to prevent them from blacking out.

This was what it was all about, he thought to himself with a wide, boyish grin. The long years of training, the unbelievable physical demands and the risks were more than made up for by moments like this. Powering through space at the command of one of the most sacred pieces of military hardware ever forged, with the power to bring righteous death to the enemies of the Emperor, was as close to perfection as life ever got.

His two wingmen were keeping station with him in a standard 'V' formation. Satisfied, he rolled his fighter slightly to make sure that Harlen was in position below him. Morten knew that despite his often cavalier attitude, Erin Harlen was one of the best pilots in the squadron, if not Battlefleet Tempestus itself. For that reason and that reason alone he was cut a little more slack than would normally be allowed in such a regimented place as an Imperial Navy starship.

As Harlen's squadron commander he was entrusted with the often troublesome job of keeping him in line and not allowing him to stray beyond his already widened boundaries of discipline.

Sure enough, Harlen's squadron of Furies were right where they were supposed to be, slightly below and behind him on his starboard wing. He rolled level again and continued on course. This intercept should take less than an hour and until then there was very little to do except sit back and keep an eye on the gauges to make sure they were flying within the tolerances of the craft. There wasn't much of anything to look at through the canopy, and, without a fixed point of reference, it was impossible to perceive their motion.

Thirty minutes of their patrol circuit had passed before the surveyor screen before Lieutenant Pelaur picked up their target.

'Target acquired, captain. Bio readings consistent with tyranid life forms. Bearing, zero-three-six right, range one thousand kilometres,' said Pelaur from his slightly elevated position in the cockpit behind Morten, 'Recommend approach vector mark four-six.'

'Affirmative, lieutenant,' said Morten, adjusting his course so as to come in from the optimum attack position in space combat – behind and above the target. Pelaur's course would also put the light of the sun behind them, such as it was, and hopefully mask their presence a fraction longer.

In space combat, where death could travel the distance between combatants in seconds, the difference between life and death could often rest on those fractions.

'Lieutenant Harlen, come in.'

'Captain Morten! My gunnery officer has a contact.'

'As does mine, Lieutenant Harlen. Approach vector mark four-six.'

'I concur,' said Caleb Martoq.

'Thirty seconds to attack run,' said Pelaur.

They were fast approaching the point where they would make their final turn before beginning their attack. From here onwards they were on a war footing.

'Confirmed,' said Morten, starting the countdown to their turn and cutting the throttle back, decelerating towards combat speed.

'Twenty seconds,' counted down Pelaur.

The pilots rapidly bled off speed from their engines, slowing so that they would be able to attack without shooting past their target.

'Lieutenant Harlen. Ten seconds, be ready.' said Morten, flexing his fingers on the control stick.

'Aye, captain. In ten.'

'Turn on my mark,' said Pelaur, his face fixed on the pict-slate before him. 'Mark!'

Morten banked the Fury sharply right and downwards, following the plot on his attack logister. The other Furies swung in smoothly behind his fighter like a flock of hunting birds.

'What do you have, lieutenant?' he asked.

The icon displayed on Pelaur's screen flashed and held a steady red.

'I have a hostile contact, captain.'

'Affirmative,' said Martoq.

'Attack pattern delta four,' ordered Morten. 'I want a volley from your squadron, Lieutenant Harlen.'

'Attack pattern delta four confirmed,' said Harlen. 'Breaking right.'

The three Furies in Harlen's squadron peeled away to the right and increased speed as they closed with the target.

'Missiles ready,' said Martoq.

'Fire at will,' returned Morten.

Morten watched the Furies of Harlen's squadron shudder as a missile detached from each of their wings and his cockpit was suddenly brilliantly illuminated as the rocket motors ignited and the six missiles flashed into the darkness.

'Missiles away!' shouted Harlen.

'Angel flight nine-zero-one, with me. Let's go,' ordered Morten.

He pushed the throttle open again and sped off after the missiles, arming his own and powering up the lascannon. If anything flew out from the target to try and intercept the missiles, he and his Furies would be waiting for them. He mouthed a quick prayer to the Emperor and checked his display. The pict-slate showed the flashing red icon of the target with two green arrowheads rapidly converging on its position.

His own flight were following the missiles in, leapfrogging Lieutenant Harlen's and leaving his flight to cover them. Any element of surprise had been lost the instant they had fired, but it had been maintained long enough.

'Impact in two seconds,' said his gunnery officer.

Morten focused his eyes beyond the canopy and saw a blossom of white fire in the distance.

'Missiles have impacted. I say again, missiles have impacted,' called Martoq over the vox-net. 'We got him!'

'Good shooting, Angel nine-zero-two!' said Morten, even though he knew that Martoq's assessment of the target's destruction was premature. They couldn't know that for certain yet.

'Did they get it, Kiell?' asked Morten.

'Looks like it, sir. I'm not getting any bio-readings any more. I think we got it.'

'You bet we got it! We blew it back to the warp!' cawed Harlen.

'Alright, we're going in for a closer look. Cut speed and we'll go in and see what we can see. Harlen, you're covering.'

'No problem, captain,' acknowledged Harlen. 'Lascannons are armed and ready. Anything that so much as twitches is going to be sucking vacuum.'

'Okay, let's take this nice and easy,' cautioned Morten. 'Kiell, keep your eyes and ears open. If we need to get out of here in a hurry I want to know about it right away.'

'Affirmative,' replied Pelaur, concentrating on the threat boards.

Morten pushed the control stick over and headed straight for the location of the explosion he had seen through the canopy. As his craft drew nearer, he saw a large, tubular object spinning in space, huge craters blasted in its side. He pulled the speed way back and moved in for a closer look. Perhaps forty or fifty metres long, the object's surface was a mottled green and pierced with undulating sphincter orifices. A tattered, fleshy frill ran the length of the creature and long, cable-like tentacles drifted behind it. Its front resembled a giant, serrated beak and ichor foamed in an expanding purple cloud from the wounds in its side, spilling into space like blood. If this thing had once been alive, it now looked very dead.

'Are you getting any bio readings?' he asked.

'No, sir. All surveyors say it's dead.'

'Good.' said Morten. 'Well, log it in the cont-'

'Look out!' screamed Lieutenant Harlen suddenly. 'Three o' clock high!'

Morten instinctively slammed the control column right and pushed out the throttles to full power. He caught a glimpse of a fleshy, toothed torpedo-like object that had spurted from the side of the supposedly life-less organism through one of the rippling orifices.

He rolled hard left, slamming them around the cockpit as it flashed over their heads.

As though in slow motion he saw the organism sail past his cockpit.

He continued his roll left, levelling off and easing up only when he had done a full circle. By the Emperor that had been close! They had almost–

'It's still on you, captain!' shouted Harlen, 'It's right on your tail!'

'Emperor's blood, this thing is persistent!'

He rolled right and dived, twisting his Fury in a looping spiral.

'Range, one hundred and fifty metres!' yelled Pelaur, 'Too close! Get us out of here!'

'What do you think I'm doing?' snapped Morten, climbing hard and pushing the throttle all the way out. If the damned thing was still with him now then it was only a matter of time before it caught them.

'Range, one hundred metres and closing!'

It was too close for any of his wingmen to shoot at and Morten could only hope that the thing, whatever it was, had to impact to detonate, or whatever it did.

'Captain!' shouted Harlen, 'Break right, Mark nine-three. Now!'

Without question Morten obeyed, hauling right and diving at full speed. He was just quick enough to see the shape of Harlen's Fury flash past his canopy, lasfire blasting from its underside.

Though he couldn't hear it, he felt the enormous pressure wave of the tyranid weapon's explosive death throes as the flurry of lasfire blew it away.

But it had been too close for them to avoid its vengeance completely. The rear quarter of the Fury lurched drunkenly sideways as hundreds of chitinous fragments scythed into the fighter's body.

Morten fought for control of the shuddering craft as it spun crazily. His helmet smashed into the side of the cockpit and his vision swam as warning lights winked into life all over the control panels. His suit expanded and despite the pressure helmet he could feel himself on the verge of blacking out. If that happened it was all over. The centrifugal forces would tear his ship apart, leaving their bodies to freeze in space.

Sparks and smoke obscured his vision and he could only just make out the shape of the throttle. Morten strained to reach it over the rising forces in the cockpit.

He could hear the squeal of tearing metal and knew that his Fury was beginning to disintegrate.

With one last effort he lunged forwards and hauled the throttle back to idle.

Almost immediately, the violent shuddering of his wounded craft ceased, to be replaced by the soft creak of twisted metal, Pelaur's rapid breathing and the protesting whine of the engines as they powered down.

The Fury drifted and spun sideways for a while, before Morten repressurised the cockpit, cleared it of fumes and gently restored power to the engines.

'You okay in the back?' he asked, craning to see how his gunnery officer was doing.

'I've been better, captain. But I'm still here. Nice work,' gasped Pelaur, obviously shaken by their close call.

'Yes, real nice work. I should have known there could be active bio-weapons.'

'We're still alive,' pointed out Pelaur.

'Yes, I suppose we should be thankful.' said Morten, making the sign of the aquila and pressing his glove to the small shrine beside him. He could see Harlen's squadron paralleling his course. From the lumps of flesh drifting past his canopy, he could see that as well as shooting down the bio-weapon, Harlen's squadron had also vaporised the original target.

He thumbed the vox and said, 'Nine-zero-two, we're allright here. A little shaken up, but other than that we're fine. By the way, thanks. That was nice shooting.'

'Don't mention it, sir' said Harlen lightly. 'Hold still now. I'm going to give you a once over, see how bad you're hurt.'

'Right. Holding steady,' replied Morten, which was easier said than done as the Fury fought his every attempt to hold her in a straight line.

Harlen's craft slid below and round the stricken fighter and came to rest off Morten's port wing.

'How bad is it?' he asked, almost afraid of the answer.

'It's not good, that's for sure. You've taken a lot of hits on the engine vectors so she's going to be hell to steer. And it looks like you're losing fuel. Not much, but we better get you home to the *Vincennes* before you run dry.'

Morten suddenly realised how close they had come to dying. If even one piece of the bio-weapon's chitin shrapnel had hit the centreline fuel tank, they'd have been incinerated in a raging fireball.

'Thanks. Get your squadron home to the *Vincennes* and we'll be back as soon as we can. If we need help we'll let you know,' said Morten. 'And let the tactical officers know about these things. I have the feeling we'll be seeing more of them.'

'Yes, sir. You sure you'll be allright?'

'We'll be late, but we'll get there. Now get out of here before I have to order you.'

'Yes, sir,' acknowledged Harlen as his three Furies accelerated to combat speed and were soon lost in the darkness.

'You ready to go home, Kiell?' asked Captain Morten.

'More than ever.'

Captain Owen Morten gingerly rolled the limping Fury towards home and slowly fed power to the engines, grimacing as the vibrations on the twisted airframe increased.

It was going to be a long ride home.

FOUR

THE UNKNOWN ARTIST had used the entire chamber as his canvas. A mosaic of enormous proportions covered the walls, the ceiling and even the floor. The workmanship was exquisite: none of the shards of coloured glass that made up the mosaic bigger than a thumbnail. Larger than the Chapel of Heroes on Macragge, the scale of such a work was breathtaking: the chamber stretched over two hundred metres long and its barrel-vaulted ceiling rose thirty metres or more above them.

Uriel and the Ultramarines walked in rapture around the perimeter of the long room, speechless in wonder at the magnificent sight, any faded expectations of Tarsis Ultra swept aside by the spectacular mosaic. Pastoral images of a rugged land of primal beauty stretched before them, the colours wondrously bright and vivid, the skill of the artist perfectly capturing the wild majesty of his subject. Glass mountains soared above glass seas of glittering azure, vibrant emerald fields teemed with proud animals.

Uriel reached out and touched the wall, half expecting to reach within the mosaic and feel the sea breeze scudding across the foaming waves that broke on cliffs of dazzling white. Atop the mountains, he recognised a majestic marble fortress with columns and golden domes that made his heart ache with longing. The Fortress of Hera, rendered in such loving detail that he could almost taste the salt of Macragge's seas and smell the sweet sap of its highland firs in his memory.

He could see the mosaic was having the same effect on Pasanius and Learchus, their faces alight with joy. Uriel craned his neck upwards, seeing a host of glass warriors at the hunt, mounted on horseback and wearing blue chitons, the loose, knee-length woollen tunics worn by men and women of Macragge in ancient times.

Leading the hunt was a giant of a man with golden curls and alabaster skin, his face alive with love and strength, carrying a long spear and oval shield. Uriel froze before this image, overcome by emotion, as he recognised Roboute Guilliman. Many times had he gazed upon the pallid, dead face of his primarch in the Temple of Correction on Macragge , where his lifeless body was held immobile in a sepulchral stasis tomb, but seeing him portrayed like this, with so much life and animation, filled Uriel with a terrible ache of sorrow for his passing. Until this moment, Uriel had never given any credence to the tales that the primarch's wounds were slowly healing, and that he would one day arise from his deathly slumber, but seeing this sight, he could now understand why people needed to believe that such a mighty warrior could return from the void.

Further along were scenes of battle, images of war from a bygone age when heroes stood as tall as mountains and could topple the earth with their strength. Here, magnificent and noble, Roboute Guilliman fought the armies of evil. Behind him, slinking from the shadows, an unseen champion of evil poised to deliver a treacherous deathblow. As Uriel's eye travelled further along the fresco he saw a warrior save Guilliman's life, masterfully rendered in chips of sapphire and glass as he thrust his bayoneted rifle deep into the enemy's belly. Sprays of rubies and garnet glittered from the wound.

Another portion of this section of the ceiling showed Roboute Guilliman on bended knee, swearing his bond of brotherhood with the warrior people of Tarsis Ultra. To see such a display of humility from one so mighty as their primarch was a sharp reminder to Uriel of everything the Ultramarines fought to protect.

Everywhere around the chamber there were new wonders and fresh visions of incredible beauty, but Uriel forced himself to tear his gaze away from the fantastical mosaic. Pasanius and Learchus stood by his side, similarly overwhelmed by this work of genius.

'It's...' began Learchus, searching for words to do this masterpiece justice.

Uriel nodded. 'I know. I have read of the Tarsis fresco, but had never believed it could be as magnificent as this.'

Footsteps echoed through the chamber and the spell was broken. The mosaic was just a wall and the images upon it nothing more than glass shards. Uriel turned as Fabricator Montante, changed into more practical plain grey robes, led the council of war into the room. The senior officers of the regiments, each with an entourage of scribes, flunkies and adjutants trailing a respectful distance behind them, followed Montante towards the centre of the chamber.

This portion of the room was sunken into the floor, where a number of marble benches and a long, low table were set, bearing clay jugs of mulled wine and wooden bowls of fresh fruit. Uriel stepped down into this sunken area and took a seat, examining his fellow commanders as they arrived.

Montante was thin and seemed pathetically eager to please. His features were delicate and ascetic, though intense. He did not look like a warrior and Uriel wondered how he had achieved his position of authority here. Was the rule of Tarsis Ultra hereditary, democratic or did it still follow the primarch's meritocratic ideals? Was Montante capable of leading his people in time of war or would he need to be replaced? Was that decision even his to make? Montante busied himself pouring wine for everyone and Uriel politely shook his head when offered a goblet.

Stagler had the look of a warrior. Uriel had heard tales of the Krieg Death Korp and how their colonels requested the most dangerous warzones for their regiments to fight in, the most lethal enemies to face. If Stagler conformed to type, then he had chosen a prime assignment for his soldiers. He sat ramrod straight and appeared deeply irritated with Montante, also declining the wine.

Rabelaq had the look of a man to whom soldiering was a way of life, though his ample gut told Uriel that the rigours of the battlefield were but a distant memory to the colonel of the Logres regiment. He enthusiastically accepted a goblet of sweet wine and sipped appreciatively.

Chaplain Astador accepted some wine and raised it in a toast.

'May this brotherhood be united in its cause,' he said.

'Hear, hear,' agreed Rabelaq draining his goblet and pouring himself another, but Astador was not finished with his salutation. 'And should any of you fall, I shall ensure that your skulls are granted a place of honour in our Gallery of Bone.'

An awkward silence fell, until Montante said, 'Thank you, Chaplain Astador. That is most gratifying to know.'

Uriel shared a glance with his sergeants as the last members of their group entered the chamber. Lord Inquisitor Kryptman limped towards their gathering, followed by a white robed acolyte wearing a cog-toothed medallion of bronze around his neck. Unusually for a member of the Adeptus Mechanicus, his hairless features were largely organic, save for the bionic attachment that covered his right eye. A number of hinged lenses of varying size protruded from the side of his skull, each capable of sliding forward to drop before his glowing red bionic eye.

Kryptman stepped down to the benches with some difficulty and as his Adeptus Mechanicus companion joined him, Uriel was shocked to see that he moved on metallic caliper-like legs that protruded from the bottom of his robes. As the acolyte descended the steps to take his place behind Kryptman, his robe parted and instead of legs and torso, Uriel caught a glimpse of a thick, flexing brass tube connecting his chest to his artificial legs.

The lord inquisitor eased himself down onto a bench, irritably shaking his head as Montante offered him some wine. He cast his gimlet gaze around the assembled company and grunted to himself, though Uriel could not tell whether it was in satisfaction or resignation.

'This is a grand adventure,' said Montante, finally sitting down. 'Most of my time involves accounts, ledgers and all manner of boring logistical work for the factories. I don't think I've ever entertained such an esteemed group in the palace.'

Kryptman gave Montante a withering stare. 'Fabricator Marshal, this is no adventure we are upon. It is a matter of the gravest urgency and most fearful nature. A tendril of hive fleet Leviathan approaches your world and you think it will be an adventure?'

'Well, no, not an adventure in the traditional sense, you understand,' said Montante hurriedly, 'but it's certainly exciting, isn't it? I mean, it's not every day we get to fight a war, and I for one am looking forward immensely to giving these beasts a bloody nose.'

'Then you are a fool, sir, and would do well to leave the defence of your world to those who understand the grave danger of a tyranid hive fleet.'

'I object to your tone of voice, sir,' protested Montante. 'I am the planetary governor, after all.'

'For the time being,' threatened Kryptman. 'Now, if we may continue? Let us be clear on one thing: I have seen, first hand, what it means to fight these aliens and it will not be an adventure, there will be no glory and little honour in their destruction.

'I declared their species Xenos Horrificus two hundred and fifty years ago and since that day I have studied, hunted and killed them, yet still know but the tiniest fraction of their xenology.'

The inquisitor indicated the Mechanicus adept behind him.

'To fight the tyranid you must first know it,' he said. 'This is Genetor Vianco Locard of the Magos Biologis, and he knows more about these xeno abominations than any man alive. He will be of great help to us. Magos, if you please?'

Locard moved to stand before them and a brass rimmed monocle whirred into place over his red eye. As he laced his hands before him, in the manner of an academic, Uriel saw they were a smooth black metal.

Without preamble, he launched into his discourse. 'The tyranids are a bio-eugenic race of xenomorphs from beyond the Emperor's light, first discovered in the 745th year of this current millennium by Magos Varnak of the Adeptus Mechanicus outpost of Tyran Primus in Ultima Segmentum, some 60,000 light years from holy Mars.'

'Bio-eugenic? What does that mean?' interrupted Colonel Stagler.

'It means that the tyranids are able to assimilate entire worlds and races, break them down into their constituent genetic building blocks and incorporate said constituents into their own physiology,' explained Locard.

Seeing Stagler's, and everyone else's confusion, Kryptman said, 'Thank you, Magos Locard, but perhaps I should explain and keep things at a level everyone here can understand.'

Uriel bristled at such a casual insult to his intelligence, and could see others frowning too, but Inquisitor Kryptman's notoriety preceded him and there were no objections as he continued: 'The tyranids are a monstrous nomadic race of predators from beyond our galaxy who ply the depths of space in vast hive fleets. Like locusts, they consume everything in their path, and as each foe is defeated it is assimilated, each future generation of tyranids becoming better adapted to hunt their prey. When they attack, they attack in their millions, swarming across a world like a plague and just as destructively. Everything, every blade of grass, every indigenous creature is engulfed by the teeming hordes. Millions of years of evolution is destroyed and uncounted millennia of hard-won development and growth are annihilated by the tyranids' insatiable hunger. The world's oceans are drunk dry, its skies boiled away and digested until nothing remains, save a barren rock, stripped bare of every living thing.'

'But can they be defeated?' asked Stagler simply.

Kryptman laughed humourlessly. 'Oh yes, Colonel Stagler, they can be defeated, but only at terrible cost.'

'The cost is irrelevant,' said Stagler brusquely. 'All that matters is that we can defeat them, yes?'

Inquisitor Kryptman arched an eyebrow before inclining his head towards Uriel saying, 'Colonel Stagler has a point. Perhaps Captain Ventris would favour us by recounting the tale of Hive Fleet Behemoth and the Battle of Macragge?'

'It would be my pleasure, lord inquisitor,' said Uriel proudly, standing and clasping his hands behind his back.

'Hive fleet Behemoth came from beyond the halo stars of the eastern fringe, its numbers too vast to count. Their alien ships descended upon Macragge, but the noble Lord Calgar, forewarned by Lord Kryptman here, had assembled a powerful fleet to defend the holy soil of our homeworld. Fearsome battle raged in space until Lord Calgar pulled back, drawing the hive fleet onto the guns of Macragge. Whilst the aliens were spread out and vulnerable, he turned and struck, his vessels crippling one of their accursed hive ships and fatally disrupting their fleet.'

'I don't understand, Captain Ventris,' said Colonel Rabelaq. 'How could the loss of one ship cause so much damage to their fleet?'

'I will answer that,' put in Magos Locard. 'To understand the motivational imperatives of the tyranids, one must first understand the nature of their consciousness. A hive fleet is made up of billions upon billions of living organisms produced in the hive's reproductive chambers by the Norn Queen. Essentially, each ship is a living creature, every organism that makes up that ship existing only to serve the ship, and each ship functioning only as part of the fleet. A gestalt consciousness links every creature in the fleet, from the mightiest warrior beast to the tiniest, microscopic bacteria of the digestion pools, creating a vast psychic consciousness we call the overmind, that is capable of exerting a monstrous will and alien intelligence. Of course these creatures have no individuality of their own and exist simply to serve the hive mind. If one can disrupt the psychic link between them, the lower organisms become confused, often reverting to their basic, animalistic natures. It is the key to defeating them.'

'Yes,' continued Uriel, 'when Lord Calgar's fleet destroyed the largest hive ship, they were able to reap a great tally in bio-ships as the aliens' attacks became increasingly uncoordinated and random. Their fleet was driven from Macragge, and though thousands of spores, each bearing a tyranid organism, had been released above the polar defence fortresses, Lord Calgar gave chase to the fleeing enemy.'

'He left his world undefended?' asked Stagler, disapprovingly.

'No, colonel, far from it,' said Uriel. 'The polar defence fortresses were held by Terminators of the First company as well as brave warriors from the defence auxilia and Titans of the Legio Praetor. Lord Calgar was confident they could hold, and pursued the tyranid fleet to the ringed planet of Circe. Together with recently arrived ships from Battlefleet Tempestus, he destroyed the tyranid fleet in a great battle. We had defeated the tyranids, but at a grievous cost. Hundreds of thousands died, the flagship of the Tempestus fleet, the *Dominus Astra*, was lost and our entire First company was killed, including my own ancestor, Lucian Ventris. Only now does it regain its full strength.'

Uriel sat back on the bench as Kryptman picked up the tale.

'Hive fleet Behemoth was no more, but the tyranids had learned from their defeat and when they returned at the head of a new hive fleet – which we named Kraken – less than a decade ago, it was on a much greater scale. Entire sectors in the eastern fringes have been swallowed by the psychic interference of the tyranid warp shadow, and yet there is worse to come. I have detected a pattern amongst a seemingly random series of attacks across Segmentum Tempestus, Ultima Segmentum and even Segmentum Solar that leads me to believe yet another hive fleet is attacking, this time from below the galactic plane. I have named it Leviathan and it appears that a splinter fleet from Leviathan threatens this world. We must stop the tyranids, gentlemen. Here and now. For if the Shadow in the Warp is allowed to smother the divine light of the Astronomican, then Humanity will surely perish. Ships will be unable to navigate the warp, communication across the galaxy will cease and the

Imperium will collapse. Make no mistake, we are fighting for the future of our very race and I am willing to make any sacrifice to ensure its survival.'

The assembled commanders were silent as they took in the scale of the coming conflict, the stakes and their part to play in it. Even Montante now seemed to appreciate the seriousness of the situation and nervously chewed his bottom lip.

'What measures have been taken to prepare this system for the tyranids' attack?' asked Astador.

'Lord Admiral Tiberius is working with Admiral de Corte to devise a strategy to delay the tyranid fleet before it reaches this world,' answered Uriel, 'but, it is apparent that the defences of this city have fallen into disrepair in many places, and we will need time to ready them for the coming assault.'

'Captain Ventris is correct,' nodded Kryptman. 'I have requested the deployment of warriors from the Deathwatch, the Chamber Militant of my ordo, and we will be able to count them amongst our forces before long. However, we must delay the tyranid advance, but we cannot deploy the fleet until we know exactly where the attack will come. Astropaths are reporting ripples and eddies in the warp, consistent with those that presage the arrival of a fleet, but the distortions caused by the Shadow in the Warp are making it impossible to pinpoint. We would end up chasing ghosts.'

'The Krieg regiment will have its men and armoured units on the ground within the next three days,' said Stagler. 'We will begin augmenting the city's defences and I have devised a training regime that will ensure our readiness for when these aliens arrive. These aliens will not soon forget the Death Korp.'

Uriel said, 'I shall assign Sergeant Learchus and a squad of Ultramarines to you to aid your training program. He is the finest instructor sergeant Agiselus has ever produced and I am sure will be of great help to you.'

'Thank you, Captain Ventris,' acknowledged Stagler. 'I welcome your aid.'

Rabelaq spoke next. 'My soldiers will be deployed by the end of the day. We have far less armour to land than Colonel Stagler's regiment and by morning I will have units moving throughout the continent to escort people back to the safety of the city. As the soldiers of the Logres regiment are raised from an ice world, this climate will present no difficulties for them, and we may also be able to teach you all a thing or two about cold weather injuries as well. To be honest, our main duties to this point have been protecting krill farmers from raiding Tarellian dog soldiers. It will do them good to have a taste of proper soldiering.'

Fabricator Montante said, 'My PDF regiments have been drilling ever since we received warning of the tyranids. As head of the PDF, I've ordered increased training over the last two months and called up all the citizen militia units to participate too. The vast majority of them have been on training exercises recently and are looking top notch, if I do say so myself. We've also begun stockpiling medical supplies, ammunition, fuel and food and drink in the caverns below the city.'

Kryptman looked surprised at this new side of the Fabricator Marshal and nodded.

'Excellent. That was to be my next point of concern.'

'Oh, don't worry about that, Inquisitor Kryptman. If there's one thing I know, its organisational logistics. I may not be a soldier, but I can organise your supplies better than anyone and make sure that every soldier has a full pack of ammunition and three hot meals a day.'

Kryptman chuckled. 'And therein lies half the battle.'

'Indeed,' beamed Montante, pleased to have something he could contribute.

The next two hours were spent in meticulous planning of the coming campaign. Everything from fleet operations to the precise deployment of men and machines throughout the city was discussed, debated and eventually decided upon. The situation was grim, but as the council of war drew to a close, there was a feeling of cautious optimism.

The lord inquisitor summed up that optimism, saying, 'Tyranids are creatures from our darkest nightmares. But remember this: they can bleed and they can die…'

Uriel poured himself a goblet of wine as the door at the far end of the chamber opened and a PDF vox-officer entered. He hurriedly made his way towards Montante, handing the Fabricator Marshal a data-slate before withdrawing.

Montante scanned its contents swiftly, his smile growing the more of the message he read. He handed the slate to Kryptman and said, 'I do believe we have them.'

Kryptman read the slate as Montante continued. 'Surveyors on listening station Trajen at the system's edge picked up an unknown contact in the Barbarus Cluster and directed fighter squadrons from the *Kharloss Vincennes* to intercept it. It seems they engaged and destroyed a tyranid scout vessel. Their astropath also reports an approaching disturbance in the immaterium. Gentlemen, I believe we now know where the enemy is coming from.'

TYREN MALLICK PUSHED forward the safety catch of his autogun and opened the breech. He lifted a clip of bullets from the pocket of his flak jacket, ensuring that the rounds were clean, and placed them in the weapon's charger guide. He pushed down on the clip until the top round was under the magazine lip then closed the breech and snapped off the safety. He lifted the rifle to his shoulder and sighted along the barrel at the three rocks he'd set up across the slope of the mountain. He breathed deeply, letting it out slowly and squeezed the trigger, expertly blasting one of the rocks from its perch.

He lowered the rifle and watched as his son, Kyle, copied his movements exactly. The crack of his shot echoed from the dark mountains, and another rock toppled from its perch. He could see several people in the township below jump at the noise before returning to erecting barricades at the town's entrance.

'Alright, son, nice work,' he said. 'Now do it again. You got to be able to do it real quick when these alien bastards come. When you can load that rifle with your eyes shut, we'll go in for supper.'

Kyle beamed at his father's praise, unloaded the rifle and began again. Tyren watched his son as he swiftly reloaded the rifle and repeated the actions they had been practising for the last two days. Though only eleven, Kyle was a natural and had the weapon loaded and ready to fire in less than six seconds. The final rock vanished in a puff of smoke as Kyle shot it dead centre.

Father and son spent another half hour practising with the rifle before a hard rain began falling and they quickly made their way down the water-logged path that led to the small mining community of Hadley's Hope. They climbed over the slippery ore barrels erected before the town's main road and made their way towards their home, taking shelter from the rain under the wide eaves of the buildings lining the road.

Tyren could see that the far end of the road was barricaded as well, timber sawhorses looped with razorwire stacked alongside ore barrels filled with rocks and sand. It wasn't much, but it was the best they could do.

Sitting alongside the town's schoolhouse, the largest building in the settlement, Tyren Mallick's home was a sturdily constructed adobe structure, built by his own hands. He'd had twenty-five good years in this house, raised three children and worked hard in the mines that made Barbarus Prime worth inhabiting. He had been as faithful an Imperial servant as he could be, attending Preacher Cascu's sermons every week down in Pelotas Ridge and also spending a month of every year helping those less fortunate than himself.

Twenty-five good years, and he was damned if some faceless adept on Tarsis Ultra was going to tell him to leave his home because there were some alien raiders approaching. Well, the people of Hadley's Hope had come together in times of crisis before now and this would be no different. Already the entrance to their mine had been sealed, the town was barricaded, and its populace ready to defend their hearth and homes.

Heavy grey clouds gathered overhead and further down the road that led to the valley below, Tyren saw the powerful tower-lights of several other communities flicker on as night drew in. Even from here he could see that the other towns had made defensive preparations similar to those of

Hadley's Hope. The shared sense of solidarity in the face of adversity was humbling, and Tyren once again gave thanks to the Emperor that he had been blessed with such fine friends and neighbours.

He and Kyle reached the heavy timber door to the house and removed their mud-caked boots before entering. Merria kept a clean house and both knew better than to dirty the place up before supper.

Warmth and the aroma of a home cooked meal enveloped him as he led Kyle inside. His wife and two daughters busied themselves with steaming plates and dishes, setting the table for supper as he hung the rifles beside the door, checking that both were properly unloaded first.

'You boys have fun up there?' asked Merria without turning from the hot stove.

'We sure did,' said Tyren, tousling his son's hair. 'Kyle here's a natural. Never missed once, did you, son?'

'Nope, not once, da,' confirmed Kyle.

His mother tutted as she turned and saw the bedraggled state of her son and husband. She cleaned her hands on her apron and shooed them towards the bedrooms.

'Both of you get out of those wet clothes before you catch your death. I'll not have you dripping all over my floor. Go on now, hurry up. Supper'll be on the table in five minutes.'

Both father and son knew it was pointless to argue and put aside their hunger while they dried off and changed into fresh clothing. They returned to the table as Merria began dishing supper, Tyren taking his customary place at the head of the table.

When everybody's plate was full, Tyren clasped his hands on the table, closed his eyes and bowed his head as he recited the Emperor's grace.

'Holy Father who watches over us all, we give thanks for this meal before us. Grant us the wisdom of your servants and the strength to prevail against the evil of sinners and aliens. This we ask in your name.'

His family echoed his amen and began tucking into their food. Hissing gas lamps hung from the roof beams provided a warm light as the family ate, the harsh glare from the arc lights outside blocked by the sheet metal Tyren had bolted over the windows.

He smiled at his wife and took a bite of his dinner.

Let these damned raiders come, whoever they were.

They would find Tyren Mallick and the people of Hadley's Hope ready for them.

SWEAT GATHERED ON Third Technician Osric Neru's brow and he wished the astropath would just shut up and give them all some peace. Her moans had been unnerving at first, but now they were just annoying, filling listening post Trajen's cramped control room with her never-ending drone. Osric's fingers beat a nervous tattoo on the console before him, as he stared in frustration at its display. The readings couldn't be right, they just couldn't. He rubbed a hand across his unshaven jaw and, even though he knew it was pointless, checked the figures once again.

The numbers scrolled across the slate once more, defiantly remaining the same as before.

He wiped the sweat from his tonsured skull and updated the parchment list beside him as his superiors on Tarsis Ultra had instructed him. Osric felt very alone and very frightened, dearly wishing he was back on Chordelis, serving in one of that world's many forge temples. If these numbers were correct, then there was an enemy fleet of unheard of magnitude approaching this system.

Vessels of the Imperial Navy were en route from Tarsis Ultra, but Osric knew they would not reach Trajen before this new fleet on his console did, and the thought terrified him. He caught the eye of the adept at the next console and tried to smile reassuringly, but failed to convince him.

He glanced over his shoulder at the senior magos and, despite his master's many augmentations, Osric could tell he was also extremely worried by what was drawing near. Repeated requests to Admiral de Corte for permission to abandon the listening post had been denied and they could only wait and hope that the approaching fleet would pass them by.

The astropath sat in a reclined couch seat next to the magos, her teeth clenched, her skin drawn and pale. She twitched and muttered, her face alive with tics and nervous flutters. Her groans filled the control room, unnerving the six man staff of the listening post further still.

Suddenly she sat bolt upright, screaming at the top of her lungs.

Everyone jumped as the girl lurched from her chair, pulling at her green robes and tearing at her face with her fingernails. She fell to her knees, shrieking piteously, digging and clawing at her skin. Blood streamed down her face as she ripped open the stitching sealing her ravaged eye sockets and plunged her fingers inside, as though trying to pluck the brain from her skull.

'They are coming!' she wailed. 'They're scratching my mind, scratching, screaming, roaring – so many voices. They're coming for us – flesh and blood, body and soul!'

Osric put his hands over his ears to shut out her screams as she staggered to her feet and reached out towards him with bloody fingers, pleading for him to stop the pain.

But he could do nothing as she pitched forward and fell to the floor.

Blood pooled around her head and her cries were silenced.

Uriel joined Lord Admiral Tiberius and Philotas, his deck officer, as they examined the system map displayed on the stone-rimmed plotting table in the transept of the command bridge of the *Vae Victus*. A bewildering amount of information filled the embedded slate, displaying a topographical representation of the Tarsis Ultra system. Curling lines of system defence ship patrol circuits, orbits of planets and local celestial phenomena were picked out, as well as the major shipping lanes. Jump points at the system's edge were marked in yellow and each planet glowed with a soft green light. Numbers scrolled across the side of the slate, though Uriel had no idea what they indicated.

'Show me,' ordered Tiberius.

Philotas adjusted the runes on the plotting table and the background information faded from the display, leaving only the planetary details illuminated.

'At the furthest extent of the Tarsis Ultra system lies the planet of Barbarus Prime,' said Philotas, as curling High Gothic script in a gold edged box flashed next to the planet.

'A mining world,' noted Uriel. 'Precious metals and gem mines mostly, though there are a few vauable minerals used in the production of the metals that make up starship hulls.'

'Population?' asked Tiberius.

Philotas checked the information box and said. 'Quite low, the last census puts it at a little over nine thousand souls, mostly scattered throughout the uplands of the eastern continental mountain ranges.'

'What is being done about getting those people off there?' asked the lord admiral.

'A warning has been issued to the local adept, and there is a bulk freighter en route from Chordelis, though it will be touch and go whether it can reach Barbarus Prime before the first tyranid organisms.'

'Damn,' swore Tiberius. 'The more worlds that fall to the tyranids, the stronger and more numerous they become.'

'Further in towards the core worlds are two uninhabited planets. The first, Parosa, has an atmosphere largely composed of a benzene-hydrogen compound. Highly toxic and though the Adeptus Mechanicus have attempted to terraform its atmosphere several times, they have thus far been unsuccessful. The second is called Yulan. It's a geologically unstable rock, wracked by volcanic storms, though it does boast several gargantuan hydrogen-plasma mining stations in permanent geo-stationary orbit.'

Philotas zoomed in on the system map as they drew closer to the core worlds.

'Next we have Chordelis, a small, but populous world, mostly given over to industrial manufacture. Population in the region of sixteen million, with a PDF strength of fifty thousand soldiers. Evacuation protocols are in effect, though I would advise giving Chordelis a wide berth. There are a great many ships arriving and departing and there have been several accidents already.

'After Chordelis, there are two agri-worlds, Calumet and Calydon, both with a largely caretaker population. These worlds are being evacuated as we speak. Then we have Tarsis Ultra itself, with a population in excess of sixty million.'

'How long before we are in a position to intercept the hive fleet?' asked Uriel.

Philotas adjusted the runes at the side of the plotting table once more and a series of lines snaked across the surface of the slate. The line began at the group of icons representing the *Vae Victus* and the ships of the Imperial fleet and quickly extended through the system to Barbarus Prime.

More numbers flashed across the slate. Philotas used a steel ruler and calipers to plot time and distance over the system map.

'At current speed, it will be seven days before we can achieve orbit around Barbarus Prime,' said Philotas. 'The tyranids will get there first.'

OSRIC NERU WATCHED the approaching cloud of objects in the viewing bay with genuine, bowel-loosening terror, prayers of protection he had not given voice to since he was a child spilling from his lips. He gripped onto his console as the alien cloud enveloped them and another explosive impact rocked the listening station. For the last twenty minutes, spore-like objects had drifted from the advancing fleet, floating aimlessly through space until they neared the listening post, whereupon they pulsated rhythmically and homed unerringly on their position.

Some exploded like mines, others burst like wet sacks of liquid, spraying corrosive acids across the structure of the station. Already there were hull breaches all over the station where acids and viruses had eaten through the hull.

The size of the approaching fleet was simply too vast to comprehend. Thousands of drifting objects surrounded the alien vessels, dead lumps that the station's pitifully inadequate turrets had managed to blast apart before running out of ammunition.

Osric checked the firing log of the various turrets, calculating how many rounds had been expended. Over twenty thousand shells had been fired into the approaching cloud though the losses they had inflicted were insignificant against a force of such scale. They were now effectively defenceless.

Osric dropped to his knees and prayed as more of the alien spores drew near.

'Neru!' barked the senior magos. 'Return to your post.'

Osric stood as yet more explosions rocked the station and a fresh clutch of warning lights flashed into life on the console.

'We're going to die!' cried Osric. 'What does it matter if I'm at my post?'

'It matters because that is what we are here for,' said the magos with a calm he did not feel. 'Yes, we will die, but we will die doing our duty to the Omnissiah and the Emperor. No man can ask for more.'

Osric nodded, bowing his head and returning to his seat as the groan of buckling metal echoed from outside the control room. Another hull breach warning bell rang and the terrified crew of the listening station heard the grinding noise of pressure doors slowly sealing off the affected area.

Then they heard the scratching of alien claws at the door to the control room.

TYREN MALLICK SHUT out the pain of his torn shoulder and painfully reloaded his rifle, the trembling of his fingers making it that much more difficult. A blood-soaked bandage wrapped his shoulder and chest where fragments of an exploding spore had ripped into his flesh. Merria had pulled out the sizzling pieces of bony shrapnel from his shoulder, but the wound had refused to heal, weeping a constant gruel of infected blood.

'Why's the sky gone a funny colour, da?' asked Kyle, his voice trembling in fear as he looked through the molten remains of the sheet metal over the windows. The normally slate grey sky boiled a loathsome, bruised purple and unnatural lightning speared through the violet sky, lighting the mountains in a lurid, unfamiliar light. A rain of dark objects fell to the plains below, amid the burning rain that ate away at the metal roofs of Hadley's Hope and had forced its people to abandon the barricades and take refuge in the schoolhouse, the only structure large enough to contain everyone.

The men of Hadley's Hope carried a mix of weapons, from ancient rifles that would be lucky not to misfire and take their wielder's hand off, to freshly oiled lasguns earned in service of the local defence forces. Twenty-three crying children huddled in the centre of the schoolhouse, their mothers and teachers doing their best to calm them with songs and prayers.

'I don't know why, son,' admitted Tyren, finally pushing the bullets home in his rifle. He rose from the table and joined his son at the window. Alien spores like grotesquely swollen and veined balloons had been falling from the sky since daybreak, and though most of them had been carried into the high peaks of the mountains by updrafts from the plains below, more were drifting back down as night fell and the air cooled.

At first, the people of Hadley's Hope had watched them with fearful curiosity, until a pulsating spore with a frill of trumpet-like cones and trailing fronds had drifted into the settlement. Pastor Upden had confidently walked up to the mysterious object and shot it at point blank range, expecting it to simply deflate. Tyren had watched in horror as the vile globule exploded, showering the pastor with a thick, viscous fluid and his screams echoed from the farthest corners of the settlement. Tyren had run to help Upden, but it was too late, his skin was already blistering and sloughing from his bones as the alien acids ate his flesh away. He screamed piteously until his throat melted and his lifeless body dissolved into a stinking slime.

Since then they had taken great care to shoot down any spores before they reached the settlement.

'You stay alert, Kyle, and holler if you see anything,' Tyren said, staring through the dripping, corroded holes in the metal. The lights from the townships below were gone, and he had been unable to reach anyone in Pelotas Ridge for several hours now.

The lights here were failing too, as the acid rain burned through the cables that didn't run underground, and Tyren knew that soon the entire community would be in darkness. He tried to ignore the sobbing of the children and the trembling voices of the women as he saw movement on the road below. The ground undulated as though it was alive and the rain glistened from the carapaces of thousands of... *things* as they ran towards the small settlement.

He knelt and fished a battered but serviceable pair of magnoculars from his pack and trained them on the road. The unnatural darkness made it hard to see much of anything, but his breath caught in his throat as he saw a sea of creatures, all fangs and talons, swarming uphill.

'Emperor save us,' he whispered, dropping the magnoculars. 'Everyone with a gun get to someplace they can shoot from,' he shouted.

He grabbed a pale-faced man next to him and said, 'Radek, take ten men upstairs and shoot from the balcony, the canopy will give you shelter from the rain.'

Radek nodded and ran off to obey Tyren's command.

Tyren looked over to his wife and daughters, giving them a wave of reassurance before finding a loophole in the wall to fire his rifle from.

Kyle shouldered his rifle and stood beside his father, a nervous smile creasing his face.

'I'm proud of you, son,' said Tyren and Kyle nodded.

Tyren peered into the gloom, seeing the rippling swarm of creatures leaping and bounding across the barricades at the end of the road.

'Here they come!' he yelled. 'Open fire!'

Children screamed as the schoolhouse was suddenly filled with noise. Gunsmoke fogged the air and the crack of weapon fire in such a confined space was deafening. Tyren saw several creatures fall, hearing more shots from upstairs.

Over the crack of gunfire, he heard a whistling scream, similar to that of incoming artillery fire, and flinched as something heavy smashed into the roof of the building. He heard timber splinter and screams from upstairs, but knew he could do nothing to help the men stationed there. The ground trembled as more objects fell from the sky and struck with incredible force.

He shot again and again into the mass of beasts, their swollen skulls and armoured carapaces deflecting all but the most accurate shots. They swarmed into the town, spreading out and closing on the schoolhouse.

A thunderous impact outside threw Tyren to the floor and blew out the windows facing the street. A section of wall collapsed and the sheet metal was blasted from the walls. Hot, reeking air blew in.

Through the hole, Tyren could see that the generator building was on fire, and there was a huge object, like a lumpen boulder, rocking in the wide crater its impact had caused.

Smaller creatures leapt towards the hole in the wall and Tyren rolled to his feet, firing wildly into the breach. Flames from across the street silhouetted the creatures and, together with another three men, they were able to kill all the monsters attempting to force their way inside. The roof of the generator building collapsed, sending sparks soaring into the darkness, a shriek of something in pain echoing from beneath the rubble.

'Get something to block this!' he yelled, firing into the mass of creatures until his rifle was empty. He fumbled for another clip as three women dragged over a heavy table and some desks, overturning them before the gap in the wall.

Gunfire and the sound of screaming children filled Tyren's senses as he reloaded his rifle. He heard impacts on the few remaining windows covered by the sheet metal and saw another give way as a horrific alien creature forced its way inside.

It leapt into the room, rain steaming from its glossy, armoured carapace. Hunched over and six-limbed, its bestial face hissed in alien hunger.

Tyren shot at it, but missed, blasting a chunk of plaster from the wall beside it. The beast ignored him, pouncing on the defenders at the northern wall. He screamed as he saw Kyle turn to face the monster and raise his rifle. But the creature was inhumanly fast and its scything claws slashed out, disembowelling his son before he could fire.

'No! No! No!' Tyren screamed, firing again. His bullet caught the creature at the base of its neck and exploded its head in a spray of dark ichor. He dropped his rifle and ran towards his son, but it was too late, his boy was already dead.

He cried out in anguish, cradling his son's body. Through a mist of tears he saw the ruins of the generator building heave upwards, as something vast hauled itself from the wreckage.

He fumbled for his rifle, as more cries filled the schoolhouse. A huge shape lumbered across the street and slammed into the side of the schoolhouse, smashing down the wall and tearing a portion of the ceiling with it. The thing's body was on fire and it shrieked in fury and pain as it battered its way inside.

Tyren felt his knees sag as a monster from his worst imaginings took a thunderous step into the schoolhouse. Larger than a mining bulldozer, it reared above him on powerful, hooved legs, two pairs of thick arms ending in long, razor-sharp talons raised above its head. Its tapered jaw was filled with hundreds of drooling fangs and its dark eyes reflected the fires that consumed it.

The horrifying creature shrieked deafeningly, lashing out with its claws and hacking men in two with every blow. It stepped further into the schoolhouse, its weight smashing the floorboards and its deadly claws killing everything within reach.

Tyren screamed and fired his rifle at the monster, its chitinous carapace absorbing every shot without effect. Another of the smaller beasts clambered through the window beside Tyren. He shot it in the head and pushed home another clip.

The giant beast continued screaming as it demolished the schoolhouse, beams crashing down as its armoured head smashed through the ceiling. The upper storey collapsed, men falling to the ground floor, only to be crushed beneath its tread. Children wept in terror. The beast's piercing shriek grew in volume, until a seething ball of greenish light vomited from its jaws, immolating the screaming women and children.

Tyren screamed in horror and ran at the alien creature, knowing it would kill him, but unwilling to live knowing his family was dead. He fired his rifle until it was empty then used it as a bludgeon, smashing it to splinters against the monster's armoured legs.

The monster struck Tyren with its powerful claws, tearing off his arm and smashing him through the wall. He splashed onto the ground outside the schoolhouse, numb with pain and loss.

The acid rain burned his skin and he could feel nothing below his neck.

Hissing aliens gathered around him, stabbing him again and again with long claws like swords. Tyren felt nothing. His life ended in a blur of razor claws and fangs.

♉

FIVE

A DYING WORLD filled the observation bay. Like monstrous, suckling parasites, the creatures of the hive fleet gathered around Barbarus Prime in a blurred, indistinct halo. Flickering lightning flashed through the atmosphere, and though the effect from space was striking, almost beautiful, Uriel knew that it signified the world was in its death throes, ravaged by storms of titanic proportions strong enough to topple mountains and drown entire continents.

The surface of Barbarus Prime heaved as its mantle cracked, split apart by gargantuan feeder tentacles that burrowed deep into its body, devouring anything capable of being broken down into its constituent organic components.

There could be nothing left alive on Barbarus Prime; soon all the world's genetic material would be absorbed by the tyranids and used as fuel for the ever-hungry reproductive chambers of the hive ships. Even now, the biological matter that had been the population of the planet would be churning within the belly of these beasts. The thought sickened Uriel and the hate he had felt on the fields of Ichar IV returned, bright and hot.

'Emperor, watch over thee,' whispered Uriel, swearing that the souls of this world would be avenged. He stood with Lord Admiral Tiberius on the bridge of the *Vae Victus*, powerless to help the world below, but ready to do anything he could to prevent any more Imperial servants losing their lives to the Great Devourer.

Tiberius strode to his command pulpit and mounted the steps that took him to his elevated commander's position. Unconsciously, he scratched at the spiderweb of scars that crisscrossed the side of his face, scars he had received fighting the tyranids at the Battle of Macragge, over two hundred and fifty years ago when he had been one of many deck officers to serve on this proud ship before rising to become its captain.

He pressed his thumb to the pict-slate on the polished mahogany lectern in front of him and the tactical plot swam into focus before him, displaying the doomed world and the Imperial fleet that had come to fight its destroyers. Alongside the *Vae Victus* was the *Mortis Probati*, the Mortifactors' ship, and to either side of them was arranged the might of an Imperial battlefleet.

They could not save the people of Barbarus Prime, but the battle to avenge them would be fought in the shadow of their dying world.

'They will be coming soon,' he said.

'How can you tell?' asked Uriel.

'See,' said Tiberius, pointing to where a gigantic creature rose ponderously from the feeding below. 'They are responding to our presence.'

Longer than the biggest battleship Uriel had ever seen, the monster's hide was gnarled and ancient, pitted with asteroid impacts and hardened by millennia travelling through the void. Its underside rippled with waving, frond-like tentacles and great, sucking orifices in its surface drooled a thick, viscous fluid as it rose to meet them. At what Uriel supposed was its rear, long feeders ending in barbed claws trailed behind it, pulsating with a grotesque motion. Nothing so huge should be capable of animation, thought Uriel, or should be allowed to manifest such a horrid mockery of life.

A host of vanguard organisms drifted up before the monster: giant, manta like creatures with vast, cavern mouths filled with teeth as large as a Thunderhawk and razor-edged wings; spinning creatures that defied any classification of form, all rippling armour plates, blades, talons and trailing tentacles. Dozens of these beasts swarmed around the larger ship, like loyal servants protecting a queen. As they rose towards the Imperial vessels Uriel was reminded of carrion beasts that hunted in packs, picking off the weakest members of a herd that, once brought down, would be guarded with tenacious ferocity while the pack leaders fed off the carcass.

'What are their tactics? How will they attack?'

'I do not know, Uriel. They will test us first, probe us for weakness and learn what they can before committing their main force. We are fortunate to have caught them feeding. We won't have to face their full strength.'

Uriel watched the multitude of organisms advancing on the *Vae Victus* and gave thanks for that small mercy. For if this was but a fraction of the strength of the tyranids, then their full might was something to be truly dreaded.

LORD INQUISITOR KRYPTMAN watched the same scene from the bridge of the *Argus*, the flagship of Admiral Bregant de Corte and this battlefleet. He watched the enormous creature detach from feeding and rise to challenge them. He had fought the tyranids for almost the entire span of his life and he could remember no emotion save hatred towards them. As he watched the planet below die, he was gratified to note that his hatred burned no less strongly than before.

The approaching hive ship was not the biggest he had ever seen, that honour belonged to the beast at the head of the hive fleet that had engulfed the world of Graia, but it was still a giant, perhaps three kilometres in length.

'Loathsome things,' observed Admiral de Corte.

'Aye,' agreed Kryptman, 'but lethal. They are armed with fearsome symbiote weaponry, sprays of acid, bio-plasma and hordes of warrior organisms that can be ejaculated from the orifices in its stony hide.'

'Our weapons are blessed by the Emperor and we will prevail,' de Corte assured him.

Kryptman nodded and pointed to the mist of spores surrounding the beast. 'Look here, admiral. That veil of spores is so thick it will protect the creature from all but the most determined of attackers.'

'Lord inquisitor,' said Admiral de Corte, his voice betraying the tension the entire bridge crew were feeling. 'I request your permission to commence the attack.'

'Yes…' nodded Kryptman, staring in macabre fascination at the wide tactics table depicting the converging fleets. 'Commence the attack.'

Blank faced logisticians connected directly to the ship's surveyor systems ringed the wide table – gridded with spatial co-ordinates – using long, flat-headed poles to move scale representations of the various ships of the fleet.

The Admiral nodded curtly and spun on his heel, marching towards his commander's lectern. Bregant de Corte was a tall, wiry man, with gaunt, pinched features and a thin, pencil moustache. His admiral's uniform hung from his emaciated frame and, upon meeting him for the first time, many found it hard to believe that this was the man who had destroyed the Ork raiders of Charadax, who had ended the piracy of Khaarx Bloodaxe and whose masterful strategy had halted the K'Nib from invading the Sulacus Rim.

He stood behind the lectern, pouring himself a glass of amasec from the crystal decanter that always sat there and taking a deep breath. He took a moment to look around his bridge, allowing seconds to pass before issuing his orders. It was important that he not appear intimidated by the alien fleet approaching and his calm demeanour would be a guide for the rest of his crew to follow.

He drained the glass of amasec and said, 'My compliments to you all, and I wish you honour in this glorious battle.'

Jaemar, the ship's commissar, nodded in approval at the admiral's words.

A naval rating, traditionally the youngest man on the ship, approached the admiral. Sweat glistened on his brow as he asked, 'Is the word given, admiral?'

Admiral de Corte replaced the glass on the lectern and said, 'The word is given. Issue all ships with the order to attack. *Gloriam Imperator.*'

THE TWO FLEETS drew closer, though the ranges between them could still be measured in tens of thousands of kilometres. The ships of the Imperial fleet spread out as the attack order filtered through to the various captains and the admiral's plan began to unfold. There appeared to be no strategy evident in the tyranids' approach, the bio-creatures rising to meet their enemy in a homogenous mass.

The Space Marine strike cruisers, together with the rapid strike cruisers of Arx Praetora squadron, advanced before the armoured behemoths of the battleship *Argus* and the Overlord battlecruiser, *Sword of Retribution*.

A trio of Sword frigates flew in a picket line before the fleet, supported by two Dauntless light cruisers, the *Yermetov* and the *Luxor*. Their fearsome lance arrays were sure to be decisive in the coming engagement and de Corte was taking no chances with their safety.

To either flank of the fleet, two squadrons of Cobra destroyers, Cypria and Hydra, surged ahead of the main fleet, their cavernous torpedo bays loaded with sanctified weapons and their pilots eager to unleash them upon the foe.

The massive hive ship at the centre of the tyranid swarm shuddered as though in the grips of a powerful seizure and expelled millions of spores, trailing glistening birth streamers as they sped away from its toughened hide.

The majestically swooping manta creatures moved as though swimming in a deep ocean, their wide, chitinous wings rippling with the motion of the solar wind. The bladed creatures that flocked around their birth queen swarmed forwards in a wave of seething claws, overcome with the instinctual urge to destroy those who threatened the hive.

The Battle of Barbarus had begun.

'ORDER THE SWORD frigates to push forwards,' said Admiral de Corte. 'Those beasts at the head of the fleet are increasing speed. I don't want them in my battle line.'

'Aye, sir,' replied Jex Viert, his senior flag lieutenant, conveying the order to the signals officer.

De Corte studied the observation bay, trying to guess how the tyranids would react to their movements. So far, he did not rate the tactical acumen of the enemy, if such a thing existed in the tyranid fleet, and he allowed himself a tight smile. He watched as the logisticians began moving the Sword frigates forward with their poles.

'These ships that approach us, Lord Kryptman, what can you tell me about them?'

The inquisitor walked stiffly along the nave of the command bridge to stand before the apse of the observation bay. He leaned closer, as though studying the creatures more closely and shook his head slowly.

'They are drone creatures, nothing more, though they are extremely resilient. I call them kraken and the will of the hive mind controls them. Do not allow them to close with you, they are filled with all manner of deadly warrior creatures.'

'I understand. Mister Viert, issue orders that no captain is to allow any alien organisms to approach to within five thousand kilometres of his ship.'

'Five thousand kilometres. Aye, sir.'

Satisfied his order would be obeyed with alacrity, de Corte returned his gaze to the observation bay. One of the larger creatures was detaching itself from the main body of the tyranid fleet, using short flaps of its wide wings to power itself forwards in sporadic spurts of motion.

'Hydra squadron to take up blocking position on the right flank. Order the *Sword of Retribution* to follow the frigates in. *Yermetov* and *Luxor* to escort her.'

'Aye, sir,' said Viert, punching in the admiral's orders. 'Might I also suggest that the strike cruisers of the Space Marines advance with the Cobras of Cypria squadron? If these alien vessels are indeed as resilient as Lord Kryptman suggests, then their heavy bombardment cannons will be of great use.'

'Your suggestion has merit, Mister Viert. Make it so, and confirm readiness of lance decks and gun crews.'

The admiral watched the dance of ships on the plotting table, seeing the plan of the battle unfold as the captains of his fleet obeyed his orders.

'All weapon decks report readiness, sir. Senior gunner Mabon reports he has a firing solution for the nova cannon.'

'Understood, inform him that he may fire when ready,' said de Corte.

He saw that the Cobras of Hydra squadron would soon be in a position to fire as well, and the Swords had rapidly closed on the first wave of the ships Kryptman called kraken.

The gap between the two fleets was closing fast and he knew it would not be long before aliens would be dying.

DEEP IN THE bowels of the Argus, the fifty-metre wide door of the nova cannon's breech groaned shut as thousands of sweating naval ratings dragged the massive weapon's recoil compensators into position. Hot steam and noise filled the long chamber, its cavernous structure fogged with the furnace heat of lifting mechanisms that hauled the enormous projectiles from the armoured magazines below.

The chamber ran almost the entire length of the ship and stank of grease, sweat and blood. A booming hymnal echoed from ancient brass speakers set into grilled alcoves in the wall accompanied by the droning chant of thousands of men.

Senior gunner Mabon watched from his gantry above the firing chamber as a series of bells chimed and a row of lights lit up along a battered iron panel before him. He couldn't hear the bells, his long service as a gunner in the Imperial Navy having deafened him decades ago.

The shell was loaded and he muttered the gunner's prayer to the warhead as he squinted through a bronze optical attachment that lifted on groaning hinges from the panel. He clamped his augmetic monocle to the optical, lining up the thin crosshairs on the red triangle that represented his target. The target was closing on them so he didn't have to make any adjustments for crosswise motion. It was a simple shot, one he could have easily made, even in the earliest days following his press-ganging on Carpathia.

Satisfied that the shell would be on target, he lifted his head and ran his gaze across the chamber, checking that his gunnery crew gangs were clear of the greased rails that ran the length of the chamber and that each had their green flag raised to indicate that all the blast dampers had been closed. He reached up and took hold of the firing chain that hung above his station.

He grunted in satisfaction and pulled hard on the chain, shouting, 'Spirits of war and fire, I invoke thee with the wrath of the Machine God. Go forth and purify!'

Steam hissed from juddering pipes and a high-pitched screech filled the weapon chamber as the gravometric impellers built up power in the breech.

Mabon rushed to the edge of the gantry and gripped the iron railings. Seeing a weapon of such power discharge was a potent symbol of the might of the Imperial Navy and he never tired of the sight.

The screeching rose to an incredible volume, though Mabon was oblivious to it, until the nova cannon fired, and the enormous pressure wave slammed through the chamber. The weapon's firing sent the three-hundred metre barrel hurtling back with the ferocious recoil. The air blazed with sparks and burning steam as the grease coating the rails vaporised in the heat of the recoil, the stench of scorched metal and propellant filling the chamber with choking fumes.

Mabon roared in triumph, gagging on the stinking clouds of gas that boiled around him.

Juddering vibrations attempted to topple him from the gantry, but he had long since grown used to them and easily kept his balance.

The smoke started to clear and his gunnery overseers began whipping their gangs into dragging the massive weapon back into its firing position once more. The armoured bays in the floor groaned open and the looped chains descended to be attached to a fresh shell.

Mabon had drilled his gunnery teams without mercy and he prided himself that he could have the nova cannon ready to fire again within thirty minutes. This time would be no different.

THE SHELL FROM the *Argus* streaked like a blur of light through space, exploding like a miniature sun in the heart of the tyranid ships. More potent than a dozen plasma bombs, the shell detonated only a few kilometres from one of the manta-like creatures, instantly incinerating it in a roiling cloud of fire, which also scattered a nearby flotilla of smaller creatures. One creature fell away from its pack, glutinous fluids leaking from its ruptured belly. It thrashed as it died, eventually becoming still as it haemorrhaged fatally.

The swarm scattered from the blast, though a host of small organisms, each no larger than a drop pod, converged on the shrinking cloud of organic debris, exploding with terrific violence as they neared the centre of the blast.

A group of creatures surged forward, as though galvanised into action by the blast, and closed on the approaching Sword frigates. Behind the frigates came *Sword of Retribution*, the Cobras of Cypria squadron and the strike cruisers of the Ultramarines and the Mortifactors.

First blood had gone to the Imperial fleet, but the battle had only just begun.

URIEL GRIPPED THE hilt of his power sword, listening to the sounds of the *Vae Victus* as her hull groaned and creaked as she manoeuvred in the battle line. The lights in the corridor were dimmed as he and his squad waited in one of the strike cruiser's reaction points. When going into battle, the Space Marines aboard a ship of war were stationed throughout the corridors of the ship in places where enemy forces were likely to try and board.

His helmet's vox-bead was tuned to the ship's bridge and he could hear the excited chatter of the various captains travelling between their ships. He listened to the cheers as it became apparent that the fleet's flagship had just scored a direct hit on an enemy vessel with her first shot. Such an auspicious beginning boded well for the coming engagement, though Uriel could not rid himself of feelings of apprehension.

He did not like the arbitrary nature of space combat, where a warrior's fate was in the hands of others, no matter how skilful or competent they might be. Uriel knew he would rather face a thousand enemies on the field of battle than wait in the sweating darkness of a starship, not knowing whether death would reach out its long, grave-dirt encrusted fingers and sweep its terrible scythe around to claim his soul. He shuddered at the thought.

Pasanius saw him shiver and said, 'Captain?'

Uriel shook his head. 'It's nothing, I just had a strange sensation of déjà vu.'

'Are you getting another one of your "feelings"?' asked Pasanius.

'No, do not worry, old friend. I just do not like the idea of waiting here for a foe who may not come. Part of me wishes I had stayed with Learchus on Tarsis Ultra.'

'Now I know you're insane,' joked Pasanius. Though the rivalry Uriel and Learchus had endured on Macragge during their training had long since been forgotten, they would never be true friends. Where Uriel had learned the virtue of personal initiative from his mentor, Captain Idaeus, Learchus seemed incapable of making that leap. He was an Ultramarine and that was to be expected, but Uriel knew that there were times when such rigid stricture was not always the answer.

Such thoughts disturbed Uriel. He knew it was but a short step from there to beginning down the path of the Mortifactors. Was that how their descent had started? Small breaches of the codex's teachings that over the centuries became greater and greater until there was nothing left of the blessed primarch's work? Astador had claimed that their Chapter venerated the primarch, but could you hold him highest above all else and yet not follow his words?

Had Idaeus been the first step towards the end of everything the Ultramarines held dear? Could he have been wrong in his teachings, and was Uriel on the path that lead to ultimate damnation? Already he had gone against the teachings laid down in the codex, most recently on Pavonis.

In the dim light of the *Vae Victus*, Uriel felt the stirrings of doubt for the first time in his life.

ABOARD THE BRIDGE of the Sword class frigate *Mariatus*, Captain Payne watched the tyranid bio-ships closing on his vessel with a mixture of anticipation and dread. It stunned him that creatures so huge could be alive, though he assumed that, in the way of the larger beasts on his homeworld, they would be as stupid as they were massive.

A clutch of drifting objects floated before the bladed ships, pulsing ahead of the alien vessel as it continued closing the distance between them.

The captain folded his arms and nodded to where his gunnery officer stood by the weapons station.

'You have a firing solution?' he asked.

'Aye, sir, the lead enemy vessel will be in range in just under a minute.'

'Very good. Order all ships to begin firing as soon as the enemy ships are in range.'

Payne marched back towards his command chair, perched atop a raised dais at the centre of the bridge. He followed the progress of the other ships in his squadron, *Von Becken* and *Heroic Endeavour*, on the pict-slate before him, satisfied that they were holding proper station – allowing their leader to take the first shot. A shiver of premonition went down his spine as he watched the creatures before his ship turn ponderously to face him and he felt he could see their dead, expressionless eyes staring deep into his soul. Such a notion was plainly ridiculous; these beasts would have been blinded by spatial debris were they to rely on sight alone. But still the notion persisted and he bunched his fists to halt the sudden tremors that seized him.

'All guns firing now,' reported the gunnery officer calmly as the ship juddered with the recoil of its powerful guns. The vibrations running along the worn teak flooring did not do justice to the violence of his guns' firing. Right now, hundreds of massive projectiles and powerful lasblasts would be hurtling through space to unleash a torrent of explosive death amongst these vile aliens.

He watched a flurry of detonations explode around the nearest bio-ship, gradually drawing in as his gunners bracketed it. Some even managed to score direct hits, their shells blasting one of the creature's giant, bladed limbs from its body. Vast streams of fluid pumped from the bio-ship's innards as the remainder of his squadron opened fire and the flash of distant explosions momentarily obscured the tyranid ships. When the viewing bay cleared, he saw that one had been completely blown apart and another was drifting listlessly in space. He surged from his chair and punched the air in triumph.

'Damn me, but that was some fine shooting. My compliments to the gun deck.'

'Aye, sir,' replied the gunnery officer, proudly.

He watched the viewing bay, seeing the remaining enemy ships shuddering, as though gripped by some form of spasm.

'What in the Emperor's name is that?' he wondered aloud.

Before he realised what he was seeing, bolts of gelatinous liquid spurted from the front section of the bio-ships.

'All ships, hard to starboard!' he yelled, suddenly understanding what was happening.

The bridge of the *Mariatus* heeled sideway as emergency power was routed to the engines, but a ship of war does not react quickly, even if her captain does. With terrifying speed the bolts hurtled towards his ships, streaking through space in a tightly focussed stream. Payne gripped the armrests of his chair as his ship fought against her forward momentum to turn away from the incoming fire.

Even as the bolts slid to the side of the viewing bay, he saw that it would not be enough. The *Mariatus* would escape significant harm, but there was no way either of her sister ships could possibly evade in time.

* * *

THREE CORROSIVE ACID bolts struck *Heroic Endeavour* on the lower section of her engine compartment. In panic, her Adeptus Mechanicus enginseers shut the engines down, venting her combustion chambers as they realised the acid was eating away at the plasma cells that powered the engines. Their quick thinking undoubtedly saved the ship and, to their immense relief, emergency procedures were able to halt the damage before the acids could breach the volatile fuel stores. Four hundred and thirty-seven men lost their lives in the attack, but her sister ship, *Von Becken*, was not so fortunate.

The full force of the tyranid weapons struck *Von Becken* broadside on, just behind her swept prow. The sheer force of impact smashed the bolts through the first layered sections of armoured panels, before the bio-acids ate through the remainder and the full force of the tyranid weapons engulfed the mid-level decks of the ship.

Hundreds died in the first moments of impact, smashed to pulp or sucked into space as explosive decompression blew out adjacent sections of the hull. The acids filled compartments with burning fluids that dissolved flesh and metal in a heartbeat, the fumes as lethal as any nerve agent devised by the Adeptus Mechanicus. Blast doors rumbled closed, sealing off the area of the impact, but the corrosive fluid liquefied the doors and spilled onwards, dissolving decks and pouring down onto the screaming men below.

The *Von Becken's* hull, already weakened by the acids and under stress from the violent manoeuvring screeched in protest, finally buckling as the venerable ship split in two.

TORPEDOES LAUNCHED FROM the Cobras of Hydra squadron streaked through space on blazing tail plumes, arcing for the nearest of the giant manta-like creatures. A cloud of spores drifted before the ship, and as the torpedoes closed the gap, a swarm of them surged forwards to intercept the missiles. Explosions rippled through the cloud of spores as the torpedoes smashed through them, some detonating prematurely, some broken apart by the acidic explosions of the spores.

Not all the torpedoes could be stopped and a handful slammed into the body of the mantis creature, the primary warheads vaporising a chunk of its hide, before the tail sections exploded, thrusting the powerful centre section of the weapons deep inside the creature to detonate.

The monster's belly heaved as the torpedoes exploded one after the other and it listed drunkenly as its lifeblood poured from its gaping wounds. But as grievously wounded as it was, the creature was by no means finished, and it could still fight back. A swelling of intercostal motion pulsed along the top of the creature and a flurry of jagged spines rippled from its flanks, thousands hurtling towards its attackers like enormous javelins. At such range, the odds of hitting a relatively fast moving target such as a destroyer were huge, but if you factored in the sheer number and density of the spine cloud the odds changed dramatically.

Two Cobras exploded as hundred metre spines hammered through their armour, smashing through the armaplas and ceramite hulls with horrifying ease. The lead vessel's bridge was destroyed upon first impact, penetrated from prow to stern by a dozen spines, while the second was reduced to a blazing hulk as three giant spines penetrated her engine core and started dozens of uncontrollable conflagrations.

The last vessel, shielded from instant annihilation by her sister ships, was nevertheless struck several glancing blows and suffered horrendous damage as several torpedoes being readied for launch exploded in her launch bays. Her crews fought to bring the damage under control, but her captain was forced to disengage from the battle. His ship's primary weapon systems were damaged beyond immediate repair and there was nothing more he or his ship could do to alter the outcome of the battle.

THE HIVE SHIP moved ponderously forward, explosions bursting around it as the incoming fire from the Imperial ships came within range. Hundreds of spores vaporised in the hail of blossoming explosions, but there were always more pumped into space from the ship's churning reproductive vats to replace them.

The Dauntless cruisers *Luxor* and *Yermetov* passed the listing remains of the frigates *Von Becken* and *Heroic Endeavour*, their lance arrays spearing towards the hive ship. Turning as a single entity, a number of smaller bio-ships sped forward, hurling themselves into the path of the burning lance beams. Three exploded, torn apart by high-powered energy weapons and another was cut in two along its length. A salvo of torpedoes launched from the Cobras of Cypria squadron slammed into the hive ship, passing through an expanding cloud of fire and spores and detonated against the craft's stony carapace.

Ichor spilled from the wound, but almost as soon as the fire of the torpedoes' explosion had faded, the tear in the creature's hide began reknitting as fresh tissue formed across the beast's flank.

Suddenly a fleshy fold in the bio-ship's underside eased open and scores of finned creatures shot from its belly, trailing sinewy streams of amniotic birth fluids. A handful were blasted to atoms by fire from the *Sword of Retribution* as it powered forward and the *Argus* angled her course around the coreward flank of the hive ship, manoeuvring into a position to bring her broadside lances to bear. But none of the fleshy creatures launched from the hive ship were bound for either of the battleships of the fleet. They converged upon the Space Marine strike cruisers that escorted them.

ADMIRAL DE CORTE watched the hive ship slip to the left of the viewing bay and counted down the minutes until his portside lances could fire. So far the battle was proceeding much as he had planned, though the durability of these alien craft had surprised him, despite the inquisitor's warning. There had been losses, but precise figures and exact information was slow to reach him.

'Mister Viert, status report,' he demanded impatiently.

'The Swords are out of action, Lord Admiral, and Von Becken has been completely destroyed. The *Heroic Endeavour's* engines have been shut down though her enginseers are attempting to relight them. Hydra squadron has lost two ships and initial reports suggest that neither will fight again without spending years in dock.'

De Corte bunched his jaw as the scale of their losses became apparent. 'I fear that we may have underestimated the cunning of these aliens,' he whispered.

'You would not be the first, admiral,' observed Kryptman.

'Did the tyranids lure us into this attack?' demanded de Corte. 'I have four ships out of action already and we have barely scratched the surface of the hive ship.'

'Fighting the tyranids, you must be prepared to accept losses, lord admiral.'

'Losses? Have you any idea how many men have died already?'

'A great many, I know. But many more will die if we fail here. We must press the attack and destroy that hive ship.'

Before de Corte could answer, Jex Viert intervened. 'Admiral! We are at optimum lance range!'

De Corte gave Kryptman a last, disgusted look before hurrying towards the tactical plot at his bridge's centre. He saw that the *Sword of Retribution* had punched a hole in the hive ship's forward screen of bio-ships with its lances and a well-placed volley of torpedoes. It raked the hive ship with its broadside guns, but only a fraction were impacting on the massive creature. A flurry of smaller craft were closing with the battlecruiser and the strike cruisers, but de Corte was confident that their close-in defences could handle them.

'Order the lance decks to fire on the craft around the gap in the tyranid line, we need space for a clear shot at that monster!'

'Aye, sir!' said Viert, punching in the admiral's orders. He placed a hand over the vox-bead in his ear and looked up, saying, 'Sir! Captain Payne on the *Mariatus* requests permission to close with the enemy. He claims to be in a position for a strafing run.'

De Corte could see that the *Mariatus* would not survive running so close to the hive ship without support. The *Argus* was almost behind the hive ship and the admiral felt the deck vibrate with the continued firing of his ship's guns.

'Tell him no, Mister Viert. We will need every ship in the coming days and I'll not allow any needless heroics. Order Payne to withdraw and come about to support the *Yermetov*!'

'Aye, sir.'

* * *

THE SMALLER FLESHY organisms fired from the belly of the hive ship sped like bullets towards the Imperial fleet, streaking past the majestic form of the Sword of Retribution and arcing towards the strike cruiser of the Space Marines. Supporting fire from the nearby battlecruiser's gun turrets obliterated the majority of the approaching organisms, and the combined guns of the Space Marine vessels and Arx Praetora squadron helped further thin their numbers. But still they kept coming.

On the bridge of the *Vae Victus*, Admiral Tiberius sweated as he watched the swarm of approaching craft. Thus far their close-in guns were holding them at bay, but it would not take much for the balance to swing against them.

'Sir!' shouted Philotas in dismay. 'The *Mortis Probati* is disengaging!'

Tiberius saw with mounting horror that Philotas was correct: the Mortifactors' strike cruiser's engines were flaring brightly as she pushed forward, her course angled upwards towards the hive ship. Her defensive guns had stopped firing and she was leaving the *Vae Victus* in her wake.

'What the hell are they doing?' demanded Tiberius, even as he saw the answer. A gap had been torn in the defences of the massive hive ship, its protective screen of drone ships stripped away by the relentless fire of the *Sword of Retribution* and her escorting Dauntless cruisers.

'They are going for the hive ship!' said Philotas.

'Can they make it before the tyranids re-establish their cover?' asked Tiberius.

Philotas consulted the plotting table, hurriedly scribbling distances and trajectories on a tablet beside him. He silently mouthed his calculations, shaking his head in exasperation.

'I think they might, lord admiral, but they will be cut off almost as soon as they breach the alien's defences.'

Tiberius slammed his fist into the lectern, cracking the glass of the slate. 'Damn them, what in the nine hells do they think they are doing? The codex clearly states that this kind of manoeuvre should only be attempted with a three to one superiority of fire.'

'I do not think Captain Gaiseric is familiar with that part of the codex, sir. And we have more pressing concerns now!' said Philotas pointing at the viewing bay.

Without the supporting fire from the *Mortis Probati's* turrets, perhaps half a dozen of the fleshy bullets fired from the hive ship had penetrated their defences and were, at best, seconds from contact.

'Emperor save us, no!' hissed Tiberius as he felt the impact of the tyranid organisms on his beloved ship.

URIEL RACED TOWARDS where the stony-surfaced object had smashed through the hull, filling the width of the corridor. Emergency bells and a hellish red glow bathed everything the colour of blood.

'Fan out!' he shouted. 'Make sure none of them get past you!' he shouted, directing his warriors to other damaged portions of the ship.

He kicked over a smouldering lump of chitin, approaching the cracked object that sat like a giant, toothed egg in the rubble of the corridor. Yellow slime dripped from its broken edges and hot steam billowed all around it. A piece of the object dropped to the deck, revealing an inner skin of a translucent, veined membrane.

'Pasanius, get up here. I need your flamer!' shouted Uriel as a ripple of motion shuddered through the membrane. He raised his bolt pistol and fired a succession of shots into the object, tearing the membrane and drawing an alien screech of pain from within.

A long claw ripped through the membrane and a grotesque creature bounded from the object. Its hide glistened wetly, dripping fluids from its bony exoskeleton, its mucus-wreathed head filled with needle-like fangs. Two pairs of arms, each ending in vicious barbed claws, clicked together as it landed lightly on the mesh deck. It hissed at Uriel, its black eyes nictating as it adjusted to its new surroundings. A trio of identical creatures followed it from the steaming chrysalis. Uriel could see many more behind them and unloaded his pistol into the mass of creatures as Pasanius finally arrived at his side.

Two of the creatures exploded as the mass-reactive shells detonated within their bodies, spattering yet more as they poured from the organism. A liquid wash of fire filled the corridor as Pasanius bathed the corridor in flame, simultaneously begging the ancient ship's forgiveness.

A burning creature bounded from the roaring flames, its teeth bared in its death fury. Uriel thrust his sword into its belly as it leapt, blasting its head from its shoulders with a single shot from his pistol. Elsewhere he could hear shots and screams of aliens as his men fought the horrific boarders.

Even as the flames died, a host of fresh creatures boiled from the object and Uriel wondered how closely packed these beasts must have been to fit within it. He swept out his sword, hacking two down with a single blow and sidestepping a third as it leapt for his head, bringing its hind legs up to rake his body with its claws.

It struck a stanchion, landing badly and Uriel stamped down on its neck, reaching for a reload for his pistol with trained economy of motion. Pasanius grappled with a pair of clawed beasts that tore at his armour with frenzied slashes of their talons. But Terminator armour had been designed with just this kind of close quarter battle in mind and they could not defeat it. Pasanius smashed their heads together, breaking their skulls open with a sickening, wet crack.

He dropped the twitching corpses, his flamer lying useless beside him, its fuel tank ruptured and leaking volatile fumes. Yet more creatures hurdled the bodies of their fallen siblings, desperate to reach their enemies. Uriel and Pasanius fought back-to-back as the alien tide threatened to overwhelm them, forced to fall back from the tide of clawed killers. They could not hold here, there were simply too many. Had they been reinforced from another boarding spore?

Uriel grunted as a razor edged claw slashed through the armour on his thigh, tearing into the muscle and ripping down to his knee. He toppled backwards, the alien's claw tearing from his flesh in a wash of bright blood. Uriel kicked out, breaking its neck and pulled himself backwards. The reek of promethium in the corridor was intense and as Pasanius helped him to his feet, he snatched a grenade from his belt.

'Run!' he shouted, pushing Pasanius down the corridor and hurling the grenade back the way they had come.

Pasanius gripped his captain's arm and pulled him to the deck as the grenade detonated, filling the corridor with lethal, scything fragments and igniting the choking promethium fumes. Roiling flames exploded with a whoosh of roaring air and the entire corridor was engulfed in a fiery explosion that billowed along its length, incinerating everything in its path. Uriel felt the flames wash over him, watching the external temperature reading on his visor rocket skywards. But neither his nor Pasanius's armour failed them and as the lethal flame wall burnt out, they found themselves in a blackened, corpse-choked passageway, littered with charred alien limbs and burning pools of promethium.

The two Space Marines struggled to their feet as the sounds of battle continued to rage throughout their ship.

There was more death yet to be done.

ADMIRAL DE CORTE watched the charging *Mortis Probati* close with the hive ship with a mixture of anger and admiration. The Mortifactors had broken his battle line, but by the Emperor they were courageous! The strike cruiser's bombardment cannon pounded the hive ship at, in spatial terms, point blank range, tearing great gouges in its hide.

The long feeder tentacles at the hive ship's rear lashed forward, swiping ponderously at the ship, but its captain swung his ship out of harm's way at the last possible second.

A host of bio-ships swung in behind the strike cruiser, blocking any escape as another cluster spun around and moved to attack. Bio acids and spurts of plasma struck the ship and flames erupted from her hull.

Inquisitor Kryptman watched the uneven battle with fierce pride, his knuckles white on the pommel of his cane. He spun to face de Corte. 'We must help them. Bring us about.'

'I cannot,' said de Corte. 'We are too far beyond them. It will be impossible to turn in time. We are manoeuvring to a position behind the hive ship as planned.'

'Do it!' snapped Kryptman, hammering his cane on the deck. 'Do it now!'

Kryptman spun to face the black uniformed Jaemar, the ship's commissar. 'You! Make him turn this Emperor forsaken ship around and support these brave warriors.'

Jaemar unholstered his pistol, cowed by Kryptman's reputation.

'The admiral is correct, lord inquisitor, commissar,' said de Corte's flag lieutenant, Jex Viert, moving to stand between Jaemar and his admiral. He placed his hand on the hilt of his sword, the threat clear. 'The image you are seeing is from our port surveyors. Even were the order given now, we will not be able to turn quickly enough to matter. In this respect, the Mortifactors are on their own.'

But Jex Viert was wrong.

CAPTAIN PAYNE, ABOARD the wounded *Mariatus*, shouted, 'For the Emperor!' as he gripped the arms of his command chair. The hive ship loomed large in the viewing bay and he knew that even if he survived this battle, he would be summoned before a court martial for disobeying a direct order. But with two of his ships put out of action by this monstrosity, he would have risked much more to avenge their gallant crews.

The *Mariatus* shuddered as blazing gouts of plasma fired from the hive ship drooled over her hull. Her guns hammered the alien monster, blowing chunks of its armoured carapace spinning into space and leaving a trail of seeping wounds along its mountainous body.

Ahead, he saw the graceful form of the Mortifactors' ship locked together with a thrashing beast with claws as big as a Battle Titan that raked its side and tore great swathes of its armour away. More bio-ships surrounded her, ready to sweep down and attack. Despite this, the massive cannon mounted on its prow continued to fire on the hive ship and though the heroism of the Space Marines was truly magnificent, there could only be one outcome.

Well, not if Payne and the *Mariatus* had anything to say about it.

URIEL RACED TO the bridge, hearing the desperate vox-traffic travelling between the ships of the fleet, dismayed at the sheer carnage unleashed. His armour was blackened and his leg flared painfully as he ran. The tyranid creatures were all dead and the damaged areas of the ship were finally secured.

He couldn't believe what the Mortifactors had done. Breaking the battle line and charging forward to engage the hive ship at close quarters was about as far from the teachings of the primarch as it was possible to get.

He mounted the steps to the bridge three at a time, sheathing his bloodied sword and sprinting through the arched entrance to the command bridge. Lord Admiral Tiberius turned as he entered, his face set in a mask of controlled fury.

'Uriel, thank the Emperor,' said the master of the *Vae Victus*.

'The boarders are repelled,' reported Uriel, staring in horror at the viewing bay as the Mortifactors' ship was slowly engulfed by the tyranid craft. Its bombardment cannon continued to fire, even as it was slowly being taken apart.

'What have they done?' he whispered.

Tiberius shook his head, words failing the ancient admiral. Then the battered shape of a Sword class frigate hove into view, trailing blazing plumes of venting plasma and golden streamers of sparks and freezing oxygen.

'Guilliman's blood, look!' shouted Philotas, as the prow of the *Mariatus* swung around and ploughed straight into the heart of the creature attacking the *Mortis Probati*.

The hull of the Imperial vessel buckled as it struck the hardened carapace of the tyranid creature, but its forward momentum could not be denied and it cracked through the flesh of the beast, spewing its bodily fluids all across the hull of the Space Marine vessel. It thrashed in its death agonies, releasing the strike cruiser and tumbled away with the *Mariatus* embedded deep within its body.

As valiant as the sacrifice of the *Mariatus* had been, there were tyranid ships aplenty to finish off the *Mortis Probati*, but before any could react to its unexpected survival, she unleashed a final shot from her bombardment cannon that struck a knotted growth tucked away at the rear of the hive ship. Bright liquid spurted from the wound like an enormous geyser and a visible shudder ran the length of the hive ship as the main synapse link to its attendant bio-ships was severed.

KRYPTMAN SAW THE great wound spew the hive ship's lifeblood into space and the listless drifting of the drone ships that surrounded it. His eyes flickered from bio-ship to bio-ship as he saw them pause in their relentless attack.

'Their connection to the hive mind is severed!' yelled Kryptman, spinning to face de Corte so quickly he almost fell. 'We must attack before it is restored! Immediately!'

Admiral Bregant de Corte nodded to Lieutenant Viert, who still stood between him and Jaemar. 'Mr Viert, order all ships forward. Let's close and finish this beast.'

WHILE THE TYRANID ships drifted in confusion, the captains of the *Sword of Retribution*, the *Luxor*, the *Yermetov* and the *Argus* all closed as quickly as possible, their gun decks loading and firing as fast as their crew chiefs could whip their gun gangs. The *Vae Victus* and Arx Praetora squadron swooped in and tore the underside of the tyranid vessel apart in a flurry of well-aimed fire. Fusillade after fusillade of explosive shells and lasblasts hammered the tyranid ship, pulverising vast sections of its carapace and spraying jets of ichor in all directions.

Feeder tentacles vainly attempted to swat away the attacking craft, but their swipes were drunken and uncoordinated. The smaller organisms protecting the hive ship threw off their lethargy, returning to their basic, instinctual desires, but by then it was too late. The Imperial ships were in textbook positions to deliver the deathblow to nearly every one of the drone ships. As though on range practice at Bakka, the *Sword of Retribution* bracketed one tyranid ship after another, annihilating them with powerful broadsides.

The battered *Mortis Probati* limped towards the listing hive ship and, in respect to her crew's reckless heroism, every other ship in the fleet hung back, allowing Captain Gaiseric to take the killing shot.

Fluid and fleshy entrails drifted from the mortally wounded beast, its alien lifeblood pumping into space from ruptured arteries and ruined organs. Those tentacles that had not been blasted off twitched spasmodically, and through a great rent in its upper carapace a vast, pulsing organ could be seen, labouring to keep the beast alive.

A single shell from the strike cruiser's bombardment cannon punched through the tough, fleshy outer layer of the hive ship's heart and detonated within its massive ventricle chambers. The explosion blasted the organ to shredded tissue and with a final, juddering spasm, the hive ship died.

ADMIRAL DE CORTE breathed a sigh of relief and his bridge crew cheered as they watched the death of the hive ship, its massive heart utterly destroyed by the Mortifactors. De Corte knew he should be furious with Captain Gaiseric for breaking the battle line, but could not deny the fact that his actions had been key to the tyranids' defeat. They went against everything taught at the naval academies, but de Corte knew that the truly great captains were the ones who could sometimes break all the teachings and still emerge victorious.

He didn't yet know if Captain Gaiseric fell into that category, or whether he had just been hugely lucky. Publicly, he would espouse the former, but privately, he suspected the latter. Had it not been for the valiant, but ultimately wasteful sacrifice of Captain Payne's ship, then the corpses of the Mortifactors would even now be joining the listing body of the hive ship. Watching the massive vessel haemorrhaging into the darkness, he mouthed a short prayer to the battle spirits that invested his ship, thanking them for their faithful service in this fight.

'Make a note, Mr Viert,' said de Corte. 'Commission a new victory seal to be added to our glorious ship's honour banner.'

'Aye sir, and perhaps a service of thanks?'

'Yes, a service of thanks to be held in the ship's chapels at vespers for all crew. Thank you, Mr Viert.'

The admiral linked his hands behind his back and returned to his command lectern as Inquisitor Kryptman shuffled along the nave to join him.

'A great victory,' said the admiral, loud enough to be heard by his entire bridge crew.

Kryptman nodded. 'A victory, yes. It remains to be seen whether it is a great one.'

The admiral leaned in close to Kryptman and whispered, 'You and I both know that this engagement has cost us dearly, but it will avail us nothing if we allow our crews to know how costly. I would appreciate your support in this matter.'

Kryptman looked ready to snap back at de Corte, but nodded curtly. 'You are correct, Admiral de Corte. Morale is crucial at this point.'

De Corte accepted Kryptman's acquiescence gracefully and began issuing the orders that would see his fleet disengage from Barbarus Prime and fall back to the orbital docks of Chordelis.

For the viewing bay was filled with a multitude of tyranid creatures rising from their feeding; a collection of hive ships and drones that dwarfed the group they had just destroyed. The Battle of Barbarus had been won, but in the face of such a vast fleet, it would be folly to fight again without first regrouping and rearming.

This had been a great victory, but it was just the tip of the iceberg. The real battles were yet to come.

SIX

LEARCHUS GAZED UP at the sloping wall that stretched to either side of him for nearly five kilometres towards the valley's flanks. Despite his disappointment in the manner in which this world upheld the ideals of Ultramar, he was pleased at the strength of its construction. Worthy of Macragge itself, he thought. Ten metres high and sheathed in smooth stone, the wall glittered like white marble in the low sun. A small revetment protected its golden gate and an icy moat drained below the level of the road into a sluggish river that wound its way to the plain below.

A foaming waterfall, pouring from the centre of the wall, roared down a copper channel embedded in its centre, fed the moat and filled the surrounding air with a chill mist of icy water. The morning was bitingly cold and his breath feathered before him, though his power armour isolated him from the worst of the frosty air.

Beside him stood a shivering officer of the Tarsis Ultra Citizens' Defence Legion, his blue, fur-collared coat and white peaked cap immaculately clean. In addition to his dress uniform, he wore a grey scarf around his lower jaw and thick mittens, thrust deep in his coat's baggy pockets. His name was Major Aries Satria and he commanded the armed forces of this city in the name of the Fabricator Marshal. His iron breastplate was polished to a silver sheen and the dress sword buckled to his gleaming leather belt shone like gold.

'When winter comes, does this moat freeze?' asked Learchus.

'This far out, yes,' nodded Major Satria, 'but as you get further into the city, the heat gets trapped by the valley sides and keeps them from turning to ice.'

'How far in do they freeze?' pressed Learchus.

'The moats at the first and second walls always freeze, and sometimes the third, but it really depends of the severity of the winter.'

Learchus nodded, setting off for the gate in the wall. 'What is the forecast for this coming winter?'

'The meteorologists say it will be a tough one,' said Satria, hurrying to keep up with Learchus, 'but then they always say that, don't they?'

The winters on Macragge had taught Learchus how tough a winter could be on soldiers, and he knew that the war could not have come at a worse time for this world. The cold weather had caused them problems already, with men reporting frostbite and other cold-related injuries. Corpsmen from the Logres regiment were instructing the men of the Krieg and local defence forces how to cope with such severe conditions, but it would take time for such practices to be adopted.

The two men crossed the moat on a crowded steel bridge. Its arching spars were limned with hoar frost and drifting floes of ice were already forming in the water below. Learchus had ordered the bridge to be rigged with explosives so that it could be destroyed upon the first attacks, though he could see that it would not be long before the moat was a solid sheet of thick ice, as easily traversable as this bridge. Nevertheless, standard practice was to destroy all approaches that the enemy could make use of and thus he had ordered it prepared for destruction.

But while the bridge still stood, many of the citizens of Erebus were making good use of it. Its metal deck vibrated with the passage of scores of vehicles, which rumbled past Learchus and Satria in the direction of the main spaceport below. All manner of vehicles, from gleaming limousines to battered agri-transports, streamed through the wall's main gate, each crammed with people carrying as many of their possessions as they could fit inside.

They stepped from the bridge onto a rutted road caked in grit that led to one of the wall's few postern gates. Tightly packed trucks filled with frightened people passed them and the sudden roar of a nearby starship engine made conversation impossible for a few seconds. Both Learchus and Satria turned, watching a cargo vessel rise from the port facilities and climb into the pale sky on smoky trails. It was the eighth vessel to leave Tarsis Ultra this morning and, judging by the crowds pressing around the walls of the spaceport, would only be one of many.

'It is unseemly that your people do not stay to fight,' said Learchus, turning back to watch the labouring men below. 'Where is their spirit? Their world is threatened and they flee before the enemy.' He shook his head in disappointment. 'No citizen of Ultramar would desert their homeworld. I believed the news of the great victory at Barbarus Prime would have put some steel in these people's spines, but it only seems to have weakened them.'

'People are frightened,' shrugged Satria. 'And I can't say I blame them. If even half of what I've heard about these aliens is true, then I can understand their desire to get away.'

'Given the chance, would you flee?' asked Learchus.

'No,' admitted Satria with a smile, 'but I swore an oath to defend this world and I don't break my word.'

'That is good to know, Major Satria. The warrior spirit of Ultramar is in you.'

Satria beamed with pride at the compliment as they eased past a madly revving supply truck. Laden with two-dozen frightened citizens of Erebus, its back wheels had sunk into the churned soil of the road and, behind it, angry horns blared continuously, as though their owners believed sheer volume of noise alone could shift the immobilised truck. Fountains of mud and chunks of grit from its spinning back wheels sprayed the limousine behind the truck, cracking its windscreen and leaving streaks of bare metal where they ripped across its pristine bodywork.

The driver of the truck continued gunning the engine, oblivious to the damage he was causing, gasoline rainbows forming in the clouds of filthy blue oilsmoke jetting from the truck's exhaust. The limousine's passenger, a tall man with a slicked widow's peak and a prominent hooked nose, climbed from the back of the vehicle and began screaming at the truck driver, delivering choice insults regarding his parents' promiscuity and bodily hygiene.

Learchus stepped forward to berate the man for his uncivil behaviour and coarse language, but Major Satria quickly shook his head saying, 'Best let me handle this one, Sergeant Learchus, I know this fellow. A gentle touch required, I think.'

'Very well,' said Learchus reluctantly.

Major Satria banged on the cab of the truck and made a chopping motion across his throat to the driver. Immediately, its engine shut down and the noise of the protesting motor faded to a throaty rumble as Satria made his way towards the limousine.

'Come now, Mr van Gelder,' said Satria, nimbly hopping across the mud of the road to address the limousine's passenger. 'There's no need for such language.'

The tall man drew himself up to his full height and tucked his thumbs into the pockets of his long frock coat. A caustic sneer spread across his features as Satria approached.

'Did you see what that imbecile has done?' he snapped.

'I did indeed, Mr van Gelder, and if you'll just bear with us, we'll get you on your way as soon as we can find some planks to put under the back wheels of this truck and get it out of the mud.'

'I want that wretched driver's name so that I can be properly compensated upon my return to Tarsis Ultra.'

'I assure you that I shall attend to the matter, sir,' soothed Satria. 'Now, if you'll just return to the lovely heated interior of your limousine, we'll soon have you out of the city.'

Before van Gelder could reply, a groan of metal sounded from behind the major. Satria turned to see Sergeant Learchus effortlessly lifting the back end of the fully laden truck from the sucking mud and push it forwards to more solid ground. The sergeant dropped the truck to the road and almost immediately it sped off to the spaceport.

Satria had heard of the great strength of Space Marines, but had thought that most were overblown exaggerations. Now he knew better.

The sergeant's face was thunderous as he marched back along the road towards van Gelder.

He pointed at the crowd that had gathered and the line of vehicles extending from the gate, shouting, 'Enough! This stops now. There will be no more departures from Tarsis Ultra. Get back in your vehicles, turn them around and get back within the city walls where you belong!'

Satria grimaced at Learchus's lack of tact and even van Gelder was momentarily taken aback. But he was not a man to be cowed easily.

'Do you know who I am?' he blustered.

'No,' said Learchus, dismissively. 'Nor do I care. Now turn this vehicle around before I do it myself.'

Having seen the Space Marine's strength demonstrated upon the truck, van Gelder was under no illusions concerning Learchus's ability to do such a thing, and reluctantly climbed into the back of his limousine.

'The Fabricator Marshal shall hear of this,' said van Gelder as a parting shot.

'I will make it my business to see that he does,' promised Satria.

Van Gelder's eyes narrowed, unsure if the major was mocking him, and slammed the door in his face. The limousine's gears ground as its driver attempted to turn it on the narrow road.

'I think we might have upset him,' smiled Satria.

'Good,' replied Learchus.

MELTED SNOW STREAKED across the fogged glass of the land train's window, running in long, wobbling lines. Lieutenant Quinn briefly wondered how fast they were actually travelling; it was hard to tell when everything he could see beyond the glass was a uniform white. He gripped the handrail as the land train swept around a bend in the track and leaned over to wipe a gloved hand across the glass, smiling at the young family seated across from him.

'No need to worry,' he said. 'It won't be long before we're in Erebus. Just one more stop to pick up the people at Prandium.'

The man nodded, his wife looking fearfully at the white-steel of the lasgun he held across his knees. It was a look he had seen many times on this journey, the terror that armed conflict had come to their once-peaceful world, but he couldn't bring himself to feel sorry for them. After all, was it not the duty of every Imperial citizen to stand against the enemies of Mankind?

He and his platoon had emptied six farming collectives of their populace and packed them on this long land train in order to bring them to the safety of Erebus. Dozens of other platoons were performing the same job all across the continent and with any luck they would be able to complete their mission without incident. Over sixty carriages snaked back from the labouring engine car and they were already nearing capacity, each carriage crammed with fearful people.

Already Lieutenant Quinn could envision the scenes of outrage when he would have to order these people to discard their belongings to make room for the people of Prandium.

Sergeant Klein, his adjutant, made his way along the carriage's central aisle with difficulty, pushing past protesting citizens, his thick jacket and combat webbing catching almost everyone he passed. Klein held his rifle raised, the sling wrapped around his arm and said, 'Sir, we're just about to pull into Prandium.'

'Excellent. Nearly done, eh, sergeant?'

'Yes, sir.'

'Order the men to stand to. I'll take First squad, you take Second.'

Klein nodded and made his way back through the carriage as Quinn felt the train's deceleration. He rose from his seat and eased his way through the crowds packing the train towards the main doors where a knot of his soldiers from the Logres regiment waited to disembark. He sketched a quick salute and wiped his hand across the glass of the doors, seeing the silver steel of the platform approaching. Something struck him as odd, but it took him a second or two to realise what it was.

The platform was empty.

Whereas some communities had been reluctant to abandon their homes, most had been only too eager to be escorted back to the safety of Erebus, their departure points thronged with anxious people, packed and ready to leave.

But not here.

Quinn sighed as he realised they were probably going to have to convince more stubborn farmers to abandon their lands and come with them. He should be used to it, he supposed. Each time the Tarellians attacked one of the sea farms on Oceanus, they would run into bull-headed krill farmers who'd be damned if they'd abandon the holdings their family had farmed for generations. In Quinn's experience, those types always ended up dead sooner rather than later.

The train slid to a graceful halt and the doors smoothly opened. Freezing air sucked the warmth from the carriage, to the groans and complaints of its passengers. Quinn stepped onto the frosted platform, feeling ice crunch under his boot.

That was unusual. He would have expected the station's servitors to have kept the platform free from ice. The windows of the station building were opaque with frost and long icicles drooped from the eaves of the main station house. The hanging sign that creaked in the low wind clearly declared that this was Prandium.

He could see Sergeant Klein's squad further down the platform and waved his adjutant over.

'This is peculiar,' he said.

'I agree,' said Klein. 'No one's been here for a while.'

'Another train hasn't passed this way before us, has it?'

Klein pulled out the small orders pad he kept in his thick winter coat's breast pocket and shook his head. 'No, not according to my information, sir.'

'I don't like it,' stated Quinn.

'What do you want us to do?'

'Move into the town,' ordered Quinn. 'And stay sharp. Something doesn't feel right here.'

Klein saluted and made his way carefully along the platform to rejoin his squad.

'Right,' said Quinn, 'let's move out.'

Using small, careful steps, he crossed the slippery platform and flicked off the safety on his lasgun as he reached the top of the steps below a sign that indicated the exit. The stone steps were slick with ice and more icicles hung from the underside of the banister. Slowly, and with great care, Quinn and his squad made their way down the stairs, emerging into the farming collective of Prandium.

Its snow-filled streets were eerily quiet, only the low moan of the wind and the crunching footsteps of his platoon disturbing the silence. Not even the lonely call of a bird sounded. The buildings were sturdy-looking, prefabricated structures, similar to those on a thousand other worlds, fashioned from local materials and built with the sweat and toil of their inhabitants. A generatorium building stood abandoned beside them and a trio of vast grain silos towered above the community at the far end of the street.

There was a tension in the air; even Quinn could feel it. Prandium reeked of abandonment. There had been nobody here for a long time and the sense of neglect was painfully evident.

'Let's go,' he said and led his squad into the settlement, crunching through the knee-deep snow. The streets felt narrow and threatening. Through a gap in the buildings, he could see Klein's squad advancing on a parallel course to their own.

A door banged in the wind and everyone jumped, lasguns swinging to face the direction the sound had come from. Quinn's feeling that there was something wrong here rose from a suspicion to a certainty. Even if these people had left on an earlier transport that he didn't know about, any farmer worth his salt would have found the time to make sure his property was closed up for the winter.

Two large harvesters stood rusting at the end of the street in the shadow of the huge grain silos and Quinn motioned his squad to follow him towards them. Even though the icy air dampened any odours he might have smelled, he could still taste the reek of rotted grain. As they circled around the harvesters, he saw something that made him pull up short and raise his fist.

At the base of the nearest grain silo, a three-metre tear had been ripped in the skin of the tower, the metal peeled back and buckled. A sloping pile of frozen grain spread from the tear.

He advanced cautiously towards the torn hole, a sudden chill enveloping him as he moved into the long shadow cast by the tower. Quinn drew his chainsword, his thumb hovering above the activation rune. He stepped onto the gritty surface of the grain, flicking on the illuminator slung beneath the barrel of his lasgun, and took a deep breath as he stared into the darkness within the silo. A thick stench, disguised by the cold air, filled his nostrils as he cautiously stepped into the silo, playing the spear of light from his illuminator around its interior. The light could only show the merest fragment of what lay within, but even that was too much.

He numbly waved his vox-operator forward.

'Get Sergeant Klein over here,' he whispered, his voice trembling, 'and tell him to hurry...'

SERGEANT LEARCHUS, MAJOR Satria and Colonel Stagler of the Krieg regiment stood atop the frosted rampart of the first wall of Erebus city, watching the soldiers of its defence force training on the esplanade between this wall and the second. Men sweated and grunted below, the sound of their training eclipsed by the ringing of hammers and clang of shovels on the frozen ground as other gangs of soldiers dug trench lines before the walls.

Learchus watched the men below with a mixture of disappointment and resignation.

'You are not impressed, I take it,' said Satria.

Learchus shook his head. 'No, most of these men would not survive a week at Agiselus.'

'That's one of the training barracks on Macragge, is it not?' asked Stagler.

'Yes, it sits at the foot of the Mountains of Hera where Roboute Guilliman himself trained. It is where myself and Captain Ventris trained also.'

Soldiers worked in small sparring groups, practising bayonet drills and close combat techniques with one another, making a poor show of the skills they would need to keep them alive in the coming battles.

Upon his first inspection of the troops, Learchus had watched each platoon fire off accurate volleys of disciplined lasfire, blasting close groupings of holes in target silhouettes. He had marched to the first platoon and grabbed a lasgun from a nervous trooper, before returning to a surprised looking Major Satria.

'You are teaching them to shoot?'

'Well, yes. I thought that might be important in a soldier,' Satria had replied.

'Not against tyranids,' said Learchus. 'Have you ever seen a tyranid swarm?'

'You know I haven't.'

'Well I have, and they come at you in a tide of creatures so thick a blind man could score a hit ten times out of ten. Any man who can hold a gun can hit a tyranid. But no matter how many you kill with your guns, there will always be more, and it is our job to teach the men how to fight the ones that reach our lines.'

Since then, the organisation of a coherent training program had fallen to Learchus and in the week since he had ordered the gates of Erebus closed, he had fought bureaucratic intransigence and years of ingrained dogma to implement a workable regime.

At dawn the men would rise, practise field stripping their weapons and perform exercises designed to enhance their stamina and aerobic strength. Corpsmen from the Logres regiment had been instrumental in instructing the soldiers in good practices while exercising in cold weather, as each activity had to be rigorously controlled, lest a soldier develop a layer of sweat beneath his winter clothes that would later condense, degrading its insulating properties dramatically.

'These men must learn faster,' said Learchus. 'They will all die in the first attack at this rate.'

'You expect the impossible from them, sergeant,' said Satria. 'At this rate they will hate us more than the tyranids.'

'Good. We must first strip them of all sense of self. We must strip away every notion of who they think they are and rebuild them into the soldiers they need to be to survive. I do not care that they hate me, only that they learn. And learn quickly.'

'That won't be easy,' said Satria.

'Irrelevant,' said Stagler. 'The weakest men will always be the first to fall anyway. When the chaff has been removed, the true warriors will remain.'

'Chaff?' said Satria. 'These are my soldiers and I'll not have them spoken of like that.'

'Your soldiers leave a lot to be desired, Major Satria,' pointed out Stagler, his hands clasped behind his back. His patrician features were pinched by the cold, and his stern gaze swept the training ground in disapproval. Learchus agreed with Stagler and though he knew that Satria's men were trying, effort had to be combined with results to mean anything.

He watched a group of soldiers practising thrusting and parrying with bayonets, their movements encumbered by thick winter clothing. Originally the soldiers had been training without their webbing and winter gear, but Learchus had swiftly put a stop to that. Where was the use in training in ideal conditions when the fighting was never going to be that way?

Learchus firmly believed in the philosophy of Agiselus: train hard, fight easy. Every training exercise undertaken by its cadets was fought against insurmountable odds, so that when the real fight came, it was never as hard.

Even after a week's training, Learchus saw that the soldiers were still too slow. Tyranid creatures were inhumanly quick, their razored limbs like a blur as they speared towards your heart, and he knew that the butcher's bill among these soldiers would be high indeed.

Without a word of explanation he turned on his heel and made his way down the gritted steps that led from the ramparts to the esplanade below. Satria and Stagler hurriedly followed him as he stepped onto its slick cobbles.

He strode into the middle of the training ground and stood with his hands planted squarely on his hips. Activity around him gradually diminished until the soldiers began to slowly gather around the Space Marine at their centre.

'You have strayed from the ideals of Ultramar that the blessed primarch left you as his legacy,' began Learchus. 'You have been seduced by the frippery and comfort that comes from lives of indulgence and peace. I am here to tell you that that time is over. Comfort is an illusion, a chimera bred from familiar things and ways.'

Learchus marched around the circumference of the circle of soldiers, punctuating his words by slapping his gauntleted fist into his palm.

'Comfort narrows the mind, weakens the flesh and robs your warrior spirit of fire and determination. Well, no more.'

He marched to stand in the centre of the circle and said, 'Comfort is neither welcome nor tolerated here. Get used to it.'

THE SKIN OF the soldier's foot was waxy-looking, a white, greyish yellow colour, and several ruptured blisters leaked a clear fluid onto the crisp white sheets of the bed. Joaniel Ledoyen shook her head at this soldier's foolishness, jabbing a sharp needle into the cold flesh on the sole of his foot. The man didn't react, though she couldn't tell whether that was a result of the frostbite or the half-bottle of amasec he'd downed to blot out the pain.

Probably a mix of both, she thought, discarding the needle into a sharps box and scrawling a note on the man's chart that hung from the end of his bed.

'Is it bad?' slurred the soldier.

'It's not good,' said Joaniel frankly. 'But if you're lucky we may be able to save your foot. Didn't you receive instruction on how to prevent these kinds of injuries?'

'Aye, but I don't read so good, sister. Never had no call for it on Krieg.'

'No?'

'Nah, soon as you're old enough you're sent to join the regiment. Colonel Stagler don't approve of educated men, says it was educated men that got Krieg bombed to shit in the first place. The colonel says that all a man needs to do is fight and die. That's the Krieg way.'

'Well, with any luck, I'll have you fighting again soon, but hopefully you can avoid the dying part,' said Joaniel.

The soldier shrugged. 'As the Emperor wills.'

'Yes,' nodded Joaniel sadly as she moved away. 'As the Emperor wills.'

So far today, she had treated perhaps fifty cases of mild hypothermia and a dozen cases of frostbite, ranging from mild blanching of the skin to this poor unfortunate, who, despite her optimistic words, would probably lose his foot.

Joaniel snapped off her rubber gloves and disposed of them as she made her way painfully back to the nurses' station at the end of the long row of beds. She favoured her right leg, pressing her palm against her hip and watching as corpsmen from the Logres regiment circulated in the long, vaulted chamber. They used thermal bandages to gradually restore heat to frostbitten limbs of the injured men in a controlled manner. Thankfully, the beds in the District Quintus Medicae facility were still largely empty – the building was designed to cope with over a thousand patients – though she knew that the steadily increasing trickle of soldiers being brought to her wards would soon become a raging torrent once the war began. Remian IV had taught her that.

She rubbed her temples and yawned, pulling out the cord that bound her ponytail and ran a hand through her long blonde hair. Tall and statuesque, Joaniel Ledoyen was a handsome woman of forty standard years, with smoky blue eyes and full features that spoke of great dignity and compassion. She wore a long, flowing white robe, bearing the crest of the Order of the Eternal Candle, one of the Orders Hospitaller of the Convent Sanctorum of the Adepta Sororitas, pulled in at the waist by a crimson sash.

Unlike the battle sisters of the Orders Militant, the sisters of the Orders Hospitaller provided medical care and support for the fighting men and women of the Imperial Guard, as well as setting up missions for the needy and impoverished of the Imperium.

Many wounded soldiers had the sisters of the Orders Hospitaller to thank for their survival and it was a source of great comfort to those on the front line to know that such aid awaited them should they be injured.

One of her junior nurses, Ardelia Ferria, looked up and smiled as she saw Joaniel approaching. Ardelia was young and pretty, fresh from her training as a novice and had only recently completed her vows on Ophelia VII. She liked her and though the youngster had yet to witness the true horrors of war, Joaniel felt Ardelia would make a fine nurse.

'All done for the night?' asked Ardelia.

'Yes, thank the Emperor. Most of these men will live to fight another day.'

'They are lucky to have you to look after them, Sister Ledoyen.'

'We all play our part, Sister Ferria,' said Joaniel modestly. 'Have the fresh supplies arrived from the upper valley yet?'

'No, not yet, though the city commissariat assures me that they will be here soon,' said Ardelia, with more than a trace of scepticism.

Joaniel nodded, sharing Ardelia's misgivings and well used to the vagaries of the city's commissariat, but knew that the supplies would be desperately needed in the coming days. She would need to contact the commissariat in the morning and demand to know what had become of them.

'I can look after the wards for the rest of the night,' said Ardelia. 'You should retire for the evening, Sister Ledoyen. You look tired.'

Joaniel tried not to be too hurt at Ardelia's remark, but supposed she did. The weight of responsibility and too many bad memories had aged her prematurely and though she still met her order's physical fitness requirements and could field strip a bolter in less than forty seconds, she knew that a life of moving from war to war had made her features melancholy.

The war on Remian IV had been the worst she had ever seen: screaming men begging for a merciful death rather than endure such pain. The stench of blood, voided bowels, antiseptic fluids and the acrid reek of war had stayed with her long after the war there had been won.

She remembered the months of counselling she had given the soldiers after the battle, bringing many of them back from the horror of their experiences on Remian. In response to her soothing words and gentle manner, the soldiers had dubbed her the Angel of Remian and that name had followed her since then. She had saved hundreds, if not thousands, of lives on Remian, but in the end, there had been no one there to soothe the horrors in her own head.

In her dreams she would find herself back there, weeping as she clamped a spraying artery, fighting to save a faceless soldier's life as he screamed and clawed at her with broken fingers. Severed limbs and the choking tang of burned human meat still filled her senses and every night she would wake with a pleading scream on the edge of her lips.

Joaniel thought of returning to her bare cell above the wards, but the prospect of such emptiness was too much for her to deal with right now.

'I shall offer a prayer to the Emperor before I retire. Call me if you need anything,' she told Ardelia, before bowing and making her way through the thick wooden doors that led from the main ward into the stone flagged vestibule.

She walked stiffly towards a low arch, stepping down into a short, candlelit passageway with a black door at its end. A carving of a hooded figure with golden wings filled the door and Joaniel pushed it open and entered the medicae's chapel.

The chapel was a simple affair, barely large enough to hold two-dozen worshippers. Three lines of hard, wooden pews ran in orderly lines from the alabaster statue at the end of the nave and scores of candles filled the air with a warm, smoky glow. Above the statue, a semi-circular window of stained glass threw a pool of coloured light across the polished wooden floor.

Joaniel bowed and made her way towards the two stone benches flanking the statue and knelt before it, bowing her head and clasping her hands together in prayer. Silently she whispered words of devotion and obedience, ignoring the dull ache that grew in her knees as the cold seeped into her bones from the bare floor. Tears filled her eyes as she prayed, the sights and sounds of Remian coming back so vividly that she could taste the smoke and smell the blood.

She finished her prayers and painfully pushed herself to her feet, the metal pins in her right thigh aching in the cold. The field hospital on Remian had taken a direct hit from an enemy artillery shell and she alone had been pulled from the wreckage, the bones of her leg shattered into fragments. The soldiers whose lives she had saved had rounded up the finest surgeons and her surgery had been performed beneath the flickering light of an artillery barrage. She had lived, but the thousands of her patients in the building had not, and the guilt of her survival gnawed at her soul like a cancer.

She rubbed the feeling back into her legs and bowed again to the Emperor's statue before turning to make her way back to her cold cell above.

'As the Emperor wills,' she said.

THE VOLCANIC WORLD of Yulan was beautiful from space, its flickering atmosphere riven with streaks of scarlet lightning and the swirls of ruby clouds painting streamers of bright colours across its northern hemisphere. A cluster of ships hung in orbit, buffeted by the planet's seismic discharges and flares of ignited gasses from the cracked surface.

Their captains fought to hold their vessels steady, their shields at full amplitude to protect them from a host of hazardous materials being ejected from the world below. Though even the smallest vessel was almost a kilometre long, they were all dwarfed by the three behemoths that hung in geo-stationary orbit above Yulan. Hundreds of pilot ships and powerful tugs from the docks above the nearby planet of Chordelis fought the miasma of turbulence in the planet's lower atmosphere to manoeuvre themselves into position at the vast docking lugs at the front of the enormous creations.

Each behemoth was a hydrogen-plasma mining station that drank deeply of the planet's violent atmosphere and refined it into valuable fuels used by the tanks of the Imperial Guard, the ships of the Navy and virtually every machine tended by the Adeptus Mechanicus. They were largely automated, as the handling of such volatile fuels was, to say the least, highly dangerous.

For several hours, and at the cost of scores of servitor drones, the first of the huge refinery ships was slowly dragged from orbit, its vast bulk moving at a crawl into the darkness of space.

Despite the danger of working in such a hostile environment, the work to moor the tug ships to the second refinery was achieved in little under three hours and it moved to join the first on the journey to Chordelis. The Adeptus Mechanicus magos overseeing the mission to Yulan was pleased with the speed with which the operation was proceeding, but knew that time was running out to recover the third refinery.

Already the tyranid fleet had reached Parosa and was heading this way.

Time was of the essence and a further six, frustrating hours passed as the tug crews tried again and again to attach themselves to the last refinery in the turbulent lower atmosphere. The tug captains moved in again, their frustration and orders for haste perhaps making them more reckless than was healthy.

But haste and a billion-tonne refinery packed with lethally combustible fuels are two things that do not sit well together.

The captain of the tug vessel *Truda* moved his vessel gingerly into position on the forward docking spar of the last refinery, eschewing the normal safety procedures regarding proximity protocols. As the *Truda* moved into final position, her captain was so intent on the docking lugs ahead that he failed to notice the *Cylla* coming around a sucking, gas intake tower.

At the last second, both captains realised their danger and attempted to avoid the inevitable collision, the *Truda* veering right and barrelling into the intake tower. She smashed herself to destruction against its structure, buckling the hot metal of the tower and crashing through the thin plates before exploding as her fuel cells ruptured.

The *Truda* could not have struck the refinery in a worse place; designed to capture the hot gasses from the planet below, the intake tower sucked a huge breath of the tug's explosion, carrying the burning plasma of its engines to the very heart of the refinery's combustion chambers, where it ignited an uncontrolled chain reaction.

Emergency procedures initiated, but blast doors not shut since the refinery's construction thousands of years ago jammed and shutdown measures failed as ancient circuits failed to close, their wiring long having since degraded to the point of uselessness.

Within minutes of the crash, the internal chambers of the refinery began exploding sequentially, with each blast blowing apart more storage chambers and multiplying the force of the blast exponentially.

From high orbit, it appeared as though the giant refinery was convulsing and before any warning could be given to the ships still clustered nearby, it exploded in a flaring corona that eclipsed the brightness of the system's star.

Everything within a thousand kilometres of the blast was instantly vaporised and the shockwave ruptured the surface of the planet below, sending plumes of fiery gasses into space.

The blast wave faded, leaving nothing of the refinery or the hundreds of men that made up the Adeptus Mechanicus detachment tasked with its retrieval, save an expanding cloud of burning plasma gas.

Oblivious to the disaster in their wake, the flotilla of tugs continued onwards to Chordelis with the two surviving refineries lifted from geostationary orbit around Yulan in tow.

Why the Ultramarines' admiral had tasked them with this dangerous duty, they did not know, but theirs was not to question, simply to obey.

THE SIX TRUCKS sat silently in the dimly lit vehicle hangar; moonlight streaming in through the high windows providing the only illumination. A dozen soldiers grunted as they loaded crates onto the back of the trucks, overseen by a supply sergeant of the Erebus Commissariat, who, despite the fact that the temperature was below zero, sweated beneath the fur-lined hood of his winter coat.

He smoked a limp bac-stick and stamped his feet to ward off the cold as the last crate was loaded onto the truck, each one marked with a scorched burn where a Departmento Munitorum shipping number and regimental crest had been stamped. The tailgates of each truck were slammed shut and secured with chained locking-pins and as his soldiers filed passed him, he pressed a wad of promissory notes into each one's hand.

'Don't do anything dumb with this,' he warned.

As the last of the soldiers left the garage, he stubbed out his bac-stick and circled the trucks, checking that all the tailgates were secured. As he rattled the last one, a group of figures emerged from the shadows at the far end of the garage.

'You all done?' asked the figure at the front.

The supply sergeant jumped, his hand reaching for the pistol below his coat.

'I wouldn't do that if I was you,' growled a hulking figure behind the first and the sergeant raised his hands.

'Snowdog,' he breathed in relief, lowering his hands as the group came into the light. He flipped another bac-stick into his mouth.

'You expecting someone else, Tudeca?' asked Snowdog, his shotgun resting on his shoulder. The leader of the Nightcrawlers wore a thick woollen coat to ward off the winter's chill and his bleached hair shone as silver as that of the girl beside him. Behind Snowdog stood the psychotic thug he called Jonny Stomp and a trio of painfully thin youths decorated with colourful, if badly drawn, tattoos across their faces. At a gesture from Snowdog, they jogged towards the cabs of three of the trucks, a redheaded girl in a tight catsuit climbing into the nearest one.

'No,' said Sergeant Tudeca. 'It's just you startled me. I wasn't expecting you so soon.'

'What can I say; I like to surprise people,' said Snowdog, nodding to Jonny Stomp. The brutish giant climbed onto the back of each of the trucks in turn, counting the number of crates in the back of each one. Sergeant Tudeca stepped nervously from foot to foot, surprised Jonny Stomp could count past his fingers, as Snowdog and Silver watched him carefully.

'It's all there?' asked Snowdog.

'Yeah, it's all there. Medical supplies and ration packs, just like you wanted. Didn't I tell you I could get them for you?'

'Yeah, you really came through for us,' agreed Snowdog, putting an arm around Tudeca's shoulders and lifting the pack of bac-sticks from his breast pocket.

Snowdog waited for a second, raising an eyebrow until Tudeca took the hint and lit the bac-stick for him, the flame wavering in his shaking hands. Snowdog reached up to steady the sergeant's hand.

'You okay, Tudeca?' said Snowdog with false concern. 'You look all jittery, man. Something on your mind?'

'It's going to cost more,' blurted Tudeca. 'I had to give my lads twice what they normally get for this. The commissariat provosts are coming down hard on anyone they catch stealing, and if they arrest me, it's a bullet in the head for sure.'

'Tudeca, Tudeca,' soothed Snowdog. 'Don't look at this as stealing; look at it as redistributing it to the people who really need it. Look, all this stuff was going to the medicae buildings for the regiments from off world. I'll make sure it gets to the people of Erebus... at a nominal charge.'

Tudeca laughed, a hoarse bray, and said, 'Nominal charge! You'll be selling this for four times its worth.'

'Hey man, it's a seller's market out there. If I can make a little money out of this war, then who's to say that's a bad thing?'

'Don't forget, you're hip-deep in this too,' pointed out Silver, her long hair glittering in the moonlight.

'Yeah, I know,' said Tudeca sourly, as Jonny Stomp dropped from the back of the last truck.

'It's all there, near as I can tell,' he said.

'Well, what the hell does that mean?' said Snowdog. 'It either is or it isn't.'

'I mean it looks right to me,' growled Jonny.

'Good enough, I guess,' said Snowdog with a shrug as Silver and Jonny Stomp each got behind the wheel of a truck. He vaulted into the cab of the truck next to him and slammed the door behind him. He rolled down the side window and leaned out, looking over his shoulder at Sergeant Tudeca as the engines of trucks roared into life. He pulled out a wad of bills, a chunk of the score from the Flesh Bar – minus what he'd paid for a stolen shipment of guns from another crooked supply sergeant the night before – and flicked it through the air towards Tudeca.

The sergeant caught the money with a lopsided grin of avarice.

'I can get more of this stuff in a little while,' he shouted, his greed overcoming his natural cowardice. 'I just got to wait until the heat dies down a little.'

Headlights speared from their mountings and the first truck moved off into the night.

'Sounds good to me,' said Snowdog as he gunned the engine of his truck.

'After all,' said Tudeca. 'Business is business.'

'Yeah,' agreed Snowdog. 'Business as usual.'

☡
SEVEN

THE ORBITAL DOCKS of Chordelis were a scene of controlled anarchy, as every technician, shipwright and able-bodied man available was pressed into service repairing the terrible damage done by the tyranids to the vessels of the Imperial Navy following the Battle of Barbarus. A perimeter of local gunboats formed a picket line around the naval vessels, isolating them from the swarm of ships that rose from the surface of Chordelis in an uncontrolled tide.

Under the supervision of the Mortifactors' Techmarines, thick sheets of steel were welded onto the damaged sections of the *Mortis Probati* and fresh shells loaded into her magazines. The crews of the *Heroic Endeavour* and the sole surviving vessel of Hydra squadron swarmed around their hulls, jury-rigging repairs that would allow them to go into battle once more. No one was under any illusions that these repairs were anything more than temporary – each ship would need many months in dock to return to full service.

The *Vae Victus* had escaped comparatively unscathed. Her hull had been breached in four places, but none of the tyranid boarding organisms had penetrated further than the outer decks and repairs would be a relatively simple matter. Not that this was any consolation to Admiral Tiberius, who had vowed that he would not forget the insult done to his ship by the Mortifactors' impetuosity. The bulk of the work on her hull had already been completed and beyond the picket line of gunboats, Arx Praetora squadron and the Dauntless cruisers *Yermetov* and *Luxor* awaited to escort her on another mission.

Since the warning of the tyranids' impending arrival had reached Chordelis, the planet had been steadily emptying and hundreds of vessels clogged the shipping lanes around the world. Wealthy citizens with their own vessels were the first to depart, closely followed by those able to book passage off-world. Those with enough money fled deeper into the galactic core while those unable to finance such a journey travelled on commercial ships crammed with refugees that shuttled back and forth between Chordelis and Tarsis Ultra. Greedy captains, scenting opportunity for profit, raised their prices accordingly until even the wealthy fled as paupers.

But though millions escaped, millions more remained. Panicked crowds flocked to every major spaceport, trying to get to safety. Desperate to escape, men offered eternal service and women offered themselves. Some were successful, more were not, and fear spread like an epidemic through the people of Chordelis.

At Berliaas, desperate crowds demonstrated outside the governor's palace, demanding action be taken to evacuate the populace. Tempers flared and thousands of angry citizens stormed the palace only to find the planetary governor had already fled Chordelis and that his missives for calm had been broadcast from off-world.

In Dremander, the crew of a rogue trader's vessel opened fire on people trying to commandeer their vessel, killing more than seventy before being overrun and torn to pieces by the angry mob.

Two days after this incident, more than eleven thousand people died at Jaretaq, the planet's largest port, as terrified crowds broke through the lines of Arbites guarding the entrance and demanded passage on the fleet of departing vessels thronging her landing platforms. As the luxury vessel *Cherrona* lifted from the planet's surface, angry crowds prevented the ground crews from releasing her mooring cables. Her starboard engine was torn free of its mountings as her captain brought her about for departure. The engine dropped and blew apart like a bomb among the milling crowds and the ponderous vessel began sliding back towards the ground, the attraction of gravity too much for its remaining engine to fight. Fully laden with refugees and thousands of tonnes of fuel, the *Cherrona* swayed drunkenly in the air, striking the nearby control tower before slamming into the landing platforms of the spaceport.

The *Cherrona* exploded with the power of an orbital bombardment, hurling blazing sheets of fire and lethal fragments in all directions, scything through thousands of people and touching off scores of secondary explosions. The devastation ripped through the spaceport until almost nothing was left standing. The blazing pyres of this terrible disaster could be seen as far away as the planetary capital of Kaimes.

All across Chordelis, the same scenes played out as its terrified population fought to escape their doomed world.

* * *

THE COMMAND BRIDGE of the Vae Victus was tense and subdued as Admiral Tiberius kept his ship a respectable distance from the mighty structure that slid through space before them and filled the viewing bay. They had all heard of the disaster at Yulan and the loss of the third refinery, and Tiberius was determined that nothing similar would happen to this one.

'How close are we, Philotas?' whispered Tiberius, as though the volume of his voice would alert the tyranids to their presence, though the aliens must surely be aware of them by now. Garbled reports from Arx Praetora squadron and the Dauntless cruisers, some thirty thousand kilometres ahead of them, had spoken of the alien fleet moving in a solid mass of creatures, several hive ships scattered throughout the swarm. They were probably too far apart to catch more than one or two, but even one was a victory.

'Hard to say, admiral,' replied Philotas. 'Surveyor returns are being scattered by the refinery vessel, but I'd say no more than fifty thousand kilometres.'

'We're cutting this very close,' observed Uriel, staring at the plotting table. 'The first engagements at Barbarus were not much closer than this.'

'I know, Uriel, I know. But we only have one chance at this. Chordelis is depending on us. We cannot fail.'

Uriel nodded, determined that Chordelis would not suffer the horrible fate of Barbarus Prime. By now there was nothing left of that world but a dead hunk of rock, its people, wildlife and very ecosystem devoured by these monstrous aliens. Chordelis also faced obliteration, but in this case the threat did not come from the aliens, but from the very people supposed to be defending it.

The thought of Kryptman's cold, steel logic sent a shiver down Uriel's spine and he was reminded of the last time he had defied the will of an inquisitor. On this very ship, Inquisitor Ario Barzano had proposed the destruction of Pavonis to prevent a madman from obtaining a weapon capable of unmaking the stars themselves. Uriel had managed to persuade Barzano to give them one last chance to act and, by the grace of the Emperor, they had been successful, and Pavonis had been spared the horror of the ultimate sanction of viral bombing.

Once again he had been forced to stand against those he would have counted as his allies in defence of the ordinary men and women of the Imperium. It astounded him that Kryptman could be so unfeeling with the lives of millions of people, consigning an entire planet to death simply to prevent the enemy from taking it.

Only two days ago in the captain's chambers on the command deck of the *Argus*, Kryptman had told them of his decision to let Chordelis die.

'We have no choice,' the inquisitor had said. 'Fighters from the *Kharloss Vincennes* have harried the vanguard of the alien fleet from

Barbarus, past Parosa and Yulan. The tyranids will be here within three
or four days at the latest. There is simply no more time to get anyone
else off Chordelis. If we stay any longer we will doom what little assets
we have, and for what? We could fight, and we would gain perhaps a
day's respite for the defenders on Tarsis Ultra. And once we are
defeated, the tyranids will devour Chordelis as they did Barbarus
Prime, swelling their numbers with an entire planet's biosphere.'

Kryptman shook his head. 'No, far better Chordelis dies by our own
hand than that of the Great Devourer. Believe me, Exterminatus is a
better, quicker death than the tyranids will offer.'

A stunned silence had greeted Kryptman's pronouncement. Admiral
Bregant de Corte blanched and took a sip of amasec before taking a
deep breath and casting his flinty gaze around the table. His assembled
captains looked shocked, but took their lead from the admiral and said
nothing. Captain Gaiseric and Astador nodded slowly.

Admiral Tiberius cleared his throat and leaned forwards, resting his
elbows on the smooth table and steepling his fingers before him.

'There must be another way,' he said slowly, and Uriel was struck by
yet another sense of déjà vu, remembering when Inquisitor Barzano
had come to a similar decision.

'Admiral Tiberius is correct,' he said. 'What is the point of us being
summoned to this system to defend it when our first reaction to these
aliens' advance is to destroy everything in their path? You would have
us stand victorious over a dead system.'

'You do not see the larger picture, Captain Ventris,' said Kryptman,
emphasising the insignificance of his rank next to his own. 'We are at
war with forces too terrible to comprehend, and one must sometimes
sacrifice the smaller battles to be victorious in the larger war.'

'Listen to yourself,' snapped Uriel. 'You talk of sacrificing smaller battles. Do you not realise that you are talking about one of the Emperor's
worlds, still populated by millions of His subjects, His soldiers? I think
that it is you who forgets the "larger war".'

'No, Captain Ventris,' said Kryptman with finality. 'I do not.'

Uriel stood and slammed his fist on the table, splintering the wood.
'Every time these aliens invade the Emperor's realm we fall back. People like you claim we cannot fight them and we hear this so often we
start to believe it. Well that stops now. I say we draw a line here and
talk no more. This time, I say we stand and fight.'

'Captain Ventris, you forget your place,' said Chaplain Astador. 'We
are here to fight the tyranids and if the learned inquisitor believes that
this is the best course, who are you to question him?'

'I am a loyal servant of the Emperor and proud son of Roboute Guilliman. As I once thought you to be, and the fact that you even ask me
that question shows me how wrong I was.'

Astador's face filled with thunder and the muscles along his jaw bunched in rage at Uriel's insult.

'While we are united in a common cause, I shall call you brother, but when this foe is defeated, there will be a reckoning between us,' promised Astador.

'I welcome it,' said Uriel, returning to his seat. 'You disgust me.'

'Gentlemen,' said Admiral de Corte. 'This is hardly the time for such discussions. The fate of an Imperial world lies before us and it ill becomes us to fight among ourselves like orks.'

'Thank you, Admiral de Corte,' said Kryptman. 'We waste valuable time in these discussions. The decision has already been made.'

'Lord inquisitor,' said Tiberius. 'I may have an alternative solution that you might consider. As we passed the orbital refineries of Yulan, I recalled my Ravensburg.'

Kryptman's eyes narrowed, his interest piqued by Tiberius's reference to the saviour of the Gothic sector, Lord Admiral Cornelius Ravensburg.

'Go on...'

And Tiberius went on to tell the story of the destruction of the *Unforgivable* and the actions of Commodore Kurtz during the defence of Delos IV. A buzz of excitement filled the room as Tiberius explained the actions he had set in motion upon passing Yulan and the potential it had.

Even now, days later, Uriel could not believe the ease with which Kryptman had decided the fate of millions. To the inquisitor these were just numbers, but to Uriel they were living, breathing people – subjects of the God-Emperor and deserving of protection. He shook himself from his reverie, focussing on the present as the sacristy bell began ringing and Tiberius descended from his command pulpit to stand beside the plotting table.

'All stop,' he ordered. 'Come to new heading zero-six-five.'

'All stop, aye,' confirmed Philotas. 'Altering heading now.'

Uriel and Tiberius shared a nervous look as the image before them slid to the left. As their engines decreased power, only the momentum of the ship kept them moving forwards. Slowly, but surely, the vast hydrogen-plasma refinery shrank in the viewing bay and a palpable sense of relief spread throughout the bridge as the distance between the *Vae Victus* and the perilous colossus increased.

As the refinery diminished, the hazy outline of an indistinct halo grew around its edges. At first, Uriel thought this was the corona of distant stars around the vast refinery, but as it drifted further away, he could see that it was actually the outer edges of the tyranid fleet's vanguard.

'Guilliman's oath,' breathed Uriel as the scale of the alien fleet became apparent. Truly they had engaged but a fraction around Barbarus Prime. The viewing bay was filled with specks of reflected light that could only be tyranid organisms and their sheer number defied counting. There seemed to be no end to the alien swarm and Uriel felt a stirring of unreasoning dread settle in his belly at the vastness of the tyranid fleet.

Even the tyranid forces he had fought on Ichar IV could not compare to the size of this fleet and, for the briefest second, he wondered if Kryptman might not have been right. Could they ever prevail against such a huge horde?

'Courage and honour,' said Tiberius, seeing the effect the size of the tyranid fleet was having on his crew. 'They are many, but we have seen they can die and we know they can be defeated. And more than this, we have faith in the Emperor. Trust in Him and the primarch and we will prevail.'

'Arx Praetora squadron is coming into view,' said Philotas. 'Some damage to all ships, but nothing serious.'

'Good. And the Dauntless cruisers?'

'*Yermetov* holding position on our portside, *Luxor* is moving forward to cover our rapid strike cruisers.'

'And the tyranids?'

'Following close behind.'

THE CREATURES INQUISITOR Kryptman had referred to as kraken drifted towards the gargantuan shape of the hydrogen-plasma refinery behind a protective screen of spores. As the spores drew near, they sped off on spurts of hot gasses towards the refinery, exploding and spraying its structure with chitinous shrapnel. But it was too vast to be more than scratched by such pinpricks.

Detecting that the spores were having little effect, a number of kraken sped forwards, spraying the colossal vessel with foaming bio-plasma and lashing its upper pylons with razor-edged tentacles. They tore huge chunks of armaplas and steel from its structure, but as vicious as their attacks were, they could do little to damage it.

More kraken surged past the refinery, speeding towards the vessels that escorted it, particularly the smaller darts of Arx Praetora squadron. Unbearably bright lances of powerful energy weapons stabbed from the prow weapons of the *Luxor*, slicing through a pair of kraken and the others scattered, abandoning their chase of the rapid strike cruisers in favour of this new, bigger prey. The *Luxor* heeled sideways as her engines fought to reverse her course and her bow swung smoothly around. More lance shots from the *Yermetov* raked the tyranid organisms as the *Luxor* made her turn until none remained close enough to threaten her.

The cruisers powered away from the creatures attacking the refinery ship as swarms of tyranids flocked towards the massive vessel. They latched on wherever they could and bit, dissolved or exploded as their genetic purpose determined. Within minutes the entire vessel was obscured by a teeming mass of frenzied creatures, each desperate to destroy this threat to their hive.

But such was the solidity of the refinery's construction that none of the creatures could penetrate its hull and soon it had drifted deep within the mass of the swarm, and a single hive ship, itself more massive than the refinery altered its course to attack. City-sized gouts of acidic sprays lashed the side of the refinery, organic matter running molten alongside inorganic as the hive ship lashed the refinery.

Giant feeder tentacles looped outwards from the hive ship's gnarled carapace and latched onto the massive vessel, effortlessly dragging it towards a cavernous orifice in its body ringed with thousands of grinding teeth.

URIEL AND TIBERUS marched to the end of the command nave and watched the massive hive ship begin to devour the vast refinery, now scarcely visible, its surface buried under a heaving mass of tyranid organisms. Tiberius paused to savour the moment before his next action.

Uriel watched the tyranid organisms attacking the refinery and felt his lip curl in a sneer of contempt. Aliens were going to die and the thought pleased him. In his mind's eye he could see the black spectre of death floating above the tyranid fleet and felt a surge of heady anticipation at the thought of the vast scale of destruction about to be unleashed. He felt the power that comes of knowing that another being lives only because you have chosen not to kill it yet, and the sensation surged like an electric charge around his body.

His fists clenched. He could feel hot anger flooding his system and the desire to strike out at these aliens, his head filling with visions of bloody fields littered with tyranid beasts.

Uriel tasted blood and realised he had bitten his own tongue, the sharp metallic taste bringing him back to the present with a jolt.

Uriel's hearts were beating a wild tattoo on his ribs and sweat beaded on his brow. He took a breath, feeling the purity of the incense-scented air run like a cleansing breath through him.

'Are you alright, Uriel?' asked Tiberius, noticing the captain's discomfort.

'Yes,' managed Uriel. 'I am.'

Tiberius nodded and returned his attention to the viewing bay.

'You have a firing solution?' he asked without turning.

'Yes, lord admiral,' said Philotas, unable to conceal the excitement in his voice.

A respectful silence enveloped the bridge as Tiberius turned and marched back to his command pulpit, leaving Uriel to stand at the viewing bay. He mounted the steps and took his place at the head of the bridge.

He placed both hands either side of the lectern and simply said, 'Fire.'

THE VAE VICTUS shuddered as her prow bombardment cannon unleashed a building-sized projectile from its flash-protected barrel. Travelling at phenomenal speed, it closed the distance between the *Vae Victus* and its target in less than a minute.

The target point had been carefully selected: the weakest point of the refinery's armour, where an explosion would cause the most damage to the internal plasma tanks. Packed with millions of tonnes of highly volatile hydrogen-plasma compound, the refinery vessel was now a gargantuan flying bomb. The shell from the bombardment cannon struck it amidships, punching through metres of thick reinforcement, a delayed fuse ensuring that it did not detonate until it was deep within the heart of its target.

The shell exploded within the largest of the plasma tanks, instantly igniting the unstable compound and setting in motion a chain reaction like the one that had destroyed the third refinery in orbit around Yulan.

As though sensing the danger, the hive ship released its grip on the refinery, but by then it was already too late. Millions of tonnes of flammable chemicals ignited and exploded like the birth of a new star. Every creature attacking the refinery was incinerated, the fireball expanding in a lethal wave front and engulfing countless other swarm creatures. Kraken, drones and spores were all burned to death in the initial fireball and thousands more suffered fatal concussive injuries from the massive blast front that followed the detonation.

The hive ship had spent millennia traversing the void between galaxies and its hide was as thick as any starship's armour, but even it was helpless in the face of so much ferocious energy. Its entire body vanished in the initial fireball, its remains blasted to atoms by the shockwave that followed in the wake of the fiery explosion.

In a fraction of a second, a creature that had taken centuries of years to grow and evolve into its current form was obliterated and wiped from the galaxy as though it had never existed.

FOR THE NINTH day in a row, the defenders of Tarsis Ultra collapsed in weary resignation. Learchus watched them, a fierce pride burning in his chest as he saw the last man drop to his haunches and remove his pack. He himself had not even broken a sweat, but his physique was such that he could have run for days before requiring any rest. He smiled as he wandered through the exhausted soldiers, aware of their angry stares and muttered curses.

The men of each regiment were performing well and a shared sense of comradeship had flourished in them all. That it had come about through a shared hatred of him did not concern him, he knew it was a passing thing. While the enemy was still distant, soldiers needed a common target for their hate and their aggression. Learchus vividly remembered Chaplain Clausel at Agiselus and how much he had hated him during his training. Clausel was now a trusted friend and mentor and had brought great spiritual solace to the men of Fourth company in the dark times of its long, proud history.

Major Satria staggered towards Learchus, his face red and streaked with sweat.

'Damn, but you're working us hard,' he gasped.

'The tyranids will work you harder,' said Learchus.

'True,' nodded Satria, bending over and resting his palms on his knees and sucking down great draughts of cool air. The major had lost weight and, since the training had begun, had shed the silver breastplate and peaked cap his rank entitled him to. His shoulder-length black hair was slicked with sweat and there was more of a swagger in his step now.

Orderlies and volunteers from the citizenry of Erebus began circulating among the panting soldiers, distributing hot food and potable water from sloshing drums. Dehydration among the soldiers had become a serious problem, with many simply eating unmelted snow, which could contain disease and dangerously lower the body's temperature.

Learchus had also put a stop to the men's rations of amasec, caffeine and bac-stics. All these vices made soldiers susceptible to dehydration and though it had almost caused a riot when first announced, Learchus knew that his decision was paying off as the number of reported dehydration injuries had dropped significantly.

Cases of foot-rot had been widespread in the early days of training, with the thick, rubberised boots of many of the soldiers trapping the moisture of their sweat and causing necrotic fungal growths to fester. Soldiers from the Logres regiment had allowed the design of their standard issue footwear to be copied by the factories of Erebus and within days, each company of soldiers was issued with dozens of pairs of socks, anti-fungal powder and brand new boots that allowed the pores of their feet to breathe.

Learchus had been impressed by the efficiency of Sebastien Montante, the Fabricator Marshal of Erebus. He had judged him an empty headed fool when they had first met. Though he was no soldier, the man's talents for organisational logistics was second to none and virtually every request Learchus had made for supplies or equipment had been met within hours.

Montante was proving to be a valuable ally, but the same could not be said for every member of the Council of Industry who helped govern Erebus. Only three days ago, Learchus had sat with the nine members of the council in the Chamber of the Mosaic, outlining his plans for the defence of the inner reaches of the valley. He remembered the shame of losing his temper at their foolishness. The foolishness of one member in particular.

Simon van Gelder.

The man Learchus had prevented from leaving the city carried the weight of his humiliation around his neck and was determined to return the favour.

'We simply cannot allow Sergeant Learchus to demolish the buildings between the walls,' said van Gelder, sipping his wine. 'Why, when the aliens are driven off, we will be penniless paupers, lords over a ruined city with nothing but its wreckage to call our own.'

'If you do not destroy them, you will have no city at all,' explained Learchus.

'The many years of peace we have enjoyed have made us complacent,' put in Montante, gesturing at the walls around them. 'Look at the mosaic here. It is clear from this that we should not have been so reckless in our building programs. The original city plans, designed by Roboute Guilliman himself, show us that there should be no structures in these areas.'

'Pah,' snapped van Gelder, with a wave of his hand. 'A faded mosaic, thousands of years old, is no basis for forcing us into economic ruin, Sebastien. What will we do when our brave defenders defeat the tyranids? How can we produce goods with no manufactories?'

'Simon, we can rebuild,' said Montante. 'But we must be alive to do so. Please listen to Sergeant Learchus.'

'Many of the buildings you own have been constructed too close to the walls, Mr van Gelder. If we are forced to pull back from a wall or the tyranids capture one, then we will be providing them with valuable cover under which to approach.'

'You speak of the regions around District Quintus? These regions are over thirty kilometres from the valley mouth. Do you mean to tell me that you expect these damnable aliens to breach our fair city that far? That you don't have the ability to stop them before that? Forgive me, but I had thought the Ultramarines to be warriors of great strength and courage. It would seem I was misinformed.'

Learchus surged to his feet and grabbed van Gelder by the front of his robes, hauling him across the table and snarling in his face. Wine spilled over the table and a goblet shattered on the stone floor.

'You dare insult our honour?' spat Learchus. 'You would do well to consider your next words, van Gelder, for if you utter such an insult again, I will kill you.'

The council sat stunned as Learchus fought to control his rage, unwilling to intervene on their fellow council member's behalf for fear that the Space Marine's anger would be turned on them. The only sounds were van Gelder's panicked breath and the drip of wine to the floor. Sebastien Montante rose slowly from the bench and put a hand on Learchus's forearm.

'Sergeant Learchus,' he said softly. 'I am sure that Mr van Gelder meant no offence, did you Simon?'

Van Gelder hurriedly shook his head.

'There, you see?' continued Montante. 'They were words spoken in haste, in the heat of the moment. Please, Learchus, if you would be so kind, would you return Mr van Gelder to his seat?'

Learchus let out a hissing breath and released his grip on van Gelder, who collapsed back onto the bench opposite with a plaintive moan. His face was ashen, though it took only seconds for his anger to return to the surface. Montante saw it coming and headed him off.

'Simon, before you say anything, I believe we have come as far as we can today and should adjourn until tomorrow morning. Agreed?'

A hurried nod of heads signalled the council's assent and after a tense pause, van Gelder had also nodded, making his way from the chamber of the mosaic without another word.

At the following day's meeting, van Gelder had been conspicuous by his absence and a missive sent to his home in the high valley inviting him to the meeting was returned unopened. A vote was taken in the matter of the demolition of his properties, the council unanimously supporting Learchus's plan.

The memory of his loss of temper shamed Learchus and he had spent every night since that moment in penitent prayer.

'How goes the work in the lower valley?' asked Learchus as Satria gratefully took a mug of water from a robed orderly, gulping it down like sweet wine.

'We've almost finished preparing the ground between the first two walls, but it's slow going. The ground's frozen solid and takes an age to break apart, even with earth moving machines.'

'We need to have the trenches completed within the next two weeks. The tyranids will be upon us by then.'

'They will be, don't worry. The men are working as hard as they can, I assure you.'

'Good. They are a credit to you, Major Satria.'

'Thank you, though you may want to tell *them* that.'

'I intend to. When they hate me more than their worst nightmare.'

'Believe me, I think they hate you more than that already,' said Satria. 'The fact that you so easily outperform them in training infuriates them. I think they feel you are showing off.'

'They are correct; I am showing off by training with them,' said Learchus. 'I want them to know that I am superior to them, for when it comes time for me to build them up, they must feel that my praise truly means something. I will make them feel like they are heroes, I will make them believe they are the greatest warriors in the galaxy.'

'You're a sneaky one, aren't you?' said Satria eventually.

'I have my moments,' smiled Learchus.

THE SMALL FLOTILLA of Imperial ships made best speed towards Chordelis, the rapid strike cruisers of Arx Praetora leading the way with the *Vae Victus*, *Yermetov* and *Luxor* following closely behind. The mood aboard the ships was cautiously optimistic. If another hive ship could be destroyed in a similar manner, might not the orbital defences combined with the fleet and system defence ships hold the tyranid fleet at bay, perhaps even prevent the aliens from putting a single clawed foot upon the soil of Tarsis Ultra?

On the bridge of the *Vae Victus*, Admiral Tiberius sipped from a goblet of water, discussing the tactical possibilities that lay before them with Uriel.

'We might yet make these damned aliens regret they came this way, Uriel,' he said.

'I think we might,' agreed the captain of the Fourth company. 'The defences around Tarsis Ultra are strong, and the last refinery should even now be rigged with lethal explosives.'

'If we can destroy another hive ship, then the overmind might decide to avoid Chordelis.'

'And that will be a victory in more ways than one,' said Uriel darkly.

'Be careful, Uriel,' warned Tiberius. 'Kryptman is not a man to cross, the power of the Inquisition is his to command. Were it not for him, Macragge might well have fallen to hive fleet Behemoth.'

'Did you ever meet him during the war?'

'Aye,' nodded Tiberius. 'He was young back then, full of the fires of an inquisitor who had found his true vocation.'

'Did he ever advocate the destruction of Macragge?'

Tiberius laughed. 'No, Uriel, he did not. I do not think that even Inquisitor Kryptman, as he was back then, would have dared voice such a thought. Lord Calgar would never have allowed it.'

'Do you think Lord Calgar would have allowed Chordelis to be destroyed?'

Tiberius rubbed a hand across his skull, considering the question before replying.

'I do not know, Uriel. Our Chapter Master is a man of great wisdom and compassion, but he is also a strategist of sound logic and I think that perhaps you and I are too fond of the idea of saving everyone we can. Lord Inquisitor Kryptman was correct when he said that sometimes you need to lose the occasional battle to win the war.'

'I cannot accept that,' said Uriel. 'The destruction of the Emperor's loyal subjects cannot be right.'

'We cannot always do what is right, Uriel. There is often a great gulf in the difference between the way things are and the way we believe they should be. Sometimes we must learn to accept the things we cannot change.'

'No, lord admiral, I believe we must endeavour to change the things we cannot accept. It is by striving against that which is perceived as wrong that makes a great warrior. The primarch himself said that when a warrior makes peace with his fear and stands against it, he becomes a true hero.

For if you do not fear a thing, where is the courage in standing against it?'

'You are an idealist, Uriel, and the galaxy can be a cruel place for people like you,' said Tiberius. 'But still I wish there were more who thought as you do. You are a great warrior, able to bring swift death to your enemies, but you have never lost sight of why you fight: the survival of the human race.'

Uriel bowed his head to the venerable admiral, pleased to have been complimented. He gripped the hilt of his sword as Philotas approached bearing a data-slate, his angular features sombre.

Tiberius took the slate and quickly scanned its contents, his mouth dropping open in horror and disbelief.

'Open the viewing bay, now!' he barked. 'Maximum magnification.'

The brass shutters concertinaed back smoothly from the bay at the front of the bridge as Tiberius descended to the table, calling up the tactical plots of the surrounding area. He muttered to himself and Uriel could see from the pulsing vein in the admiral's temple that his fury had built to an incandescent level. He had never seen Tiberius so angry before.

'Admiral, what is it?' he asked.

Tiberius handed Uriel the data-slate as the shutters of the viewing bay finally folded back. He read the words at the same time as what they said was displayed on the viewing bay.

Even at maximum magnification, the planet before them barely filled the viewing bay, reflected light from the distant sun rippling across its heaving, fiery surface. Firestorms were raging across the dead planet as flammable gasses released from oceans of decaying organic matter enveloped it, scouring the surface to bare, lifeless rock.

The tyranids themselves could do no more thorough a job.

'Sweet heavens, no...' breathed Uriel, the data-slate dropping from his fingers. 'How?'

'The Mortifactors,' said Tiberius sadly. 'Kryptman lied to us. He had no intention of making a stand here.'

Uriel said nothing as the world of Chordelis burned.

PHASE III – ATTACK

☊
EIGHT

THE QUARTERS OF Captain Uriel Ventris were spartan and clean, as befitted the leader of the Fourth company of the Ultramarines. A simple cot bed with a single linen sheet sat in one corner of the cell below the Ventris family shield. Next to the bed stood a thin-legged table upon which sat a clay jug filled with wine and a pair of silver goblets. Various recording crystals sat in neat piles next to the jug and at the foot of the bed lay an open, gunmetal grey footlocker containing simple blue robes and exercise garments.

Uriel poured himself a generous measure of wine from the jug and sat on the edge of his bed, swirling the crimson liquid around the goblet. He tipped his head back and drained the glass in one long swallow. The strong flavour made him grimace as the sight of the burning world in the viewing bay returned to him. He wondered how many people had been on Chordelis when the virus bombs hit. How many hundreds of thousands had Kryptman sacrificed in the name of the larger war?

The thought saddened him and he poured another glass, raising it in a toast to the dead of Chordelis. He downed the drink and poured yet another, suddenly desiring the oblivion that only alcohol could provide.

He had been able to stop Inquisitor Barzano from destroying Pavonis, but he had not saved Chordelis and the weight of that failure was now a dark stain upon his soul. Had the people even known what was happening when the first bombs had exploded in the atmosphere?

The life-eater virus was quick to act and utterly lethal in its effects. Perhaps some had an inkling of what was being done to their world, but most would probably have succumbed without realising the magnitude of the betrayal visited upon them. The atmosphere would be saturated with mutagenic toxins that attacked the biological glue that held organic matter together, breaking it down with horrifying rapidity. Within hours there would be nothing left alive and the virus would be forced to turn on itself in an unthinking act of viral self-cannibalism. The planet's surface would be covered by a thick layer of decayed sludge, wreathed in vast clouds of toxic waste matter. All it would take was a single shot from orbit to ignite the fumes and firestorms of apocalyptic magnitude would sweep the entire surface of the planet bare.

Uriel had seen the horror of Exterminatus and had even been part of an expedition to administer the ultimate sanction once before, on a Chaos tainted planet whose population had become base savages practising human sacrifice to their dark gods. Under certain circumstances, such destruction was appropriate, even necessary, but this act of murder sat badly with Uriel and he could not find it in himself to forgive what Kryptman and the Mortifactors had done.

His mind was filled with contradictions and doubt as he pondered the ramifications of what had happened at Chordelis. In following the plan of Admiral Tiberius, they had exercised initiative and reacted to the developing situation with an original idea. They had not referred to the Codex Astartes and, much as he hated to admit it, the Mortifactors were closer to the correct procedure as laid down in that holy tome. What then did that tell him?

A knock came at his door and Uriel said, 'Enter.'

The door slid open and Pasanius stood in the doorway, his bulk filling the frame. He wore his devotional robes; his armour – like Uriel's – being repaired in the company forge three decks below. The silver of his bionic arm reflected the flickering candlelight from the passageway outside.

'I have a problem, captain,' began Pasanius, 'I've got a jug of wine and if there's one thing I know, it's that it's not good to drink on your own. Care to help me finish it?'

Uriel managed a wan smile and waved Pasanius inside. There was nowhere to sit, so Pasanius sat on the floor, resting his back against the wall. Uriel handed him two goblets, and he filled them with wine. Pasanius handed one back to Uriel and raised the other to his nose. He closed his eyes and smelled the heady aroma of wild berries and blackcurrants laced with a subtle hint of aged oak.

'This is the good stuff,' said Pasanius. 'Bottled on Tarentus in the year seven hundred and eighty-three, which, I'm reliably informed, was a good year for the vineyards on the southern slopes of the Hill of the Red Blossoms.'

Uriel sipped the wine, nodding appreciatively and the pair lapsed into a companionable silence, each lost in his own thoughts.

Eventually, Pasanius said, 'So do you want to tell me what's bothering you, or do I need to wait until you're drunk?'

'I have not been drunk since Agiselus, you remember?' said Uriel.

Pasanius laughed. 'Aye, Chaplain Clausel shut us out on the mountains and left us there for three days.'

'Emperor save me, but he was a hard bastard back then.'

'He still is, it's just he's on our side now.'

'Clausel would assign you a month of fasting if he heard you say that.'

'Maybe, but I know you won't tell him.'

'True,' agreed Uriel, taking another drink. The wine would not get either of them remotely drunk thanks to the preomnor, an implanted pre-digestive stomach that analysed and neutralised virtually any toxins, including alcohol. Nevertheless the two friends still enjoyed the taste of a fine wine.

'I have been having doubts, Pasanius,' said Uriel finally.

'About what?'

'A lot of things,' said Uriel. 'I was thinking about Captain Idaeus and everything he taught me about thinking beyond the scope of the codex. At the time I could not make the leap of initiative to believe what he said, but the more we fought together, the more I could see what he said put into practice.'

'Aye, he was a wild one, was Idaeus,' agreed Pasanius. 'But clever too. He knew when to bend the rules and when not to.'

'That's the problem, Pasanius. I don't know if I can do what he did... if I can understand when to follow the codex and when to think laterally.'

'You're doing fine, captain. The men of the company trust you and would follow you into the very fires of hell. Isn't that enough?'

'No, Pasanius, not by a long way. I thought Captain Idaeus was right, but now I see the Mortifactors and I wonder where his line of thinking will lead. If we follow his beliefs to their logical conclusion, will we end up like them?'

'No, of course not. Chaplain Astador said it himself: he and his Chapter are a product of their homeworld. He told me all about Posul and, if you ask me, it sounds like a vision of hell. Permanently shrouded in darkness, with each tribe fighting to kill one another so they can prove that they're the most brutal and be chosen to become Space Marines of the Mortifactors. A culture like that breeds a contempt for life and we should have seen it the moment they sided with Kryptman.'

'But we didn't.'

'No,' shrugged Pasanius. 'Hindsight is a wonderful thing.'

'I know, but look at what happened to Chordelis. We broke with the Codex Astartes to send that refinery into the swarm, the Mortifactors followed an inquisitor's direction and an Imperial world died. But I know we did the right thing, morally, in trying to save Chordelis, despite the logic of Kryptman's argument.'

Uriel slammed his goblet down on the table, spilling wine across his data crystals and bedsheet. 'I feel like a blind man who cannot feel the path before him.'

'Well, nobody ever said that the Emperor's service was supposed to be easy,' said Pasanius, pouring another two goblets of wine.

LORD INQUISITOR KRYPTMAN watched the *Vae Victus* dock with the northern pier of the star fort through its central basilica's main viewing bay, feeling a surge of unfamiliar excitement pound through his veins. He stood with his hands laced behind his back, wearing the formal robes of an inquisitor of the Ordo Xenos. Captain Ventris would know by now that he had lied to him about giving Chordelis a chance to live, but there was no use now in pointless recriminations. The tyranids had to be defeated by any means necessary.

Admiral Tiberius would understand that, but Ventris was the protégé of Captain Idaeus, a captain he had seen on Macragge following the defeat of hive fleet Behemoth. He would need to be wary of Ventris's puritannical anger.

Fortunately, he had sufficient force to ensure that Ventris would be kept in line.

The blue and white curve of Tarsis Ultra shone at the bottom of the viewing bay, dozens of system ships and defence monitors hanging in orbit around the planet. There was a formidable force arrayed here and the Ultramarines' demonstration of how effective a weapon the refineries could be as floating bombs had not gone unnoticed. The last refinery hung in high orbit, a fleet of servitor-manned tugs ready to drag her into the heart of the tyranid fleet and unleash fiery destruction.

The inquisitor limped to his desk and sat behind its sweeping nalwood expanse. It had been commissioned hundreds of years ago for his mentor from a world whose name he could not now remember, and was a work of impressive craftsmanship. It never failed to intimidate those who came before him – not that he expected a Space Marine to be intimidated by a mere desk – but it gave him a sense of place whenever he sat behind it.

He knew that the Ultramarines would even now be on their way to his chambers.

Kryptman touched the vox-bead at his collar and said, 'Captain Bannon, could you and Chaplain Astador come in here.'

URIEL MARCHED PAST frightened-looking naval ratings and techs as he, Tiberius and Pasanius made their way towards the basilica of the star fort. The orbital space station was a massive construction, impossibly ancient and, together with the others in the linked chain, powerful enough to defeat a battleship together with any attendant escorts, and even through his anger, Uriel could see that they would be potent weapons in the fight against the tyranids.

As they had drawn closer to the star fort, he had seen the vast shape of the last refinery anchored thousands of kilometres away from the nearest vessel, remotely piloted ships packing its structure with even more explosives. Proof positive that Kryptman had never intended to save Chordelis.

The trio passed through the northern quadrant of the star fort, entering the central basilica where Inquisitor Kryptman awaited. A black uniformed armsman directed them to the chambers the inquisitor had requisitioned and as they approached the door, Admiral Tiberius took hold of Uriel's arm and said, 'Remember, Uriel. Kryptman is not a man to cross, so be mindful of what you say.'

'I will,' promised Uriel and rapped his gauntlet on the door, pushing inside without waiting for an answer. Tiberius nodded briskly to Pasanius, who swiftly followed his captain inside.

Uriel pulled up short as he saw Kryptman seated behind an ugly desk of a dark wood, two Space Marines flanking him. He recognised Astador and took the other for one of the Mortifactors until he saw the silver inquisitorial symbol on his left shoulder guard. The yellow of the Imperial Fists Chapter on his other shoulder was a stark contrast to the midnight black of his armour, his skin deeply tanned and his hair a close-cropped blond.

'Ah, Captain Ventris,' said Kryptman. 'Allow me to introduce Captain Bannon of the Deathwatch.'

'Deathwatch...' breathed Uriel. The Chamber Militant of the Ordo Xenos, the elite alien fighters in which he himself had once served for a decade. Kryptman had said that he had requested a Deathwatch kill team, but Uriel had not expected them to arrive in time for the coming conflict.

Formidable killers of xeno creatures, each member of the Deathwatch was chosen from the finest warriors of his Chapter to serve for a time with the Ordo Xenos to combat the threat of aliens throughout the galaxy. There were none better qualified to join this fight than the Deathwatch, and seeing the stylised skull symbol on Bannon's shoulder guard immediately filled Uriel with fresh hope.

He marched towards the gaudy desk and leaned forwards, resting his fists on its surface. He locked eyes with the inquisitor and said, 'You lied to us.'

'You allowed yourself be lied to, Uriel,' said Kryptman. 'Did you really think I was a man who changes his mind on a whim?'

'No, but I thought you were a man of your word. Everything I have learned of you has led me to believe that you were a man of honour.'

'Then you are naïve indeed,' said Kryptman. 'I am a man who gets the job done.'

'Even if that means murdering innocent people?'

'If it proves necessary, then yes.'

'I do not know who I hate more just now. You do not see the tyranids killing one another to achieve victory.'

'Not yet,' answered Kryptman with a sly smile.

'You would do well to watch your tone, Captain Ventris,' said Astador, circling the desk to stand face to face with Uriel. 'Your Chapter owes this man its very existence.'

'Get away from me, Astador,' warned Uriel.

'You will mind your place, Captain Ventris,' said Astador. 'We all have a part to play in this war. You must accept yours as I accept mine.'

Uriel felt his anger towards Astador flare and before he knew what he was doing, he hammered a thunderous right cross against the Chaplain's jaw. Astador spun backwards, crashing into the wall, but before Uriel could capitalise on the surprise of his attack, he felt a powerful grip encircle his neck and a burning heat prickle the skin beneath his jawline.

'If you so much as move, I will plunge this power knife up through your soft palate and into your brain,' said Captain Bannon. Astador surged to his feet, a killing light in his eyes, and in them, Uriel could see the feral tribal warrior he had been on Posul.

But before he could move, Pasanius was there, his massive hand wrapped around the Mortifactor's neck. He held the struggling Chaplain in a grip of steel.

'Don't,' he said.

'All of you, stop this madness now!' bellowed Tiberius, stepping into the centre of the room. He stared at Bannon and said, 'Take that knife away from my captain's throat,' before turning to Pasanius.

'Sergeant, let go of Chaplain Astador and step away from him.'

Pasanius looked round at Uriel, who nodded, the movement almost imperceptible due to the glowing amber blade at his neck, and released the Mortifactor. Astador's eyes blazed fury, but he made no aggressive moves and Pasanius stepped back, radiating threat and the promise of fresh violence should the Chaplain attempt anything further.

Bannon withdrew the knife from Uriel's neck and said, 'I know of you, Captain Ventris, and I have a great respect for what you have done in the past, but we must be united in this common cause. It ill becomes us to fight amongst ourselves when there is a terrible foe who seeks to destroy us all.'

Uriel nodded and unconsciously rubbed his neck where the burning edge of Bannon's power knife had singed his skin.

'Captain Bannon speaks true,' said Tiberius. 'We are all servants of the divine God-Emperor and must comport ourselves accordingly. We are not animals or blasphemers who have cast off the codes of moral behaviour. There is to be no more violence between us.'

The tension in the room slowly ebbed away and Bannon offered his hand to Uriel.

Uriel took a deep, calming breath before taking Bannon's hand, feeling the killing rage drain from his body, leaving him vulnerable and ashamed. Deep inside he felt the touch of an ancient being within him and heard its diabolical laughter echoing within his soul.

'Come,' said Kryptman, when he sensed his audience had calmed. 'We have much to discuss. While we have been fighting the tyranid fleet, Magos Locard has been busy in the biologis research labs on Tarsis Ultra and his findings are most illuminating...'

BLINDING CLOUDS OF hot steam filled the train platform as another land train pulled into its designated berth and Pren Fallows, the platform over-seer, cursed as his snow goggles fogged with condensation. He pulled off the goggles and wiped the inner face clear with the sleeve of his overalls. There was precious little snow here anyway, the heat generated by the land trains and the hundreds of milling people soon turned the snow and ice to a shin deep mucky slush.

Trains had been arriving daily for the past month, each laden with frightened farming communities from the outlying regions and, as the largest city on Tarsis Ultra, Erebus had been receiving the majority of these refugees. As if the city wasn't crowded enough already. Pren shrugged, pushing his way through the crowds and making his way to the control booth that overlooked the platform.

Seventeen train berths and fifty track lines radiated from the docking bays. He and his staff of seventy men had pulled double shifts for the last two months, ensuring that each train had deposited its human cargo and then departed on time to pick up yet more. It was thankless, dirty work and there was precious little reward to be had, but it was the life the Emperor had chosen for him and though he knew it would do no good to complain, Pren Fallows was not the kind of man to let that stop him.

Powerful arc lights mounted on steel towers bathed the platforms in a ghostly white light, and despite the heat, his breath fogged before him. Yellow coated provosts from the city Commissariat directed people from the docking station, taking names on clipboards and directing them to the Ministorum camps further up the valley.

It was a scene of organised chaos, but this train had been the last of the day and there were no more scheduled until noon the following day, which would allow Pren and his crew to enjoy a well-earned break.

As the provosts escorted the last of the refugees from the station, a blessed calm descended. Pren stopped and smiled, enjoying the dead quiet of a winter's night and an empty station.

He climbed the rusted iron ladder to the control booth, stamping the slush from his boots before pushing open the door.

'Close the damn door!' shouted Halan Urquart, his deputy controller, who sat before a bank of controls, his feet up on the table, drinking a cup of hot caffeine. 'You're letting all the damn heat out.'

'Sometimes I wonder if you understand who's in charge here, Halan,' replied Pren, unfastening the wax-lubricated zipper on his winter coat and hanging it on a hook on the back of the door.

'Yeah, I wonder that sometimes too.'

'Anything to report?' asked Pren, brushing the ice from his beard.

'Nah, it's been real quiet. The provosts seem to have finally got the hang of moving people out of here without bothering us.'

'About bloody time,' commented Pren, pouring himself a mug of caffeine. It was lukewarm, but beggars couldn't be choosers. He pulled up a seat next to the window, watching as another flurry of snow began to fall, coating the platforms in a fresh blanket of pristine white.

Pren lifted the station logs from the basket tray beside Halan and began flicking through his deputy's scrawled handwriting. He sipped his caffeine, noting that the turnaround times for the land trains was as quick as it had been even before the war. He'd need to remember and say a few encouraging words to his staff come the morning.

He flipped over to another page, glancing up as a shiver passed down his spine. He put down his mug and stared out the misting window, squinting through the fogged glass at the twin pinpricks of light that were approaching the station.

'What the hell...' he muttered.

'What's up, chief?' asked Halan.

'Look,' said Pren, pointing in the direction of the mysterious lights.

'What the hell...' said Halan.

'I know,' said Pren. 'I thought we were all done for today.'

'We are, I don't know what that is.'

The men watched as the two points of light drew closer through the night's darkness, their sense of apprehension growing with their brightness. As the lights got closer, they came within the glow cast by the tower lights. Halan and Pren both breathed a sigh of relief as they saw the sleek shape of a land train glide smoothly into the station, its sides and roof coated in a thick layer of frost.

The train slowed and came to a complete halt at the end of the furthest platform, its doors jerkily sliding open. Pren and Halan waited for the inevitable crowds to emerge, but nobody disembarked from the train. It simply sat, silent and unmoving on the far end of the platform, steam venting from the grilles around its engines and the track.

Both men shared an uneasy glance.

'I guess we should go down and have a look,' suggested Pren.

'I just knew you were going to say that,' said Halan, pulling on his winter coat and gloves.

Pren grabbed a portable illuminator and donned his winter gear, following his deputy outside into the biting cold. He clambered down the frosted ladder and trudged alongside Halan through the fresh snow towards the unmoving land train. As they drew nearer, they could see the windows of the train were dark and opaque with frost, even those of the driver's cab, and their sense of unease grew stronger.

The darkness and silence of the docking station, normally a relief after the hectic bustle of a day's work now pressed in around them and Pren wished some of the provosts were still left in the station. At least they were armed.

He gripped Halan's arm and the man nearly jumped out of his skin.

'Guilliman's oath!' swore Halan. 'Don't do that!'

'Look, you can see the train's number on the engine.'

'So?'

'Well we can tell which bloody train this is and why it's here now, you idiot.'

'Oh, right,' said Halan, pulling out a data-slate from his coat and scrolling through a list of numbers, eventually stopping at the train's designation.

'Got it. This was due in last week.'

'Last week? And no one noticed it was missing?'

'I guess not, we've been pretty busy here you know.'

'True,' said Pren. 'Well, where's it come from?'

'According to this, it was under the supervision of a Lieutenant Quinn from the Logres regiment. They were picking up refugees from across the north-eastern districts. Their last stop was at Prandium and they should have been here six days ago. I guess the train must've come in on auto.'

Halan tucked away the slate and the pair gingerly continued towards the train, their steps cautious, hearts beating faster. The train's doors stood open, but still no one got off. A light flickered inside, briefly illuminating the train's interior and a tinkle of broken glass made both men jump.

Steam gusted from the engine, melting the ice coating the train and cold water dripped from around the opened doors. Pren and Halan reached the doors and warily stepped into the darkness of the train.

Pren flicked on the illuminator and swept the beam around the interior of the carriage.

He heard Halan cry out in horror and fell to his knees as his mind attempted to cope with the butchery he saw all around him.

Bodies. Hundreds of gutted, flensed, dismembered and partially devoured bodies filled the carriage, like hunks of meat in a coldroom. Strung from the walls on resinous streamers of glistening mucus, their dead flesh hard and unyielding, their frozen eyes staring down in mute accusation at the station operators.

Stalactites of frozen blood reached down to the uneven floor and Pren felt a suffocating fear swell in his chest. He dropped the illuminator and it rolled down the carriage floor, casting lunatic shadows across the interior of the frozen charnel house, the spinning beam giving the rictus features of the corpses a hideous animation.

'Sweet Emperor–' wept Pren. 'What happened here?'

But the dead had no answers to give him, merely frozen eyes, emptied bellies, shorn limbs and gnawed flesh.

And further back along the train, a creature that had first come to Tarsis Ultra many months ago ghosted from its lair and vanished into the warm labyrinth of Erebus city.

THE COMBINED NAVAL might of the Imperial defenders of the Tarsis Ultra system hung in orbit around the world that gave it its name. A chain of linked space stations ringed the planet's equatorial belt, towed into position to face the approaching tyranids by a host of tugs and pilot boats. Dozens of defence monitors and system ships lumbered into their position in the battle line alongside Admiral de Corte's flagship *Argus*, the battlecruiser *Sword of Retribution*, and the Dauntless cruisers *Yermetov* and *Luxor*.

Gathered around the hulking form of the carrier *Kharloss Vincennes* were the Cobras of Cypria squadron, together with the one surviving vessel of Hydra squadron. The two strike cruisers of the Space Marines anchored in the shadow of the *Argus*. Lord Inquisitor Kryptman and the Space Marines had already deployed to the surface of Tarsis Ultra, their presence there deemed more vital than aboard their vessels. As a result, the *Mortis Probati* and the *Vae Victus* would stand off from the main engagement and utilise their fearsome bombardment cannons, rather than entering into the thick of the battle. With only a limited number of thralls and servitors to defend them, there would be no possibility of them repelling boarders and such ancient craft were too valuable to be lost in such a manner.

The tyranid fleet first appeared as a sprinkling of light against the velvet backdrop of stars, its scale magnificent and terrible. Reflected starlight gleamed from city-sized chitinous armour plates and glittered on trailing tentacles that drooled thick, glutinous slime. Swarms of smaller creatures, their fronts crackling with twisting arcs of electrical discharge, surrounded the hive ships, surging ahead of the main fleet with a speed hitherto unseen among the organisms that made up the alien fleet.

Under the power of dozens of straining servitor-crewed tugs, the hydrogen-plasma refinery drifted forward to meet the tyranids. Its hull was packed with yet more explosives and volatile plasma cells, and the magnitude of the resultant explosion was sure to dwarf the detonation of the previous refineries.

* * *

ADMIRAL DE CORTE watched the tyranid creatures close on the refinery with a feral smile on his lips. Though tens of thousands of kilometres away, the refinery still dwarfed everything around it, and de Corte knew that the blast was certain to kill hundreds, if not thousands, of alien organisms. If they were lucky, perhaps another hive ship would be drawn to attack the refinery and yet another of the masters of this fleet could be destroyed.

Swarms of aliens surrounded the refinery, many passing close, but none yet attacking. De Corte resisted the temptation to order the *Argus's* nova cannon to fire until one of the larger beasts moved in to attack. His practiced eye watched the vanguard of the alien creatures smoothly part as they swept past the refinery, their movements as precise as the finest naval squadron's display manoeuvres.

'They're not attacking it,' said Jex Viert.

De Corte chewed his bottom lip, pondering whether to order the nova cannon to fire. So long as the refinery drifted before his fleet, he was reluctant to order a general advance and the damned aliens weren't taking the bait.

Something was wrong. The tyranids had reportedly swarmed all over the refinery the Ultramarines had sent towards them beyond Chordelis, so why weren't they doing the same now?

Four enormous creatures approached the massive construction, rippling orifices on their elongated prows filled with rotating blade-like fangs. They surged past the refinery, their long, trailing tentacles snagging on its superstructure. Whether their actions were accidental or deliberate, de Corte was unsure, but he did not like the synchronicity with which they had moved into position. Hordes of creatures with spined crests rippling upwards from their bodies like bizarre, reflective organic sails, emerged from the swarm, moving with a grotesque, peristaltic motion to take up position before the refinery.

'What in the name of the warp are they doing?' wondered de Corte aloud as another group of alien creatures, with crackling arcs of electricity spitting before them moved to surround the tentacled leviathans.

'Sir,' prompted Jex Viert, 'The kraken in the vanguard of the alien fleet are approaching engagement range.'

De Corte snapped his gaze to the plotting table and the automaton-like logisticians moving the markers representing the tyranid fleet forward towards his battle line. The refinery would have to wait. 'Mister Viert, order the monitors forward and issue clearance to engage to all ships. My compliments to each captain, and wish them all good hunting.'

'Aye, sir,' nodded his flag lieutenant.

LORD ADMIRAL TIBERIUS watched the same scenes from the bridge of the *Vae Victus*, his own confusion matching that of de Corte.

'This is damned peculiar,' he said, rubbing a hand across his jaw. 'Why doesn't de Corte shoot?'

'I believe he is waiting for one of the hive ships to attack the refinery,' said Philotas.

'Then he has underestimated the ability of these creatures to adapt to new battlefield situations.'

Tiberius did not know how right he was.

THE TENTACLED LEVIATHANS whose trailing appendages had caught on the refinery strained against its massive weight, their bodies little more than a colossal series of powerful, interlinked muscles. Though internal fibres ruptured within them, and each creature burned so much energy in halting the refinery's forward motion that they would soon be consumed in the process, they continued hauling on its gargantuan bulk.

The vast overmind cared nothing for the individual creatures that made up the majority of its mass and directed its monstrous will at the muscle beasts. Even in death, the muscle beasts would not be wasted, their organic mass would be reabsorbed by the hive fleet and used to produce fresh warrior creatures.

The hive ships lurked in the centre of the swarm, keeping a safe distance from the dangerous intruder in the midst of the fleet.

Slowly at first, but with greater speed as they overcame the refinery's inertia, the dying muscle beasts began dragging it behind them.

Fluids and muscle fibre was shed from their bodies as the single-minded purpose of the hive mind continued to destroy them.

And the refinery followed behind them, gaining more and more speed as it returned to the Imperial battle line.

ADMIRAL TIBERIUS SUDDENLY realised what was happening and shouted, 'Philotas, open a channel to Admiral de Corte. Now!'

'Admiral?'

'Hurry, Philotas!' shouted Tiberius, descending from his command pulpit and running to the communications station as Philotas held out the brass headset and hand-vox.

The vox officer nodded as the clipped tones of Admiral de Corte and hissing static crackled from the gold-rimmed speaker on the panel.

'Admiral Tiberius, make this quick, I have pressing concerns just now.'

'Destroy the refinery. Now. The tyranids are pulling it back towards our battle line.'

'What? Are you sure?'

'I'm sure, admiral. Check your auguries if you must, but do it quickly.'

'You must be mistaken, Tiberius. How could the tyranids possibly even have the capacity to understand our intentions?'

'They learn, admiral. I should have known that we could not pull the same trick twice with these beasts. Please, admiral, we don't have time for debate. Destroy it now!'

'I shall have my surveyor officers confirm what you say, but I am unwilling to destroy so potent a weapon on a whim. De Corte out.'

Tiberius handed the headset back to the Space Marine at the vox station and marched back to the plotting table. Quickly he scanned the positioning of the Imperial fleet and felt his skin crawl as he realised the scale of the disaster that could soon befall the Imperial fleet unless they took swift action. Philotas joined the admiral, furiously entering figures into his navigational slate.

'If we move now, we can intercept the refinery, lord admiral,' he said.

'Do it. All ahead full, divert all available power to the auto loaders for the prow cannon. I want to be able to hit that refinery with everything we've got. And contact Captain Gaiseric on the *Mortis Probati* and get him to join us, we'll need his ship too.'

'Aye, sir. All ahead full,' shouted Philotas, relaying the admiral's order.

Tiberius felt the deck shifting and prayed that they were in time.

'WELL?' ASKED ADMIRAL de Corte, impatiently.

'It would seem Admiral Tiberius is correct,' replied Jex Viert, his voice betraying his anxiety. 'The refinery does appears to be closing with us now.'

Hot fear dumped into Bregant de Corte's system as he realised the ramifications of this new information. He nodded to his flag lieutenant.

'Order the nova cannon to fire!' shouted Jex Viert. 'Signal all ships to open fire. Now, for the Emperor's sake, now!'

No, thought Admiral de Corte, not for the Emperor's, for ours.

COLOSSAL ENERGIES HURLED the explosive shell from the breech of the nova cannon on the prow of the *Argus* and sent it streaking on a blazing plume towards the tyranid fleet. Travelling at close to five thousand kilometres per second, the shell closed the gap between the foes in a little under twenty-five seconds. As it closed to within fifteen thousand kilometres, blazing arcs of blue lightning surged outwards from the rippling plates of the creatures that surrounded the muscle beasts dragging the refinery, enveloping the missile's shell. Instantly, the shell exploded in an expanding cloud of burning plasma, its shattered remnants spinning off into space.

The crackling, lightning spitters and the beasts with giant sail-like appendages took up station before the refinery as a flurry of shells and energy blasts slashed towards it. A thick morass of spores and tyranid creatures swarmed forward, exploding and spilling their lifeblood as they absorbed the mass of firepower directed at the refinery. Lance beams cut through spores and burned alien flesh before finally striking the reflective sails of the winged beasts that escorted the lightning spitters. The sails' honeycombed structure dissipated much of the lance beams' strength, rendering them harmless as they scored the structure of the refinery, but failed to penetrate its metal hide.

Starhawk bombers and Fury interceptors surged from the launch bays of the *Kharloss Vincennes*, attempting to punch a hole through the tyranid screen, but every gap they blasted was soon filled with even more alien beasts. Eventually, the commander of the furies, Captain Owen Morten, pulled his surviving craft back to the carrier to refuel and rearm. Just because a task was impossible was no reason to give up.

No matter how hard the Imperial Navy hit, they could not penetrate the screen of tyranid creatures protecting the refinery and without the drag of friction, its speed increased until it was hurtling towards the Imperial battle line.

'NOTHING IS GETTING through!' shouted Philotas.

'Keep firing,' ordered Tiberius, his voice strained.

'Aye, sir.'

Tiberius's jaw muscles bunched in anxiety as he watched the rippling series of explosions bursting before the *Vae Victus*. Her firepower, normally so fearsome in battle, was availing her nothing as every shell from her bombardment cannon was intercepted by a tyranid creature sent to its death by the alien imperative of the hive mind.

Hundreds of beasts were dying, but they were achieving what the hive mind desired.

Nothing could touch the refinery.

ADMIRAL DE CORTE gripped the arms of his command chair as the *Argus* canted to starboard. The massive vessel was slowly moving from the path of the oncoming refinery, but even without asking, he could tell they weren't going to make it. The fleet was scattering from its path as quickly as it could, but even at cruising speed a vessel as vast as a Victory class battleship took time to turn, and even longer from anchor.

Withering salvoes of massed gunnery from the defence monitors and system ships had prevented the approaching kraken from breaking their battle line, but nothing could halt the inexorable approach of the refinery.

'Estimated time to lethal range, Mr Viert?'

'Forty seconds, sir.'

'GET US CLEAR, Philotas,' ordered Tiberius. The closure speeds of the refinery and the *Vae Victus* was such that, in the time it would take to load and fire another shell from the bombardment cannon, the massive structure would be past them before the shell could arm itself.

Tiberius angled his stance as the prow of the strike cruiser rose and the refinery swiftly vanished from the viewing bay. The admiral could feel the deck shudder beneath him as its hull groaned under the pressure of such violent manoeuvring and the thump of fire from her broadsides and close-in guns as smaller tyranid organisms shearing from the refinery's protective swarm threatened to overwhelm her. Without her complement of Space Marine defenders, Tiberius knew that to allow the tyranids to board the *Victus* would seal its fate.

'Estimated time to lethal range, Philotas?'

'Twenty seconds, Lord admiral.'

SALVOES OF TORPEDOES exploded amongst the vanguard of the guardian swarm, killing alien organisms in their fiery blasts, but nothing could penetrate the thick mass of creatures forced to give up their existence in service of the hive mind. Less than sixty thousand kilometres separated the fleet from the refinery now.

And at its current speed, that meant about ten seconds.

'ALL HANDS, ABANDON ship!' bellowed Admiral de Corte as the proximity alarms of the *Argus* began blaring. The sacristy bell chimed again and again, warning – as though warning were needed – of the imminent collision of the refinery. He knew it was a wasted breath, none of the ship's lifeboats would be able to get clear of the blast radius of the refinery, but he had to try. Their doom filled the viewing bay, hurtling towards them with awful finality and, in the few seconds left to him, he stood and marched to the centre of the command nave.

He saluted his bridge crew and said, 'It has been an honour to serve with you all. The Emperor protects.'

As THE REFINERY flew into the midst of the Imperial fleet, the lightning spitters that had protected the gargantuan construction turned, whipcord fast, and lashed their former charge with raw tongues of blue fire. Metal ran molten beneath the assault and, like bloated ticks, the lightning spitters bored their way within the softened plates of the structure.

Once inside, each creature pushed its magma-hot discharge before it like a drill bit, slashing through metre after metre of sheet metal to reach the storage chambers at its heart. The heat from their crackling arcs of energy rippled around them, melting their own armoured carapaces and scorching the flesh from their bones, but driven by the implacable will of the hive mind, each beast continued onwards until it reached its goal.

As the first beast punched through the armoured chemical tanks, the flaring, electric arcs flashed across the fuel chamber, instantaneously igniting the volatile hydrogen-plasma mix. Others penetrated fuel chambers across the length and breadth of the refinery and in a heartbeat, the colossal bomb of the refinery was ripped apart in a cataclysmic explosion.

HUNDREDS WERE BLINDED by the dazzling brightness of the explosion as it ripped across the heavens above Tarsis Ultra. The *Argus* vanished in the corona of the blast, its shields no protection against the violence of the detonation. Metres-thick sheets of adamantium were vaporised in an instant as the plasma fire engulfed the ancient vessel. Compartments vented into space, the oxygen igniting as the heat tore through the ship and its massive structure sagged as her keel melted in the incandescent heat. Thousands of men died instantly as their blood flashed to steam and the skin was scorched from their bones in the time it took to draw breath to scream.

The fires of the explosion expanded rapidly, quickly eclipsing the doomed *Argus* and smashing into the other vessels of the Imperial fleet. Six defence monitors and as many system ships vaporised as their magazines and fuel stores exploded. The Cobras of Cypria squadron broke apart as their store of torpedoes cooked off in the launch bays, though the ill-fated Cobra of Hydra squadron miraculously survived.

The launch bays of the *Kharloss Vincennes* blazed as fuel stores caught light, the blast doors melting shut and rendering them unable to recover previously launched squadrons of fighters and bombers. Well-practiced fire drills saved the ship and her captain's quick manoeuvring put her prow-first into the detonation and lessened the buffeting shockwave's effect.

The *Sword of Retribution*, the *Yermetov* and the *Luxor*, shielded from much of the blast's force, were spared the worst of the damage, though their corridors echoed to the sound of hull breach klaxons and yelling damage control gangs.

BLOOD-RED LIGHT bathed the control bridge of the *Vae Victus*, the sacristy bell ringing as though the ship herself was screaming. Sparks and jets of hydraulic fluid spurted from shattered control panels, but Tiberius knew they were lucky still to be in one piece.

The *Vae Victus* had been stern on to the explosion and its force had hurled her about like a leaf in a hurricane, but Admiral Tiberius's quick thinking had put her clear of the main destructive energies of the hell that had engulfed the majority of the Imperial fleet.

'Damage report!' bellowed Tiberius.

'We've got hull breaches on decks six, seven and nine,' reported Philotas. 'The engines are operating at fifty per cent efficiency and we've lost most of the turrets on our rear quarters'

'What of the rest of the fleet?' asked Tiberius, dreading the answer.

'I don't know sir. The surveyors are having trouble penetrating the electromagnetic radiation released by the blast.'

'Get me Admiral de Corte, we need to get control of this situation, now.'

'Aye, sir.'

Tiberius lurched across the buckled deck to stand beside the plotting table, trying to make sense of the confused hash of imagery displayed there. A red haze filled the bottom of the schematic, the slate unable to display enough symbols to represent the tyranid fleet. Scattered blue icons faded in and out of focus as the surveyors fought to lock down the positions of the Imperial vessels.

'Emperor save us,' whispered Tiberius as names of vessels began flickering up next to the blue icons. Precious few, he saw. He frowned, scanning the table for the icon representing the *Argus*. Tiberius looked up as Philotas said, 'The *Argus* is gone, sir.'

'Gone–' echoed Tiberius.

'She caught the full force of the blast. There's nothing left of her.'

The lord admiral fought down his shock at the destruction of so mighty a vessel as the *Argus* and the death of her crew.

'And the rest of the fleet?' he asked, quietly.

'It looks like the local ships took the worst of the blast, but we've lost the Cobras and the Argus. The *Sword of Retribution* is damaged, but under power, and the *Kharloss Vincennes* is still with us though her launch bays are out of action.'

Tiberius nodded curtly, assessing the scale of the catastrophe and knew that the campaign in space was over.

'Issue a general communication to all vessels. I am taking command of the fleet. Order all ships to disengage. Get clear of Tarsis Ultra and rendezvous at Calydon.'

'Admiral?'

'Do it!' snapped Tiberius. 'Fighting an unwinnable battle is of no value if by doing so we lose the war. Now do as I say.'

Philotas nodded and dispatched the admiral's orders as Tiberius gripped the edge of the plotting table. Nothing now could be gained by fighting the advancing tyranids in space and he would not be responsible for dooming every man of the Imperial fleet.

Whatever came next, the defenders on Tarsis Ultra would have to face it on their own.

U
NINE

A COLD WIND blew across the tops of the Cullin Mountains, howling across the rocky ground below and stripping any lingering warmth from the bright morning. The air was crisp, but the sun was bright and low, preventing the foaming waters of the mountain springs from freezing over. Splashes of emerald green forests dotted the lower slopes of the mountains and, here and there, herds of shaggy yrenbacks made their way back down slope to the warmer plains from their drinking grounds.

Suddenly, the motion of the herds halted, each animal raising its long, furry neck into the air, as though scenting a predator. The herds milled in confusion, drawing closer to one another, agitated at their inability to identify the threat they all felt. The animals brayed in confusion, ears flat against their skulls.

A scattershot darkness covered the flanks of the mountain as a host of shapes flashed across the sky. All across the mountains, puffs of snow and rock were thrown skyward by the tremendous impacts of falling objects. The herds scattered as more and more objects dropped from the sky, churning the surface of the mountains with their numbers.

The clouds above flashed with purple lightning as spores burst within them, dispersing a multitude of contaminants and viruses that instantly began working to alter the climatological balance of the planet's atmosphere. Heat built up rapidly, increasing the air pressure and causing actinic bolts of lightning to arc from cloud to cloud, dispersing them as a viscous, toxic rain.

In minutes, the newly risen sun was obscured by the sheer mass of spores falling from the heavens. Terrified yrenbacks ran backwards and forwards across the mountain sides, leaping through the deep snow in their blind panic. Churning motion erupted from the steaming spores that had landed in their midst, flashing claws and alien screeches as the creatures within them emerged and sought something to kill. Driven into a frenzied killing fury by the hive mind and bio-engineered, super-adrenal chemicals, the first wave of tyranid invaders hacked entire herds of the grazing animals to bloody ruin before collapsing and dying, spent by the fury of their assault and their inability to survive the freezing temperatures.

Thousands of tyranid organisms in the first wave perished as the numbing cold of Tarsis Ultra froze them within minutes of their arrival. After burning virtually all their bodily energies in their initial surge of violence, and without reserves of fat, none could survive more than a few minutes before perishing.

But none of this mattered, for as each creature died and the hive mind became aware of the local conditions on the prey planet, it simply adjusted the biological physiology of its warrior organisms, enabling them to produce more insulating tissue and energy reserves that would allow them to survive for longer periods.

AMID THE LOAMY earth of the lower forests, the thick, biological rain soaked into the tree canopy and saturated the earth with its bacteria-laden substance. Microbes containing the genetic blueprint of tyranid fauna spread rapidly through the ground, assessing and digesting the chemical content of the soil before turning that energy into horrifyingly fast growth spurts.

Multicoloured fronds ripped their way through the silver bark of the trees and twisting vines and creepers surged from the moistened ground. Again, the cold of Tarsis Ultra dramatically shortened the plants' lifespan, but as each leaf and creeper died, it vomited a host of fresh spores into the atmosphere and the cycle began again.

As each generation of plant went through its brief life cycle, the chemical reactions fermenting in the ground began raising the temperature of the surrounding air. Streamers of heated air drifted from the ground, warming the burgeoning plant life until the rate of growth was rising exponentially. Jagged spore chimneys of thick, vegetable matter broke through the hot earth and pushed skyward, their root structure burrowing through the permafrost to the nutrient-rich soil below. Hot steam and exhaust gasses from the biological conflagration below belched from the chimneys, sending yet more spores high into the atmosphere to be spread by the prevailing winds. As the atmosphere heated even more, strong updrafts of warm air rose, meeting the cold air descending from the mountaintops to create freak weather patterns that spread the contamination of the tyranid organisms even further.

The invasion of Tarsis Ultra had begun.

* * *

DESPITE THE INABILITY of the Imperial fleet to hold back the tyranid invaders, Tarsis Ultra was not without defences of her own. Ground-based batteries of defence lasers fired skyward and hundreds of orbital torpedoes roared into the upper atmosphere on blazing tail plumes.

The defence lasers slashed through the sky, but the rapidly mutating content of the air had one more adaptive surprise for the defenders of Tarsis Ultra.

One of the greatest problems for ground-based laser weapons was the reduction in power they suffered over long distances, called 'thermal blooming'. As a laser beam travels through the air, small quantities of its energy are lost to the surrounding atmosphere as heat, which causes disturbances in the air and disrupts the optical path of the beam. Not only does this impair accuracy, but it spreads the beam wider, thus weakening the energy delivered to its target. For the colossal energies produced by the defence lasers, this was not normally a problem, but each beam was passing through dozens of rapidly fluctuating temperature patches in the air, causing them to impact with greatly reduced power.

Many of the smaller organisms suffered at the hands of the defence lasers, but the majority of the tyranid creatures had little to fear from them.

But torpedoes have no such barriers to performance and these weapons reaped a fearful tally amongst the gathering predators. Hundreds of torpedoes exploded amongst the bloated spore ships of the tyranid fleet, destroying some and fatally wounding others. Scores of alien creatures perished and fell through the atmosphere as bright, fleshy meteors, haemorrhaging their lifeblood like comets' tails.

The skies above Tarsis Ultra were what Imperial strategos referred to as 'target-heavy' and every torpedo found its mark in a tyranid creature. Within two hours, over five hundred confirmed kills had been reported by the silo commanders, along with desperate requests for additional ordnance to fire. Faced with so many targets, each silo exhausted its supply of weapons after another hour of firing.

Against any conventional invaders, the defences of Tarsis Ultra would have caused utter devastation and crippled any attempt to invade.

But the tyranids were far from conventional invaders.

FROM THE AIR, the hydro-skiff resembled a speeding silver bullet as it roared along the frozen surface of the hydroway. Its passenger compartments were laden with soldiers of the Logres regiment making their way back to Erebus, its speed approaching two hundred kilometres per hour as its giant, prop-driven engines hurled it along the frozen canal surface.

A mist of ice crystals billowed in its wake as the hydro-skis angled to take the skiff around a bend in the canal, rounding a series of low hills capped with a thatch of evergreen firs. Sparks flew as the offside ski grazed the mag-rails on the side of the canal, the pilot having taken the turn a little too fast for comfort. But concerns of safety were now outweighed by the need for speed. They had seen the heavens criss-crossed by bright streaks of lasfire, and the pale blue of the sky to the west was laced with cloudy pillars from firing torpedo silos. No one needed to tell the men of the Logres regiment what was happening, and that it was time to head for the safety of Erebus.

Unnatural twilight was falling as tyranid spores filled the sky above, long shadows cast by chittering black clouds that spun and swooped like flying oil slicks. Soldiers peered nervously through the steamed windows at the gathering darkness, willing the skiff's pilot to coax his machine to yet faster speeds.

A pair of the black clouds dropped through the air, looping downwards to fly parallel to the skiff, a third descending in a lazy spiral ahead of it. Officers watching through the roof periscopes shouted at their men to stand to, chivvying them to the windows and bellowing orders to fire at will.

Blasts of freezing air filled the skiff as windows were forced open and barrels of lasguns pushed through. Lasbolts snapped upwards, punching into the black flocks that pursued the skiff. Occasionally, a twisted shape would tumble to the snow, but such precious victories were few, and despite the terrific speed of the skiff, the flocks drew nearer still.

Cries of fear echoed along the length of the passenger compartments as the flocks began to overtake the skiff and the soldiers had their first glimpse of the enemy. Grotesque, membrane-winged creatures with leering, fang-filled maws and clawed limbs surrounded them. Lasbolts tore amongst the aliens, but for every one that was downed, a hundred more remained. They swooped over and around the skiff, spitting black gouts from weapon orifices that peppered its metal skin like handfuls of thrown stones. Glass smashed and men screamed as the aliens' fire struck them, their armour cracking and dissolving under the impacts.

Medics ran to the wounded, peeling off bloody flak vests and applying pressure to the ragged holes in the soldiers' bodies, then recoiled in horror as they saw clutches of writhing, beetle-like creatures boring deep into the men's flesh.

Scrabbling claws tore at the skiff's roof, gouging long tears in the thin metal. The skiff swayed from side to side, throwing more sparks as the pilot fought to compensate for the additional weight and drag of the attackers. Soldiers fired through the roof, killing the flying beasts in their dozens, but unable to dislodge them all.

Muscular taloned arms reached in and dragged a screaming soldier through a hole in the roof, his cries cut off as the rushing wind snatched away his breath. His comrades fought to pull him back, but another volley of the flesh-eating creatures slew the would-be rescuers in a hail of fire.

The skiff screamed around another bend in the icy canal, only to be faced by yet another flock of the winged monsters, swirling in an impenetrable cloud and blocking the skiff's path with their bodies. The pilot reacted instinctively, slamming on the air brakes and wrenching the controls to one side. Barbed brakes deployed from the skis, throwing the skiff into an uncontrollable skid.

The rear end of the skiff fishtailed, the passenger compartment slewing around until it was travelling sideways. Wider than the canal, its back end caught the edge of the mag-rails and flipped it over onto its side. At such high speeds, the impact ripped the passenger compartment open and tore the coupling to the engine with it, sending it spinning into the air to crash down onto the ice a hundred metres further down the canal where it exploded in a searing orange fireball.

Flames billowed skywards as the wreckage skidded along the canal for another six hundred metres, the heat from the flames melting the ice as it slid. Amid the carnage of the crash, a few pitiful survivors crawled from the wreckage, battered, bloodied and dazed.

Even before they had a chance to freeze to death, the winged gargoyles were upon them, biting and clawing at their helpless prey until there was no one left alive.

The first victims of the land war of Tarsis Ultra had been claimed.

FROM THEIR PERCH high on the roof of their warehouse hideout, Snowdog and Silver watched the distant contrails of torpedoes as they climbed through the purple skies into the upper atmosphere.

The devotional holos, normally full of nameless preachers demanding prayers to the Emperor, had been displaying a non-stop procession of warnings against the dangers of contact with xeno species.

Snowdog didn't know what was happening with the war, but was pretty certain that there must have been a screw-up somewhere along the line, because you didn't start firing ground based weapons except to prevent an imminent invasion.

'This does not look good,' said Snowdog.

'Nope,' agreed Silver, 'It sure doesn't.'

LORD INQUISITOR KRYPTMAN stood in an armoured viewing bay atop the Governor's Palace, watching the same scenes with a similar feeling. With the news that the fleet had been forced to disengage, his hopes that this invasion could be stalled before it reached the surface of the planet had been shattered. He cast his gaze across the landscape one last time, knowing that even were they able to defeat the aliens, this world would never be the same again.

Orders had been issued to all officers on tactical doctrine and the proper conduct to be followed during conflict with the tyranids. Experience bought with uncounted lives was even now circulating amongst the soldiers of Tarsis Ultra and Kryptman hoped that the sacrifice of those who had died to gather that information would not have been in vain.

As he watched the beginning of the tyranid invasion, Magos Locard joined him in the bay, hands clasped before him and mechadendrites swaying gently above his head.

'So it begins again,' mused the inquisitor, watching the swirling, multi-coloured sky.

'Indeed,' said Locard. 'Were it not such a monstrous thing, it might be considered aesthetically pleasing. It is nature driven into paroxysms of creation.'

'Creation, yes, but there is nothing natural about this. It is creation designed to destroy and consume.'

'An interesting dichotomy, yes?' observed Locard.

'Yes, but one for another time perhaps. How goes your research?'

'It progresses. The facilities here are lacking in some regards, but they are sufficient for my needs. The samples taken from the xeno creatures recovered from the *Vae Victus* have helped immensely, but their genetic structure shows evidence of mutation. Evidently, the tyranids have entered another iteration of evolution since the consumption of Barbarus Prime.'

Kryptman turned to face the magos and nodded. 'I had suspected as much.'

'To achieve our goal, it seems clear we will need to somehow obtain a gene sample that is as close to the hive's original structure as possible, one that has not been subjected to mutation at the behest of the overmind.'

'And how do you intend to obtain such a specimen?'

'Ah, well that I do not yet know,' admitted Locard.

'Find a way,' ordered Kryptman.

URIEL WATCHED LEARCHUS and Pasanius march along the front lines of the city's defences and fought the urge to join them. Little time had passed since he had been a veteran sergeant himself, and the old desire to check on the men under his command still came to the fore on the eve of battle. He had greater concerns now, he reminded himself, as he checked the data-slate to ensure that everything in his sector of responsibility was as it should be.

From above, the plain before the city walls resembled the top of a race-track with curved trenches linking the two sides of the valley. Three entrenchments crossed it, progressively narrowing as they neared the city walls, but Uriel knew that these were nothing more than temporary defences. The first wave of tyranids would come at them from the air, pinning them down while the bulk of the tyranid army approached on foot.

Sebastien Montante had assured him that the valley sides were well defended with enough guns to make any aerial attack unfeasible. Uriel had his doubts, knowing that the sheer scale of a tyranid invasion was beyond the comprehension of most people who had never seen one.

Seven thousand men occupied the first trench, six thousand the second and another two thousand the third. The remainder of the soldiers waited within the walls of Erebus itself, held in reserve until needed. Rumbling before the wall, its armoured flanks bristling with guns and its crenallated battlements swarming with soldiers, was the Capitol Imperialis of Colonel Octavius Rabelaq. Emblazoned with the heraldry of the Logres regiment, the massive rhomboid-shaped command vehicle rose nearly fifty metres from the ground. From here, Rabelaq could direct his soldiers and maintain command and control over the battle. Its tracks were wider than a road and four Leman Russ battle tanks could fit within the barrel of its main gun. It was a fearsome reminder of Imperial power and its might was plain for all to see. Smaller tanks surrounded the Capitol Imperialis, like ants around an elephant, passing through the gates in the wall towards the front line.

Those tanks that had already taken position idled in well-sited berms, with flared aprons of flattened snow behind them to allow them to reverse out and withdraw to the next line.

Soldiers in dirty overwhites huddled in their dugouts, clustered around plasma-wave generators, cooking their rations. The men clearly relished what might be their last hot meal for some time, and Uriel knew that little improved morale more than hot food and beverages. Here, Montante had excelled himself, handling the logistical nightmare of feeding and equipping tens of thousands of soldiers with the skill of a veteran quartermaster. He had organised vast kitchens to supply the soldiers defending his city with regular hot food and ensured that the commanders had a reliable supply train.

Everything had been organised with admirable efficiency and he could see the teachings of the Codex Astartes in the precise layout of the defences. Uriel was reminded of the schematics he had seen depicting the defences of the northern polar defence fortress on Macragge during the First Tyrannic War, though he hoped to avoid the outcome of that battle.

Satisfied that all was as it should be, he marched along the slush-covered duckboards of the trenches towards the front line. A thick, two-metre berm of snow had been built before the trench to absorb any incoming fire, since, rather than exploding away from projectiles like sand, snow would anneal under the impact and become a stronger, more effective barrier.

Buckets of water had been repeatedly poured down the slope of the snow barrier before the lip of the trench, making a glass-smooth surface that would hopefully prove extremely difficult for the aliens to scale.

'Any word on when we can expect to see them?' asked Pasanius, joining Uriel on the trench's firing step.

'Soon,' answered Uriel as Learchus marched over.

'You have done fine work, Learchus,' said Uriel, gripping his sergeant's hand in welcome.

Learchus nodded. 'The soldiers here are good men, brother-captain, they just needed reminding of the teachings of the Codex Astartes.'

'I'm sure you gave them a very pointed reminder,' noted Uriel.

'Where necessary,' admitted Learchus. 'I was no harsher than any other Agiselus drill sergeant.'

Both Pasanius and Uriel winced as they remembered the severity of their training on Macragge. Neither had any doubt that Learchus had put the soldiers here through hell in order to prepare them for the coming war. But if it made them better soldiers, then it was a price they should be thankful for.

'Where are the Mortifactors and the Deathwatch to be stationed?' asked Learchus.

Uriel pointed towards the southern reaches of the trenches, his brow furrowing at the memory of the confrontation with Astador and Kryptman in the orbiting space station. He had lost control and the shame of that lapse still burned inside him. He was a Space Marine in the service of the Emperor and was above such petty considerations as temper. But the death of so many innocents on Chordelis and the stain left within his soul by the Bringer of Darkness had overcome his normally unbreakable code of honour.

The thought of losing control and becoming little more than a killer without a conscience frightened him greatly. Briefly he thought of confessing to the growing darkness within him, but bit back the words, unsure of how to articulate his feelings. Such weaknesses were foreign to a Space Marine and he had not the humanity to reach out and express them.

The three Space Marines watched the boiling sky in the far distance with trepidation. None would ever forget the horrors they had witnessed on Ichar IV and the thought of facing such a foe again brought nothing but apprehension.

While they knew they could fight any foe and triumph, they were but a hundred warriors and, against such a numberless horde, there was only so much they could do.

The soldiers around them were numerous, though nowhere near as numerous as the tyranids. But where the defenders of Tarsis Ultra had the advantage over the alien horde was in their basic humanity, the courage that came from defending one's hearth and home.

The very thing Uriel and his sergeants lacked.

* * *

THE WESTERN MOUNTAINS writhed with motion. Thousands upon thousands of mycetic spores hammered the ground, each disgorging a mucus-covered creature that hissed and screeched in animal hunger. Swarms of beasts gathered in the shadow of the twisting, smoke-wreathed forests, the natural beauty of the ecology perverted into monstrous, alien flora that consumed the nutrients in the soil and spread a dark stain of necrotic growth across the landscape. Bubbling pools of acids and enzymes formed in sunken patches of ground, small devourer organisms plunging into the acid baths to give up the energy they had consumed to feed the voracious appetite of the alien fleet.

When enough creatures had gathered in a snapping, biting mass, the horde set off at some unseen signal, powerful hind limbs propelling the bounding swarm through the deep snow of the mountains and onto the plain below. Larger creatures stamped through the snow, their bestial jaws snapping and clawed hands sweeping aside the smaller aliens as they moved through the swarm. Tens of thousands of aliens charged down the mountains, directed to their prey by invisible cords of psychic hunger that connected them with thousands of flying gargoyles that swept ahead of the swarm and reeled them closer to their prey.

All across Tarsis Ultra, the beasts of the tyranid invasion closed on their targets.

GUARDSMAN PAVEL LEFORTO of the Erebus Defence Legion nervously licked his lips, then wished he hadn't as he felt the cold freeze the moisture within seconds. He desperately needed to empty his full bladder, but the latrine pits were three hundred metres behind his platoon's section of the forward trench. He cursed the need to drink so much water. At his age, his bladder wasn't the strongest in the world, and the need to drink five canteens of water every day to stave off dehydration – a very real danger in this cold climate – was a constant pain.

But the corpsmen of the Logres regiment were all humourless bastards when it came to cold weather injuries, and it was now a court martial offence to suffer from dehydration, frostbite or hypothermia.

The trench was not as cold as it had been in the weeks previous to this, though high on the periscope platform, a cold wind chilled him to the marrow despite the many-layered thermal overwhites he wore. The presence of so many soldiers raised the temperature by several degrees and the tanks had become a magnet for cold soldiers who basked in the heat radiating from their engine blocks. This section of trench alone was home to over three hundred soldiers, a mix of squads from the Logres and Krieg regiments. None of the off-world soldiers were that friendly, and treated the majority of the Defence Legion soldiers like weekend warriors, amateurs playing in the big boys' arena. This combined with fraying tempers caused by the miserable conditions, had made relations between the defenders of Tarsis Ultra strained to say the least. The initial excitement of leaving his regular post in the Erebus smelteries had long-since evaporated and he missed the predictable monotony of his work.

But more than that, he missed returning home to his wife and children at the end of the day and the cramped, yet homely hab-unit that they and three other families shared high on the north face of District Secundus. Sonya would be readying the evening meal about now and his two children, Hollia and little Solan, would be on their way back from the scholam. The ache of their absence was painful and Pavel looked forward to an end to this war when he could be reunited with them.

Banishing thoughts of home and family, he pressed his face to the rubberised eyecups of the bipod-mounted periscope magnoculars and pressed the button that flipped open the polarised lens covers. He shifted his balaclava under his helmet to get a good look through the magnoculars. The heat from his skin momentarily fogged the glass before the image resolved into clarity before him.

The bleak, unbroken whiteness of the landscape was empty as far as he could see, though he knew that the freezing temperatures reduced his depth perception and visual acuity. Still, he wasn't the only one watching this sector, so he wasn't too bothered that he couldn't see much. Seeing nothing was a good thing anyway, wasn't it?

'Anything?' asked his squad mate, Vadim Kotash, holding out a steaming tin mug filled with caffeine towards Pavel. At forty-five years old, Vadim was a year younger than Pavel and together, they were probably the oldest men in the platoon. His friend's face was obscured by his balaclava and snow-goggles, a scarf wrapped around his mouth muffling his words.

'Nah,' said Pavel, snapping the covers back over the magnoculars. He took the mug and, pulling the scarf from his mouth, sipped his hot drink. 'Can't see anything worth a damn in this weather.'

'Aye, I hear that. Con tells me that Kellis got taken back to the medicae yesterday. Snow blindness got him. The young fool kept taking his goggles off.'

'The provosts will haul him over the coals for that.'

'I wouldn't mind being hauled over the coals, it might warm my old bones up,' chuckled Vadim.

'It would take the furnace back in the smeltery for that now,' said Pavel.

Vadim nodded as an officer in a long, mud-stained Krieg greatcoat and a thick, furred colback studded with a lieutenant's pips stalked down the trench. He carried his lasgun slung over his shoulder and he scowled in displeasure as he marched.

'Uh-oh, it's Konarski,' hissed Vadim, tapping Pavel's shoulder, but it was already too late.

'You!' snapped Konarski. 'Why the hell aren't you watching for the enemy?'

Pavel started at the sharp bark of Konarski's voice, spilling caffeine onto his overwhites.

'Uh, sorry, sir. I was just–'

'I don't give a damn what you were doing, you are supposed to be watching for the enemy. You might single-handedly condemn us all to death with your carelessness. I'll have you on report for this, you mark my words.'

Pavel groaned in frustration as Konarski fished out a battered, and obviously well-used, disciplinary infractions notebook and a worn-down nub of a pencil.

'Right then, soldier, name, rank and serial numb–'

Konarski never got a chance to finish his question as the alert sirens blared into life all along the front line. Wailing klaxons screamed a warning to the soldiers and the trenches erupted in panicked motion as troopers fumbled for their weapons and scrambled to the trench's firing step. Pavel dropped his mug and pressed his face to the trench periscope, the altercation with Konarski forgotten.

He snapped up the covers and gasped as he saw the swarming black shapes knifing through the air towards the trenches. The entire upper half of the viewer was filled with alien creatures and he could hear the rustling roar of thousands of beating wings as they drew nearer.

Realising he no longer needed the scope, Pavel dropped to the firing step and lifted his rifle to his shoulder. Engines belched smoke as Hydra flak tanks drove forward, sending frozen mud and snow flying as their tracks churned the ground. Ammunition trucks followed the tanks, each carrying three thousand shells in easy-to-load ammo panniers, since a Hydra could pump out up to a thousand rounds a minute.

Pavel watched the approaching cloud of flying aliens with a mixture of terror and anticipation. Never having journeyed far beyond the walls of Erebus, he was excited to have the chance to see real aliens from afar. But if even half of the information given in the platoon briefings on these creatures was true, then he knew that in all probability he wouldn't enjoy too close an encounter with a tyranid organism.

The noise of the sirens died, and the awful sound of the aliens' flapping wings echoed from the valley sides along with a brittle, high-pitched noise of millions of claws clicking together.

'Hold your fire until they get closer,' ordered a captain of the Logres regiment, calmly walking behind them with his sword drawn, the blade resting on his shoulder. 'Don't waste any of your shots, you'll need every one of them.'

Pavel caught Vadim's eye, seeing the fear behind his friend's nervous smile.

'Don't worry, Vadim,' said Pavel. 'Just keep a fresh power cell handy and you'll be fine.'

Vadim nodded shakily as the Hydras began firing and the noise of the quad-barrelled weapons as they began pumping shells into the approaching swarm was deafening. Hundreds of explosions burst among the flying creatures, painting the sky with dirty smears, and the distant screeches of dying creatures drifted through the cold air. Steam billowed from the air-cooled barrels and robed enginseers circled each tank, sprinkling their hulls with blessed water from their aspergillum as the guns sprayed the air with explosive shells.

Pavel watched the swarm above convulse as fire from the Hydras ripped through it, blasting apart hundreds of creatures with every passing second. The carnage wreaked among them was fearsome and hundreds of falling black objects drifted from the swarm. He wondered how they could possibly take so much punishment and still keep coming.

In perfect synchrony, a portion of the swarm dipped and flowed from the sky as another climbed, heading for the high peaks of the city. The lower swarm rapidly lost altitude to skim the ice and race towards the trenches like dark bullets.

The Hydras continued to spray the air with shells, the barrels depressing as the swarm heading for the trenches descended. The range was closing rapidly, the chittering screeches of the aliens clawing at the nerves of the thousands of men facing them.

Pavel watched the aliens through the scope of his lasgun, the blinking red crosshairs flashing to green as the aliens entered the weapon's lethal range.

'Fire! Fire at will!' bellowed an officer, and thousands of lasguns opened fire simultaneously. The black swarm jerked, hundreds upon hundreds of the beasts cartwheeling into the ice. Disciplined volleys pierced the swarm. Pavel fired without aiming. It simply wasn't necessary when the enemy came at you in such numbers.

The alien screeches rose to a howling gale and suddenly they were upon them.

Vadim ducked as a flying monster smashed into the lip of the trench, vestigial rear limbs scrabbling for purchase on the ice. Membranous wings flapped as its ribbed arms pointed towards him, a slime-dripping symbiotic weapon aimed at his heart.

Pavel shot the beast in the head and its thrashing carcass fell into the trench. A pair of hissing monsters swooped low, gobbets of black slime spattering the trench walls as Pavel pushed Vadim to the slush at the bottom of the trench. He rolled as the beasts came at him, oblivious to the screams and sounds of battle echoing from all along the trench line. He opened up on full-auto, filling the trench with bright lasbolts and cutting the creatures in two.

Vadim shot another beast as it clawed its way over the snow berm. He dragged Pavel to his feet. The air was thick with gargoyles, swooping and diving at the trenches, clawing and biting and firing their disgusting bio-weapons. Screams tore through the hissing of the monsters and the air reeked with the stench of blood and fear.

A clutch of the screeching beasts swooped down from the thinning swarm, bright spurts of bio-plasma melting snow and flesh with equal ease. Vadim screamed as he was lifted into the air by a gargoyle, his legs thrashing and his cries piteous as he was carried from the trench. Pavel jumped, grabbing hold of Vadim's legs, but his thick mittens couldn't get a grip and his friend was carried into the sky. Pavel fell back into the trench as another gargoyle swooped towards him. He dived to one side, desperately bringing up his lasgun to block its sweeping claws. Sparks flew as the alien's talons hacked through the barrel, ripping through his overwhites, but tearing free before cutting into his chest. He stumbled, falling to his rump on the firing step. He hurled his useless weapon aside, reaching for his war-knife as the beast spun in the air and came back for another pass.

Alien gore spattered him as the gargoyle exploded in midair, detonating from within as it was struck by a burst of fire from a Space Marine's bolter. He wiped dripping ichor from his goggles in time to see an Ultramarines captain and sergeant fight their way down the length of the trench, killing aliens and shrugging off their attacks as if they were on the parade ground.

'Thanks,' blurted Pavel, but the warriors had already moved on.

He dropped to his knees, retching as the reality of his near death flared and shock began to take hold. Sick dread filled him and hot fear dumped into his system as he realised how close he had come to leaving Sonya a widow.

He felt his limbs shake and rooted amongst the dead on the floor of the trench for a weapon, realising that action was his only hope of staving off the onset of this paralysing fear.

Pavel hurriedly loaded the lasgun, and surged to his feet. He clambered back to the firing step and fired into the mass of creatures boiling in the air above him. He fired and reloaded, losing count of how many power packs he slammed home, resorting to taking more from the pouches of the fallen when his own ran out. But even he could see that the swarm's numbers were diminishing.

Unable to land and fight, the gargoyles could never capture the trenches, and Pavel wondered what exactly the point of this attack was.

The answer was horrifyingly clear. The aliens were probing them… learning. This attack was nothing more than an exploration of their prey's capabilities, the merest hint of what was to come. This vanguard was a diversion only, and the beasts that died here in their thousands were expendable, fodder to be used in order to decide how best to defeat the creatures that defended this world.

The thought of such a cold, unfeeling logic chilled him to the core. If thousands might be sacrificed for the merest scrap of information, what more horrors might the aliens' leaders unleash?

The sounds of battle were beginning to diminish and here and there, Pavel could see the armoured forms of the Ultramarines and the Mortifactors despatching the last elements of the swarm, moving and firing their cumbersome weapons with an efficiency that came from decades of constant practice.

He steadied himself against the side of the trench as a crippling wash of sensations flooded him. Relief at his survival, an ache for his family and grief for Vadim – though he had no idea whether his friend was alive or dead.

He slumped to the trench's firing step as exhaustion filled his limbs with cold lead and his hands started to shake.

Pavel wept for his lost friend and the tears turned to ice on his cheeks.

SNOWDOG LET RIP with a huge burst of fire from the heavy stubber, the shells cutting a hissing gargoyle in two and sending it tumbling from the boarded-up window it had been attempting to batter its way through. Silver calmly double-tapped another as it tore at a hole in the ceiling and Tigerlily spun and wove her way through the aliens, tearing wings and plucking out eyes with her thin daggers.

Jonny Stomp and Trask fought back to back, blazing away with their purloined weapons at the bizarre-looking creatures that were trying to bust into their warehouse hideout. The guns' reports were deafening, and cries of panic and fear from those civilians who'd been lucky enough to reach the safety of the warehouse dopplered in and out of perception between the blasts of fire.

The doorway timbers finally splintered and half a dozen screeching monsters fought to get through the opening. Snowdog spun and braced himself, keeping his stance wide as he depressed the firing stud on the textured grip of the heavy stubber. A metre-long tongue of fire leapt from the perforated barrel and annihilated the aliens in a blood-and-smoke stained cloud. Even braced, the recoil staggered Snowdog, the stream of shells ripping upwards and blasting chunks of the plaster ceiling loose.

He swung the gun back down again, searching for fresh targets, but, for the moment, finding none. The panicked whimpers and muffled sobs from the two-dozen civilians at the back of the warehouse were already irritating him and he let out a deep, calming breath, running to the edge of the shattered window frame to risk a glance outside.

Since early evening, the roaring of defence guns had echoed from the valley sides and he'd watched the tops of the rock faces erupt in a furious storm of gunfire. At first he couldn't see what they were shooting at, but pretty soon a billowing cloud of creatures came into view. Trailing the monsters came a black rain, spores in their thousands, dropping towards the city at a terrific rate.

Explosions painted the sky, shells bursting amongst the dropping organisms and killing thousands of aliens. Snowdog had never seen such a magnificent display of the city's defences before, and the firepower they brought to bear on the spores was nothing short of incredible.

The scale of the tyranid invasion was of an order of magnitude greater than the city's architects had ever bargained for, and scattered pockets of the aerial bombardment were able to penetrate the umbrella of flak, mostly in the lower reaches of the city, far from where the extra guns studding the walls of the Imperial Palace of Sebastien Montante defeated the first wave.

Curious onlookers surrounded the spores that did manage to land, eager to see, first-hand, this threat to their world, most paying with their lives as the spores erupted with alien killers: slashing beasts and sickle-armed monsters with pitiless eyes and voracious appetites.

Snowdog had watched as a handful of spores had smashed through the thin, corrugated iron roofs of nearby dwellings, wincing at the impacts and knowing that the inhabitants were already dead. People scattered, shocked into action by the violence around them.

Nearly a hundred of the leaping, hissing beasts thronged the narrow streets before the warehouse building serving as their base. Screaming people, carrying children and pathetic bundles of personal possessions had fled before the aliens and, in a moment of weakness that he just knew he was going to regret, Snowdog had allowed them sanctuary in the warehouse.

Since then, he and his gang had been fighting for their lives as aliens fought tooth and nail to get inside. Jonny had held them at bay long enough for Snowdog to break out the weaponry they'd snagged from one of the many crooked supply sergeants at the busy port facilities, and with everyone carrying such powerful guns, they'd sent the aliens packing with their tails well and truly between their legs.

It pained Snowdog to use these guns, because the resale value would be a hell of a lot less now they'd been fired. Still, he figured, he had crates and crates of ration packs and medical supplies in storage and would bet the sun and the moon that there'd be a hell of a demand for them in the coming days.

He coughed as sudden quiet descended on the hab-unit, his lungs filled with acrid smoke from the heavy calibre weapons' fire. Trask and Jonny Stomp high-fived.

'You see that one I got between the eyes?' snarled Trask. 'Blew its Emperor-damned head clean off!'

'Aye. But what about the one I nailed with the grenade launcher? That was sweet,' said Jonny, miming firing his weapon again and again.

Snowdog left them to their bragging, shouldering the smoking heavy stubber and smiling at Silver, who nodded back and reloaded her pistols.

Lex and Tigerlily slumped to the floor, sparking up a couple of obscura sticks and Snowdog let them, figuring the threat was over for now.

Silver sidled next to him and rubbed the back of his neck, leaning up to kiss his cheek. She smiled and nodded towards the crowd of terrified people at the back of the warehouse, her normally icy demeanour melting.

'That was a good thing you did, letting those people in,' she said.

'Yeah, ain't I the hero?' snapped Snowdog.

'No,' replied Silver, 'but I think maybe you're a sentimentalist.'

'Me? Don't bet on it, honey. I don't even know why I did it. If I'd had time to think about it, I'd have shut the door in their faces.'

'Really?'

'Really.'

Silver searched his eyes for any sign that he was joking, then removed her hand from his neck when she found none. He saw her aloof exterior reassert itself as her stare penetrated his apparent altruism to the white heat of his self-interest.

She turned away and said, 'I just bet you would have.'

Snowdog returned his gaze to the snow-covered city through the window. He didn't blame Silver for thinking the best of him; he could be charming when he wanted to be, but he knew that he was basically a guy whose selfishness was too deeply ingrained for him to change. He knew his faults and they weren't his defining characteristics, they were casual attributes – a monument to his desire to look out for number one.

He cursed softly to himself as he remembered how Silver had looked at him when she believed he had let the fleeing people into the warehouse through unselfish motives. There was no guile in that look and its naked honesty scared him with how it made him feel. Snowdog rested the stubber against the wall and pulled a pack of bac-sticks from his trouser pocket, lighting one as he considered what would happen next.

He'd have to feed these people, and keep them safe, a duty that went against every instinct in his body. He looked out for his nearest and dearest and that most certainly did not include civilians. Damn. He glanced over at Silver, feeling the chill of her eyes and cursed again.

He ran a hand through his bleached hair, hearing the sound of screams and gunfire as more aliens ran into resistance in other parts of the city. He looked at the huddled people and shook his head.

What had he been thinking? What *was* he thinking?

Stacked crates stretched all the way back into the darkness of the warehouse; it was a veritable treasure trove of weapons, medical supplies, food, clothing, blankets – all the things a city in the grip of winter and invasion would desperately need.

He switched his gaze from the crates to the huddled people and as he saw the desperate longing in their eyes, he pictured the contents of the crates.

Snowdog smiled, suddenly scenting opportunities multiplying.

U
TEN

URIEL AND LEARCHUS surveyed the wreckage of the trench lines with practiced eyes, realising that against another aerial assault they would probably hold, but against a combined assault of land and airborne creatures, they would not. Reconnaissance provided by the Fury pilots stranded on Tarsis Ultra after the *Kharloss Vincennes* had been unable to recover them had indicated that a chitinous tide of unimaginable proportions was barely sixty kilometres to the west.

A conservative estimate of their speed of advance put the tyranid horde less than hour away. Three aircraft had been lost to discover this information, brought down by roving packs of gargoyles lurking in the coloured clouds that billowed up from the mutant growths propagated by the alien spores.

'We will not hold this line, brother-captain,' said Learchus.

'I know, but it will be a bitter blow to morale to have to pull back so soon after the first attack.'

Stretcher bearers and field medics moved along the trenches, applying battlefield triage where they could and marking those who needed immediate removal to the medicae facilities with charcoal sticks. The soldiers of all the regiments had performed heroically, but Uriel knew that heroics alone were not enough to win this war.

Further along the trenches, Uriel could see Chaplain Astador of the Mortifactors, kneeling in prayer within a circle of his brother Space Marines. Smoke from an iron brazier set before Astador drifted skyward and even over the stench of today's battle, Uriel's enhanced senses could pick out the scent of boiling blood.

Learchus followed his captain's gaze, his lip curling in distaste as he too caught the scent of blood in the dark smoke.

'What devilment are they about now?' wondered Learchus.

'I do not know, sergeant, but I'll wager that you will not find its like within the pages of the Codex Astartes.'

Learchus grunted in agreement as Major Satria of the Erebus Defence Legion and Captain Bannon of the Deathwatch made their way towards the two Space Marines. Bannon moved with the leisurely stride of a born warrior; his armour was bloodstained, the yellow and black symbol of the Imperial Fists obscured with purple ichor. Satria's features were bloody and exhausted. A red-stained bandage bound his left arm and his helmet bore deep grooves, scarred by alien claws.

'Sergeant Learchus,' he said.

'Major Satria. Your men have fought bravely,' said Learchus.

'Thank you,' replied Satria. 'There's steel in these lads. We won't let you down.'

'Your fighting spirit is commendable, Major Satria, but I fear this is but a taster of what is to come,' said Uriel.

'You may be right, Captain Ventris, I've just received reports that seven other cities have been attacked already. And we can't raise many of the smaller settlements.'

'They are already dead,' said Bannon.

'You can't know that,' protested Satria.

'But I can, Major Satria,' answered Bannon. 'I have fought the tyranids before and we can expect more attacks very soon, launched with even more ferocity and cunning.'

'So what do we do?'

'We will fight,' stated Bannon, his tone brooking no argument. 'This is the largest settlement on Tarsis Ultra and the tyranids will see it as the most vital organ of their prey to strike. They will attack throughout Tarsis Ultra, of course, but their greatest effort will be directed at us.'

Uriel nodded, his blood flaming with the certainty and passion of Bannon's voice, feeling the killing rage and hatred of the tyranids boil upwards through his veins.

'Where are your men?' asked Learchus.

'I have stationed them at key points in the defence line,' answered Bannon. 'Each has the Litany of Hatred of the Xenos carved on his breastplate and will recite them to the soldiers around them as they fight. The Emperor's holy wrath will infuse every man with the courage to do his duty.'

'They will do so anyway,' promised Satria.

Uriel let the words of his companions drift over him as the scent of blood in his nostrils suddenly leapt in clarity, swelling to fill his perception until he could see and feel nothing beyond the desire to see it shed.

He could feel the pace of his heart rates increase until he realised he was in danger of hyperventilating.

'Captain Ventris?' asked Bannon. 'Are you alright?'

With an effort of will, Uriel dragged his perceptions back to the present, feeling the real world suddenly snap back into focus and the overpowering stench of blood recede like a forgotten dream. He unclenched his fists and nodded.

'Yes, yes, I am fine,' he said slowly. 'I am simply eager to spill more alien blood.'

Uriel swore he could feel the amusement of a dark spirit lurking just behind his eyes.

IN ANOTHER SECTION of the trenches, Pasanius wiped black streaks of alien blood from his silvered bionic arm, a frown of consternation creasing his features. He picked up a handful of snow and smeared it over the gleaming metal, watching as it melted and washed yet more of the blood from his arm. Finally, he stooped and picked up a fallen scarf, wiping the surface of his arm clean.

The metal beneath was gleaming like new, its surface smooth and unblemished by so much as a scratch.

Pasanius caught his breath and closed his eyes.

He held his arm close to his body and prayed.

AGAIN THE WARNING klaxons blared and soldiers rushed to man the trenches. Distant swarms of gargoyles swooped in the sky as a swelling, rustling noise built from a whisper to a roar. Uriel recognised it as the sound of millions of creatures frantically jostling together as they churned forwards in an unstoppable mass, driven to kill and fight by the implacable will of the hive mind.

A rippling black line appeared on the horizon, an undulating tide of claws, armoured carapaces and leaping monsters. He flexed his fingers on the grip of his sword, his thumb hovering over the activation rune, willing the tyranids closer so that he might slake this bloodlust in their ripped entrails.

The horizon seethed with motion, the entire width of the valley filled with alien monsters intent on killing. Imperial artillery pieces, placed nearer the city walls, boomed and plumes of black smoke and explosions of ice fountained on the ice plain. Defence turrets and hastily constructed pillboxes opened fire, filling the air with deafening noise and lethal projectiles. Howling Lightning and Marauder aircraft streaked over the trenches to strafe the forward elements of the tyranid swarm or send high explosive bombs to crater the ice and incinerate tyranid creatures in their hundreds. Imperial Guard tanks lobbed shells on a high trajectory, their commanders knowing they would find targets without the need to aim.

The vast cannon on the frontal cliff of Colonel Rabelaq's Capitol Imperialis fired, its thunderous shot sounding like the crack of doom. Sheets of ice and snow fell from the mountains as the thunderous barrage of a well dug-in force unleashed the full fury of its firepower against the enemy.

Thousands of tyranid organisms were killed, their carcasses trampled in the furious rush of the surviving creatures to reach their prey, but Uriel could see that the actual damage inflicted was negligible. Thousands were dead, but a hundred times that number remained.

Among the swarm, he could see larger, more threatening looking beasts, their shape suggesting giant, living battering rams. Creatures that felt no pain and whose nervous systems were so rudimentary that it could take their bodies many minutes to realise that they were in fact dead. Crackling arcs of blue energy sparked amongst the swarm and the screeching wails of the aliens echoed from the valley sides, plucking at the strained nerves of the soldiers.

He glanced at the nervous faces around him, seeing the regimental insignia of Krieg, Logres and Erebus Defence Legion units. Every face was wrapped in snow goggles, scarves and helmets, but he could sense the fear in all of them.

'Place your trust in the Emperor,' shouted Uriel, 'He is both your shield and your weapon. Trust to His wisdom that there is purpose in everything, and you will prevail. Kill your enemies with His name on your lips and fight with the strength that He has given you. And if it is your fate to give your life in His name, rejoice that you have served His will.'

Uriel activated his power sword, coils of energy wreathing the blade in deadly energy.

'Let the aliens come,' he snarled. 'We will show them what it means to fight the soldiers of the Emperor.'

CHAPLAIN ASTADOR FELT the pulse of the world through the ceramite plates of his armour, sensing the planet's pain at this invasion in every strand of life that took its sustenance from its spirit. The scent of his own burning blood filled his senses and allowed his ghost-self to commune with those who had gone before him, who had worn the holy suit of armour in ages past, whose perceptions of the universe were uncluttered by the fetters of mortal flesh.

He could feel the flaring energies of the soldiers around him, fear radiating hot and urgent, but also courage and determination. It was a potent combination, but Astador could not yet tell whether it would be enough to stand before these creatures that gave neither thought nor obeisance to the spirits of the dead and all that they could know.

Though he could sense individual intelligences lurking within the swarm, he could feel a single keening voice that lanced through the swarm, a single driving imperative that gave them great strength of purpose, but no will of their own. It felt like cold steel, a glacial spike driven through his ghost-self. The sheer horror of this utterly alien consciousness threatened to overwhelm Astador, and the awesome scale of such domination of the self beggared belief.

There was no hunger, no anger, no courage, or ambition in that imperative, only a single-minded desire to consume.

There was strength in that, to be sure, but also great weakness.

But should that cold steel imperative be broken, what then could such slave creatures achieve with no will of their own?

Casting his ghost-self further into the chill of the ghastly tyranid psyche, Astador probed for ways to do just that.

CAPTAIN OWEN MORTEN hauled violently on the stick of his Fury interceptor, pulling a hard dive for the deck. Whiteness flashed past his canopy and he levelled his wings as he pulled out some forty metres above the ice. He feathered the engines, pulling around and craning his neck over his right shoulder. A trail of bright explosions bloomed in his wake, alien carcasses cartwheeling through the air and Morten's icy countenance hardened even further.

Hastily reconfigured to carry air-to-ground munitions following their landing on Tarsis Ultra, Captain Morten's squadron of Furies were taking the fight back to the tyranids. His last sight of the *Kharloss Vincennes* was of her launch bays in flames before the violence of the refinery's explosion had eclipsed her death throes. A blood price had to be paid for all their shipmates and the Angel squadrons were reaping it in the blood of these damned aliens.

Erin Harlen's Fury looped overhead, the bombs on his centre pylon pickling off in sequence to impact in a string of detonations that merged into one continuous roar.

Morten rolled his Fury, screaming back across the trenches below and checking that his two wingmen were still on station with him. High above, Lightning interceptors looped in lunatic acrobatics with packs of gargoyles, their pilots keeping the flying creatures busy while they delivered their explosive payloads. Even a cursory glance told him that the Lightnings would not be able to hold the flocks of aerial killers off their backs for much longer.

He thumbed the vox-link on his control column.

'We're going in again,' he said. 'Low altitude strafing run. Follow on my lead.'

'Captain,' warned Kiell Pelaur, his gunnery officer, 'we're all out of missiles. We don't have anything left to drop.'

'I know, lieutenant. Switching to guns.'

Morten pushed the nose of the aircraft towards the ground, the swarm rushing towards him through the canopy. The shuddering of the airframe increased and a red light flashed on the panel before him as the proximity alarms shrieked as the Fury's altitude dropped to a mere thirty metres. Flying at such height required the steadiest of hands on the stick, as the slightest error would smear the Fury across the ice.

But the commander of the Angel squadrons was amongst the best pilots the *Kharloss Vincennes* battlegroup could put in the air and his control was second only to that of Erin Harlen. The tyranids rushed towards them, plumes of ice crystals foaming in the wake of the screaming Furies.

Captain Morten pulled the trigger on his control column, sending lancing bolts of energy from the Fury's lascannon into the horde. Explosions of blood and ice tore through them as the powerful weapon fired again and again. Morten screamed as he fired, feeling the burning desire to kill every single one of these abominations in one fell swoop. He pictured a blooming red fireball, the destruction he could achieve by simply letting go of the Fury and allowing her a final, glorious death in the heat of battle.

Another red light began blinking as the last energy cell for the lascannon was ejected from the Fury's underside and the frequency of the proximity alarm rose to a shrill new height.

'Captain!' screamed Pelaur, 'Pull up! For the Emperor's sake pull up!'

Pelaur's shout snapped Morten from his visions of death and he took a deep breath, pulling back and hauling the Fury into a looping climb.

'Imperator, captain! That was some real close flying,' breathed Pelaur. 'That's the kind of thing I expect from Harlen.'

Captain Owen Morten didn't reply, picturing a giant valedictory explosion.

PAVEL LEFORTO FIRED into the mass of aliens, terrified beyond thought at the scale of what he was seeing. Giant monsters lumbered through the charging mass of beasts, their snapping talons bigger than the claws on the lifting rigs that hauled girders in the smeltery.

The alien advance had faltered about ten metres from the trenches, the smooth ice coating the snow berm defeating their attempts to close the final gap. But already the smaller beasts were chopping into the ice to pull themselves closer. They died in droves, but following creatures used the corpses to push even closer. The advance had stalled, but it had granted the Imperial forces only the briefest of respites.

The noise of battle was tremendous: roaring guns, explosions, screaming and the inhuman rasping of the tyranids. A huge mushroom cloud erupted in the centre of the aliens as the Capitol Imperialis fired again, throwing ice and alien bodies hundreds of metres into the air.

The platoon briefings told him to shoot at the larger tyranid creatures, the sergeants claiming that this would disrupt the smaller beasts. Quite how that would work was a mystery to him, but he had spent his entire adult life obeying orders and wasn't about to stop now.

He ejected a spent power cell and slotted home a fresh one with trembling hands. Raising the rifle to his shoulder, he sighted along the barrel at a towering monster with a flaring bone crest rising from the back of its skull. Powerful, clawed arms held a long gristly tube that dripped slime, and surrounding the monster were dome-skulled creatures with bony protuberances growing from their upper limbs. He aimed a shot at the largest creature's skull, his bolt ricocheting from the thick fringe of bone. A missile streaked from behind him towards the giant monster, exploding against the bony growths of one its chitinous protectors.

Realising there wasn't much he could do to scratch this monster, he switched targets as a hissing alien, having finally climbed the carpet of dead, planted its claws in the top of the snow berm. He shot it full in the face, blowing its head off and leaving its body anchored to the trench by its long talons.

Soldiers all around him fired frantically into the masses of aliens, knowing that to survive they had to prevent them from reaching their lines.

But Pavel could already see they wouldn't succeed.

URIEL SLASHED HIS sword through a hormagaunt's midsection and kicked another's head from its shoulders as it clawed its way over the snow berm. Beside him, Pasanius's flamer seared a clutch of aliens as they attempted to scale their dead. Snow and ice steamed in the heat and droplets of promethium melted small holes in the ice.

Uriel saw a brace of monsters drop into the trench further along the line and shouted to Pasanius, 'With me, sergeant!'

He dropped from the firing step and sprinted towards the breach in the lines, firing his bolt pistol as he ran. The explosive shells blasted apart a handful of the creatures and he burst amongst the rest like a thunderbolt, slashing left and right with furious strokes of his power sword. Aliens died by the score as the two Space Marines smashed their way through their hissing bodies.

Claws scraped at their armour, their speed blinding, but these warriors were the very best of the Emperor's soldiers and none of the aliens' blows could halt them. Uriel felt ancestral hatred of these beasts pound in his veins as he slew, attacking, always attacking, with no thought to his own defence.

A pack of hormagaunts landed atop him, driving him to his knees. Chitinous claws hammered his armour, one penetrating the joint of his breastplate and hip. Blood burst from the wound, clotting instantly as his enhanced bloodstream formed a protective layer over the tear in his flesh. He rolled, crushing several of the beasts beneath his weight and thrashed like a madman to dislodge the others. He slammed his elbow downwards, feeling bone break, and swung his arm in a wide circle, leaving severed alien limbs and opened bellies in the wake of his blade.

He clambered to his feet, spinning with his sword raised as he felt a powerful grip encircle his arm. He roared in hate, diverting his stroke at the last second as he saw Pasanius before him, hammering his sword into the packed snow of the trench wall.

Pasanius ducked past Uriel and poured a tongue of fire down the length of the trench from his flamer. Duckboards caught light and aliens screeched as the fire consumed them. More were pouring over the top of the berm and dropping into the trench.

The Space Marines turned and fought with all the skill and ferocity the Adeptus Astartes were famed for, shrugging off blows that would have killed a normal man twice over and fighting beyond the limits of courage and endurance.

Then the tide of smaller beasts parted and a giant beast with massive clawed arms stomped across the mass of dead aliens towards them. Three metres tall, the warrior organism was all rippling armour plates and glistening organs, layered beneath a bony exo-skeleton coated with an encrusted layer of fatty tissue. Its jaw opened, letting loose a terrifying screech as its scythe-taloned arms raised to strike. A drooling bio-weapon spat a phlegmy wad of slime.

Uriel dived aside, the sparkling slime blasting a huge chunk of ice from the wall behind him. He sprang to his feet as the monster smashed its way through the snow berm, standing at the lip of the trench. He fired his last remaining bolts at the huge creature, blowing off chunks of its chitinous armour, but failing to stop its murderous progress. Pasanius bathed the creature in fire, the insulating fat on its bones sizzling and filling the trench with a disgusting odour. Dozens of hormagaunts followed in its steps.

Uriel leapt to meet the monster, swinging his power sword at its thorax. A bladed limb swept down, blocking the blow as another slammed into his breastplate, cracking the ceramite and knocking him from his feet. He rolled with the blow and dove around the side of the beast, hacking his blade through its legs just above its giant hooves. The beast howled in pain, crashing to its knees and toppling forwards into the trench where it lay thrashing its clawed arms impotently.

Pasanius fought the hormagaunts back as yet more poured through the gap their larger sibling had battered.

'Captain!' bellowed Pasanius.

'I know!' shouted Uriel, leaping onto the bucking monster's back. The giant tyranid beast struggled to right itself, but Uriel reversed the grip of his sword and drove the blade downwards through its skull.

Instantly its motion ceased and Uriel roared as he ripped his blade free in an arc of black blood. He jumped from the monster's back as Pasanius cut his way through the suddenly dazed-looking hormagaunts. Uriel and his sergeant didn't give the disorientated creatures time to recover their wits, hacking them down without mercy.

Uriel killed them without pity, hating them for driving him to this frenzy of slaughter. His blade rose and fell, its surface coated with blood as he waded in alien gore. The battle around him receded until he could see nothing beyond the death that surrounded him, the blood and the sudden fear of creatures that had no will of their own, having had the blanket of connection stripped away from them.

Thunderous footfalls shook him from his reverie of blood. He saw Pasanius hurled through the air and the shadow of another gigantic monster rear up through the mist of ice and blood.

Larger than a dreadnought, the carnifex shrieked with a rasping of plates deep in its shark-like maw. Its carapace was battered and cracked, alien blood pouring from numerous wounds punched through its body. Rearing up, it blocked the sun and four massively clawed arms reached towards him.

Then its jaw opened wider still and an emerald green torrent of bio-plasmic fire vomited from inside it.

Uriel threw up his arms to ward off the energised plasma, but the force of the alien's discharge smashed him to the ground.

He fought to stand, the hissing green ichor coating his visor and rendering him blind. He lashed out with his sword, feeling it bite through alien flesh.

The ground shook as the carnifex towered over him and Uriel felt the heat of its breath on his face.

ASTADOR FELT HIS grip on his ghost-self slip as he neared the cold fire at the centre of the swarm's mind. A giant presence like the chill at the heart of a glacier bathed his soul in ice-water and he could feel its presence echo from the sides of the valley like a cavern-deep river. This was it, this was the control, this was the heart of the cold mind.

He could sense its awareness only as a fragment of something unimaginable vaster, and deep on the edges of its perception, he knew that it too was aware of him. Cold ripples of horror reached for him, but his ghost-self was already returning to his body.

Astador opened his eyes and smoothly rose to his feet.

The warriors who had loaned him their strength did likewise and he blinked as his normal sight restored itself. All around him battle raged, but he felt disconnected from it, his spirit resisting the imprecations of flesh and the limitations that imposed.

Mortifactors and members of the Deathwatch battled the tyranids all around them, fighting to keep the alien creatures from breaking his trance.

Captain Bannon marched towards him, his armour bloody.

'Well?' he asked. 'Do you know?'

'I know,' said Astador.

PAVEL HURLED HIS last grenade into the mass of creatures, ducking as the concussive force of the detonation dislodged a section of the trench. He had passed beyond fear now, acting simply on adrenaline and training. So many things had happened to him that he could not function were fear to take hold. His body's own sense of self-preservation clamped down on his fear and drove him ever onwards.

He shot, stabbed and hacked his way through the alien creatures, scavenging whatever munitions and weaponry he could find when his own ran out. He tripped, rolling over the dissolving corpses of two soldiers wearing Krieg greatcoats, slamming his face against the cold steel of their fallen weapon. Hissing slime ate away their flesh and Pavel recoiled, spitting blood as he pushed himself upright.

Jade light lit up the trench and he saw a hulking monster with a vividly patterned carapace smash its way through the trench barricades, green fire spewing from between toothed mandibles. Dozens of hissing beasts gathered behind the massive creature, ready to pour into the trench. An Ultramarines sergeant lay unconscious on the snow and the same captain who had saved his life from the gargoyles sprawled in a steaming pool of the creature's green fire.

Pavel acted without thinking and lifted the Krieg gunners' weapon onto his shoulder, praying that they had loaded the missile launcher before they'd died.

URIEL SCRAMBLED BACKWARDS, desperately wiping hissing bio-plasma from his visor.

He looked up and saw death in the black eyes of the carnifex. They were black, lidless and devoid of life, like a doll's. He felt the wall of the trench at his back and knew there was nowhere else to go.

His sword arm came up, but he knew it was too late.

Then a blistering streak flashed through his vision and struck the carnifex square in the centre of its skull. A powerful shockwave buffeted Uriel and he felt bony shrapnel spray him. As the echoes of the explosion faded, he looked up through the cloud of smoke at the massive organism and saw that its head had vanished, leaving nothing but a charred blood basin, oozing brain and skull fragments.

The carnifex swayed for a second until its body registered the fact that it was dead and its knees buckled. The massive creature collapsed and Uriel rolled aside as it fell, the impact throwing up blood-streaked bio-plasma and ice.

Further along the trench he caught sight of a soldier with the insignia of the Erebus Defence Legion stencilled on his helmet, a smoking missile launcher cradled on his shoulder.

He pushed himself to his feet as a tide of hormagaunts poured through the gap bludgeoned by the carnifex.

Raising his sword, he leapt to meet them.

PAVEL TOSSED ASIDE the smoking missile launcher and swiftly rolled over one of the Krieg gunners, searching for more weapons. He unholstered the man's laspistol and drew his sword from a wide scabbard. The blade was toothed and heavy, and Pavel recognised a chainsword, though he had never used such a weapon before.

He searched for an activation stud, finding it on the base of the pommel, and the sword roared into life, the toothed blade spinning like a chainsaw. He rose and sprinted to where the Ultramarines captain was desperately fending off a horde of beasts that were pouring into the trenches.

He swung the heavy chainsword, feeling the blade judder as it tore through alien bones and sprayed him with alien fluids. He fired into the mass of creatures, blasting another to death and ripping his sword free in the same instant.

Pavel fought without the skill of the Ultramarines captain, but his fear and the desire to protect his home empowered him with fury and courage.

Together he and the Space Marine captain fought the aliens like heroes of legend. His arm ached from swinging the sword and he switched to using it two-handed when the laspistol ran out of charge.

He hacked a screeching beast in half as another giant figure in blue armour joined him and the captain, a sergeant with a gleaming silver arm. He grinned as he killed another alien, picturing the stories he'd be able to tell Hollia and Solan when this was all over.

He tried to pull the chainsword free from the creature's chest, but the toothed blade was jammed in its bony exo-skeleton. He desperately tugged again as another monster bounded over the trench barricade.

Its claws slashed for his head and he swayed aside.

But not quickly enough as a scything blade hammered into his helmet, tearing it from his head. A lower set of clawed limbs stabbed at him, tearing through his overwhites and hot pain shrieked along his nerve endings. Blood sprayed from the wound and he collapsed, feeling gore-melted snow slam into his face.

Pavel rolled, drawing his war-knife and, through a blur of red water and tears of pain, raised it in time to skewer the beast's throat as it leapt at him. It claws scrabbled at him as it died. Pavel wrenched the knife upwards, impaling its skull on the blade.

Releasing the knife, he weakly pushed himself to his feet, using the side of the trench for support. His vision swam and he felt his legs turn to water as a wave of sick dizziness swamped him. He numbly peeled the sodden fabric of his torn overwhites from his shoulder. Sticky blood oozed wetly from a deep gash and a glistening black claw was wedged in the cut. Strange, he thought dreamily.

His wound didn't seem to hurt. There was no pain.

He wondered why, but was saved from the answer by collapsing, face first, into the bloody snow.

He was unconscious before he hit the ground.

URIEL RAN THROUGH the twisting passages of the trench, racing towards where he could see a group of black armoured warriors mounting up in five Rhino armoured personnel carriers. Colonel Rabelaq was feeding in reserves from the second trench to stabilise the front and yet more troops were moving up from the third line. The defences were holding, but only just. If the tyranids kept up this ferocious assault, then it was only a matter of time until the front line was breached.

He vaulted mounds of the dead, hurrying past desperate combats to reach the southern salient, where the Rhinos growled as the drivers gunned the engines. He could see Captain Bannon of the Deathwatch and the bone-rimmed armour of Chaplain Astador as he made his way through his kneeling men, administering the Mortis Astartes blessing to each one.

Captain Bannon rose to his feet as he caught sight of Uriel approaching, and moved to intercept him.

'What are you doing?' demanded Uriel.

'What must be done to hold the line,' answered Bannon, blocking Uriel's route.

'You are taking the fight to the aliens, aren't you?'

'Yes. Chaplain Astador has located the beast he believes is controlling this element of the tyranid swarm.'

'What? How?'

'The spirits of his ancestors have guided him to it.'

'Are you serious?'

'Deadly serious,' stated Bannon. 'I trust his judgement on this implicitly.'

Uriel was stunned. To hear a brother Space Marine place such faith in ritual and superstition was beyond belief, but it was happening right here in front of him. He wondered what Idaeus would do.

Uriel nodded, his expression hardening. 'Very well then, I'm coming with you.'

Bannon's eyebrows arched. 'Really?'

'Aye. If we can end this now, then you'll need all the help you can get.'

Bannon searched Uriel's face for any sign of an ulterior motive, but finding none, slapped a palm on his shoulder guard and said, 'So be it. Find a transport and let's go.'

Uriel jogged towards the Rhinos and, realising there would be no room for him inside, clambered onto the roof of the nearest one. Its every panel was black, fastened with rivets stamped with tiny brass skulls and a grinning skull topped each exhaust, blue oilsmoke jetting from each jaw. The engine roared and Uriel gripped the edge of the roof as the rest of the Mortifactors and seven members of the Deathwatch climbed aboard the five transports.

The Rhino spun as the tracks fought for purchase on the slushy ground, before lurching forward as they finally bit. Thick timbers had been laid across the trench and the Rhino reared upwards as it hit the edge of the snow berm, slamming down hard onto the ice on the other side. Uriel's Rhino took the lead at the head of a wedge of transports, crushing those aliens not quick enough to get out of the way.

Alien screeches rose to new heights as they reacted to the interlopers in their midst, and a section of the swarm smoothly altered the direction of its charge to intercept the Rhinos. Scores of bounding, clawed monsters drew close and Uriel pulled himself along the roof as the front hatch opened and a warrior of the Mortifactors pulled himself up to man the pintle-mounted storm bolter. He snapped back the action and checked that it was equipped with a full load, before pulling the trigger and working the bucking weapon left and right, clearing a path for the Rhino to follow.

Uriel hung on for dear life as the Rhino swayed crazily through the aliens, gripping his sword in his other hand as the vehicles crushed a path towards a monstrous, humped creature lurking in the centre of the swarm. Its glistening, segmented body rippled with motion and, even from here, Uriel could feel a sickening sense of dread permeate his soul as the Rhino drew nearer.

A flash of gleaming claws brought him back to the present with a jolt as a hormagaunt leapt from the swarm towards him. He brought his sword up in the nick of time, hacking the creature in two with one sweep.

The Rhino's speed was dropping. Dozens of beasts clambered across the vehicle's hull as it sped closer to its objective, alien bodies clogging the tracks and allowing others to climb over them to reach the prey on top.

Uriel stabbed and slashed with his sword, keeping the monsters from reaching the gunner who continued spraying bolts into the mass of creatures. Wind whipped by him as the Rhino ploughed onwards.

An explosion behind him rocked the vehicle with its force. He risked a glance over his shoulder, seeing the second Rhino burning fiercely, bright flames leaping from its ruptured hull. Blazing Space Marines stumbled from the wreck, still fighting as they burned. Hissing creatures surrounded them and soon the warriors were lost to sight as hundreds of clawing, biting creatures buried them beneath their bodies.

Uriel looked to see where the shot had come from, and saw a grotesque monster drifting above the ice, its long, sinuous tail whipping beneath its bulbous head. Withered limbs hung uselessly beneath its hissing maw and a crackling haze surrounded the rippling frill of skin beneath its armoured skull.

As though sensing his scrutiny, the monster hissed, slowly turning its unnatural gaze towards the speeding Rhino. Uriel leaned forwards and rapped his fist across the shoulder guard of the gunner.

'One o'clock!' he yelled, jabbing his sword towards the floating beast.

The gunner nodded, and the storm bolter roared, spitting a hurricane of mass-reactive bolts at the monster. Uriel saw a firefly blossom of purple light flare around the creature and cursed as he saw that the volley had left it unharmed. Almost immediately, a flaring corona of psychic energy built around the creature's head, and Uriel gripped the edge of the Rhino, realising what would come next.

A bolt of pure white light streaked from the creature's overlarge head, slamming into the front of the Rhino. Uriel was hurled from his perch by the impact. He sailed through the air, just barely grabbing onto the edge of the roof panel, his feet scrabbling for purchase on the running boards.

The Rhino slewed sideways, but its recently blessed armour held firm against the abomination's attack. Ichor-slick ice hurtled beneath Uriel's feet as he fought for grip.

A screeching creature leapt for him and he kicked out as yet more hormaguants closed in. He lashed out with his feet and sword, breaking bones and splitting skulls.

Finally gaining his balance, he sheathed his sword and swung himself back onto the roof as he felt the Rhino veer off to the side. Uriel knew that they would not be lucky enough to survive another blast from the warp creature and as he looked up, he realised that the Rhino's driver had reached the same conclusion.

The floating beast was directly before them, drifting backwards in an attempt to get clear, but there was no escape as the Rhino's spiked bull bar slammed into its withered body and dragged it beneath the armoured tracks of the transport. Uriel heard a satisfying crack as it was crushed beneath the weight of the vehicle, seeing the giant stain on the ice of its crushed carcass as the Rhino drove onwards.

Their charge had been broken up, but the four surviving Rhinos were now within striking distance of their prey. From his vantage point on the Rhino's roof, Uriel could see a swirling motion amongst the swarm as its leader alerted its minions to the danger. With a precision unseen except on the parade ground, whole swathes of the alien beasts altered direction, abandoning their attack on the trenches to come to the aid of their master.

Gunfire from the Rhinos hammered the disgusting beast, its antlered head retreating within its carapace as bolts exploded all around it. Crackling energies flared from its head and the sense of dread Uriel had felt earlier grew stronger still. His innate horror at this creature threatened to overwhelm him with its alien otherworldliness, until thoughts of the Bringer of Darkness surged, unbidden, into his mind, and the sheer evil of its existence made him laugh at the insignificance of this creature.

Guardian warrior organisms rushed to the alien's defence as the Rhinos skidded to a halt beside the lumbering beast and the Space Marines debarked with speed and precision. Uriel leapt feet first from the roof of his transport, hammering into the face of the closest monster. He felt fangs snap under his boots and rolled to his feet.

He stabbed his glowing sword through its bloody head and charged across the snow to face the next beast. Giant claws scythed towards him and he dived beneath them, aiming a gigantic, disembowelling sweep at the organism's belly. Black blood sprayed and its alien screech was cut short as Uriel hammered his blade through its neck.

More creatures closed in around him as he fought his way towards the giant master of the horde. Claws and razor-edged hooves bludgeoned him, but he cared not for the pain as a dark mist closed on his sight and he hacked about him, severing limbs and opening bellies in his frenzied charge.

He could hear a roar of animal hate and spun, searching for the source of such an atavistic howl, before realising that it was his own. Shocked at his loss of control, the battle snapped into a slow-moving ballet of utter clarity. He could see the Mortifactors forming a cordon around the seven members of the Deathwatch who jammed melta charges into the flesh of the thrashing, segmented body of the swarm leader.

And he could see the soulless, black eyes of the monster as it realised its doom was at hand. Even as he watched, its horned, beetle-like head surged from its carapace and hammered into his chest, digging deep and lifting him high into the air. A massive, toothed orifice opened beneath its horns and Uriel was powerless to prevent himself from sliding into its fanged maw. He gripped its bony horns with one hand and desperately tried to pull himself free.

The monster's eyes rolled back as a nictitating membrane blinked and the orifice closed on his body. He felt the fangs bite into his armour, and knew that the incredible strength of the beast would soon break open its toughened plates. Uriel spun his sword, holding it blade downwards.

He felt fangs pierce his flesh. Blood flowed.

He stabbed the blade into the beast's chitin-plated skull, roaring as he drove it into its brain as a dazzling brightness suddenly lit up the world.

Sudden, intense heat flared as the Deathwatch's melta bombs detonated, and he could feel the death-grip on his body relax. The snowy ground rushed up to meet him and he grunted as he slammed into the

ice. A deathly silence fell across the valley and even Uriel could feel a
keening sense of loss rip through the tyranid swarm.

Swiftly he cut himself free of the giant tyranid beast's maw and dragged
his legs from the glutinous, sucking orifice. He felt a hand on his shoulder
and pushed himself to his feet in time to see Bannon and the rest of the
Space Marines backing away from the charred carcass of the monster
towards the Rhinos.

'Come on,' snapped Bannon, his tone angry. 'It is dead. We must get
away.'

'Aye,' gasped Uriel, staggering after the captain of the Deathwatch.

As he climbed inside the scorched and ichor-stained Rhino he felt nothing but shame as he pictured his frenzied, uncontrolled raging attack.

DARKNESS WAS SEVERAL hours old by the time the all clear sounded. With
the death of the swarm leader, the tyranid attack had foundered, the alien
creatures milling in panicked confusion as the controlling will was
stripped from the majority of them. Furious counterattacks from the Space
Marines and disciplined firing protocols soon despatched any remaining
creatures that still appeared capable of independent action and as the temperature dropped to twenty below freezing, most of the tyranids froze to
death where they stood.

Some survived by burrowing into the depths of the snow, where their
increased reserves of fat allowed them to enter a form of short-lived hibernation, but these were few and far between. There were not, however, the
resources to hunt them down as the subzero temperatures prohibited all
but the most essential movements among the defenders.

Such a manoeuvre was even now being undertaken as the Imperial
forces retreated to the second trench line. Realising that the first line would
not hold against another attack, Colonels Stagler and Rabelaq had decided
to pull back on the heels of what was being promoted as a great victory.

But with aerial reconnaissance promising yet more incoming swarms, at
least triple the size of this vanguard, and each counting towering beasts
that rivalled the size of Battle Titans among their number, there were no
illusions among the high command that this victory was anything other
than a stay of execution.

ELEVEN

A BLUE GLOW filled the command bridge of the Capitol Imperialis, throwing the faces of the command staff into stark relief. Hooded servitors sat immobile before their consoles, insulated bundles of cables snaking from the backs of their robes to sockets in the grilled floor. A lilting chant of imprecations to the machine god drifted from bronze speakers on the ceiling. Sputtering recyc-units tried to keep the atmosphere cool, but the temperature in the command bridge was still stifling.

Uriel did not like being in this armoured leviathan: it ill-suited the Space Marine way of war to be so static and the Codex Astartes frequently pointed out the need for mobility on the battlefield. But recently he had paid little more than lip service to the teachings of his primarch's holy tome. Learchus had made no secret of his disapproval of Uriel's helter-skelter journey on the roof of a Mortifactors' Rhino, claiming it was a foolish stunt more in keeping with the Sons of Russ than a proud Ultramarine, and Uriel was inclined to agree with him.

He shook his head clear of the memory and returned his attention to matters at hand.

The situation was not good.

A holo-map with a rippling green representation of the landscape surrounding Erebus filled the centre of the columned chamber, grainy static washing through the image every few seconds. Information received from various sources fed into the display, picking out Imperial units and positions of incoming swarms. Colonel Rabelaq stood at the end of the map, flanked by his aides and adjutants, while Uriel and Colonel Stagler stood on one side of the map with Chaplain Astador and Captain Bannon on the other.

'It appears that Hera's Gate and Parmenis have both fallen,' began Rabelaq. 'We've been unable to raise Imperial forces in either one of them, and the squadron of Lightnings we sent to obtain visual reports on Konoris and Inyiriam have failed to return. We must assume that the forces that destroyed them are now inbound on our position.'

'And what of the forces that are already moving towards us?' asked Stagler, still wearing his Krieg greatcoat and colback despite the heat.

Rabelaq didn't answer immediately, his consternation evident. 'Ah, well, that we're not sure of. It appears a great many of them have scattered or gone to ground, and we're assuming that they've burrowed into the snow for shelter, as animals are wont to do in winter, to await the arrival of the other swarms. A great many of our reconnaissance assets have already been lost and I felt it would be unwise to lose any more for what would in all likelihood not gain us much more information than we already know.'

Stunned silence greeted his pronouncement, before Bannon leaned over the map and said, 'It is a mistake, Colonel Rabelaq, to assume that these aliens will behave like animals, and if there is one thing I have learned about the tyranids, it is that you do not want to let them out of your sight, even for a second.'

'Yes, well, that's as maybe, Captain Bannon, but if you look at the map, you'll see that we have three distinct swarms of creatures closing on our position. Originally, the southernmost swarm would have reached us first, but it appears as though it has altered the speed of its advance so that all three will arrive together.'

'Clever,' mused Astador, 'very clever. They have learned that we can defeat one swarm, and gather to overrun in one massive charge.'

Uriel watched the icons on the holo-map crawl slowly across the flickering representation of the surface of Tarsis Ultra. Something nagged at the back of his mind, but he could not put his finger on what. He knew it was something simple, but of great import.

'And what is happening in space?' asked Captain Bannon. 'Have we been able to make contact with the fleet?'

Uriel said, 'The Shadow in the Warp is still making astropathic communication impossible, but we have been able to make brief contact with Lord Admiral Tiberius over the long-range vox-caster. Communications are still very fragmentary and we are having trouble maintaining the link through the electromagnetic interference generated by the hive fleet.'

'And what is his situation?' said Astador.

'The admiral has the fleet at anchor around the agri-world of Calydon, though he tells me that a great many vessels are heavily damaged.'

'Have the tyranids not tried to engage him?' asked Bannon.

'Not in any strength, no. It would appear that there are only two hive ships remaining in orbit, so the aliens do not have the capability to effectively control their forces here and despatch an expeditionary force to destroy the fleet.'

Bannon asked, 'Then is the fleet in any shape to offer us support?'

'Potentially,' said Uriel. 'Admiral Tiberius has suggested a plan of attack, but I need to confer with the Fabricator Marshal before expounding further on this. For the moment, no, we are on our own.'

Heads nodded around the map table as each commander digested Uriel's information.

'Then, in short, gentlemen, we have no other choice but to pull back behind the city walls,' said Rabelaq. 'The trenches simply can't hold against these numbers. The walls will prevent the smaller brood organisms from attacking and we have ample guns positioned there to pick off the larger beasts.'

'I agree with Colonel Rabelaq,' said Astador. 'We must accept that the city will suffer under the attack. Better to fight on our terms than theirs.'

Reluctantly, Colonel Stagler nodded, though Uriel could see it irked him to give ground, even when it would be suicide to stand and fight.

'The Krieg regiment will provide the rearguard for the retreat,' he said, almost spitting the words. Uriel looked at the map again and suddenly his nagging worry came to the fore of his mind.

'Were there not four swarms approaching us earlier?' he asked.

'Yes, Captain Ventris,' nodded Rabelaq, 'but we believe that the smaller northern swarm has simply merged with the one moving in from Parmenis. They were, after all, less than thirty kilometres apart.'

'Are you sure about that?' asked Uriel.

'Well, no, but where else could they be? The northern mountains are impenetrable, Fabricator Montante has assured me.'

'With all due respect to Fabricator Montante, he is not a soldier. Can we trust our security to the conclusions of a logistician?'

'He has local knowledge, Captain Ventris. Major Satria concurred also and having seen hololithic topography of the region in question, I am in agreement.'

Uriel could see the others around the room were alarmed at the prospect of a potentially missing swarm, but since there was no proof as to its existence, none had any answer as to what could be done about it.

'How long do we have before they reach us?' asked Bannon.

'Five, maybe six hours at most,' said Rabelaq.

'Then let's get to work,' said Stagler.

SNOW SWIRLED IN obscuring blizzards around the crumbling hab units of District Secundus, gathering in windblown drifts and deadening the sounds of the column of refugees that trudged through the knee deep white carpet that enveloped Erebus.

Displaced by the rain of organic bombs and those creatures whose cocoon spores were able to penetrate the flak umbrella protecting the city, nearly six hundred people trudged through the blizzard towards a nondescript collection of buildings constructed against the rocky sides of the southern slopes. Armed men stood watch at the splintered timbers barring the entrance and a ragged tarpaulin flapped behind them.

Since the first days of the tyranid attack, word had spread of the hero Snowdog who had saved the people of the Secundus shanties from the tide of alien beasts that dropped from the skies. That his reputation as a murderer and thief were well known was secondary to the fact that people said he had food and medical supplies.

The winters of Tarsis Ultra were harsh and those without wealth or dwellings would soon perish without shelter.

And there was a brutal killer on the loose somewhere in Erebus.

Even amid the chaos of an alien invasion, its depredations could not go unnoticed: small, isolated groups of citizens found butchered like livestock, their bodies hacked to pieces and their flesh devoured. Fear whipped through the poorest quarters of the city, and those that could not escape to the high valley, where the soldiers of the Fabricator Marshal patrolled the streets and thoroughfares where the monied citizens of Erebus dwelled, were forced to band together for mutual protection.

As the fear of this mysterious butcher grew, so too did its violence, as though the very terror it spawned drove it to new heights of slaughter. Whole communities were murdered in their homes and only the ruthlessly patrolled area around the territory of the Nightcrawlers seemed to escape the killer's attention.

For people with no hope, Snowdog was their only hope.

Papa Gallo, the unofficial but acknowledged leader of the group, pulled back his hood and approached the two men guarding the door. The shorter of the pair racked his shotgun and jammed it in his face.

'We've come for shelter from the monsters,' explained Papa Gallo.

'Shelter's not cheap,' came the muffled reply.

Pappa Gallo laughed, turning to face the wretched people behind him. 'Look at us. What do you think we can offer you? We don't have anything left.'

'Oh, I don't know,' laughed the other man, eyeing the younger women. 'What do you say, Lomax? I bet we could come to some arrangement with these good people.'

'Shut up, Trask,' said the man who had spoken first. 'That's for Snowdog to decide.'

Pappa Gallo sighed. They might live through this winter, but if they did, they would emerge more desperate than before.

DEEP IN THE shadows of the ruined habs, crouched beneath a buckled sheet of corrugated iron, a creature watched the column of refugees through multi-faceted eyes, scenting the fear and despair as coloured washes through its various senses. Its flesh rippled a silvery grey as its chameleonic scales mirrored the surfaces around it and, with a stealth surprising for such a large creature, it slipped away from its shelter.

Its reserves of fatty tissue were low and it would need to kill again to replenish them, the freezing temperatures of Tarsis Ultra almost too much for even its fearsome adaptive qualities to cope with.

Since its virtual hibernation in the grain silos of Prandium, the beast, a species known by Imperial troops as a spook or mantis stalker, but more correctly as a lictor, smoothly loped across the snow to shadow the shambling people. It leapt onto the wall of a crumbling brick building, powerful intercostal muscles lashing fleshy barbs towards the top of the wall, which retracted to pull the beast rapidly up the sheer surface.

Long scythe-like claws unsheathed from chitinous hoods on its upper arms and dug into the wall as it smoothly swung its muscled bulk onto the roof.

Worm-like tendrils surrounding its jaw scented the air, and the beast set off again, following the column of refugees from on high.

Pheromone sacs situated along the ridge of its armoured spine atomised powerful attractants that would serve to lure more tyranid creatures to this place. Thus far it had roamed the city unmolested, careful to avoid the many dangers in such a heavily populated place.

But now the overmind, for whom it had travelled far ahead, was upon this place and it could afford to throw off its stealthy mantle and kill with all the ferocity it had been bred for.

The lictor stalked to the edge of the roof, squatting on its haunches as it watched a figure detach from the column and approach a building that stank of prey.

TRASK LET LOMAX do the talking as his eyes roamed over the women, though it was hard to spot the lookers thanks to the winter clothing most were wearing. He rested his shotgun on his shoulder and wondered again how the hell Snowdog had managed to pull one over on all these people. One moment of foolish altruism had spread the word throughout the city that he was running some kind of refuge from the cold and the aliens.

It made Trask want to laugh fit to burst at the thought of how wrong people could be. Those that had been allowed to stay were paying through the nose for everything they needed: shelter, food and even basic medical supplies. Some wanted narcotics, an escape from the terror, and that was available too. Also at a price. And if someone couldn't pay with hard currency or in valuables, then there were always other ways. A man with a comely wife or daughter could obtain things a single man could not, and amongst Snowdog's gang, there were plenty willing to accept that currency.

Snowdog had put a stop to that because it didn't bring any profit, which hadn't stopped Trask of course, he'd just had to become more circumspect.

In a group this size there was sure to be some money to be made and a few fillies to pluck. As he was contemplating the prospect of fresh conquests, a blur of motion caught his eye atop the smashed ruins of the old munitions factory. He raised a hand, squinting against the glare and through the flurries of snow.

What the hell was that?

He couldn't see anything now, but he was sure his eyes weren't playing tricks on him.

There! There it was again! Something dropped from the roof of the building, landing in a snowdrift with a piercing shriek. Whatever it was, it moved like quicksilver, charging into the mass of refugees before he could shout a warning. He brought his shotgun down and racked the slide as the screaming began.

Bright arcs of blood sprayed the snow and Trask caught sight of a neatly severed head fly across the street. Screams of terror echoed from the side of the valley as people scattered from the deadly killer in their midst. Trask saw a clear space form around a collection of gory rags that only superficially resembled human remains. A blurred creature pounced from the bloodbath onto the back of man carrying a swaddled infant.

The man went down in a tangle of limbs as a giant set of bony claws stabbed downwards, skewering him to the street. His death cry made Trask flinch in terror.

The thing moved fast, darting through its feast of victims and eviscerating anyone within reach of its claws.

Papa Gallo grabbed Trask's long coat and shouted, 'You've got a gun damn you, use it!'

The old man's hands shook him from his paralysis. Trask punched the old man away and stepped onto the road. He levelled his shotgun. Screaming people streamed past, too many to stop and he let them go, figuring Snowdog could sort out this mess later.

Lomax joined him. 'What the hell is it?' he yelled.

'Damned if I know,' replied Trask as more and more people buffeted him. A knot of people trying to escape down a side street were brutally hacked down by the murderous assailant and Trask levelled his shotgun as he saw the murderer clearly for the first time. Its hide was slathered in blood and gore and whatever chameleonic properties it might once have had were now rendered moot.

It stood on two legs, nearly three metres tall, its body powerfully muscled and ridged with bony armour plates. It was bigger than any of the beasts Trask had seen so far and its upper claws were gargantuan, hooking blades that clove people in two with each swipe. Beneath those monstrous claws, muscular arms ending in fierce, taloned fists lifted shrieking victims to its fang-filled jaws.

It spun quickly, its stock of victims exhausted, moving rapidly across the icy ground towards him and Lomax.

Suddenly he was struck by the absurdity of what he was doing. Why the hell was he risking his neck for these dumb people?

He turned tail and sprinted back for the warehouse as the beast charged.

Lomax spun and shouted, 'Where the hell–' as Trask ran, but was cut off as something shot from between the bony plates of the creature's chest and punched clean through his body. Lomax dropped his gun and stared in shocked disbelief at the barbs protruding from his chest before being yanked off his feet and stabbed to death by the monster's claws.

Trask ran like he'd never run before, tossing aside his gun, arms pumping. He took the steps to the warehouse two at a time, slipping on the ice on the top step and falling face first onto the concrete.

It saved his life. Gigantic blade talons smashed through the wall of the warehouse where his head would have been. He whimpered in fear, rolling aside as the talons came at him again, striking sparks from the ground as he desperately evaded the alien's attacks. He squeezed shut his eyes, feeling his bladder empty in naked terror.

A shotgun blast fired, deafeningly close, and he screamed. More gunshots sounded. A howling screech of pain echoed.

Something whipped by his face, a spatter of warm liquid splashed his face and neck. He curled into a ball and waited to die.

After long seconds, he plucked up the courage to open his eyes. The creature was gone, and relief washed over him. He wiped stinking slime from his face, looking up to see Snowdog and Silver staring down at him, disgust clear on their faces. Wisps of smoke curled from the barrel of Snowdog's shotgun and Silver had both her pistols drawn.

'Man, I don't know why the hell I keep you around,' snapped Snowdog, offering him a hand up. He smiled weakly at Silver, who didn't even deign to look at him, too busy taking in the horror of the massacre before them.

'Where's Lomax?' asked Snowdog.

Trask tried to answer but the words wouldn't come.

'I asked you a question, man,' said Snowdog.

'He's… he's gone,' managed Trask. 'That thing got him.'

'No thanks to you, I'll bet,' sneered Silver.

He tried to shoot her a venomous look, but it came off as merely petulant.

'Did you see what it was?' asked the albino-haired gang leader.

'No,' said Trask, shaking his head. 'I didn't, but it was big, man, real big. Bigger than anything we've seen. It was fast too, fast like on spur or something, you know?'

'It was fast all right,' shot back Silver, 'but not fast enough to catch you, eh, Trask?'

'Frag you, Silver,' said Trask, some of his cocksure attitude returning now that the monster was gone.

'Not this lifetime,' she said, spinning on her heel and heading back inside the warehouse.

'Get yourself cleaned up, Trask,' snapped Snowdog. 'We got work to do. These people ain't gonna get fleeced all by themselves, now are they?'

Snowdog turned and left him standing on the icy steps, the wetness in his crotch beginning to freeze.

Feeling his earlier fear turn to anger and resentment, Trask followed Snowdog inside, rubbing at a stinging patch of skin on his neck and face.

THE DOORS WERE emblazoned with the caduceus, a staff with two winged snakes entwined around it, and even before Uriel pushed them open he could hear screams and smell the stench of death and blood.

The walls of the District Quintus Medicae facility rang to the agonised cries of over a thousand wounded men, the reek of antiseptic sprays and camphorated oils unable to mask the bitter stench of infected flesh and weeping wounds. His breath misted before him, the temperature of the room close to freezing. Sisters of the Order Hospitaller scurried through the long, vaulted chamber, their flowing white robes stiffened with dried blood. The desperation and fear in this place was palpable and it tore at Uriel's heart to see so many brave men brought low by the vile aliens.

Shrieks of wounded men and sobs of those soon to go under the bone saw echoed. Three orderlies held down a screaming Krieg Guardsman, his legs nothing more than thrashing stumps, as they attempted to clamp the spray of blood from his femoral artery. Stretcher bearers passed Uriel, carrying a woman whose arm was severed just above the elbow and Uriel could see the wound had festered, no doubt frostbitten as she had lain awaiting rescue. The stump wept pus onto the rough blanket that covered her.

Droning priests chanted the *Finis Rerum* from high pulpits, but their words were inaudible over the screaming.

It seemed that the screaming would never stop. He watched one of the sisters pull a sheet over a dead man's face and nod to the orderlies. Uriel was no stranger to death, but this simple evocation of human suffering touched him in a way he could not explain.

The woman looked up from the corpse and saw him. She wiped a dirty sleeve across her eyes and limped around the bed towards him. Her blonde hair was pulled in a greasy ponytail and Uriel could see she had not slept in days. Her smoky blue eyes were dull and bloodshot, but she had strength in her, that much was obvious.

'Brother-captain,' she said. 'Sister Joaniel Ledoyen, senior nursing officer at your service, but we are sorely pressed, so whatever you need, please be quick.'

'Why is it so cold in here?' asked Uriel.

'Because one of those damned... things hit our generator before the first attack and the blasted tech-priests haven't been able to get us a new one,' snapped Joaniel. 'Now do you have any more stupid questions, or can I get on with trying to save some lives?'

'I am sorry, sister, I am weary from the battle and my manners escape me. I am Brother-Captain Uriel Ventris and I need to find a soldier I had brought here. His name is Pavel Leforto and he belongs to the Erebus Defence Legion. He saved my life and I wish to offer my thanks.'

Joaniel's expression softened and she pointed to a nurses' station in the centre of the chamber.

'There. My deputy, Ardelia, will try to find him for you, though you should be prepared for the fact that he may be dead.'

'As the Emperor wills,' said Uriel. The corner of the woman's mouth twitched at the familiar phrase and she nodded.

'Now, if you will excuse me, I have work to do,' she said and turned away.

Uriel watched Sister Joaniel Ledoyen limp towards the next bed and the next bloodstained soldier, then turned on his heel and marched to the nurses' station.

IT TOOK AN hour to locate Pavel Leforto. The bed Ardelia first indicated held only a pitiful wretch whose burned face was encased in gauze bandages, but was obviously not Pavel as his shoulder was uninjured. Eventually, Uriel located him on the second floor of the building, his upper shoulder and neck wrapped tightly in a plasflesh bandage. An intravenous drip bag was wedged under his arm – presumably to keep it from freezing – which in turn was draped outside the sheets to allow the liquid in the bag to flow.

His eyes were closed, but his breathing was deep and even. Even Uriel's limited knowledge of human physiology told him that Pavel Leforto would live, though he would have a vivid scar to remind him of his battle with the tyranids. Uriel remembered the last time he had seen Pavel's face, screaming and contorted in agony as Pasanius had rushed him back to the triage station. His features were at peace now, oblivious to the cries echoing from the floor below and the miasma of death that filled this place.

Clutched in the sleeping man's hand was a hololithic slate, and Uriel bent to lift it, seeing the image of a homely, but attractive woman with two beaming children clutched close to her. Uriel stared at the picture for several minutes, seeing the love these people had for this man through the grainy image. Pavel Leforto had a family to cleave to, a home to defend and a future to protect...

Things he could never have.

Replacing the picture, Uriel removed a purity seal from his armour and set it on Pavel's chest, before retreating from the bed, unwilling to disturb the wounded soldier's rest. He left the upper floor and made his way down to the medicae building's vestibule. Through a low arch to his left he saw a small passageway that led to an open doorway, from which a warm, softly glowing light spilled. He caught the soothing scent of incense over the stench of blood and stepped through the arch and into the medicae building's small chapel.

Simple and elegant, the chapel was spartanly furnished, the only concession to ostentation a semi-circular stained glass window depicting sisters of the Order Hospitaller ministering to the sick and providing alms to the needy. Uriel felt a peace and serenity he had not experienced in many months, as though a dark shadow that smothered the better angels of his nature could not violate this holy place.

He closed the door and walked to the end of the nave, bowing to the effigy of the Emperor and kneeling beneath His majestic gaze.

'Emperor of Mankind, in this time of war I seek the solace that only you can provide. Too often I feel hate poisoning my dreams. A darkness gathers in me and I fear for my soul in the coming days. Help me to overcome the taint that was placed within me and save me from becoming that which I have spent my entire life fighting in your name.'

Uriel took a shuddering breath and said, 'I am afraid that I may soon lose sight of what it is to serve you, that I am not worthy of your love.'

'No, Captain Ventris,' said a voice behind him. 'All who serve the Emperor are worthy of that.'

Uriel spun, rising to his feet. Sister Joaniel stood framed in the light from the window, the warm colours imparting a ruddy, healthy glow to her skin.

'Sister,' said Uriel. 'I did not notice you.'

'I know, I'm sorry for disturbing you. Would you like me to go?'

'No, no, of course not.'

'Then may I join you?'

'Yes, please do.'

Sister Joaniel nodded and limped to the end of the nave, genuflecting before the Emperor's statue and wincing as her hip joint cracked noisily. She sat on the front pew and said, 'I often come here when I have time. It is very peaceful.'

'It is,' agreed Uriel moving to join her on the pew, dwarfing the Adepta Sororitas nurse. The timber creaked under his bulk. 'I felt as though a great weight might unburden itself from me here.'

'You carry a burden?' asked Joaniel.

Uriel did not answer, his eyes cast down at the polished wooden floor. Eventually he said, 'You heard what I was saying when you came in.'

'True, but I do not know what you were referring to. Would you like to talk about it? I have counselled a great many warriors who carried emotional wounds as well as physical. Trust me, it can be very cathartic to give voice to thoughts that trouble you.'

'I do not know, sister... I am... not good at expressing such things.'

'Does it have something to do with the soldier you came to see?'

'No, more to do with a monstrous alien I fought on a distant world.'

'What kind of alien, a tyranid?'

Uriel shook his head. 'No. To this day I am not exactly sure what it was. All I know is that it was an ancient creature, old when the galaxy was young, that lived for slaughter and revelled in murder. An inquisitor I knew called it the Bringer of Darkness, and such a name was aptly given, for it could reach into a man's thoughts and drag his basest instincts to the fore.'

Uriel's hands began to shake as he relived the battle beneath the world on Pavonis. 'I saw men rend and tear themselves apart in an orgy of bloodletting and I felt my own urge to kill driven to new heights that sicken me to this very day. Visions of madness and death surrounded the creature and when its mind briefly touched mine, I saw everything, all the slaughter in the universe, and it bathed my soul in blood.'

'But you defeated it?'

'After a fashion. We drove it away and lived to tell the tale, though what became of it, I do not know.'

'You are haunted by the things it showed you,' stated Joaniel.

'Aye,' nodded Uriel, placing his head in his hands. 'I close my eyes and all I see is blood, death and mutilation. When I fight, I can barely hold back the killing rages born from the taint of the Bringer of Darkness.'

'I do not pretend to understand the nature of this monstrous being, but I feel you are tormenting yourself needlessly, Uriel. To have your mind touched, however briefly, by something of such power is bound to leave scars. To believe otherwise is folly.'

Joaniel reached out and took Uriel's hand. 'Every injury, whether physical or psychological, leaves behind its mark and sometimes they come tumbling out like daemons in the dark. Scars heal, Uriel, but only if you let them.'

'You do not think I am tainted?'

Joaniel smiled. 'No, I do not, Uriel. The power of this Bringer of Darkness must have been prodigious, but you defeated it. Yes, it showed you the depths to which man can sully himself with blood and death, but such barbarity is in all of us. You must accept that aspect of yourself and understand that part of the Bringer of Darkness will always be with you. With acceptance will come release. That you feel such pain tells me you are not tainted.'

Uriel nodded, already feeling the shadow within him recede at Joaniel's words. The two sat in companionable silence for many minutes until the vox bead in his ear crackled into life and the clipped tones of Learchus said, 'Brother-Captain, your presence is required at the main wall.'

He stood, acknowledging the message and bowed to the seated woman. 'My thanks for your understanding, Sister Joaniel,' said Uriel. 'But I must go now.'

Joaniel pushed herself from the pew and offered him her hand. Uriel shook it, his gauntlet swallowing her delicate hand utterly.

'I am always here, Uriel, should you feel the need to talk some more.'

'Thank you, I should like that,' said Uriel, bowing once more and marching quickly from the chapel.

MOVING THOUSANDS OF men and machines along with their attendant supplies, munitions and vehicles was potentially a nightmare, but with the well-drilled provosts of Erebus directing the soldiers of the Imperial Guard, there were precious few snarl-ups on the roads leading back to the city.

A thousand men of the Krieg regiment manned the second line of trenches as the Logres regiment and the Erebus Defence Legion pulled out. Those supplies that could not be brought back within the city walls were torched, bright pyres burning in the late afternoon sun. Supply trucks ferried troops back to barracks within Erebus at an admirable speed, and high in his Capitol Imperialis, Colonel Rabelaq was satisfied that the evacuation of the trenches was proceeding about as well as could be expected.

But random chance and misfortune have always played a part in any military operation and two things were to happen that would cost the Imperial defenders greatly.

On the high road to the northern gate, trucks laden with ordnance for the tanks bounced along a road which had become heavily rutted due to the immense volume of traffic passing along it and a supply truck loaded with this volatile payload dropped into a pothole, bouncing out with a teeth rattling jolt. Whether one or more shells had a faulty fuse mechanism or a careless soldier had accidentally removed one of the arming pins would never be known, but as the shells clattered around inside, the truck suddenly exploded in a devastating fireball. Secondary blasts ripped apart what little remained of the truck as the full complement of ordnance cooked off in the heat and detonated in a string of concussive booms that obliterated the road and everything within a hundred and fifty metres. Those vehicles spared the horror of the blast halted, backed up for half a kilometre and trapped on a narrow road with little room to turn around and head for another gate.

As the provosts attempted to sort out the logjam of vehicles, a swirling black cloud, fully a kilometre wide, appeared on the horizon far to the east, swooping and screeching low over the peaks of the high valley. Warning sirens blared and the city's guns opened fire. Fearing they were under attack, many of the Imperial units immediately adopted a defensive posture, slamming down the hatches of their tanks and readying their weapons to fire.

In many cases, this undoubtedly saved their lives.

From the ridges of the northern mountain slopes, hundreds of tyranid organisms poured down the treacherous, rocky slopes to fall upon the strung-out Imperial forces.

Soon, fierce battles were raging before the city walls as a tide of alien killers, having traversed the supposedly impassable mountains, fell upon the unsuspecting Guardsmen.

Alien and human blood flowed in rivers as the two forces clashed.

But there was worse to come.

'OH, SWEET EMPEROR, no…' moaned Colonel Rabelaq as the images on the holo-map suddenly leapt forwards. Fresh enemy icons appeared on the northern mountains and he realised that Captain Ventris had been right to doubt Fabricator Montante's word regarding their impassability. Fear settled in his belly and the blood drained from his face. The tyranids had fooled them all. The calculus-logi of the Capitol Imperialis had projected the speed of the advancing swarms and assumed that they were moving at optimum speed. Naively, he had fallen to thinking the same thing, but as he watched the icons of the three swarms closing rapidly with Erebus, he realised that he had fatally underestimated the cunning of these aliens.

He rushed towards the vox-station, and grabbed the carved nalwood handset from the console.

'All Krieg units, be advised that the tyranids will be on you imminently! I repeat, the tyranids will be attacking your position within minutes! Get out of there now!'

'WHAT THE HELL are you talking about?' snapped Lieutenant Konarski, grabbing the headphones from the vox-operator and jamming them to his ear. His eyes widened as he heard the panicked voice of Colonel Rabelaq screaming for them to evacuate the trenches.

He tossed back the handset and ran to the trench periscope, pressing his face to the viewing plate. Biting back a curse he swung the scope from left to right and felt a cold band of iron close around his chest as he saw a tide of alien monsters hurtling towards their position.

'Shit,' said Konarski and unslung his lasgun from his shoulder.

He ran along the trench, shouting at his men to stand to.

'Sir!' called his vox-operator. 'We're not evacuating?'

Casting his gaze along the line of the trench and seeing other Krieg officers pushing their men onto the trench's firing step, he said, 'No, son, we're
not.'

'But Colonel Rabelaq's orders…'

'Damn Rabelaq!' snapped Konarski. 'We're the Death Korp of Krieg, son.
Did you think that was just a pretty name? We never retreat. We fight and
we die, that's the Krieg way.'

As TERRIFYING AS the first attacks on the trenches had been, they were but a
shadow of this assault. A massive, multi-limbed beast stamped forwards,
smashing giant craters in the ice as it charged. Steaming jets of scalding
acids sprayed from grotesque organic tubes slung beneath its massive jaws,
dissolving snow, ice and flesh in smoking conflagrations. Hundreds of
spines fired with monstrous muscular contractions hammered the
trenches, punching through metres of snow to skewer both men and tanks.

A boiling tide of creatures swarmed around the legs of the gargantuan
beast. Chitin-clad organisms with bony prows and curled forelimbs hurled
fleshy pods which burst in lethal sprays of razor-sharp bone and bio acids.
Slow moving, each creature excreted another organic missile as it slithered
across the ice.

Similarly bulky creatures, with fused, bony forelimbs that resembled
long, organic cannons spat crackling chitin shells that hammered the
retreating tanks with sprays of corrosive viruses and acids. Crackling electric energy leapt from the giant claws of thick, serpentine creatures that
hurtled across the ice, their rasping armoured hides throwing up clouds of
ice crystals in their wake.

But leading the charge, faster even than the multitude of ravening organisms that made up the bulk of the tyranid swarm, was a clutch of enormous
creatures that smashed their way forwards on gigantic claws that dragged
their bloated bodies across the ice with terrifying rapidity. Brood nests
pulsed with a grotesque peristaltic motion between the bony plates of their
hides and rippling muscle contractions hurled razor-edged spines towards
the trenches.

A dark cloud of gargoyles massed above the attacking aliens, a massive
black brood-mother moving amongst them, its monstrous wings flapping
ponderously as it descended towards the men of Krieg.

LIEUTENANT KONARSKI RETCHED as he pushed the dissolving remains of his
vox-operator from his legs to fall into a pool of smoking acids that melted
its way through the trench's duckboards. He tried to stand, but the acrid
stink of seared flesh doubled him in up with a fierce coughing fit. Blood
and smoke filled the trench as tyranid missiles burst around their shattered
defences. Here and there shots were returned, but it was a drop in the ocean
compared to the fire they were receiving.

Finally overcoming his nausea, he shouted, 'For Krieg!' and fired over the lip of the trench. A dark shadow blotted out the light from the sun and Konarski looked up in time to see a gigantic monstrosity with wings tens of metres wide swooping low towards the trenches. Scores of smaller beasts clung to its belly and a swirling fire built between its jaws.

He risked a glance over his shoulder to see why no one was shooting the damn thing down. As he saw the nearest Hydra he realised why.

Its frontal section was a molten, twisted mass, thick armour plating liquefied by corrosive viruses and acids. Gory slime oozed from the vehicle's interior, the disintegrating flesh of its crew steaming in the cold air. But Konarski saw the Hydra's gun section was still intact.

He dropped his rifle and sprinted towards the quad-barrelled gun. He had to get it firing again. Huge, shrieking creatures with scything arms and horrific organic weapons poured over the trenches, tearing his men apart. Swarms of smaller creatures leapt and killed around them.

Desperate hand-to-hand combat raged as troopers vainly attempted to stem the alien tide. Giant, fleshy monstrosities disgorged hordes of clawed monsters that he recognised as genestealers. Everywhere, they were being overrun.

Konarski crouched low and held his gloved hand across his nose and mouth as the stench of melted human flesh assailed him. He scrambled across the stinking remains of the crew, sliding up into the gunner's compartment.

'Yes!' he shouted as he saw that the guns were still powered up and fully loaded. Gripping the firing handles, he slewed the four-barrelled turret around to face the giant flapping monster. Konarski punched the firing studs and a four-metre tongue of flame roared from the muzzles to strafe the sky with fiery explosions. The gun rocked with powerful recoil, pumping out hundreds of shells every few seconds. Konarski screamed as he fired, the horror of the last few days washing from his body in a storm of adrenaline.

Through the vision blocks he saw the flying beast torn apart as the close range blasts ripped through its bony armour plates to detonate within its vital organs. Screeching, it tumbled from the sky, rolling in a flurry of snow and alien blood to crush the broods it carried with its bulk. Explosions of coloured fumes erupted from its belly, noxious clouds of alien toxins blanketing the ground and green tendrils spilling into the trenches.

Working the gun left and right, he shredded every alien he could see, keeping the firing studs depressed long after the ammunition had run out.

COLONEL RABELAQ WATCHED through the viewing bay of the Capitol Imperialis and immediately saw that the Krieg rearguard was sure to be annihilated unless they were reinforced. Cries for help and desperate pleas for fire missions clogged the vox-circuits. The scale of the disaster staggered him.

The elements ambushed on the road to the city were holding, and in many places driving the tyranids back. Given time, Rabelaq guessed they could probably fight their way behind the walls. But time was the one thing they did not have.

The soldiers of Krieg could not hope to hold the tyranid advance long enough.

There was only one thing to do.

He marched to the centre of his command bridge and buttoned his frock coat, pulling the collar straight and brushing a piece of lint from his epaulettes.

'General advance, ready main gun,' he ordered.

'Sir?' queried his adjutant.

'You heard me, damn you! General advance, I'll not leave those brave lads to fight and die on their own. That's not the Logres way. Now do as I order!'

'Aye, aye, sir,' nodded the man, hurrying to obey.

Colonel Octavius Rabelaq came to attention as he felt the rumbling vibrations of the gigantic tracks and the Capitol Imperialis began its ponderous advance.

THE GROUND SHOOK, the charge of hundreds of alien monsters dislodging snow, ice and timber from the walls of the trenches. Konarski grabbed whatever men he could find through the stinking clouds of alien fumes, hauling them back towards the city wall. They had done as much as they could, and it was time to get his men to safety.

Huge vibrations rumbled through the ground, and briefly he wondered if they were in the grip of an earthquake. A screeching roar behind him echoed with alien hunger and he turned to raise his lasgun in a final show of defiance.

Suddenly the earth heaved and a thunderous string of explosions filled the world with noise. Bright light flared behind him and the crack of displaced air threatened to deafen him. He felt himself flying through the air as massive tremors split the ground before him. He hit hard and rolled, swallowing snow as stars burst before his eyes.

Flames leaped before him and he pushed himself dizzily to his knees.

What the hell had just happened?

Then the smoke parted and he saw a towering cliff of steel rising before him. Grinding forward on lumbering tracks that crushed the earth, it split the very bedrock with its mass, throwing up tank-sized chunks of ice and rock. The blessed sight of the aquila was emblazoned on the soaring leviathan, just below the gigantic, smoking barrel of the Behemoth cannon mounted on the Capitol Imperialis. Konarski laughed as the mammoth war-machine rumbled past him, his cry of exultation snatched away as its cannon fired again, the concussive force hurling him through the air once more.

The landing knocked the breath out of his body, but fuelled by adrenalin, he quickly staggered to his feet and lurched off in the direction of the city.

Colonel Rabelaq had bought them time and he wasn't about to waste it.

COLONEL STAGLER KEPT the compress bandage tight against his stomach, dizzy from blood loss, but unwilling to accept medical attention until he knew the fate of his men. Even from his vantage point on a snow-capped gun tower atop the main wall, billowing clouds of smoke and fumes obscured his view of the trenches. He could get nothing from the vox-caster, simply screams and alien howls. His men were probably lost, but they had died in the Krieg manner: fighting hard and dying well.

The fool Rabelaq had surprised him, pushing his precious mobile command post into the alien mass. He'd bought the men fighting the ambushing aliens enough time to break free of the noose and escape to the transient safety of the city. Entire broods of aliens had circumvented the walls, dropping from the high cliffs and into the depths of the city, but he couldn't worry about them right now.

The Capitol Imperialis fired again and more snow tumbled from the highest peaks of the mountains. Hundreds of aliens swarmed up the flanks of the mighty vehicle, many more slamming their bulk into its tracks. Electrical discharges erupted around its hull and bright explosions surrounded it. Its close-in defences stripped away whole swathes of attacking aliens, but could not cope with the sheer volume of attackers.

Stagler snapped his fingers in the direction of his vox-operator.

'Get me Colonel Rabelaq,' he ordered as he saw a sight that would stay with him until his dying day.

'WHY ARE WE slowing, damn you?' demanded Colonel Rabelaq.

'Sir, the track units are jammed. We can't move,' came the reply.

The commander of the Logres regiment rushed to the surveyor station, where dozens of small pict-slates displayed images from the external viewers. Flickering scenes of carnage filled every one, thousands of tyranid brood creatures swarming around the Capitol Imperialis. Hundreds of short-range bolters fired a continuous stream of explosive shells into the alien horde, but could not stop them all.

He felt the recoil-dampened vibration of the main gun and even through the thick hull of his command vehicle, he could hear the shrieks of the deadly aliens as they fought to get at the humans inside his armoured behemoth.

Hundreds, perhaps thousands of aliens had thrown themselves into the mighty tracks of the Capitol Imperialis to prevent it from escaping, and the scale of such unthinking devotion terrified Rabelaq to the soles of his boots. Not even the ruthlessly driven Macharius or the charismatic Slaydo had inspired such obedience from their warriors.

A horrified intake of breath lifted him from his reverie and he looked up to see the gargantuan beast emerge from the billowing clouds of ice and poisonous clouds, crushing everything before it.

Multiple mandibles slavered around a cavern-sized sphincter mouth ringed with thousands of thick fangs. Dripping ichor spilled from the orifice in thick ropes of corrosive drool. Chitinous legs, reverse jointed like a spider's, dragged its bloated body across the ice, hundreds of scuttling organisms crawling across the thick bony plates of its upper armour.

'Great saints,' whispered Rabelaq. 'All power to the auto loaders! Fire the main gun, for the Emperor's sake. Now!'

'Sir! Colonel Stagler on the vox!'

'I don't have time for that fanatic now,' he snapped. 'Fire the main gun!'

Even through metres of adamantium deck and noise suppressors, he felt the thunderous recoil of the Behemoth cannon. The monster rocked under the impact and a huge cheer filled the command bridge. Huge chunks of excised flesh sailed through the air and parade-ground sized sheets of blood sprayed from a huge crater in the beast's flank.

It sagged to one side, its foreleg hanging by gory ribbons of torn muscle. Dark blood gouted from the wound, flooding the trenches below and melting the ice with its heat. A split opened along the sac of its belly, tearing wider as the screaming monster continued to drag itself towards the Capitol Imperialis. Thousands of leaping, snapping creatures and bloated egg sacs tumbled from the wound, only to be crushed beneath the massive beast's weight.

'Come on, come on,' hissed Rabelaq as he watched the indicator lights on the main panel charting the reloading process far below on the gun decks. He willed the gunnery overseer to whip his men harder and get the damn gun loaded. Forcing himself to look away from the panel, he watched in horror as the tyranid monster reared up again, the flesh already reknitting where their shells had struck it. Ichor no longer spilled from its belly and already new strands of muscle and tissue were slithering along the wounded leg to reconnect severed tendons and bone.

'Sir, hull breaches on decks two, three and five!'

'Sir, engine room reports intruders!'

'Colonel, close-in defences are out of ammunition!'

Rabelaq listened to more incoming reports, each more damning than the last, and knew that his career as a soldier in the Emperor's armies was finally over. This was one battle he would not walk away from and raise a toast to in the officers' mess in years to come.

Strangely, the thought did not discomfort him as much as he thought it might.

He felt a terrific impact rock the command bridge as the gigantic tyranid creature slammed into the side of the Capitol Imperialis. He grabbed onto the brass rail that surrounded the holo-map table as the deck lurched sickeningly.

Servitors slid from their chairs, dangling on the cables that attached them to the deck, and his fellow officers screamed as they were thrown to the walls as the mighty leviathan was pushed over. He could see nothing through the viewing bay, simply a heaving mass of purulent flesh. Warning bells chimed and flames leapt from shattered consoles. Glass splinters flew as buckled metal fell onto the map table and steam spurted from ruptured pipes.

The deck continued to tilt and Rabelaq snatched the vox-handset from the side of the sparking map table.

'This is Colonel Octavius Rabelaq,' he said calmly. 'Colonel Stagler, if you can hear this, then you know what to do. Rabelaq out.'

The colonel dropped the handset, finally losing his grip on the map table as the Capitol Imperialis passed its centre of gravity and slammed into the ice. He sailed across the control room and smashed into the corner of a twisted console. He lay immobile in the exploding control bridge, blood and brain leaking from his ruptured cranium.

The only thing that consoled him as he slipped into unconsciousness was the fact that they would talk of his death for years to come in the regimental messes.

URIEL WATCHED THE enormous bulk of the bio-titan attacking the fallen Capitol Imperialis with a mixture of horror and sorrow. Colonel Rabelaq had been a good man and the soldiers of the Logres regiment would feel his loss keenly.

They had all heard Colonel Rabelaq's valedictory order and watched as Colonel Stagler passed the order to fire to the gun towers. Alien shrieks echoed from the valley sides as the bio-titan ripped open the toppled Capitol Imperialis with its gigantic claws, tearng open its thick armour as easily as a child might unwrap a gift.

Then the dusk was transformed into daylight as every heavy artillery piece on the walls opened fire on the fallen vehicle's engine section. Fiery explosions blasted from the shattered wreck, incinerating hundreds of the smaller creatures as they clawed their way inside the vehicle. Uriel knew that there may have been survivors within, but knew that this was a more merciful death than anything the tyranids would offer.

A huge mushroom cloud blossomed skyward as the combined weight of fire finally penetrated into the heart of the Capitol Imperialis and detonated the plasma reactor deep inside.

Streamers of unbearably bright light streaked from the wreck as the plasma chambers ignited and vaporised everything within half a kilometre. As the light faded, Uriel saw a deep crater, filled with hissing, molten flesh. The fatally wounded bio-titan floundered in a magma-hot soup of plasma, ice flashing to superheated steam and scalding its bones bare of flesh. Not even this monster's fearsome regenerative capabilities could save it and it screeched in agony, thrashing madly in its death throes.

Melting snow and ice poured into the crater, forming a lake of rapidly freezing water. Hissing clouds of steam billowed as the plasma boiled away much of the water, but within minutes there was nothing left to mark this titanic encounter save a frozen, ice-filled crater entombing the bodies of thousands of aliens and the mortal remains of Colonel Octavius Rabelaq.

'In Mortis est Gloriam,' whispered Uriel.

TWELVE

For the next four days the tyranids threw themselves at the walls of the city, each time losing thousands of their number, but their attacks never diminished in volume or ferocity. Ramps of dead aliens were piled so high at the base of the wall that their mass cracked the ice of the moat. Flamer units torched their remains as best they could, but the sheer volume of corpses could never be cleared in time before the next attack.

Each assault would begin with a barrage of crackling bio-shells fired from bloated creatures with pumping bony frills around their heads, whose fused forelimbs had evolved into vast, ribbed cannons. Huge chunks of the wall were blown away, but as it was built as a stepped structure into the slope of the ground, these did little more than blast the bedrock of the mountain. Following this, a rain of fleshy pods fired from the back of lumpen monsters with long, bony limbs would fall on the defenders.

Each missile would explode in the air, disgorging drifting clouds of poison that engulfed the front line and killed scores of soldiers and wounded hundreds more. As the medicae facilities filled with troopers blinded by corrosive fumes or coughing up their dissolving lungs, it became necessary for the first assaults to be met by the warriors of the Adeptus Astartes. They alone could hope to withstand the deadly toxins in the opening moments of the attack.

Following the bombardment, the plain before the city rapidly filled with hissing alien killers as they emerged from their snow caves, scooped out by sightless, burrowing creatures. Few tyranid species could survive at night without protection when the temperature plummeted to forty

447

below zero, and the darkness was the only respite from the horror for the defenders of Erebus.

Electrical fires and gouts of poisonous flame, chittering devourer creatures and bony shrapnel bombs pounded the walls relentlessly and as casualties spiralled into the tens of thousands, the decision was made to abandon the first wall.

Barely anything remained of its parapet and the smaller creatures had entered another evolutionary iteration, spontaneously developing fleshy tendons equipped with jagged hooks that enabled them to scale the sheer surfaces of the walls. The many guns mounted on the sides of the valley were keeping the majority of the aerial creatures at bay, and after the ambush at the city wall, no one was dismissing the possibility of the tyranids attacking from avenues previously considered impossible.

Pockets of aliens had penetrated the city through drainage culverts, forgotten caves and even over the high peaks of the mountains, and, while they were wreaking havoc among the civilian population, not a single man from the front line could be spared to hunt them down.

For now, the people of Erebus would need to look to their own defence.

URIEL FELT THE cold against his skin as a burning sensation, but welcomed the pain as a sign he was still alive. His armour was dented, torn and gashed in innumerable places, stained with so much alien blood that its original colour was scarcely visible. The actuators in his left shoulder guard wheezed as he walked, the result of the none-too-tender ministrations of a gigantic tyranid warrior organism. Techmarine Harkus had done what he could to allow the auto-reactive shoulder guard to move freely, but without the proper blessed instruments, he had been forced to beg the armour's forgiveness and effect a temporary repair.

He had not slept since the destruction of Colonel Rabelaq's Capitol Imperialis, and while his catalepsean node had allowed him to continue to function, influencing the circadian rhythms of his brain and his response to sleep deprivation, he felt a marrow-deep tiredness saturate his body.

Looking at the thousands of men gathered around the lines of flaming braziers he felt his respect for them soar. If he was this tired, he could not imagine what the human soldiers must be feeling. Learchus, his armour similarly brutalised, looked well rested, his eyes bright and his stride sure as he marched beside his captain.

'Guilliman's oath, these men are weary,' said Uriel.

'Aye,' agreed Learchus. 'That they are, but they'll hold. I know they will.'

'You trained them well, brother-sergeant.'

'As well as the codex demands,' said Learchus, a hint of reproach in his tone.

Uriel ignored his sergeant's gentle rebuke as they emerged from the buildings of District Quatros and onto the ruined plain before the second wall.

Where once the area had been thronged with factories, production hangars and dwellings, there was now only iced rockcrete rectangles to indicate where they had once stood. Lines of burning oil drums packed with whatever flammable materials were to hand burned and kept the air just above freezing. Already scores of soldiers had perished in the cold nights, frozen to death where they lay, their comrades forced to pry their corpses from the ground as dawn broke.

The council of Erebus, initially supporting Learchus's decision to demolish the buildings so as to deny the tyranids cover between the walls had balked as the reality of the proposition had hit home. Simon van Gelder led the most vocal group of opposition and, in a move of surprising boldness, Sebastien Montante had dissolved the council of Erebus, giving command of his city to Colonel Stagler until such time as the tyranids were driven off.

It amazed Uriel to think that on the brink of annihilation, men could still squabble over such petty concerns as property and wealth. This world might bear the name of the Ultramarines, but its leaders had long since forsaken the teachings of the primarch.

But as he and Learchus marched towards the wall, he was filled with love for the soldiers who stood defiant before the tide of alien invaders. Here was the spirit of Ultramar best exemplified. In the common man, who stood tall against the horrors of the galaxy and was willing to die to protect what he believed in.

The two Space Marines stopped by one of the blazing fires on the edge of the wall, nodding in greeting to the soldiers clustered around its fleeting warmth. Uriel cast his gaze out over the ruined ground between the first two walls at the masses of aliens gathered before him. The collective exhalations of millions of creatures breathing in concert filled the valley, sounding like a single slumbering monster.

It would likely not be that simple, but if Lord Admiral Tiberius's plan succeeded then there was a chance that it might be. He had conferred with Sebastien Montante following his dissolution of the council, finding him awkwardly climbing into a suit of thermal overwhites and pulling on a webbing belt of ammunition.

'What are you doing, Fabricator Montante?' Uriel had asked.

'Well, now that the council has been dissolved, I think it's about time I picked up a gun and started fighting, don't you?'

Uriel folded his arms and said, 'When was the last time you fired a weapon, fabricator?'

'Ah, now let me think… probably during basic training, when I did my regulation service in the Defence Legion.'

'And how many years ago was that?' pressed Uriel.

Montante had the decency to look abashed as he said, 'About thirty years ago, but I *need* to fight, don't you understand?'

'I do, Sebastien, have no fear of that. You are one of the finest logisticians I have met, and your place is here. You have kept the soldiers supplied with food and ammunition, invested time, effort and money to ensure that all our military needs are met. But you are not a soldier, Sebastien, and you will die in the first minutes of an assault.'

'But–'

'No,' said Uriel firmly, but not unkindly, 'You can best serve your city in other ways.'

'Like how?'

'Well, you can start by telling me all about the orbital defences of Erebus: where they are, their status and how we get them firing again.'

Montante looked confused, 'But there's nothing left of them, Uriel. The torpedo silos expended their stocks of ordnance and the defence lasers fired until their power capacitors were dry.'

'Indulge me,' said Uriel.

And he had. Uriel and Montante spent the next two hours poring over maps, computing ranges, fuel to weight ratios, introducing all manner of variables into their discussions until they settled on the optimum course of action. Satisfied that the admiral's plan was indeed workable, Uriel had left, forcing Montante to swear an oath that he would not attempt to join the fighting men on the walls until the end came.

Then he had explained his idea to the other commanders. Initially sceptical, a cautious excitement gripped the senior officers as he outlined the results of his and Montante's labours, and they began to appreciate the scope of the plan.

Preparations were already underway and all they could do was hold until the battered remnants of the fleet were in position to strike. The operation was planned for the day after tomorrow and Uriel was anxious to begin. For too long they had retreated before the aliens. Now they had a chance to strike back.

Kryptman's pet Mechanicus had promised them a weapon to use against the tyranids, but had yet to deliver. Time was running out for Locard, and Uriel knew that the admiral's plan was the best shot they had at ending this war. It was a long shot, but as he looked down at the immensity of the tyranid swarm, he knew it was the only one they had.

He turned from the wall to see Learchus standing beside the brazier, his palms outstretched towards the flames. Uriel's brow furrowed in puzzlement, knowing Learchus was perfectly insulated from both the heat and cold within his power armour, before realising his sergeant was unconsciously copying the men around him. He smiled and listened to what Learchus was saying as he saw Chaplain Astador and Major Satria approach from further along the length of the wall. More men began drifting over from other fires as Learchus raised his voice to carry further.

'You have fought with courage and honour,' said Learchus, 'giving your all for the fight and no man can do more than that. Vile aliens assail us from all sides, yet amidst the death and carnage not one amongst you is willing to take a backwards step. I am proud of you all.'

'You taught us well, Sergeant Learchus,' shouted Major Satria.

'No, greatness was in all of you, I just knew where to look for it. You are known as the Erebus Defence Legion, the protectors of your people. But you are more than this. The oath of brotherhood sworn between your world and mine at the dawn of the Imperium binds us together more surely than the strongest chains of adamantium.'

Learchus raised his fist and shouted, 'You are warriors of Ultramar, and I am proud to call you brothers.'

A huge cheer echoed from the sides of the valley.

SNOWDOG FISHED OUT the last pair of guns from a crate before kicking it to splinters. Tigerlily and Lex collected the smashed timbers in large plastic bags, for sale as firewood to the thousands of people that now filled the warehouse and its adjacent buildings. He handed a freshly stamped lasgun with a pair of power cells fixed to the stock with duct tape to Jonny Stomp. The weapon looked absurdly tiny in Jonny's shovel-like hands and Snowdog grinned.

'I'll try and find something better for you soon, big man,' he promised.

'Good,' grunted Jonny. 'These pipsqueak guns just don't cut it, Snowdog.'

'Hey, it's all we got.'

The ammo for Jonny's grenade launcher had long since run out and he'd been unhappy with anything less destructive. And they could certainly do with something more powerful: the attacks on the warehouse had increased in ferocity and number over the last few days, as though the aliens knew there was a smorgasbord of prey just sitting here.

So far the guns they'd heisted from the Guard were doing the job adequately, and Lex's bombs were proving to be as effective against aliens as they were against the Arbites. But Snowdog knew that soon they'd need more.

He said, 'Hey, Trask, catch,' and tossed him a gleaming autogun with a bag of clips. Trask fumbled the catch, too busy scratching at an ugly red rash he'd developed on the side of his face and neck.

It made his dog-ugly features even more unpleasant to look at and he never stopped clawing at his flaking, mottled skin.

'Damn it, Trask, you gotta pay more attention,' said Snowdog.

Trask made an obscene gesture and turned away, heading back into the noisy interior of the warehouse. Snowdog put Trask from his mind and made his way to where those men he'd deemed relatively trustworthy were guarding the remainder of his purloined supplies.

Still plenty left and there were more people coming in every day. His stash was growing steadily as desperate people gave him all they had for what they needed. Analgesic spray? That'll cost you. Ration packs to feed your children? That'll cost you.

It was simple economics really, supply and demand.

They wanted his supplies, and he demanded their money.

When this was over, he was going to be rich, and then there'd be nothing he couldn't do. Take the Nightcrawlers legit or dump them and move on – he didn't know which yet, but with his pockets bulging with cash, there was no limit to the opportunities. Maybe even get off this planet and hit some virgin territory that was just waiting for a man with his talents to open it up.

Satisfied that all was as it should be, he slung his shotgun and made his way back into the warehouse. Crammed in tight, nearly three thousand people covered virtually every square metre of floor space. Smouldering braziers kept the worst of the night's biting chill away and stolen, high-calorie Imperial ration packs designed for winter operations were stretched to feed entire families. Ragged tarpaulins offered a little privacy to those who could scavenge them. Only the cold kept the stench of so many unwashed bodies from stinking the place up.

Tigerlily made her way through the crowded warehouse and, though he knew she was giving away firewood without taking anything in return, he let it go, figuring it was as well to keep her sweet. There was no one better with a knife and he'd seen her handiwork often enough to know that pissing her off wasn't a good idea. Soft sobbing and low voices filled the warehouse. Glares of hostility followed him everywhere, but he didn't care.

They might hate him, but they needed him. Without him, they were all as good as dead. It was that simple, and if he made a killing along the way, well that was just fine and dandy.

As he made his way to the front of the warehouse he heard a strangled cry from behind a tied-down tarp.

It was a common enough sound in here and Snowdog ignored it until he heard a familiar voice hiss, 'Shut your mouth, girl. Your man agreed to this, so shut your damn mouth and lie still.'

Immediately, Snowdog spun on his heel and racked his shotgun. He ripped aside the tarp, snarling in rage as he saw Trask holding down a weeping girl, her dress hitched up over her knees.

'Trask, damn you! I said no more of this!'

'Frag you, Snowdog,' snapped Trask, rising to his feet. 'They ain't got no money!'

'I said no,' repeated Snowdog. He stepped forwards and hammered his shotgun into Trask's face. The thick wooden stock broke his nose with a sharp crack. He followed up with a boot to the groin. Trask dropped, hands clutched to his crotch and blood spurting from his nose. Snowdog spun the shotgun and jammed the blue-steel barrel between Trask's legs.

'I even think you've done this again and I pull the trigger next time. You get me?'

Trask coughed a wad of blood and phlegm.

'I said, "do you get me?",' bellowed Snowdog.

'Yeah, yeah,' coughed Trask. 'I get you, you bastard.'

'Get out of my sight, Trask,' snapped Snowdog.

His face a bloody mask, Trask painfully picked himself up and lurched away, shouting at sniggering people to shut the hell up. Snowdog took a deep breath and held out his hand to the crying girl. She shook her head, tears cutting clear streaks down the dirt on her face.

'Whatever,' shrugged Snowdog, fishing out a couple of crumpled bills from his trousers. He tossed them to her and said, 'I might be many things, but I won't stoop that low. You understand?'

The girl nodded hurriedly, tucking the cash into her dress and scurrying away.

Snowdog watched her go as Silver came up behind him and slid her arms around his waist.

'He's gonna kill you if you don't kill him first,' she said.

'Not Trask,' said Snowdog, 'he ain't got the guts to come at me face to face.'

'I know, that's why you'd better watch your back.'

'I will,' promised Snowdog.

LORD INQUISITOR KRYPTMAN shivered, despite the thick robes he wore and the thermal generator burning brightly beside him. His breath misted in the air and the stench from the huge pile of corpses gathered on the esplanade behind the wall on the orders of Magos Locard was beginning to make him nauseous. He had studied, dissected and killed tyranids for over two centuries, but could never get used to their disgusting alien smell. The sooner this race was exterminated the better.

His personal retinue of Storm Troopers as well as two members of the Deathwatch led by Captain Bannon formed a cordon around them, hellguns and bolters pointed outwards into the night.

'Anything?' he shouted to Locard, who was waist-deep in tyranid viscera. His robes were filthy, his mechadendrites sifting through the organic waste and a genoprobe chiming softly in his hands.

'No, my lord. All the creatures I have examined so far are at least sixth generation iterations and therefore useless.'

'Damn,' swore Kryptman. 'Very well, burn them. Burn them all.'

* * *

CONCEALED BY THE night's darkness, the lictor slid through the darkness of the city, making its way towards where the pheromone signature of its alien kin was strongest.

Drawn towards the valley mouth, the lictor moved with stealth and speed, like a flickering shadow that darted from cover to cover, unseen and unheard, even by those it killed. On occasion it had encountered prey and killed them to bolster its energy reserves before moving onwards.

The lictor rounded the corner of a ruined building, feeling the scene before it wash through its sensory receptors in a heartbeat. It sensed heat, dead kin and a pheromone signature that surely indicated a leader beast of prey.

CAPTAIN BANNON'S EYES scanned from side to side as Inquisitor Kryptman and Locard performed their grisly autopsies on the tyranid corpses they had been ordered to gather. For what purpose, Bannon didn't know and didn't care, so long as it helped the defenders exterminate these xenos. He and his men had travelled the length and breadth of the city's armed forces, instructing every squad in the best methods of combating tyranids, pointing out weak spots in their natural armour, vulnerable organs and the correct hymnals to recite both prior to and following combat.

It was slow work, but it was paying off, as the daily casualty rosters, while still horrifying, were not as high as they might have been. Bannon understood that this could partly be accounted for by the weakest men having already fallen and the strongest remaining, but the men of Erebus had learned quickly and he knew that alien losses were much higher.

He had been impressed by the Ultramarines and the Mortifactors, though he found it hard to believe that both were descended from the same gene stock. His proud lineage came from the blessed Rogal Dorn and he briefly wondered how many of the successor Chapters of the Imperial Fists had deviated from their original teachings. Not many, he surmised, if the Black Templars were anything to go by.

'Captain Bannon,' said Inquisitor Kryptman.

'My lord?'

'There is nothing here of value. Burn it all.'

Bannon said, 'Aye,' and nodded to Brother Elwaine, originally of the Salamanders Chapter, who raised his flamer and sent a sheet of burning promethium over the mound of cadavers. His mouth twitched in a smile of satisfaction as he watched them immolate.

'Brother-captain,' snarled Henghast of the Space Wolves. 'Enemy near!'

Bannon knew better than to doubt the Space Wolf's senses, but before he could do more than face outwards, it was upon them.

One of the inquisitor's Storm Troopers was lifted from the ground, multiple barbs bursting from his back in a spray of blood and bone. Hellguns fired blindly into the dark, the soldiers having lost their night vision looking into the fire. Another soldier fell, his legs shorn from his body by a massive swipe of chitinous claws.

He saw it in the flickering glow of the flames. A lictor, its upper claws unsheathed and bloody. He raised his bolter, aiming for the junction of thorax and legs, and fired a hail of shells. The lictor spun away from his shots, speeding around the edge of the burning pyre of alien corpses.

Bannon ran around the fire, shouting, 'Henghast, go left! Elwaine, cover!'

Elwaine widened his stance, bracing his flamer as Henghast made his way around the other side. Kryptman had his pistol drawn and Locard twisted his head left and right, chattering excitedly to the inquisitor.

He scanned the ground before him, shutting out the screams of those wounded by the lictor. Damn, but it was quick. Where had it come from?

Bannon heard it a second before it attacked.

Powerful muscles hurled the lictor straight over the pyre, its claws aimed at his heart. He dropped, rolling and firing in one motion. Its claws ploughed the rockcrete, shearing through his shoulder guard and drawing blood. His shots went wild as a tongue of flame washed over the lictor.

But it was no longer there, vaulting from Elwaine's line of fire and smashing the Space Marine from his feet. Clawed hands ripped the flamer from his grip and tore his arms from his sockets in a flood of crimson. Elwaine dropped with a grunt of pain, still kicking at beast as it dismembered him.

Bannon fired again, this time drawing a screech of pain from the lictor as his bolts penetrated its chitinous hide. It spun, blindingly quick, and barbed tendons lashed out, skewering his bolter. The weapon exploded as the propellant in the ruptured shells ignited and Bannon fell back, his gauntlets melted in the blast.

Hellgun fire slashed at the lictor and over the screams Bannon head Kryptman's voice.

'Don't kill it! For the Emperor's sake, don't kill it!'

He rolled to his feet as the lictor came at him. drawing his combat knife and leaping to meet it.

As he leapt he realised that the lictor wasn't coming for him.

It was going for Inquisitor Kryptman.

Kryptman fired his pistol at point blank range, blasting clear a portion of the lictor's upper thigh. It stumbled, but its mantis-like upper claws swept down to eviscerate the inquisitor.

Then Henghast was there, his power sword sweeping down to intercept the blow. The former Space Wolf spun low and slashed his blade through the lictor's upper claws, drawing twin spurts of black blood. It roared in alien rage and once again its barbed hooks lashed out, entangling the Space Marine's sword arm. Its lower arms punched out, ripping through Henghast's armour and hurling him through the air. Blood pumped from its severed claws as Bannon fought to draw his own sword with his scorched hands. His power armour dispensed pain retardant drugs into his system.

The lictor spun away from the fire, its wounds driving it from the fight before he could reach it. He stumbled towards the inquisitor and Locard. Both were alive. Shaken, but alive.

'Get it, Bannon!' hissed Kryptman, 'but for the love of the Emperor, don't kill it. We need it alive!'

He stumbled after the monster as it sped towards the city walls, shouting into the vox, 'Uriel, Astador, anyone! I need help. I am in pursuit of a lictor heading north-westwards to the walls. Close on my position, and if you see it subdue it. I repeat, subdue it, do not kill it!'

URIEL, PASANIUS AND ten warriors from the Fourth company ran from the walls towards the source of Bannon's desperate call for aid. Leading his men in prayer, he had been amazed at the last portion of Bannon's message. A lictor on the loose and they were not to kill it?

'Spread out,' ordered Uriel.

'Why in the name of all that's holy can't we kill the damned thing?' said Pasanius.

'I don't know, but Bannon must have a good reason.'

'How are we supposed to see it, I thought these things were chameleons?'

'Just follow the screams,' said Uriel as he heard cries of pain a hundred metres or so to his left. His armour's auto-senses penetrated the darkness with ease and he saw the shimmering outline of the creature as it butchered its way through the picket line of squads protecting the army's rear.

'With me, now!' shouted Uriel and took off towards the lictor. He opened a channel to Bannon. 'I see it, it's in north sector delta!'

Whether the monster needed to kill or simply took pleasure in the act, Uriel didn't know, but it had stopped to slaughter the men stationed there. Uriel raised his gun, his finger tightening on the trigger before he remembered he was not to kill the creature. It spun away from him and leapt for the side of the rock face, its lashing hooks digging into the rock and hauling it rapidly upwards.

'It's getting away!' shouted Pasanius.

'Not if I can help it,' snarled Uriel, switching his bolter's shot selector to single shell. The lictor scaled the mountainside in jerky leaps, several of its fleshy grapnels hanging useless at its side.

Uriel said, 'Bolter-link,' and sighted carefully along the barrel of his weapon. Range vectors and an aiming reticule appeared on his visor, designating the point his shell would impact. He waited until the dot flashed red and pulled the trigger.

The weapon bucked in his hand and a portion of the rock face exploded as his shell blasted it apart. The lictor screeched in frustration as its flesh hooks were blown clear of the rocks and it tumbled hundreds of metres down the side of the mountain to slam into the ground with a sickening thud.

The lictor pushed itself groggily to its feet as Uriel and Pasanius leapt on it, pinning it to the ground with their weight. It thrashed weakly, tearing at their armour, but as more Ultramarines arrived, they eventually grappled the struggling monster to immobility.

Bannon skidded towards the battling Ultramarines with more of the Deathwatch behind him. Three of his men carried high-tensile cabling, capable of bearing the weight of a Land Raider.

'Bind it,' he ordered.

☡
THIRTEEN

IN A CAVERNOUS hangar built into the rock face of the van Gelder family's mountain estates, a veritable army of lifter-servitors and indentured servants loaded a long, silver-grey starship named Magnificence with scores of sealed crates. The ship's sides were emblazoned with heraldic crests depicting heroic van Gelders of history and her worth beyond measure.

Unwilling to entrust the loading of his entire estate to mere workers, Simon van Gelder, former councillor of Erebus City, watched impatiently from a high gantry as his harried overseers checked off each crate as it was wheeled up the ramp into the *Magnificence's* capacious hold. The operation to load her had been underway for several hours now, and Simon knew that the abundance of his possessions would mean he would be here for some time yet.

Well, no matter. All that concerned him was that the loading be done before this invasion progressed any further. He was damned if he was going to stay and die with these fools for the sake of some outmoded notion of honour. An oath sworn with some long-dead – and probably mythical – figure was no oath at all and certainly didn't bind him.

No, he was going to survive this war and if by some mischance these fools were actually able to drive the aliens from Tarsis Ultra, then he would return with his wealth intact, not flattened in the name of military strategy. Those meek sheep who blindly followed Montante's fawning over these Space Marines were sure to be bankrupted by this war and even if they survived, they would have no one to turn to for their continued economic life but him.

The thought of Montante begging him to return to the council and pledge his financial support to prop up his ineffectual regime pleased him mightily and he wondered how long it would be before he would be in a position to manoeuvre Montante from office. Not long, he was sure. The industrial blocs were notoriously fickle and with the right palms greased and pockets filled, it would be child's play to ensure that his nomination was successful.

Simon pulled out a thick cigar from his long frock coat, lighting it with a small gold lighter and puffing an expansive series of smoke rings.

Scenting the smoke, a safety protocol servitor marched stiffly towards him.

A red light flashed on its chest panel as it said, 'This area is a protected zone and the ignition of combustible materials is prohibited. Extinguish all flames and prepare for censure.'

Simon waved the servitor away, snapping, 'Go away. Authorisation code Gelder nine-alpha-prime.'

The servitor turned and marched away as Simon shook his head and strolled along the gantry to an armoured blast door that led onto a balcony overlooking the city. Another servitor opened the door, wired into the rock of the wall, its arms augmented with powerful pistons that turned the heavy locking wheel with ease.

The door ground open and cold air rushed in. Simon gathered his insulated coat about himself and walked into the fading light of evening. This high on the valley sides, the wind whipped by like a scalpel, cutting him to the marrow with its icy blade. Far to the west he could hear the faint metallic ring of battle, the cries of fighting men carried eastwards on the wind that howled through Erebus. His contempt for what these men of war had led them to knew no bounds and his desire to live through this surged through him once more.

A chattering blast of gunfire sounded from further up the valley, close to Montante's palace. Simon watched as a flock of the flying aliens darted through the air above the source of the River Nevas. The servitor-manned guns on the valley sides tracked their movement, filling the air with explosive projectiles that burst in lethal clouds of shrapnel and shredded dozens of the beasts before they withdrew. They were clever these aliens, saw Simon. Testing each area of the valley for weak points to find a way in.

But Simon knew there were no weak points. His consortium, in conjunction with the Adeptus Mechanicus, had supplied and built the weapons as well as the servitors that controlled the guns and he knew that their coverage was nigh-on impenetrable.

Anything that flew above a certain altitude was interrogated by the machine spirits bound within each gun and should there be no response to that interrogation, the guns would open fire. Without clearance, flyers would be mercilessly engaged and destroyed the moment they entered the guns' coverage.

Simon smiled, his fingers playing over a plain metallic box in the pocket of his coat.

Unless you knew how to shut them down.

TECHS SWARMED AROUND the Ultramarines' Thunderhawk, stripping armoured panels from its hull and removing ammo hoppers from its frame under the watchful eye of Techmarine Harkus. His features were anxious and Uriel could hear frequent angry tirades passing between Harkus and the Adeptus Mechanicus cutters.

Sparks flew as extra weight was removed from the Thunderhawk with heavy cutting gear, thick plates of armour stripped and weapons removed to try and reduce the overall weight of the gunship from seventy-six tonnes to a mere forty.

A giant crane groaned as it lifted off the main battle cannon, tracked lifter-servitors unloading the shells through the front ramp. Adeptus Mechanicus tech-priests worked atop scaffolding built around the cockpit to remove the fore-mounted heavy bolters, while below them a procession of enginseers stripped out every unnecessary fitting. Teams of welders surrounded the stricken gunship, blue sparks flaring as they replaced its heaviest plates of armour with thin sheets of lightweight metal.

The sheets bent as augmented servitors lifted them into place to be welded and Uriel knew that they would be scant protection from even the most glancing of impacts.

'It breaks my heart to see such a noble vehicle so cruelly treated,' said Uriel. 'We must make our obeisance to its war-spirit that it might know we only do this out of the direst of circumstances.'

Beside him, Captain Bannon nodded in agreement. 'Aye, but your Techmarine will ensure that the correct supplications are made and prepare us with the proper prayers to offer.'

Crouched by the engine cowlings Harkus looked distraught at the drastic measures being taken to lighten his charge.

'I wonder who he is more terrified of just now?' wondered Bannon. 'The war-spirit of the Thunderhawk or his Master of Forges?'

'A little of both would be my guess,' chuckled Uriel, thinking of the irascible Fennias Maxim back on Macragge who had balked at the idea of him forging his own blade when there were dozens of skilled artificers who could do a better job.

Harkus rose from the engine and jogged around his wounded gunship, his distress plain to see. He waved a hand at the Thunderhawk.

'These... these butchers are destroying my craft. Nine hundred years old, over two thousand campaigns and this is how we treat her. There will be words had when this is all over, mind. She can't take this kind of treatment.'

'How heavy is she?' asked Uriel.

'Too heavy,' snapped Harkus, 'she's still over fifty tonnes.'

'We need her at forty, Brother Harkus,' reminded Bannon.

'Don't you think I know that!' said Harkus in exasperation. 'But I'm a Techmarine, not a miracle-worker; I can't change the laws of aerodynamics. We can only take off so much before she'll become unflyable.'

'Find a way, brother,' said Uriel gently. 'Strip her down to her bare bones if you have to. Everything depends on you getting this honourable craft down to forty tonnes and still flyable.'

Harkus shook his head. 'I'll try, but I can't guarantee anything. I can feel her war-spirit's anger and it won't be easy to placate.'

'I know you'll do your best, Brother Harkus,' said Uriel as the furious Techmarine returned to yelling at the cutting crews as yet another armour plate clanged to the landing platform.

'Can he do it?' asked Bannon. 'Much depends on it.'

'He was an apprentice of Sevano Tomasin, one of our finest who died on Thracia. If anyone can achieve the impossible, it is Harkus.'

Bannon nodded. 'Even if we succeed, we may not make it back. You know this.'

'I know,' said Uriel slowly. 'But if we can end this, then it will be worth it.'

Bannon nodded, then paused before saying, 'You do not have to come on this mission, Uriel. We are the Deathwatch and this is what we are trained for.'

'I have served in the Deathwatch also, and if you go, I go. Besides, Harkus will want another Ultramarine there to make sure the Deathwatch treats his gunship with proper respect.'

SNOWDOG QUICKLY CHANGED power cells on his lasgun, his rate of reloading putting many veteran Guardsmen to shame. He fired over the barricade they'd built around the entrance to the warehouse, pitching another bladed killer backwards into the bloody snow. Jonny Stomp blazed away on full auto, and Silver blasted the aliens with carefully aimed shots from her twin pistols.

He'd drafted perhaps a hundred or so of the most able-bodied refugees and stuck guns in their hands, before bundling them outside to the barricades to fight. Some had complained that since they were paying him for protection, they shouldn't have to fight. Snowdog explained down the barrel of a gun that they didn't have an option.

Aliens poured from every street into the open ground before the warehouse, charging through the hail of fire that awaited them without fear or thought for their own lives. Before this had all gone nova he'd heard on some of the devotional vids that there were supposed to be large creatures that controlled the smaller ones, but thankfully they hadn't seen any of them yet. Perhaps they were all at the front line, which, judging by the noises coming from the west, was getting closer every day.

He wondered why no soldiers had come to their aid, but figured that they knew this was a Stank ghetto and that the city would be better off if the tyranids conveniently wiped out a few thousand Stankers. So it looked as though they'd have to do this on their own. So far, each attack had been sent packing by Snowdog and his gang, leaving more and more alien dead on the ground.

What he couldn't figure was why the hell were they so furiously attacking this place?

Trask fired his shotgun into the midst of the charging aliens, and even with one eye swollen shut by the rash that covered half his face, he still couldn't fail to hit something. A knot of aliens attacked that section of the barricade, and Snowdog opened up on full auto, cutting two in half and blowing another one's legs clean off.

Tigerlily, Rentzo and a dozen other members of the Nightcrawlers waited at the doors to the warehouse in reserve, fear etched on every face.

Another wave of screeching aliens poured into the square and now Snowdog knew he wasn't imagining things; the attacks on the warehouse *were* getting more frequent and more ferocious. It seemed as though every alien in the city was coming for him. What the hell was the matter with these aliens? Did they resent him making some money of the back of their invasion or something?

Silver crouched down to reload her pistols and raised her eyebrows. 'Some day, huh?' she said.

'Yeah, some day,' he agreed.

THE THUNDERHAWK WAS a dark shadow against the blackness of the night, the blue of its armoured hull visible only on the leading edges of its wings and tailfins, the rest having been stripped off to reduce its weight. Uriel and the members of the Deathwatch stood in a loose circle, their hands clasped in prayer. Each had made his peace with the Emperor and was prepared for the mission.

Uriel had cleaned and repaired his armour as best he could, but its fabric was still beaten and in need of months in the forge. Teams of struggling lifter-servitors carried the last of the Thunderhawk's cargo on board, the landing skids creaking under the strain.

As they finished loading the gunship, Harkus emerged from within and gave Uriel a nod of affirmation. Everything was loaded and securely locked down. The Thunderhawk was going to be doing some hard flying and the last thing they needed was loose cargo spilling in the back. Looking at the thin panels on the sides of the gunship, Uriel knew that the cargo would go straight through it.

'We are ready,' said Bannon, slinging his weapon.

'Aye,' agreed Uriel, checking the action on his own weapon and ensuring his sword was secure in its scabbard. The remainder of the Deathwatch silently checked over their own and each other's armaments with the silence of the elite soldiers they were. Satisfied, each man recited the first five verses of the Catechism of the Xeno before turning and marching aboard the gunship.

Uriel took a deep breath and looked around the soaring peaks of the mountains. Distant specks spun in the starlit sky far to the west. He shook his head as a sudden premonition of doom passed through him and followed the Deathwatch into the gunship's crew compartment.

There was barely room for the Space Marines to move inside, with creaking pallets stacked to the roof and the gunship's other passengers taking up a great deal of room. There were no armoured benches to sit on, their weight deemed unnecessary, so he crouched with his back to the rumbling fuselage.

The ramp whined closed, shutting out the starlight, and Uriel's autosenses took over.

A screaming whine built as the engines spooled up to vertical take-off power and Uriel offered a quick prayer that Harkus had not let them down and that Lord Admiral Tiberius was near. He felt the Thunderhawk lurch as it lifted easily into the air, and turn on its axis as Harkus set their course. He was surprised at the ease with which the gunship had lifted off before remembering that the problem was not now its weight, but its range.

It was all a question of whether they could reach their objective, carry out their mission and still have enough fuel to get them back.

Uriel felt the acceleration of the gunship as the engines built up to full power, pushing them eastwards across the mountain tops. There was cloud cover higher up and while nap-of-the-earth flying might keep them safe from being spotted, it was hugely inefficient and burned up vast quantities of fuel.

As the gunship sped eastwards, Magos Gossin, the most senior of their Adeptus Mechanicus passengers, tapped him on the shoulder and pointed through the vision port.

'Even if we succeed here, will this world ever truly be ours again?'

Uriel twisted his head to look outside.

Purple clouds boiled in the distance and streamers of multi-coloured smog hugged the horizon, reaching into the upper atmosphere like a smeared painting.

Uriel wanted to lie, but felt he would choke on the words.

'No,' he said. 'No, it will not.'

The Thunderhawk streaked through the night sky.

THE VAE VICTUS was a far cry from the gleaming vessel that had set out from Macragge so many months ago. Her central nave was buckled and splintered, the polished timbers blackened and scorched. Many of her previously manned console stations sat empty, their systems damaged beyond repair without months of time in dock. Wisps of steam gusted from hastily sealed pipes and many of her weapons were unable to fire.

Her surveyors were functioning at minimum capacity, most of the external auguries having been incinerated in the fiery blast of the refinery's destruction. Much of her hull had been melted or stripped away in the explosion and her engines would only allow her captain to perform the most basic of manoeuvres.

And Tiberius knew that they had escaped relatively lightly.

They had lost the *Argus*, most of the local fleet and the *Kharloss Vincennes* would never launch fighters again. He had been forced to order all hands to abandon the Dauntless cruiser *Yermetov*, when it became apparent her warp drives had been damaged in the blast and would soon implode. Her crew had escaped to the *Sword of Retribution* and sent her into the warp on her last voyage.

The two remaining vessels of Arx Praetora squadron and the *Mortis Probati* of the Mortifactors limped alongside the *Vae Victus*. Captain Gaiseric and his crew were eager to exact a measure of revenge against the tyranids.

One Overlord battlecruiser, two battered Space Marine strike cruisers and a carrier that could not launch any strike craft was not much of a fleet to take on the full might of a hive fleet, but it was all they had.

Tiberius ran a hand over his scarred, hairless skull and chewed his bottom lip.

'Any word from Uriel?' he asked.

Philotas looked up from the cracked plotting table. Its slate was dark and his deck officer had rolled star charts spread across its surface.

He shook his head. 'No, lord admiral. The last message we were able to receive was over an hour and a half ago saying they were on schedule.'

'I don't like this, damn it. We could be sailing into a trap!'

'Indeed we could.'

'You're sure there's nothing from Uriel?'

'As sure as I can be. Most of our vox-casters were smashed in the explosion or had their internal workings fried by the electromagnetic pulse. We were lucky to make contact at all.'

'Then we're going to have to do this the old fashioned way,' said Tiberius.

Philotas nodded and returned to his charts as Tiberius stared in anticipation at the viewing bay. The world of Tarsis Ultra spun gently before him, tainted with several bruised areas of colour that were spreading across its surface. He could see distant specks of tyranid organisms and felt his hate grow. Like parasites, they suckled on this world, draining it of its life without thought for the billions of creatures that called it home. Even as he watched them, several of the vanguard drone creatures altered direction to face the incoming Imperial fleet.

'All ships, this is Tiberius. Battle stations. They're coming.'

He closed his eyes and muttered a prayer that Uriel was currently hurtling towards his objective.

Whether he was or he wasn't, there was nothing Tiberius could do about it.

All he could do was lead his ships into battle and fight.

SPOUTS OF MUD and water were thrown up as the Thunderhawk touched down on the upper slopes of the eastern mountains in a cloud of shrieking jetwash. Its skids slid briefly on the slippery ground before finally finding purchase. The front ramp slammed down into the mud and the five members of the Deathwatch and Uriel surged from its interior.

Uriel jogged to a covering position and crouched low behind a jagged black boulder, resting his bolter on it as he surveyed the slopes below him for threats. A thick, viscous rain fell and Uriel could tell that the tempera ture here was many degrees higher than at Erebus. Already tyranid mutagenic viruses were working to raise the temperature of Tarsis Ultra for ease of consumption.

The thick sheets of rain cut visibility dramatically and he could see no more than three hundred metres through it. Thunder rumbled, followed shortly by jagged bolts of lightning that speared the sky, throwing patchy illumination onto the plains below. He cursed as he realised they would have little or no warning of any attack.

He signalled to one of the Deathwatch to take his place and climbed the mud-slick slope to where Bannon co-ordinated the unloading of the Thunderhawk's cargo. Another whip of lightning seared the sky and Uriel saw what they had come for, thrown into shadow by the bright atmospheric discharge.

From the outside it was nothing remarkable, simply an oversized rockcrete bunker some thirty metres square, with an armoured blast door leading within. A hemispherical dome topped with eight long gun barrels squatted atop the bunker, its bronze surface streaked with oxides.

Four lifter-servitors struggled under the weight of cargo pallets while Magos Gossin and his three drenched Adeptus Mechanicus tech-priests hitched up their robes and hurriedly made their way towards the bunker. Behind them, the servitors carried the precious cargo, fully charged capacitors to power the defence lasers, into the bunker with the utmost care.

Bannon strode downhill to meet Uriel, his black armour glossy in the heavy rain.

'Anything?'

'No, but they could be right on top of us and we wouldn't know,' replied Uriel, having to shout to be heard over the rain and whine of the Thunderhawk's engines.

Another tense half an hour passed until eventually the last of the charged capacitors was unloaded from the belly of the Thunderhawk and taken inside the bunker. By now the Adeptus Mechanicus should be hooking them up to the main power grid. Silently Uriel prayed they would work fast.

He slid downhill through the thick mud to his earlier vantage point and squinted down into the murk. Movement rippled below him, but was it incoming tyranids or a trick of the light and rain?

Then a sheet of lightning flashed in conjunction with booming peals of thunder and the night was suddenly and vividly illuminated.

The slippery slopes of the mountain teemed with tyranid creatures, swarming uphill in their thousands. Leaping hormagaunts led the charge, but in his brief glimpse he saw a trio of lumbering, crab-clawed carnifex and a great winged beast with a long, barbed tail and a huge bony crest that stretched high above its bellowing jaws. Giant blades on its upper limbs cut the rain and a steaming bio-weapon oozed from its midsection.

He scrambled back uphill, fighting through the thick, sucking mud.

He opened a channel to the captain of the Deathwatch and Techmarine Harkus.

'Bannon, ready your men! Harkus, get the Thunderhawk off the ground,' he yelled.

Seconds later, the gunship's engines roared as it lifted off to assume a holding pattern until the Space Marines were ready for extraction.

Uriel looked back down the slopes of the mountain.

'And tell Gossin to work faster,' he said. 'They're here...'

'FIRE BOMBARDMENT CANNON!' shouted Tiberius as the two pincered kraken moved slowly across the viewing bay. Without many of their targeting auguries, gunnery was a far from exact science and only his and Philotas's experience gave them any chance of scoring hits on their foe.

The bridge shuddered as the ship's main gun fired and Tiberius winced as a fresh batch of red runes began flashing on the damage control panels.

'Hull breach reopened on deck six!'

'Come to new heading, zero-five-seven,' ordered Tiberius. 'Flank speed. We've got to get past their cordon.'

The entire bridge groaned as the battered ship forced itself into the turn, her buckled keel squealing in protest.

'Come on, hold on,' Tiberius whispered to the spirit of the *Vae Victus*.

Sprays of ichor burst before his ship as the bombardment cannon's shells impacted on the kraken's hide, detonating in a giant fleshy burst of gore. An angular prow slid into view as the *Mortis Probati* crossed the bow of the Ultramarines' ship. Her starboard guns hammered the listing remains of the kraken, blasting its thrashing body to expanding clouds of scorched flesh.

The second kraken ponderously moved to engage the Mortifactors' ship, its blade wings rippling as it changed course. Behind it, Tiberius could see the outline of one of the massive hive ships, limned in the glow of the planet's atmosphere.

'All ahead full,' shouted Tiberius. 'Twenty-degree down angle. Take us through the gap!'

Tiberius gripped the cracked timbers of his command pulpit as the *Vae Victus* shook violently and accelerated through the gap the strike cruisers had blasted.

Smaller drone creatures peeled off from their attack on the *Sword of Retribution*, swooping around to come for Tiberius's vessel.

'Lord admiral!'

'I see them, Philotas. Engage with port batteries.'

'We won't hit much without the targeting surveyors.'

'Fire anyway.'

'If they board us, we will be unable to repel them.'

'Damn them! Our only priority is the hive ships. Stay on target!'

THE *Sword of Retribution* pushed deeper into the swarming tyranid creatures, firing devastating broadsides from its many gun decks, filling the space around it with vast explosions. It had suffered the least of the Imperial fleet and its captain had volunteered to take the lead position in the attack.

Lethal strikes from the dorsal lances punched a hole in the tyranid fleet through which the smaller vessels of the fleet sailed. Alien vessels surged to close the gap, but the Space Marine vessels were too fast, slipping past the vanguard organisms on a course for the hive ships.

The *Kharloss Vincennes* limped behind the *Sword of Retribution*, her ruptured hull and damaged engines causing her to fall behind the speeding Space Marine ships. As the tyranid creatures closed the gap in their forces, they also closed inexorably on the wounded carrier. Unable to launch fighters or bombers to defend herself, she was easy prey. Close-in turrets and broadside batteries kept the alien creatures at bay for a time, but as more and more closed with her, there was no doubting the outcome of the battle.

Snaking tentacles drifted forwards from a dozen cone-shaped drones, latching limpet-like to the hull of the battling carrier. Acidic secretions bound the creatures to the ship and their maws irised open, revealing caverns of giant teeth that burrowed into their prey at a horrifying rate.

Larger ships closed, then suddenly altered course to head back towards the planet, recalled by the hive mind to catch its attackers in a trap.

As the *Kharloss Vincennes* fought the losing battle for its life, the remainder of the Imperial fleet pushed on into the swarm.

THE NEAREST HIVE ship lay before the *Vae Victus*, its gargantuan shape filling the viewing bay before him. Attendant guardian creatures formed an impenetrable barrier between her and her escorting ships.

'All ships, fire all weapons!' shouted Tiberius. 'We have to break through.'

Massive projectiles hurtled through space, exploding in vivid blossoms of fire ahead, but none were reaching their target. Kraken and drones moved in an intricate ballet that would have been virtually impossible for the Imperial Navy to emulate, screening the hive ship from the incoming firepower. Tiberius saw a handful of shots penetrate the living shield, but precious few were causing any real damage.

Tiberius opened a vox-link to the captain of the *Sword of Retribution*.

'Captain, you must clear us a path! Use whatever means are necessary.'

He snapped off the link without waiting for an answer and said, 'Philotas, try and raise Uriel. Tell him that whatever he's doing, he'd better do it fast, because we won't last much longer here.'

RAIN HAMMERED THE mountainside and lightning provided stroboscopic illumination across the rocky slopes as the thousands-strong horde scrambled up towards the bunker. Rivers of foaming water flooded downhill, sweeping great swathes of the aliens with it.

For once, the tyranids' metamorphosis of a planet's surface was working against them, saw Uriel. The glutinous mud was as much of a hindrance to them as it was to the Space Marines. Bolter fire raked the slopes, blasting apart hormagaunts and other nameless horrors in stuttering blazes of shells. Uriel hurled a pair of grenades, ducking back behind a rock as they detonated, sending up showers of mud and alien body parts.

Screeching carnifex struggled in the mud, their bulk causing them to sink knee deep. The winged monster flapped above the horde, buffeting winds keeping it from advancing for now.

The Deathwatch picked off aliens with single shots to their vulnerable organs, careful to conserve their ammunition. Bannon scrambled across the slopes to Uriel's position, his armour caked in clods of mud, the symbol of the Imperial Fists barely visible.

'They're circling around behind us. We need to get inside!'

Uriel looked up into the filthy downpour, seeing indistinct shapes bounding across the rocks towards the bunker. Bannon was right, given a few minutes, they would be surrounded.

'Let's get going then,' he said, rising from behind the rock.

Uriel felt the ground shift under his feet and leapt backwards as a huge portion of mud suddenly detached from the slope, sliding downhill as the torrential downpour washed it from the side of the mountain. He landed on his back and rolled, grabbing onto the rock as he felt himself slipping. His bolter clattered behind the rock.

He heard Bannon cry out and saw the captain of the Deathwatch desperately scrambling in the mud to keep from sliding into the mass of aliens below. Uriel braced himself on the rock and held out his hand towards Bannon. The two warriors gripped wrists and Uriel began pulling.

'Uriel!' shouted Bannon.

He looked up, seeing a monstrous beast with a fang-filled maw clawing its way up the slope. Its long, taloned fist clamped around Bannon's ankle and squeezed. The ceramite cracked under its awful strength and its black eyes locked with Uriel's. Bolter shells burst around the battle as the Deathwatch bought time for Uriel to rescue their captain.

Uriel roared as he fought against the tyranid's strength, knowing that he could not defeat it. Bunching the muscles in his thighs, he braced his boots against the rock and gave a herculean pull, reaching down to sweep up his bolt-gun with his free hand.

Feeling the tendons in his arm crack, he straightened his legs, the counterbalance of the tyranid warrior pulling him to a standing position. Gripping his bolter in one hand he aimed at the creature's head.

'Let go,' he said simply and emptied the magazine into its face, its brains mushrooming from the back of its skull as his bolts detonated within its cranium. Its grip spasmed and Uriel hauled Bannon to the rock, pulling him to his feet as another streak of lightning lit up the sky.

The two Space Marines slipped and stumbled their way towards the bunker through the torrents of water and mud. Twice, tyranid creatures came close to overtaking them, but each time the unerringly accurate bolter fire of the Deathwatch kept the aliens at bay. Uriel heard static-filled words in his helmet vox, but could make little sense of them. He recognised the voice as that of Philotas, the deck officer of the *Vae Victus*, but whatever he was saying was unintelligible.

Eventually they reached the rockcrete apron surrounding the bunker and slammed into its reassuringly solid bulk. As more lightning burst overhead, tyranid creatures slid downhill from the slopes above, skidding in the mud as they tried to find their footing. Silhouetted in the glare, Uriel saw the carnifex and the monstrous winged beast finally crest the plateau and lumber towards the bunker.

'Everybody inside, now!' yelled Bannon, firing at the carnifex as he limped backwards. Uriel stood beside him, loading and firing off another magazine to little effect. The monster's screeching roar echoed from the mountains as it charged through the rain. Uriel ducked inside the bunker, grabbing the giant locking wheel and shouting, 'Bannon! Get inside, now!'

The Deathwatch captain kept firing and Uriel was about to repeat his order, when Bannon turned and ran inside, dropping his bolter and helping Uriel with the door. Armoured and sheathed in double layers of adamantium, the door weighed over four tonnes, and was normally closed by means of hydraulic pistons, but Uriel and Bannon pulled it shut in seconds, desperation lending their limbs extra strength.

The door slammed closed and Uriel spun the locking wheel.

'That was too close,' breathed Uriel.

'Aye,' agreed Bannon, scooping up his weapon.

The steel of the door buckled inwards with a resounding clang. Thunderous impacts rocked it and dust fell from the ceiling. Glow-globes on the ceiling flickered with each impact.

'Come on,' said Bannon, 'This door will not hold them for long,' and marched along the bare rockcrete corridor. Casting wary glances at the booming door, Uriel followed him, eventually arriving in the humid fire-control chamber. Banks of ancient technology lined the edge of the octagonal room and an iron ladder led up to a brass rimmed hatch in the ceiling.

Magos Gossin sat before what was presumably the main firing panel with his head bowed in prayer, his tech-priests kneeling behind him and chanting in counterpoint to their master's words. Mud-caked Deathwatch Space Marines stood at attention as the droning mantra continued, with no sign of drawing to a close.

'Magos Gossin,' snapped Bannon. 'When can you fire these guns?'

Gossin turned in his seat, his displeasure at having been interrupted plain. 'The capacitors are linked to the main grid, but the necessary prayers to begin the firing sequence are lengthy and intricate. It would be preferable if you did not interrupt me as I perform them.'

Bannon marched towards Gossin as another impact slammed into the main door.

'Do you hear that?' he demanded. 'We have minutes at best before the tyranids are upon us. Fire these guns now or they will not fire at all. Do you understand me?'

A tortured metallic screech echoed through the bunker. Gossin stared fearfully along the corridor and nodded.

'Deathwatch, with me!' shouted Bannon, heading back towards the door.

THE VIEWING BAY of the *Vae Victus* lit up with the destruction of the *Kharloss Vincennes*, reflected light from the explosion flaring from the glossy carapaces of the tyranid bio-ships.

'Emperor watch over thee,' whispered Tiberius as another impact rocked his vessel. Deathly red light bathed the command bridge as more and more tyranid weapons scored hits. Their defensive capabilities had been degraded comprehensively by hundreds of drifting spores and there was nothing he could do to stop it.

The *Sword of Retribution* still fought, her captain performing brilliantly in evading the tyranid creatures and hammering the hive ship's escorts.

'He's fighting to reach the second hive ship,' said Philotas.

But Tiberius could see he wouldn't make it. Already organisms were swarming over her hull and suffocating her firepower.

They had come so close! The first hive ship was right in front of them. The *Vae Victus* and the *Mortis Probati* had stripped away a huge portion of its defences, diverting much of the defences previously protecting it from attack from the planet's surface.

But there was no attack from the planet and Tiberius felt his heart sink at the thought that they had failed.

'All ships, prepare to disengage,' he said.

THE DOOR BLEW inwards, ripped in two by a massive pair of claws. Rain and wind howled inside the bunker as a dozen hormagaunts fought to squeeze past the screaming carnifex that smashed its claws into the rock-crete around the door in an attempt to squeeze its massive bulk inside.

A volley of disciplined bolter fire brought down the first and second waves

A giant crack split the ceiling, the carnifex bludgeoning its way forwards.

Screeching howls and deafening blasts of gunfire filled the narrow corridor.

Uriel aimed at the carnifex's head, its blunt features expressionless as it hammered its way inside. His shot put out its eye, blasting a chunk of skull clear. The beast flinched, but simply lowered its bony head and slammed harder on the bunker's structure.

Leaping hormagaunts filled the corridor, screeching with alien fury as the Space Marines slowly fell back before them. Glow-globes shattered and the ceiling split apart with a booming crack. Huge chunks of rock dropped into the corridor. Uriel hurled himself clear as tonnes of rock collapsed and billowing clouds of dust filled the air.

He dragged himself to his feet, scrabbling for his fallen bolter as a mud-covered warrior organism leapt atop the steel-laced rubble. Its fangs spread wide and a secondary set of jaws lashed out, biting deep into Uriel's helm. His visor shattered and he felt blood on his face as the jaws withdrew. He dropped to his knees against the wall, disengaging the vacuum sockets on his gorget and tearing the helmet loose.

The tyranid warrior pounced and a hail of bolter shells stitched across its thorax, exploding wetly within and spraying Uriel with its blood. Bannon hauled him to his feet as the tyranids clambered over the rubble and the Deathwatch hammered them with more shells.

Without the protection of his helmet's auto-senses, the noise was deafening. Gunfire and thunder combined with the lightning to form a cacophonous backdrop to the battle. Dimly Uriel heard Bannon calling the Thunderhawk down as they fell back towards the control chamber.

As the Space Marines withdrew, Uriel was suddenly aware of a bitter, metallic taste on the air as a powerful static charge built around him. His scalp tingled and even over the noise of battle he could hear a deep, bass thrumming build beneath him.

He looked up through the shattered ceiling in time to see an incandescent streak of light spear skywards, looking like the manifest wrath of the Emperor

ONCE AGAIN THE viewing bay lit up, and it took Tiberius a moment to realise why. Another streak of light slashed past the *Vae Victus* blasting clean through the body of the hive ship. Another shot fired, followed closely by another and he surged from his command pulpit and punched the air.

'Damn you, Uriel. I knew you could do it!' he yelled over the ringing of alarm bells.

With atmospheric conditions more or less stable in the region selected by Uriel and Sebastien Montante, the beams from the defence laser silo were unaffected by the thermal blooming that had so hamstrung the defences in the opening stages of the invasion.

In low orbit, and with its planetward defences engaged in protecting it from the Imperial fleet, the hive ship was horribly vulnerable and was now paying the price. Explosions of flesh rippled across the hive ship's body as blasts from the defence lasers destroyed it.

'All ships, belay my last order!' he shouted. 'Target everything you can at that hive ship! We've got it, by the Emperor, we've got it!'

URIEL CLIMBED THE ladder in the centre of the control chamber, hauling on the rusted opening lever and pulling aside the hatch. The static hum was even stronger here and a soft blue glow illuminated the dome above the control chamber. Then a dazzling light flared and Uriel blinked away blistering afterimages as the flash of the defence laser's fire filled the interior of the dome. The guns were firing automatically now and would continue to do so until the capacitors they had brought ran dry.

'All clear!' he yelled.

The sounds of bolter fire intensified as the tyranids, perhaps sensing their prey was escaping, intensified their attack.

Uriel hauled himself up into the dome, reaching back and pulling up the tech-priests as they scrambled up the ladder. Outside the dome he could hear the roar of the Thunderhawk's engines as it hovered overhead.

One by one, the Deathwatch climbed to the dome, until only Bannon remained. He fired a last burst from his bolter before dropping it and leaping for the ladder. He climbed fast as the tyranids flooded the chamber below. Uriel and another Space Marine pulled Bannon through the hatch and slammed it shut.

'Time to get out of here, wouldn't you say?' said Bannon breathlessly.

'Way past time,' agreed Uriel, as the guns fired again.

With Uriel leading the way, the exhausted group made their way onto the roof of the bunker. The wind and rain had diminished and the scale of the swarm surrounding the bunker now became apparent. Howling jetwash from the hovering Thunderhawk's engines threatened to hurl them from the roof. Hormagaunts frenziedly tried to climb to the roof of the bunker as the carnifexes battered its walls. They had seconds at best.

Thick, rappelling cables hung from the crew ramp of the gunship and Uriel quickly grabbed them, distributing a cable to each of the Deathwatch as he saw swarms of gargoyles hurtling through the air towards the gunship.

'Look,' he said, pointing.

'I see them,' nodded Bannon, grasping a cable.

The Deathwatch gathered up the tech-priests and Magos Gossin as Harkus activated the winch to pull them up. Uriel wondered how the fleet had fared as he swung through the air below the gunship and the ramp above drew nearer. The flocks of gargoyles were closing rapidly and he silently urged the winch to haul them faster.

Deciding that he couldn't wait any longer, Harkus spun the gunship, feathering the engines to gain altitude. Uriel didn't blame him. The ground slid below him, thousands of aliens hissing with malevolence towards the sky as their prey escaped.

Then the world turned upside down.

Something huge buffeted him, smashing into his back and spinning him crazily.

He heard a screech of rage and a grunt of pain. Flapping wings spun him around. His vision swum, but he could see the giant, winged monster thrashing in the cables below the Thunderhawk's open crew ramp.

Its wings spurted blood, slashed to ribbons by the cable as it mauled a black-armoured figure who fought it with equal ferocity. As the combatants fought spinning on the cable, Uriel caught a flash of the yellow Imperial Fists insignia.

Captain Bannon stabbed the creature with his power knife, plunging it again and again into its hard, bony carapace. In return the monster's claws tore at his armour, ripping ceramite plates free and gouging bloody chunks from his body.

Swarms of gargoyles swooped down, closing to attack.

The Thunderhawk swayed in the air, unable to make its escape.

Hands reached down to grip Uriel's armour and pull him aboard. He collapsed exhausted onto the armoured deck, breath coming in great heaving gulps as he rolled over to the edge of the ramp.

Below him, man and monster fought in a battle the likes of which Uriel had never seen. The gunship altered course, attempting to put as much distance between it and the hundreds of approaching gargoyles. But with its crew ramp open, it could not accelerate fast enough.

Uriel could see the realisation of this pass through the Deathwatch captain.

He saw what Bannon intended and shouted, 'No!'

But it was too late. Bannon reached up and slashed his power knife through the cable.

He and his monstrous opponent plummeted to the mountainside below, landing amid the swarming creatures.

Cursing the tyranids with all his heart, Uriel pulled himself up the Thunderhawk's fuselage and hammered the ramp's closing mechanism. Now able to achieve escape velocity, Harkus spun the gunship on its axis, punching the engines and kicking in the afterburners. Flocks of gargoyles snapped at the gunship's wings, but he was able to break clear and the aircraft banked around, heading back towards Erebus with hundreds of flying monsters in hot pursuit.

Uriel stared through the vision port.

Below him, Captain Bannon fought his last battle against thousands of screeching killers.

PHASE IV – SUBDUAL

♅

FOURTEEN

THE THUNDERHAWK STREAKED through the lightening sky, vaporous contrails streaming from the trailing edges of its wings. The flight from the gargoyles had burned much of their precious fuel and Harkus was forced to climb to where the air was thinner and every kilometre of range could be squeezed from what little fuel the gunship's tanks still contained.

Should that not prove sufficient, then there was no way they would survive to reach Erebus.

The interior of the gunship was eerily empty, the five members of the Deathwatch, the tech-priests and Uriel all that filled its now spacious storage bays. Without the heavy capacitors, the Thunderhawk could fly much faster and had quickly outdistanced the pursuing gargoyles, concealing itself among the cloud layer.

The howl of the wind was deafening, but even over the tremendous noise, Uriel could hear the valedictions of the Deathwatch and though he too felt Captain Bannon's loss keenly, he respected their need to say their farewell privately.

Uriel closed his eyes and offered a short prayer for the departed captain of the Deathwatch.

It was the least he could do to honour his memory.

HEAVY BLAST DOORS slid smoothly aside, the freezing chill of an Erebus morning rushing in to fill the wide hangar as the *Magnificence* lifted from her moorings in a haze of screaming jets, heavy blast deflectors venting her exhaust fumes into the cold air.

The vessel ponderously nosed out of the hangar, its pilot proceeding with extra care since the owner of the starship was seated directly behind him and with the hold filled with such a vast array of wealth, she handled less deftly than usual. Hardwired into the controls of the ship, he was aware of every aspect of the *Magnificence*, but with a master as volatile as Simon van Gelder it never paid to take chances.

Simon watched the rocky interior of the hangar slide past through the viewing bay, to be replaced by the pristine white of the sky. He smiled as he saw his mountain estates below the ship, still guarded by his privately funded army. Though he expected Erebus to fall any day, there was no reason to leave his property unprotected. If he did return, he would require to reside in prestigious lodgings once again.

The ground slowly fell away as the pilot gained altitude. Simon could see tiny figures lower down the valley pointing at his ship and felt a smug glow of satisfaction as he pictured their dismay at his escape.

A buzzing warning sounded from the speakers, drawing his attention away from the rapidly diminishing landmarks of Erebus.

'The valley defence guns are interrogating us,' said the pilot, with a nervous edge to his voice.

Simon nodded, looking up through the viewing bay to see the massive defence guns rotating in their housings to acquire his ship. He smiled and removed a plain, metallic box from his long coat, unwinding an insulated cable from one end and plugging it into the pilot's console. He pressed a black button on its side and said, 'Broadcast this signal on all frequencies. It will shut down the protocols controlling the guns.'

'We shall be quite safe,' said Simon, deciding to retire to his sumptuous quarters in the upper levels of the ship.

'HANG ON TO something,' shouted Harkus as the Thunderhawk banked sharply around the highest peak to the east of Erebus. 'We have incoming hostiles!'

Uriel strode through the crew compartment to join the pilot in the cockpit. Ahead he could see the gouge in the mountains that was Erebus. Rising from mountain roosts, black flocks of gargoyles and other, more lethal, flying beasts clustered around the highest peaks.

They sped through the air towards the Thunderhawk and Uriel saw it would be a close run thing whether they reached the covering fire of the city's guns before they were caught.

'How are we for fuel?' he asked.

'The reserve tanks are virtually dry. We're flying on fumes and prayers now,' answered Harkus testily.

'Not enough to use the afterburners?'

'Barely even enough to land safely.'

Uriel nodded, watching as the valley of Erebus grew in the windshield. So too did the growing flock of flying monsters that raced to intercept them.

The Thunderhawk's speed increased as Harkus dipped the nose and the mountainside raced up to meet them. Snow-covered rocks flashed beneath them. What he wouldn't have given for some of the gunship's weapon systems right now.

Suddenly the ground dropped away and Harkus hauled back on the controls, deploying the air brakes and pulling the gunship into a screaming turn. Daylight speared inside as bio-weapons fire punched through the thin sheets of lightweight metal welded to its side. Uriel heard one of Gossin's tech-priests screaming as alien organisms ate away his flesh.

He gripped onto the empty co-pilot's chair as the gunship swayed violently in the air and a warning light flashed on the controls.

'We're under the cover of the guns, but they're not firing!' yelled Harkus.

Uriel let out the breath he'd been holding, watching as flying aliens closed in around them. Dozens of impacts perforated the thin hull of the gunship. Fresh screaming echoed.

'Emperor's blood!' shouted the Techmarine, and Uriel looked up in time to see a silver behemoth with heraldic crests emblazoned along the length of its hull rising through the air directly in front of them.

SIMON HEARD HIS pilot's shout of alarm and turned, ready to rebuke him, but the words died in his throat as he saw the roaring Thunderhawk hurtling towards them and the thousands of black, winged monsters that pursued it.

His legs sagged and he dropped to his knees.

'No,' he moaned, 'not like this...'

THE THUNDERHAWK BROKE left and dived, Harkus pushing the weakened airframe beyond the limits of its endurance. The pressure tore the thin sides free and hurricane-force winds roared through its interior. Uriel saw the reflective silver hull of the vessel before them streak past, so close he could have reached out and touched it. The Deathwatch managed to grip onto the bars and struts of the frame, but the three tech-priests were swept screaming to their deaths.

Uriel slammed into a thick stanchion, grabbing onto it as he slid along the violently heaving deck. Over the howling air he heard Harkus swearing and invoking the name of the machine god in equal measures.

The deck lurched again and Uriel saw the ground terrifyingly close through the gaps in the Thunderhawk's flanks. It raced past then vanished from sight as Harkus brought them level again. Uriel pulled himself upright, still clutching the stanchion tightly.

The noise of rushing air diminished, Harkus easing back on the thrusters and bringing the gunship level.

'Imperator, that was close!' breathed Uriel.

'Brace yourselves!' yelled Harkus. 'We're coming into land and it's going to be a rough one!'

THOUSANDS OF GARGOYLES swarmed across the *Magnificence*, clogging air intakes and smashing into control surfaces. Larger creatures skidded across its hull, tearing and biting through her metal hide with acidic saliva and diamond-hard teeth.

Scores of creatures attached themselves to the underside of the hull, clawing and biting open access panels and climbing through the open undercarriage ports. Within seconds, tonnes of extra weight had been added and the already overburdened craft began to list drunkenly to starboard.

Simon's pilot pushed the engines out in an attempt to dislodge the creatures, but with so much of the craft overbalanced and clogged with alien flesh, one simply flamed out, causing the vessel to yaw uncontrollably.

The ship's windshield blew out. Screeching creatures swarmed in and Simon screamed as they tore the flesh from his bones.

A sweeping silver wing struck the rock face and sheared from the hull.

The *Magnificence* tumbled from the skies, gaining speed as she fell until she crashed in a spectacular fireball amid the buildings of District Secundus.

STREAKING BLACK SHAPES spun in the sky above Snowdog as he made his way through the ruins of the destroyed warehouse. Smoking rubble tumbled from the shattered walls and the baleful orange glow from the twisted piles of blazing wreckage more than resembled his vision of hell.

Weeping families hugged the crushed bodies of loved ones and dazed survivors wandered through the ruins, blinded and burned by the crash of the falling starship. A silvered wing pointed towards the sky and a burning section of its hull was embedded in the ground before the warehouse.

Broken crates from the ship's hold littered the ground, spilling smashed porcelain and gilt-edged finery to the snow. A framed portrait of an ancient nobleman lay smashed in the ruins, rolled rugs and tapestries burned in a pool of fuel and fluttering pages from a library's worth of books filled the air. Fabulously expensive clothing soaked in pools of melted snow, ruined beyond repair, and valuables of all description lay scattered throughout the fiery hell of District Secundus.

There was a small fortune just lying on the ground, and Snowdog helped himself to as much as he could fit into his backpack, all the while keeping an eye on the wheeling shapes above and cursing the damn pilot who'd brought his vessel down on top of them. The rear of the warehouse was gone, obliterated by the impact of the plummeting starship. Every one of the crates of supplies he'd heisted, scammed from crooked supply sergeants or killed for was gone, burned to ashes in the searing conflagration.

Tigerlily stood numbed at the scale of the destruction unleashed by the crash, while Lex and Trask scooped up handfuls of gems and stuffed them into their pockets. Jonny helped himself to a vast hunting rifle that poked from a smashed crate, the size of the shells now looped around the big man's body in crosswise bandoliers simply staggering.

'You could bring down an angry grox with that, Jonny!' shouted Snowdog.

Jonny laughed and raised the rifle, miming the rifle's colossal recoil.

The grin fell from Snowdog's face as he saw Silver lying under a pile of cracked stones, her face bloody and arms outstretched. He ran over to her and checked her pulse. It was thready, but strong. She groaned, and Snowdog saw a length of reinforcement bar impaling her side. Blood leaked from the wound and he gently eased her off the steel bar, grimacing as he saw fully fifteen centimetres had stabbed into her.

He removed his scarf and plugged the hole in her side, tying it around her body. It wasn't much, but it was the best he could do for now.

A hand gripped his upper arm and spun him around. He reached for his pistol, but relaxed as he found himself facing a weather-beaten old man.

'What you want, grandfather? Can't you see I'm busy?'

Papa Gallo slapped Snowdog hard in the face.

'You owe these people, Stanker. You took their money and possessions in exchange for safety.'

'What?' snapped Snowdog, pulling his arm free of the old man's grip. He pointed to the sky and said, 'Hey, I gave 'em a place to stay out of the cold and kept these damned things from killing them. I think I done my share. I got problems of my own now.'

Tigerlily moved up to stand behind him and nudged him in the ribs, but Snowdog ignored her, too intent on the confrontation with the old man and the wounded Silver.

'I don't think so,' said Papa Gallo, folding his arms.

'Tough,' retorted Snowdog, 'Anyway, all the stuff they gave me's gone up in smoke.'

'Not our problem. You owe us.'

Tigerlily nudged him again and this time he shot her an irritated glance. She nodded in the direction of the blazing warehouse. He followed her gaze and felt a hot thrill of fear slide around his body. Hundreds of soot-stained civilians, gathered silhouetted in the flames, many of them armed. Armed with weapons Snowdog himself had given them.

They were on edge and looked ready to use them.

Snowdog locked eyes with Papa Gallo and saw the fierce determination there.

He saw Jonny slide a shell for his rifle from the bandoliers and shook his head.

'Okay, man, you win,' said Snowdog, kneeling beside the unconscious Silver. 'What do you want? But be quick.'

'There's a lot of wounded here and you don't have the supplies to deal with them any more.'

'And?'

'And we need to get these people some help. I want you to lead them to the nearest medicae facility,' stated Papa Gallo.

'Shit, man, the nearest one still standing's in District Quintus,' protested Snowdog.

'Not my problem,' repeated Papa Gallo, and as Snowdog looked at the bleeding girl beside him and the many weapons facing him, he realised he had no choice.

'Okay then,' he shrugged, shucking his backpack onto his shoulders and gathering up Silver in his arms. 'Let's get gone. We don't wanna be hanging around with those things flying overhead.'

THE LICTOR THRASHED against its restraints, flesh hooks lashing out at the armoured glass that separated it from those who observed it. Bound to three upright dissection tables pushed together, its powerful muscles bunched as it attempted to break free, but the restraints rendered it immobile. Even so, it had killed two magos-biologis who had unwisely failed to observe full xeno-containment procedures and wounded a third who had subsequently been put to death for his lapse.

With the lictor's capture, Magos Locard's work had progressed with a new urgency following the failed attempt to destroy both hive ships between the defence lasers and the Imperial fleet. Things had gone from bad to worse when the cowardly Simon van Gelder had attempted to flee Tarsis Ultra and treacherously shut down the valley's defences.

The aerial exclusion zone had eventually been re-established, but not before hundreds of gargoyles and their monstrous brood-mothers had penetrated deep into the valley of Erebus. It appeared that they were without the controlling influence of the hive mind, as the majority of the creatures had reverted to their basic, animalistic instincts, nesting in the caves of the valley sides and attacking small groups of civilians. Others had rampaged through the densely-populated quarters of the city, killing in an orgy of random violence for two days before being hunted down by volunteer groups from the Erebus Defence Legion.

The fighting at the District Quintus wall raged with undiminished ferocity, the tyranid swarm almost doubling in size with the addition of yet more creatures as they were drawn to Erebus by the single remaining hive ship. Time was running out for the defenders of Tarsis Ultra and Magos Locard was their last, best hope.

Deep in one of the Adeptus Mechanicus vivisectoria, Magos Locard held forth to an assembled audience of Colonel Stagler, Major Satria, Lord Inquisitor Kryptman, Chaplain Astador and Uriel. A blank-faced servitor with augmented bionics grafted to its head and upper body stood in attendance to the magos, carrying a silver pistol case. They watched the lictor through the armoured glass with revulsion, its physiology repugnant, its mental processes beyond their comprehension.

'As you can observe,' began Locard, 'the lictor organism, even restrained by level three xeno-containment – unfortunately the highest level available in these facilities – is still 45.43% lethal.'

'So why are you keeping the damned thing alive?' demanded Stagler. 'Why not just kill it?'

'To defeat these aliens, we must first understand them,' explained Kryptman. 'When fighting the ork, the hrud, the galthites, the lacrymole we do so armed with knowledge of their undoing. To fight one tyranid is not to know another. Their adaptive nature is what makes them such superlative predators. It is their greatest asset and, potentially in this case, the one weakness we might exploit.'

'In what way?' asked Uriel.

'Tell me, Captain Ventris, have you heard the phrase "to turn an enemy's strength against him"?'

'Of course.'

'That is exactly what we intend,' said Kryptman with a sly smile. 'Magos Locard, if you please.'

Locard nodded and turned to the servitor, his mechadendrites unlocking the pistol case with precise turns of cog-toothed keys that slid from their tooled digits. He lifted a magnificently crafted silver pistol and a large calibre glassy bullet from the foam interior. With exaggerated care he slid the bullet into the breech and handed the weapon to the servitor as his mechadendrites relieved it of the case. At a nod from Kryptman, he spun the locking wheel that led into the lictor's cell and said, 'Proceed with instruction one.'

The servitor turned and pushed open the heavy door, marching to stand beside the dissection tables. Locard sealed the door as the lictor renewed its efforts to break free. The servitor approached and raised the pistol, pressing it against the fleshy portion of the lictor's midsection.

'What in the name of the Emperor is it doing?' asked Uriel.

'Observe,' said Locard, with more than a hint of pride in his voice. He pressed a thumb to the intercom and said, 'Perform instruction two.'

The servitor pulled the trigger, firing the glassy shell into the lictor. Ichor spilled from the wound, hissing on the vivisectoria's floor. Without pausing, the servitor placed the pistol carefully on the floor as Locard released the dissection table restraints.

In a blur of motion the lictor pounced, its severed upper claws smashing the servitor across the room. Its heavily augmented body cracked the glass, drawing cries of alarm from the observers.

Uriel and Astador unholstered their bolt pistols and aimed them through the glass.

'Wait!' cried Kryptman.

The lictor charged the servitor, its lower arms tearing into its grey flesh in a frenzy of violence. Blood sprayed the walls as the beast ripped its victim to shreds, tearing and gouging its body until there was nothing even remotely humanoid remaining. The beast reared up and hammered against the glass. Fresh cracks spread wider, rapidly spiderwebbing across its surface.

'Kill it! Kill it!' shouted Colonel Stagler.

Before Uriel and Astador could fire, the lictor doubled up, dropping to the floor of its cell. The beast let out a keening wail, its entire body convulsing as a frenzy of rippling motion undulated within its flesh.

'Ah yes, now it begins,' noted Locard. 'Resilient, but I expected that, what with its genome being relatively fixed.'

'What's happening to it?' said Uriel, staring in disgust at the convulsing monster.

The lictor fell onto its back, wracked by massive spasms, its body heaving into a giant inverted 'U'. Even through the glass, Uriel heard a loud crack as its spine snapped. The lictor's flesh split and monstrous growths erupted from within, its flesh writhing in uncontrolled evolution. Semi-formed limbs writhed from its viscera and other unnameable organs swelled from its mutating body.

The monster let out a final, tortured screech as an explosion of black blood vomited from its every orifice. Finally it was still.

Uriel was repulsed beyond belief. The lictor was undoubtedly dead, but what had killed it? Simple poison? Sudden hope flared in him as he realised that they might have a weapon with which to defeat the entire tyranid race.

'Excellent work, magos,' said Kryptman as the servitor's blood dripped from the cracked glass.

'Thank you, my lord.'

'What did you do to it?' said Astador.

Locard smiled. 'Using the lictor's genetic sequence, I was able to isolate the base strands of this splinter fleet's original mutation. With that "key", if you will, I was able generate a massive over-stimulation of its adaptive processes. In effect, I drove it into a frenzy of hyper-evolution that not even a tyranid's body could stand. A lictor's genetic structure is normally extremely stable, hence the infection took a little longer to take effect than

I anticipated, but I think you'll agree that the results speak for themselves.'

'This is incredible,' breathed Uriel.

'Indeed it is, Captain Ventris,' agreed Locard, with no hint of false modesty.

'With this weapon we can finally defeat the entire tyranid race!'

'Ah, regrettably, that is not the case,' explained Locard. 'Each hive fleet's gene sequence is vastly different and it was only due to the capture of such an early generation of creature that we were able to isolate this hive fleet's genetics at all.'

'So we can only utilise this weapon on this fleet?' said Stagler.

'Regrettably so, and it may not prove effective against these aliens either. Many of the creatures on Tarsis Ultra have evolved to the sixth or seventh iteration and may have deviated too far from the base strand to be affected.'

'So it may not work at all?' asked Uriel.

'I believe it will, though of course I cannot be certain,' answered Locard.

'We should distribute this ammunition as soon as possible,' said Major Satria excitedly.

Uriel saw a look pass between Kryptman and Locard and suddenly the purpose of the demonstration became clear.

'It it not that simple, Major Satria,' he said.

'No?'

'No, it is not. Is it, lord inquisitor?'

Kryptman stared at Uriel for long seconds before nodding sombrely.

'Captain Ventris is correct. It would be pointless to manufacture ammunition with this gene-poison at this stage in the battle. No, this must be taken to the heart of the enemy where it will do the most damage.'

'And what does that mean?' asked Satria.

'It means,' said Uriel, 'that we are going to have to fight our way into the hive ship. It means we must infect the hive queen.'

IN THINE EVERLASTING Glory had always been one of Sister Joaniel's favourite prayers, speaking as it did of the joy and duty of service to the Emperor. She had dedicated her life to the preservation of life and the healing of those whose frail bodies and minds had come back broken from the horrors of war. On Remian she had lived when those in her care had died and she wept as she prayed, feeling the same guilt burn within her at she thought of the poor unfortunates who lay bleeding and dying throughout the medicae building.

As she had known would happen, the flood of casualties had risen to a raging torrent, with hundreds of men being brought in every day. No matter how hard she scrubbed, she could not get the stench and taint of blood from her hands. No matter how many soldiers they mended, there were always more being brought in by the stretcher-bearers.

And as the front line had drawn ever closer to District Quintus, she and her staff had worked under the noise of artillery and gunfire. The noise of war, screams, explosions and sobbing was always with her, and the sight of so many wounded men haunted her dreams.

Their faces blurred together so that she could no longer tell who lived and who died. So many times she had thought of just giving up, driven to tears by the sheer impossibility of their task. But each time, she recited her favourite prayer and the doubts and guilt were pushed back for a time.

She began the prayer for a fourth time and was midway through the second verse when she heard slamming doors and sounds of a commotion from the vestibule. Rising painfully to her feet, she limped from the chapel to see what all the fuss was about.

Climbing the steps to the vestibule, Joaniel saw a throng of injured people gathered before the doors to the wards. Uniformed orderlies were barring their way, arguing with a youngish man with bleached hair who carried a silver-haired girl whose midriff was a bloody mess.

'What in the name of all that's holy is going on here?' she said, her voice cutting through the babble of voices that filled the vestibule.

The man with the girl in his arms turned and ran his gaze up and down her. A woman with her flame-red hair shaved into stripes flanked him, her face lined with exhaustion.

'I got injured here, figured you could take care of her,' said the man.

'And who are you?' asked Joaniel.

'Me? I'm Snowdog, but that don't matter. I got saddled with bringing these people here and that's what I did. This girl's hurt bad, can you help her?'

One of the orderlies pushed his way towards her through the crowded vestibule, his annoyance plain. He waved a hand at the crowd, more of whom were gathered outside the medicae building, and said, 'They're not military personnel. We can't take them. We're too crowded as it is.'

'Hey, man, you gotta help,' said Snowdog. 'Where the hell else am I gonna go?'

'Not my problem,' snapped the orderly.

'I have heard of you,' said Joaniel. 'You are a killer and a dealer in guns and narcotics.'

'So?'

'So why should I help you, when there are thousands of men risking their lives every day against the tyranids?'

'Because that's what you do. You help people,' said Snowdog, as though it were the most obvious thing in the world.

Joaniel smiled at Snowdog's simple sentiment, ready to rebuke him for such naivety, before it hit her that, yes, that was what she did. It was that simple and she suddenly realised that she could not turn these people away. To do so would betray everything her order stood for. And that she would not do.

Joaniel nodded to Snowdog and pointed to a wide set of stairs that led to the upper levels of the medicae building.

'The top level is not as crowded as the others. I will send food and corpsmen to see to your wounded. We have few staff and even fewer resources thanks to our supplies being stolen, but I promise we will do what we can.'

'But they're not military personnel!' protested the orderly.

She turned to the orderly and snapped, 'I don't care. They will be given shelter and all the care we can spare. Is that understood?'

The orderly nodded, taking the wounded woman from Snowdog's arms and carrying her inside to the wards.

'Thank you, sister,' said Snowdog.

'Shut up,' said Joaniel. 'I'm not doing this for you, it's for them. Let me make myself quite clear. I despise you and all that you are, but as you say, there are wounded people here, so let's get them in out of the cold.'

GIGANTIC YELLOW BULLDOZERS finished clearing the worst of the rubble from the long boulevard that led to the front line, teams of pioneers of the Departmento Munitorum overseeing the final sweeps of the makeshift runways for debris. A stray rock or pothole could spell doom for any aircraft unlucky enough to hit it and this mission was too important for a single craft to be lost. Fuel trucks and missile gurneys crisscrossed the rockcrete apron, delivering final payloads to the multitude of aircraft whose engines filled the air with a threatening rumble. Everywhere there was a sense of urgency as pilots and ground crew prepared their airborne steeds for battle.

Captain Owen Morten, commander of the *Kharloss Vincennes'* Angel squadrons, made a final circuit of his Fury interceptor, checking the techs had removed the arming pins on his missiles and that the leading edges of his wings were free from ice. The greatest danger in flying in such cold conditions was not the additional weight of any ice, but the disruption of the airflow over the wing and subsequent reduction in lift. Satisfied that the aircraft was ready for launch, Morten zipped his flight suit up to his neck and patted the armoured fuselage of the Fury.

'We'll do this one for the *Vincennes*,' he whispered to himself.

'You say something?' asked Kiell Pelaur from the cockpit where he was finishing his ministrations to the Fury's attack logister.

'No,' said Morten, watching as the enginseers continued their inspection of the ice ramp that would hopefully allow them to take off without the length of runway they were used to. The plazas, squares and streets surrounding him were filled with a veritable armada of craft. Every cutter, skiff, fighter, bomber or recon craft that could be put in the air was right now being prepped for immediate launch.

Owen knew that most of them would never return, sacrificed to ensure the Space Marines got through to their objective. The thought did not trouble him. He had long since resigned himself to the fact that this would be his final flight. The skies above him were where he was meant to be and where he had always known he would die.

The thought that he would soon see all his dead shipmates was a great comfort to Owen Morten as he clambered up the crew ladder and vaulted into the cockpit.

THE BLACK THUNDERHAWK was devoid of insignia or ornamentation. Or so it appeared until closer inspection. Every square centimetre of its hull was inscribed with filigreed scriptwork, carved by hand with painstaking care. Catechisms and prayers of hatred for the xeno decorated the aircraft's body from prow to stern.

Chanting tech-priests circled the aircraft and blessed armourers inscribed words of ire onto the seeker heads of the wing-mounted missiles. Each heavy calibre shell loaded into the ammo hoppers of the autocannons was dipped in sanctified water before being slotted home with chants that would ensure detonation.

The five surviving members of the Deathwatch knelt in prayer before the gunship, entreating it to see them safely to their destination. Henghast led the prayers, his wounds still paining him, but recovered enough from his battle with the lictor to accompany his battle-brothers. Brother Elwaine of the Salamanders had also survived, and was even now undergoing augmetic surgery to replace his arms. Despite Elwaine's protests, Henghast had not permitted him to join the mission.

Five men against the might of a hive ship. It was of such things that the legends of the Deathwatch were made and thoughts of the battle to come filled Henghast's Fenrisian soul with fire. Should they survive, it would make for a fine saga for the Rune Priests to tell around the feast tables of the Fang.

Henghast clasped his hands to his chest and said, 'We mourn the loss of Captain Bannon, and revere his memory. He was a fine leader of men and a worthy brother in arms. I dearly wish he could be here to lead us into battle once more, but wishes are for the saga poets and we will bring honour to him by fighting this battle in his name.'

A long shadow fell over Henghast and his lip curled over his fangs as he smoothly rose to his feet, ready to rebuke whoever had interrupted his men's devotions.

But the words died in his throat as he saw the figure standing before him.

A Space Marine, his armour painted midnight black, with a single bright blue shoulder.

'Ready your warriors, Brother Henghast,' said Captain Uriel Ventris of the Deathwatch, 'we go into battle.'

₢ FIFTEEN

URIEL FELT THE lurch of the Thunderhawk lifting off and rested his helmeted head against the rumbling side of the roaring aircraft. A soft blue light filled the crew compartment, and a beatific choir of angels drifted from humming recyc-units that circulated sacred incense inimical to the xeno. The Deathwatch sat along the opposite fuselage, their heads bowed as they readied themselves for the coming fight.

Brother Henghast, the Space Wolf, led their prayers, and Uriel was not surprised to hear pious imprecations that were the mark of a warrior preparing himself for death in battle. He allowed his gaze to wander over the brothers he would be sharing his final battle with, knowing that their service in the Deathwatch already meant that they were amongst the best and bravest warriors their Chapter could boast.

Brother Jagatun of the White Scars sat sharpening a long, curved tulwar, a horsehair totem dangling from its skulled pommel. Brother Damias, an Apothecary of the Raven Guard, taciturn and solitary, his power fist etched with bizarre scars that reminded Uriel of those inflicted by zealous priests who worked themselves into a self-mortifying frenzy of devotion. Beside him sat Brother Alvarax of the Howling Griffons and Brother Pelantar of the White Consuls. Both individually loaded the hellfire shells of their heavy bolters, the mutagenic acids contained in each silver-cased bolt deadly to xeno organisms.

Seated beside Uriel was the final member to make up their number. He alone of this band of warriors retained his Chapter's original colours and his presence was as much of as reassurance to Uriel as the Deathwatch itself.

Veteran sergeant Pasanius gripped the barrel of his heavy flamer tightly in his silvered bionic hand, silently awaiting the coming battle.

Uriel had tried to dissuade his oldest friend from coming, but Pasanius was having none of it, and since Brother Elwaine and his flamer were unable to fight, Henghast had been only too glad for Pasanius to accompany them. In the close confines of the tyranid hive ship, a flamer was sure to be a vital element of their attack.

Seeing that Pasanius was absolutely entrenched in his position, Uriel knew he would need to have his sergeant dragged away to prevent him from coming and had reluctantly, but inwardly gratefully, allowed him to come. Astador and Learchus were more than capable of holding the defenders together and his presence would not affect the fate of Erebus one way or another.

Astador had embraced him, promising his mortal remains a place of honour in the Gallery of Bone. Uriel had not liked the finality in the Chaplain's voice as he intoned the Emperor's blessing upon him.

Learchus had offered no such blessings, his fury at what he saw as his captain's desertion of his men incandescent. 'Your place is with your men, not leading the Deathwatch!' he had argued.

'No, Learchus, my place is wherever I can do the most good,' he had replied.

'Show me where it says that in the codex,' snapped Learchus.

'You know I cannot, sergeant. But this is just something I have to do.'

'Lord Calgar shall hear of this.'

'You must do what you feel is right, Learchus, as must I,' said Uriel before leaving his furious sergeant to ready the Ultramarines for the last battle.

Uriel was saddened by Learchus's inability to see beyond the letter of the codex, feeling sure that Roboute Guilliman would have approved of his decision to lead the Deathwatch into battle. He knew that there was great wisdom in the pages of the Codex Astartes, but knew also that it was wisdom to learn from, that such dogmatic adherence to what its pages contained was, as Astador had said, not wisdom, but repetition.

But there was a danger in this: that such thoughts would lead inevitably to the path the Mortifactors walked. Uriel had no wish to pursue that path, but knew now that there was a balance to be had in following the spirit of the codex, if not the letter. He smiled as he imagined the silent approval of Captain Idaeus and watched through the vision port as the view darkened from the violet sky of Tarsis Ultra to the blackness of space.

He looked around the crew compartment once more at his comrades. Seven magnificent warriors going into battle.

A battle that would decide the fate of a world.

* * *

LEARCHUS WATCHED THE Thunderhawk blast into the upper atmosphere, surrounded by hundreds of escorting aircraft as bright spots of light against the darkness. Dawn was already lightening the horizon with a diffuse amber light and he could see the first stirrings beneath the snow as the tyranids emerged from the ground.

The cracked remnants of the wall were sagging in many places, but there was little that could be done about it. Some work had been done to ready it for the coming assault, but the bulk of work undertaken throughout the night had been in preparing the runways for the aircraft to launch.

He gripped the hilt of his chainsword tightly, his anger at Uriel and Pasanius still bright and hot despite their departure. He and the remaining eighty members of the Fourth company stood at parade rest behind the northern segment of the District Quintus wall, ready to receive the attack of the tyranids. Chaplain Astador and the sixty-three warriors of the Mortifactors held the southern portion of the wall, and Learchus made a mental note to keep an eye on these reckless descendants of his Chapter.

Astador had already offered him the chance to partake in one of their barbaric blood rituals before the battle, but he had refused, marching away in disgust before doing something he might regret.

'Courage and honour!' he bellowed as the first bloated creatures moved sluggishly forward, tensioned, bony arms stretching back to launch their organic bombs.

THE TASTE OF blood still strong in his mouth, Chaplain Astador watched the unyielding figure of Learchus as he stood ramrod-straight with his warriors. He knew Learchus was a great warrior, but Astador knew he could never be anything beyond that.

His ghost-self had only recently returned to his body and his spirit still rebelled at its incarceration in the prison of flesh. Briefly Astador considered telling Learchus what the spirits of his ancestors had shown him, but shook his head and returned his gaze to the advancing tyranids.

What would be the point in telling him?

He would not be thankful for the knowledge that his captain was going to die.

A PUNISHING TWO-HOUR barrage of spores hammered the District Quintus wall, wreathing the ramparts in drifting clouds of toxic vapours. High winds channelled down the length of the valley dispersed much of the poisonous filth, but interspersed with the gaseous spores were those that sprayed acidic viruses upon detonation. Huge portions of the parapet dissolved into puddles of molten rock, sliding down the face of the wall like thick rivulets of wax.

A section of the southern rampart slid from the liquefying ground, sending a trio of Mortifactors tumbling to the base of the wall. They smashed through the thin ice of the moat, plunging beneath the icy waters only to rise minutes later as they swam to the surface.

Learchus watched the black-armoured Space Marines take up firing stances as the hordes of aliens surged forwards in one homogenous mass. Immediately, he could see this was no normal attack, but a concerted hammer-blow designed to smash through their defences. The smaller, leaping organisms streamed forwards, a chittering black tide that covered the ground. Gunfire hammered their numbers, but such casualties were insignificant next to the size of the overall attack.

The weight of so many creatures broke the ice of the moat with an almighty crack and thousands of organisms plunged into its subzero waters. They kept coming, the vast numbers of frozen bodies in the moat providing a means of crossing for those behind.

Giant clawed beasts with entire broods of hissing aliens encased in their armour plates charged, throwing up great chunks of ice as they powered forward. Scorpion beasts that Learchus had not seen before scuttled forward, streaming weapons formed from bony outgrowths in their midsections firing at the wall.

Lightning-sheathed beasts with vast, slashing claws slithered, snakelike, towards them, arcs of energy lashing the wall and blasting free tank-sized chunks of rockcrete.

Learchus opened a channel to Major Satria of the Erebus Defence Legion.

'Lead your men forwards now, Major. Pattern alpha one.'

'ARE YOU SURE you're ready for this, sir?' asked Major Satria as he jogged towards the wall.

'I'm sure, major. Now stop fussing,' chided Sebastien Montante as he breathlessly tried to keep up with the major and the five thousand Defence Legion troopers. His webbing was loose and he was sweating profusely in his overwhites.

His lasgun felt like it weighed as much as a lascannon, but he was glad of its reassuring feel. He felt powerful just carrying it and only hoped he remembered how to fire it when the time came to fight.

DEEP IN THE many caves that riddled the high peaks of the eastern valley a keening screech built to a deafening howl that echoed around the upper echelons of the city. Many of the gargoyles that had penetrated the aerial cover of Erebus thanks to Simon van Gelder's treachery had been hunted down and killed, but a great many had not. The majority of these had been simple warrior organisms bred to fly, but nine had been much more.

Secreted in the deepest caves, the gargoyle brood-mothers had obeyed the overmind's command to nest and produce more of its kin. Driven into a frenzy of reproduction, the brood mothers had since expired, but not before giving birth to thousands upon thousands of offspring.

As the assault began on the wall, an implacable imperative seized the nesting gargoyles who took to the air in their thousands, and a black tide of monsters screeched from their hiding places to attack.

'You GOT THEM, lieutenant?' asked Captain Morten, tensing his fingers on the Fury's control column.

'Yes,' snarled Keill Pelaur. 'The attack logister can't keep up with all the signals it's getting. The bio-ships are altering formation to face us, but they're slow. We'll be on them before they're properly aligned.'

Morten grinned beneath his oxygen mask.

The target information on Pelaur's slate was being echoed on his own display and the sheer numbers they were about to face were beyond anything in the squadron's history.

Fitting then, that this should be its last battle.

A rune on Morten's armaments panel flashed, indicating that he was within his missiles' optimum kill range.

He opened a channel to the aircraft he led.

'All craft open fire!'

He pulled the trigger on the control column twice in quick succession, shouting, 'For the *Vincennes!*' Scores of missiles leapt from beneath the wings of hundreds of aircraft, streaking upwards towards the tyranid fleet. They had to punch a hole through the screen for the Thunderhawk. All other concerns were secondary.

The gap was rapidly closing between the two forces and Morten knew it would get real ugly, real quick. Even as he watched, the enemy creatures smoothly moved into blocking positions, scores of smaller, faster creatures moving to intercept them.

'Stay sharp,' called Morten, 'the enemy is turning into us.'

The initial volley had cut a swathe through the outer screen of tyranid spores, but hundreds more remained, all closing on his aerial armada. A lesser man might have been cowed, but Owen Morten was a born and bred Fury pilot who lived for combat.

He pulled into a shallow climb and armed his last missiles.

Almost as soon as he'd done so, he and his squadron were tangled up in a madly spinning dogfight with dozens of fleshy, spore creatures that spun and wove almost as fast as the Furies. Morten rolled hard left, catching sight of a speeding organism and followed it down.

'I'm too close for a missile shot!' he yelled, switching to guns as the creature tried to shake him.

Every move the creature made, the Fury was with it, spinning around like insects in a bizarre mating ritual. The beast flashed across his gunsight and he pulled the trigger.

'Got you, you bastard!' he roared as bright lasbolts ripped the tyranid beast in two.

'Captain! Break right!' screamed Pelaur as a spuming bolt of light speared past the Fury's canopy.

He pulled around and breathed deeply, amazed at how close their near miss had been. He eased back on the throttle and switched back to missiles.

A warbling tone in his ear told him the missile's war-spirit had found a target and he pulled the trigger again.

'Captain!' called Erin Harlen. 'You've got one right behind you!'

Morten hauled right and checked his rear, twisting his Fury in an attempt to shake the pursuing organism.

'I can't get rid of it!' swore Morten as the beast matched his wild manoeuvrings.

'It's firing!' shouted Pelaur.

'Breaking left!' answered Morten, rolling hard and kicking in the afterburner. He felt his flight suit expand and his heartbeat race.

A bolt of crackling energy spat below him and he spun the plane round in a screaming, tight turn, chopping the throttle and almost stalling the engine.

The creature tried to match his turn, but was too slow.

Morten rolled inverted and pulled in behind the pulsing organism, lining it up in his sights and firing.

Bolts from the lascannon shredded the creature and it exploded in a bloody spray.

Listening to the vox-chatter, he heard screams and imprecations from the rest of the aircraft. The tyranids were slaughtering them, but he couldn't think about that just now. Not while there was a battle still to be fought. But as he scanned the space before him, he could see they'd blown a gap. The Thunderhawk was streaking through it, the blue glare of its plasma engines bright against the darkness of the massive hive ship's stony carapace.

Then he saw a giant, winged creature with spitting, electrical mandibles powering after the Space Marine gunship. Arcs of crackling energies lashed the Thunderhawk again and again, and Morten could see it wouldn't survive much longer.

His flight suit was soaked with perspiration and he knew he was at the edge of exhaustion, but he pushed out the engines to follow the Thunderhawk.

URIEL FELT THE gunship lurch, and leaping streaks of blue energy sparked from the fuselage. The pilot threw them in a series of wild turns, but Thunderhawks had never been designed for dogfights and Uriel knew it was only a matter of time before whatever was pursuing them was able to destroy them. Weapons and ammo packs tumbled from the lockers above him.

He pushed clear of the restraint harness and rose to his feet, turning to retrieve the weapon Inquisitor Kryptman had given him. To lose it now would end their mission before it had begun. He staggered as another impact smashed into the gunship. Flames erupted from a shattered fuel line and warning klaxons screamed.

Yet another hammer-blow struck the rear quarter of the Thunderhawk and one of the vision ports blew out with a decompressive boom.

Rushing air howled from the gunship, and Uriel felt his rage growing. They could not fail. Not after coming so close.

But as further impacts rocked the Thunderhawk, he knew they could not survive another.

CAPTAIN OWEN MORTEN pushed the Fury as fast as it could go. His fighter streaked past the tyranid organism pummelling the Thunderhawk as he armed the last of his missiles.

A flickering blue glow illuminated the interior of the Fury as bolts of lightning lashed from the mandibles of the creature. Fully six times the size of the Fury, Morten knew that only a direct hit on its most vulnerable location would destroy it.

'Captain!' shouted Pelaur, 'ease back on the throttle or we won't have enough fuel to get back to the planet.'

'We're not going back,' said Morten calmly as he neatly slotted the Fury between the giant tyranid beast and the Thunderhawk.

'What the hell are you doing?' screamed Pelaur.

'What needs to be done,' answered Morten, cutting the engines and spinning the Fury on its axis until it had turned a full one hundred and eighty degrees.

The crackling maw of the tyranid beast filled his canopy. Giant arcs of lighting enveloped the Fury. Sparks and flames filled the cockpit.

Captain Morten pulled the trigger, sending his last missile straight down the monster's throat.

URIEL FELT A huge detonation behind the gunship, and awaited the inevitable destruction of the Thunderhawk. But the fatal blow never landed and the Thunderhawk levelled out, weaving through the hail of spores that gathered around the monstrous hive ship.

He made his way up the central aisle of the gunship towards the cockpit. All he could see ahead was the craggy cliff of the hive ship's hide. Inquisitor Kryptman had shown them the most likely locations of possible entry points, and he scanned the grey moonscape before him for one.

The aerial armada had got them through and now it was time to make good on that sacrifice.

'There!' he said, pointing to a rippling, fleshy orifice on the side of the gargantuan creature, organic waste venting through it into space by peristaltic motion of flesh. A ribbed sphincter muscle expanded as more waste was expelled and Uriel knew they had found what they had come for.

'Hurry! If what Inquisitor Kryptman says is true, it will close in seconds!'

The pilot deftly guided the gunship forward, increasing power to the engines as the fleshy orifice began to contract. Only as they approached did Uriel realise how vast it was, fully sixty metres in diameter.

Before it could close completely, the Thunderhawk sped into the ribbed, fleshy tunnel beyond.

Truly they were in the belly of the beast, thought Uriel as the sphincter vent closed and the faint light of the stars was snuffed out.

LEARCHUS SWEPT HIS chainsword through the neck of yet another tyranid creature, his blade clogged with alien meat and gristle. His bolter had long since run out of shells and he fought two-handed with his blade.

Clotted blood caked his shoulder where a screeching monster twice the height of a man had gained the walls and torn through his armour. The wall was a charnel house of alien and human dead. Cracked pillars and columns clustered at the wall's edge were hung with gory spatters of blood and entrails that spilled over the icy ground, making it treacherous underfoot. Learchus fought for balance with every step he took.

Major Satria fought alongside him, stabbing with his bayonet and firing with his lasgun whenever he had the chance to reload. Beside him, Fabricator Montante fought with desperation and courage, if not skill. Learchus had already saved his life on numerous occasions and though it was foolish of Montante to be here, he was forced to admire his bravery.

'Warriors of Ultramar hold fast!' bellowed Learchus.

Drifting spores exploded amongst the battling warriors, but they refused to give way. He kicked out at a screeching hormagaunt as it scrabbled over the lip of the wall, sending its shattered skull spinning to the heaving mass of aliens below.

Over the deafening clash of battle at the wall, Learchus heard the roar of guns behind him and risked a glance over his shoulder to see who was shooting. The few remaining Hydra flak tanks were firing eastwards and his hearts skipped a beat as he saw the impenetrable black cloud of gargoyles sweeping down the length of the valley.

'Guilliman save us...' whispered Learchus as he took in the numbers of enemy now closing on their rear.

'Astador!' he yelled over the vox.

'I see them!' replied the Chaplain.

The Hydras punched holes in the swarm, but Learchus could see the sheer scale of the attack would defeat them.

* * *

SEBASTIEN MONTANTE FOUGHT with a strength and courage he never knew he possessed. His arms ached from the fighting, but he was filled with elation at finally having proven himself worthy of the mantle of leadership of this world. He ducked behind a fluted pillar as he reached for a fresh energy cell for his lasgun. A Space Marine fell beside him, a smoking crater blasted in his armour where his chest had been.

Sebastien hastily reloaded and spun around the pillar, opening up on a swarm of scuttling creatures with wide, webbed hands circling behind Learchus and Major Satria.

He felled three with a single burst of full auto and crippled a fourth as a giant shadow reared over him.

Sebastien spun and raised his rifle. A lashing, spined whip hacked his gun in two and spun him from his feet. He scrambled upright, using the pillar for support and fumbled for his sabre as the huge warrior organism towered above him. Its bony carapace was brightly patterned with crimson streaks and its hissing jaws seemed to leer at him as the writhing whips on the end of its upper limb lashed out again.

Sebastien screamed as the razor-edged tendril gouged his flesh, binding him to the pillar as it tightened. The monster's claws reached out towards him...

Then Learchus was there, hacking through the fleshy lash with his sword and spinning inside the monster's guard. Its claws closed around his body as he stabbed his blade through its hard, chitinous plates. It screamed and gouged great holes in Learchus's armour.

Sebastien struggled to free himself, but gave up as the talons embedded in the whip's length continued to bite deep into his flesh.

Learchus roared as he finally drove his sword through the beast's throat and Major Satria rushed over to help.

A black shadow passed overhead and Sebastien saw a teeming multitude of creatures descend on the defenders at the wall. The carnage was terrible as men were lifted up and clawed to death by this new foe. As the resistance at the wall began to disintegrate, Major Satria unsheathed his knife.

'Soon have you free, my lord,' he said, moving around the back of the pillar.

Sebastien nodded, in too much pain to reply.

Then he saw a massive set of ridged claws hammer into the rampart and a vast, gurgling beast haul its incredible bulk over the wall. A flock of creatures, red and black, with the same webbed fists as those he'd killed, scuttled from the folds of its flesh and raced towards them.

'Major...' he croaked, too quietly to be heard.

The beasts paused, raising their bizarre looking hands, as though they were waving at him and the ridiculousness of the thought almost made him want to laugh.

Their fists expanded, as though filling with air and suddenly dozens of sharp spines blasted from their hands and slashed towards him.

He screamed as he felt them penetrate his flesh. How many he didn't know, all he could feel was pain and fire racing around his body. He sagged against the barbed alien cord binding him to the pillar, his body pierced by dozens of long organic spines. His head sagged on his neck and he saw a spreading pool of blood expanding around his boots.

He heard someone shout his name, but everything was growing dim and he couldn't make out who.

Then everything went black and consciousness slipped away.

URIEL CLIMBED DOWN from the battered Thunderhawk and stepped onto the soft, spongy flesh of the hive ship's interior. Inquisitor Kryptman's weapon was stored in a holster at his hip. It didn't fit exactly, but was close enough not to matter.

A diffuse green light lit up the ribbed chamber they found themselves in, its vastness filled with pungent fumes and knee-deep organic effluent. The stench was indescribable and Uriel turned down his olfactory auto-senses before his disgust overwhelmed him.

He waved forward the rest of his warriors, Pasanius taking the lead with the blue flame of his flamer burning brightly in the rich atmosphere of the hive ship. Uriel felt motion around his boots and saw grotesque, beetle-like creatures scuttling across the ribbed walls of the chamber, feasting on the waste embedded there.

They were no threat and he ignored them as they pushed deeper into the chamber. A pulsing rumble thumped from the walls like a gigantic heart-beat, or a series of heartbeats. Kryptman had said that a hive ship was a massive agglomeration of creatures blended into one gestalt beast that formed the overmind.

'This place is cursed,' said Brother Pelantar, moving up to take a flanking position, his heavy bolter slung low and ready to fire. Alvarax took up the same position on the opposite flank.

'You might be right,' agreed Uriel, remembering the depths of Pavonis where he had fought the Bringer of Darkness and how evil echoes of past horrors could saturate a place with their power.

Brother Damias moved to the centre of the group, reading from a specially modified auspex Inquisitor Kryptman had furnished him with. Its blue light reflected from the base of his helm, its soft chiming loud in the warm chamber.

Hissing gusts of steam vented from slitted orifices and a tremor ran through the floor of the chamber as the walls rippled with motion. Uriel saw the scurrying organisms speed into fleshy caverns set in the depths of the wall and said, 'Come on, let us be about our business. I do not believe we should linger in this place.'

With Pasanius leading the way, the Deathwatch moved off into the depths of the hive ship.

SNOWDOG SPRINTED DOWN the stone stairs of the medicae building as the sound of alarm bells rang throughout the facility. Sisters of the Order Hospitaller hurried through the building, directing those wounded men who could walk towards the upper levels. Others carried stretchers or boxes of medical equipment.

He skidded to the bottom level, finding the vestibule thronged with nurses as they guided those without their sight through the armoured door at the base of the stairs. Snowdog could almost taste the panic in the air.

'What's going on?' he demanded.

No one answered him, too wrapped up in their own fear to reply. He pushed his way through the crowds towards the main wards, finding many more wounded men being chivvied to their feet by tearful sisters. Straight away he could see that there were far too many wounded for them to cope with.

As he realised this, he saw Sister Joaniel marching towards him.

'You!' she yelled, 'come here!'

He made his way along the ward, dodging wounded men as they limped towards the main doors.

'What's going on?' he asked again.

'We've received the evacuation order,' said Joaniel desperately. 'We need to get these men out to safety. The front line is about to fall.'

'What? But it's less than half a kilometre from here!'

'I know, that's why we can't waste any time. I need your help.'

'*My* help? What do you think I can do?'

Joaniel gripped Snowdog's arms and said, 'The medicae facility is built against the rock face of the valley's southern wall. There is an entrance to the caves on the upper levels that lead further up the valley.'

'And?'

'And I want you to lead these people out of here to safety,' explained Joaniel.

'What? I just got them here!'

'I don't care, just do it,' snapped Joaniel.

'Okay, okay,' said Snowdog. 'What about you? What are you gonna be doing?'

'I'm going to be making sure that my patients get out of this building alive.'

OOZING SLIME DRIPPED from the ceiling, hissing as droplets pattered against the shoulder guards of the Deathwatch. The fleshy passageways of the hive ship were a cornucopia of biological horrors, fleshy folds of muscle and gristle lining every wall and suppurating pools of digestive juices filling every footprint they left. Tiny slave organisms hurried along every passageway, ignoring the Space Marines as they pushed deeper into the body of the beast.

The omnipresent rumble drifted from every orifice and the noise of biological processes was thick in the air.

Uriel could feel a nascent claustrophobia as the walls of the ribbed passage contracted in time with the rumble, expanding again as though they were in some great breathing organ. Steaming jets of liquid sprayed them as they passed from the passageway into a wide, necrotic chamber of crackling gristle and pulped meat.

Row upon row of ruptured egg sacs and niches with cancerous organic pipes hanging inert within them lined the walls of the chamber from floor to ceiling.

'What is this place?' asked Henghast.

'They slept here,' said Damias, sweeping his softly chiming auspex around. 'They slept away the years while they travelled to Tarsis Ultra from wherever they came from.'

Uriel saw Damias was right as he spotted a tyranid warrior organism in one of the niches, its flesh withered and dead. Its four arms hung limply at is side, its bony head slumped over its shoulder.

A sudden hissing motion rippled through the walls, a greenish glow building from the smoke that drifted at ankle height. At the far end of the chamber, a fleshy fold of bone lifted aside and a wash of stinking chemicals spilled into the chamber carrying a tide of screeching tyranid creatures.

'Captain!' yelled Pasanius as he bathed them in flames.

Alvarax and Pelantar braced themselves and sprayed the creatures with shells from their heavy bolters. Uriel fired into the mass of aliens as a host of the ventricle valve doors rippled open and yet more beasts poured into the chamber.

A giant beast bounded towards them, its armoured carapace low and armoured like a scorpion. It bounded towards Jagatun, who ducked and slashed its soft underbelly with his razor-edged tulwar. Looping organs spilled from the wound.

Henghast howled and slashed his power sword through its body, dragging Jagatun to his feet while firing his bolter with his free hand. Pasanius fell back, each step accompanied by a spray of liquid fire into knots of screeching aliens.

Uriel blazed away at the creatures as they poured from the walls to assail them. He didn't know how many beasts the hive ship had at its disposal, but he knew they could not afford to find out.

'Deathwatch, fall back!' he ordered.

Alvarax and Pelantar backed away, firing as they went and closing on Uriel.

'Brother Damias!' yelled Uriel. 'Which way?'

Damias was blood-streaked, his power fist coated in alien gore. He consulted the auspex and said, 'This way.'

He set off through an oval hole in the wall as Uriel called, 'Everyone through here!'

Henghast dived through the hole, followed by Jagatun. The roar of heavy bolters covered them before Pelantar ducked into the gap. Uriel pushed Pasanius through and shouted, 'Alvarax! Come on, we are leaving!'

Alvarax raked his fire over the attacking beasts, his aim sure. Dozens of aliens fell, blown apart by his sanctified shells.

Then the ground opened up beneath him and he was gone, sucked into the depths of the ship.

Uriel shouted, 'Alvarax!' and moved to go to his battle-brother's aid, but a strong hand gripped him and hauled him back.

'He's gone,' yelled Pasanius, 'Come on!'

Uriel nodded and pushed into the close confines of the new passageway, feeling his way by touch rather than sight. He heard an oozing sound behind him as muscular contractions pulled the passage way wider to allow more of their pursuers to chase them. Pasanius pushed him ahead and turned to fill the passageway with flames. Screeching howls followed them as aliens burned. The fleshy passage shuddered in sympathy with their pain and Uriel was suddenly reminded of something Kryptman had told him before they left Tarsis Ultra: 'As you penetrate deeper into the ship, its nervous system will become more sophisticated. It will feel pain the closer you get to its centre.'

He followed his warriors as the passageway sloped downwards, the soggy texture of the ground squelching as he ran. He heard gunfire and saw a glow from up ahead as the passage widened into a vein-ridged chamber with a pulsing, mushroom shaped organism at its centre.

A score of dead creatures littered the ground before the thing. 'What is that?' asked Henghast.

'Does it matter? They were guarding it so it must be important to them,' said Jagatun, slashing his tulwar through its stem. Plumes of spores erupted from the organisms severed stalk and enveloped Jagatun like a cloud of buzzing insects. He batted them away before doubling up as the surface of his armour began corroding before Uriel's eyes.

He heard the White Scar's screams over the vox as the spores devoured him from within, his filters and rebreathers no defence against such a deadly attack. The Deathwatch backed away from the clouds of corrosive spores, unable to help their stricken battle-brother. Pasanius fired his flamer, consuming them in a cleansing burst of promethium.

Chittering screeches from the sucking passageway they had just come from echoed towards them.

'This way,' said Uriel plunging into a ridged opening in the far wall, emerging into a long, curving passage, knee-deep in sloshing fluids. Fronds of cilia dangled from the roof and walls of the passage, waving as though in a gentle breeze. The sludgy liquid flowed away to the right and Uriel waited for Brother Damias to join them.

As the Deathwatch assembled, Damias led them to the left, splashing through the foetid ordure against the flow. Worm-like organisms swam through the sludge, latching onto their armour and attempting to feed.

The Space Marines plucked them from their armour in disgust. They were annoying but hardly dangerous. Uriel pushed onwards through the circular tunnel, the fronds above him brushing against his helmet.

He halted as he heard a strange sound over the constant rumble of the hive ship. It sounded like distant thunder, like standing at the end of the Valley of Laponis on Macragge and listening to the noise of the far-off Hera's Falls.

As he realised what it was he shouted, 'Hold on to something!'

He punched his fist through the tough walls of the veined passage and gripped a handful of the hive ship's substance as hundreds of tonnes of organic waste thundered along the passageway towards them.

SNOWDOG HUSTLED THE wounded men up the stairs to the upper levels of the medicae building, wondering how long they had before the tyranids got here. The damned alarm bells were still ringing and he smashed the butt of his gun against one until it shut up. Jonny was on the landing above him and Lex was busy wiring the main door of the building with the mother of all explosive devices. Tigerlily was keeping an eye on Silver who was now stable, but still unconscious. He had no idea where Trask was, but didn't much care one way or another. He still carried the back-pack filled with valuables taken from the crashed starship, so it wasn't as though Trask was off stealing that.

He pushed his way down to the vestibule, seeing the skinny shape of Lex still working at the door.

'Lex, whatever you're doing, do it quicker, man,' he said.

'Hey, I'm going as fast as I can. You know, if you helped, I could get done quicker.'

'No way, man. Me and explosives? Forget about it.'

'Well thanks for offering anyway,' sneered Lex.

'No problem. Everyone off this floor?'

'Yeah, I think so. Everyone except that crazy sister.'

Snowdog pushed his way into the main ward area. The place was deserted except for Sister Joaniel, who stood behind the central nursing station with a plain wooden box before her.

Snowdog jogged towards the nursing station and slung his lasgun. 'Hey, sister, we don't have time to hang around here. Time we was gone.'

'Is everyone safe?' asked Joaniel, tears streaking her face.

'Yeah, more or less. They're all on their way upstairs if that's what you mean.'

'Good,' nodded Joaniel. 'I couldn't save them before.'

'What? Save who?'

'All of them. On Remian. They called me the Angel of Remian because I put them back together after the war had broken them, but in the end I couldn't save them. They all died.'

Joaniel held up the wooden box and said, 'They gave me this for all the good work I'd done. It's a medicus ministorum... I don't deserve it.'

'Okay,' said Snowdog in puzzlement, 'as fun as it is to trip down memory lane, Sister Joaniel, I think we need to get going.'

As if to underscore his words, a thudding boom impacted on the thick wooden doors of the medicae building. Even through the thick walls, Snowdog could hear the scrape of hordes of aliens swarming around the building.

Lex stuck his head in the door to the wards and shouted, 'Come on, let's get the hell out of this place.'

Snowdog turned to Joaniel. 'You heard the man, now come on.'

She gathered up the wooden box, but didn't move. Cursing himself for a fool, Snowdog grabbed her by the arm and pulled her along the ward.

'Why the hell do I let myself get into these situations?' he wondered aloud.

Together they emerged into the vestibule, the doors already splintering under repeated blows from something massive. They skidded across the stone flags of the floor, sprinting for the armoured door that led to the stairs. Jonny Stomp stood at the bottom, his massive hunting rifle slung over his shoulder.

'Come on!' he yelled.

With a crash of shattered timbers, the main doors were ripped from their frame and scores of snarling creatures poured in around a massive battering ram of a monster. Its claws were massive, sheathed in splintered wood and its jaws screeched with burning fires.

It took a thunderous step into the medicae building, the stone cracking under its weight, just as Lex's bomb went off.

Snowdog gathered Joaniel in his arms and threw himself flat as the detonation slammed them both into the wall. Fire and dust and stone filled the air as the blast took out the aliens as well as the columns supporting the roof and walls of the entrance. The giant beast staggered, but didn't fall, its armoured hide painted with the gory ruin of its smaller kin. It reeled at the edge of a crater gouged in the ground, blocks of stone tumbling from the walls around it.

Snowdog rolled onto his stomach, his body one giant mass of pain. Strangely, his back felt fine, but then he remembered his backpack of valuables and figured it must have protected him from the worst of the blast. He tried to push himself to his feet and cried out in pain, feeling at least one rib broken.

Joaniel pushed herself up against the stone wall, still clutching her medicus ministorum. Snowdog groaned beside her as the gigantic monster recovered its wits enough to take another stamping step towards them.

Jonny Stomp stepped down into the vestibule, his enormous hunting rifle wedged tightly against his shoulder.

The massive beast was almost upon him, the fire building between its gnashing mandibles.

Jonny sighted along the barrel and pulled the trigger.

And the beast's head vanished in an explosion of blood and bone.

Jonny was hurled through the stair door by the recoil and landed in a sprawling heap. He whooped with glee, thumbing another shell into the breech.

The monster crashed backwards into the crater blown by Lex's bomb as Joaniel pulled Snowdog to his feet. He cried out in pain as she pushed him into Jonny's arms.

'Go on!' she shouted. 'Get him out of here!'

'What you gonna do?' said Jonny.

'I'm right behind you,' said Joaniel, crouching by the medicus ministorum and flipping open its lid.

Jonny saw hundreds more of the smaller beasts gathering outside. 'Whatever you say,' he shrugged and half-carried, half-dragged Snowdog after him.

Joaniel lifted a gleaming bolter from within the box and slid home a magazine of shells.

She glanced upstairs, seeing Jonny and Snowdog rounding the first landing.

And closed the door, hearing the heavy clang of the lock as it slammed home.

Hissing monsters cautiously stalked into the medicae building, wary of more traps.

Joaniel cocked her bolter and smiled to herself. She hadn't been able to save those on Remian, but here and now she was going to do everything that was expected of a Sister Hospitaller of the Order of the Eternal Candle.

'Come on!' she screamed. 'Are you going to make me wait all day?'

She smiled beatifically as she opened fire, blasting the nearest creatures apart in controlled bursts. She fired and fired, killing dozens until finally the hammer slammed down on an empty chamber.

She dropped the weapon and spread her arms wide as the beasts leapt forward.

The Angel of Remian died with the last of her guilt washed away in blood.

LEARCHUS RAN THROUGH the ruins of District Quintus, the last remnants of the defenders of Erebus falling back in disarray alongside him. Swooping creatures dived from above, tearing at the routing soldiers and even the formidable strength of the Space Marines was sorely tested.

The Ultramarines and the Mortifactors fought side-by-side, buying time for the Krieg, Logres and Defence Legion troops to rally at the next wall. Learchus could see it was hopeless, but he had the soul of a warrior and fought on. The tyranids had closed every avenue of escape, as though they knew every possible route through the city or they could anticipate every move the Space Marines made.

He fired a bolter he had taken from a dead Marine, bringing down a host of winged monsters carrying off a Krieg soldier and hacked down a pair of hissing beasts that were devouring the corpse of a fallen Ultramarine.

He reached down and grabbed the armour of his dead comrade and began dragging him backwards. Chaplain Astador stumbled alongside him and lent his strength to the task, smashing an alien's skull with his crozius arcanum as he did so. The warriors of the Fourth company and the Mortifactors gathered around their leaders, forming a defensive perimeter around them. Learchus saw how pitifully few they were now.

Less than forty Space Marines still fought.

But fewer than this number had won against impossible odds before and Learchus knew that while there was still blood pumping round his body, he would never surrender.

Together the Space Marines dragged the corpse back towards a wide plaza from where a great many aircraft had launched earlier. It crossed his mind to wonder how close Captain Ventris had come to succeeding, but supposed it didn't matter much now.

'Wait,' said Astador.

'What?' snapped Learchus. 'We have to keep moving.'

'No,' said Astador, pointing to the base of the next wall. 'It is already too late.'

Learchus saw hundreds of tyranid beasts sweeping around their flanks, cutting off their escape. Giant creatures, three times the height of a Space Marine, and hordes of warrior beasts filled the area between them and the next wall.

Astador was right. It was too late for escape.

PHASE V – CONSUMPTION

℧
SIXTEEN

THOUSANDS OF LITRES of stinking bio-fluids roared past the Space Marines with the force of a tidal wave, pummelling their armour and ripping them from the walls of the pipe. Uriel felt alien flesh tear under his gauntlet and cursed as he was swept along.

He spun crazily in the flow, slamming into the sides of the tunnel and his battle-brothers, losing his orientation as he tumbled along with the waste matter. All he could see was murky fluids and occasional glimpses of the tunnel walls. He tried to grip the sides of the tunnel, but the waving cilia had withdrawn into the meat of the walls.

Uriel flipped upright for a second, seeing an outthrust gauntlet. He grabbed onto it, an iron grip clamping around his wrist and halting his headlong tumble. Thundering fluids threatened to rip him from his saviour's grip, but he found his footing in a fold of flesh and hauled himself upright.

His head broke the surface and he saw the Deathwatch clustered on a bony ledge above the raging torrent of filth. Pasanius hauled him from the tunnel and he collapsed wearily onto the reassuringly firm surface.

'Thank you, my friend,' he gasped.

Pasanius nodded, too exhausted to reply. Uriel pushed himself to his knees, taking a closer look at their surroundings. They lay in an oval chamber that obviously fed into the fluid-filled tunnel. Damias, Henghast and Pelantar crouched beside a mesh of sinew that blocked their passage from this chamber and Uriel speculated that they were perhaps in some form of filter chamber. Noxious gusts of gas soughed from beyond the mesh of fibres and the rumble of multiple hearts was even stronger.

'How close are we, Brother Damias?' asked Uriel.

'I do not know, brother-captain,' replied Damias, his voice full of reproach. 'I was careless enough to lose my grip on the auspex as I was swept along. I shall perform whatever penance you deem suitable upon our completion of the mission.'

Uriel cursed quietly, but contented himself with the thought that so long as they headed in the direction of the hive ship's heartbeats, they couldn't go far wrong. It had been a long-held belief of Kryptman's that the reproductive chambers of the Norn Queen, the brood mother of the hive, would be close to the hearts, where the nutrients and vital fluid flow was purest.

'Do not worry, brother. The Emperor shall guide us,' said Uriel, drawing his power sword and hacking through the fibrous mesh that blocked the chamber's exit. Once he had managed to relight his flamer, Pasanius took point again, leading them along the glistening passageway. Mucus-like saliva dripped from the walls and more of the slithering, worm-like beasts burrowed in and out of the walls and floors.

'By the Emperor, this is worse than Pavonis, and I thought that was bad,' said Pasanius.

Uriel nodded in agreement. The darkness beneath the world had been terrible, but this grotesque mockery of the gift of life was almost too much to countenance. The blasphemy of the tyranids was beyond measure and he could not fathom how a race that gave nothing back to the universe, that lived only to consume, could be allowed to come into existence.

'What is Pavonis?' asked Henghast.

'A world on the eastern fringe, but that is a tale for another day,' said Uriel.

'I shall hold you to that promise, brother-captain. I will need a saga of your bravery to take back with me to the Fang.'

Uriel was struck by the undiminished optimism of the Deathwatch. Despite their losses and the scale of the task before them, not one had uttered a single sentiment that suggested that they did not believe utterly that they would prevail.

He slapped a palm on Henghast's shoulder guard and said, 'When we return to Tarsis Ultra I shall share the victory wine with you and tell you all about Pavonis.'

'Wine! Pah, wine is for women. We will drain a barrel of Fenrisian mead and you will wake with a hangover like continents colliding.'

'I look forward to it,' said Uriel as Pasanius raised his hand.

Uriel joined his sergeant at the head of their column, listening as the boom of multiple hearts and other, less obvious organs rumbled close by. A low-ceilinged chamber with a heaving sphincter muscle at its centre rasped with tendrils of ochre vapours gusting through it. Booming echoes rang from the fleshy walls.

'I believe we are close, brother-captain. The sounds converge on this place' said Pasanius.

'I think you're right, my friend, but where is it coming from?'

Brother Henghast entered the chamber and removed his helmet, coughing briefly before his enhanced resiratory system was able to adapt to the toxic atmosphere.

'What are you doing?' demanded Uriel. 'Put your helmet back on!'

Henghast cocked his head to one side and whispered, 'Auto-senses are all well and good, but my own are better.'

The Space Wolf sniffed the air, his features twitching as he filtered the smells and sounds of the hive ship with senses more sensitive than even Uriel's. The Ultramarine's senses had been enhanced by the Apothecaries of his Chapter, but were still no match for those of a Space Wolf.

'The heartbeats are strongest from this passage,' said Henghast, replacing his helmet and standing clear to allow Pasanius to proceed. Uriel said, 'Well done, Brother Henghast.'

As they proceeded along this new passage, wisps of smoke filled the air and the sound of monstrous hearts beating in counterpoint grew louder and louder. The glow of Pasanius's flamer silhouetted his sergeant and cast a flickering blue glow around the dripping walls of the passage.

They followed the twisting passage for several kilometres until a sickly green glow replaced that of the flamer. The passageway angled downwards, gradually widening until Uriel could see and hear the booming organs whose noise they had been following.

Larger than super-heavy tanks, the pair of thudding hearts pulsed with massive intra-muscular motion, pumping life-sustaining fluids around the hive ship. Uriel fought the urge to open fire. Kryptman had warned him that these organs would be protected by metres of tough, fibrous skin and that there were sure to be others that could take over.

Hissing organisms prowled the chamber beyond, but whether they were aware of them yet, he could not say.

Uriel and the Deathwatch crouched at the end of the smoky passageway, staring into the heart of the hive ship.

They had reached the reproductive chambers of the Norn Queen.

SNOWDOG GRIMACED IN pain as Jonny hauled him upstairs, hearing the booming impacts against the door below. His head hurt and his ribs felt like he'd gone ten rounds with a Space Marine. He glanced down the stairs.

'Where's Sister Joaniel?' he gasped.

'Dunno,' said Jonny without breaking his stride. 'I guess she's dead.'

'What?'

'Yeah,' confirmed Jonny, 'she shut the door behind us.'

'She shut the door?'

'Yeah.'

Snowdog mentally shrugged. It was a shame she was dead, but if she was crazy enough to try and take on the entire tyranid race, then that was no concern of his. Crashing thumps on the door below made him glad she'd shut the door. He wasn't sure he'd have trusted Jonny to remember to do it. The door was armoured, but with these monsters, you couldn't count on any barrier holding for too long.

'Where are the others?'

'Upstairs I guess. Why you got to ask so many questions?' said Jonny.

'Because that's how I find things out,' snapped Snowdog, regretting it instantly as the pain in his ribs flared bright and urgent.

They rounded another landing and Snowdog could have sworn that there hadn't been this many stairs before. As his senses began returning to normal, he heard a soft pattering, like a wind-chime in a strong breeze, and wondered what it was. He realised a second later and cried out in alarm.

'Jonny! Stop! Stop!' he yelled. 'Turn around!'

'Huh?' said Jonny, but complied.

Snowdog moaned in frustration as he saw a cascade of gold, silver and precious stones forming a glittering trail back down the stairs. He wriggled free from Jonny's grasp and painfully shucked the backpack from his shoulders as the crashes on the door below became even more frenzied.

The backpack had saved him from the worst of Lex's bomb sure enough, but it was in a hell of a mess for having done so. Everything he'd taken from the wreck was spilling through long, burnt tears in the canvas. There was barely anything left.

He began transferring the remainder into his pockets, hearing the scream of buckling metal from below. He heard a footfall on the stairs behind him, but ignored it as he continued to stuff precious stones into his pockets.

'Hey, Trask,' said Jonny.

Snowdog felt his blood chill and reached for his pistol, but it was too late.

He heard the rack of a shotgun slide and rolled to one side, yelling in pain as the splintered ends of his ribs ground together.

But the shot wasn't aimed at him. Jonny Stomp toppled to the stairs, a halo of blood splattered on the wall behind him.

Snowdog squinted through a haze of tears of pain and raised his pistol.

Trask kicked him in the face. He felt teeth break and spat blood.

'You and me got some unfinished business, Snowdog,' said Trask.

THE SIGHT OF the Norn Queen was something that Uriel would never forget for as long as he lived. The creature was massive, easily the size of a Battle Titan, its bulk filling the chamber with countless means of producing its monstrous offspring. A vast, mucus-ribbed tube hung from the walls, pulsing with disgusting motion and dripping great swathes of egg sacs to a slime filled pool where nurse organisms carried them away in great, scooped pincers.

Huge pools of protoplasmic ooze bubbled and burst with motion as screeching infant beasts were drooled from its surface along bony chutes to begin growing almost as soon as they hit the ground. Thousands of gelatinous incubation larvae hung from resinous mucus on the great arched ceiling, supported on huge ribs of bone, each thicker than the columns in the Temple of Correction on Macragge. Stinking fluids coated the floor and foetid steam gusted from millions of tiny orifices in the walls. Ropes of dripping intestine and nutrients pumped viscous fluids into the belly of the Norn Queen, its vast, bloated head fused with the ribbed ceiling of the chamber. Six-legged creatures that resembled fat spiders crawled all over its body, cleaning, feeding and ministering to their queen. Huge javelin-like spines protruded from her bony carapace, each dripping with hissing poisons.

The Norn Queen itself was as much a part of the bio-ship as an individual creature. Warrior organisms patrolled the chamber, snapping their glossy claws at any of the slave-beasts that approached too near the queen. Bigger than the largest tyranid warrior Uriel had ever seen, these warrior beasts were bred for once purpose and one purpose alone – to defend their queen to the death.

'How do we proceed?' asked Damias.

'With this,' said Uriel, unholstering the weapon Kryptman had given him. It was the silvered pistol with which the servitor had administered the gene-poison to the lictor, but with an added refinement. Fitted atop the barrel was a long, metallic tube, its blue-steel sheen subtly crystalline. At the end of the tube was an offset ring of nine small spines that slotted over the barrel of Kryptman's pistol. It was always distasteful to use the weapons of the xeno, but Inquisitor Kryptman had assured him that hrud fusil technology was simply a symbiosis of melta and plasma technology. A product of vile alien heresy to be sure, but one that, in this case, would prove useful in administering the gene-poison.

'What is it?' asked Pelantar.

He slid the gun back into its ill-fitting holster and said, 'It is the means by which we can end this. Just get me to the hive-queen.'

Uriel rose to his feet and said, 'But first we need to fight our way in, and we'll have to do it the old-fashioned way, with flesh, blood and steel.'

The Deathwatch followed their captain as he marched into the Norn Queen's chamber, Pasanius beside him, Henghast on his left and Damias on his right, Pelantar covering them with his heavy bolter.

Almost immediately, a warning screech sounded from one of the nurse organisms and the guardian warriors spun to face the intruders. A cacophonous wailing echoed throughout the chamber, a furious beat thrashing the walls as the tyranids rushed to defend their queen.

Pasanius bathed the first attackers in fire, the guardian creatures howling in anger at such destructive energies being unleashed in their queen's chambers. Pelantar fired a hail of mutagenic bolts into the mass of aliens, chanting the rites of firing as he slew.

Uriel ran forwards, the energised blade of his power sword cleaving through alien flesh and bone with ease. The smaller beasts fell like wheat before the scythe and though he felt the killing rage building behind his eyes, he made his peace with it, turning the taint of the Bringer of Darkness into a positive force.

Flames lit up the hellish glow of the chamber and crackling arcs of energy flared from Damias's power glove as he battered his way forward. Henghast howled in fury as he charged the alien creatures. Pelantar's heavy bolter ripped a path through them.

Uriel spun under a scything blow from a leaping beast that was more fanged maw than anything else, hacking it in two as he sensed the presence of something huge behind him. He threw himself forward, barely avoiding being sliced in two by a guardian organism.

The alien beast towered above him, larger than a carnifex, but more slender and quick. Its jaw was filled with dripping fangs and its upper pair of limbs ended in flashing talons that slashed for his head. Uriel rolled aside as they gouged the floor and slashed his sword at its legs.

The creature bounded over his blow, smashing its claws against his armour. Ceramite parted under the blow and blood washed down his side before the larraman cells halted the flow. Pain-suppressors pumped into his body and he staggered as the beast struck him again. He flew through the air, landing on the edge of a bubbling pool of stinking ichor. Whipping tentacles burst from the pool and wrapped around his midriff.

Uriel cried out and slashed his sword through them, rolling to the base of the pool.

The guardian organism bounded across to him, its hooves throwing up gouts of stinking fluids. Uriel rolled desperately, pushing himself to his knees and raising his sword to block just as the claws hammered down towards him.

Sparks flew and he grunted as he held the strength of the beast at bay.

He rolled beneath the claws, releasing his block and thrust his sword upwards into the creature's groin. It howled and collapsed to one knee, driving the blade deeper into its flesh.

Uriel ripped the weapon clear and hacked it through the monster's midsection. It thrashed as it died, insectile creatures swarming over its corpse to devour it as food for their queen. Uriel staggered towards his target as Pasanius joined him. His sword was bloody and the armour of his silvered arm was missing.

Brother Damias fought with skill and cunning, his power fist reaping a bloody tally in the furious battle. Henghast killed with all the ferocity he and his Chapter were famed for as Pelantar sprayed shells throughout the chamber, bursting egg sacs and perforating the gristly tube that snaked across the chamber walls.

Three warrior organisms blocked their path, each as deadly as the one Uriel had killed.

Damias and Henghast fought their way towards the two Ultramarines.

'The old fashioned way,' he breathed. 'Straight through them, eh? Pasanius, Henghast and I will hold them, you get to the queen!'

Uriel nodded and the four Space Marines raced towards the guardian beasts.

Pelantar saw what they intended and fired a carefully aimed blast towards the tyranids. Two reeled from the fusillade, their carapaces no match for the blessed ammunition of the Deathwatch.

But in doing so, he neglected his own defence for a fraction of a second.

And that was all his foes needed.

With a snap of claws, the heavy bolter was smashed apart and Pelantar was lifted from his feet in a massive set of powerful talons. He fought with every last bit of strength, punching bloody holes in the beast's carapace, but it was too late. With a bellowing roar, the beast ripped Pelantar in two, tossing the shorn halves away for the scavenger beasts to feed on.

Damias and Pasanius attacked while the beasts Pelantar had given his life to wound still staggered from his shells. One burned in the flames as Damias punched through the other's carapace with the lethal energies of his power fist. Henghast joined Pasanius in attacking the burning monster.

Uriel ran for the bloated belly of the Norn Queen, his sword raised to strike down the final beast between him and his goal. Its claws snapped shut and Uriel swept his sword through them. He leapt to meet the creature, ducking inside its guard as it flailed its razored claws at him, slashing its own flesh to ruin.

Uriel pulled himself up the creature's body, its bony exo-skeleton providing ready-made handholds. The creature thrashed as it sought to dislodge him, hacking itself bloody as its claws tried to pluck him from its body. Secondary jaws punched down through his breastplate, biting a fist-sized chunk of flesh from his chest and tearing free a portion of his pectoral muscle.

Uriel roared in pain, but kept his grip on the beast's ribs. He pulled himself to the armoured plates of its shoulders and drove his sword into its neck. Black blood spurted and the beast screeched in agony as it died. The monster's death spasm wrenched the sword from his grip.

Before it collapsed, Uriel vaulted from its shoulders onto the glistening walls of the chamber, his fingers closing on the hardened flesh of the Norn Queen's hide. Hordes of the scavenger organisms closed on him as he climbed, biting and clawing him. They clambered all over him, even squeezing inside his armour, their weight alone threatening to prise him loose.

Despite the pain-suppressors, his chest was bathed in agony. He batted clear the scavengers long enough to draw Kryptman's pistol and press it against the belly of the Norn Queen.

Feeling his grip on the queen's flesh sliding free, he pulled the trigger.

He felt a blast of unimaginable heat as the hrud mechanism activated, lancing a column of fire, hotter that the heart of a star, through the thick flesh of the Norn Queen. A fraction of a second later the pistol bucked in his hand as the shell containing the gene-poison fired into its body.

He dropped the pistol and felt himself sailing through the air as he finally lost his grip on the queen's hide. Uriel twisted as he fell, splashing into the slimy floor of the chamber. He screamed in pain as noxious fluids spilled into the wound on his chest.

He rolled, crushing the scavengers beneath his weight and weakly tried to rise to his feet. He saw Damias destroy the creature he fought with repeated blows of his power fist. Pasanius was hauled from his feet by his blazing foe and lifted high above the ground. Henghast hacked at the beast's legs, but it refused to die.

The beast's claws crushed Pasanius's silvered arm, the metal buckling under the creature's incredible strength. Uriel reached for his sword, before realising it was still embedded in the tyranid warrior creature.

He looked up at the hissing shape of the Norn Queen's head and felt a terrible despair flood through him.

The gene-poison had had no effect on the monster.

They had failed.

TRASK LIFTED THE backpack, its contents spilling from the tears like glittering, precious rain. His ugly swollen features were twisted in hate and anger.

He kicked Snowdog in the ribs and again in the face.

'You stupid bastard,' he snarled. 'Did you really think I was gonna take all the crap you kept shovelling me? Two years I gave you and this is all I get?'

Snowdog looked up through a mist of tears and his own swelling features. Over Trask's ranting he could hear the door several floors below finally give in to the inevitable. He pressed his back to the wall in an attempt to push himself to his feet. Trask kicked out at him again, but Snowdog rolled aside and Trask's boot smashed into the stone of the wall.

He howled in pain, but recovered before Snowdog could do much more than slide over on his side beside the supine Jonny. The big man was still alive, saw Snowdog. Bleeding badly, but still alive.

Not for much longer if he couldn't deal with Trask.

Hideous screeching filled the stairs below, and he could imagine the aliens scrambling over one another as they leapt and bounded towards the upper levels. He fumbled around beneath Jonny's body, smiling to himself as he felt metal and wood in his grip.

He twisted his head to look at Trask.

And suddenly it all made sense. The swelling on Trask's face wept a purple pus and Snowdog knew that the lone creature that had attacked the column of refugees must have sprayed Trask with some kind of scent that drew these aliens to him like flies to shit.

He smiled at the aptness of the phrase.

'What the hell you smiling at?' said Trask, reaching for fresh shotgun shells.

'You, man. It's been you they've wanted all along.'

'Huh?' said Trask as Snowdog rolled to face him, Jonny's hunting rifle held out before him.

'You want him?' he yelled to the aliens below. 'Well, here he is!'

Snowdog fired the huge rifle, feeling the monstrous recoil crack yet another rib. The impact hurled Trask back down the stairs, a huge portion of his torso simply blasted away by the shell. He crashed down onto the landing below, his body a mangled mess. Tyranid beasts swarmed over the landing, but halted at Trask's body, hacking and slashing it to shreds.

While the scent of whatever was on Trask was keeping the aliens busy, Snowdog used the rifle as a crutch and painfully got himself to his feet. Briefly he considered trying to lift Jonny, but quickly dismissed the idea as insane.

He heard more footsteps above him and laughed in relief as Tigerlily and Lex sprinted downstairs.

'What the hell's going on?' yelled Tigerlily.

'Later,' said Snowdog as he fought through the pain and climbed the stairs. Between them, Tigerlily and Lex managed to lift Jonny and the battered foursome limped up the final set of stairs to the top level of the medicae building.

Snowdog had never been so glad to reach somewhere in all his life.

'Where's Silver?' he said.

'She's safe,' said Tigerlily, pulling him onwards. 'Come on, the entrance to the caves isn't far. Let's get the hell out of here.'

'Best idea I've heard all day,' said Snowdog.

LESS THAN TWENTY Space Marines remained. Heroism the likes of which Learchus had only read about in history had kept them alive for nearly forty minutes, but the end was drawing near. Horrified men of the Guard watched the Space Marines' last stand from the District Sextus wall, unable to help them. Learchus would not have wanted their help anyway.

This was a glorious battle, a fitting way for any servant of the Emperor to meet his end. He and Chaplain Astador fought back-to-back, killing aliens with ferocity and skill.

A mound of alien corpses surrounded the Space Marines, hundreds deep, and the shrinking ring of fighting warriors stood atop the mound, battling like heroes of legend.

Another warrior fell, dragged down by alien claws and Learchus felt the spirit of the martyr move within him. As he hacked down another hissing beast, he began to sing, a rousing hymnal from the dawn of the Imperium, a battle song to stir the hearts of all who heard it.

Astador joined him and soon every one of the Space Marines was raising their voices to the heavens in praise of the Emperor as the tyranids closed in for the kill.

PASANIUS KICKED THE guardian beast in the face, crushing its skull and pulverising its brain as Henghast finally drove his sword through its guts. Its claws spasmed and released him. He fell to the floor with a splash.

Uriel saw the golden hilt of his sword protruding from the corpse of the warrior organism. He struggled to his feet to reach it, wishing no more than to die on his feet with a weapon in his hand. He wrenched it from the dissolving flesh of the beast and limped to stand beside Pasanius and the gore-streaked Damias and Henghast.

The four Space Marines stood with their weapons facing outwards, ready to fight and die like men. Hissing creatures closed in on them, fangs bared and claws poised to strike.

A sudden, violent tremor shook the chamber and a tormented, animal wail built from behind Uriel. The smaller creatures dropped to their haunches in terror as the throat of the Norn Queen, silent for hundreds of years, gave voice to a screech of unimaginable pain.

Its body convulsed, tearing free of its egg sac and mucus-hardened limbs fused to the walls broke with the violence of the spasms. Huge tears in the queen's belly ripped open, mutant growths erupting from every one. The queen's flesh boiled and ripped as her evolutionary genome was thrown into anarchy and stimulated beyond all control by Magos Locard's gene-poison.

Every creature in the chamber took up the wailing screech of agony as evolutionary imperatives were passed through the gestalt consciousness which linked every creature in the hive ship and every creature connected to the overmind.

The chamber shook, the very structure of the ship screaming as every creature was driven into a frenzy of uncontrolled mutation.

Uriel watched as creatures convulsed so violently they snapped their own spines, frothing at the mouth with aberrant growths and genetic deviancy.

'It's working!' shouted Uriel as portions of the chamber erupted in white-hot fluids and acidic slime fell from the ceiling in enormous clumps.

'Aye, it worked,' agreed Pasanius, cradling his mangled arm, 'but let's get out of here before it claims us as well.'

The Space Marines fought their way through the rapidly disintegrating chamber of the Norn Queen, the aliens jerking spastically as they died.

Uriel felt a tremendous sense of vindication as they fled the chamber, knowing that he had made the right choice to lead this mission.

He never saw the javelin-like spine shoot from the carapace of the Norn Queen as it slashed through the collapsing cavern. The two-metre barb hammered through his back and exploded from his stomach in an explosion of ceramite and flesh.

The jagged missile passed clean through him, juddering in the necrotising floor.

He slumped forward, the pain beyond anything he had ever felt before.

'Uriel!' screamed Pasanius.

He looked down at the wound. Strange that there was no blood. A hard red scab formed around the exit wound, but there was no blood. A sluggish feeling permeated his body and a sharp pain blossomed in his left side, spreading throughout his body.

Pasanius lifted him from the ground.

'Damias, you're an Apothecary! Help him!'

Uriel felt his vision grey, his limbs becoming heavier and heavier.

He couldn't understand. He'd been hurt worse than this before and not felt like this. He saw his heart rate spiralling downwards in the corner of his visor.

'Bones of Corax,' swore Damias. 'It's phage-cell poisoning. It's sending his larraman cells into overdrive and his blood is clotting throughout his body!'

'Then do something about it!' bellowed Pasanius.

Uriel felt their words fading and tried to open his mouth, but his vision greyed and he felt his hearts stop pumping as they clogged with coagulated blood.

He closed his eyes and the pain went away.

LEARCHUS KILLED ANOTHER tyranid creature and started another verse before he realised that the attacks were not coming with the same fury as before.

In fact, they were not coming at all.

The alien beasts thrashed in violent fits, their screeching roars rising to new heights. He saw packs of creatures turn on one another, slashing each other's bodies to red ruin without cease. Thrashing monsters filled the plaza, howling in pain as the overmind died, their bodies unable to survive the psychic shockwave of its death.

Tyranid organisms scuttled and ran through the streets of District Quintus, howling in berserk fury and falling on one another in an orgy of senseless bloodletting.

The Space Marines forgotten, the tyranids tore themselves to pieces.

Before any of the larger creatures were able to regain control, the sixteen surviving Space Marines made their way towards the wall of District Sextus. Very few creatures opposed them and those that did attacked with no cohesion or purpose and were butchered without mercy.

THE INTERNECINE SLAUGHTER continued throughout the rest of the day, the defenders watching with elation as the alien menace that had threatened their world for so long tore itself to pieces.

As night drew in and the temperatures plummeted, whole swathes of organisms perished as they succumbed to the freezing temperatures, unable to seek shelter without the control of the hive mind to direct them.

Some creatures survived, larger creatures with a degree of autonomy from the hive mind, and soon they accumulated small packs of desperate beasts, taking refuge in the warmer parts of the ruined city.

Night finally closed on Tarsis Ultra as a speck of light descended from the heavens, a battered Space Marine gunship, its wings dipped in mourning.

EPILOGUE

PASANIUS SAT ALONE on the ruins of the District Quintus wall, staring out into the white expanse of the plain before the devastated city. Stripped of his armour, he wore a simple chiton of blue cloth and cradled his silver arm close to his chest. He watched as a transport flashed overhead; returning from another ruined city with more bad news no doubt.

It had been six days since their return from the dying hive ship and Pasanius had spent much of his time in prayer, offering his thanks for their victory and his sorrows for those who had fallen in battle. There were so many dead, so many prayers to say. The vast chamber of the mosaic held a candle for every soldier dead or missing, and the glowing light from the crystal dome was visible from the far end of the valley.

Among the honoured dead was Sebastien Montante, his spine-pierced body discovered on the ruins of the very wall Pasanius now sat upon. His body lay in state in the Imperial palace and the priests of this world were already calling for his beatification. Pasanius knew it probably wouldn't be long before Sebastien was made into a saint and he chuckled, thinking how amusing the Fabricator Marshal would have found that idea. Saint Sebastien, it had a nice ring to it.

Colonel Stagler's body had been found by his men atop a mound of tyranid creatures, his frozen corpse brutally hacked to pieces. His men did not mourn him. He had died in the Krieg way and that was enough. With both Stagler and Rabelaq dead, Major Aries Satria of the Erebus Defence Legion assumed control of the Imperial Guard forces until such time as a more senior Guard officer could be appointed.

And such a time would not be long in coming. With the destruction of the hive ship, the Shadow in the Warp had lifted from the Tarsis Ultra system and a flood of astropathic communiqués were received by those telepaths who had not been driven insane by the tyranids' infernal psychic noise.

Imperial Navy vessels were less than a week away, ponderous battle-cruisers and vast transports bringing in fresh troops to bolster the weakened defences.

The Mortifactors had left Tarsis Ultra yesterday, Chaplain Astador offering to take the mortal remains of the fallen Ultramarines and inter them within the ossuaries of the Basilica Mortis. Learchus, who had taken command of the surviving warriors of the Fourth company, had politely, but firmly, declined.

Inquisitor Kryptman and the Deathwatch still prowled the ruins of the city, gathering alien carcasses for Magos Locard to study. The gene-poison might only have worked on this hive fleet, but there was still much to learn about the tyranid race.

Volunteer kill teams were being assembled to hunt down the surviving tyranid monsters that had gone to ground in the depths of the ruined city and caves of the high valleys. The shadow of destruction had been lifted from this world, but Pasanius knew that there would be trouble with the tyranids for many years to come if his experiences on Ichar IV had taught him anything.

The winds from the plain were cold and Pasanius extended the silver fingers of his right arm, the metal gleaming and pristine.

Already more than one tech-priest had commented on the skill of the artificer who had repaired his bionic arm following the battle on the hive ship.

Pasanius shivered, closing his eyes as he tucked his arm inside the fabric of his chiton.

He could tell them nothing, because there had been no artificer.

The arm had repaired itself.

THERE WAS PAIN. He supposed pain was good, it meant he was still alive.

Uriel opened his eyes, gummed with so long spent unconscious. He blinked away the residue and tried to push himself upright, but fell back, exhausted, unable to do much more than turn his head.

He lay on a sturdy bed in a stone chamber with a vaulted roof. It was warm and he felt a comfortable numbness that could only be the result of pain balms. He pulled back the sheet to look at his bandage-wrapped body. Scars crisscrossed his chest and he could feel the ache of recent surgery. Whatever had happened to him, it had been serious.

Uriel drifted in and out of consciousness for several hours until he was aware of a figure standing beside his bed, adjusting a drip feed attached to his arm.

He tried to speak, the words coming out as little more than a hoarse croak.

'You'll find it hard to speak for a while, Uriel,' said a voice he recognised as belonging to Apothecary Selenus. He managed to say, 'What happened?'

'You were poisoned by tyranid phage cells that attacked the larraman cells in your bloodstream. The poison caused your blood to clot on a bodily scale and your hearts failed, clogged with agglomerated blood. Clinically, you were dead, but the Deathwatch were able to get you back to the Thunderhawk in time for Brother Damias to administer a massive dose of anti-coagulants and begin infusions of fresh blood. Pasanius almost killed himself providing you with enough blood to keep you alive long enough to get you here. You are lucky indeed to have such a friend as he.'

Uriel nodded, trying to take in the information, but drifted off into unconsciousness. When he awoke again it was to see a man in the uniform of the Erebus Defence Legion with his arm in a sling sitting beside him. He wore a Space Marine purity seal pinned to his breast.

'You're awake,' he said, standing and extending his hand.

'Yes,' managed Uriel. 'You're–'

'Pavel Leforto, yes. You saved my life in the trenches.'

Uriel smiled in recognition. 'You saved mine too as I remember.'

'Yes, well, I was lucky with the missile launcher. On any normal day, I'd probably have hit you,' said Pavel.

'Well, thank you anyway, Pavel.'

'You're welcome, Captain Ventris. Anyway, I just came to say thank you, but I have to report to my unit now. You know, plenty more work to be done,' said Pavel.

Pavel came to attention and saluted before turning and marching from the room.

Uriel watched him go, thinking back to the picture of his family Pavel had hel when he had lain injured.

When it came time for Pavel Leforto to die he would have the legacy of his wife's memories and his children's lives to proclaim that he existed, that he had enriched the Emperor's realms for a brief span with his labours.

What would Brother-Captain Uriel Ventris leave behind?

A lifetime dedicated to the service of the Emperor, to the service of Humanity, even though he was no longer part of it? He only dimly remembered his parents, they had been dead for almost a century now, their memory a distant shadow, eclipsed by decades of devotion to the Chapter and the Emperor. There was nothing left to remind him of his humanity, no family and few friends. Once he was gone it would be as though he had never existed.

Uriel had sacrificed his chance to experience such a life the instant he had become an Ultramarines novice.

And knowing this, would he have been so willing to become a Space Marine had he realised the enormity of what he was sacrificing to become one of the Emperor's elite?

Uriel smiled, his features softening as the answer was suddenly so clear that he was amazed he had even questioned it.

Yes. He would have. In giving up the chance for a normal life, he had gained something far greater. The chance to make a difference. The chance to stand defiant before the enemies of Mankind and hold back the tide of degenerate aliens, traitorous heretics and servants of Chaos that sought dominion over the Emperor's realm.

That was something to be proud of. His strength came from ancient technology that made him stronger, faster and more deadly than any warrior had ever been before. He had sacrificed his chance to be truly human and, yes, he stood apart from the mass of Humanity, but countless lives would have been lost but for his sacrifice.

That was a noble gift and he was thankful for what and who he was.

Uriel smiled to himself as he drifted into a dreamless sleep.

SNOWDOG WINCED AS he limped over to the bed where Silver lay asleep. His side hurt like a cast-iron bitch and the swelling on his face didn't seem to want to go down. He pulled the blanket up over Silver and brushed a strand of white hair from her face.

She stirred, opening her eyes and reaching up to touch his bruised face.

'Hey,' she said.

'Hey, yourself. How you feeling?'

She groaned as she pushed herself upright. 'Terrible. Next dumb question?'

Snowdog leaned down to kiss her, his cracked ribs flaring painfully.

She saw the pain in his eyes and chuckled.

'Some time, huh?'

'Yeah,' he agreed, 'some time.'

'So what's next for us, then?'

Snowdog didn't reply immediately, glancing over his shoulder into the front room of the abandoned hab-unit they'd commandeered as a temporary base. Lex and Tigerlily played dice and Jonny Stomp snored loudly on a bed of rolled-up coats.

He'd lost most of what he'd lifted from the wreck of the crashed ship and as he looked at the shotgun and lasgun lying on the floor he smiled.

'Looks like it's business as usual, honey,' he said. 'Business as usual.'

DEAD SKY, BLACK SUN

PROLOGUE

DISTANT HAMMER BLOWS from monstrous engines reverberated through the chamber, echoing from the Halls of the Savage Morticians far below, rising alongside noxious tendrils of acrid vapours and agonised screams. Leering gargoyles of pressed and riveted iron ringed the chamber's dizzyingly high, arched ceiling and the tops of impossibly huge, pillar-like pistons, each one wreathed in greasy steam, ground rhythmically up and down through wide, skull-rimmed holes that ran along its edges.

A great chasm in the obsidian floor billowed scalding steam in roiling waves of heat and was crossed by a gantry of studded iron decking that rested upon massively thick girders, which in turn were supported on chains whose oily links were as thick as a man's torso.

Lit by a hot, orange glow from a snaking ribbon of molten metal at the chasm's base, many hundreds of metres below, the chamber reeked of sulphurous fumes and the searing, bitter taste of beaten metal. The gantry led towards a massive, cyclopean wall of dark-veined stone, pierced by a great, iron gate that had been tempered in an ocean of blood during its forging. Studded with jagged black spikes, the inner gate of the fortress of Khalan-Ghol was flanked by two armoured colossi, whose burnished iron hides were scarred by millennia of war. The gate led to the inner halls of the fortress's new master, and both daemon-visaged Titans, hung with the blighted banners of the Legio Mortis, raised fearsome guns – capable of laying waste to cities – to track a dozen figures who dared approach the gate.

The terrible enormity of the chamber did not faze the warriors who marched towards the groaning bridge; they had seen such sights before.

Indeed, the leader of this group of warriors hailed from a citadel far more ancient and monolithic than this.

Lord Toramino, warsmith of the Iron Warriors, curled his lip in contempt as he raised his altered eyes to stare down the barrels of the Titans' weapons. If the half-breed thought such a vulgar display of power would intimidate him, then he was even more foolish than his inferior lineage would suggest. They had passed through the fortress's gatehouse three days ago, travelling unchallenged by any of the half-breed's warriors, though Toramino had felt supernatural eyes upon them ever since. No doubt warlocks of the kabal were watching them even now, but Toramino could not have cared less, marching with his head held high and hands clasped behind his back.

Alongside him, Lord Berossus growled as he watched the Titans' guns train upon them, spooling up his own weapons. Toramino looked up at Berossus and shook his head at his vassal warsmith's lack of restraint. None here could face a Titan and live, but such were the ingrained responses of Berossus that no other reaction was possible.

Toramino stepped onto the iron bridge, the metal hissing beneath his armoured boot and rippling like mercury, reflecting his massive, armoured form in its glistening lustre. Standing well over two metres tall, Lord Toramino wore a suit of exquisitely tooled power armour, handcrafted on Olympia itself and burnished to a mirror sheen. Its trims were edged with arabesques of carven gold and onyx chevrons and its every surface wrought with terrible sigils of ruin. An ochre cloak of woven metallic thread, stronger than adamantium, billowed around his wide frame, partially obscuring the skull-masked symbol of the Iron Warriors on one shoulder guard and his own personal heraldry of a mailed fist above a plan view of a breached redoubt on the other.

An Iron Warrior from his most trusted retinue carried his elaborately carved helm, and another carried his blasted standard, an eight-pointed star of blackened bone set upon a spiked, brass-rimmed wheel and woven with sinew extracted from a thousand screaming victims. Long white hair, pulled into a tight scalp-lock, trailed down his back and his stern, patrician features were pinched and angular – speaking of long years of bitter experience. His eyes were opalescent orbs of gold, smouldering with suppressed rage beneath thick brows.

As they approached the wall, huge blasts of stinking, oil-streaked gases jetted from the pistons either side of the gate and with a groan and squeal of grinding metalwork, the colossal locks disengaged with percussive booms that shook the dust from the chamber's ceiling.

The Titans lowered their mighty weapons and the upper portions of their bodies twisted around on bronze joints to grip the spiked gateway and pull. Steam jetted from wheezing fibre-bundle muscles, and slowly the awful gate groaned open, spilling an emerald light into the chamber as Toramino and Berossus passed between the mighty death machines and into the sanctum sanctorum of the lord of the fortress.

Toramino remembered this place from the many times he had come to pay homage to Khalan-Ghol's former castellan – a great and terrible warrior who had now ascended to the dark majesty of daemonhood. The walls within were of a plain black stone, threaded with gold and silver and glistening with moisture, despite the heat radiating from the terrazzo floor of powdered bone. Sickly white light reflected as pearlescent streaks on the floor from a score of tall and thin arched windows that pierced the eastern wall, draining the chamber of life and imparting a deathly pallor to its occupants.

A score of Iron Warriors stood to attention at the far end of the chamber, gathered about a polished throne of white and silver upon which sat a warrior in battered power armour.

It galled Toramino that he came before the fortress's new lord as a supposed equal. The half-breed was a bastard mongrel, not fit to wipe the blood from an Iron Warrior's armour, let alone command them in battle. Such an affront to the honour of the Legion was almost more than Toramino could bear, and as he watched the lord of the fortress rise from his throne of fused iron and bone, he felt his hatred rise in a venomous wave of bile.

The half-breed's appearance matched Toramino's opinion of him in that he was unclean and had none of the nobility of the ancients of Olympia. His close-cropped black hair topped a rugged, scarred face with bluntly prosaic features, and his armour was dented and scarred, still marked with the residue of battle. Did the half-breed not care that he was now receiving two of the most ancient and noble warsmiths of Medrengard? That this upstart's warsmith could have appointed such a low mongrel as his successor beggared belief.

'Lord Honsou,' said Toramino, forcing himself to bow before the half-breed while keeping his hands clasped behind his back. His tone was formal and he spoke in low, sibilant tones, though he was careful to include a mocking inflection to his words.

'Lord Toramino,' answered Honsou. 'You honour me with your presence. And you also, Lord Berossus. It has been many years since the walls of Khalan-Ghol shook to the tread of your steps.'

The floor cracked under the weight of Lord Berossus, a hulking monster of dark iron and bronze with a leering skull face. Fully twice the height of Toramino, the living remains of Warsmith Berossus had been fused within the defiled sarcophagus of a dreadnought many thousands of years ago.

The grotesque machine hissed and a grating voice, muffled and distorted by a bronze vox-unit, said, 'Aye, it has, though I feel sullied to stand within its walls knowing a bastard mongrel like you is its new lord.'

Augmented and extensively engineered since his interment, Berossus's mechanical form towered above the other dreadnoughts of his grand company, his leg assemblies strengthened and widened to allow him to carry heavier and heavier breaching equipment. The dreadnought's upper body was scarred and pitted, the testament of uncounted sieges engraved on its adamantium shell. One arm bore a mighty, piston-driven siege hammer, the other a monstrous drill ringed with heavy calibre cannons.

Four thick, iron arms ending in vicious picks, blades, claws and heavy gauge breachers sprouted from behind Berossus's sarcophagus and hung ready for use over his armoured carapace.

Toramino saw Honsou bite back a retort and his soulless, golden eyes sparkled with amusement at the directness of Berossus. Honsou must already know what had brought them both here. There was only one thing that would make both him and Berossus deign to step within the walls of the half-breed's lair and he smiled, easily able to imagine Honsou's chagrin at having to share what his former master had won.

'You must forgive Berossus, Lord Honsou,' said Toramino smoothly, stepping forward and extending his hands before him. Unlike the rest of his armour, his gauntlets were fashioned from a brutal, dark iron, pitted and scarred with innumerable battles. Steeped in carnage, Toramino had long ago vowed never to clean a death from his hands and his gauntlets were gnarled with aeons of blood and suffering. As his armoured gauntlets came into view, the Iron Warriors behind Honsou snapped their bolters upright, every one aiming his weapon at Toramino's head.

Toramino grinned, exposing teeth of gleaming silver, and said, 'I come before you to offer my congratulations on the victory at Hydra Cordatus. Your former master executed a masterful campaign; to carry the walls of such a formidable stronghold was a truly great achievement. And your fellow captains, Forrix and Kroeger? Where are they that I might fete them with honours also?'

'They are dead,' snapped Honsou, and Toramino took pleasure in the vexation the half-breed took from his exclusion from the honours of victory. He scented the mongrel's pathetic desire to be accepted by them and closed on the true purpose of their journey here.

'A pity,' said Toramino, 'but their deaths served a greater purpose, yes? You were successful in capturing the prize that lay beneath the citadel?'

'A pity?' repeated Honsou. 'It is only a pity that I was not able kill them myself, though I did have the pleasure of watching Forrix die. And yes, we took the spoils of war from the cryo-facility beneath the mountains – what the Imperials hadn't managed to destroy at least.'

'Stable gene-seed?' breathed Toramino, unable to keep the hunger from his voice.

'Aye,' agreed Honsou. 'Biologically stable and without mutation. And all of it for the Despoiler. You know that, Toramino.'

Lord Berossus laughed, a grainy wash of feedback-laced static, his massive armoured body leaning down as he said, 'Do not think us fools, half-breed. We know you kept some for yourself. You would be foolish not to have.'

'And if I did, what business is it of yours, Berossus?' snarled Honsou.

'Whelp!' roared the dreadnought, taking a crashing step forward as the clawed servo-arms on his back snapped to life. 'You dare speak in such tones to your betters!'

Before Honsou could reply, Toramino said, 'Though he speaks bluntly, Lord Berossus also speaks true. I know you kept some gene-seed for yourself. So listen well, half-breed: your former master was a sworn ally of Berossus and myself, and we expect you, as his successor, to honour these oaths and share the spoils of victory.'

Honsou said nothing for long seconds then laughed in their faces. Toramino felt his hatred for this insolent half-breed burn hotter than ever.

'Share?' said Honsou, turning and receiving a long, broad-bladed axe from an Iron Warrior behind him and nodding to another, who bent to lift a heavy iron cryo-chest from behind the throne as scores of warriors from Honsou's grand company marched into the hall from behind them.

The Iron Warrior with the cryo-chest held it out before Toramino as Honsou said, 'In that cryo-chest is all that I am willing to share. It is my only offer so I advise you to take it and leave.'

Toramino's eyes narrowed as he reached a battered gauntlet out to lift the lid, wisps of condensing air ghosting from within the chest. His every instinct told him that this was a trap, but he could not show weakness before the half-breed.

He opened the container and stiffened as he saw that it was empty.

'Is this some pathetic attempt at a jest, half-breed?' hissed Toramino. 'You turn your back on your master's oaths?'

Honsou took a step towards Toramino and spat on the warsmith's gleaming breastplate. 'I spit on those oaths as I spit on you,' he said. 'You and your idiot monster. And no, it is no jest. Understand this, Toramino, you will get nothing from me. None of you will. What I took from the Imperials on Hydra Cordatus I fought and bled for, and neither you or any one else, is going to take from me.'

Toramino seethed with anger, but bit it back. The muscles of his neck bunched, and it was all he could do to quell the rage boiling within him. He snarled an oath and nodded to Berossus, who roared and slammed his mighty siege hammer down upon the Iron Warrior carrying the cryo-chest, obliterating him in an explosion of flesh and armour. A blazing corona of electrical discharge flared around the cratered floor and gory matter drooled from the crackling hammer.

Incredulous that this vile half-breed had the nerve to behave in this manner before one such as he, Toramino bellowed, 'You dare insult me like this?'

'I do, and you are no longer welcome in my halls. I give you leave to depart as befits warsmiths of your station, but you will never set foot within this fortress again while I draw breath.'

'To defy me means death,' promised Toramino. 'My armies will tear this place down stone by stone, girder by girder, and I will feed you to the Unfleshed.'

'We shall see,' said Honsou, gripping his axe tightly. 'Send your armies here, Toramino, they will find only death before my walls.'

Without deigning to reply, Lord Toramino spun on his heel and marched from the chamber, his retinue and Lord Berossus following close behind.

If the half-breed wanted war, then Toramino would give him war.

A war that would stir the mighty Perturabo himself from his bitter reveries.

PART I – DEATH OATH

U
ONE

URIEL KEPT HIS breathing smooth as he stepped through the last moves of his attack routine, every action in perfect balance and focus, his body and mind acting in absolute synchronicity. Slowly and deliberately, he performed the strikes, first his elbow then his fist striking an imaginary foe, keeping his movements precise. He kept his eyes closed, his stance light and balanced, with all parts of his body starting and ending their movements at the same time.

Completing his steps, Uriel took an intake of breath as his fists crossed before him, then exhaled, maintaining his concentration as he returned his arms smoothly to his sides, centring his power within himself.

He could feel the potentiality of the lethal force in his limbs, sensing the strength grow within him and feeling a calmness he had not felt in many weeks enfold him as he completed the last of the prescribed movements.

'Ready?' asked Pasanius.

Uriel nodded and shook his limbs loose as he dropped into a fighting crouch, fists raised before him. His former sergeant was much larger than him, hugely muscled and wearing a sparring chiton of blue cotton that left his legs and arms bare. Even though it had been nearly two years since Pasanius had lost his arm fighting beneath the world against an ancient star-god, Uriel still found his eyes drawn to the gleaming, silver-smooth augmetic arm that replaced his lost limb.

Pasanius wore his blond hair tight into his skull and though his face was capable of great warmth and humour, it was set in a deathly serious expression as they prepared to fight. Pasanius launched a slashing right cross towards his head and Uriel swayed aside to avoid the blow. He

529

deflected Pasanius's follow-up punch and spun inside his guard, hammering his elbow towards his opponent's throat. But the big man pivoted smoothly away and deflected Uriel's strike, pulling him off balance.

Uriel ducked beneath a scything punch and leapt backwards in time to dodge a thunderous kick to his groin. Despite his speed, the heel of Pasanius's foot still hammered into his side, and he grunted in pain as the breath was driven from him.

Uriel dodged away from the next blow, bouncing lightly on the balls of his feet as his opponent came at him again, blocking and countering everything Pasanius threw at him. The big man was faster than he looked and Uriel knew he could not avoid being hit forever. And when Pasanius landed a clean blow, very few got back up.

He threw murderous punches towards Pasanius, pivoting his hips and shoulders to get his full weight behind his blows, while ducking in to deliver rapid-fire punches to his opponent's ribs. Pasanius stepped back, untroubled by such strikes, and Uriel swiftly followed him, throwing a hooking punch at his head. It was a risky gambit and easily blocked, but instead of Pasanius's gleaming forearm coming up to block the blow, Uriel's fist smashed home against his right temple.

Pasanius stumbled and dropped to one knee, bright blood weeping from where the skin had split above his right eye. Uriel stepped away from Pasanius, dropping his fists and easing his breathing as he stared in puzzlement at the gash on his former sergeant's forehead.

'Are you all right?' asked Uriel. 'What happened? You could easily have blocked that.'

'You just caught me by surprise,' said Pasanius, wiping away the already clotted blood with his fleshy hand. 'I expected you to go for the legs again.'

Uriel replayed the last few seconds of their bout again in his mind, seeing again his and Pasanius's positions and movements as they sparred.

'The legs? I wasn't in a strong position to attack your legs,' said Uriel. 'If I wanted to attack from that position, I had to go for the head.'

Pasanius shrugged. 'I just didn't get my block up in time.'

'You didn't even try, not even with the other arm.'

'You won. What are you complaining about?'

'It's just that I've never seen you miss such an easy block, that's all.'

Pasanius turned away, picking up a towel from where it hung on the brass rail that ran around the circumference of the geodesic viewing dome Captain Laskaris had given over to them for sparring and training. The blackness of space filled the view from the dome: stars spread across it like diamond dust on sable. Reflected light from the distant star of Macragge glittered on the dome's many facets and cast a soft pall of ghostly light throughout the viewing bay.

'I'm sorry, Uriel, this whole situation has me a little... off balance,' said Pasanius, draping his towel over his augmetic arm. 'To be exiled from the Chapter...'

'I know, Pasanius, I know,' said Uriel, joining his sergeant at the edge of the dome. He gripped the rail as he stared through the toughened arma-glass at what lay beyond.

The gothic, cliff-like hull of the bulk-transporter, *Calth's Pride*, stretched away into the darkness of space and beyond sight as the vessel journeyed from Macragge towards the Masali jump point.

URIEL STEPPED INTO his quarters, throwing his towel onto the gunmetal grey footlocker at the foot of his bed and walking into the small ablutions cubicle set into the steel bulkhead. He pulled off his sweat-stained chiton and hung it from a chrome rail, turning the burnished lever above the chipped ceramic basin and waiting for it to fill. He scooped up a handful of ice-cold water, splashing it over his face and letting it drip from his craggy features.

Uriel stared at the foaming water in the basin, its spray reminding him of his last morning on Macragge, kneeling on Gallan's Rock and watching the glittering spume in the rocky pool at the base of the Falls of Hera. He closed his eyes, picturing again the distant seas, shimmering like a blanket of sapphires beyond the rocky white peaks of the western mountains, themselves sprinkled with scraps of green highland fir. The sun was set-ting, casting blood-red fingers of dying light and bathing the mountains in gold. It had felt as though the homeworld of his Chapter had been grant-ing him one last vision of its majesty before it was denied to him forever.

He would hold onto that vision each night as he lay down on his sim-ple cot bed, recalling its every nuance of colour, sight and smell, anxious that it should not fade from his memories. The stale, recycled taste to the air made the memory all the more poignant, and the harsh, spartanly fur-nished quarters he had been allocated aboard the *Pride* were a fond reminder of his captain's chambers back on Macragge.

Uriel lifted his head and stared at the polished steel mirror, watching as droplets trickled like tears down his reflection's cheek. He wiped the last of the water from his face, the grey eyes of his twin watching him, set beneath a heavy, brooding brow and close-cropped black hair. Two golden studs were set upon his brow and his jawline was angular and patrician. His physique dwarfed that of the ordinary human soldiers who filled this enormous starship, genetically enhanced by long-forgotten technologies and honed to the peak of physical perfection by a lifetime of training, dis-cipline and war. His arms and chest were criss-crossed with scars, but greater than them all combined was a mass of pale, discoloured flesh across his stomach where a tyranid Norn-queen had almost slain him on Tarsis Ultra.

He shuddered at the memory, turning and sitting on the edge of his bed, remembering his last sight of Macragge as the shuttle had lifted off from the port facility at the end of the Valley of Laponis. He had watched his adopted homeworld shrink away, becoming a patchwork of glittering, quartz-rich mountains and vast oceans that were soon obscured as the shuttle rose into the lower atmosphere.

Slowly the curve of the world had become visible, together with the pale haze that marked the divide between the planet and the hard vacuum of space. Ahead, *Calth's Pride* had been an ugly, metallic oblong hanging in space above the planet's northern polar reaches.

He had reached out and placed a gauntleted hand against the shuttle's thick viewing block, wondering if he would ever set foot on Macragge again.

'Take a good look, captain,' Pasanius had said gloomily, following Uriel's gaze through the viewing block. 'It's the last time we'll see her.'

'I hope you're wrong, Pasanius,' said Uriel. 'I don't know where our journey will take us, but we may yet see the world of our Chapter again.'

Pasanius shrugged, his massive armoured form dwarfing his former captain. The late Techmarine Sevano Tomasin had forged the armour upon Pasanius's elevation to a full Space Marine, its armoured plates composed of parts scavenged from suits of tactical dreadnought armour that had been irreparably damaged in battle.

'Perhaps, captain, but I know that *I'll* never lay eyes on Macragge again.'

'What makes you so sure? And you don't need to call me "captain" any more, remember?'

'Of course, captain, but I just know I will not return here,' replied Pasanius. 'It's just a feeling I have.'

Uriel shook his head. 'No, I do not believe that Lord Calgar would have placed this death oath upon us if he thought we could not honour it,' he said. 'It may take many years, but there is always hope.'

Uriel had watched his former sergeant, understanding his grim mood as his eyes drifted to the huge shoulder guard where the symbol of the Ultramarines had once been emblazoned. Like his own armour, all insignia of the Ultramarines had been removed following their castigation by a conclave of their peers for breaches of the *Codex Astartes* on Tarsis Ultra and they had taken the March of Shame from the Fortress of Hera.

Uriel sighed as he thought of all that had happened since he had first taken up his former captain's sword to take command of the Ultramarines Fourth Company; so much death and battle that was a Space Marine's lot. Battle-brothers, allies and friends had died fighting renegades, xenos creatures and entire splinter fleets of tyranids.

He sat back against the bulkhead, casting his mind back to the carnage the tyranids had wreaked on Tarsis Ultra. He still had perfect recall of the horrific battles fought on that ice-locked industrial world, the fury of the extra-galactic predators' invasion indelibly etched on his memories. The battles on Ichar IV – another world ravaged by the tyranids – had been terrible, but the gathering of Imperial forces there had been magnificent, whereas those assembled on Tarsis Ultra had been horrifically outnumbered, and only desperate heroism and the intervention of the legendary Inquisitor Lord Kryptman had brought them victory.

But it was a victory won at a cost.

To save the planet, Uriel had taken command of an Ordo Xenos Deathwatch squad – in defiance of his duty to his warriors and the tenets of his primarch's holy tome, the *Codex Astartes* – and fought his way to the heart of a tyranid hive ship. Upon the company's return to Macragge, Learchus, one of his most courageous sergeants, had reported Uriel's flagrant breaches of the *Codex's* teachings to the High Masters of the Chapter.

Tried before the great and good of the Ultramarines, Uriel and Pasanius had waived their right to defend themselves, instead accepting the judgement of Marneus Calgar to prevent their example passing down the chain of command. The penalty for such heresy could only be death, but rather than waste the lives of two courageous warriors who might yet bring ruin to the enemies of the Emperor, the Chapter Master had bound them to a death oath.

Uriel could vividly remember the evening they had set out from the Fortress of Hera, accepting the judgement of Lord Calgar and showing the Chapter that the way chosen by the Ultramarines was true. They were bound to the death oath that the Chapter might live on as it always had.

Chaplain Clausel had read verses from the Book of Dishonour and averted his eyes as Uriel and Pasanius marched past him towards the doors of the gatehouse.

'Uriel, Pasanius,' said Lord Calgar.

The two Space Marines stopped and bowed to their former master.

'The Emperor go with you. Die well.'

Uriel nodded as the huge doors swung open. He and Pasanius had stepped into the purple twilight of evening. Birds were singing and torchlight flickered from the high towers of the outermost wall of the fortress.

Before the door closed, Calgar had spoken once again, his voice hesitant, as though unsure as to whether he should speak at all.

'Librarian Tigurius spoke with me last night,' he began, 'of a world that tasted of dark iron, with great womb factories of daemonic flesh rippling with monstrous, unnatural life. Tigurius told me that savage morticians – like monsters themselves – hacked at these creatures with blades and saws and pulled bloodstained figures from within. Though appearing more dead than alive, these figures lived and breathed, tall and strong, a dark mirror of our own glory. I know not what this means, Uriel, but its evil is plain. Seek this place out. Destroy it.'

'As you command,' said Uriel as he had walked into the night.

The chilling vision of Librarian Tigurius could be anywhere in the galaxy, and though the thought of venturing into such a hideous place filled Uriel's soul with dread, part of him also relished the chance to bring death to such vile monsters.

It had been five days since the bulk lifter had broken orbit with Macragge and used its conventional plasma drives to journey to the Masali jump point.

All Uriel's enemies had been met blade-to-blade and defeated, yet here he and Pasanius were, aboard a vessel rammed to the gunwales with regiments of Imperial Guard bound for Segmentum Obscurus and the wars that had erupted in the wake of the Despoiler's invasion of Imperial space.

'Courage and honour,' he whispered bitterly, but there was no reply.

PASANIUS PRESSED THE point of his knife into the centre of his chest, the skin dimpling under its razor-sharp tip. The skin broke and blood welled from the cut, dripping down his chest before swiftly clotting. Pasanius pushed the blade deeper, dragging the knife across the bulging pectoral muscle on the left side of his chest and cutting a long, horizontal slice in his skin.

He ignored the pain, altering the angle of the blade and cutting diagonally down towards his solar plexus, forming a mirror image of the cuts on the opposite side of his chest. Quick slashes between the heavy cuts formed the final part of his carving and Pasanius dropped the knife onto his bed, falling to his knees before the makeshift shrine set up on the floor beside his bed.

Candles burned with a scented, smoky aroma, flickering in the breeze wafting from the recyc-units and long strips of prayer papers covered in Pasanius's spidery handwriting lay curled at their bases. Pasanius lifted a strip of gilt-edged paper with bloody fingertips, reading the words of penance and confession written there, though he knew them by heart. He raised his gleaming bionic hand, spreading his fingers and placing it palm-down upon his bloody chest, cut with the form of an eagle with outstretched wings.

Pasanius dragged his hand down his chest, smearing the congealed blood across its gleaming metal while mouthing the confessional words written on the paper. As he finished the words, he lowered the paper into the wavering flame of the candle and held it there until it caught light. Hungry flames licked up the length of the prayer paper, greedily consuming the words written there and scorching the tips of his fingers black.

The paper crumbled to flaking, orange-limned embers, disintegrating in his hands and drifting gently to the floor. The last ember fell from his hand and Pasanius slammed his clenched silver fist into the wall of his quarters, punching a deep crater in the bulkhead.

He brought his hand up in front of his face to stare at the terrible damage. His metal fingers were cracked and bent by the force of the impact, but Pasanius wept bitter tears of disgust and self-loathing as he watched the tips of his fingers shimmer and straighten until not so much as a single scratch remained.

'Forgive me...' he whispered.

URIEL EJECTED A spent magazine from his bolter and smoothly slapped a fresh one into the weapon as another enemy came at him from the doorway of the building before him. He rolled aside as a flurry of lasbolts kicked up the sand and rose to a shooting position beside a pile of discarded ammo crates. The movement so natural he was barely conscious of making it, he sighted along the top of his bolter and squeezed off a single round, blasting his target's head off with one well-aimed shot.

Another shooter snapped into view on the building's parapet and he adjusted his aim and put another shell squarely through the chest of this latest threat. Pasanius ran for the building's door as Uriel scanned the upper windows and surrounding rooftops for fresh targets. None presented themselves and he returned his attention to the main door as Pasanius smashed it from its hinges in a shower of splinters.

Uriel broke cover and ran for the building as Pasanius gave him covering fire, hearing the distinctive snap of lasgun shots and the answering roar of a bolter. As he reached the building, he slammed into the wall. Pasanius hurled a grenade through the door before ducking back as the thunder of the explosion blasted from within.

'Go!' shouted Pasanius. Uriel rolled from his position beside the door and plunged within the smoke-filled hell of the room. Bodies littered the floor and acrid smoke billowed from the explosion, but Uriel's armour's auto-senses penetrated the blinding fog with ease, showing him two enemies still standing. He put the first one down and Pasanius shot the second in the head.

Room by room, floor by floor, the two Ultramarines swept through the building, killing another thirty targets before declaring it clear. Since the door had been broken down, all of four minutes had passed.

Uriel removed his helmet and ran a hand across his scalp, his breathing even and regular, despite a training exercise that would have had even the fittest human warrior gulping great draughts of air into their lungs.

'Four minutes,' he said. 'Not good. Chaplain Clausel would have had us fasting for a week after a performance like that.'

'Aye,' agreed Pasanius, also removing his helm. 'It is not the same without his hymnals while we train. We are losing our edge. I do not feel the necessity to excel here.'

'I know what you mean, but it is an honour to have the skills we do and it is our duty to the Chapter to hone them to the highest levels,' said Uriel, checking the action of his bolter and whispering the words of prayer that honoured the weapon's war spirit. Both men had offered prayers, applying the correct oils and rites of firing before even loading them. Such devotion to a weapon was common among the fighting men and women of the Imperium, but to a Space Marine his boltgun was much more than simply a weapon. It was a divine instrument of the Emperor's will, the means by which His wrath was brought to bear upon those who would defy the Imperium.

Despite his words, Uriel knew that Pasanius spoke true when he talked of losing their edge. Four minutes to clear a building of such size was nothing short of amazing, but he knew they could have done it faster, more efficiently, and the idea of not performing as well as he knew he could was galling to him.

Since he had been six years old and inducted to the Agiselus Barracks, he had been the best at everything he had turned his hand to. Only Learchus had equalled him in his achievements and the possibility that he was not the best he could be was a deeply disturbing notion. Pasanius was right – without the constant drilling and training they were used to as part of a Space Marine Chapter, Uriel could feel his skill diminish with every passing day they travelled from Macragge.

'Still,' continued Pasanius. 'Perhaps we need not be the best any more, perhaps we no longer owe the Chapter anything at all.'

Uriel's head snapped up, shocked at the very idea and shocked at the ease with which Pasanius had voiced it.

'What are you talking about?'

'Do you still feel that we are Space Marines of the Emperor?' asked Pasanius.

'Of course I do. Why should we not?'

'Well, we were cast out, disgraced, and are no longer Ultramarines,' continued Pasanius, staring vacantly into space, his voice wavering and unsure. 'But are we still Space Marines? Do we still need to train like this? If we are not Space Marines, then what are we?'

Pasanius lifted his head and met his gaze, and Uriel was surprised at the depths of anguish he saw. His former sergeant's soul was bared and Uriel could see the terrible hurt it bore at their expulsion from the Chapter. He reached out and placed his hand on Pasanius's unadorned shoulder guard.

Uriel could understand his friend's pain, once again feeling guilty that Pasanius shared the disgrace that should have been his and his alone.

'We will always be Space Marines, my friend,' affirmed Uriel. 'And no matter what occurs, we will continue to observe the battle rituals of our Chapter. Wherever we are or whatever we do, we will always be warriors of the Emperor.'

Pasanius nodded. 'I know that,' he said at last. 'But at night, terrible doubts plague me and there is no one aboard this vessel I can confess to.

Chaplain Clausel is not here and I cannot go to the shrine of the primarch and pray for guidance.'

'You can talk to me, Pasanius, always. Are we not comrades in arms, battle-brothers and friends?'

'Aye, Uriel, we will always be that, but you too are condemned alongside me. We are outcast and your words are like dust in the wind to me. I crave the spiritual guidance of one who is pure and unsullied by disgrace. I am sorry.'

Uriel turned away from his friend, wishing he knew what to say, but he was no Chaplain and did not know the right words to bring Pasanius the solace he so obviously yearned for.

But even as he struggled for words of reassurance, a treacherous voice within him wondered if Pasanius might be right.

URIEL AND PASANIUS made their way back down through the bullet-riddled training building and the mangled remains of thirty-seven servitor-controlled opponents, their plastic and mesh bodies torn apart by the Space Marines' mass-reactive bolter shells. Exiting the training building, they made their way through the packed gymnasia, heading towards one of the vessel's many chapels of veneration. With their firing rites complete, their rigidly maintained routine now called for them to make obeisances to their primarch and the Emperor.

The lights in the gymnasia began to dim, telling Uriel that the starship was close to entering its night-cycle, though true night and day were meaningless concepts aboard a starship. Despite that, Captain Laskaris enforced strictly timetabled lights out and reveille calls to more quickly acclimatise the passengers of *Calth's Pride* to the onboard ship time. It was a common phenomenon that many soldiers had trouble adjusting to life aboard a space-faring vessel; the enforced claustrophobia along with dozens of other privations caused by ship-board life resulting in vastly increased instances of violence and disorder.

But the regiments currently being transported within the ship's gargantuan hull had been raised in Ultramar, and those trained within the military barracks of the Ultramarines' realm were used to a far harsher discipline than that enforced by the ship's crew and armsmen.

The gymnasia was a vast, stone columned chamber, fully ninety metres from sanded floor to arched ceiling and at least a thousand wide. An entire regiment or more could comfortably train in shooting, close-quarter combat, infiltration, fighting in jungle terrain or the nightmare of city-fighting. These dedicated arenas were sectioned off throughout the gymnasia, fully realised environments where thousands of soldiers were receiving further training before reaching their intended warzone far in the galactic north-west. Row upon row of battle-flags hung from the ceiling, and huge anthracene statues of great heroes of Ultramar lined the walls. Stained-glass windows, lit from behind by flickering glow-globes, depicted the life of Roboute Guilliman as looped prayers in High Gothic echoed from flaring trumpets blown by alabaster angels mounted on every column.

'Good men and women,' noted Uriel as he watched a group of soldiers practising bayonet drills against one another.

Despite their discipline, Uriel could see many of the training soldiers casting confused glances their way. He knew that their armour, bereft of the insignia of the Ultramarines, would no doubt be causing endless speculation amongst the regiments billeted within the ship.

'Aye,' nodded Pasanius. 'The Macragge 808th. Most will have come from Agiselus.'

'Then they will fight well,' said Uriel. 'A shame we cannot train with them. There is much they could learn and it would have been an honour for us to pass on our experience.'

'Perhaps,' said Pasanius. 'Though I do not believe their officers would have counted it as such. I feel we may be a disappointment to many of them. A disgraced Space Marine is no hero; he is worthless, less than nothing.'

Uriel glanced round at Pasanius, surprised by the venom in his tone.

'Pasanius?' he said.

Pasanius shook his head, as though loosing a quiet unease, and smiled, though Uriel could see the falsity of it. 'I am sorry, Uriel, my sleep was troubled. I'm not used to having so much of it. I keep waiting for a bellowing Chaplain Clausel to sound reveille.'

'Aye,' agreed Uriel, forcing a smile. 'More than three hours of sleep a night is a luxury. Be careful you do not get too used to it, my friend.'

'Not likely,' said Pasanius, gloomily.

URIEL KNELT BEFORE the dark marble statue of the Emperor, the flickering light from the hundreds of candles that filled the chapel reflecting a hundredfold on its smooth-finished surface. A fug of heavily scented smoke filled the upper reaches of the chapel from the many burners that lined the nave, smelling of nalwood and sandarac. Chanting priests, clutching prayer beads and burning tapers, paced the length of the chapel, muttering and raving silently to themselves while albino-skinned cherubs with flickering golden wings and cobalt-blue hair bobbed in the air above them, long lengths of prayer paper trailing from dispensers in their bellies.

Uriel ignored them, holding the wire-wound hilt of his power sword in a two-handed grip while resting his hands on the gold quillons. The sword was unsheathed, point down on the floor, and Uriel rested his forehead on the carven skull of its pommel as he prayed.

The sword was the last gift to him from Captain Idaeus, his former mentor, and though it had been broken on Pavonis – a lifetime ago it seemed now – Uriel had forged a new blade of his own before departing on the crusade to Tarsis Ultra and his eventual disgrace. He wondered what Idaeus would have made of his current situation and gave thanks that he was not here to see what had become of his protégé.

Pasanius knelt beside him, eyes shut and lips moving in a silent benediction. Uriel found it hard to countenance the dark, brooding figure Pasanius had become since leaving the Fortress of Hera. True, they had been cast from the Chapter, their homeworld and battle-brothers, but they still had a duty to perform, an oath to fulfil, and a Space Marine never turned his back on such obligations, especially not an Ultramarine.

Uriel knew that Pasanius was a warrior of courage and honour and just hoped that he had the strength of character to lift himself from this ill disposition, remembering sitting in a chapel not dissimilar to this in one of the medicae buildings on Tarsis Ultra, vexed by torments of his own. He also recalled the beautiful face of the Sister of the Order Hospitaller he had met there. Sister Joaniel Ledoyen she had been called, and she had spoken to him with a wisdom and clarity that had cut through his pain.

Uriel had meant to return to the medicae building after the fighting, but had been too badly injured in the final assault on the hive ship to do anything other than rest as Apothecary Selenus struggled to remove the last traces of the tyranid phage-cell poisoning from his bloodstream.

When he had been well enough to move, it was already time to depart for Macragge, and he had not had the time to thank her for her simple kindness. He wondered what had become of her and how she had fared in the aftermath of the alien invasion. Wherever she was, Uriel wished her well.

He finished his prayers, standing and kissing the blade of his sword before sheathing it in one economical motion. He bowed to the statue of the Emperor and made the sign of the aquila across his chest, glancing down at Pasanius as he continued to pray.

He frowned as he noticed some odd marks protruding from the gorget of Pasanius's armour. Standing above him, Uriel could see that the marks began at the nape of Pasanius's neck before disappearing out of sight beneath his armour. The crusting of scar tissue told Uriel that they were wounds, recent wounds, instantly clotted by the Larraman cells within their bloodstream.

But how had he come by such marks?

Before Uriel could ask, he felt a presence behind him and turned to see one of the priests, a youngish man with haunted eyes, staring at him in rapt fascination.

'Preacher,' said Uriel, respectfully.

'No, not yet!' yelped the priest, twisting his prayer beads round and around his wrists in ever tighter loops. 'No, no preacher am I. A poor cenobite, only, my angel of death.'

Uriel could see the man's palms were slick with blood and wondered what manner of order he belonged to. There were thousands of recognised sects within the Imperium and this man could belong to any one of them. He scanned the man's robes for some clue, but his deep blue chasuble and scapular were unadorned save for their silver fastenings.

'Can I help you with something?' pressed Uriel as Pasanius rose to his feet and stood by his side.

The man shook his head. 'No,' he cackled with a lopsided grin. 'Already dead am I. The Omphalos Daemonium comes! I feel it pushing out from the inside of my skull. He will take me and everyone else for his infernal engine. Deadmorsels for his furnace, flesh for his table and blood for his chalice.'

Uriel shared a sidelong glance at Pasanius and rolled his eyes, realising that the cenobite was utterly insane, a common complaint amongst the more zealous of the Emperor's followers. Such unfortunates were deemed to exist on a level closer to the divine Emperor and allowed to roam free that their ravings might be grant some clue to the will of the Immortal Master of Mankind.

'I thank you for your words, preacher,' said Uriel, 'but we have completed our devotions and must take our leave.'

'No,' said the cenobite emphatically.

'No? What are you talking about?' asked Uriel, beginning to lose patience with the lunatic priest. Like most of the Adeptus Astartes, the Ultramarines had a strained relationship with the priests of the Ministorum; the Space Marines' belief that the Emperor was the mightiest mortal to bestride the galaxy, but a mortal nonetheless, diametrically opposed to the teachings of their Ecclesiarch.

'Can you not hear it, son of Calth? Juddering along the bloodtracks, its hateful boxcars jolting along behind it?'

'I don't hear anything,' said Uriel, stepping around the cenobite and marching towards the chapel's iron door.

'You will,' promised the man.

Uriel turned as a monotonous servitor's voice crackled from the electrum-plated vox-units mounted in the shadows of the arched ceiling, announcing: 'All hands prepare for warp translation. Warp translation in thirty seconds.'

The cenobite laughed, spittle frothing at the corners of his mouth as he raised his torn forearms above his head. Blood ran from his opened wrists and spattered his face before rolling down his cheeks like ruby tears.

He dropped to his knees and whispered, 'Too late... the Lord of Skulls comes.'

A spasm of sickness sheared along Uriel's spine as the last words left the cenobite's mouth and he stepped towards the man, ready to chastise him for uttering such blasphemies in this sanctified place.

The lights in the chapel dimmed as the ship prepared for warp translation.

Uriel dragged the young preacher to his feet.

And the cenobite's head exploded.

TWO

BLOOD GEYSERED IN slow motion from the ragged stump of the cenobite's neck and Uriel pushed his spasming corpse away in disgust, backing away and wiping the sticky fluid from his face. The body remained upright, jerking and thrashing as though in the grip of a violent seizure. The cenobite's arms flailed wildly, yet more blood flickering from his opened wrists and spattering the statuary and altar.

Even as he stared in horrified fascination at the corpse's lunatic dance, Uriel felt the familiar sensation of his primary stomach flipping as the ship jumped into the treacherous currents of the warp. He gripped one of the chapel's pews as he felt a sudden dizziness, which vanished seconds later as his Lyman's ear adjusted for the sudden spatial differentiation between dimensions.

The hideous corpse continued to thrash and convulse, refusing to fall despite its lack of a head, and Uriel tasted the unmistakable sensation of warp-spawned witchery on the air. The man's fellow priests wailed in terror, dropping to their knees and spilling prayers of protection and mercy from mouths open wide in horror. Some, made of sterner stuff, drew pistols from beneath their robes and aimed them at the dancing corpse.

'No!' shouted Uriel, drawing his sword and leaping towards the hideous revenant. It lunged towards him, arms outstretched, but a sweeping stroke of Uriel's blade clove it from collarbone to pelvis and the shorn halves of the man fell to the marble floor, twitching, but mercifully free of whatever monstrous animation had possessed it before.

'Guilliman's blood!' swore Pasanius, backing away from the dead cenobite and making the sign of the aquila over his chest. 'What happened to him?'

'I have no idea,' said Uriel, kneeling beside the corpse and wiping his blade on the cenobite's chasuble as the lights in the chapel began flashing urgently. Wailing klaxons and ringing bells could be heard from beyond the chapel door.

Uriel smoothly rose to his feet, saying, 'But I have a feeling we'll find out soon.'

He turned and ran back to the chapel door, grabbing his bolter from the gun rack beside the entrance to the vestry. Pasanius scooped up his flamer and followed him out into the corridor, drawing up sharply as he saw what lay beyond the chapel door.

BOTH MEN STOOD transfixed as the arched passageway before them swelled and rippled, as though in a diabolical heat haze, its dimensions swelling and distorting beyond the three known to man.

'Imperator!' breathed Pasanius in terror. 'The Geller field must be failing. The warp is spilling in!'

'And Emperor alone knows what else,' said Uriel, his dread of the unknown terrors of the warp sending a shiver of fear along his spine. Without the Geller field to protect the ship from the predatory astral and daemonic creatures that swam in the haunted depths of the immaterium, all manner of foul entities would have free rein within the vessel's halls, ethereal horrors and shadowy phantoms that could rip men to shreds before vanishing back into the warp.

'Come on,' shouted Uriel. 'The gymnasia. We need to gather as many soldiers as we can before it's too late.'

Uriel and Pasanius lurched their way along the passageway, stumbling like a pair of drunks as they fought to hold their equilibrium in the face of this spatial insanity. Screams and roars came from ahead, but Uriel found himself unable to pinpoint exactly where ahead was as sounds echoed and distorted wildly around him. The floors and ceilings of the stone passageways seemed to run fluid, swirling as though their very fabric was being unravelled before his eyes.

The sound of a tolling bell rang out, ponderously slow and dolorous one second, tinny and ringing the next. Using the wall as a guide, though it was a treacherous one, the two Space Marines fought their way onwards, each step bringing fresh madness to their surroundings.

Uriel thought he saw a tall mountain, wreathed in smoke, form from the floor before it vanished and was replaced by a roiling sea of snapping mouths. But even that disappeared like a fever dream as soon as he tried to look upon it. He could see Pasanius was having similar difficulties, blinking and rubbing his eyes in disbelief.

A grainy static filled Uriel's vision and an insistent buzzing, like an approaching swarm of insects, filled his skull. He shook his head, trying to clear the distortion and unable to comprehend the things he saw before him.

'How close are we?' yelled Pasanius.

Uriel steadied himself on a bulkhead, grateful for its transitory solidity, and shook his head again, though the movement made him want to vomit. 'How can we tell? Everything changes the moment I look at it.'

'I think we are almost there,' said Pasanius, pointing to where the passageway widened into a marble-flagged atrium, though at present, it appeared that the chamber had been inverted, its domed ceiling swirling below their feet, its dimensions skewed completely out of true.

Uriel nodded and pushed himself forward, an intense and nauseous sensation of vertigo seizing him as they stumbled into the flipped atrium. Uriel's eyes told him he was crossing the floor, but he could tell that his every step found him crossing the shallow concave bowl of the inverted dome. His booted feet trod the shielded glass of the atrium's dome that was all that lay between him and the warp.

Uriel looked down through the dome, the nauseous sensation in his gut surging upwards, and he dropped to his knees, vomiting explosively across the glass. A sickly mass of bruised colours foamed and swirled beyond the glass, the very stuff of the warp itself, noxious and toxic to the eye. Its bilious malevolence went beyond its simple hideous appearance, violating some inner part of the human mind that dared not comprehend its nightmarish potential.

Uriel found his eyes drawn to a loathsome stain of the warp, a vile, filthy sore of ash-stained yellow, he was unable to drag his sight from. Even as he stared at it, the warp shifted, stirred into life by the mere attention and echoes of Uriel's thoughts. Vile, terrible things began shaping themselves from the foul soup of raw creation and Uriel knew that were he to see what horrific thing would be born from its hateful depths, he would go mad.

Gauntleted hands gripped him and hauled him upright, and he could feel the warp's blind, impotent rage at being denied such a morsel as his sanity.

'Don't look at it! Keep your eyes closed!' shouted Pasanius, dragging Uriel over the surface of the dome. Uriel felt its insistent call; the seductions of its fecundity and the promises of power that could be his were he but to surrender to it. His eyes ached to see the awful magnificence of the warp, but Uriel kept them screwed tightly shut, lest they betray his soul to the immaterium.

Breathless and disgusted, Uriel and Pasanius clambered from the atrium and crawled away from the false seductions of the warp, the feelings of sickness diminishing the further they went.

Uriel looked up, coughing stringy, vomit-flecked spittle and said, 'Thank you, my friend.'

Pasanius nodded and said, 'There. The entrance to the gymnasia should be through that cloister!'

'Aye, it should be,' agreed Uriel pushing himself weakly to his feet. 'Let's just hope it is still there.'

Uriel stumbled through the cloister and turned towards the entrance to the gymnasia.

'Oh no...' he whispered as he saw what lay before him.

Where he had expected to find the carven marble archway of the gymnasia, there was now a gargantuan gateway of brazen metal: bronze and laced with razorwire that led into a rectangular, earthen arena which was fully a kilometre wide and twice that in length. More incredible still, there was no roof to this arena, simply a lacerated crimson sky, flecked with cancerous, melanoma clouds. What new madness was this?

Screaming, mad and insane like the wails of the damned in torment, echoed from within and pierced Uriel's skull with lancing, glass shards of pain.

His stomach knotted in horrified disgust as the overpowering reek of fresh blood filled his senses.

The soldiers of the 808th Macragge they had come to find were still here, but where there had once been a proud regiment of men and women ready to fight for the glory of the Emperor, there was now nothing more than the screaming, bloody shreds of those yet to die.

Hundreds of soldiers writhed on the ground, splashing great gouts of blood around them as though fighting some subterranean attacker. Fleshless, bony hands reached up through the dark earth, clawing and grasping at their bodies and dragging them below the surface. Uriel ran through the gate, sword in hand, and felt his boots sink into the soft and loamy ground, crimson liquid oozing from the waterlogged earth.

Bones and grinning skulls gleamed whitely through the red earth and Uriel saw that the ground was not waterlogged at all, but flooded with fresh-spilled blood.

His mind reeled at the prospect. How many must have been drained of their life's blood to irrigate such a vast space so thoroughly? How many arteries had been emptied to slake the vile thirst of this dark, dark earth?

Uriel was shaken from his disgust by the nearby screams of a man half submerged in the earth and weeping tears of agony.

'Help me! For the love of the Emperor help me!' he shrieked.

Uriel sheathed his sword and ran over to help the man, who reached up with pleading arms. The man's gore-slick hands slid from his gauntlets, but Uriel gripped his tunic and hauled him clear of the ground, staggering back in horror as he saw that the man had been stripped of flesh below the waist, his entire lower body flensed of muscle, meat and blood. Even as he watched, the hungry earth swallowed what remained of the dying man, unwilling to be cheated of its fleshy morsel.

A sense of utter helplessness filled Uriel as he watched men and women devoured by the bloody ground, the monstrous sound of marrow being suckled from the bone echoing from the monolithic sides of this gory arena.

'Blessed Emperor, no!' wailed Pasanius, fighting to save a howling woman from a similar fate. Laughing shadows ran like black mercury along the walls of the arena, a capering dance of souls that flared into the blood-red sky as the slaughter of thousands concluded.

A sudden silence descended upon the arena as the last of the bloody ground's helpless victims were dragged beneath its thirsting depths. No sooner had the last body vanished from sight, when a throaty gurgling erupted from the centre of the arena and Uriel saw a long strip of rock-crete slowly rise from the soaking ground. Dull, bloody rail tracks arose with it, running across the middle of the arena and ending at opposite walls.

The hateful silence was broken by a sibilant moaning, as of a thousand voices trapped in a nightmare they know they will never wake from.

'Holy Emperor, protect us from evil, grant us the strength of spirit and body to fight your enemies and smite them with your blessing,' prayed Pasanius.

'Too late,' whispered Uriel, drawing his sword and standing ready to fight whatever new monstrosity the warp might unleash. 'We failed.'

No… you have not yet begun…

Both Uriel and Pasanius spun, searching for the source of the voice.

'Did you hear that?' said Uriel.

'Aye,' nodded Pasanius, 'I think so, but it felt… felt as though it was inside my head. Something terrible is coming, Uriel.'

'I know. But whatever comes, we will fight it with courage and honour.'

'Courage and honour,' agreed Pasanius, firing the igniters on the nozzle of his flamer.

'Let's go,' said Uriel grimly, nodding towards the dripping platform in the centre of the arena. 'Whatever is coming, we'll meet it head on!'

Pasanius followed his former captain as they made their way across the hideously squelching ground towards the platform.

As they mounted its steps, the source of the sibilant moaning was finally revealed.

Each sleeper laid between the rail tracks was a jigsaw of bodies and limbs, writhing in agony and knotted together by some dark sorcery. They screamed in lunatic delirium, their voices piteous and heartbreaking. Though he knew none of the faces, the cast of their features told Uriel that they were of the stock of Ultramar and that the souls of those consumed by this abominable place were suffering still.

Eyes and mouths churning in the fluid matter of each sleeper gave anguished voice to their suffering before being forced from form to formlessness that another soul might vent its endless purgatory.

Uriel's hatred swelled within him at such horror and he closed his eyes...

Splintering crystals of alternate existences clash and jangle, detaching from the walls of one plane and shifting their position to resonate at a different frequency. Echoes in time allow the planes to shift and change; altering the angles of reality to allow the dimensions to unlock, dancing in a ballet of all possibilities.

...then opened them as he felt a sickening vibration deep in his bones and a restlessness ripple through the air. The jagged stumps of bone jutting through the ground retreated into its sanguineous depths and the moaning sleepers wept with renewed anguish.

Where the rail tracks vanished into the walls of this vast courtyard, streamers of multi-coloured matter were oozing from the stonework.

Rippling spirals of reflective light coiled from the mortar, twisting the image behind like a warped lens. The walls seemed to stretch, as though being sucked into an unseen vortex behind, until there was nothing left but a rippling veil of impenetrable darkness, a tunnel into madness ringed with screaming skulls sent out to die.

Warped realms, a universe and lifetimes distant, flow together, joining all points in time on the bronze bloodtracks. On a journey that leads everywhere and begins nowhere, the Omphalos Daemonium pushes itself from nothingness to form. Snaking from its daemonic womb and leaving nothing but barren rape and death in its wake.

And the Omphalos Daemonium came.

THOUGH THE CENOBITE had raved of the might and power of the Omphalos Daemonium's evil, they had been but the merest hints of the thing's diabolical majesty. Roaring from the newly formed tunnel mouth like a brazen juggernaut of the end times, the Omphalos Daemonium shrieked along the bloodtracks towards the horrified Space Marines.

Vast bone-pistons drove it forward, iron and steel flanks heaving with immaterial energies. Bloody steam leaked from every demented, skull-faced rivet as wheels of tortured souls ground the tracks beneath it to feast on the oozing blood of the dead earth.

Deep within its insane structure, it might have once resembled an ancient steam-driven locomotive, but unknown forces and warped energies had transformed it into something else entirely. The thunder of its arrival could be felt by senses beyond the pitiful five known to humankind, echoing through the planes that existed and intersected beyond the veil of reality.

Behind it came a tender of dark iron and a juddering procession of box-cars, their timbers stained with aeons of blood and ordure. Uriel knew without knowing that millions had been carried to their deaths in these hellish containers, carried to whatever loathsome destination this horrifying machine desired before finally being exterminated. The vast daemon engine slowed, the sleepers driven beyond sound in their torment as the towering machine halted at the edge of the platform.

Uriel thought he heard booming laughter and the grinding squeal of warped timber doors sliding open on runners rusted with gore.

Gusts of blood-laced steam hissed from the armoured hide of the Omphalos Daemonium and malevolent laughter rippled through them as they writhed on evil business of their own. Each tendril thickened and became more solid as they wormed towards the Space Marines and Uriel said, 'Stand ready.'

The tendrils of smoke vanished without warning and in their place stood eight figures, each wearing a featureless grey boiler-suit and knee-high boots with rusted buckles along the shins. Each carried a fearsome array of knives, hooks and saws on their leather belts.

Their faces were human in proportion only, flensed of the disguise of skin and glistening with revealed musculature. Crude stitches crisscrossed their skulls, and when they turned their heads as though hunting by scent, Uriel saw they were utterly featureless save for distended and fanged mouths. They had no eyes, nose or ears, only discoloured swellings that bulged and rippled beneath their fleshless skulls.

'Daemons!' shouted Uriel. 'Foul abominations! Come forth and die on my blade.'

A daemon's patchwork face swung towards him, tumourous tissue in its neck bulging with horrid appetite. None of the foul creatures moved, content merely to watch the two Space Marines as a billowing cloud of steam vented from the side of the vast daemon engine. With a clang of locks disengaging, a thick iron door squealed open and a gigantic figure stepped onto the platform.

Standing head and shoulders above them, the giant wore a clanking, mechanical suit of riveted iron plates and thick sheets of melted, vulcanised rubber. Over its rusted armour it wore a charred apron, and a crown of blackened horns sprouted from a conical helmet with a raised visor. For all its crude fabrication and disrepair, Uriel recognised the armour as impossibly ancient power armour, such as had been worn by warriors of legend many thousands of years ago. The stench of scorched meat enfolded it, together with a crackling sensation of depraved evil and unquenchable rage.

One shoulder guard was studded with star-shaped rivets, the other emblazoned with a symbol of ancient malice that both Ultramarines recalled from the depths of righteous anger instilled in them by Chaplain Clausel's daily Litanies of Hate. A grinning, iron-visored skull that once was the heraldry of a Legion that had fought for the Emperor in hallowed antiquity, but was now a symbol of unending bitterness and hatred. It was a symbol that now belonged to the most lethal foes of the Imperium: warriors of unutterable evil and malice – the Chaos Space Marines.

'Iron Warriors…' hissed Uriel.

'The Betrayers of Istvaan,' growled Pasanius.

The figure carried a long, iron-hafted billhook, the broad, curved blade rusted and pitted with reddish brown stains. A pair of burning yellow eyes, like sickly, dying suns, shone from beneath the helmet as the figure took a heavy step towards them, the skinless daemons moving to stand behind it.

'Deadmorsels feed the new fire, blood is supped by the faceless Sarcomata, and flesh of man will come with me,' said the figure, its voice like rusted metal on their skulls.

It gripped its enormous billhook in one blackened, burned hand and beckoned them impatiently towards the hissing daemon engine with the other.

'Come!' boomed the giant. 'I have purpose for you. Obey me or the Slaughterman turn you into deadmorsels! I am the Omphalos Daemonium and my will drives this suit of flesh, and it will turn you into deadmorsels! Now come!'

Uriel felt sickened even being near this thing of Chaos. Could it really believe that they would willingly have truck with such evil? The featureless daemons, which Uriel guessed were the Sarcomata the Omphalos Daemonium spoke of, spread out on the platform, unhooking long, serrated knives from their belts.

'Courage and honour!' yelled Uriel, leaping towards the nearest of the Sarcomata and stabbing for its belly. His sword passed straight through the creature, its form transforming into a cackling pillar of red steam. He pulled up in surprise, grunting in pain as the beast's form coalesced beside him and its blade slashed across his cheek. Another darted in, its rusty blade stabbing into his neck. He twisted free of the weapon before it could penetrate more than a centimetre and swung at his new attacker. Once again, his assailant flashed to steam before his blow could land and Uriel found himself off balance as another knife blade laid his cheek open to the bone.

'Burn, Chaos filth!' roared Pasanius and sprayed a blazing gout of promethium at the giant Iron Warrior. The volatile chemical flames licked hungrily at the giant, but no sooner had the fire taken than it guttered and died.

The creature's booming laughter echoed from the sides of the arena. 'I have been a prisoner in flames for aeons and liveflesh thinks it can burn me!'

Pasanius slung his flamer and reached for his pistol, but, with a speed that belied its ungainly form, the Chaos creature stepped forward, wrap-

ping its blackened fingers around Pasanius's throat and hauling him from
his feet.

Uriel slashed at the Sarcomata as they surrounded him, each thrust and
sweep of his sword hitting nothing but chuckling tendrils of steam that
vanished only to reappear elsewhere to cut him. Clotted blood caked his
face and he knew that he could not fight such foes for much longer.

He saw the giant in the rusted armour lift Pasanius from his feet and
hurl him through the iron door the Omphalos Daemonium had first
stepped from, and surged towards the Chaos creature. He could not fight
foes that could disappear at will, but he swore that this traitor from the
elder days would die by his hand. He swung his sword towards the Iron
Warrior, the blade wreathed in pellucid flames able to cut through armour
and flesh with equal ease.

The sword struck his enemy full square on the chest, but the blade simply clanged from the heavy iron plates of his armour. Uriel was amazed,
but drew his arm back to attack again. Before he could strike, the Iron Warrior's fist slammed into his face, sending him sprawling across the
platform.

He fought to regain his senses, but the Sarcomata surrounded him, their
blackened fingers reaching hungrily for him. Their touch felt like rotted
meat, wriggling with the suggestion of maggots and freshly hatched larvae.
Their dead skin masks were centimetres from his face, their breath like a
furnace of cadavers. They moved their undulating faces around his, as
though tasting his scent, their fearsome strength pinning him to the
ground.

'The Sarcomata favour you, Ultramarine…' laughed the giant, striding
across the platform towards him. 'They are corruption of spirit given form
and purpose. Perhaps they sense a certain kinship?'

Uriel waited for death as one of the Sarcomata lowered its mouth to his
bared neck, but the Omphalos Daemonium had greater purpose for him
than mere murder, and roared in impatience.

The skinless daemons hissed in submission, hauling Uriel from the platform and carrying him towards the iron door of the massive daemon
engine.

Burning air and the stench of cooked meat gusted from within, and as
he was carried inside, Uriel knew that they were truly damned.

℧ THREE

BLOOD. THE STENCH of it filled his nostrils, overpowering and sickening, the bitter, metallic taste catching in the back of his throat. His neuroglottis sifted hundreds of different blood-scents and the searing tang of burning flesh made his eyes water before his occulobe compensated and secreted a protective membrane across the surface of his eye.

He blinked away the moisture, twisting in the grip of the Sarcomata and trying to get a bearing on his surroundings. Despite what his eyes told him, he knew he must be seeing things, for the interior of the daemon engine confounded his senses and flouted any notion of reality. It defied geometry, impossibly arching beyond the limits of vision to either side: a sweltering, red-lit hell cavern. A wide-doored firebox roared and seethed at one end of the chamber and long lines of dangling chains and pulleys, each with a limbless human torso skewered on a rusted hook, hung from the darkened, dripping roof.

He and Pasanius were dragged past scattered mounds of human limbs, each piled higher than a battle tank, the flesh rotten and stinking. Two of the Sarcomata slithered away from Uriel to lift a headless torso and thrust it into the firebox.

They stoked the daemon engine with flesh and blood, its belching stacks spewing ashen bodies into the air. The giant in the armour of the Iron Warriors dragged Pasanius behind it, the mighty sergeant helpless against such power.

'No!' shouted Uriel as the Omphalos Daemonium dropped its billhook and easily lifted Pasanius with one hand while reaching for an empty hook with the other. The iron giant took no notice of him and rammed the rusted hook into the backplate of Pasanius's armour, drawing a grunt of pain from him.

Uriel struggled all the harder as he saw an empty hook hanging beside Pasanius, but the Sarcomata held him firm and he could not break their hold. Fleshy, wriggling hands lifted him high and he gritted his teeth to stop himself from crying out as he too was spitted on a hook, the barbed point went through his armour and pierced his back. The Sarcomata hissed and drew back, the lumpen growths beneath their exposed flesh rippling in monstrous hunger.

The clang of mighty pistons echoed through the impossible structure, hissing spigots belching stinking clouds of oil-streaked steam and iron-grilled furnaces flaring with blue and green flames. Moans and the creaking of molten metal mingled with the chittering glee of the Sarcomata, and Uriel could imagine no more complete a vision of hell.

The Omphalos Daemonium watched their futile struggles and stepped forward, gripping Uriel's jaw in one blackened gauntlet. Uriel could taste the ash on its fingers and smell the cooked meat beneath. The creature... was it an Iron Warrior or some daemonic entity within the flesh of one? Uriel could not tell, and as it leaned close, its breath like the air from an exhumed grave, he kicked out, his boot ringing harmlessly from its ancient breastplate.

'You waste your energy, Ultramarine. It is not within your power or destiny to destroy me. Save your strength for the world of iron. You will need it.'

'Get away from me, you bastard abomination,' shouted Uriel, struggling in his captor's grip, despite the fiery pain from the hook gouging his back.

'It is pointless to resist,' said the Omphalos Daemonium. 'I have travelled the bloodtracks between realities for countless aeons and all things are revealed there. What has been, what is and all the things that might yet be. I have snuffed out lives yet to be born, changed unwritten histories and travelled paths no others may walk. And you think you can defy my will?'

'The Emperor is with us, yea though we walk in the shadows–' began Pasanius.

The Omphalos Daemonium smashed a gauntleted hand across Pasanius's chin, swinging him wildly around and drawing a hiss of pain from him as the hook in his back dug deeper into his flesh.

'Prayers to your corpse of a god mean nothing here. His power has gone out of the world and nothing now remains of him.'

'You lie,' snapped Uriel. 'The power of the Emperor is eternal.'

'Eternal?' snarled the Omphalos Daemonium. 'You would do well not to use such words so lightly until you have experienced such a span, trapped and helpless and tormented beyond reason.'

The yellow eyes of the Omphalos Daemonium burned into Uriel's and he saw the depthless rage and madness within them. Whatever the malign intelligence that lurked within the ancient suit of power armour was, it was clearly insane, the torments it spoke of having driven it into a depthless abyss.

'What are you?' said Uriel eventually. 'What do you want with us?'

The Omphalos Daemonium released its grip and turned from him as the Sarcomata began gathering up more body parts and carried them towards the furnace, hurling legs, arms and heads into the flames.

'That is unimportant for now,' it said, pulling a thick chain that hung beside the firebox and hauling on a rusted lever with a thick, rubberised handle. 'All that matters is that you are here and that, at this time, our journeys follow the same path.'

Uriel felt the impossible room judder as the lever was drawn back fully, the iron door they had been carried through shutting with a squeal of tortured metal. Pain flared in his back as the hook twisted between his ribs and the massive daemon engine began to move. Cadavers on other hooks swung on their jangling chains and Uriel felt the familiar churning sensation in his belly of a warp translation. Was this infernal engine somehow capable of traversing the currents of the warp? Was that how it had managed to intercept *Calth's Pride* within the treacherous shoals of the immaterium?

He knew not to dwell too long on such things. The asking of such dangerous questions led to the path of deviation, the very thing that had seen them condemned to this fate.

The churning sensation in Uriel's stomach grew and he gritted his teeth against the growing pain. The Omphalos Daemonium turned from its labours and retrieved its billhook as the Sarcomata continued feeding the fires with corpses.

'Where are you taking us?' hissed Pasanius through gritted teeth.

'Where you need to go,' said the giant. 'I know of your death oath and what has led you here. The Lord of Skulls has more artifice to him than simply the art of death.'

'You are a daemon!' snarled Uriel. 'You are an abomination and I will see you destroyed.'

'Your skull will be laid before the throne of the Blood God before that happens, Space Marine. I have already seen the manner of your death; would you know of it?'

'The words of a daemon are lies!' shouted Pasanius. 'I will believe nothing you say.'

The Omphalos Daemonium slashed its billhook around, the blade flashing towards Pasanius's neck. Blood welled from a shallow cut across the sergeant's throat.

'You seek death, Ultramarine, and I would gladly rend and tear your soul. I would rip your flesh screaming from your bones and garland this body with your entrails, but your death is to be far worse than even one such as I could devise. Your skull will be honoured with a place in one of the bone mountains within sight of the Blood God.'

Another shudder, more intense, passed through the chamber and Uriel felt as though red-hot skewers were being pushed through his skull.

'You should honour me, for you travel in ways no mortal has dared for aeons.'

The Omphalos Daemonium raised its arms to the ceiling and laughed.

'We travel the bloodtracks. The Heart of Blood and the daemonculaba await!'

And the daemon engine roared into realms beyond existence.

URIEL SCREAMED.

Space folded, the currents of the warp vanishing; the arena, the daemon engine, the firebox, Pasanius. All disappeared, ripped away as everything around him turned inside out and became meaningless concepts. He felt himself simultaneously explode into a billion fragments and implode within himself, compressed to a singularity of hollow existence.

Faces floated before him, though as a dense ball of nothingness and a fragmented soul he knew not how he recognised them. Worlds and people, people and worlds, flashing past in a seamless blur, yet each as clear as though he examined each one in detail. Time slowed, yet rushed, splintering crystals sounding from far off as fractured realities ground and shifted like tectonic plates.

He saw the daemon engine spiral through the cracks between dimensions, snaking a path that wound through the shifting glass shards of reality, existing outside of everything, travelling in the slivers of null-space between all that was and all that ever could be.

He saw worlds of choking fumes, people in walking comas shuffling from one banal day to another, grey and dead without even the awareness to scream at the frustration of their pointless lives. Worlds where twisting numbers fell upon mountains of implausibility before running in molten rivers of algorithms to a sea of integers. It was gone in a heartbeat, replaced by a towering world of mountains and seas, white, marble and gold. Flames roared and seethed from every surface as the world burned, its people ashes on the wind, all life extinguished. Uriel, though he could no longer be sure he even knew who that was any more, saw with mounting horror that he knew this world. He saw the Fortress of Hera cast down, her once proud walls splintered and broken, the Temple of Correction no more than a shattered ruin. Daemons made sport in the Shrine of the Primarch, gnawing on his holy bones and defiling his sacred corpse.

He wept at such vileness, furious at his helplessness and incapable of wreaking his vengeance upon those who had visited such wrath upon Macragge.

Black, howling things closed on the daemon engine, unseen, slithering guardians of nothingness worming their way through the cracks to close on them.

The daemon engine had travelled the bloodtracks for millennia and knew that these blind sentinels were no threat to its terrifying power. Such guardian creatures fed on the souls of those unwitting fools who breached this realm by accident; madmen who pored over forgotten lore and forbidden magicks to unlock the gates between dimensions. Mortals who dared to travel to realms not meant for souls were devoured and made into yet more of the dark worms. The bloodtracks carried the daemon engine away from the toothless, questing mouths of the guardian creatures, its evil and power burning those that managed to approach too close.

Clockwork worlds, worlds taken by evil, worlds of elemental madness, worlds of chaos, worlds of insanity and worlds of arcing lightning. Everything was here. Every action that spawned a new realm of possibility could be found here and Uriel felt the knowledge of such things fill him as he hung from his hook, bleeding and raw.

The glue that held his fragile mind from sundering into pieces began to come undone, awful knowledge of the insignificance of being and the pointlessness of action tore at his sense of who he was and he desperately fought to hold onto his identity.

He was Uriel Ventris.

He was a warrior of the Emperor; sworn to defend His realm for as long as he lived.

He was a Space Marine.

His will was stronger, his purpose and determination greater than any other mortal man. He was in the belly of the beast and he would fight its corrupting touch.

He was... who...? His existence flickered and despite the protection of the daemon engine, he knew the madness that claimed the minds of the ignorant fools who sought such places out was enfolding him. He struggled to hold on as shards of his life began spiralling away from him, each spawning fresh realities within this terrifying multiverse.

Visions of potential and unwritten pasts floated past Uriel's eyes and he gasped as he saw alternate histories...

slide past

his eyes

He saw himself as a wrinkled ancient,

He saw himself as a young man,

Lying prone on a simple cot bed and

but one who was no longer a

surrounded by grieving family members.

Space Marine. He was a lean,

Here was his son, dark haired like him,
muscled farmer, toiling in the
but taller and with the look of a warrior.
cavern farms on his homeworld of
Uriel's heart swelled in pride and regret;
Calth. His features were soft and
pride in his son and regret
tinged with great regret
that this vision of his life could never be...
that this vision of his life could never be...

Both faded from his mind, though he craved to see more of them, to know the consequences of his life having travelled the road not taken. But such was not to be and other visions intruded on his sight.

Pavonis.

Black Bone Road.

Tarsis Ultra.

Medrengard?

What were these? Names of places or people? Memories or invention? Had he journeyed to these places? Was he from them? Were they his friends? He could taste the meaning on every jagged syllable, but none made sense, though he knew he should recognise them. Except... except there was one that did not have the subtle flavour of recognition. One that tasted of dark iron, that reeked of ashen pollutants, burning oil and echoed to the hammer of mountainous pile-drivers and pistons of hellish engines.

This world, that reality, was alien to him. Why now should it then intrude on his fracturing consciousness? It swelled in his perception, growing and filling what remained of his mind before it too vanished and his mind began to collapse inwards.

Nothing made sense any more; all was... dissolvingintamorassofinformation.Hecouldnolongerholdontoanythingcoherent,feelinghisthoughtsblurandsoften,runninglikeahundredtributariesofathousandriversthatempteidintoaseaofoblivionandhewelcomedit,knowingitwouldendthisscreamingmadnessinhishead.Aneternityoraninstantpassedthoughhecouldnottellwhich–timewasnowameaninglessconcept,bereftofmeaningandreference.

AvoicesoundedamidsttheinsanityandwhatlittleremainedofUrielVentrisclutchedatit,asadrowningmangraspsforalifeline

'Fear not, Ultramarine,' it said. 'This journey is like all mortal life.'

The daemon engine roared back into the realm of existence.

'It ends...'

URIEL DREW BREATH, his hearts hammering fit to break his chest, his blood thundering around his body and his face streaked with crimson that wept from his eyes and nose. He had bitten his tongue and his mouth was filled with a coppery taste.

He spat, tasting the reek of fumes and the acrid, iron stench of industry. He lay still for long seconds as he tried to work out where he was. Above him was an unending vista of white, without depth or scale, and he blinked, reaching up to wipe the congealed blood from his face. His hand passed before his face and he was struck by a lurching sense of vertigo. He had a sudden sensation of falling and cried out, scrabbling around him for purchase.

His hands closed on a fine shale of metallic shavings and his vertigo vanished as he realised he was lying on his back and looking up into the sky – a dead sky, featureless and vacant without so much as a single cloud or speck to blight its horrid emptiness. He ached everywhere, his muscles weary to the point of exhaustion and a searing pain in his back from where his flesh had been gouged by the hook. His thoughts tumbled over themselves as he tried to piece together what had just happened.

He pushed himself upright, seeing Pasanius next to him, retching onto the metallic ground. His friend's face was drawn and hollow, as though the weight of the world had settled upon his shoulders.

'Get up,' said a grating voice behind him and a flood of memory filled Uriel's skull. Daemon. Daemon engine. He fought to stand, but his flesh was still adjusting to its return to existence and he could only stumble to his knees.

Before them stood the Omphalos Daemonium, gigantic and monstrous in its blackened and ancient suit of power armour. Behind their captor was a shimmering, impossible rectangle of seething red light, a doorway back to the hellish interior of the daemon engine.

It carried its billhook and stood ankle deep in the powdery shale of the ground. Their weapons, Uriel's sword and bolter together with Pasanius's pistol and flamer rested against the rocks beside it. White reflections of the dead sky glittered on its shoulder guards and it seemed to Uriel that the grinning, visored skull there burned with even more malice than before.

'You will need to restore your equilibrium soon, Ultramarines,' said the daemon thing with an echoing chuckle. 'The delirium spectres will hear the pounding beats of your hearts and such morsels as you shall not go unnoticed for long.'

'The what?' managed Uriel at last.

'Monsters,' said the giant.

'Monsters?' repeated Uriel, gritting his teeth and finally climbing to his feet. Pasanius picked himself up and stood beside him, his face ashen, but angry.

'The skins of murderers stitched across desecrated frames by the Savage Morticians and filled with the mad souls of those who have died by their hands,' explained the Omphalos Daemonium. 'They hunt in these mountains and you will know them by the cries of the damned at your heels.'

'Where are we?' said Pasanius. 'Where have you brought us?'

'This is Medrengard, world of bitter iron,' said the Omphalos Daemonium, pointing at something behind the two Space Marines. 'Domain of the daemon primarch, Perturabo. Can you not feel his presence on the air? The malice of a being who once walked with gods and is now cast down to dwell beyond the realm he once bestrode. Look upon this ashen world and despair!'

Uriel turned to where the Omphalos Daemonium was pointing, the breath catching in his throat as he saw the desolate vista before him.

They stood on a high, rocky plateau above a sweeping, grey hinterland of utter wretchedness. Far below them on the dismal steppe was a world of death. Uriel had thought the sweltering cavern of the daemon engine had been a vision of hell, but it had been no more than a prelude to this soul-destroying desolation. Vast expanses of industrial heartland sprawled across the surface of the world: steel skeletons of factories, mountains of coal and reddish slag and mighty, belching smoke stacks. Flames burned from blasted refineries, the pounding of mighty hammers and the clangourous screech of iron on stone audible from hundreds of kilometres away.

Uriel had seen pollution-choked hive worlds, planets teeming with uncounted billions who toiled ceaselessly in filthy, smog and soot-choked death worlds, but they were garden paradises compared to Medrengard.

He had even set foot on the iron surfaces of Adeptus Mechanicus forge worlds, the hallowed domains of the priests of the Machine God. He had been awed by the scale of their pounding infrastructure, their every surface given over to colossal manufactorum and cathedral forges, but even the mightiest of these worlds was but a village smithy compared to Medrengard.

Rivers of molten metal snaked like channels of lava and evil clouds of smoke wreathed each tall tower and fanged chimney in a halo of lethal fumes.

A vast, dark range of mountains towered over it all, blasted black rock where no living thing had ever lived or ever would. The peaks seemed to scrape the sky itself; the jagged stumps of the mountains a dozen or more times taller than the highest summit of Macragge. Uriel felt his blood chill as his eyes travelled up the terrifying heights of the enormous crags, seeing vile tendrils of noxious black smoke writhing from behind the mountains and clawing impossibly into the sky.

Strange turrets reared beyond the peaks and Uriel knew with awful certainty that some nightmare city lay concealed and brooding in the deep, dark valleys of that damnable mountain range. A city where walls and bastions spread across the ground and distant domes fouled the rock like fungi after the rain. It was a hideous, dead-ringed outpost of malice that was rightly abhorred by all living things. Tarnished steeples and stained walls, deathly weed-tangled spires and empty halls were filled with limping and shuffling ghosts in rags who blindly obeyed the loathsome will of the city's diabolical master: the daemon primarch Perturabo, lord and master of the Iron Warriors.

'The hate...' whispered Uriel. 'So much hate and bitterness.'

'Yes,' said the Omphalos Daemonium. 'Imagine all the rank bitterness I smell within you – poisoned and grown strong by millennia of vengeful brooding, and it is still but the merest fraction of how much a living god can hate.'

Uriel closed his eyes to shut out this nightmare vision, understanding that to take even a single step towards the dreadful city was to die, but its cyclopean immensity was etched forever in his mind such that nothing could ever remove it.

The futility of existence in the face of this nameless horror was almost too great to bear and he raised his eyes to the dead sky, its soul-destroying emptiness preferable to Perturabo's baleful city. The ghostly black tendrils squirmed through the sky and he saw that they poured towards the solitary thing to stain its emptiness.

A vast black sun, its surface so dark that its darkness was not simply the absence of colour and light, but such that its fuliginous depths sucked all life and soul from the world.

Pasanius wept at its horrible, crushing weight and Uriel was not surprised to find that he too shed tears at the sight of such an abomination against nature.

'Emperor protect us,' he whispered. 'This is...'

'Aye,' said the Omphalos Daemonium. 'This is the place you call the Eye of Terror.'

'Why...?' gasped Uriel, tearing his gaze from the morbid sun. 'Why here?'

'This is the end of your journey. The place where you will fulfil your oath.'

'I do not understand.'

'That matters not. The things you seek to destroy, the daemonculaba, are on this world, shuttered away in the darkness, far from the sight of man in a great fastness fashioned from madness and despair.'

'Why would you bring us here?' demanded Uriel, a measure of his self-control returning. 'Why would a creature of Chaos seek to aid us?'

The Omphalos Daemonium laughed its booming, discordant laugh and said, 'Because you are to do my bidding, Uriel Ventris.'

'Never!' snapped Uriel. 'We would die before aiding a beast such as you.'

'Perhaps,' agreed the giant warrior. 'But are you willing to sacrifice all that you have fought to protect by defying me? Everything you have sacrificed and everyone you have bled to save will be washed away in an ocean of blood if you do.'

'You lie,' growled Pasanius.

'Foolish morsels. What need have I of lies? The Architect of Fate has lies enough for this universe; the Lord of Skulls demands no such pretences. I know what you saw as we travelled the bloodtracks, your world afire and your people dead, ashes on the wind as it burned to death.'

The Omphalos Daemonium took a ponderous step towards them, its billhook lowered to aim at Uriel's chest.

'I can make that happen,' it promised. 'All the splintered futures you saw can be shaped and I can ensure that your precious home dies screaming in the flames. Do you believe that?'

Uriel stared into the leprous yellow eyes of the daemon and knew with utter certainty that it could do the things it spoke of – Macragge destroyed, Ultramar gone...

'Yes, I believe you,' he said at last. 'What would you have us do?'

'Uriel!' cried Pasanius.

'I do not believe we have a choice, my friend,' said Uriel slowly.

'Think of what you are saying,' said Pasanius in disbelief. 'Whatever this bastard thing wants us to do can only be for evil. Who knows what we might unleash if we agree to do what it wants?'

'I know that, Pasanius, but what else can we do? Would you see Ultramar destroyed? The Fortress of Hera brought to ruin?'

'No, of course not, but–'

'No, Pasanius,' said Uriel evenly. 'Trust me. You have to trust me. Do you trust me?'

'You know I do,' protested Pasanius. 'I trust you with my life, but this is madness!'

'Then trust me now,' pressed Uriel.

Pasanius opened his mouth to speak once more, but saw the look in Uriel's eyes and simply nodded curtly.

'Very well,' he said sadly.

'Good,' hissed the Omphalos Daemonium, revelling in their defeat. 'There is a fortress many leagues from here, high in the southern mountains, and its master has something deep in his most secret vault that belongs to me. You will retrieve it for me.'

'What is it?' asked Uriel.

'It is the Heart of Blood, and that it is precious to me is all you need know.'

'What does it look like? How will we recognise it?'

The Omphalos Daemonium chuckled. 'You will know it when you see it.'

'Why do you need us for this?' demanded Pasanius. 'If it's so damned important, why the hell don't you just get it yourself?'

The Omphalos Daemonium was silent for a beat, then said, 'I have seen you with it and it is your destiny to do this. That is enough.'

Uriel nodded, hearing a distant, shrill cry on the air.

The Omphalos Daemonium heard the noise too and cocked its head, turning and marching back to the rectangle of red light that led back into the daemon engine and the hissing Sarcomata.

As it reached the shimmering doorway, it said, 'The delirium spectres come. They hear the beat of your hearts and their hunger tears at them. It would be wise not to be found by them.'

'Wait!' said Uriel, but the Omphalos Daemonium stepped through the doorway and he watched helplessly as it faded and vanished from the mountainside, taking their daemonic captor from sight.

A leaden weight of despair settled on Uriel's soul as the Omphalos Daemonium disappeared, and he dropped to his knees as he heard the cries of what sounded like a skirling chorus of air raid sirens.

He looked into the dead sky and saw a flock of hybrid, winged... things, flapping rhythmically on fleshy pinions towards them from the high peaks of the mountains.

'What the hell...?' said Pasanius, squinting into the sky.

'The delirium spectres,' said Uriel, scrambling over the ashen ground to retrieve his weapons.

'What do we do?' said Pasanius, belting on his pistol and slinging his flamer over his shoulder.

'We run,' said Uriel, as the madly screeching flock drew closer.

FOUR

BLACK SHAPES AGAINST the white sky screeched as they descended from the heights of the mountains and streaked towards the two Space Marines. The delirium spectres filled the air with the wails of murder victims and Uriel could hear their agony in every shriek torn from their bodies.

He scanned the plateau for obvious hiding places, hating the idea of flight, but knowing that the Omphalos Daemonium had not lied when it had told them that it would be wise not to be found by these creatures.

'Uriel,' said Pasanius, pointing further up the steep slopes of the mountain to a narrow defile in the rockface. 'There! I don't think they will be able to get in there.'

'Can we make it?'

'Only one way to find out,' said Pasanius, setting off for the scree slope.

Uriel buckled on his sword and ran after Pasanius, his breath ragged and strained in the toxic atmosphere. His back felt as if it was on fire, but he pushed aside the pain as he reached the slope and began climbing after Pasanius. The slope was rough, composed of dusty iron filings, craggy lumps of coal and twisted scoria. Pasanius's prodigious strength enabled him to scale the slope, albeit with great difficulty, but the loose incline gave Uriel no purchase and the harder he struggled, the further he slid back.

Screeching wails of obscene hunger echoed from behind and he risked a glance over his shoulder as the first of the delirium spectres dived from above.

'Uriel!' shouted Pasanius from a ledge above. 'Go left!'

He rolled to the left as the creature dropped from the sky, welded iron claws on its wings gouging the ground where his head had been.

He kicked out and the creature skidded down the slope, its fleshy wings beating the air in fury as it righted itself. Its shape was like that of some great, ocean-dwelling manta ray, an external skeleton formed of iron struts with its flesh a billowing sheet of patchwork human skin stitched to the metal. Screaming faces bulged across its leathery hide, a vicious 'o' of a mouth edged in hundreds of needle-like teeth.

Another three creatures swooped from above, their jaws stretching across the entire surface of their skin and billowing wings flaring out to arrest their dives as they smashed into Uriel. The creature Uriel had knocked aside leapt into the air with a discordant howl as he struggled with the beasts that enfolded him, their teeth gnashing against his armour.

Pasanius shot the airborn delirium spectre, but his bolt passed clean through its flesh before detonating and it altered its course to swoop further up the slope to attack him with a deafening screech.

Uriel gripped the greasy flesh of the monsters attacking him and wrenched it from his armour, seeing anguished faces bulge from the surface of the skin and reach out to him. He punched through a thrashing jaw, his fist ripping through the taut skin as a flare of heat washed over him from above and he heard Pasanius shout, 'Get back!'

The beast thrashed in his grip as the others snapped and bit at him. He forced his other hand through the wound he had punched, rolling down the slope and dislodging the others. He gripped the flapping skin to either side and tore it from the iron frame, feeling the souls trapped within scream of their release.

Flickering lights and joyous cries erupted from the dying beast, and as the last soul departed, Uriel was left with an inanimate pile of torn flesh and metal in his hands. He hurled its remains aside as yet more of the creatures circled lower. Uriel drew his sword, slashing the energised blade through the flesh of the nearest delirium spectre, drawing a hysterical shriek of freedom from its jaws before it collapsed.

The last beast leapt towards him and he dived forwards, rolling and slashing high with his blade and hacking it into two halves as it passed overhead.

He heard another cry of release and saw a lifeless pile of iron struts and burning skin lying further upslope. Pasanius had his flamer out, spraying burning gouts of promethium into the air to discourage the other creatures from approaching too closely.

'Come on!' shouted Pasanius. 'I don't know how much longer this will hold them!'

Uriel sheathed his sword and stopped to grab two shorn lengths of iron from the corpse of the nearest monster before heading once more for the treacherous slope.

Driving the lengths of iron bar deep into the powdery shale like crude pitons, Uriel was able to climb the slope without too much difficulty while Pasanius kept the delirium spectres at bay with his flamer.

At last he reached the ledge and rolled onto his back as the delirium spectres closed in again. He drew his sword once more and slashed the first apart, feeling a grim satisfaction as it screamed in gratitude before its dissolution. Others burned in the fire, child-like laughter rippling from their blazing flesh as they died.

The two Space Marines edged backwards to the sanctuary of the defile, killing the shrieking, swooping beasts every time they came near. Though they killed dozens of them, Uriel could see hundreds more gathering around the mountaintops and knew that unless they found cover soon, they were as good as dead. They could not hope to hold off that many forever.

The defile was behind them and Uriel glanced along its length as it wound further and deeper into the mountain. Flocks of the delirium spectres circled lower and Uriel prayed they would not be able to follow them.

'I can't tell where it leads!' he said.

'It doesn't matter, does it?' replied Pasanius, bleeding from a patchwork of shallow cuts across the side of his head. 'We don't have much choice.'

'Give them one more blast, then follow me in!'

Pasanius nodded and shouted, 'Go!' and sent another stream of blazing liquid towards the shrieking monsters. Uriel darted into the defile, the narrow basalt walls glassy, black and reflective. It scraped against his shoulder guards, cutting grooves through the paint, and Uriel offered a whispered prayer of forgiveness to the armour's battle-spirit at such careless treatment.

Pasanius backed into the narrow defile, having to force his way sidelong through its narrow length and Uriel had a sickening vision of the pair of them trapped here and waiting to be picked off by these vile creatures.

'Damn, but it's tight,' grunted Pasanius stoically.

Frustrated screeches rang from above and Uriel saw scores of the monstrous beasts flashing overhead across the narrow strip of sky at the top of the defile. He pushed further along its twisting length, the ground sloping upwards and the distance between them and the open sky diminishing with every step.

'We're running out of room!' he called back, as a desperate scrabbling of claws and clanging of metal on stone sounded from above. Hissing beasts, fleshy wings thrashing, forced themselves down into the defile, their screeches echoing deafeningly in the enclosed space. Wails of frantic hunger and longing spat from their bodies and Uriel stabbed upwards, skewering the first of the delirium spectres on his blade.

More forced themselves into the defile, clanging and beating against one another as they struggled to reach their prey.

Unable to fire his flamer in such a confined space, Pasanius ripped them apart with his bare hands, tearing the skin from the desecrated frames with angry bellows. Uriel stabbed and cut blindly, dead flesh enfolding him and sharp teeth snapping at his face. The sound of tearing skin mingled with their grunts of pain and the incongruous noise of joyful souls escaping their hideous torment as each beast died.

'Keep going!' shouted Pasanius in a lull between the ferocious attacks.

'I don't know what's ahead,' answered Uriel.

'It can't be any worse than this!'

Uriel couldn't disagree and forged onwards, wiping clotted blood from his forehead and desperately seeking somewhere that would offer better shelter. The delirium spectres resumed their circling above the defile, patiently waiting for another chance to attack.

The defile twisted and turned, each step winding further into the mountain until at last it turned downwards and led out onto a narrow path that ran along the side of a sheer cliff.

The rockface fell away for hundreds of metres on one side of the path and at its end Uriel could see a narrow cave, its entrance surrounded with a forest of long iron spikes hammered into the rock.

'There's a cave ahead,' said Uriel. 'Looks like someone has used it to hide from these things already.'

'How can you tell?'

'There are spikes around the cave mouth. I doubt these beasts could get near the entrance without fouling their wings.'

'That just begs the question–'

'Who put them there?' finished Uriel.

Pasanius looked towards the sky, hearing the delirium spectres clanging from the rock and their shrill cries drawing closer as they circled down to attack once again.

'We will have to make a break for it,' said Uriel.

'We'll never make it,' pointed out Pasanius. 'They'd be on us before we got halfway.'

'You think I don't know that?' snapped Uriel. 'But we have to try.'

Uriel bit his lip as he wondered how far they could get before the creatures caught them. They might be able to fight some of them off, but not all of them, and even if the monsters didn't kill them, it would be only too easy for them to hurl them from the path.

And to fall such a distance would be fatal, even to one as mighty as a Space Marine.

One of the monsters flew overhead, its blind hunger loathsome and utterly alien.

'Wait...' said Uriel as a memory struggled to the surface of his mind.

'What?'

'When the Omphalos Daemonium spoke of these creatures it said something about how they hunted, something about our hearts and how we wouldn't go unnoticed for long.'

'And?'

'And that's how they are hunting us, they can hear our heartbeats,' said Uriel.

Pasanius was silent for a moment before saying, 'Then we take away what they need to hunt us.'

'You still remember the mantras that trigger the sus-an membrane?'

'Aye, though it's been decades since I've needed to recite them.'

'I know, but we damn well better get them right,' said Uriel. 'I don't want to fall into a coma halfway along that path.'

Pasanius nodded in understanding as Uriel slowly crept to the edge of the defile. The delirium spectres were high above them, but still too close for them to have any hope of reaching the cave entrance unmolested.

Uriel turned to Pasanius and said, 'Go when I go. Slowly, but not too slowly, I don't want you dying on the way.'

'I'll try not to,' replied Pasanius dryly.

Uriel closed his eyes and recited the verses taught to him by Apothecary Selenus that began the hormonal activation of the sus-an membrane, an organ implanted within his brain tissue during his transformation into a Space Marine. He took deep breaths, regulating his breathing and forcing his heart rate to slow. What he was doing was extremely dangerous, normally requiring many hours of meditation and the correct prayers, but Uriel knew they didn't have time for such preparations.

Uriel could feel his hearts pounding in his chest, their rhythmic beats slowing.

Forty beats a minute, thirty, twenty, ten...

He could hear Pasanius repeating the same mantras, knowing that they had to move and reach the cave before the organ activated fully and plunged them into a state of complete suspended animation and their hearts stopped beating completely.

Three beats a minute... two...

Uriel stood, his vision greying at the edges and his limbs feeling leaden.

He nodded to Pasanius and walked from the transient cover of the defile, moving as quickly as he dared along the path towards the cave mouth. Pasanius followed, the piercing shrieks of the daemonic furies above him almost breaking his concentration and icy sweat streaking his pale face. Both Space Marines hugged the cliff face as they inched their way along the path.

The winged beasts swooped towards them, their shrieks ringing from the cliff-face as they circled and climbed in confusion, unable to pinpoint them.

They were almost at the cave as the flocks above wheeled aimlessly in the air.

Two of the delirium spectres flapped noisily past Uriel, their wings flaring as they landed with a scrape of claws on the path before him. Their cries were low and hideous as they turned slowly, their rippling, fleshy skins trying to discern their quarry.

Uriel slowed as he inched his way past the monsters, fighting to hold his body in the limbo between life and a self-induced coma.

He stumbled, his boot scraping against the nearest beast's claws...

He froze.

But whatever other senses it may have possessed, the creature did not register the touch and ignored him.

Uriel edged past the oblivious monster.

The second beast took to the air as he drew near the end of the path and–

One beat...

The delirium spectre twisted in midair, giving voice to an ear-splitting shriek as it heard the thudding beat of his heart. The flocks above ceased their confused wheeling and turned as one towards them, screeching in triumph.

'Move!' shouted Uriel, abandoning all subterfuge and running for the cave mouth, ducking below the first spike and threading his way between the others to reach the entrance. He staggered inside, gasping a great lungful of air. His chest was a raging inferno as his hearts suddenly leapt from a virtual standstill to their normal rhythm in a matter of moments.

He pushed into the stygian darkness of the cave, dropping to his knees as he fought to stabilise his internal organs and willed himself not to slip into a sleep he knew he would not wake from.

Pasanius backed into the cave, his flamer billowing out a cone of blazing fuel.

The delirium spectres flapped noisily around the entrance to the cave, screaming in anger at being denied their prey. Several darted in to attack, but only succeeded in skewering themselves on the sharp spikes protecting the entrance. Their thrashing bodies ripped apart, their torn skins and iron frames tumbling down the cliff as they died.

Uriel let out a juddering breath, knowing how close they had come to death.

'Pasanius, are you all right?' he gasped.

'Barely,' wheezed Pasanius. 'By the Throne, I never want to have to do that again. It felt like I was dying.'

Uriel nodded, pulling himself upright using the walls of the cave. His returning vision easily penetrated the gloom of the cave and he saw that they were in a long, arched tunnel carved into the rockface, but by who or what he could not tell.

'Well, at least we are safe for the moment,' said Uriel.

'Don't be too sure about that,' replied Pasanius, kicking over a cracked human skull that lay on the floor.

THE TWO SPACE Marines made their way carefully along the tunnel, the screeching wails of the delirium spectres fading the further they penetrated into the mountain. Their enhanced eyesight magnified the glow from the hissing nozzle of Pasanius's flamer such that they walked through the utter darkness as though their steps were illuminated by glow-globes.

'Who do you think made these tunnels?' asked Pasanius, staring at the marks of picks and drills cut into the rock.

'I have no idea,' said Uriel. 'Perhaps slaves or the populace of this world before it was taken by Chaos?'

'I still can't believe we have travelled so far,' said Pasanius. 'Do you really think this is Medrengard? Can we really be in the Eye of Terror?'

'You saw the dark city beyond the mountains. Can you doubt that one of the fallen primarchs dwells there?'

Pasanius made the sign of the aquila over his chest to ward off the evil that went with even thinking about such things. 'I suppose not. I felt the evil as a poison in my bones, but to come so far... it is impossible, surely.'

'If this is truly the Eye, then nothing is impossible,' said Uriel.

'I had always believed that the stories of worlds taken by daemons and the Ruinous Powers were nothing more than dark legends, exaggerated tales to scare the unwary into obedience.'

'Would that they were,' replied Uriel. 'But as well as destroying these daemonculaba that Librarian Tigurius saw in his vision, I believe that we have been brought to this place to test the strength of our faith as well.'

'And have we failed already?' muttered Pasanius. 'To truck with a daemon...'

'I know, I have put our very souls at risk, my friend,' said Uriel. 'And for that I am sorry. But I could see no choice other than to make the Omphalos Daemonium believe we would do as it wished.'

'Then you don't plan on getting it this Heart of Blood, whatever that is?'

'Of course not,' said Uriel, appalled. 'Once we find it, I intend to smash the vile thing into a million pieces!'

'Thank the Emperor!' breathed Pasanius.

Uriel stopped suddenly. 'You thought I would acquiesce to the desires of a daemon?'

'No, but given how we ended up here and what it threatened...'

'Breaking faith with the *Codex Astartes* is one thing, but trafficking with daemons is quite another,' snapped Uriel.

'But we have been cast out by the Chapter, banished from the Emperor's sight and are probably trapped forever in the Eye of Terror,' said Pasanius. 'I can see why you might have thought it could have been an option.'

'Really?' demanded Uriel angrily. 'Then pray explain it to me.'

Pasanius did not meet Uriel's gaze as he said, 'Well, it seems likely that the Heart of Blood is some daemonic artefact meant to bring ruin upon an enemy of the Omphalos Daemonium here in the Eye, so might not we be doing the Emperor's work by stealing it from its current master?'

Uriel shook his head. 'No. That way lies madness and the first step on the road to betraying everything we stand for as Space Marines. By such steps are men damned, Pasanius, each tiny heresy excused by some reasonable explanation until their souls are irrevocably blackened and shrivelled. With no Chapter to call our own, some might say that our only loyalty now is to ourselves, but you and I both know that is not true. No matter what becomes of us, we will always be warriors of the Emperor in our hearts. I have told you this before, my friend. Do you still doubt your courage and honour?'

'No, it is not that…' began Pasanius.

'Then what?'

'Nothing,' said Pasanius eventually. 'You are right and I am sorry for even thinking such things.'

Uriel locked his gaze with that of his friend. 'Do you remember the story of the ancient philosopher of Calth who spoke of a stalactite falling in a cave and asked if it would make a sound if no one was there to hear?'

'Aye,' nodded Pasanius. 'It never made sense to me.'

'Nor I, at least until now,' said Uriel. 'Though we have been exiled, we retain our honour and though it is likely that the Chapter will never hear of our deeds, we will continue to fight the enemies of the Emperor until our dying day. Yes?'

'Yes,' agreed Pasanius, slapping his hand on Uriel's shoulder guard. 'And that's why you were captain and I was just a sergeant. You know all the right things to say.'

Uriel chuckled. 'I don't know about that, I mean, look at us, tens of thousands of light years from Macragge and stuck in a cave in the Eye of Terror…'

'…filled with corpses,' finished Pasanius.

Uriel turned and saw that Pasanius was right. The tunnel had widened into a domed cave with rough walls and a number of shadowy passageways leading away. The remains of a long dead fire filled a deep firepit at the centre of the cave, a thin shaft of weak light spearing down from a smoke vent in the roof. Skeletal bodies littered the floor of the cave, splayed and broken, scattered throughout the cave, the bones dusty and cracked.

'Throne! What happened here?' whispered Uriel, circling the firepit and kneeling beside a rag-draped skeleton.

'Looks like they were attacked while they cooked a meal,' said Pasanius, poking around in the remains of the fire with his silver arm. 'There are pots still in the firepit.'

Uriel nodded, examining the bones before him, wondering who they had belonged to and what malicious twist of fate had seen him condemned to such a death.

'Whoever did this was incredibly strong,' said Uriel. 'The bones are snapped cleanly.'

'Aye, and this one has had its skull ripped from its shoulders.'

'Iron Warriors?' asked Uriel.

'No, I don't think so,' said Pasanius. 'There was a madness to this attack. Look at the stains on the walls. It's blood, arterial spray. Whoever killed these people did it in a frenzy, ripping out throats and tearing their victims apart in seconds. They didn't even have time to arm themselves.'

Uriel crossed the chamber to join Pasanius, stepping over the bones of the dead as he noticed something metallic lying partially buried in the dust. He bent down to retrieve it, his fingers closing on a crude, thick-handled knife, the blade long and flexible. He turned to look at the splayed bodies and a sickening realisation came to him.

'They were skinned,' he said.

'What?'

'The bodies,' said Uriel, holding up the knife. 'They were skinned. They were killed and then their killers flayed them.'

Pasanius cursed. 'Is there no end to this world's evil?'

Uriel snapped the blade of the skinning knife and hurled it away from him, the broken pieces clattering from the rocky walls of the cave. What manner of beast would track its prey deep into the mountains to attack with such speed and frenzy before taking the time to remove its victims' hides? He hoped they would not find out, but a sinking feeling in his gut told him that there was a good chance they had already stumbled into its territory.

'There's nothing we can do for them, now, whoever they were,' he said.

'No,' agreed Pasanius. 'So which way onwards?'

Uriel crossed the cave, stopping to examine each passageway and hoping to discern some clue as to which direction offered the most hope of a way out.

'There are tracks leading away at this one,' he said, kneeling and examining the ground at the middle passage. 'A lot of them.'

Pasanius joined him, tracing the outline of a huge footprint in the dust. There was no telling how old it was, but, despite its size, there was no doubt that it was human.

'Are you thinking these might lead to the monsters' lair and that we should avoid it?'

'No, I think that they might lead to a way out of these tunnels,' said Uriel.

'I *knew* you were going to say that,' sighed Pasanius.

URIEL AND PASANIUS set off down the tunnel, its course meandering through the mountains for what felt like many kilometres, until they completely lost track of which way they were headed. As the ground underfoot became rockier, the tracks vanished and Uriel knew they were hopelessly lost.

But just as he began to think that they might never again see the surface – not an unappealing prospect in itself – he caught a hint of something on the air. A breath of motion, the faintest gust of a breeze on his skin.

He held up his hand and quieted Pasanius as he opened his mouth to speak.

Just on the threshold of audibility he could hear a soft rumble, like a distant crackle of white noise. Though it took all his concentration, he followed a twisting path through the tunnels, doubling back, stopping and retracing his steps every now and then as he followed the noise.

As it grew louder, his path became surer and within an hour of first hearing the noise, he saw a bright sliver of white sky ahead.

'I never thought I would be grateful to see that sky again,' said Uriel.

'Nor I, but it is better than that accursed darkness.'

Uriel nodded and the two Space Marines emerged from the tunnel, blinking in the perpetual daylight of Medrengard. As they stepped out onto the mountainside, Uriel saw the source of the noise he had been following.

'Guilliman's oath!' swore Pasanius.

Many kilometres ahead over the mountain was a fortification built from dark madness and standing in defiance of all reason. Its steepled towers and mighty bastions wounded the sky, its massive gateway a snarling void. Its walls were darkened, bloodstained stone, veined with unnatural colours that should not exist and which burned themselves upon the retina.

Lightning leapt between its towers and the clanking of great engines and machines echoed like thunder from beyond its walls.

Pillars of smoke and fire leapt from the walls where explosions blossomed against them, hurling great chunks of black stone from the colossal fortress. The distant rumble of artillery crashed and boomed, bright muzzle flares of innumerable great howitzers and siege guns firing upon the fastness from the jagged rocks below.

The primal battle cries of thousands, tens of thousands of warriors – perhaps even more – were carried on the wind from the distant battle, together with the smell of burnt iron and war.

Clouds of ash and smoke from the blazing pyres surrounding the fortress flickered and twitched with the fury of the siege below, and Uriel felt his soul blacken in the face of such savagery.

Nothing could reach that fortress and live.

But that was exactly what they had to do.

PART II – BENEATH A BLACK SUN

FIVE

A BLAST OF superheated air whooshed between the stumps of the merlons, hurling Honsou from his feet and vaporising the top half of one of his Iron Warriors. He rolled to one side as the smoking legs collapsed beside him and leapt to his feet, leaning over the ragged remains of the fortress wall and waving his mighty toothed axe.

'Come on, Berossus, you will need to do better than that!' he shouted.

Far below, the metallic coughs of massed artillery fire echoed from the dark mountains, shelling the lower bastions of Khalan-Ghol to oblivion. The screams of dying men drifted up towards him, but Honsou paid them no mind. They were but slaves and those too badly injured for skinning in the flesh camps, and there were plenty more of them to expend.

He wiped dust from his armour as more Iron Warriors marched forward to plug the gap the stray shot had blasted in the upper levels of his fortress. It had been a lucky impact and Honsou felt a thrill of adrenaline course through his body at the near miss. Ever since the siege on Hydra Cordatus, he had craved the fire and thunder of battle once more. The fighting on Perdictor II upon his return to the Eye of Terror had been desultory and unsatisfying, the warriors of the Despoiler proving no match for his advance forces.

But now his 'fellow' warsmiths were attacking him, and this was sure to be a battle worthy of the name. Once again he was forced to prove his mettle to those who thought him no better than the Imperial dogs they fought the Long War against. The bile rose in his throat at the thought that even though his predecessor had named him warsmith, he was still not considered their equal.

573

'Lord Berossus is thorough in his attentions,' said Obax Zakayo, his grating, static-laced voice snapping Honsou from his bitter reverie. 'The lower bastions will be nothing but dust and bones soon.'

Honsou turned to face his lieutenant, a huge, wide-shouldered Iron Warrior with yellow and black chevrons edging the plates of his dented power armour. Hissing pipes wheezed from every joint, leaking stinking black fluids and venting puffs of steam with his every step. Like Honsou, he carried a fearsome war-axe, but he also wielded a crackling energy whip, writhing on the end of a mechanised claw attached to his back.

'If Berossus thinks he is achieving anything by killing such chaff, then he is even stupider than I believed,' sneered Honsou, wiping grey dust from his visor with his glossy black augmetic arm. His former master had gifted the mechanical arm to him after his own had been hewn from his body by the late castellan of Hydra Cordatus. It had once belonged to Kortrish, a mighty champion of ancient days and had been a physical indication of his master's favour.

'What he lacks in imagination, he makes up for with determination,' said Honsou's personal champion, a tall, slender warrior in power armour so dark and non-reflective that he moved like a liquid shadow. His voice was a ghostly monotone, his face a crawling mass of bio-organic circuitry that ran like mercurial fire beneath his dead skin and made his eyes shine with a lifeless, silver sheen.

'Berossus is irrelevant, Onyx. He'll shell the lower bastions to rubble and not be able to move his artillery up. No, it is Toramino that we must keep a careful watch on,' replied Honsou, turning from the battlements as fresh explosions and the roars of charging warriors rippled up from below.

'Agreed,' said Onyx, long bronze talons unsheathing from the grey flesh of his hands. 'Do you wish me to destroy him?'

Honsou had seen some of the most hideous things in this galaxy – having perpetrated a great many of them himself – but even he was unsettled by the malefic presence of Onyx. The Iron Warrior, if he could even still be called such, was a shunned figure, the daemonic presence within him making him outcast even amongst his own warriors. Though his human side still held sway in the symbiotic relationship with the daemon bound to his flesh, its diabolical presence was unmistakable.

'No,' said Honsou. 'Not yet, anyway. I'm going to break these vermin against my walls first. I can defeat Berossus easily enough, but I want Toramino to see this half-breed beat him, to know that the warsmith was right to name me his successor. Then you can kill him.'

'As you wish,' said Onyx, a barely-perceptible haze of power surrounding him.

When the creature had bound itself to Honsou's service, as master of Khalan-Ghol, it had spoken its true name as a sign of its fealty, but its pronunciation had been beyond Honsou, so he had settled for the closest approximation of the part he had been able to understand: Onyx. Honsou had seen, first hand, just how lethal Onyx could be when the warp-spawned part of him rose to the surface and he unleashed the full terror of his inner daemon.

Onyx was his dark shadow, his protector, and he could think of no better a creature to be his champion and bodyguard.

'Berossus is proud though,' said Obax Zakayo, 'and not to be underestimated. He has great strength and many warriors in his grand company.'

'Let them come,' said Honsou.

'They already do,' pointed out Obax Zakayo, gesturing over the edge of the wall.

Honsou followed Obax Zakayo's pointing gauntlet and grinned with feral anticipation.

Tens of thousands of soldiers swarmed across the smoking, cratered hell of the lower bastions, screaming like beasts as they slaughtered the few, mangled survivors of the shelling. Their victims begged for mercy, but their attackers had none to give and the carnage was on a truly grand scale.

Banners with the devotional heraldry of Berossus were raised high and sacred standards that proclaimed the glory of Chaos in its most raw, visceral aspect were planted in the bloody soil. Within minutes, disembowelling racks were set up and the soldiers who were still alive were ritually butchered before the walls to taunt those who watched from above.

'So like Berossus,' scoffed Honsou, shaking his head and watching as another hundred screaming soldiers had their entrails dragged from their bellies and looped around rotating drum mechanisms.

'What?' asked Obax Zakayo.

'He doesn't even have the wit to allow some of his prisoners to live to show his honourable mercy.'

'I fought with Lord Forrix at the side of Lord Berossus before,' said Obax Zakayo wistfully, 'and I know there is no such quality left within him.'

'You know that and I know that, Zakayo, but if Berossus had any sense, he'd try and convince the soldiers of Khalan-Ghol that he does.'

'Why?'

'Because if our soldiers could be made to believe that Berossus would be merciful, the thought of surrender might enter their heads,' answered Onyx. 'But since they now know that only hideous death awaits them should they be taken alive, they will fight all the harder.'

'To breach a fortress you need to break the men inside, not the walls. And to break a besieging army you must wear its warriors down to the point where they would rather turn their guns upon themselves than take another step forward,' said Honsou. 'We must make every one of Berossus's soldiers feel he is living beneath the muzzle of one of our cannons; that he is nothing more than meat for the guns.'

Obax Zakayo nodded in understanding and said, 'We can do that. My guns will sow the ground before the walls with their shredded flesh and the rocks will flow with waterfalls of their blood.'

'To the warp with that, Zakayo, so long as they die!' snarled Honsou, pleased to see the ember of fear smouldering within Obax Zakayo flare to life once more. 'Or else you will be down there with the scum next time. Ever since you lost those slaves bound for my forges to the damned renegades, your promises have been as worthless as the filth I scrape from my boot.'

'I will not fail you again, my lord,' promised Obax Zakayo.

'No, you won't,' said Honsou. 'Just remember that Forrix is no longer your master, I am, and I know that you are a true protégé of his. He may have become so jaded that he tolerated your lack of vision, but do not think for one second that I will.'

Suitably chastened, Obax Zakayo returned his gaze to the slaughter below. 'What will Berossus do now that he has the lower bastions?' he asked.

'He will send the daemon engines,' said Honsou.

As though on cue, the monstrous silhouettes of scores of hulking, spider-legged war engines and clanking dreadnoughts could be seen advancing through the pillars of smoke and blazing wreckage. Berossus's daemonic war engines stalked through the ruined bastions, forcing their way through the fields of corpses, and began clambering across the rocks towards the battered slope of the next level of redoubts.

'Just as you predicted he would,' said Onyx, watching the approach of the daemonic machines.

Honsou nodded, listening as the ululating shrieks of the terrifying war engines echoed towards the next level of defences, hundreds of the clawed and snapping monsters hauling their spiked bulk towards the defenders above them. The next rampart was some five hundred metres above the lower bastions, many levels below where Honsou and his lieutenants watched, but the daemon engines would not take long to reach the defenders. They poured their fire into the climbing machines, but nothing could stop them.

The artillery fire from below resumed with a thunderous crescendo, the first volley exploding against the rock between the defenders and the climbing daemon engines. Boulders the size of tanks tumbled down the sloping rockface, smashing a number of dreadnoughts to flattened hunks of metal as the bombardment continued, the gunners shifting their aim as they found their range.

'Now?' asked Obax Zakayo.

Honsou shook his head. 'No, let the dreadnoughts get closer first.'

Obax Zakayo nodded, watching as the first of the spider-like daemon engines reached the next level, their massive, clawed pincers snatching up soldiers and ripping them apart. They howled as they killed, revelling in the slaughter and hurling the corpses from the battlements.

'Now,' said Honsou.

Obax Zakayo nodded and spoke a single word into his power armour's vox unit.

Honsou watched with relish as the ground of the bastions below shook and trembled as though an earth tremor had struck. Huge, gaping cracks ripped across the bastions, splitting the rock with a hollow boom that rivalled the thunder of the guns. Smoke and flames blasted from the cracks as the ground beneath the entire front half of the bastions sagged and splintered. With a groaning creak, millions of tonnes of rock exploded and detached from the side of Khalan-Gol, sliding ponderously down the face of the mountain.

Thousands of Khalan-Gol's soldiers were carried screaming to their deaths, the avalanche of rubble and debris smashing every one of the daemon engines from the mountainside, crushing them beneath the unstoppable tide of rock. Hundreds were buried beneath the mountain; their shrieking roars billowing from the rubble as their mystical bindings were smashed asunder and the daemons within them were shorn from their iron vessels.

Honsou laughed as he watched the dreadnoughts and the thousands of enemy soldiers below turn to flee the avalanche, knowing that they were already doomed. The tide of rock swept over them all, pouring down the slopes they had fought and bled to capture.

The rumble of grinding rock slowly faded, as did the bellowing roar of the guns, Berossus realising that their fire would be wasted without an escalade.

Honsou turned from the mass destruction he had unleashed.

Now Berossus would know he had a fight on his hands.

THE UNCHANGING SKY and static sun made it impossible to discern the passage of time through their surroundings, and the internal chronometer on Uriel's visor had only displayed a constantly fluctuating readout that he eventually disabled. Days must surely have passed, but how many was a mystery. He had heard that time flowed differently in the Eye of Terror, and supposed he should not have been surprised at such affronts to the laws of nature.

'Emperor, I hate this place,' said Pasanius, picking his way over a pile of twisted iron jutting from the rock of the mountain. 'There is not one natural thing here.'

'No,' agreed Uriel, tired and hungry despite his armour's best efforts at filtering and recycling his bodily excretions into drinkable water and nutrient pastes. 'It is a wasteland of death. Nothing could live here.'

'I think something lives out here,' said Pasanius, glancing at the darkened peaks all about them. 'I'm just not sure what or that I even want to find out.'

'What are you talking about?'

'Haven't you felt it? That we're being watched? Followed.'

'No,' said Uriel, ashamed that his instinct for danger appeared to have deserted him. 'Have you seen anything?'

Pasanius shook his head. 'Nothing for sure, no, but I keep thinking I can see, I don't know, something.'

'Something? What kind of something?'

'I'm not sure, it's like a whisper in the corner of my mind's eye, something that vanishes as soon as I try to look at it,' said Pasanius, darkly. 'Something red...'

'It is this place,' said Uriel. 'The lair of the Enemy will attempt to mislead and betray your senses. We must be strong in our faith and resist its evil magicks.'

Pasanius shook his head. 'No, it is something not of the Enemy, but something that lives here. I think it's what killed those people in the cave.'

'Whatever killed and skinned those people was evil and an enemy of all living things. Let them come, whatever they are, they will find only death.'

'Aye,' agreed Pasanius as they climbed onwards. 'Death.'

The besieged fortress was lost to sight for now, the path from the tunnels leading them down into the rocky gullies and crevasses of the mountains. The white sky beat down upon them, harsher than the fiercest sun, and Uriel deliberately kept his eyes averted from its flat emptiness. Once, he thought he caught a glimpse of the red things Pasanius claimed were following them, but they defied his every attempt to see them properly. Eventually he gave up, unable to catch sight of them, and concentrated on simply putting one foot in front of the other.

The harsh, metallic shale of the mountainside grated beneath his boots and every now and then they saw grilled vents piercing the rock that disgorged a hot steam that tasted of beaten metal. The vents plunged down into the mountain, the darkness impenetrable, even to a Space Marine's enhanced eyesight.

Uriel saw billowing smoke stacks hundreds of metres above them, thousands of blocky chimneys lining the ridge like great pylons that spewed corrosive fumes into the atmosphere. Yet no matter how much black waste was released into the air, the dead sky was always above them, blank and oppressive.

Over the tops of the mountains before them, Uriel could see what looked like bloated dirigibles, drifting above somewhere ahead in the mountains. Long cables drooped from their bellies, but whether these were simply anchoring them to the ground or acting as some form of barrage balloon, Uriel could not tell. Perhaps they were designed to keep the delirium spectres at bay from some facility as yet unseen?

As their weary trudge through the reeking air of the mountains continued, the two Space Marines passed a shorn quarry of shattered stone, where the side of one of these cyclopean smoke stacks was exposed. Reddish-brown stains spilled from the joints between the massive, curved blocks making up the stack and a monstrous heat radiated from the stonework in pulsing waves.

'Where do you think it goes?' said Uriel.

'I don't know. Perhaps there is some manufactory below the mountains.'

Uriel nodded, wondering what diabolical production line was at work beneath their very feet. Were men and women dying even now to forge weapons, armour and materiel for the dread legions of Chaos? It galled him that he could do nothing to prevent such abomination, but what choice did they have? The sacred task of the death oath placed upon them by Marneus Calgar took precedence over all other concerns. The daemonic womb creatures... these daemonculaba were in the besieged fortress they had seen as they climbed from the darkness of the tunnels beneath the mountains and nothing would stand in Uriel's way of reaching that damned place.

Pressing on, Uriel and Pasanius climbed a jagged, saw-toothed ridge, its sides sheer and corrugated, as though gouged by some gargantuan bulldozer blade. A blackened depression of splintered stone and iron, thousands of metres in diameter, fell away from them on the other side, crags of iron columns and twisted girders protruding from the mountain like clawed fingers. The depression appeared to be perfectly circular, though it was difficult to tell, whipping particles of sand and iron filings filling the air and lashing round the circular valley in spiteful, howling vortices. A narrow sliver of white sky was just visible on the far side of the depression, but all Uriel's attention was fixed on the sight that filled the centre of the depression.

'In the name of the Emperor...' breathed Uriel in disgust.

A huge grilled platform filled the centre of the depression. Agglomerated layers of dust coated its every surface and its perforated floor dripped and clogged with jelly-like runnels of fat and viscera. Tall poles jutted from the platform, held in place by quivering steel guys that sang as the unnatural wind whistled through them. Hooked between the poles were billowing sails of flesh, stretched across timber frames that the scouring, wind-borne particles might strip them of the leavings of their former owners.

Monstrous, debased creatures in vulcanised rubber masks with rounded glass eye sockets and ribbed piping running into tanks carried on their backs scraped at the stretched skins with long, bladed polearms. They lurched across the platform with a twisted, mutated gait and gurgled monotone commands to one another.

'What are they doing?' said Pasanius, horrified at the sight before him.

'It looks like they're curing the hides, scraping them clean,' said Uriel.

'But the hides of what?' said Pasanius. 'They can't be human, they're too large.'

'I don't care what they are,' snarled Uriel, setting off down the treacherous slope towards the platform and drawing his golden-hilted sword. 'This ends now.'

Pasanius set off after Uriel, unlimbering his flamer and checking its fuel load.

If the mutant creatures were aware of them they gave no sign, the howling wind and rumble of distant artillery masking the sounds of their approach. But whatever they lacked for in awareness, they made up for in thorough diligence, dragging their bladed polearms up and down the length of the billowing skins to clear them of whatever the lashing winds left behind. Uriel saw a carven set of stone stairs leading to the platform and took them two at a time as his anger continued to build.

The first of the mutants died with a strangled screech on the point of Uriel's sword, the second fell without a sound as Uriel hacked its head from its body with one blow. Now aware of the killers in their midst, the remainder scattered in terror. A sheet of flame incinerated more of the mutants, their screams ululating as their rubber bodysuits melted on their corrupted flesh.

The slaughter was over in a matter of moments, the twisted mutants no match for the power and fury of the Adeptus Astartes. Most turned to flee, but there was nowhere to hide from Uriel's wrath. As the last mutated creature fell beneath his blade, Uriel took a deep breath, taking profound pleasure in the butchery of such worthless wretches. Whatever deviant beasts they had been in life, they were only so much dead flesh now.

He turned as Pasanius said, 'Uriel, look…' and pointed at the nearest of the skins.

Uriel felt his heart tighten in his chest as he saw the dead features of a man atop the huge expanse of skin. Stretched almost beyond recognition, but a man's nonetheless.

'Holy blood. But how could a man become so vast?' said Pasanius.

Uriel shook his head. 'Not by any natural means.'

'But why?'

'The ways of the Enemy are unknown,' said Uriel. 'Better that some remain so.'

'What shall we do?'

Uriel turned in a circle, seeing row upon row of faces in the skins circling the platform – dead, slack features of men and women staring down at him as though he were the subject in an anatomist's theatre.

'Burn it,' he said. 'Burn it all.'

Ʊ
SIX

WITH THE SCORCHED reek of burning flesh still in their nostrils, Uriel and Pasanius left the depression in the rock, leaving the smouldering remains to the scouring wind and whatever passed for carrion on Medrengard. Invigorated and filled with purpose from the slaying of the mutant things, their step was quick and energised, but by the time they passed through the narrow slice in the rock face and began climbing worn steps carved into the rock, the leaden weight of the daemon world had settled upon them once more.

Uriel glanced back down at the blazing sheets of skin, feeling his hate at what had been done to these people burn as brightly. He knew that the image of the skinned man's features would haunt him forever, and was reminded of the horror of the disassembled flesh sculpture created by the loathsome xeno surgeon beneath the estate of Kasimir de Valtos on Pavonis.

Just by being here he felt polluted, as though his very soul was becoming hardened or being drained from his body to nourish the dead rock underfoot, and he was becoming less himself. The emptiness of Medrengard was leaving him hollowed out, a shell of his former self.

'What will be left,' he whispered, 'when this world takes the last of me?'

He could tell Pasanius was feeling the same way, his cheeks hollow and his eyes glazed as he trudged up the winding stairs. Even as he watched, Pasanius stumbled, his silver arm reaching out to arrest his fall, but at the last minute his friend snatched his arm back and he fell to his knees instead.

'Are you all right?' asked Uriel.

581

'Aye,' nodded Pasanius. 'Just hard to keep focussed without an enemy to fight.'

'Fear not, my friend,' said Uriel. 'Once we reach this fortress, I am sure we will have enemies aplenty. If what the Omphalos Daemonium has told us is true, then we will have a surfeit of them.'

'Do you think a daemon of the Skull Lord is capable of telling the truth?'

'I do not know for sure,' said Uriel honestly, 'but I believe daemons only cloak what they need to in lies, wrapping kernels of truth in shrouds of deceit. Part of what it told us is true, I am sure, but which part... well, who knows?'

'So what do we do?' asked Pasanius, trudging after Uriel.

'Whatever we can, my friend,' said Uriel. 'We will act with courage and honour and hope that that is enough.'

'It will need to be,' said Pasanius. 'It is all we have left.'

THE HIKE THROUGH the mountains seemed never-ending, their path through the blackened, rocky desolation draining their spirits with every step they took. They saw more of the steam-venting grilles and the acidic reek of the great smoke stacks was their constant companion as they neared the summit of yet another toothed crag of rock.

The further they travelled, the more signs of death they saw. Bleached bones lay strewn all about in the rocks, but Uriel could not discern how they had come to be here. Not a scrap of meat remained on the bones, but it was impossible to tell whether they had been picked clean by scavengers or boiled free of flesh. Toxic clouds of smog and ash hugged the ground; noxious and polluted, lurking in cracks in the rock like predators with coiling tendrils of fog questing through the air like undersea fronds.

Uriel briefly removed his helmet to cough up a mouthful of brackish phlegm, its substance black and stringy. His enhanced metabolism enabled him to survive such pollutants in the air, but didn't make them any less unpleasant.

Several times they had been forced to traverse hissing rivers of molten metal as they flowed along great basalt culverts towards the smelteries and forges on the plains below. The heat of the mountains was growing and great geysers of scalding steam and hot ash spewed from vents and cracks in the rock. Were it not for their blessed power armour and bio-engineered physiology, neither Uriel nor Pasanius could possibly have survived the journey.

Again, Uriel thought he caught sight of the reddish things Pasanius believed were following them, but each time they would vanish into the rocks and remain unseen. Flocks of the delirium spectres wheeled far overhead, but Uriel suspected that only the heat of the lava-hot rivers of metal and spouting plumes of boiling water kept them at bay.

As he passed near a zigzagging crack in the ground, a whooshing tower of boiling liquid suddenly erupted from it. Steam billowed around him, blinding him, and he stumbled away as a rain of objects began clattering around him, falling from somewhere above. Coughing and spluttering, feeling the heat scorch his oesophagus, he wiped moisture from his visor and watched a rain of bones fall upon the mountain, ejected from somewhere deep below the earth by the spouting geysers.

'Well, at least we know where the bones are coming from,' said Pasanius.

The strange objects Uriel had seen in the sky before they had discovered the scouring platform came into sight once more as they neared the summit, swollen leathery balloon-like objects with drooping cables that hovered in the sky over something beyond the ridge of black rock. Now that they were nearer, Uriel could see that his initial assumption that these were some form of crude barrage balloon looked to be accurate. Dozens of them floated ahead, their surfaces a patchwork of uneven fabric and, after what they had seen thus far on Medrengard, Uriel did not want to think too hard as to what they had been fashioned from.

The sound of the siege was not so distant now, the rumble of artillery drawing closer with every step they took.

'Whoever is attempting to take that fortress is determined indeed to keep up such a prodigious expenditure of ordnance,' said Uriel as he clambered up another sheer slab of rock. His gauntlets were battered and scarred, the razor-like rocks of Medrengard tearing at them with every handhold.

Pasanius nodded, his breath heaving as he climbed to join Uriel. The massive sergeant removed his helmet and spat the taste of the world from his mouth. 'Yes, I don't think we're the only ones interested in this Heart of Blood.'

'You think that's what the besieger is after?'

'I don't know, but it's certainly one explanation. Like you said, he's determined.'

'The forces of the Dark Powers make war upon one another for their own amusement. It doesn't necessarily mean anything.'

'True, but all I have learned of the Iron Warriors from Librarian Tigurius leads me to believe that they are consumed by bitterness and malice, not given to capricious whims. Whoever is attacking this fortress is doing so for more than their amusement.'

'You could be right,' agreed Uriel. 'Come on, there is only one way to find out. The summit is near.'

Once again they set off, and after what could have been no more than another hour's climb through drifting banks of stinking steam and yet more piles of bones, they crested the summit before them. Uriel had expected the ground to drop away from them, descending to the plains below, but instead the ground flattened into a rubble-strewn plateau of jagged spikes of rock and snaking cracks that drooled a yellowish fog. One of the bloated balloons was almost directly overhead and Uriel now saw that the cables dangling from it were barbed and as thick as a man's thigh, scraping great furrows in the grey powder of the ground as it drifted.

'Listen,' said Uriel, dropping to one knee.

Pasanius was silent, cocking his head and listening for what Uriel had heard.

Amid the bass rumble of artillery fire and the hammering of distant forges, there was a pulsing, mechanical sound, such as might be made by a host of generators. Though it was hard to pick out any one sound from the omnipresent background noise of Medrengard, Uriel was certain it was coming from up ahead and was near.

'What do you think it is?' he asked.

'Engines perhaps?' suggested Pasanius.

'Maybe,' nodded Uriel.

'Maybe something we can steal.'

'My thoughts exactly,' grinned Uriel, pushing himself to his feet and moving cautiously through the rolling banks of stinking fog while hugging the tall pillars of rock. The noises grew louder as they approached, and as the clouds of smog parted, Uriel saw their source.

A sprawling complex of corrugated metal buildings, each the size of a large warehouse, squatted atop the plateau, surrounded by a high fence of razorwire topped with forests of iron spikes. Bodies hung draped from thick lengths of timber along the fence, their flesh desiccated and their limbs twisted at unnatural angles around the spars. Pillars of ashen smoke curled from a building of black brick near the centre of the camp and a low moaning permeated the air. A greasy, fatty residue coated the rocks and Uriel smelled a loathsome stench that reminded him of spoiled meat.

'This place reeks of death,' he whispered.

In the centre of the camp, a tall, armoured tower reared into the sky, thick iron girders and cable stays supporting a monstrous assembly that resembled the head of some gargantuan daemonic creature. Flames spouted from its eyes and nostrils, and its gaping mouth was filled with long gun barrels. Two bunkers guarded the entrance to the camp, their roofs sloped and festooned with spikes. Uriel could see the glint of heavy guns through the firing slits and knew that to approach this death camp, they would need to cross the interlocking fields of fire of both bunkers.

Beyond the razorwire barrier, Uriel could see warriors in iron grey armour patrolling the interior of the camp, and felt his instinctual hatred rise to the surface.

'Iron Warriors!' hissed Pasanius.

'Iron Warriors,' repeated Uriel, gripping the hilt of his sword tightly.

Traitors. Abominations. Chaos Space Marines... was there any other foe so vile?

These warriors sought the ruination of everything Uriel believed in and the destruction of the Emperor's realm. Every aspect of his soul cried out for vengeance.

'What is this place?' asked Pasanius as the shutter doors of one of the warehouse buildings screeched open and a host of the shambling mutant things they had killed earlier emerged. Behind them came a pathetic, shuffling mass of humanity, their heads cast down and their bodies swathed in baggy, flesh-coloured robes.

'Some kind of prison?' ventured Uriel, as the mutants herded the prisoners towards the gates of the camp. Were all these buildings filled with prisoners? The great daemonic head on the tower turned on grinding cogs to face the hundreds-strong column, huge streams of flame belching from its eyes. A booming voice roared from its mouth, speaking a language Uriel did not understand, but which sent aching spasms through his joints and muscles, as though the sound resonated within the darkest recesses of his brain.

The prisoners marched through the camp, the mutants stabbing at them with crackling prods and beating them with iron-tipped cudgels. The Iron Warriors marched ahead of the column, hideously perverted bolters carried across their breastplates. As they approached, the gate squealed open, the corpses hanging from it jittering in a grotesque imitation of life.

'Where are they taking them?' wondered Uriel.

'Oh, Emperor, no,' whispered Pasanius. 'They're taking them–'

'To be skinned alive...' finished Uriel as he saw that the prisoners were not swathed in baggy robes at all, but were all completely naked to the elements. Their flesh hung in huge flaps from their bodies, stretched beyond all normal proportions by some unknown means. Encrusted dewlaps drooped from emaciated arms, chests, legs and buttocks. Men and women clutched fold upon fold of stretched skin to their bodies for fear it would trip them, sagging bellies and drained teats hanging like empty sacks of dried leather from their wasted frames.

'They're taking them to the skinning platform. No, no...' said Uriel. 'But why?'

'Does it matter?' snarled Pasanius, gripping his flamer tightly, his silver finger hovering over the ignition key. 'We can't let this horror go unpunished!'

Uriel nodded, feeling his hatred for the Iron Warriors reach new heights, but he forced himself to try and remain calm. To attack this column was suicide, they were directly in front of the bunkers and the gun tower, not to mention three Iron Warriors.

But to let such an affront against humanity go unmolested? To allow these traitors to butcher these people as though they were no more than animals?

Pasanius was right, such evil would not stand.

He could see righteous anger in Pasanius's eyes, but also something else, something darker. Uriel saw the light of a zealot in his battle-brother's eyes, the light of one who goes to battle with a death wish, where survival is irrelevant.

Was there more to Pasanius's desire to fight than the obvious reasons of humanity?

It seemed to Uriel that there was, but such were questions for when, or if, they lived through the next few minutes.

Uriel drew his sword, his thumb hovering over the activation rune.

He gripped Pasanius's shoulder guard and said, 'If we do not survive, then it has been an honour to call you my friend.'

Pasanius nodded, but did not reply, his gaze never wavering from the approaching column of slaves, mutants and Iron Warriors.

His eyes suddenly narrowed and he nodded at something over Uriel's shoulder. 'What in the name of the Emperor?'

Uriel turned and saw a number of figures moving stealthily through the high crags that surrounded the camp.

'Are these the things that have been tracking us through the mountains?'

'No,' said Pasanius. 'I don't think so. They look like...'

'Space Marines!' breathed Uriel as he saw two figures in green power armour rise from behind a cluster of boulders and aim missile launchers towards the camp. The Iron Warriors below had not noticed the figures moving above them and Uriel realised with wild enthusiasm that this must surely be an ambush!

A pair of missiles shot from the Space Marines' weapons and slashed towards the leftmost bunker, slamming into the rockcrete and obscuring it in a bright explosion of fire and smoke. Another flashing pair of contrails hammered into the opposite bunker from somewhere high above Uriel and Pasanius and the second bunker vanished in a fiery explosion.

Prisoners screamed and Iron Warriors bellowed commands at the mutant herders as more warriors in power armour emerged from hiding now that the trap was sprung. Bolter shells stitched an explosive path through the prisoners, blood and screams filling the air as they died. More missiles shot out and exploded against the bunkers, and Uriel heard the crack of stonework collapsing under the onslaught.

'Let's go!' shouted Uriel, activating his sword and charging from cover towards the panicked column of prisoners. Pasanius was quick to follow him, a blue flame leaping to life on the end of his weapon.

Uriel saw an Iron Warrior clubbing a prisoner with the butt of his gun and aimed his charge towards him. The warrior was a full head and shoulders above Uriel, his armour spiked and daubed with unclean symbols. A pair of curved and looping horns sprouted from his helmet and he carried a brutal sword with screaming, serrated teeth. He spun, hearing Uriel's wild charge and raised his weapon, but it was already too late.

Uriel slashed his sword through the Iron Warrior's breastplate, drawing a spray of black blood and a roar of pain from his foe.

Pasanius sprayed a sheet of flame across a second Iron Warrior, one with mechanised, snapping claws for hands and an explosion ripped through the prisoners as a fuel-filled tank on the Chaos Marine's back detonated.

Uriel heard the roar of bolter fire from above, seeing scores of warriors in different coloured power armour charging from their concealment. He swayed aside as the Iron Warrior swung his sword in a graceless arc meant to behead him and slashed his sword around at his flank, cutting a full handspan into his armour. More missiles speared out from the spires, slamming into the towering daemon head and rocking it back. Thick cable stays snapped and whipped around in slashing arcs as the daemon tower roared.

Heavy calibre shells ripped from its mouth, tearing great gouges in the earth as they sprayed through the camp, striking friend and foe alike. The mutants in rubberised body suits jabbed the prisoners back to the camp, drawing blood and piteous cries from their wretched charges.

The Iron Warrior roared in anger, stepping forward to smash his fist against Uriel's chest. His strength was phenomenal, even for one genetically engineered to be stronger, and Uriel was hurled back, skidding through the ash as his attacker raised his sword two-handed to deliver the deathblow. He drew his pistol and squeezed off two shells, both ricocheting from the Iron Warrior's armour.

'Now you die, renegade!' bellowed the traitor.

Uriel rolled aside as the screaming sword hacked into the ground, kicking out at the Iron Warrior's kneecap. He roared as he struck, putting his entire strength behind the blow, feeling his foe's armour splinter and the knee shatter into fragments. The Iron Warrior howled and dropped to the ground. Uriel didn't give him a chance to recover and stepped in, driving his sword clean through the Iron Warrior's chest.

The warrior seized his neck and chuckled, a throaty death rasp, and Uriel felt the immense strength in the grip. He twisted the blade, spurts of blood spraying his hands as the wound tore wider. The Iron Warrior's grip on his neck tightened and he heard a joint in his gorget pop and crack as his dying foe sought to choke the life from him. Uriel slammed his fist into the side of the warrior's helmet again and again, pounding his skull to destruction until he finally released his grip.

Uriel staggered back from the dead Iron Warrior, seeing the Space Marines storming through the open gateway in the razorwire fence. The bunkers were smoking ruins, their interiors like abattoirs. Gunfire blasted from the daemonic tower, ripping through the ranks of the attacking Space Marines. Some fell, but most picked themselves up before ducking into whatever cover they could find. Mutants fled before the wrath of the attackers, but they were cut down without mercy, hacked to death with swords or beaten to death with armoured gauntlets.

The fire from the tower was punishing the attackers and as its fiery gaze swept across the plateau, Uriel had a sickening sensation that it *saw* him, saw him and recognised him...

Even as he watched, he saw a warrior in midnight black power armour leap from a spire of rock to one side of the camp. A searing fire erupted from his back and Uriel saw the warrior was wearing a jump pack. Smoke and flames fired from its vents, propelling the warrior through the air to land on the head of the daemon tower. Flames burst from its eyes and the tower shook violently, but whether that was in response to the Space Marine landing on it or the daemon's own fury, it was impossible to tell.

The warrior slashed at the daemonic head with lightning sheathed claws, crackling arcs of blue energy flaring where he struck, before swinging one-handed from the side of the head and clamping something to its side. The tower shook violently, as though seeking to dislodge its attacker, but the dark armoured warrior drove his lightning claws into the daemon head and hung on. He swung around the tower, slashing at the thick cables that held it in place before bracing his feet against its cheek and pushing off. His jump jets fired as the melta charge he had placed on the daemon head detonated and he flew clear on the bow wave of an explosion that vaporised the top of the tower in a pluming mushroom cloud of incandescent energy.

With a shrieking roar, the tower swayed drunkenly, the few remaining cable stays twanging loudly as they pulled taut before snapping with the crack of a gunshot. The tower toppled majestically, crashing through the corrugated tin roof of the nearest warehouse and sending up plumes of dust and smoke.

Gunfire sounded sporadically from the camp as the last of the mutant labourers were rounded up and killed, and Uriel let out a deep breath as he saw that the battle was over.

He dragged his sword from the chest of the body before him, looking around to see an Iron Warrior on his knees, blood flooding down his breastplate as Pasanius slashed at him with his own chainblade. Both his arms had been hacked off and his belly had spilled its contents across the dark earth.

The fight was gone from the Iron Warrior, but still Pasanius took his measure of vengeance from him. A mob of Space Marines had the last Iron Warrior surrounded and shot him to death without mercy, their bolts penetrating his torn armour and exploding wetly within his flesh.

Only now, with the battle over, did Uriel really pay close attention to the armour of the Space Marines he had fought alongside. No more than two or three were alike in colour or design, and each bore testament to many hard fights, with ancient battle scars hastily and imperfectly repaired with crude grafts and filler. Almost all bore a different Chapter symbol on their shoulder guards and many had painted over them with jagged red saltires.

Wailing slaves squatted in their folds of flesh or cradled each other in their misery. Uriel ran over to Pasanius as he continued to hack the fallen Iron Warrior into pieces.

'Pasanius!' shouted Uriel.

He grabbed Pasanius's arm as he drew back for another blow. 'Pasanius, he is dead!'

Pasanius's head snapped round, his eyes ablaze with fury. For the briefest second, Uriel feared that something terrible had possessed his friend, then the killing light went out of him and he dropped the Iron Warrior's weapon and let out a deep, shuddering breath. The sergeant dropped to his knees, his face ashen at the fury he had unleashed.

'Your comrade's anger does him credit,' said a voice behind Uriel and he turned to see the warrior in black who had destroyed the tower. His armour was a far cry from the usual gleaming brilliance of a Space Marine's power armour, being ravaged with dents, scars and patches. Hot vapours vented at his shoulders from the nozzles of his jump pack, and a white symbol – a bird of prey of some kind – had been painted over with a jagged red cross. His helmet bore a similar symbol across his visor.

'You kill Iron Warriors well, both of you,' he said.

Uriel took the measure of this Space Marine before answering, seeing a confident, almost arrogant swagger to his posture.

'I am Uriel Ventris of the Ultramarines, and this is Pasanius Lysane. Who are you?'

The warrior sheathed the lightning claws on his gauntlets and reached up to release the vacuum seals on his gorget. He removed his helmet and took a lungful of the stale air of Medrengard before answering.

'My name is Ardaric Vaanes, formerly of the Raven Guard,' he said, running a hand over his scalp. Vaanes's hair was long and dark, bound in a tight scalp lock; his features angular and pale, with deep-set hooded eyes of violet. His cheeks were scarred and he bore a trio of round scars on his forehead above his left eye, where it looked as though long service studs had been removed.

'Formerly?' asked Uriel warily.

'Aye, formerly,' said Vaanes, stepping forward and offering his hand to Uriel.

Uriel eyed the proffered hand and said, 'You are renegade.'

Vaanes held his hand out for a second longer before accepting that Uriel was not going to take it and dropped it to his side. He nodded. 'Some call us that, yes.'

Pasanius stood next to Uriel and said, 'Others call you traitor.'

Vaanes's eyes narrowed. 'Perhaps they do, but only once.'

The three Space Marines stared at one another in silence for long seconds before Vaanes shrugged and walked past them towards the wrecked camp.

'Wait,' said Uriel, turning and following the renegade. 'I don't understand. How is it you come to be here?'

'That, Uriel Ventris, is a long story,' replied Vaanes, as they passed through the gate into the blazing camp. 'But we should destroy this place and be gone from here soon. The Unfleshed are close and the scent of death will draw them here quickly.'

'What about all these people?' asked Pasanius, sweeping his arm around to encompass the weeping prisoners outside the camp.

'What about them?'

'How are we going to get them out of here?'

'We're not,' said Vaanes.

'You're not?' snapped Uriel. 'Then why did you come to rescue them?'

'Rescue them?' said Vaanes, gesturing to his warriors, who began methodically working their way around the warehouse buildings and placing explosive charges. 'We didn't come to rescue them, we came to destroy this camp and that is all. These people are nothing to me.'

'How can you say that? Look at them!'

'If you want to rescue them, then good luck to you, Uriel Ventris. You will need it.'

'Damn you, Vaanes, have you no honour?'

'None to speak of, no,' snapped Vaanes. 'Look at them, these precious people you want to save. They are worthless. Most do not survive to reach the skinning chasm anyway and the ones that do soon wish they had not.'

'But you can't just abandon them,' pressed Uriel.

'I can and I will.'

'What is this camp anyway?' asked Pasanius. 'A prison? A death camp?'

Vaanes shook his head. 'No, nothing so mundane. It is much worse than that.'

'Then what?'

Vaanes grabbed the handles of the roller shutter door of the nearest warehouse and hauled it open, saying, 'Why don't you find out?'

Uriel shared a wary glance with Pasanius as Ardaric Vaanes gestured that they should enter the building. A powerful reek of human waste gusted from within, mixed with the stench of rotted flesh and the stink of desperation. Flickering lights sputtered within and a low sobbing drifted on the stinking air.

Uriel stepped into the brick building, his eyes quickly adjusting to the gloom within. Inside, the warehouse was revealed to be a mechanised factory facility, with iron girders running the length of the building fitted with dangling chains and heavy pulley mechanisms on greased runners. Mesh cages on raised platforms ran along the left-hand side of the building, a mass of pale flesh filling each one, with gurgling pipes and tubes drooping from bulging feed sacks suspended from the roof.

A trough that reeked of human faeces ran beneath the cages, clogged and buzzing with waste-eating insects. Uriel covered his mouth and nose, even his prodigious metabolism struggling to protect him from the awful stench. He walked forwards, his boots ringing on the grilled floor as he approached the first cage.

Inside was a naked man, though to call him such was surely to stretch the term. His form was immense, bloated and flabby, and his skin had the colour and texture of bile, with a horrid, clammy gleam to it. Rusted clamps held his jaw open while ribbed tubing pulsed with a grotesque peristaltic motion as nutrients and foodstuffs laced with growth hormones were pumped into him as another tube carried away his waste. Coloured wires and augmetic plugs pierced the flesh of his sagging chest, no doubt artificially regulating his heart and preventing the cardiac arrest that his vast bulk should have long ago brought on.

His limbs were thick, doughy lumps of grey flesh, held immobile by tight snares of wire, his features lost in the flabby immensity of his skull, his eyes telling of a mind that had long since taken refuge in madness. Uriel felt an immense sadness and horror at the man's plight – what manner of monster could do this to a human being?

He moved on to the next cage, finding a similar sight within, this time a naked woman, her body also bloated and obscene, her belly scarred and ravaged by what looked like repeated and unnecessary surgery. Unlike the occupant of the previous cage, her eyes had a vestige of sanity and they spoke eloquently to Uriel of her torment.

He turned away, appalled at such hideousness, seeing that there were hundreds of such cages within this darkened hell. Repulsed beyond words, yet drawn to explore further, he crossed the chamber to see what lay on the other side of the building. More cages occupied the right-hand side of the building, but these were narrower, occupied by splayed individuals who looked like the poor wretches Uriel had once seen on a hive world that had been cut off from the agri world it had relied upon for foodstuffs. Starving men and women were hung from iron hooks, wired to machines that kept them in a hellish limbo between life and death as their body fat was forcibly sucked from them by hissing pumps and industrial irrigation equipment.

Their skin hung loose on their bodies and drooped from their emaciated frames in purulent sheets. Uriel now knew the fate of those in the cages behind him. Fattened up artificially so the skin might stretch to obscene proportions, then ultra-rapidly divested of their bulk that they might be skinned to provide swathes of fresh skin.

But why? Why would anyone go to such lengths to harvest such vast quantities of human skin? The answer eluded Uriel and he felt an all-consuming pity well up within him at the plight of these prisoners.

'You see?' said Ardaric Vaanes, standing behind him. 'There is nothing you can do for them. Freeing these… things is pointless and their death will be a blessed release.'

'Sweet Emperor,' whispered Uriel. 'What purpose does this cruelty serve?'

Vaanes shrugged. 'I do not know, nor do I care. The Iron Warriors have built dozens of these camps in the mountains over the last few months. They are of importance to the Iron Warriors, so I destroy them. The "why" of it is irrelevant.'

'Are all the buildings like this one?' asked Pasanius, his face lined with sorrow.

'They are,' confirmed Vaanes. 'We have already destroyed two such camps, and they were all like this. We must destroy it now, for if we do not, the Unfleshed will come and there will be a feasting and a slaughter the likes of which you cannot imagine.'

'I do not understand,' said Uriel. 'The Unfleshed? What are they?'

'Beasts from your worst nightmares,' said Vaanes. 'They are the by-blows of the Iron Warriors, abortions given life who escaped the vivisectoria of the Savage Morticians to roam the mountains. They are many and we are few. Now, come, it is time we were gone.'

Uriel nodded wearily, barely listening to Vaanes, and followed the renegade back out into the remains of the camp. Numbly he took in the scale of the camp: two dozen of these buildings filled it, each one a darkened hell for those farmed within them. For all that he hated to admit it, Vaanes was right, the sooner this facility and all within it were destroyed the better.

A Space Marine in the grey livery of a Chapter Uriel did not recognise jogged up to Vaanes and said, 'They're here. Brother Svoljard just caught their scent!'

'How far?' demanded Vaanes, clamping on his helmet and calling to the remainder of his warriors over his armour's vox.

'Close, perhaps three or four hundred metres,' answered the warrior. 'They approached from downwind.'

'Damn, but they're learning,' hissed Vaanes. 'Everyone clear out. Head south into the mountains and make your own way back to the sanctuary.'

'What is it?' asked Uriel.

'The Unfleshed,' said Vaanes.

♈ SEVEN

GALVANISED BY THE urgency in the renegade's tone, Uriel quickly followed him through the camp as the first of the charges detonated with a hollow boom. Debris and flesh rained down as one of the human battery farms exploded, freeing the prisoners from their agonies in a fiery wash of release.

More charges blew and more of the infernal buildings collapsed inwards. Uriel prayed that the souls within them would forgive them and find their way to the Emperor's side. Flames and smoke billowed from the blazing wreckage of the camp as it was destroyed and the Space Marines ran for the safety of the mountains.

Uriel and Pasanius followed Ardaric Vaanes and his renegades southwards, climbing away from the camp as Uriel heard a mad chorus of howls from the mountains either side of them.

The breath caught in his throat and his pace slowed at the sight of the Unfleshed as they shambled from the mountains towards the burning camp with a twisted, lop-sided gait. Monstrously huge, they were a riot of anatomies, a carnival of the grotesque with no two alike in size or shape. Hugely built and massively tall, they were grossly swollen, glistening red and wet, the rippling form of their exposed musculature out of all proportion to their bodies. Uriel saw that, over and above their enormity and lack of skin, every one of them was deformed in other nightmarish ways, resembling the leavings from a mad sculptor-surgeon's table.

Here was a creature with two heads, fused at the jawbone, with a quartet of cataracted eyes that had run together into one misshapen orb. Another bore a monstrous foetal twin from its stomach, withered, and metastasised arms gripping its parent tightly.

Yet another shambled downhill using piston-like arms, its legs atrophied to little more than grasping claws. A trio of beasts, perhaps related somehow, shared a similarity in their deformities, with each clad in flapping sheets of leathery skin. Their skulls were swollen and distended with long fangs, and bony crests erupted from their flesh all across their bodies.

But supreme amongst the tide of roaring horrors charging towards the camp was a gargantuan beast that led them. Taller and broader than all the others, its physique was greater even than the largest of its monstrous followers, its lumpen head hunched low between its shoulders. Though some distance from Uriel, its skinless features bore the unmistakable gleam of feral intelligence, and the thought of such a creature possessing even the barest glimmer of self-awareness repulsed Uriel beyond reason.

'Come on, Ultramarine,' shouted Vaanes. 'No time to gawp at the monsters!'

Uriel ignored Vaanes and stared at the creatures as they smashed their way through the razorwire fence, unheeding of the barbs that tore at their red-wet bodies. Were they impervious to pain, wondered Uriel?

'What are they?' he said.

'I told you,' shouted back Vaanes. 'Come on! There's enough meat down there to keep them busy for a while, but once they've eaten their fill, they'll try to hunt us. If you don't come now, we will leave you here for them.'

Uriel continued to stare at the grisly spectacle below with morbid fascination, watching as the Unfleshed ripped their way through the ruins of the warehouses, tossing aside massive girders like matchwood and gorging on the scorched meat within. Horrific sounds of snapping bone and tearing flesh sounded from below as the Unfleshed fell upon the prisoners who had remained outside the camp when the renegades had first attacked.

Most died in the first instants of the attack, torn to pieces in a frenzy by the Unfleshed. Others were devoured alive, limbs and slabs of meat flying as the monsters fought for every morsel, their terrible roars of loathsome appetite echoing from the mountains.

Pasanius gripped his arm and said, 'We have to go, Uriel!'

'We let them die,' said Uriel darkly. 'We abandoned them. We might as well have killed them ourselves.'

'We couldn't have saved them, but we can avenge them.'

'How?' said Uriel.

'By living,' answered Pasanius.

Uriel nodded and turned away from the hideous spectacle below, shutting out the roaring feasting and orgiastic howls of pleasure, and feeling a part of his heart grow colder and harder as he left these people to die.

KHALAN-GHOL WAS in flames. Its spires were in ruins and its bastions pounded to dust by the relentless bombardment. Square kilometres burned in the fires of Berossus's shelling, but it was still the merest fraction of the scale of the fortress. Unnatural darkness swathed the fortress, black clouds of lightning-shot smoke hanging low and blotting out the dead whiteness of the sky for leagues around. Snaking kilometres of trenches topped with razorwire surrounded the darkened peak, newly constructed redoubts, bunkers, pillboxes and towers whose mighty guns deafeningly shelled Honsou's fastness, strobing the landscape with their red fire.

Belching manufactorum had been erected on the plains and the pounding clang of industry was a constant refrain in the air. Glowing, orange-lit forges constantly churned out shells, guns and the materiel of war, and Honsou knew that their production rates would put the finest Imperial forge world to shame. He saw the huge silhouettes of Titans on the horizon, their diabolical forms dwarfing everything around them. They could do little but act as gun platforms for now, the leviathans unable to climb the mountainous slopes of Khalan-Ghol until the massive ramp Berossus was building was complete.

He and a hand-picked cadre of his finest warriors clambered down the jagged slopes towards the forces arrayed below them. Honsou slid down a fallen pile of broken boulders, rotted, skeletal arms jutting from the cracks between them, but whether they belonged to one of his warriors or one of his foes he neither knew nor cared.

Berossus had been nothing if not thorough in his attentions; the lower bastions were gone, shelled until it was as though they had never existed, and the outer ring of forts had fallen before his onslaught.

Tens of thousands had already died in the battle, but Berossus had not been so stupid as to waste his best warriors in the battle thus far. Chaff, slaves and rabble bound to the service of Chaos, had charged his walls only to be met and hurled back by fire and steel.

Combined with the soldiery of Toramino's grand company, the two warsmiths had enough manpower to drag down the walls of Khalan-Ghol eventually; it was simply a matter of time.

Time Honsou did not intend to give them.

'Berossus is a fool,' he had said, when broaching the plan that now saw him cautiously approaching the sentry lines of the enemy's furthest advanced trenches. 'We will take the fight to him.'

'Beyond the walls?' asked Obax Zakayo.

'Aye,' replied Honsou. 'Right to the very heart of his army.'

'Madness,' said Zakayo.

'Exactly,' grinned Honsou. 'Which is why Berossus will never expect it. You know Berossus! To him, sieges are simply a matter of logistics. As a former vassal of Forrix, I would have thought you would have appreciated that, Zakayo.'

'I do, but to leave the protection of our walls...'

'Berossus is a slave to the mechanics of a siege. *This* course of action results in *that* result – that's how he thinks. He is too hidebound by the grand tradition of battle from the ancient days to think beyond the purity of an escalade, to expect the unexpected.'

'It has not failed him before,' pointed out Obax Zakayo.

'He hasn't fought me before,' said Honsou.

The trenches ahead were lit by drumfires, and the clang of digging shovels and the rumble of earth-moving machines was all but obscured by the thunder of guns.

'Onyx,' whispered Honsou, unsheathing his black bladed axe. 'Go.'

Onyx nodded, a fluid shadow and all but invisible in the darkness, slithering on his belly towards the trenchline, his outline blurring and merging with the night. Obax Zakayo said, 'If he is discovered, we will all die here.'

'Then we die,' snarled Honsou. 'Now be silent or I will kill you myself.'

Suitably chastened, Obax Zakayo said nothing more as he heard the sound of gurgling cries and slashing blades from ahead. Honsou saw a fountain of blood spurt above the line of the trench and knew that it was now safe to approach.

He crawled to where Onyx had cut a path through the razorwire and dropped into the trench. A score of corpses filled the trench and adjacent dugout, blood, glistening and oily in the firelight, coating the walls and seeping between the well laid duckboards. Each body lay sprawled at an unnatural angle, as though every bone had been broken. Each bore a long gash up the centre of their backs where their spinal column had been ripped out. Onyx himself stood immobile in the centre of the trench, slowly sheathing bronze claws into the grey flesh of his hands as the silver fire of his veins burned even brighter than normal. The daemon within him revelled in the slaughter and allowed the human part of him to return to the surface once more.

'Good kills,' said Honsou as his Iron Warriors dropped into the trench, spreading out and securing their entry point. He ran over to the communications trench at the back of this widened area and ducked his head around the corner. Just as he had expected, he could only see partway along it, the trench following a standard zigzagging course. Further down its length, he could see red-liveried soldiers and slaves.

'Have you no imagination, Berossus?' he chuckled to himself. 'You make this too easy.'

He turned away and gathered his warriors about him. 'It is time. Let's go, and remember, as far as anyone here knows, we are loyal Iron Warriors of Berossus. Let no one challenge that.'

His warriors nodded and, with Honsou in the lead, they set off down the communication trench. They walked with the confident, easy swagger of warriors who know they are without equal, and all the human and mutant labourers of Berossus abased themselves before them as they passed.

They passed dugouts filled with twisted mutant creatures gathered in chanting groups around shrines to the Dark Gods, their mutterings overseen by sorcerers in golden robes. None questioned them, none had any reason to, honoured to have ancient warriors of Chaos pass by. Honsou saw bright arc lights suspended on baroque towers of iron that reared into the night and were hung with all manner of bloody trophies. Chanting groups of robed figures surrounded them,

Honsou stopped and asked, 'Zakayo, what are these towers? This doesn't look like something Berossus would do.'

'I am not sure,' replied Obax Zakayo. 'I have never seen their like.'

'They seek to break the walls of Khalan-Ghol with sorcery,' said Onyx. 'The towers are saturated with mystical energy. I can feel it, and the daemon within me bathes in it.'

'What?' hissed Honsou, suddenly wary. 'Are their magicks strong enough to overcome the kabal and the Heart of Blood?'

'No,' said Onyx. 'Not even close. There is great power here, but the Heart of Blood has endured for an eternity and no power wielded by a mortal can defeat it.'

Honsou nodded, reassured that the mystical defences of his fortress would hold. He glanced at the towers.

'This smells of Toramino,' he said. 'Berossus would not have thought of it.'

'Aye,' agreed Obax Zakayo. 'Lord Toramino has great cunning.'

'That he does, but I'll see that arrogant bastard dead before he takes Khalan-Ghol, sorcery or not.'

Passing beyond the towers, Honsou and his warriors emerged from the trench lines without incident, watching as the sweating, straining army of Berossus sought to bring his fortress to ruin. Tracked dozers laden with shells rumbled past behind high earthworks and Honsou was forced to admire the thorough completeness of the siegeworks. Forrix himself would have been proud.

Plumes of fire shot up from an iron refinery. The thunder of processing plants producing explosives and the hammering of forges filled the plains; millions of men working to bring him down. Stockpiles of ammunition and brass-cased shells were stored in armoured magazines and as they passed each one, Obax Zakayo would enter and place an explosive charge from the dispenser on his back. Honsou knew that Obax Zakayo was, in all likelihood, a liability, too entrenched in the old ways of his former master to be part of Honsou's cadre of lieutenants, but no one knew demolitions and explosives like he did.

And he had a cruelty to him that appealed to Honsou's sense for mayhem.

The further back they travelled from the front trenches, the greater the risk of discovery became. He saw sturdily constructed barrack-bunkers and great artillery pits that had obviously been built by Iron Warriors, and heard roaring bellows of madness that could only mean the cage-pits of the dreadnoughts were near.

'It is folly to continue, my lord, we should retreat now,' said Obax Zakayo. 'We have placed enough explosives to disrupt Berossus for months.'

'No, not yet,' said Honsou, a reckless sense of abandon driving him onwards as he caught sight of a familiar banner flapping in the wind atop an armoured pavilion. It squatted in the shadow of one of the colossal Titans, beyond a forest of razorwire and a staggered series of bunkers. 'Not when we have a chance to deliver something a little more personal to Lord Berossus himself.'

Obax Zakayo saw the banner and said, 'Great gods of Chaos, you cannot be serious!'

'You know I am, Zakayo,' said Honsou. 'I never joke about killing.'

DUG SEVEN METRES down into the rock, the sides of the artillery pit were reinforced with steel-laced rockcrete, at least two metres thick. Angled parapets, designed to deflect enemy artillery strikes swept up over the embrasure the huge siege gun would fire through. Honsou knew that none of his artillery pieces could reach this far and that such endeavour was wasted effort, but it was so like Berossus to have them built anyway.

The mighty cannon's bronze barrel was silhouetted against the roiling clouds above, etched with great spells of ruin and hung with thick, drooling chains of desecrated iron. It sat at the base of an incline on rails, so that after each shot it would roll back into its firing position.

Perhaps a hundred human soldiers surrounded the huge cannon, guards to protect the mighty siege gun. Honsou and his warriors brazenly marched towards the artillery pit, daring the soldiers to stop them. Though he and his warriors proudly displayed the heraldry of the Iron Warriors, it would not take the soldiers long to realise that they did not belong here and raise the alarm.

Honsou could see they were attracting stares, but pressed on, pushing the bluff to the limit as an Iron Warrior with a heavily augmented head and arms climbed from the artillery pit. Red lights winked on his helmet, fitted with range-finders, trajectorum and cogitators, and Honsou knew he looked upon one of Berossus's Chirumeks. More machine to him than man, the practitioner of the black arts of technology scanned him up and down before a huge gun affixed to his back swung around on a hissing armature and aimed at them.

Onyx never gave him a chance to fire the weapon, leaping forward with the speed of a striking snake. His outline blurred, becoming oily and indistinct as he moved. A flash of bronze claws and a rip of flesh and the Chirumek collapsed, his spinal column held aloft by the daemonic symbiote.

'Hurry!' shouted Honsou, running for the artillery pit now that all hopes of subterfuge were gone. He dropped into the artillery pit, firing his bolter at its other occupants. Loader slaves died in the hail of fire, blasted apart by his explosive shells and Chirumeks dived for cover as the Iron Warriors stormed in.

Yells and shouts of warning sounded from the human soldiers, but as the bark of gunfire continued, most were soon silenced. Honsou knew they didn't have much time and shouted, 'Zakayo, get down here!'

The lumbering giant climbed down into the pit as Honsou and his warriors slaughtered the remainder of the gun's crew. The huge cannon hissed and rumbled, revelling in the bloodshed around it and he could sense the daemonic urge to kill bound within it. Obax Zakayo climbed to the gunner's mount and began hauling at the bronze levers there.

Laughing at the irony of the moment, Honsou also climbed the ladder to the gunner's position as the turret emitted a bass groan and the barrel began turning from Khalan-Ghol towards the pavilion of Berossus.

The growling barrel depressed until it was virtually horizontal as bolter fire rattled from the sides of the artillery pit and Iron Warriors from Berossus's grand company poured from their barracks – together with their human auxiliaries – to launch a counterattack.

'Can't you hurry this up?' snapped Honsou.

'Not really, no!' shouted Obax Zakayo, pulling thick levers and heavy chains fitted to the daemon gun's breech. Honsou leaned over the railings of the gunnery platform and shouted down to his warriors. 'Get ready to reload this gun when we fire! I want at least a couple of shots before we have to escape!'

Four warriors broke from the defence of the gun pit and began hauling on the pulley chains that led down through a great iron portal in the floor of the artillery pit to the armoured magazine below. Within seconds, the iron gate groaned open and an enormous shell emerged. Grunting with the effort, the Iron Warriors manhandled the shell onto the gurney that would deliver it to the gun. It was extremely dangerous to have the magazine open while firing, but Honsou figured that since it wasn't their gun anyway, it didn't matter whether it got blown up or not.

'Ready to fire!' shouted Obax Zakayo.

Honsou sighted along the aiming reticule and laughed, seeing the roof of Berossus's pavilion and the gold and black heraldry of his banner.

'Fire!' he yelled and Obax Zakayo yanked the firing chain. Honsou swayed as the gun's massive recoil almost hurled him from the gunnery platform, the roar of its firing nearly deafening him. Thick, acrid smoke belched from the barrel as the great cannon screamed in pleasure. The daemonic breech clanged open of its own accord and his Iron Warriors ran the next shell along the rails and into the weapon.

As they fetched another shell from the magazine, Honsou saw that the first shot had been uncannily accurate. The banner of Berossus was no more, destroyed utterly by the explosion. The top portion of the pavilion was gone, nothing but a saw-toothed ruin left of its upper half. Even as he watched the debris rain down, secondary explosions were touched off by the burning wreckage as the gun fired again.

This time he was ready, but even so, was again almost dislodged by the recoil. Once more the pavilion vanished in a sheet of flame as their second shell impacted. Another shell was rammed home, but as the breech clanged shut, Honsou felt a huge tremor pass through the earth, swiftly followed by a second.

He looked up through the murk in time to see a massive shadow moving through the darkness and saw with a thrill of fear that one of the Titans was making for them. The ground shook to its tread, the footsteps of an angry god of war come to destroy them.

'Come on!' he shouted to Obax Zakayo. 'One more shot, then it's time we were gone!'

Obax Zakayo nodded, casting fearful glances over the gunner's mantlet with each booming footstep of the approaching Titan. Once again the mighty daemon gun fired, this time striking the barrack block beside the pavilion and reducing it to flaming rubble.

'Everyone out!' shouted Honsou, leaping from the gun and running towards the ladders that led from the artillery pit. Honsou wrenched open the iron door to the magazine as he passed and lobbed a handful of grenades inside. He leapt for the ladder as a huge shadow enveloped the artillery pit and looked up in time to see the massive, clawed foot of the Titan descending upon him.

He scrambled up the ladder and rolled aside as its thunderous footstep slammed down, obliterating the daemonic gun in a heartbeat and missing him by less than a metre. He rolled away and lurched to his feet, still dazed from the concussive impact of the Titan's foot when the grenades he had dropped into the magazine detonated.

The ground heaved and bellowed, huge geysers of flame and smoke ripping from the ground as hundreds of tonnes of buried ordnance exploded in a terrifyingly powerful conflagration. Honsou was lifted into the air and swatted for a hundred metres or more by the blast, slamming into an earthen rampart and rolling into a pile of excavated soil.

He picked himself up, coughing and reeling from the impact to take stock of his surroundings. He turned as he heard a groaning sound and saw the Titan that had destroyed the gun pit sway like a drunk, its leg destroyed from the knee down by the magazine's explosion. Sparks and plasma fire vented from shattered conduits and sparking cables. Even as he watched, the massive daemon engine began to slowly topple over, its piston-driven arms flailing for balance as it fell.

He turned away, laughing as dismayed soldiers and horrified Iron Warriors watched one of their mightiest daemon machines destroyed before their very eyes. The ground shook as the Titan hit the ground and was smashed asunder, but Honsou was already making his way back to Khalan-Ghol. He had no way of knowing what had become of the rest of his warriors, but trusted that they were experienced and resourceful enough to get back to Khalan-Ghol on their own in all this confusion.

A dark form emerged from the smoke beside him and he recognised the sinuous form of Onyx. The daemonic symbiote's claws were unsheathed and bloody, the glittering fire of his eyes shining with a deathly lustre. He had hunted well.

'A successful foray,' said Onyx with typical understatement.

'Aye,' agreed Honsou. 'Not bad. Not bad at all.'

THE SANCTUARY ARDARIC Vaanes had spoken of turned out to be secreted in a shadowed valley overlooking the plains before the mighty fortress shrouded in dark clouds and explosions. The sounds of battle still raged from below and Uriel could see a tremendous blaze deep in the besieger's camp. Their flight from the Unfleshed had been a helter-skelter journey of false trails and looping attempts to prevent the beasts from following their tracks.

Uriel could not shake the sound of the Unfleshed feasting on the prisoners, but was surprised at how little it bothered him now. Perhaps Vaanes had been right, there was nothing anyone could have done for those poor unfortunates, and death was the best thing for them.

The renegades had split up once clear of the death camp and now returned to their base in ones and twos, climbing down the valley sides or hiking up from below.

'Our sanctuary,' said Vaanes, pointing towards a series of crumbling bunkers and blockhouses that had fallen into disrepair and had clearly seen better days. Partially filled-in trenches and rusted coils of razorwire were angled before the dilapidated constructions, but Uriel's practiced eye could see that this place was not without its defences. Barely visible gun nests overlooked the approaches and he doubted that anyone could approach without some warning being given.

'What was this place used for?' asked Pasanius.

Vaanes shrugged. 'An old ammunition store, a barracks, a construction exercise? Who knows? All I know is that when we found this place it was abandoned and no one ever came near it. That's good enough for me.'

Uriel nodded as they crossed a trench via a series of iron sheets and Vaanes moved ahead of them towards the blockhouse beyond the bunkers.

Pasanius leaned close to Uriel and whispered, 'What are we doing? These Space Marines are renegades! Are we to damn ourselves even more in the sight of the Emperor?'

'I know,' said Uriel bitterly, 'but what choice do we have?'

'We can strike out on our own.'

'Aye, and maybe we will, but they have been here longer than us and we may learn something of this world and its dangers.'

Pasanius looked unconvinced, but said nothing more as they reached the armoured doors to the blockhouse. Whatever mechanism had once opened and closed them obviously no longer operated and Vaanes hauled them open with brute strength before disappearing within and indicating that they should follow.

Uriel ducked inside the blockhouse, the interior surprisingly well-lit by numerous holes pierced in the roof. Shafts of dead white light pooled on the rockcrete floor and reflected from the peeling, flakboard walls.

'I realise that this might be a little more luxury than you're used to as Ultramarines, but it's the nearest thing we have to a home just now,' grinned Vaanes as he walked ahead of them into the blockhouse's main chamber.

Light streamed in through the firing slits and Uriel could see that the chamber was full of the same Space Marines who had attacked the camp earlier. Most were engaged in cleaning their weapons or repairing their armour and Uriel was shocked at the sheer number of different Chapter symbols he saw on display.

Howling Griffons, White Consuls, Wolf Brothers, Crimson Fists and many others he did not recognise.

But most surprising of all were two figures crouched in the corner of the main chamber cleaning lasrifles. Dressed in the battered fatigues and torn uniform jackets of the Imperial Guard, they looked up as Uriel and Pasanius entered. Both men were so filthy and dishevelled that it was impossible to tell what regiment they had belonged to, but both wore expressions of tired, proud courage.

'Two new warriors for our band!' called Vaanes before slumping against one wall and removing his helmet.

Uriel refrained from qualifying that statement as the leaner of the two Guardsmen rose to his feet and limped towards Uriel. His skin was pale and wasted looking, blotchy and unhealthy, his eyes bloodshot.

The man extended a palsied hand and said, 'Lieutenant Colonel Mikhail Leonid of the 383rd Jouran Dragoons.'

'Uriel Ventris, and this is Pasanius Lysane.'

'What kind of Space Marines are you?' asked Leonid, stifling a cough. 'I don't see any markings.'

'We are Ultramarines,' replied Uriel. 'Sent from our Chapter to fulfil a death oath.'

Leonid shrugged. 'A better reason than most for being here.'

'Perhaps,' nodded Uriel. 'And how is it that a colonel of the Imperial Guard comes to be here?'

'That,' said Leonid, 'is a long story...'

⎈
EIGHT

LEONID AND SERGEANT Ellard, the softly spoken companion of the colonel, spent the next hour and a half regaling Uriel and Pasanius of how they had ended up in slavery on the bleak daemon world of Medrengard, beginning with the devastating assault of the Iron Warriors on the world of Hydra Cordatus just prior to the Despoiler's invasion through the Cadian Gate.

He spoke of weeks of constant shelling, of tanks and Titans and of the lethal cancers that base treachery had infected the men and women of his regiment with. But more than this, he spoke of noble courage. He spoke of a warrior named Eshara, a Space Marine of the Imperial Fists, and the sacrifice he and his men had made before the Valedictor Gate. Uriel felt a fierce pride well within him at the thought of such a noble warrior standing before impossible odds, and wished he could have met such a brave hero.

But ultimately, the story did not end well. The Iron Warriors finally took the citadel before Imperial reinforcements could arrive and Leonid wept as he spoke of the brutal slaughter that took place upon its final fall.

'It was a nightmare,' said Leonid. 'They showed no mercy.'

'The Iron Warriors serve the Ruinous Powers,' said Uriel. 'They do not know the meaning of the word.'

'Captain Eshara bought us some time, but it wasn't enough. The cavern below was too large and there was too much gene-seed to destroy. We–'

'Wait,' interrupted Uriel. 'Gene-seed? There was Space Marine gene-seed beneath your citadel?'

'Yes,' nodded Leonid. 'An Adeptus Mechanicus magos told me that it was one of the few places in the galaxy where it could be stored. The Warsmith

Honsou stole it and brought it to this world along with the slaves he took for his forges at the battle's end.'

'Who is Honsou?' asked Pasanius.

'He is the warlord who dwells in the fortress you saw as we came into this valley,' said Ardaric Vaanes.

'It is this Honsou's fortress that is besieged?' said Uriel, unable to mask his interest.

'It is,' confirmed Vaanes, wandering over to join the conversation and squatting down on his haunches. 'Why are you so interested in Honsou?'

'We have to get to that fortress.'

Vaanes laughed. 'Then you truly are here on a death oath. Why do you need to get to Honsou's fortress?'

Uriel paused, unsure as to how much he could trust Vaanes, but realised he had no choice and said, 'Our Chief Librarian was granted a vision from the Emperor, a vision of Medrengard and bloated, daemonic womb creatures called daemonculaba giving birth to corrupt, debased Space Marines. We are here to destroy them and I think that more than mere happenstance has brought us to this place.'

'How so?' asked Vaanes.

'Can it be coincidence that this Honsou has returned here with quantities of gene-seed for these daemonculaba and that we should learn of it from a man who was there to see him take it?'

Vaanes looked Ellard and Leonid up and down. 'I wondered why I hadn't left you to die with the other slaves on the Omphalos Daemonium. Perhaps something other than curiosity stayed my hand.'

Uriel started. 'You know of the Omphalos Daemonium?'

'Of course,' said Vaanes. 'There are few on Medrengard who do not. How is it you know of it?'

'It brought us here,' said Pasanius. 'It appeared within our ship when we made the translation to the immaterium. It killed everyone on board and then brought us here.'

'You willingly travelled within the Omphalos Daemonium?' said Vaanes, aghast.

'Of course not,' snapped Uriel. 'Its daemon creatures overcame us.'

'The Sarcomata...' nodded Vaanes.

'Aye, then the iron giant within the daemon engine brought us here.'

'The iron giant?' asked Leonid. 'The Slaughterman?'

'Slaughterman? No, it said that it only wore the flesh of the Slaughterman, that it was the will of the Omphalos Daemonium that commanded.'

'Then the daemon is free!' breathed Vaanes.

'What is it anyway?' asked Uriel.

'No one knows for sure,' began a sallow-skinned Space Marine of great age wearing armour of deep red and bone, with a raven's head on his shoulder guard. 'But there are tales aplenty, oh yes, tales aplenty.'

'And would you care to share any of them?' asked Vaanes, impatiently.

'I was just about to,' growled the Space Marine, 'if you'd given me half a chance.'

The Space Marine turned to Uriel and said, 'I am Seraphys of the Blood Ravens, and I served in my Chapter's Librarium in the years before my disgrace. One of the greatest driving forces of my Chapter is the seeking out of dark knowledge and forbidden lore, and over the millennia of our existence we have discovered much, and all of it gathered it aboard our Chapter fortress.'

'Your Chapter knew of the Omphalos Daemonium?'

'Indeed we did. In fact, it was a source of particular interest to many of our secret masters. Over the centuries I read much of this daemonic entity, and though much of what was said I believe to be false, there are some things I believe are true. It is said that once it was an ancient and powerful daemon prince, a servant of the Blood God that existed only for slaughter. The skulls it piled before its dark master were legion, but always one creature ever outdid it, one of the Blood God's most favoured avatars, a daemon known as the Heart of Blood; so terrible it was said to have the power to summon bloodstorms and drain the vital fluid from its victims without even laying a blade to their flesh.'

Uriel and Pasanius shared a start of recognition as Seraphys continued. 'This avatar was a daemon of deadly artifice who forged for itself a suit of armour into which it poured all of its malice, all of its hate and all of its cunning, that even the blows of its enemies would strike them down.'

'What became of these daemons?' said Uriel.

Seraphys leaned closer, warming to his tale. 'Some say they fought a great battle that sundered the very fabric of the universe, hurling the debris across the firmament and thus were the galaxies and planets born. Others say that the avatar of the Blood God outwitted the Omphalos Daemonium, and trapped it within the fiery heart of a mighty daemon engine bound to the service of the Iron Warriors, becoming the dread chariot of the Slaughterman – ever to hunger in torment for vengeance.'

'Then how is it that it is free?'

'Ah, well, that the ancient legends do not tell,' said Seraphys sadly.

'I think I might know,' said Leonid.

'You?' said Seraphys. 'How could a lowly Guardsman know of such things?'

Leonid ignored the Blood Raven's patronising tone. 'Perhaps because when Ardaric Vaanes and his warriors freed us from captivity, we were able to defeat the Slaughterman and drive him into the firebox of the daemon engine. We thought we had destroyed him.'

'But all it did was free the daemon within the firebox to take the Slaughterman's flesh for its own,' said Vaanes.

'Does anyone know what became of the Omphalos Daemonium's rival, the avatar?' asked Sergeant Ellard hesitantly.

'There is nothing in the tales I have read of its ultimate fate,' said Seraphys. 'Why?'

'Because I think I have seen it.'

'What? When?' asked Leonid.

'On Hydra Cordatus,' explained Ellard. 'Sir, do you remember the stories that went around when the Mori Bastion fell?'

'Yes,' nodded Leonid. 'Mad stuff, ravings about a giant warrior killing everything in the bastion by his voice alone and a whirlwind that... fed on blood.'

By now a sizeable crowd had gathered to hear these tales and the synchronicity of these revelations was lost on no one.

Ellard nodded. 'I saw it too, but... I didn't say anything. I thought they'd section me for sure if I said what I'd seen.'

'Don't keep us in suspense, sergeant, what happened to it?' demanded Vaanes.

'I don't know for sure,' said Ellard, 'but once it killed Librarian Corwin, it opened up some kind of... gateway... I think. I'm not sure exactly. It was some kind of black thing that it stepped through and vanished. That was the last I saw of it.'

Vaanes rose from his squatting position and said, 'I think you bring trouble with you, Uriel Ventris of the Ultramarines. This is a deadly world, but we can survive here. We steal what we need from the Iron Warriors, and they in turn try to hunt us. It is a fine game, but I think your coming to Medrengard has just skewed that game.'

'Then perhaps that is a good thing,' pointed out Uriel.

'I wouldn't bet on it,' cautioned Vaanes.

PASANIUS SAT ALONE on the rocks outside the blockhouse, more tired than he could ever remember being. He had been awake now for... days, weeks? He couldn't tell, but he knew it had been a long time. The sky above was still that damnable white, and how anyone could live on such a world, where there was no change to mark the passing of time, was beyond him. The crushing monotony of such a bleak vista made him want to weep.

He held his arms out before his chest, turning both hands before his face. His left gauntlet was torn and scarred, ruined by the constant climbing over razor-sharp rocks, but his right was as unblemished as the day it had been grafted to the flesh and bone of his elbow. Thus far he had been able to keep its unique ability to repair itself secret from his battle-brothers, but he knew it was only a matter of time before its miraculous powers became known. Pasanius hammered his fist into the ground, pounding a powdered crater in the rock, smashing his fingers to oblivion then watching in disgust as they reknitted themselves once more.

The shame of concealing such evil from his brethren had almost been too much to bear and the thought of disappointing Uriel terrified him. But to admit to such weakness was as great a shame, and the guilt of this secret had torn a hole in his heart that he could not absolve.

There was no doubt in his mind that it had been beneath the surface of Pavonis, facing the ancient star god known as the Nightbringer, that he had been cursed. He remembered the aching cold of the blow from its scythe that had severed his arm, the crawling sensation of dead flesh where once there had been living tissue. Was it possible that some corruption had been passed to him by the Nightbringer's weapon and infected his body with this terrible sickness?

The adepts of Pavonis had been quick to provide a replacement arm, the very best their world could produce, for Techmarine Harkus and Apothecary Selenus to reattach. He had never been comfortable with the idea of an augmetic arm, but it was not until the battles aboard the *Death of Virtue* that he had begun to suspect that there was more to his new limb than met the eye.

What crime had he committed to be so punished? Why had he been visited by such an affliction? He knew not, but as he removed his breastplate and took out his knife, he vowed he would pay for it in blood.

URIEL LAY BACK and tried to sleep, his eyelids drooping and heavy. At least in the blockhouse there were areas out of the perpetual light of the dead sky, where darkness and sleep could be sought. But sleep was proving to be elusive, his thoughts tumbling through his head in a jumble.

Uriel now felt sure that there was more to this quest than he had initially thought. He knew he should not have been surprised to learn that the Heart of Blood was more than just an artefact, that the schemes of daemons were never straightforward. Were he and Pasanius part of some elaborate vengeance the Omphalos Daemonium had planned for its ancient rival? Who knew, but Uriel vowed that he would not allow himself to be used in such a way. Dark designs were afoot and a confluence of events had come together to bring them to this point. Despite the dangers around him, he felt on some instinctual level that the will of the Emperor was working through him.

Why then did he feel so empty, so hollow?

Uriel had read of the many saints of the Imperium and had heard numerous sermons delivered with impassioned oratory from the pulpit of how the Emperor's power was like a fire within that burned hotter than the brightest star. But Uriel felt no such fire, no light burned within his breast and he had never felt so alone.

Sermons always spoke of heroes as shining examples of virtue: pure of heart, untainted by doubt and unsullied by self aggrandisement.

Given such qualifications, he knew he was no hero, he was outcast, denied even the name of his Chapter and cast within the Eye of Terror with renegades and traitors. Where was the bright light of the Emperor within him here?

He shifted his position, trying to get comfortable on the hard rockcrete floor so that he might be rested enough to press on to the fortress. He knew that the chances of their surviving the journey to the fortress of Honsou were minimal, but perhaps there was some way to entice these renegades to join them. In all likelihood they would all die, but who would miss such worthless specimens as them anyway?

As he turned over, he caught sight of a silhouetted Space Marine in the doorway and pushed himself into a sitting position as Ardaric Vaanes entered and sat resting his back on the wall opposite Uriel.

Thin light spilled in through the doorway, a fine mist of dust floating in the air where Vaanes's footsteps had disturbed them. The two Space Marines sat in silence for long minutes.

'Why are you here, Ventris?' said Vaanes, eventually.

'I told you. We are here to destroy the daemonculaba.'

Vaanes nodded. 'Aye, you said that, but there's more isn't there?'

'What do you mean?'

'I saw the way you and your sergeant looked at one another when Seraphys mentioned the Heart of Blood. That name has some meaning for you doesn't it?'

'Perhaps it does. What of it?'

'Like I said, I think you bring trouble with you, but I can't decide whether it is trouble I want to be part of yet.'

'Should I trust you, Vaanes?'

'Probably not,' admitted Vaanes with a smile. 'And another thing. I noticed that you very deliberately shied away from explaining why the Omphalos Daemonium went to such lengths to bring you here.'

'It is a daemon creature, who can say what its motives were?' said Uriel, reluctant to reveal the pact, even a false pact, he had made with the Omphalos Daemonium.

'How convenient,' said Vaanes, dryly. 'But I still want an answer.'

'I have none to give you.'

'Very well, keep your secrets, Ventris, but I want you gone once you have rested.'

Uriel pushed himself to his feet and crossed the room to crouch beside Vaanes.

'I know that you have no reason to, but trust me. I know we are all here on the Emperor's business – too much is happening to be mere accident. Come with us, we could use your help. Your men fight well and together we can regain our honour.'

'Regain our honour?' said Vaanes. 'I had no honour to lose, why do you think I am here and not with the battle-brothers of my Chapter?'

'I don't know,' replied Uriel. 'Why? Tell me.'

Vaanes shook his head. 'No. You and I are not friends enough to share such shames. Suffice to say, we will not go with you. It is a suicide mission.'

'Do you speak for everyone here?' demanded Uriel.

'More or less.'

'And you would turn your back on a brother Space Marine in need of your strength?'

'Yes,' said Vaanes. 'I would.'

Suddenly angry, Uriel rose and snapped, 'I should have expected no less from a damned renegade.'

'Don't forget,' laughed Vaanes, getting to his feet and turning to leave, 'that you too are a renegade. You're no longer one of the Emperor's soldiers and it's time you realised that.'

Uriel opened his mouth to reply, but said nothing as he remembered a line from the last sermon he had heard Chaplain Clausel deliver outside the Temple of Correction.

Softly he whispered that line as Vaanes left the room: 'He must put a white cloak upon his soul, that he might climb down into the filth to fight, yet may he die a saint.'

URIEL AWOKE WITH a start, startled and disorientated. He had not been aware of falling asleep, an awareness of his surroundings giving him a strange sense of dislocation as he blinked away sleep. He pushed himself upright, repeating a prayer of thanks for a new day and feeling his mind focus and sharpen as the Catalepsean node of his brain reawakened his full cognitive functions.

Allowing a Space Marine to sleep and remain awake at the same time by influencing the circadian rhythms of sleep and his body's response to sleep deprivation, the Catalepsean node 'switched off' areas of the brain sequentially. Such a process did not replace normal sleep entirely, but allowed a Space Marine to continue to perceive his environment whilst resting.

He ran a hand across his scalp and left the shadowed room, catching the mouth-watering scent of hot food. He entered the blockhouse's main chamber, the same lifeless light spilling in through the firing slits and groups of Space Marines gathered around a cookfire upon which bubbled a large pot of a thick gruel-like porridge. It looked like poor food at best, but right now it was as desirable as the tenderest morsel of roast boar.

Several figures lay sprawled around the chamber, Space Marines resting and Leonid and Ellard asleep beneath the firing slit, using their rifles as pillows.

'I'd say "good morning", but that's not really a term I can use on this world,' said Ardaric Vaanes, spooning some porridge into a crude bowl of beaten metal and handing it to Uriel. 'It's not much, just some stolen ration packs made to go a long way.'

'It's fine. Thank you,' said Uriel, accepting the bowl and sitting next to Pasanius, who nodded a greeting as he scooped the greyish food into his mouth. 'Aren't you worried about the smoke of the fire being seen?'

'On Medrengard? No, rising smoke isn't anything unusual on this planet.'

'No, I suppose it isn't,' said Uriel between mouthfuls. The porridge was thin and he could taste watered down nutrients, the gruel barely enough to stave off starvation, let alone provide any nourishment. But still, it had more taste than the recycled paste his armour provided him.

'Have you thought any more about what I asked before?' said Uriel, finishing the bowl of porridge and setting it down beside him.

'I have,' nodded Vaanes.

'And?'

'You intrigue me, Ventris. There is more to you than meets the eye, but I'm damned if I know what. You say you are here to fulfil a death oath, and I believe you. But there is something else you are not telling me and I fear it will be the death of us all.'

'You're right,' said Uriel, seeing that he had no choice but to tell these renegades the truth. 'There is more and I will tell you all of it. Gather your warriors together outside and I will speak to you all.'

Vaanes narrowed his eyes, wary at letting Uriel speak directly to his men, but realising that he could not refuse. 'Very well. Let's hear what you have to say.'

Uriel nodded and followed Vaanes and his men into the still air and burning glare of the black sun. Space Marines filed out of the block-house and descended from their posts in the peaks surrounding the bunker complex as they were called down. Yawning and blinking, Leonid and Ellard stepped into the brightness of the valley, cradling their lasguns over their shoulders.

When the entirety of the renegade warrior band had gathered, some thirty Space Marines of various Chapters, Vaanes said, 'The floor is yours, Ventris.'

Uriel took a deep breath as Pasanius whispered, 'Are you sure this is wise?'

'We don't have a choice, my friend,' replied Uriel. 'It has to be this way.'

Pasanius shrugged as Uriel moved to the centre of the circle of Space Marines and began to speak, his voice strong and clear. 'My name is Uriel Ventris and until recently I was a captain of the Ultramarines. I commanded the Fourth Company and Pasanius was my senior sergeant.

We were cast from our Chapter for breaking faith with the *Codex Astartes* and to our brethren we are no longer Ultramarines.'

Uriel paced around the circumference of the circle and raised his voice. 'We are no longer Ultramarines, but we are still Space Marines, warriors of the Emperor, and we will remain so until the day we die. As are you, and you and you!'

Uriel jabbed his fist at Space Marines around the circle as he spoke. 'I do not know why any of you are here, what circumstances drove you from your Chapters and led you to this place, and nor do I need to know. But I offer you a chance to regain your honour, to prove that you are true warriors of purpose.'

'What is it you are asking of us?' said a huge Space Marine in the livery of the Crimson Fists, his battered skull scarred and shaven.

'What is your name, brother?'

'Kyama Shae,' said the Crimson Fist.

'I am asking you to join us in our quest, Brother Shae,' said Uriel. 'To penetrate the fortress of Honsou and destroy the daemonculaba. Some of you already know that, but there is more. The Omphalos Daemonium, the daemon that brought us here did so for a reason. It spoke to us of the Heart of Blood and told us that it resides within the secret vaults of Honsou's fortress.'

A muttered ripple of horrified surprise travelled the circle as Uriel continued. 'It charged us with retrieving the Heart of Blood for it, and we agreed.'

'Traitors!' hissed a White Consul. 'You consort with daemons!'

Pasanius surged to his feet and shouted, 'Never! Say such a thing again and I will kill you!'

Uriel stepped between the two Space Marines and said, 'We agreed because our homeworlds were threatened with destruction, brother, but fear not, we have no intention of honouring such an agreement. When I find this Heart of Blood in that fortress I will destroy it. You have my word on that.'

'How can we trust you?' asked Vaanes.

'I have only my word to offer you, Vaanes, but think on this. The warlord Honsou has recently returned from campaign and is laden with stolen gene-seed. What do you think he is using it for? How do you think the daemonculaba are producing these newly-birthed abominations? With enough gene-seed, Honsou can create hundreds, perhaps even thousands, of new warriors for his armies. Soon they will come and destroy you. You know this, so why not strike now before they are able to?'

Uriel could see that his words were reaching the assembled Space Marines and pressed on. 'You say that what hurts the Iron Warriors is at the heart of all you do, well what will hurt them more than this, to have their newest warriors destroyed before they can fight? At the very least, we can cause the Iron Warriors such grief that they will not soon forget us. If we are to die in this, then at least it will be with our honour!'

'What use is honour if we are all dead?' asked Vaanes.

'Death and honour,' said Uriel. 'If one brings the other, then it is a good death.'

'Easy for you to say, Ventris.'

Uriel shook his head. 'No, Vaanes, it is not. You think I *want* to die? I do not. I wish to live for a long time and bring death to my enemies for many years to come, but if I am to die, I can think of no better an end than fighting alongside brother Space Marines for a noble cause.'

'Noble? Who do you think cares?' snapped Vaanes. 'If we die on this suicide mission of yours, what will any of this matter? Who will even know of your precious honour?'

'I will,' said Uriel softly. 'And that will be enough.'

Silence fell and Uriel could see that the renegade Space Marines were torn between the status quo of their current existence and this chance for redemption. He could not yet tell which way they would lean.

Just as he was beginning to believe that no one would rise to the challenge he had offered them, Colonel Leonid and Sergeant Ellard stood and crossed the circle towards him.

Leonid saluted him and said, 'We will fight alongside you, Captain Ventris. We're dying anyway and if we can kill Iron Warriors before that happens, then so much the better.'

Uriel smiled and accepted Leonid's hand. 'You are a brave man, colonel.'

'Perhaps,' said Leonid, 'or a man with nothing to lose.'

'I thank you both anyway,' said Uriel as Brother Seraphys also came forward to join them.

'I will come with you, Uriel,' said Seraphys. 'If I can learn more of the machinations of the Ruinous Powers then that can only be for the good.'

Uriel nodded his thanks as first one Space Marine, then others came forward to join him. They came in ones and twos, until every one of the renegade Space Marines stood beside Uriel and Pasanius save Ardaric Vaanes.

The former Raven Guards Space Marine chuckled to himself and said, 'You have a way with words, Ventris, I'll give you that.'

'Join us, Vaanes!' urged Uriel. 'Take this chance for honour. Remember who you are, what you were created to do!'

Vaanes rose and approached Uriel. 'I know that well enough, Ventris.'

'Then join us!'

The renegade sighed, casting his gaze around the ruined bunker complex he had called home and the Space Marines who now stood with Uriel.

'Very well, I will help you get into the fortress, but I'm not getting killed to help you carry out your death oath. So long as you understand that.'

'I understand that,' assured Uriel.

Vaanes suddenly grinned and shook his head. 'Damn, but I knew you were trouble…'

NINE

THE WARRIOR BAND gathered up their weapons and equipment, filled with a new sense of purpose as they prepared to leave the sanctuary. Uriel cleaned his armour as best he could and knelt to give thanks to his battle gear, placing his gun and sword before him and asking them to help him do the Emperor's bidding.

Pasanius filled his flamer with the last of his promethium and though it pained him, he knew he was going to have to leave it behind soon. A weapon with no ammunition was no weapon at all.

At last the warriors were ready and Uriel proudly led the ragtag band of Space Marines away from the crumbling bunkers towards the mouth of the shadowed valley. Ardaric Vaanes marched alongside him and said, 'You realise you're probably going to get every one of us killed.'

'That is a distinct possibility,' admitted Uriel.

'Good, I just wanted to make sure you understood that.'

THE SKY DARKENED when they finally reached the end of the valley, an unnatural darkness of low, threatening smoke clouds. Briefly Uriel wondered if there were such a thing as weather on Medrengard, but dismissed the notion. What need had the Iron Warriors of weather? Nothing grew here or needed nourishment from the heavens.

Ahead was their ultimate destination, and now that Uriel could see it clearly, he understood Vaanes's assertion that to attempt to penetrate the defences of such a fastness was a suicide mission.

The fortress of Honsou was a nightmarish black fang against the sky, ebony towers of dark, bloodstained stone piercing the clouds of ash and crackling with dark lightning. The towers and arched halls of the fortress were surrounded by scarred bastions with walls hundreds of metres tall. The upper levels stood inviolate against the besieging army below, but the lower reaches were a cratered hell of flames and war. A haze of powerful energies surrounded the fortress as though it were not quite real. Uriel had to blink away stinging moisture from his eyes if he gazed too long at its lunatic architecture.

The world itself echoed to the snarl of mighty machines, and the rhythmic drumming of hammers sounded like the beat of some monstrous mechanical heart. Like a malignant fungus, the armies of Honsou's attackers were spread around the fortress in jagged lines of circumvallation, zigzagging approach saps snaking through the lower foothills of the fortress and ending in heavily fortified parallels, studded with enormous bunkers and redoubts. Blooms of explosions swathed the fortress and the plains before it flickered and flashed with the constant muzzle flares of monstrous cannons and howitzers.

A huge ramp was under construction from kilometres back that would allow heavy tanks and Titans access to the upper levels of the fortress and Uriel could see that the plain was teeming with millions of warriors. Sprawling camps and entire cities had been built to barrack these soldiers, and how they were going to successfully get through so many enemies to reach the fortress was beyond him.

'Having second thoughts?' asked Vaanes.

'No,' said Uriel.

'Sure?'

'I'm sure, Vaanes. We can do this. It will not be easy, but we can do it.'

Vaanes looked unconvinced, but pointed to where the plateau narrowed to become a near-vertical shear in the rock that carved a path down the flank of the mountain, 'That's the way down that leads to the plains below. It's steep, very steep, and if you fall you're dead.'

'How the hell are we meant to get down that?' breathed Leonid.

'Very carefully,' said Vaanes. 'So don't fall.'

'It's all right for you,' said Ellard, slinging his lasgun and making his way towards the path. 'If you fall you have a jump pack!'

'What? You want me to announce our presence here?' returned Vaanes.

Uriel followed the renegade and was seized by a dizzying lurch of vertigo as he saw the route they must take.

The plain was thousands of metres below them, steaming waterfalls of molten metal splashing along basalt channels towards lakes of glowing orange below.

'You need to go down facing the rock,' explained Vaanes, edging onto the path, barely half a metre across and gripping onto cracks in the rock for handholds. Gingerly, he edged out onto the path, leaning into the rockface and sliding sideways along and down.

Uriel went next, gripping the rockface and easing himself out onto the narrow path. He kept his weight forward, knowing that to overbalance even a little would send him plummeting thousands of metres to his death. Cold wind whipped at him and he felt his heartbeats hammering in his chest.

He edged out, following Vaanes's example and utilising the same hand-holds wherever he could. Within the space of a few hours, his muscles ached, his fingers burned with fatigue and they were barely half way down. His breath came in short, hard gasps and it was all he could do to not look down.

Hand over hand followed hand over hand and shuffling step to the side followed shuffling step to the side until they reached a point where the slope became shallower and it was possible to climb directly downwards for a short distance.

As Uriel climbed down to a narrow ledge, he flexed his fingers, the textured pads of his gauntlets torn and useless. His arms were leaden weights and he hoped he had the strength to make it to the bottom. With a little more room to manoeuvre on the ledge he carefully eased round and gazed at the terrifying scale of the siegeworks below.

What had brought this siege about anyway? Was it some internecine conflict or was there some other, darker purpose to the slaughter going on below? Did the attackers have some knowledge of the Heart of Blood or the daemonculaba?

He supposed it didn't matter why the followers of the Dark Powers made war upon one another; the more they killed each other, the fewer were left to attack the Emperor's realm.

A startled cry from above snapped him from his reverie and he looked up in time to see a hail of stones skitter down the slope, closely followed by Colonel Leonid, who screamed in terror as he tumbled downwards.

Uriel pressed himself flat against the rockface and leaned dangerously to one side to snatch at Leonid as he plummeted past.

His fingers closed on Leonid's uniform jacket and he gritted his teeth, gripping the rocks tightly as the colonel's weight threatened to pull them both from the ledge. Under normal circumstances, Uriel would have had no problem with catching Leonid like this, but off balance on the edge of a crumbling corbel of rock he felt himself being pulled from the cliff as his agonised fingers slipped from their transient handhold.

'I can't hold on!' he yelled. The ledge crumbled at the edge, dirt and pebbles spiralling downwards to the plains far below.

'Don't let go!' screamed Leonid. 'Please!'

Uriel fought to hold on, but knew that he could not. Should he just let go? Surely the presence of Leonid would not affect their mission one way or another. He was a normal man amongst Space Marines, what good could he possibly do?

But before he could release his grip he felt a hand take hold of his shoulder guard and pull him back. Above him, Sergeant Ellard had hold of his armour and strained to pull him back. Uriel was too heavy for him to hold, but Ellard's strength was prodigious and held Uriel long enough for him to shift his grip to a better handhold with firmer balance. Centimetre by centimetre, Uriel eased himself back onto the firmer ground of the ledge and was able to deposit Leonid back onto the slope.

The colonel was hyperventilating, his face pallid from shock and terror.

'You are safe now, Mikhail,' said Uriel, deliberately using the colonel's first name.

Leonid took great gulps of air, keeping his eyes averted from the drop behind him. His body shook, but he said, 'Thank you.'

Uriel did not reply, but looked up to see a breathless Sergeant Ellard clinging to the rockface by what looked like his fingernails. Uriel respectfully nodded at the man, who nodded back.

'Sir, are you able to go on?' asked Ellard.

'Aye…' wheezed Leonid. 'I'll be all right, just give me a minute or two.'

The three of them waited as long as they dared before moving onwards, Uriel in the lead with Ellard bringing up the rear. The colonel's steps were hesitant and unsure at first, but eventually his confidence returned and he made good time.

The journey down the mountains blurred into a painful series of vignettes: traverses across terrifyingly narrow spurs of rock and heart-pounding drops onto splintered ledges. Uriel continued down the slope of the mountain, pressing himself flat against the rock until he felt a tap on his shoulder and looked around to see that he had reached the base of the shear in the rock, that he was on a wide, screed slope of ash and iron debris. A churned mass of broken earth sloped gently to the darkened plains below.

The warrior band were spread around, breathless from their climb, and as Uriel looked up to see Leonid and Ellard completing the descent, his admiration for their endurance and courage soared as did his shame at the thought of even considering letting Leonid fall to his death.

Ardaric Vaanes approached him and said, 'You made it then.'

'You were right,' said Uriel. 'That was not easy.'

'No, but we're all here. Now what?'

That was a very good question. They were still many kilometres from the fortress, and Uriel could not even begin to guess how many enemy soldiers lay between them and its lower slopes. He scanned the ground below him, picking out scores of work parties and earth-moving machines hauling hundreds of tonnes of earth to build the ramp that led towards the fortress. A hissing lake of molten metal pooled at the base of the slope, bathing everything in a hellish orange glow and the rumble of engines and cursing voices drifted up from the construction sites.

'You know there's no way we can just walk through that many soldiers. Even if the vast majority are only human.'

'I know,' replied Uriel, eyeing the huge bulk-haulers. 'But perhaps we will not need to.'

THE HEAT RADIATING from the molten lake was stifling, filling the air with stinking fumes and making each breath hot and painful. Uriel edged around a tall mound of piled steel sheeting and waited for the latest work party to shuffle past, chained together at the neck by spiked collars and dressed in filthy rags. Servants of the Iron Warriors in all-enclosing vacuum suits shouted gurgled commands to the slaves, beating and whipping them as they pleased.

The rumble of heavy, tracked bulk-haulers and booming gunfire covered the Space Marines' approach down the lower slopes of the mountain, the darkness of the smoky clouds only helping them to approach the construction site unobserved. The huge machines were bigger than the largest super-heavy tank Uriel had ever seen, controlled via a cab mounted high on a massive, tracked engine unit that pulled a huge container on wheels with the diameter of three tall men.

Laden with tonnes of earth and rock, they plied their stately way up the ramp before depositing their cargo on its forward slope and then turning around and making their way back down again to refill. Millions of tonnes had already been poured out, yet the ramp was barely halfway towards the upper levels of the fortress. Uriel watched as a trio of bulk-haulers made their way towards the bottom of the ramp, and turned to Pasanius.

'They're coming,' he whispered through his armour's vox unit.

'I see them,' confirmed Vaanes.

Across the construction site from Uriel, he could see Vaanes climbing the side of the ramp, gaining height from where he could use his jump pack to better effect. Other Space Marines were poised ready for the word to attack.

The first of the bulk-haulers completed its wide turn and ground off into the smoke for more earth and Uriel bit his lip in nervous anticipation.

'Second one's almost round,' said Pasanius, and Uriel could sense the anticipation in his sergeant's voice.

'Aye,' he nodded. 'Ready?'

'As I'll ever be.'

'At times like this, I wish Idaeus was still here,' said Uriel.

Pasanius chuckled and said, 'This attack would be just his kind of thing.'

'What? Against impossible odds and with no recourse to the *Codex Astartes*?'

'Precisely,' said Pasanius, nodding in the direction of the ramp. 'Last one's down.'

Uriel returned his gaze to the hauler as it described a wide arc at the bottom of the ramp and the massive machine turned towards the fortress. When the cab had levelled out, but the huge trailer portion was still curved around, he rose to his feet and shouted, 'Go! Go!' over the vox and ran out into the open.

Scattered groups of slaves looked up at them as they ran for the enormous machine, but otherwise paid them no mind. Up close, the bulk-hauler was even larger than it had first appeared, fully nine metres tall and constructed of dented sheets of thick iron and bronze girders. Its wheels were solid and tore deep furrows in the ground as it rumbled onwards. Fortunately, it was still moving slowly enough to catch and Uriel leapt for the iron ladder that led to the cab above.

Space Marines jogged alongside the bulk-hauler and clambered onto the running boards, beginning to climb the craggy sides of the trailer. Uriel swiftly ascended the ladder towards the platform bolted to the side of the driver's cabin, hearing a heavy thump of something landing on the cab's roof. Metal tore and he heard screams.

He continued climbing, seeing the door above him burst open and a creature in a vacuum suit and leather harness emerge from the interior of the cab. Harsh, static trills of fear emitted from a copper faceplate as it saw Uriel, but he didn't give it time to react, reaching up and gripping its harness.

It tried to draw a pistol, but Uriel pulled hard and sent it spinning from the driver's cab to the ground below. Kyama Shae, the Crimson Fists Space Marine riding the running boards, shot the mutant in the head and the groups of slaves clustered around this part of the ramp cheered as it died.

Uriel scrambled up the ladder and swung into the driver's cabin, ready to fight, but saw that there would be no need. Another two creatures, clad in the same black vacuum suits as the one Uriel had thrown to the ground, lay dead in their bucket seats, torn open from neck to groin by Ardaric Vaanes's lightning claws.

The renegade sat awkwardly before a control panel, the bulk of his jump pack almost filling the cabin. He struggled with an array of levers and a giant wheel beneath a great rent in the steel roof, and said, 'Do you know how to drive this thing?'

'No,' said Uriel. 'But how hard can it be?'

'Well, we're about to find out,' said Vaanes.

Uriel wiped a hand across the blood-smeared windscreen and peered through at the rear ends of the two bulk-haulers in front of them.

'Just keep it straight, and try to stay with the two ahead for as long as you can.'

Vaanes nodded, too intent on working out the controls to the bulk-hauler to reply. Uriel left him to it and swung out onto the platform on the side of the cab.

The Space Marines of the warrior band were making their way along the running boards to the ladders at the sides and rear of the bulk-hauler, climbing up towards concealment within the empty trailer.

Satisfied they could actually get close without significant risk of discovery, Uriel clambered back into the driver's cab and dragged out the dead bodies of the mutant drivers. He hurled them from the cab, those slaves chained nearest to where the bodies fell tearing them apart with wanton abandon.

'It's not actually that difficult,' said Vaanes as Uriel closed the door behind him.

'No?'

'No, a Rhino's harder to control than this. It's just a little bigger.'

'Just a little,' agreed Uriel.

He left Vaanes to wrestle with the controls and stared through the dirty windscreen at the siegeworks beyond, the scale of the battle taking his breath away.

They passed great artillery pits, enormous guns, bigger by many times than the heaviest artillery pieces of the Imperial Guard, hurling tank-sized shells towards the fortress. Tall towers hung with bodies and spiked bunkers were spread throughout the camp and a sprawling infrastructure had arisen to support the massive effort of taking Honsou's fortress. Dark wonders and monstrous sights greeted them at every turn, the myriad horrors of a daemon world at war.

The bulk-haulers drove along corpse-hung roads, skull-paved plazas where naked madmen capered around tall idols hung with entrails and pillars of iron that crackled with powerful energy. They watched mutants hurl crippled slaves into bubbling pools of molten metal, laughing as they did so, and Uriel turned away. He could not save them all, so he would save none of them. It scarred his soul to let such atrocities go unpunished, but he was coming to believe that Vaanes was right – better to let them die than to be killed trying and failing to save them.

As the bulk-hauler swallowed up the distance between the outskirts of the camp and the siege lines, they drove over great bridges of iron that crossed deep trenches, through kilometres of razorwire and around deep pits containing screaming mechanical monsters. Shadows of great, clawed limbs swayed in the firelight and Uriel felt a shiver of dread at the thought of even laying eyes on such daemon engines.

The heat in the cab was oppressive, but he didn't dare open the door for fear of discovery. So far they had been able to continue following the bulk-haulers ahead of them, but as soon as the lead hauler turned away from the fortress, it would only be a matter of time before their ruse was discovered.

The bulk-haulers rolled onwards through the Iron Warriors' camp, driving through great shanty towns of red-garbed soldiers and blazing drumfires. Soldiers chanted in praise of their masters and fired off shots into the air as they danced around the flames.

'These are the warriors of Lord Berossus,' said Vaanes, pointing to a gold and black standard raised high at the edge of the camp.

'And who is he? A rival of Honsou's?'

'So it would seem. He is the leader of a grand company of the Iron Warriors, a vassal of Lord Toramino, one of their most powerful warlords.'

'How do you know all this?' asked Uriel.

'We have sometimes taken prisoners,' replied Vaanes, 'and did not shirk from their interrogation. If Berossus is here, then so too is Toramino. Whatever the reason they lay siege to Honsou's fortress, it must be powerful indeed.'

'Perhaps they know what Honsou brought back from Hydra Cordatus and desire a share in his spoils of victory.'

'Gene-seed? Yes, that would probably do it.'

'We can't let that happen.'

Vaanes laughed. 'We are but thirty warriors and you would have us topple this world.'

'Why not?' said Uriel. 'We are Space Marines of the Emperor. There is nothing we cannot do.'

'I don't know why, since you are probably going to get me killed, but I like you, Uriel Ventris. You have an absurd sense for attempting the impossible that appeals to me.'

Uriel returned his gaze to the siegeworks outside, pleased at the compliment, as the lead truck reached a wide crossroads and began making a wide turn towards a huge spoil heap.

'Damn it, they're turning,' cursed Vaanes as he saw the same thing.

'We are too far away to make it on foot,' said Uriel. 'There are whole regiments ahead of us.'

'What do you think?'

'Push it!' said Uriel. 'Head straight for the fortress and we will kill anyone that gets in our way. We'll drive over them or shoot them, just get us as close to that fortress as you can.'

'I'll try!' shouted Vaanes, pushing the hauler into high gear and slamming his foot to the floor. 'We won't get far before we run into trouble, so get ready to give me some covering fire.'

Uriel nodded and left the driver's cab, calling to the other Space Marines in their band and alerting them to their plight. Acknowledgements flickered on his visor and Uriel readied his sword and bolter as the bulk-hauler rumbled towards the crossroads. The main route travelled by the bulk-haulers was clearly visible, curving off to the left, but instead of slowing to take the turn, their transport increased speed and roared straight ahead, bucking madly on surfaces not designed for such a heavy vehicle.

Screams and shouts of alarm rose in their wake as tents, stores and prefabricated huts were flattened beneath their tracks. Red-liveried soldiers, slaves and mutants scattered before them, those not quick enough crushed to death by their wild charge.

Shots ricocheted from the sides of the bulk-hauler, but they were sporadic, hastily aimed and Uriel knew that they need not be concerned about such small-arms fire. It would be when word was passed on ahead that they would need to worry.

Sure enough, he could see fire teams ahead of them, swinging round static weapon platforms that would tear their vehicle to shreds.

'Warriors, engage!' he shouted over the vox.

Space Marines who had been waiting for his command rose from behind the shelter of the trailer's sides and opened fire, bolter shells raking the gunners of the weapon teams and ripping their guns to pieces. The bulk-hauler crashed into the trench lines, ploughing a huge furrow in its wake as it slowed going across the softer ground.

Yelling soldiers leapt into their trenches, but there was no refuge to be found there, as the massive weight of the hauler collapsed their trenches and buried scores of men beneath tonnes of earth and rubble. Uriel watched without compassion, relishing the destruction they were causing. He fired his weapon into the soldiers, yelling encouragement to the other Space Marines of their warrior band as they killed the enemy.

He looked up in time to see a brilliant flash of light and ducked as a huge explosion hammered the ground beside them. The bulk-hauler swayed, and for a moment Uriel felt sure it would tip over.

But the Emperor was with them and the hauler righted itself, slamming back to the ground with teeth-loosening force. Uriel pulled himself upright and saw several artillery pieces aiming for them with their gun barrels lowered. Another explosion burst next to them, showering the hauler with debris and earth and smoke. The gunners were finding their range, heedless of however many of their own men they killed to get it, and Uriel knew that they had seconds at best before one of the guns got lucky and blew them to atoms.

'Everybody off!' he shouted. 'Now!'

After two such close calls, none of the Space Marines needed any encouragement. They clambered over the sides of the bulk-hauler and leapt from the vehicle. Uriel saw Pasanius hit the ground and roll, and hauled open the driver's cab.

'Vaanes! Come on, let's go!' he shouted over the din of gunfire and explosions.

'Go!' he shouted. 'I'm right behind you!'

Uriel nodded and vaulted from the platform outside the cab. He hit the ground hard and rolled, smashing a dozen soldiers aside as he landed. In a heartbeat he was on his feet, slashing with his sword and running for the mountain. Shots kicked up dust around him and ricocheted from his armour as he ran.

He saw Ardaric Vaanes leap from the driver's cab as a shell from one of the guns finally struck the bulk-hauler. The engine section vanished in a sheet of flame and the wreckage ploughed onwards for another few seconds before slamming through a razorwire fence and exploding with the force of a cluster of demolition charges. Secondary explosions quickly followed as fuel bladders and siege shells cooked off in the huge blast. Uriel realised Vaanes must have used those last few seconds to guide the hauler towards a valuable target before escaping the cab.

The earth shook as shells arced through the air and burning sheets of fuel sprayed in all directions. Enemy soldiers ducked and ran for cover in the maelstrom of exploding shells and blazing plumes of scorching fires, but Uriel and the Space Marines kept running.

Ahead, he saw the lower reaches of the mountain, where Berossus's engineers had constructed vast funicular rails onto the rock that climbed towards the higher peaks of the mountains. A giant, angled car, bounded by iron railings, ascended the rails, bearing hundreds of the Iron Warriors' soldiers towards the battle high above.

Thousands of soldiers clustered at the base of the mountain, awaiting their turn to travel up the mountainside and join the assault. The sounds of explosions and gunfire were nothing new to them and they had not yet noticed the charging Space Marines behind them. Uriel saw Pasanius and Vaanes up ahead and called to them over the vox.

'The platform on the right!' he called. 'There's an empty car just coming down. We need to take it!'

'I see it,' replied Vaanes.

The Space Marines of the warrior band struck the milling soldiers like a freight train, cutting down scores in the first seconds of their attack. Grimly they forced their way onward, hacking, cutting and slaying their way forward in an orgy of bloodshed.

Caught unawares by the killers in their midst, the soldiers fought to get out of their way and Uriel soon found himself with a clear run to the platform. Vaanes was there before him and had already killed them a path up to the approaching funicular car.

Uriel took the steps up to the platform two at a time, glancing over his shoulder to see the rest of their warriors right behind him, keeping low to avoid the worst of the gunfire directed at them. The car docked at the platform with a huge, ringing clang and barely had it done so before the Space Marines swarmed over it.

The car was empty save for a grey-fleshed servitor creature, fused with the mechanism of its controls, whose only function appeared to be pulling the levers that sent it up or down the mountain. Uriel and Pasanius, together with Kyama Shae, moved to the edge of the platform and fired into the approaching enemy soldiers whose courage now began to return.

'Ventris!' shouted Vaanes. 'Come on, the car's leaving!'

Uriel slung his bolter and slapped the shoulder guards of his two companions before running for the funicular car. Grinding cogs and wheezing engines lifted it from the platform, but it was slow to get moving and Uriel clambered aboard before it had climbed more than a metre. He turned to help Pasanius, gripping his silver arm and hauling him up, noticing with surprise that it was utterly pristine, without so much as a scratch on it. How could that be, when his own gauntlets were torn and battered to the point of uselessness?

Pasanius moved past him to take up a firing position at the railings and Uriel turned to help Kyama Shae aboard the moving car.

Small-arms fire spanged from the sides of the car and the railings, but as it rapidly picked up speed they were soon beyond the range of the soldiers' rifles.

Uriel glanced over at Pasanius before transferring his gaze to the mountain above. Black, smoky clouds wreathed the higher slopes, lightning and explosions flaring in the darkness from the battle above.

'Well, we're here,' said a breathless Vaanes.

Uriel turned to watch the swiftly diminishing ground as they rose into the clouds and darkness swallowed them.

'Getting here was the easy part,' said Uriel. 'Now we have to storm the fortress.'

TEN

'It would seem your attempt to antagonise Lord Berossus by shelling his pavilion was successful,' said Obax Zakayo needlessly, as another flurry of shells impacted against the walls. Plumes of flame and smoke soared skyward and Honsou laughed as he watched bodies rain down amid the rubble. Dust enveloped them, chunks of debris clattering down on the cobbled ramparts, and Honsou coughed as he swallowed a mouthful of ash. It was perhaps foolish to be this close to the front lines, but he was not so far removed from the sharp end of battle that he did not relish the cannon's roar in his ear.

'Yes, it does, doesn't it? He's so predictable it almost takes the fun out of crushing him.'

'But, my lord, he is within days of breaching the inner walls of Khalan-Ghol,' said Onyx, standing slightly behind Honsou. 'How can this be to our advantage?'

'Because he is dancing to my tune, Onyx, not his own. Get an enemy to react to your designs and he is as good as lost. I almost have him exactly where I want him. But Toramino… Toramino is not so easy. He is the one we need to be wary of. I don't know what he is doing.'

'Our scryers have seen nothing of note regarding Toramino,' said Obax Zakayo. 'It seems he waits, simply husbanding his warriors while Berossus grinds his men to dust against our walls.'

'I know, and that's what worries me,' snapped Honsou, waving his arms at the carnage taking place on the walls below him. 'Toramino is too clever to simply hurl his men at us like this. He knows that Berossus has no other stratagems and is waiting for his moment to strike. We must anticipate that and pre-empt him. Or else we are lost.'

Onyx leaned over the parapet and cast his gleaming silver eyes to either side of where he, Honsou and Obax Zakayo stood. Iron Warriors were ready to defend the ramparts should the bastions below fall, which if the projected strength of the assault below was correct, was entirely likely.

'We are too close to the battle,' he said.

Honsou shook his head. 'No, I need to be here.'

'I can protect you from an assassin's blade or a killer's bullet,' said Onyx, 'but I cannot say the same for an artillery shell. An eternity of torment awaits my essence should I allow you to die while under my protection.'

'Why should I care about your eternal torment?'

'You wouldn't, you'd be dead.'

Honsou considered this for a second and said, 'You may have a point there, Onyx.'

The daemonic symbiote nodded respectfully as more screaming shells exploded against the walls below. Honsou turned, content that the bastion here was as secure as he could want. The warriors he had chosen to accompany him into the camp of Berossus commanded this section of the walls, and there were no better warriors in his grand company.

He had taken one step when a flash of dark prescience made him look up and he yelled, 'Down!'

Whether it was by sheer luck or great artifice, Honsou would never know, but a salvo of shells from the guns below impacted on the edge of the ramparts upon which he and his warriors stood, shearing the rock clean from its supports in a cataclysmic hammerblow. Honsou picked himself up and desperately scrambled for the safety of the esplanade behind the ramparts, but it was already too late.

With a grinding crack of splintered stone, he and hundreds of his finest warriors were swept down the mountainside in a raining avalanche of rubble and blocks of sundered stone.

EMERGING FROM THE smoke was like being born into hell, thought Uriel. At first he had been frustrated not being able to see their ultimate destination, but upon passing through the dark clouds of the mountain and seeing it up close for the first time, he soon wished for the sight of it to be snatched away from him.

Stretching up to pierce the dead sky, the fortress of Honsou was a madman's conceit made real, stone laid upon stone so that each angle was subtly *wrong* and violated the senses on a deep, instinctual level. Its dark veined walls reared up in defiance of the laws of perspective, looming and huge with pierced garrets leaning from the wallhead and spiralling, lightning-sheathed spires. Blades and spikes stabbed from its glistening fabric, and black rain, like the very lifeblood of the fortress, spilled from where artillery shells had struck. Fast-flowing rivers of molten metal poured from glowing culverts and ran down the mountainside like streams of lava from an erupting volcano.

Guns fired from daemon-visaged portals and burning, daemonic blood spilled from vast iron cauldrons onto the screaming soldiers below. Flames danced on the ramparts and in the mass of struggling soldiers. Death and destruction stalked the battlefield this day, and they hunted well.

Tens of thousands of soldiers thronged the rubble-strewn reaches of the fortress, fighting their way up a ruined screed slope that had once been a bastion. Explosions tossed corpses through the air as buried mines swept hundreds to their deaths and the monstrous forms of a pair of Titans struggled in the rubble, crushing men and machines beneath their great footsteps as they fought amid the flames.

Uriel and the Space Marines watched the terrifying battle rage above them, the car grinding as it approached the upper platform where it would deposit them and begin the journey back down the mountain.

'Emperor protect us,' breathed Vaanes. 'It's like nothing I've ever seen before.'

'I know…' agreed Uriel, drawing his sword as the car clanged home against the platform and the bronze gate in the railings squealed open.

'How can we hope to survive this?'

Uriel turned to Vaanes and said, 'Remember what I told you: death and honour. If one brings the other then it is a good death.'

'No…' hissed Vaanes. 'No death is a good one. Not like this.'

None of the Space Marines moved, too in awe at the terrible and magnificent spectacle of war on a scale few had ever experienced. Uriel realised he had to get them moving before the vastness of this battle and their impulse for survival overcame the newly-rekindled sense of honour and duty he had instilled in them.

He was saved when Pasanius shouted, 'Come on, get moving! Everybody off!'

Ingrained reflexes took over and the Space Marines swiftly debarked from the funicular car, chivvied all the way by a bellowing Pasanius. Only Uriel and Ardaric Vaanes remained on board.

'Come on,' said Uriel. 'We have work to do.'

Vaanes said nothing, but nodded and followed Uriel from the car, climbing up past the platform and unsheathing the crackling claws from his gauntlet.

'What are you doing?' called Uriel.

'Funicular cars work on the principle of counterbalancing one another,' explained Vaanes, slicing his claws clean through the thick cables that held the car.

The platform groaned and the cable snapped with a metallic twang, whipping around and sending the car plummeting back downhill through the smoke. The sound of screeching metal and showers of fat orange sparks followed it down.

'No one will be coming up here in a while,' said Vaanes, climbing back to join Uriel.

'Clever,' said Uriel.

The two Space Marines jogged over to where the rest of the warrior band had sequestered themselves, hidden in a fold in the rock below an overhanging bastion where they could observe the battle in relative safety. Missiles and shells crisscrossed the air, and the noise of explosions and gunfire was deafening. The mountain trembled to the footsteps of the Titans, both of which lurched heedlessly through the battle as they grappled and struck at one another. Snarling daemon heads slammed together and massive blades tore at each other's armour as whipping, barbed tails brought down whole swathes of the wall.

'Now what?' shouted Pasanius, barely audible over the cacophony.

'Now we have to get in!' said Uriel.

'You mean we join the assault?' asked Vaanes. 'Impossible!'

'What choice do we have?' yelled Uriel.

'We can get the hell off this mountain! I told you I'd help you get in, Ventris, but I also told you I wasn't going to get killed for your death oath!'

'Damn it, Vaanes, we're here now! We have to keep going!'

Vaanes looked set to reply when a salvo of shells streaked overhead and struck the lip of the overhanging bastion directly above them. Dust and debris showered them, rocks tumbling down the slopes as it split from the mountain with a splintering crack.

'Look out!' shouted Uriel as the bastion crumbled and toppled, falling towards them in an avalanche of rubble and blocks of sundered stone.

HONSOU FELT ROCKS pummelling him as he fell, battering him and threatening to crush him utterly. He tumbled end over end, his senses whirling in a kaleidoscopic flurry of noise and light. The breath was driven from him as he landed, and he rolled aside as huge, tank-sized blocks of rubble smashed down around him. Choking clouds of black dust and smoke billowed, and though he felt painfully battered by the fall, he didn't feel any broken bones or ruptured organs.

'Onyx!' he yelled hoarsely. 'Zakayo!'

'Here!' coughed Zakayo. 'I am alive!'

'As am I,' said Onyx, 'but I require assistance.'

Honsou struggled over to where his champion lay almost completely buried beneath a pile of jagged lumps of rockcrete with twisted iron bars protruding from them. Onyx's torso and lower body were trapped beneath a volume of rubble that would have crushed even a power-armoured warrior flat, but immaterial energies had saturated the daemonic symbiote's flesh and it was proof against such things.

Honsou gripped the debris and strained against its massive weight, but it was too great even for one as enhanced as he. Obax Zakayo joined him, the hissing mechanical arms sprouting from the armature of his back to grip the reinforcement bars.

Iron Warriors began picking themselves up from the rubble, those who hadn't been crushed beneath falling masonry or otherwise killed in the bastion's collapse lending their strength to freeing Onyx.

Honsou moved out of the way and looked around him as glowing after-images of the battle flashed on his visor. He shook his head to clear it and get a better idea of where their fall from the fortress had brought them.

More rubble had been dislodged from above by the thunderous battle of the nearby Titans and Honsou saw that they would have little difficulty in getting back to the fortress. The lucky artillery strike had collapsed a good portion of the wall beneath the bastion that now formed a ready-made slope that led straight to the walls.

That was if they survived to get back to the fortress, he thought, watching as blurry shapes approached through the swirling clouds of dust and smoke.

URIEL TORE OFF his helmet, its visor cracked and useless; the pressure seals that clamped it to his gorget smashed and irreparable. He muttered a prayer of unction for the helmet's spirit and placed it on the ground. Without his auto-senses, he could only see hazy outlines through the smoke and debris of the bastion's fall, but blinking away motes of dust from his eyes, he saw that the Emperor had blessed them once more.

'There!' he shouted, pointing to the great gash torn in the side of the fortress where the bastion had fallen. A steep but practicable slope of rubble and rebar-laced rockcrete led upwards towards the ramparts. Uriel knew they would never get a better chance than this to penetrate the fortress.

Leading the way, he picked his way upwards, seeing indistinct, power-armoured forms also clambering to their feet. At first he assumed that these were the Space Marines of the warrior band, but as the dust began to settle, he saw they were not.

They were Iron Warriors.

HONSOU WATCHED A Space Marine emerge from the smoke, his blue armour dust covered and battered. His heart lurched as the warrior snarled and drew a shimmering blade. One of the False Emperor's warriors? Here? His surprise almost cost him his life as the blade sang for his neck and he was barely able to parry it with his axe, dodging away from the return stroke of the Space Marine's blade.

His axe screamed as its warrior soul roared to life and Honsou saw that the attacking warrior's blue armour was devoid of all insignia or markings. A renegade? A mercenary?

Was this Toramino's doing? Rallying the renegade scum that skulked in the mountains to his cause? But he had no more time to wonder at the warrior's origins as his blade stabbed for him once more.

'Iron Warriors!' he bellowed. 'With me!'

URIEL SLASHED AT the Iron Warrior again, but his every stroke was parried by a huge war-axe with a glossy, black-toothed blade. His foe shouted to his warriors and more shapes emerged from the dust, swords and axes raised and bolters piercing the smoke with barking muzzle flashes.

'Emperor guide my blade!' he shouted as he attacked again.

'He has no power here,' retorted the Iron Warrior as he spun his axe and attacked.

Uriel sidestepped and brought his sword around in a beheading stroke, but his opponent was not there, rolling beneath the blow and swinging his axe for his back. Uriel hurled himself flat, the screaming axe blade slashing centimetres from his armour. He rolled aside as the axe hammered down, the earth shaking in fury at its impact.

Uriel kicked out, driving the Iron Warrior to his knees and slicing his sword in a wide arc towards his head. The tip of his blade caught the Iron Warrior's helm and sent him tumbling down the slope. He scrambled to his feet as more Space Marines joined the fray and the vast shadow of the battling Titans engulfed them. The fury of the devil machines' combat dwarfed this one, but for all that, it was equally brutal and merciless. Vicious, short-range firefights and melees broke out, bolters roaring and grunts of pain and anger sounding as explosive shells cracked open armour and blades tore at flesh. He drew back his sword to gut an Iron Warrior, but a lashing coil of energy snaked out and ensnared his arm.

Pain roared up his arm and it was all he could do to keep hold of his sword as flaring bursts of agony coursed along the length of the energy coil. Uriel dropped to his knees as a giant, wide shouldered Iron Warrior drew near, massive mechanised arms snapping from his shoulders and the snaking whip of energy attached to yet another of his hunched claws.

'You dare attack the master of Khalan-Ghol! You will die!' roared the warrior, his voice ugly and crackling. A wash of flame shot through the combat and Uriel caught the sickening stench of cooked meat. Once again the earth heaved and a gargantuan foot slammed down against the mountainside not three metres from Uriel, leaving a deep crater in its wake.

He saw the massive Titans towering above them as he fought against the crippling pain lashing in waves from the energy whip. While the whip-armed claw held him immobile with agony, the lumbering Iron Warrior's free hands unsheathed a crude, brutal, but no doubt effective chainsaw-bladed axe.

'Obax Zakayo!' screamed a voice, but Uriel could not see who shouted through the pain screeching around his nervous system. Gunshots burst against the Iron Warrior's armour and he lashed out with his axe.

'You?' laughed the Iron Warrior. 'You were under my blade once, slave, and escaped. You will not do so again.'

For the briefest second, his attention shifted from Uriel and it was all the distraction he needed. He swept up his sword, hacking through the energy whip, and the pain vanished, leaving him drained, but free of its incapacitating agony. Uriel pushed himself to his feet, seeing Colonel Leonid and Sergeant Ellard facing off against the Iron Warrior.

Lasbolts hammered his bulky body, but his debased power armour could withstand such trifles and he roared, swinging his axe for Leonid's midriff. The colonel jumped back, stumbling on loose rubble, and fell to the ground. Obax Zakayo closed for the kill, but Ellard leapt upon the Iron Warrior, pummelling his fists against his head.

Ellard was a big man, but next to the Iron Warrior he was a child, and Obax Zakayo ripped him from his back and hurled him away. Uriel stepped in and hammered his sword across the Iron Warrior's shoulders. The blade crackled as it hacked though the ceramite plates of his armour, but slid free before connecting with flesh.

Obax Zakayo swung his axe in a vicious arc at Uriel's groin, but the blow never landed as the ground shook and cracked, molten metal spewing up as the crashing footsteps of the battling Titans finally split the mountain. White hot metal hissed and spat as it spilled out onto the rocks, rendering them down to slag in seconds. Uriel scrambled away from the widening crack in the ground, sheathing his sword as he saw that there was no way his opponent could reach him across the gulf of liquid metal.

Roiling clouds of bitter smoke gusted from the river of molten metal and Uriel scrambled away from its intolerable heat, Leonid and Ellard clambering over the rocks to join him.

'This is Uriel Ventris!' he shouted, hoping that the vox-bead attached to his larynx was still functioning. 'If anyone can still hear me, make for the breach above us now!'

Bolters roared behind him and the crash of explosions almost drowned his order, but as he climbed through the blinding clouds of steam and smoke, he could see the shadowy forms of the warrior band climbing towards him.

The breach was above them, barely thirty metres away, the rubble-strewn sides of the fortress a beacon that called him onwards.

They had done it. They had found a way in.

BLOOD BLINDED HIM and a grating static filled his senses. Honsou removed his helmet, tossing it aside in anger, and wiped blood from his eyes. Banks of hot steam sent runnels of moisture down his face and he pushed himself upright as the thunder of battle returned to him with all its fury.

'What in the name of the Dark Gods is happening?' he shouted to no one in particular.

'My lord!' returned Obax Zakayo, picking his way carefully through the rocks. Moisture and blood ran from his armour, his energy whip crackling with sparks where it had been severed. 'The–'

'Renegades!' roared Honsou. 'Is this what Toramino has been reduced to?'

'Aye, renegades,' agreed Obax Zakayo. 'Renegades and runaway slaves, they–'

'I was wrong to fear him, Obax Zakayo,' said Honsou, a measure of calm returning to him. 'They are all dead?'

'No, my lord. The mountain sundered and we were separated.'

Honsou looked up sharply. 'Then where are they?'

'That is what I am trying to tell you. They broke past us and made for the breach!'

'Damn!' cursed Honsou. 'Then why in the name of Chaos are you still standing here?'

'My lord, a river of molten metal separates us. For now, there is no way across.'

'For you, perhaps,' sneered Honsou, striding through the battle to where he had left his trapped champion. 'Onyx!'

Iron Warriors still struggled with the debris that buried the symbiote, but seeing their master's fury and urgency, redoubled their efforts. Within minutes, they had shifted enough of the rubble to allow Onyx to pull himself free of the debris. Lithe, supple and showing no signs of having been almost crushed to death, Onyx made his way gracefully towards Honsou. His black armour bore not a single scratch and Honsou saw Onyx's daemonic powers rippling just below the surface of his crawling, silver-etched skin. His eyes blazed with deadlights as Honsou pointed to the breach.

'Find the renegades,' he ordered Onyx. 'Find them and bring them to me.'

The daemon creature nodded and set off up the slopes of the mountain.

THE SHATTERED REMNANTS of this part of the ramparts were eerily deserted, the noise of battle muted from here, as Uriel pulled himself over the tattered lip of stone with the aid of the orange-steel rebars. He rolled to his feet, alert for danger, but finding none. The brooding presence of the fortress still towered above him, but he kept his eyes averted from its monstrous geometries for now, turning and helping the remainder of their force onto the battlements.

The walls swept around the mountain, curving and angled, seemingly at random, hordes of human soldiers and mutants firing from the embattled ramparts into the masses of attackers below. Thousands of warriors fought in the breach, looking from here like some great serpent that heaved and convulsed as it pushed its way, metre by metre, up the rubble slopes.

Pasanius and Vaanes climbed up, followed by Leonid and Ellard and the rest of the warrior band. Uriel could scarce believe it. They were within the walls of the fortress!

'Throne of Terra,' breathed Pasanius. 'That was bloody work!'

'It's not over yet,' cautioned Uriel, turning and more fully surveying their surroundings. A row of great archways led deeper into the fortress, each one as tall as a battle Titan and ringed with grotesque carvings that squirmed within the rock, as though the unquiet matter of the blocks was reshaping itself as they watched.

'Which way?' asked Vaanes as the last of the Space Marines climbed to the ramparts.

'I don't know,' admitted Uriel. 'There is nothing to choose between them.'

'Then we've nothing to lose, whichever one we take,' pointed out Vaanes, heading towards the middle archway.

'I suppose,' said Uriel, though a gut feeling told him that there *was* something different about this archway. He could not put his finger on what, but since he had no better idea of which one to take, he set off after Vaanes. The Space Marines followed him, bolters levelled in cautious apprehension.

Vaanes waited for him at the entrance to the archway, and as Uriel passed beneath its stygian immensity, he sketched the sign of the aquila across his chest, hearing a distant pounding, like the slow heartbeat of a sleeping monster.

'We are in the belly of the beast once more, Uriel,' said Pasanius, the guttering blue tip of his flamer throwing their faces into stark relief and causing the carvings on the inner faces of the archway to leer and dance across the walls.

'I know,' nodded Uriel, praying that the white cloak he had put over his soul would protect it from the vile things they were sure to see in the heart of the Enemy's lair.

ONYX GHOSTED OVER the lip of the ruined bastion, his bronze claws sliding slowly from his flesh. His silver eyes scanned the battlements for any sign of the renegades, but they were nowhere to be seen. Moving like a shadow, Onyx tasted the air, the crawling silver veins beneath his skin burning brighter as he channelled the daemonic energy within him into tracking the intruders.

His vision shifted into realms of sight beyond the ken of mortal men, where that which had already come to pass could be seen by listening to the echoes in the air. He watched as shadowy forms climbed over the ramparts, in much the same way as he had just done: many warriors, led by one whose soul burned brightly with purpose and another whose soul was withered and dead.

As though formed from swirling particles of smoke, their forms were ethereal and insubstantial, but Onyx could see them as clearly as though he had been here to watch them arrive. They had passed this way but minutes ago, their phantasmal echoes walking from the battlements and heading in the direction of the monstrous archways carved into the mountainside.

Onyx watched as the ghostly figures were swallowed up by the whispering darkness of the archways and sheathed his claws. He would need to take another route into the fortress to hunt the intruders, for if Khalan-Ghol had lured them into the bedlam portals, there was a good chance they were already dead.

ʊ
ELEVEN

THE JOURNEY THROUGH the darkened archway was one that Uriel knew he would never forget. The sensation of being spied upon by every square centimetre of wall was intolerable and he was sure he could hear a susurration of whispered voices, just on the threshold of hearing. Their words, if such they were, were unintelligible, but on some primal level, Uriel knew that they whispered of vile, terrible things.

...dishonour, disgrace and failure...

This at least he felt he could bear, having already seen the most terrible things imaginable in the presence of the Nightbringer, but still...

The twilit darkness seemed to go on forever and Uriel soon lost track of how long they had been travelling along the damnable tunnel.

...it doesn't ever stop, it goes on and on...

'Imperator! Does this ever end?' growled Vaanes as they delved further and further into the never-ending darkness.

'I know,' said Uriel. 'I get the feeling that we do not travel normal paths here. We can trust nothing, not even the evidence of our own senses.'

'Then how will we find what we're looking for?'

...you won't...

'We will have to trust that the Emperor will show us the way,' said Uriel, irritated by Vaanes's constant questions.

Vaanes shook his head in exasperation. 'I knew I should have never come on this mission. It was doomed from the start.'

...yes, doomed, only death awaits...

'Then why did you come?' snapped Uriel, rounding on the former Raven Guard, his temper fraying.

...he hates you and will betray you...

'Damned if I can remember,' snarled Vaanes, his face centimetres from Uriel's. 'Perhaps I thought you had more of an idea about how you planned to get in here and find what we came for!'

...he doesn't, he will see you dead soon...

'Damn you, Vaanes. Why must you always undermine me?' said Uriel, hearing soft, malicious laughter and the whispers of the walls growing louder in his ears. 'Every step of this journey you have done nothing but tell us that we are on a fool's errand. That may be so, but we are Space Marines trapped on a daemon world and it is our sacred task to fight the enemies of mankind wherever they may be.'

...not any more. Give in, you are worthless...

'Don't you understand? We are not Space Marines,' shouted Vaanes, the reflected blue light of the tunnel glittering in his eyes. 'Not any more. We are all outcasts, shunned and banished from our Chapters. We owe neither them nor the Emperor anything any more. And I, for one, am getting sick of hearing your sanctimonious voice telling me what I ought to be doing.'

...yes, kill him, what is he to you anyway...?

Uriel shook his head as Vaanes slapped a gauntleted hand on his shoulder guards and said, 'Where is your Chapter badge, Ventris? I don't see it, does anyone else?'

'What happened to you, Vaanes?' asked Uriel, angrily shrugging off the hands on his shoulders and gripping the hilt of his sword. 'How did you become so damaged?'

...because he has no honour, he deserves to die...!

'Because I let myself get put in situations like this once too often,' hissed Vaanes. 'And I swore I would not blindly follow another to my death. Damn me, but I let myself get fooled again.'

Uriel drew his sword, his anger boiling over when he heard the soft susurration of the whispering walls once more and the words and feelings behind them wormed their way into his brain.

...more, say more, give vent to all your secret doubts and fears and frustrations...

The voices insinuated themselves within his head and lodged upon his tongue, just *aching* to be said for the sake of malice and spite. Uriel clamped his hands to his ears as a measure of understanding forced its way past the fog of bitterness that filled his mind.

The voices clouded his head, louder now that their subterfuge was unmasked. Uriel stumbled and reached out to steady himself, his hand brushing against the wall, its undulating substance wet and fluid. He dropped to his knees and shouted, 'Get out of my head!'

...no, worthless you, meaningless you, insignificant you, unremembered you...

'Uriel? Are you all right? What's going on?' shouted Pasanius, running over to where his captain knelt. Vaanes backed away from Uriel, shaking his head and clutching his temples in pain.

'What the hell is going on?' he yelled as the roar of voices, thousands of them, swelled in volume and filled the tunnel.

...kill, it's such a friendly word... it's the only way...

'Don't listen to them!' shouted Uriel. 'Shut them out!'

The other Space Marines now felt the full power of the lunatic voices, dropping their weapons as the urge to turn them upon themselves grew unbearable. A shot rang out and one of their warrior band, a Doom Eagle, toppled forwards, his skull little more than a charred blood basin, spilling brain and skull fragments as he fell.

Uriel threw away his gun as he felt the muscles of his arm twitch in response to the voices, fighting their urgings

...it is hopeless, no point in fighting, nothing can stand against the majesty of Chaos...

He squeezed his eyes shut, repeating the Litanies of Hate as preached by Chaplain Clausel from his umbersap pulpit; catechisms of loathing and the Rites of Detestation he had been taught when in the service of the Ordo Xenos.

...it is pointless to resist the inevitable. Join us! Give in and kill yourself...

Uriel fought the urge to curl up and give in, remembering past glories where victory *had* meant something concrete, where the defeat of terrible foes had achieved something meaningful. He pictured the great victory on Tarsis Ultra, the defeat of Kasimir de Valtos and the capture of the alpha psyker on Epsilon Regalis. With each victory remembered, the power of the voices diminished, the despair they fostered kept at bay by his powerful sense of worth and purpose.

He staggered to his feet, seeing Pasanius disengage the promethium unit from his flamer and flip a fragmentation grenade from his dispenser into his hand.

'No!' shouted Uriel and kicked the grenade from his sergeant's hand.

Pasanius rose up to his full height, his face twisted in a snarl of anger and tears coursing down his face.

'Why?' he yelled. 'Why won't you let me die? I deserve to die.'

...he does! Let him die, you hate him anyway...!

'No!' gasped Uriel, fighting the deadly power of the voices. 'You have to fight it!'

'I can't!' wailed Pasanius, holding his silver arm up before him. 'Don't you see? I have to die.'

Uriel gripped his friend's shoulders as another shot echoed in the tunnel and another warrior succumbed to the suicidal lure of the voices.

'Remember how you got that arm?' shouted Uriel. 'You helped save the world of Pavonis. You stood before a star god and defied it. You are a hero, Pasanius! All of you, you are heroes! You are the greatest warriors this galaxy has ever seen! You are stronger, more courageous and more resourceful than any mortal man!'

...no, no, no, no, no, no, no, no, no, no, no, no, no, no, no, no, no, no, no...

Uriel released Pasanius and moved from warrior to warrior, shouting at them as he went, his voice growing louder as he warmed to his theme.

'Do not forget who you are!' he yelled over the furious whispers. 'You are Space Marines. Warriors of the Emperor of Mankind and you fight the Dark Powers wherever you find them. You are strong, proud and you are warriors. You have fought for centuries and your honour is your life, let none dispute it!'

He drew his sword and activated the blade, which rippled with fiery energies, and raised it high.

'Every foe we slay means something!' shouted Uriel, slashing at the walls of the tunnel with every word. 'Every battle we win means something. *We* mean something! Remember every battle you have fought, every foe vanquished, every honour won. They stand for everything we were created to serve. Remember them all and the voices will have no power over you!'

The slithering carvings within the walls screeched in frustration, retreating into the depths of the rock before Uriel's bright blade as his words undid their masquerades. A new sound arose to banish the hateful whispers: the sound of voices being raised in honour of great victories of the Imperium.

The Storming of Corinth, the Iron Cage, Phoenix Island, the Liberation of Vogen, Armageddon, the Fall of Sharendus, the Eleggan Salient, the Battle of Macragge... and a hundred others rang out against the foul temptations of the voices, the walls becoming dark and solid as the volume of the warrior band's shouts grew.

Uriel almost wept in triumph as the darkness of the walls retreated and the illusory nature of the tunnel fell away to reveal the softly glowing exit before them. The soulless light of Medrengard filled the tunnel and though it promised nothing but death and emptiness, Uriel rejoiced to see it.

'This way!' shouted Uriel, scooping up his bolter before staggering exhaustedly towards the tunnel's exit.

The warrior band gathered their weapons and followed him from the hellish mouth of madness.

ONCE CLEAR OF the tunnels of despair, Uriel saw that they had barely penetrated the walls of the fortress at all. The Iron Warrior with the coruscating energy whip had called this place Khalan-Ghol, and as Uriel cast a wary glance towards the hungry maw of the tunnel they had just left, he wondered if it was a name given to the fortress or one it had taken for itself. A potent malice saturated the air, a sense of ancient sentience lurking in the very rocks and mortar of this place.

The Space Marines, Colonel Leonid and Sergeant Ellard collapsed as they fled the dark of the mountain, shaking their heads clear of the last vestiges of the tunnel's evil. It had led them out onto a high ledge at the head of a long, winding set of carven black stairs overlooking the madness of the interior of Honsou's fastness.

Sprawling towers, manufactories and darkly arched cloisters jostled for space amid tall statues and spike-fringed redoubts. Dark-tiled roofs and insane structures of non-Euclidian geometries that hurt the eyes and violated the senses were crammed within the jagged, hostile architecture of the fortress, twisting, and gibbet-hung boulevards winding between them in impossible ways. A wan emerald light held court over it all, pierced with streamers of sickly orange fires burning from forges and melancholy temples. Streams of liquid metal ran in basalt troughs through the fortress, the reflected heat bathing everything in droplets of glistening, metallic condensation.

Copper, verdigris-stained gargoyles vented clouds of steam and tall, crooked towers of black brick spewed choking clouds of pollutants into the atmosphere from great, piston-heaving power plants. Grey figures shuffled through the city and dark, slithering things slipped like shadows through the nightmare streets of the fortress towards the heart of the mountain, where a single, rearing tower of iron stood, its dimensions immense and impossible.

It speared the clouds above, a swirling mass of bruised vaporous energies circling its tallest peak. Thousands of arched firing slits pierced the tower, its base out of sight behind the belching forges clustered before it. Uriel knew that the master of this horrible place must dwell within that awful tower and understood with utter certainty that this was their ultimate destination.

Flocks of the delirium spectres wheeled above the dread tower, their raucous cries echoing weirdly from its tall spires and nameless garrets. Tall peaks of the black mountains swooped high above them, and though it had seemed they walked for many kilometres through the rock of the mountain, the noise of the battle was close, as though they had travelled only a little way.

'How can that be?' said Vaanes, guessing Uriel's thoughts.

'I don't know,' replied Uriel. 'We cannot trust that our senses are not deceived at every turn in this dark place.'

'Uriel, listen, about that tunnel and the things that were said...'

'It doesn't matter. It was the voices, they got inside us and made us say these things.'

Vaanes shook his head. 'What were they? Daemons? Ghosts?'

'I do not know, but we defeated them, Vaanes.'

'_You_ defeated them. You saw through what they were trying to do to us. I almost gave in... I wanted to.'

'But you had the strength to defeat them,' said Uriel. 'That came from inside _you_, I just reminded you of it.'

'Maybe,' said Vaanes, in a rare moment of confession. 'But I am weak, Ventris. I have not been a Space Marine of the Emperor for many decades now and I do not think I have the strength to be one again.'

'I believe you are wrong,' said Uriel, placing his hand in the centre of Vaanes's breastplate. 'You have heart, and I see courage and honour within you, Vaanes. You have just forgotten who you really are.'

Vaanes nodded curtly, pulling away from his touch without replying, and Uriel just hoped he had been able to convince the former Raven Guard of his own worth. This hellish place would test them all to the very limits of their courage and would seek out any chink in their armour and destroy them if they let it.

He caught Pasanius's eye, but his friend broke the contact just as quickly, turning his back upon Uriel.

'Pasanius,' said Uriel. 'Are you ready to move on?'

The sergeant nodded. 'Aye, there's no telling what might follow us through those tunnels. The sooner we're gone the better.'

Uriel reached up to stop Pasanius as he moved off. 'Are you all right, my friend?'

'Of course,' snapped Pasanius, pushing past Uriel and marching to the top of the winding, uneven stairs. Smooth, black and glassy, they would require careful negotiation if they were to avoid slipping and breaking their necks.

Pasanius led the way down, the Space Marines and the two Guardsmen following gingerly in single file. The clanking workshops of the fortress spat flames and smoke; the pounding of hammers the size of tanks echoing from the blackened walls of the windowless buildings. But over everything hung the leaden weight of the spirit of the iron tower, its dead-windowed stare crushing the soul by its very existence.

As they descended into the fortress, Uriel saw strange creatures of light moving between the vast structures, tall, elegant beings walking on golden stilts that trailed streamers of lambent amber fire. Bizarre carriages were suspended between them, filled with glowing ripples of light and a swirling latticework of cogs and pistons. A procession of these creatures passed through the fortress, but they were soon lost to sight in the illogical maze of the streets.

Huge bulldozers, similar to the bulk-hauler they had commandeered, rumbled through the wider thoroughfares, red and hateful, with tall banner poles hung with eight-pointed stars and iron tenders hitched behind them. Blood sloshed from the tenders, leaving a filthy stream of red in their wake as they made their way from the fighting on the walls to the tower at the centre of the fortress. Twisted limbs jutted from the blood-filled tenders, the corpses in each one jostling against one another as the bulldozers ploughed onwards. As the bodies moved, it was clear from their size and muscle mass, that they were those of Iron Warriors.

'Where are they taking them?' said Leonid.

'For burial perhaps,' suggested Uriel.

'I didn't think the Iron Warriors cared too much about honouring the dead.'

'Nor did I, but why else bring the fallen back inside the walls?'

'Who knows, but I have a feeling we'll be finding out soon,' said Vaanes, gloomily.

'If it is connected to our mission, then yes, you're right,' said Uriel continuing down the stairs to the interior of the fortress. The stone steps reflected the light from the purple clouds above the iron tower and Uriel wondered what dark practices and plans had been hatched within its cold depths. The stairs curled down the cliffside of the mountain, widening until they formed a long processional that opened into a bone-flagged esplanade with iron execution poles spaced at regular intervals.

Corpses hung from three of the poles, dry and desiccated, their skin sagging and blotchy. Uriel ignored them, staring into the dark mass of hammering buildings and winding, haunted streets that led towards the tower.

The same emerald glow that suffused the mountain's interior from above was stronger now that they had reached the bottom of the stairs though, the source of its sickly glow was invisible. The manufactories towered above them, the noise of grinding pistons, hissing valves and clanging hammers echoing from all around them and Uriel tasted ash and hot metal on the air.

'Let's go,' said Uriel, as much to galvanise himself into action as to issue an order.

He set off with his bolter at the ready, the Space Marines of the warrior band following close behind him, instinctively falling into a defensive formation with Leonid and Ellard at their centre and all their guns pointing outwards.

A chill of the soul pierced every warrior as they entered the evil shadows of Khalan-Ghol, the chill of plunging into the black waters of an underground lake that has never known the warming touch of a sun. Uriel shivered, feeling a thousand eyes upon him, but seeing nothing and no one moving around them.

'Where are all the people we saw from above?' asked Vaanes.

'I was wondering the same thing,' said Pasanius. 'This place looked well occupied.'

'Perhaps they are hiding from us,' replied Ellard.

'Or perhaps it just seemed occupied,' suggested Uriel, casting wary glances all around him, catching fleeting snatches of movement from in the shadows. 'This place will confound our senses and try to mislead us with illusions and falsehoods. Remember what happened in the tunnel.'

The streets and narrow alleys of Khalan-Ghol twisted at random, zigzagging and twisting around until Uriel could not say for sure which way they were even heading any more. He wished he still had his helmet, but wasn't sure that even its direction finding auspex would be any use here. He couldn't see the iron tower in the cramped streets and had to trust that his instincts were leading them towards it.

Tall shadows danced on the walls, capering along the sides of the black brick buildings, as though racing them through the interior of the fortress. The darkness pressed in around them, and Uriel found himself absurdly grateful for fleeting snatches of the white sky above them. He could feel the power of the black sun above him, but kept his eyes averted for fear of the madness it promised in its fuliginous depths.

Tinny laughter, like a child's, seeped from the walls and shadows and Uriel could see the Space Marines were greatly unsettled by such a plaintive sound. He was reminded of the joyous cries the delirium spectres emitted on their death and wondered if there were similar creatures lurking somewhere nearby.

It seemed that for hours they wandered, lost and misdirected by the insanities of the daemon city. Uriel could find no landmarks upon which to base his choice of direction, the iron tower obscured by the looming sides of the windowless forges and the impenetrable shadows cast by the black sun.

Eventually, he called a halt to their march and ran a hand across his sweat-streaked scalp. There was no rhyme or reason to the layout of the fortress, if even such a thing truly existed. Travelling down the same street was no guarantee of arriving at the same place and doubling back did not return them to whence they had begun.

Impossible physics misdirected them at every turn and Uriel was at a loss as to how to proceed. He squatted on his haunches and placed his gun across his thighs, resting his head against the crumbling brickwork of the building behind him.

He could feel the pounding of heavy industry through the building's fabric, but of all the weirdly angled structures they had passed, they had seen neither window nor entrance to them, simply smoking chimneys and steaming vents.

'What now?' asked Vaanes. 'We're lost aren't we?'

Uriel nodded, too weary and soul sick to even reply.

Vaanes, slung his bolter across his shoulder, as though he had expected no other answer. He looked towards either end of the narrow, enclosing street, its surface black and oily, with the rainbow sheen of spilt promethium to it.

'Is it just me or is it getting darker here?' he asked.

'How can it be getting darker, Vaanes?' snapped Uriel. 'That damned black sun never sets, never even so much as moves in the sky. So I ask you, how can it be getting darker?'

'I don't know,' hissed Vaanes. 'But it is. Look!'

Uriel rolled his head around and saw that Vaanes was right. Creeping liquid shadows were slithering up the walls, swallowing the light and obscuring the surfaces of the buildings they climbed. Inky black, the shadows rippled from the walls, spreading like slicks across the ground and rearing up at the ends of the cobbled street to enclose them.

'What the hell is going on?' gasped Uriel as the sinister, impossible shadows began to coalesce before them, nightmare pools of foetid black iridescence that crept across the walls and street towards them from both front and back.

They drove stinking clouds of vapours straight from the abyss itself before them, vile toxic fumes and indescribable pollutants. Shapeless congeries of protoplasmic bubbles erupted across their amorphous forms, and Uriel now saw the source of the pallid, emerald glow that suffused the city as myriad temporary eyes formed and unformed in the hideous depths, glowing with their own luminescence.

'What are they?' he cried as the slithering mass of filthy, stinking creatures – or creature – oozed forwards.

'What does it matter?' shouted Vaanes. 'Kill them!'

Bolters fired explosive bolts into the heaving mass of corruption, exploding within the jelly-like mass of the things' bodies and the overpowering stench of chemical and biological pollutants gusted from the wounds.

Uriel caught a breath of the fumes and immediately dropped to his knees and vomited copiously across the ground. Even the formidable biological enhancements of a Space Marine were unable to overcome the sickening, horrific stench their bolters had unleashed.

More and more Space Marines dropped to the ground, retching and convulsing at the foulness of the creatures.

'Pasanius!' gasped Uriel. 'Use your flamer!'

He could not tell whether his battle-brother had heard his exclamation, but seconds later Pasanius bathed the advancing beasts in sheets of flame from his hissing weapon. The fires engulfed the beasts, leaping high and burning with terrifying force, as though they contained every flammable substance known to man.

Crackling ooze burned with a white flame and Pasanius switched his aim to the approaching shadow creatures behind them. More liquid flame sprayed and the deafening cries of the burning creatures reached new heights as they burned. Insensate eyes immolated and new ones formed in the fluid flesh of the beasts as the flames burned them. Eye-watering fumes were released from the conflagration, but even though it seemed the beasts were in pain, they did not retreat, holding them trapped within the narrow street.

The heat was intense, but protected by power armour, the Space Marines were immune to the lethal temperatures. The Space Marines sheltered the two Guardsmen as best they could from the killing heat, but Uriel could see that both Leonid and Ellard were on the verge of collapse. The fires killed the worst of the stench and Uriel pulled himself to his feet using the wall.

'Why don't they die?' cursed Vaanes. He held his bolter at the ready and Uriel could see he desperately wanted to fire, but kept his finger clear of the trigger guard, having seen how little effect their initial volley had had. Space Marines picked themselves up, forming a defensive cordon between the walls of flame at either end of the street.

'And why aren't they attacking?' wondered Pasanius. 'Until they went up in flames, it looked like they were ready to overrun us.'

'I'm not sure,' answered Uriel, as an unsettling suspicion began to settle in his gut. 'I think that maybe they never intended to kill us, that maybe they intended something else.'

'What?' asked Vaanes.

'Maybe they just intended to trap us here,' said Uriel, watching as a warrior in glossy black power armour and glowing silver traceries for veins marched through the leaping flames, the oozing matter of the beasts parting before him.

Bronze claws unsheathed from both his grey-fleshed hands and his eyes burned with a soulless silver light.

'Found you,' said the warrior.

♅
TWELVE

'You survived the bedlam portals,' said the warrior, sounding faintly impressed as he walked towards the Space Marines. His armour was utterly black, not even the bright flames reflecting on its mirror-smooth surfaces. Uriel saw that the warrior did not carry a gun, but that did not put him any more at ease. After all, how supremely confident must a warrior be to come before more than two-dozen Space Marines unarmed?

Though to call this warrior unarmed was a misnomer, thought Uriel, seeing his long, glittering bronze claws.

'Who are you?' called Uriel.

The warrior smiled, dull silver light spilling from his mouth as he spoke. 'You have not the aural or vocal configurations to hear or speak my name, so you will know me as Onyx.'

The Space Marines turned their guns on Onyx, the crackling flames beginning to die as more ripples of shadow slithered into the street and quenched them in darkness.

'Are these your creatures?' asked Uriel, raising his own weapon.

'The Exuviae? No, they are nothing more than the polluted filth of Khalan-Ghol, waste matter shed by its industry that mutated to idiot life. They infest this place, but they have their uses.'

'You would do well to let us pass,' snarled Vaanes.

Onyx shook his head. 'No, my master has commanded me to bring you to him.'

'Your master?' said Uriel. 'Honsou?'

'Indeed,' said Onyx.

Uriel could see that there was no they were going to get past Onyx without violence. He had no idea how fearsome the enemy warrior Onyx was in blade-to-blade combat and had no desire to find out.

Calmly, he said, 'Kill him.'

Bolter fire ripped along the street, but Onyx moved like quicksilver, a darting shadow that slipped between the shells and pirouetted above the hail of gunfire. Bronze claws slashed for Uriel's belly and he threw himself back against the wall, only just avoiding being disembowelled by Onyx's stroke.

Pasanius stepped in and hammered his boot towards Onyx, but the black warrior spun away and cracked his elbow into Pasanius's face before leaping over him and delivering a spinning kick to Ardaric Vaanes. Kyama Shae fired his bolter at point blank range, the shells ricocheting from the gleaming black armour of his target.

Onyx lunged close and hammered his fist into Shae's gut, the bronze claws tearing through the Crimson Fist's armour and ripping upwards. Onyx spun away from his victim with a tortured crack of bone, Shae's spinal column clenched in his fist. The Space Marine collapsed to his knees, blood flooding from the great wound torn in his body. His eyes stared in horrid fascination at his spinal column in another's hands for the briefest second before he pitched face first to the ground.

Uriel's jaw dropped open in horror at the sight, as the dripping, bloody spinal column was enveloped within the glassy darkness of Onyx's armour, and the silver-eyed killer leapt upwards as more bolter fire raked the wall behind him. He pushed off from the wall, twisting in midair to lash out with his claws and feet, crushing windpipes and decapitating Space Marines with every blow.

As he landed, he plunged his bloodstained blades into each victim, ripping their spines out with the awful sound of splintering bone. Five Space Marines were down and they hadn't managed to shed a drop of this thing's blood. Uriel sprayed bolts towards Onyx, but no matter how he anticipated the killer's movements, he was always just that little bit too slow to hit him.

'Emperor save us, he's too fast!' shouted Vaanes.

Another Space Marine fell, ripped open from groin to sternum and Uriel could see that Onyx was not going to be too particular in how he carried out his master's wishes. The black-armoured warrior spun through the air, his blazing silver veins and eyes leaving molten trails as he moved with preternatural speed.

Uriel raised his bolter as Onyx leapt for him, but knew that he wouldn't be quick enough. Onyx's fist hammered into his throat, the claws on the furthest extremities of his fists pinning him to the wall behind. Uriel's head cracked painfully against the brickwork and he felt blood matt his hair. He saw that Onyx's middle claw was partially retracted into his flesh, the point pricking the skin of Uriel's throat.

'Anyone else moves and your leader dies!' shouted Onyx, bathing Uriel in silver light as he spoke. The flames from the burning Exuviae had died and the renewed oily, shadow beasts slithered forward, rearing up on amorphous bodies that now achieved a semblance of solidity. The survivors of the warrior band surrounded Onyx and Uriel, their weapons aimed squarely at the symbiote's back.

'I thought you said your master wanted you to bring us to him,' gasped Uriel.

'He did,' nodded Onyx. 'But he didn't say if you were to be alive.'

'He's not our leader,' said Vaanes. 'So go ahead and kill him, but you will follow him into death!'

'I beg to differ,' said Onyx. 'I can see his soul burning with the light of purpose.'

'Vaanes, shoot him!' shouted Uriel, twisting in Onyx's grip and closing his eyes as bolter shells filled the air around him with a deafening roar. He felt Onyx shudder as the bolts struck him. Amid the gunfire, he heard the warrior laugh, and cried out in pain as he felt Onyx's middle talon stab forwards to punch through his throat and embed itself the wall.

The talon was ripped free and he slid down the wall, blood pouring from his neck and armour in a scarlet wash before the Larraman cells were able to clot his blood and stem the wound. Uriel gasped, the breath rasping in his throat, and he realised his trachea had been completely severed. Uriel closed his eyes as his vision greyed and his body fought for oxygen, his chest hiking convulsively. He fought to stay focussed, knowing that to slip into unconsciousness was to die, and shifted his breathing to the third lung grafted to his pulmonary system. His altered breathing pattern shut off the sphincter muscle that normally took in air and he gulped down a great breath as his enhanced physiology took over.

Onyx spun beyond the hail of shells, landing behind the Space Marines with an atavistic howl of bloodlust. His claws swelled to become monstrous golden swords and three Space Marines were hacked apart in as many blows. His face swelled and rippled, black horns curling from his temples and gleaming lines of augmetic body parts becoming visible within his form as the daemonic entity within Onyx took complete command of his body.

His eyes blazed and Uriel could see the beast he had become was eager to do them more harm, but before he could enact it, his entire body shuddered and the daemon-thing Onyx had become retreated back into his flesh, the golden swords writhing and sliding back into his hands.

Even as Uriel watched, Onyx's original form was restored before his eyes.

Onyx let out a long breath and dropped to one knee, but before any of the warrior band could take advantage of his momentary vulnerability, the undulating forms of the Exuviae roared like black tidal waves and bore down upon them. Uriel struggled to rise, but the bubbling, animated pollutants swept over him, pinning his arms and holding him fast within their grip.

Dull, mindless eyes ruptured from the toxin-flecked matter, blinking idiotically at him and he heard the repulsed cries of the surviving Space Marines as the Exuviae swallowed them in their stinking, foetid embrace.

WITH ONYX LEADING the way through the interior of Khalan-Ghol, the delirious architecture seemed to resolve itself in response to his very presence. Where the chaotic nature of its plan had led Uriel and his battle-brothers a merry dance through its shadow-haunted streets, it eased the path of the daemonic creature and his shambling, slithering following. The Exuviae roiled along the cobbled streets with a grotesque, rippling motion, bearing their immobile charges within their odious, fluid bodies.

Only Uriel, Pasanius, Vaanes, Seraphys, Leonid, Ellard and nine other Space Marines had survived to reach this far within the fortress, but Uriel knew that so long as he drew breath he could not forgo his death oath. The soot-stained thoroughfares of the fortress soon fell away to reveal their ultimate destination: the centre of the fortress and the great tower of iron.

Whether it had been a trick of perspective or the illusory power of Chaos, Uriel did not know, but he was shocked speechless by its sheer immensity. Its summit was lost to sight beyond the writhing purple clouds above and it was impossible to see the entirety of its width. Twisting, crooked towers sprouted from its sides, overhanging forges spewed thick toxins into the air, swooping winged things clustered around dark rookeries and evil lightning crackled from slitted windows. A high wall surrounded the base of the tower, its ramparts thick with Iron Warriors and gun turrets.

A huge gate of black iron with a tall, armoured barbican to either side defended the entrance to the tower and as Onyx led them towards it, the dread portal swung open with a scream of deathly anguish. The Exuviae carried them through the dark gate, and as they were borne along the passageway, Uriel saw scalding steam gusting from the spiked murder holes in the roof.

Emerging from the oppression of the gateway, Uriel gaped in dark wonderment as he saw that the tower did not sit upon the rock of the mountain at all, but was impossibly suspended over a giant void that mirrored the dead sky above on hundreds of immense chains. Each link was as thick as the columns that supported the great portico before the Temple of Correction and as they were carried towards a bridge, Uriel saw that the tower also plunged deep into the void for thousands of metres.

'Emperor protect us...' breathed Uriel.

'You waste your breath,' said Onyx. 'You think *he* has any power in this place?'

Uriel disdained to reply, unwilling to further bandy words with one touched by the fell powers of the immaterium. A long basalt slab spanned the void, its surface worn smooth by the passage of uncounted marching feet, leading to an enormous gateway that pierced the tower itself. As they crossed the bridge, Uriel saw that it was fashioned from some deathly material, hissing and spitting as though fresh from the forge. Its scale was colossal: entire regiments would be able to march through and the tallest of Titans could pass beneath it without fear.

Onyx led them towards the gate, a smaller, rivet-studded postern granting them access to the tower's echoing interior. Uriel felt the power of ages past within the tower and its ancient malice was a potent breath on the air.

'Khalan-Ghol,' said Onyx proudly. 'The power and majesty of a living god helped forge this fortress, shaping it into a form pleasing to him, unfettered by any of the laws of nature.'

'It is an abomination!' snarled Pasanius.

'No,' said the daemonic symbiote. 'It is the future.'

THE INTERIOR OF the tower was no less horrifying than its exterior – vast dusty halls of bronze statues, huge, sweating forges that spat sparks and orange rivers of metal. A parching, stifling heat infused the tower, black moisture dripping from the shadowed vaults of the ceiling. Uriel could hear distant screams and heavy hammer-blows far below, louder and more powerful than he had heard thus far on Medrengard.

Crawling shadows, perhaps more of the Exuviae, lurked in the high cloisters, though the most numerous inhabitants of the tower appeared to be figures swathed in black robes, walking with a wheezing mechanical gait.

Red augmetic eyes scanned them with interest as Onyx led his coterie of Exuviae deeper into the tower, clicking brass limbs grasping towards them with a hissing hunger. Warped cog symbols combined with the eight-pointed star of Chaos were burned into their robes and gurgling algorithmic voices clicked between them as they tended to vast, dusty machines whose purpose was lost on Uriel.

As they passed a hulking, bronze construction with pumping, greased pistons and an armature-mounted pict-slate, a huge, hissing monster stepped from the shadow of the great machine to bar their way.

Onyx stiffened as the black-robed creature shuffled painfully into a pool of light and Uriel felt a creeping horror scrape its way up his spine at the sight of it. It moved awkwardly on six, spider-like legs of riveted iron, its body braced within an oil-stained exo-skeleton at its centre. Where its flesh was exposed, Uriel could see that it was withered and dead, a patchwork of sutures running along raised ridges of bone. Its head was heavy and hung low on its shoulders, brass rods piercing the width of its skull and scaffolded by a cage of brass bolted to its temples.

Its hooded face was a loathsome, parchment-coloured skull, the lower half gleaming metal and flensed of skin, its eyes replaced with whirring mechanical optical feeds.

Myriad transparent tubes pierced its flesh, running in gurgling loops around its body and hissing valves released noxious gusts as its chest heaved with the effort of breath. It reached forward to lift Uriel with long, augmetic arms, bulky with scalpels, drills and blowtorches.

Onyx stepped in front of the creature, his claws unsheathing.

'No,' he said. 'These ones are for the master of Khalan-Ghol.'

The beast hissed in anger, its clawed hands snapping in frustration and its drill bits whirring dangerously close to Onyx's head. It reached down to push Onyx out of its way, but the black-armoured warrior refused to be moved.

'I said no,' he repeated. 'It may be that the Savage Morticians will have them in time, but that time is not now.'

The creature appeared to consider this for a moment, before its hideous skull face nodded and it retreated into the shadow of the machine once more.

Onyx watched it go and, while his attention was elsewhere, Uriel struggled within the stinking prison of the beast that bore him, Pasanius and Vaanes, but it was no use, they were held utterly immobile. At last, sure the Savage Mortician was not waiting in ambush, Onyx sheathed his claws and led the Exuviae bearing his prisoners onwards.

Uriel's frustration grew with every darkened hall they traversed and every impossibly angled staircase they climbed or descended, unable to move so much as a single muscle. The maddening sound of hammering grew louder the further they travelled and the same emerald light that permeated the city beyond the tower grew brighter as their journey led them from passages and chambers raised by the hands of men into a vast fiery cavern edged with great steam-venting pistons.

A gleaming silver bridge crossed a great chasm in the floor, through which rose banks of hot, sulphurous fumes and the taste of beaten metal. Beyond the bridge was a colossal wall of dark, green-veined stone pierced by a great, iron gate. Studded with jagged black spikes, the gate was flanked by two daemon-visaged Titans, their armoured plates scarred by millennia of war. Uriel saw with loathing that the rippling kill banners hanging from their weapons bore the damnable symbol of the Legio Mortis.

'Behold, the inner sanctum of the fortress of Khalan-Ghol! You are honoured indeed!' cried Onyx, leading them across the bridge spanning the chasm. As they drew near the gate, it unlocked with a reverberating boom that shook the dust from the leering gargoyles clustered around the chamber's roof, and the Titans reached around to open the spiked portal.

Onyx led them through the gateway and at last Uriel and his companions came face to face with the master of Khalan-Ghol.

THE WALLS WITHIN the inner sanctum of the fortress were of a dressed black stone, threaded with gold and silver and glistening with moisture. A score of tall, arched windows pierced one wall and the dead light of the sky was reflected as milky lines on the floor.

Surrounded by two score Iron Warriors and seated on a throne of silvery white sat a scarred warrior with close-cropped black hair, clad in a dented and heavily battle-scarred suit of armour. His face was cruel, set in an expression of arch interest, a long, recently healed scar on his right temple. Behind him stood the giant Iron Warrior who had incapacitated Uriel with the writhing energy whip.

'Get rid of the Exuviae, Onyx,' said the warrior.

Onyx nodded and turned to face the slithering monsters, the silver lines on his face flaring brightly and a silver sheened hiss escaping his mouth. Uriel felt the solidity of the creatures become less constrictive and toppled to the floor as their form became sticky and liquid once more. Their substance retreated from the light on the floor, reverting to their sinuous shadow forms. Like whipped dogs, they slipped into the dark corners of the hall before sliding out of sight through the great gateway and back into the mordant darkness of the fortress.

Briefly Uriel considered reaching for his sword, but when he looked up, he stared into the barrels of some forty bolters, their plated sides carved with obscene sigils and decorated with the eight-pointed star of Chaos. The Iron Warriors divested them of their weapons and indicated that they should approach the warrior on the throne.

As they neared, Uriel saw that the warrior carried a huge black war-axe across his lap and recognised him as the Iron Warrior he had first fought on his ascent up the breach. His sword had come within centimetres of beheading this fiend.

'I know you,' said the warrior, recognising him also.

'You are Honsou?' said Uriel.

An Iron Warrior stepped in and hammered the butt of his weapon across the back of Uriel's skull. He dropped to one knee, the wound on the back of his head opening once more and fresh blood soaking his armour.

Honsou nodded. 'You know of me, but I do not know you. What are you called?'

'You will learn nothing from us by force,' said Uriel, rising to his feet and massaging the back of his head.

'It is a simple question,' said Honsou, rubbing his fingers across the scar on his temple. 'I would know the name of the warrior who drew my blood.'

'Very well. I am Uriel Ventris and these are my warriors.'

Honsou looked beyond Uriel. 'You keep strange company, Uriel Ventris – renegades, traitors and runaway slaves.'

Uriel did not reply, realising that Honsou believed him to be nothing more than a renegade himself. Without insignia or markings, there was nothing to indicate that he was still a warrior of the true Emperor of Mankind.

His mind raced as he tried to think of some way to exploit the traitor's mistake as Honsou continued: 'How is it you know of me? Did Toramino tell you?'

'Who?'

'Do not play the innocent with me,' cautioned Honsou. 'You'll find I have no patience for it. You know who Toramino is.'

Still Uriel did not reply and Honsou sighed. 'There is no point in trying to be noble, I will learn what I want to know. If not now, then the Savage Morticians will extract it from you soon enough. Trust me, you would do better to tell me what I want to know now than to suffer at their hands.'

'I learned of you from Toramino, yes,' Uriel said at last.

Honsou chuckled. 'See Zakayo, Toramino has sunk so low that he stoops to the employ of mercenaries. So much for his high ideals of purity, eh?'

'Indeed,' said Obax Zakayo, circling Honsou's throne and lifting Leonid and Ellard with the powerful, hissing claws that hunched over his shoulders. Both men struggled in his grip, but were powerless to resist the giant's strength.

'I told you that you would be beneath my blade again, slaves.'

'Put them down, Zakayo, their blood is not worth spilling here. Put them to work in the forges.'

Obax Zakayo nodded and dropped the two Guardsmen, but remained beside them, his desire to wreak bloody harm upon them plain.

'Why are you within the walls of my fortress, Ventris?' said Honsou.

'As you say, we are mercenaries,' replied Uriel.

'They had passed through the bedlam portals and were attempting to make for the inner keep when I found them,' said Onyx. 'I believe them to be assassins.'

'Is that it, Ventris? Are you an assassin?'

'I am but a simple soldier.'

'No, you are not,' stated Honsou, rising from his throne and walking towards Uriel with a relaxed, confident stride. 'A simple soldier would not have brought his warriors alive through the bedlam portals or penetrated this far into Khalan-Ghol.'

Honsou took hold of Uriel's chin, turning his head from side to side, and Uriel saw that the traitor's arm was a black metal augmetic, its surfaces smooth like an insect's carapace. Its touch felt loathsome on his skin.

'Why are you on Medrengard?' asked Honsou, looking into Uriel's eyes.

Uriel met Honsou's gaze and the two warriors stared at one another, each daring the other to break the contact first. Uriel was a warrior of the Emperor of Mankind and Honsou a traitor; one just over a century old, the other having bestrode battlefields thousands of years past. Though a gulf of time and faith separated them, Uriel saw a warrior spirit within Honsou and a core of bitterness that was unsettlingly familiar.

Whether his presence in the Eye of Terror had heightened his senses or he felt some form of dark kinship with the master of Khalan-Ghol, he didn't know, but he saw with horror that there was not so great a difference between them as he might have thought.

He saw the same drive to prove himself the equal of his peers, the same frustration at being denied his rightful place through the blindness of others. Part of him admired Honsou's single-mindedness at pursuing his goals.

But for an accident of birth, might they have stood together on the battlefield as brothers? Might Uriel have fought in the Black Crusades or might Honsou have stood shoulder to shoulder with brother Space Marines in defence of Tarsis Ultra?

He saw the recognition and admiration in Honsou's face, seeing that he too had understood their shared heritage.

'We are on Medrengard to fight,' said Uriel simply.

'So I see,' nodded Honsou. 'You fought well before my walls. I take it I have you and your warriors to thank for destroying Berossus's troop elevators?'

'Aye,' said Vaanes proudly. 'I cut the cable.'

'Then it is certain you do not serve Berossus, perhaps only Toramino...' said Honsou with relish. 'In any case, you have done me a great service! Without reinforcements, Berossus was unable to carry the walls. But for you, Khalan-Ghol might now be in his damn fool hands.'

Honsou circled the warrior band of Space Marines, taking the measure of each of them in turn. He stopped beside Pasanius and lifted his silver arm to more carefully examine its unblemished surfaces.

'This is fine workmanship,' he said. 'Your own?'

'No,' said Pasanius through gritted teeth. 'The adepts of Pavonis fashioned it for me.'

'Pavonis? I have not heard of that world. Is it a world of the Mechanicum?'

'No.'

Honsou smiled. 'You hate me, don't you?'

Pasanius turned to stare at Honsou. 'I hate you, yes. You and all your traitorous, bastard kin.'

Honsou circled behind Pasanius and wiped black dust and the filthy residue of the Exuviae from his armour, taking a closer look at the colour of the plates below. He returned to Uriel's side and examined his armour too.

'I see no insignia,' he said. 'What Chapter were you from?'

'What does that matter here?' said Uriel.

'I like the way you answered that.'

'How did I answer it?'

'Very carefully,' chuckled Honsou. 'Shall I tell you what I think?'

'Would it matter if I said no?'

'Not really, no. For what it is worth, then, I think you are Ultramarines, though I dread to think what heinous crime an Ultramarine must commit to be banished to the Eye of Terror. Did you turn left instead of right on the parade ground? Forget to say your prayers in the morning?'

Uriel felt his anger grow, but forced himself not to react to Honsou's mockery. 'Yes, we are Ultramarines, but the reasons we are here are unimportant. We are here to fight.'

'Then do you care who you fight for?'

Uriel considered the question before answering. 'Not particularly,' he said.

'Then I could use warriors like you,' said Honsou, extending his hand. 'I can offer you so much more than Toramino or Berossus. Will you join me?'

Uriel stared at the Iron Warrior's hand, a tumble of emotions racing through his head. He and Honsou shared many qualities as warriors, but they could never reconcile their differences in faith... could they?

With no Chapter to call his own, might he not be better served by finding a warrior leader of courage and vision he could fight alongside?

Everything he had been brought up to believe and everything he had been trained in as a Space Marine warred with the bitterness at their expulsion from the Ultramarines, and as he locked eyes with Honsou once again, he saw the only course open to him.

PART III - IN THE REALM OF THE UNFLESHED

U

THIRTEEN

URIEL LUNGED TO the side and hammered his elbow into the throat of the Iron Warrior holding his sword and caught the falling scabbard as the traitor clutched for his shattered windpipe. The blade hissed from its sheath as he shouted, 'I am a warrior of the Emperor of Mankind and a Space Marine. I will never join the likes of you!'

Honsou didn't move and Uriel's blade sang for his neck, but the bronze claws of Onyx were there first, intercepting the blow. Onyx's other fist hammered into Uriel's chest, sending him sprawling across the powdered bone floor and driving the breath from him. He dropped his sword and gasped for breath as he momentarily tried to take oxygen in through his severed trachea before his autonomic functions reverted to his third lung.

He reached for his fallen sword, but a booted foot slammed down on the blade.

'How stupid do you think I am, Ventris?' snarled Honsou. 'Do you think I became the master of this fortress by blind luck? No, I earned this by being better than everyone who tried to take it from me!'

Honsou's boot lashed out, smashing into his jaw and cracking the bone. Uriel rolled away from Honsou's kicks, the Iron Warriors closing on the warrior band with their bolters raised as they made to come to Uriel's assistance.

Uriel struggled to rise, but Honsou was giving him no chance, dropping his knee into the small of his back and hammering hard, economical punches into his ribs. Honsou gripped the back of his head and slammed Uriel's face into the floor. Uriel felt his nose break and his cheekbone crack under the assault, twisting his head to try and avoid the worst of the blows.

But Honsou was a gutter fighter and trapped his head with his elbow while pounding his face in fury.

'Damn, but you will wish you had accepted my offer!' raged Honsou as he stood and wiped Uriel's spattered blood from his face. 'I will give you to the Savage Morticians and they will rape your flesh and show you agony like you have never known. Your body will be their canvas and once they are done violating you, they will render you down to flesh their wasted frames.'

Uriel rolled onto his back, blood filling his mouth, and he coughed, spattering his armour with red. He pushed himself onto one elbow and said, 'I am Uriel Ventris of the Ultramarines, loyal servant of the beneficent Emperor of Mankind and foe to all the traitorous followers of the Ruinous Powers. Nothing you can do will change that.'

Honsou snarled and crouched over Uriel's breastplate, hammering his fists against Uriel's face once more. Blood sprayed the floor as he yelled. 'Damn you, how dare you refuse me! You are nothing, no one. Your Chapter has disowned you! You are nothing to them. What can you possibly have to gain by honouring them?'

Uriel's hand shot out and caught Honsou's descending fist.

'I would have my honour and my faith!' he spat, lashing out with his other fist and smashing Honsou aside. Uriel rolled to his feet and staggered to join the remainder of the warrior band. The Space Marines and the two Guardsmen formed a circle of defiance before the Iron Warriors. Uriel spat blood and teeth, leaning on Pasanius for support.

'You had me worried there for a moment,' said Pasanius. His tone was light, but even in his battered state, Uriel caught the concern in his friend's tone.

'I am a warrior of the Emperor, my friend,' he gasped. 'I would never turn to the Dark Powers, you know that.'

'I know that,' agreed Pasanius.

'Well you certainly had that bastard fooled,' said Vaanes, moving to stand beside them, his lightning claws sliding from his gauntlet. 'And me too. Damn it, Ventris, I won't die like this!'

'Neither will I, if I can help it,' said Uriel.

The Iron Warriors surrounded them, bolters aimed at their hearts as Honsou rose, wiping blood from his face.

'I'll make sure you're broken in two, Ventris,' he promised. 'I'll let them feed you the filth of the daemonculaba then have you thrown to the Unfleshed. Let's see how your precious ideals hold up then.'

'Nothing you can do will ever break my faith in the Emperor,' said Uriel.

'Faith?' scoffed Honsou. 'What is that but hopeful ignorance? The Iron Warriors once had faith, but where did that get them? Betrayed by the Emperor and cast into the Eye of Terror. If that's what faith in the Emperor gets you, then to hell with it, you're welcome to it!'

Pasanius roared in anger and leapt for Honsou's throat, but again Onyx darted in to protect his master, hammering his bronze claws towards his throat. For such a big man, Pasanius moved surprisingly swiftly and he batted aside Onyx's blow, backhanding his massive fist into the daemon symbiote's face.

Onyx roared and fell back, silver fire spurting from his ruptured flesh. Pasanius gripped Honsou's armour, drawing back his gleaming fist to deliver a killing blow.

But before he could strike, a biting claw closed on his arm and Obax Zakayo wrenched him back. The hydraulic claw snapped shut on Pasanius's forearm, crushing the limb and virtually severing it completely. Obax Zakayo lashed out with his sledgehammer fist and smashed the sergeant from his feet, closing to finish the fallen sergeant with his own dread axe. He raised the weapon high, but the blow never landed, the Iron Warrior incredulous as what he saw before him.

Uriel watched in horror and amazement as the crushed and mangled metal of Pasanius's arm ran like liquid mercury and the destruction Obax Zakayo had done to it vanished utterly, every single dent, scrape and imperfection renewed until the arm was as unblemished as the day it had first been grafted to the sergeant's stump of an elbow.

'Pasanius...' breathed Uriel. 'What... how?'

His friend rolled onto his side, hiding his newly healed silver arm from Uriel's sight.

'I'm so sorry...' he wept. 'I should have...'

Honsou loomed over Pasanius, pulling the sergeant's silver arm away from his chest where he cradled it. He slid his own augmetic fingers across the silver perfection of Pasanius's mechanised arm and looked at his own glossy, mechanical limb in leering anticipation.

'Take them to the Halls of the Savage Morticians and give them to the Savage Morticians, but tell them to keep this one alive... I want this arm.'

Honsou rose and walked over to Uriel, his features twisted in betrayed anger. 'But give Ventris to the daemonculaba, he's not worth anything else. Let them abuse his body and take what they want from him before shitting him out.'

THE JOURNEY TO the Halls of the Savage Morticians was as fraught with insane visions and delirious apparitions as the one towards its inner sanctum. The interior of the tower flaunted the laws of nature and physics with nauseating perspectives and impossible angles that fought the evidence of Uriel's senses.

They descended winding spiral stairs that looped around others in a dizzying double helix pattern, with shuffling slaves, gold-robed acolytes and Iron Warriors climbing or descending – Uriel wasn't sure which – above them in defiance of gravity.

Obax Zakayo, Onyx and the forty Iron Warriors had marched the warrior band from Honsou's chambers, back through the chasm-split chamber and Titans towards the dirge-echoing cloisters of the tower. Beyond that, Uriel could not say what route their captors led them, the chaotic architecture of the tower defeating his every attempt to remember their route of travel.

Battered, without weapons and heads bowed in defeat, the Space Marines and Guardsmen were herded through darkened, dusty corridors – though Pasanius kept his distance from Uriel and would not meet his eyes. Such passivity chafed on Uriel's sense of honour, but to attack their captors now would see them all slaughtered. And while he still had a death oath to fulfil and continued to draw breath, he knew there would be time enough to fight.

Their march led ever onwards to what Honsou had called the Halls of the Savage Morticians, where dwelt the Savage Morticians. Uriel had caught more than a little fear at the mention of these individuals, and did not relish discovering the reason for that fear. Was the creature that had tried to take them from Onyx as they had entered the tower one of these beings? Uriel had a horrible suspicion they would find out all too soon.

Their march came to an abrupt end when Obax Zakayo hesitantly approached a low, red-lit archway, its edges delineated with hooks, long needles and gory meat racks hung with cuts of dressed human flesh. Plaintive cries and the hiss of sizzling meat gusted from within, carried upon the stench of blood and despair. Something moved within the glowing arch, a shambling, misshapen thing.

Obax Zakayo hesitated before passing beneath the archway, the click, click of metal claws on stone and the echoes of a booming heartbeat echoing from the dripping archway ahead. The Iron Warriors' apprehension was plain to see. Onyx displayed no such hesitancy, passing the threshold into the domain of the Savage Morticians without fear.

Uriel felt foetid warmth as he passed through the arch, glancing around to see what could so discomfit the Iron Warriors. The silver fire of Onyx's eyes and veins cast a faint glow around the chamber, and Uriel was suddenly grateful for the dimness of the light as he saw macabre hints of all manner of grotesque experimentation hung from the walls and displayed within jars of milky fluid. The chamber's occupant limped towards Obax Zakayo, its every step obviously painful.

Uriel saw its naked body was a mélange of limbs and appendages from Emperor alone knew how many other bodies. Its head was stitched on backwards, with rusted copper augmetics replacing its eyes and ears. It bore itself up on legs that had obviously belonged to two people of greatly differing size and its torso was a spiderweb of poorly healed surgical scars. Perhaps it had once had a gender, but nothing remained of its groin to tell. The thing's arms dangled before its chest in an asymmetrical loop, its hands grafted together in one lumpen mass of fused flesh and bone.

'What want you?' it slurred from a mouth thick with ropes of drool. 'Not welcome.'

'Sabatier,' said Onyx. 'We bring offerings for your masters. New flesh.'

The creature named Sabatier transferred its gaze from Onyx to the warrior band and dragged itself painfully towards Ardaric Vaanes. It reached up to rub its fused fists against his face, but Vaanes pulled away from its bruised flesh before it could touch him.

'Don't touch me, you monster,' he snarled.

Sabatier chuckled – or gargled, it was hard to be sure – and turned back to Onyx.

'Defiant,' it said as Vaanes lunged forwards and grabbed its neck, twisting its head around with a loud crack of bone. It sighed once and dropped to the ground. Obax Zakayo stepped in and gripped Vaanes's armour with his mechanised claws, lifting him from the ground with a roar of anger.

'And strong...' said Sabatier from the ground as it awkwardly picked itself up. Its head lolled on its shoulders, a sharp-edged shard of bone jutting from its patchwork skin.

It waved the fleshy loop of its arms at Obax Zakayo. 'Leave him be, masters always prefer flesh be strong, than weak, starved things normally get. Maybe defiant one get lucky and masters make him like me. Dead, but not cold in ground.'

'He should be so lucky,' said Obax Zakayo, dropping Vaanes back to the ground.

'No, will not be,' said Sabatier, raising its head and speaking a guttural incantation.

At the sound of its phlegm-filled voice, the far wall of the archway shimmered and vanished, the noise of screams and the pounding heartbeat filling the chamber. A great, iron-meshed cage lay beyond, and the Iron Warriors pushed them into its centre with brutal clubbings from their bolters.

Once they and their captors had entered the cage, Sabatier looped its arms around a yellow and black chevroned bar and, with some difficulty, pulled it shut across the cage's door. As the door clanged shut, the cage lurched and a grinding squeal built from above as ancient mechanisms engaged and the cage began to descend into the depths of the tower.

Uriel looked down through the grilled floor of the cage, seeing only a dimly glowing shaft constructed of oily sheets of beaten iron. The bottom was lost to perspective, and Uriel saw that there was no way that this shaft could be physically contained within the tower. The fact of the shaft's spatial impossibility did not surprise him any more.

Vaanes sidled close to Uriel as the shaft continued its descent, gaining speed as it went until the metal sides were screaming past.

'We have to get out of here soon. I don't like the sound of these Savage Morticians.'

'Nor I,' agreed Uriel. 'Anything that worries an Iron Warrior cannot be good.'

'Perhaps your sergeant with that self-repairing arm can fight his way clear. Where in the hell did he get that?'

'I wish I knew...' said Uriel as the speeding cage finally slowed before coming to a juddering halt. Sabatier hauled open the doors on the opposite side of the cage.

The Iron Warriors beat them from the cage into a gradually widening tunnel hacked through the rock. At its end was a pulsing red glow, a chorus of screams, hissing, clanging and thumping engines. But drowning everything beneath its thudding, regular hammering was the pounding of a deafening heartbeat.

The red glow and hateful cacophony of noise swelled until they passed into the colossal cavern beyond.

'Oh, no...' breathed Uriel as he finally laid eyes upon the Halls of the Savage Morticians.

'What the hell...?' said Vaanes, his face lit by the diabolical, blood-red glow of the cavern.

Its far side was lost to sight, the ribbed iron walls soaring to distant heights where throbbing machines and mighty turbines roared and seethed. Great cables and looping tubes ran across the walls and curving ceiling, dripping a fine mist of bodily fluids to the stinking rocky floor. Tiered levels of darkened cages, similar to the ones Uriel had seen in the mountain flesh camp, circled the walls of the cavern, troughs running below each one and pipes running from heavy bladders suspended from the roof.

As he was forced into the cavern, Uriel felt a sudden dullness assault his senses, feeling as though under the effects of a massively powerful pain balm. Everything seemed bleached of its colour and taste and smell, as though every sensory apparatus of his body was being smothered.

The floor of the cavern was rough and irregular, random structures and gibbets built upon one another with mortuary tables – some occupied, some not – scattered in a haphazard fashion around the chamber. Drawn by the noise of the elevator cage, black-robed monsters threaded their way through the cavern, scuttling forwards on an assortment of wildly differing forms of locomotion. Some came on spidery limbs, others on long assemblies of stilts, while others rumbled forwards on spiked track units. Their waving arms were an eclectic mix of blades, claws, clamps, bone saws and whirring cranial drills. No two were alike, but each one bore the scars of massive, self-inflicted surgeries, their forms repugnant and evil.

Each displayed a corrupted version of the skull and cog symbol of the Adeptus Mechanicus upon its robes, though Uriel found it hard to reconcile these abominations with the priests of the Machine God. Their skins were dead and they babbled in a series of unintelligible clicks that sounded like gibberish to Uriel.

Onyx stepped into the cavern, closely followed by Sabatier. The Savage Morticians quickly surrounded them, prodding Onyx with pincer arms and stabbing at him with needles.

'A gift from Lord Honsou,' said the daemon symbiote, ignoring the examination. Finding nothing of worth on his daemonic frame, the fell surgeons moved on, approaching the warrior band with a sick, skeletal lust in their soulless eyes. One of the nightmare monsters turned back to Onyx and Uriel recognised it as the one they had seen upon entering the tower. Its mouth opened and a hissing, clicking language emerged.

'Your gift acceptable,' translated Sabatier. 'You get to leave unsurgeried.'

Onyx nodded, as Uriel took in more of the dark wonders displayed throughout the cavern. But immediate and terrifying as the forms of the Savage Morticians were, it was to the centre of the chamber that Uriel's gaze was irresistibly drawn.

Held suspended over a bubbling lake of blood by a trio of thick chains and gleaming silver awls piercing its chest and torso was a bloated red daemon, ancient and swollen with crackling energies. The flesh of its body was scaled and thick tufts of shaggy, matted hair ran from its horned skull down the length of its back. Its cloven hooves clawed the air and as it thrashed impotently against its fetters, Uriel could see great wounds on its back where a pair of wings had been surgically removed. Its chest heaved violently in time with the booming echo that filled the chamber and Uriel knew that this imprisoned daemon must be the source of the noise.

'"You will know it when you see it…"' said Pasanius.

'What?'

'That's what the Omphalos Daemonium told us, isn't it?'

'About what?' asked Uriel.

'The Heart of Blood,' said Pasanius. '"You will know it when you see it."'

Uriel looked up at the bound daemon, realising that Pasanius was right. This could be none other than the Heart of Blood, the daemon thing that according to the tale Seraphys had told, had outwitted the Omphalos Daemonium and bound it to an eternity of torment within the firebox of a terrifying daemon engine.

Surrounding the lake of blood were hundreds of upright coffins of black iron with gurgling red tubes piercing their tops. In each coffin lay a chanting, gold-robed sorcerer, their withering bodies pierced by scores of exsanguination needles that fed the hissing lake beneath the imprisoned daemon with their blood. A pulsing tube rose from the lake, penetrating the daemon's chest as the psykers' blood was forced into its immaterial flesh. The daemon writhed in agony above the lake, a rippling haze of psychically dead air rising from the warp entity's skull and filling the pinnacle of the chamber. The daemon's torment at its confinement was plain and now that he focussed on it, Uriel could clearly see that this was the source of his deadened senses.

'Lord Honsou requests that this one,' said Onyx, indicating Uriel, 'be fed to the daemonculaba, while the one with the silver arm has it removed and brought to his inner sanctum. Is this acceptable?'

The creature lurched forwards, lifting Pasanius with a hissing claw that sprouted from its pneumatic leg assembly. A whining blade snapped from the armature on its wrist and with brutally efficient cuts, sawed the armour from Pasanius's upper arm, exposing the muscled flesh of his bicep and the junction of flesh and metal.

'Put me down, Chaos filth!' yelled Pasanius, kicking out at the withered chest of the Savage Mortician. It hissed, as though unused to such defiance and a thick needle extended from beneath the saw-blade and stabbed through Pasanius's breastplate. Within seconds the sergeant's struggles had ceased and the monster handed him on to another of its surgical brethren.

Uriel surged forward as Pasanius was borne away, but his lethargic senses slowed him and Onyx stopped him with a bronze blade at his neck.

'Don't,' he said simply. 'His fate will be nothing next to yours.'

Uriel said nothing as the Savage Morticians surrounded them and gathered them up in their mechanical claws.

'I will kill you,' promised Uriel as he was lifted, struggling, from the ground. 'You had best shoot me now, for I will see you dead if you do not.'

'If the powers decree that is my fate, then so be it, but I think you are wrong. You will die in this place, Uriel Ventris,' shrugged Onyx before turning on his heel and re-entering the tunnel that led to the elevator cage with a grateful-looking Obax Zakayo.

Uriel fought uselessly against the claws of the Savage Mortician, but its strength was enormous and he could not move. Its dead face hissed as it examined his body in detail. Gleaming arms of bronze held him immobile while pincers and needles pierced his flesh.

A clicking arrangement of spindly rods extended from the monster's hood, telescoping outwards and bearing a meshed mouthpiece that snicked into place before its toothy jaws. Sharp drill-bits clicked from the mouthpiece and burrowed into the Savage Mortician's metal jaw, sending dusty flurries of metallic flesh flying.

The mesh unit hissed with static and the Savage Mortician said, 'You are to be fed to daemonculaba. Waste of flesh. Much surgeries could be done with you. Things unknown become known. Others will do.'

'What are you going to do with us?' shouted Vaanes, struggling helplessly in the grip of a tall, black-robed monster that travelled on hissing mechanical legs, reverse jointed like those of a Sentinel.

'We are the surgeons of demise,' said the monster. 'Monarchs to the king-dom of the dead. Will show you the meaning of pain. Abacinate you then open you up with knives. Take what we want. Make your flesh our own.'

The dark priests of flesh and machine stalked off through the red-lit cavern, carrying the members of the warrior band towards the experimentation tables, animatedly discussing their proposed surgeries with one another in their clicking, machine language.

The Savage Mortician holding Uriel set off in a different direction entirely, its rolling, multi-legged stride carrying it swiftly through the chamber. Uriel saw horrific sights as he was borne through the hellish cavern; stripped down bodies, chains of prisoners sewn together, screaming madmen with their skulls pumped full of fluid, the internal pressure forc-ing it through their bulging eyes.

Men and women turned above slow-roasting fires, burning flesh drip-ping away and hissing on the iron skillets below. More mutants like Sabatier, deformed and reassembled without reason or recourse to the laws of anatomy, tended to the more mundane experiments, feeding on the screams of their subjects and recording every aspect of their suffering on long sheaves of parchment.

Several times they were forced to make diversions through the cavern to avoid the hateful red bulldozers he had seen from atop the stairs that led down into the fortress. They still hauled the blood-sloshing tenders filled with the corpses of Iron Warriors behind them, and threaded their way through the experimentation chamber taking the bodies to some unknown destination.

Uriel lost sight of the bulldozers as the Savage Mortician climbed a long grilled ramp that led up to the first tier of cages that ran around the cir-cumference of the chamber. A number of conduits suspended on cruel iron hooks followed the curve of the cavern walls, laden with groaning, spitting pipes, crackling electrical cables and a clear tube filled with a viscous, gristly substance. As they reached the top of the ramp, Uriel saw that the cages were indeed filled with hideous victims that resembled those poor unfor-tunates who had died in the flesh camp in the mountains. But as horrific as that had been, this was a horror beyond anything he had seen before.

Each vast, bloated creature in these cages was female, their bodies swollen beyond all resemblance to humanity. Shackled into their cages, they gurgled and drooled in voiceless madness and torment, their vocal chords having long since been cut. Engorged as they were by unnatural means, Uriel saw that their size was not simply due to monstrous infu-sions of growth hormones and dark magicks.

These gargantuan females were pregnant.

No normal pregnancies though, saw Uriel. Their swollen bellies rippled with numerous tumescent growths, giant squirming things, easily the size of a Space Marine...

With repulsed horror, Uriel realised that he looked on the daemonculaba, vile, terrible, daemonic wombs from which were ripped newly created Chaos Space Marines. Each cage was filled with these horribly pregnant monsters and Uriel wept at their terrible fate.

Here was the ultimate goal of his death oath, the destruction of which would see him restored in the grace of his Chapter. He struggled harder in the grip of the Savage Mortician as it began cutting his armour from his body with a brutally efficient mix of blades and plasma cutters.

This was no delicate surgery, and he screamed as his flesh was cut, pierced and burned black by the procedure. Shards of his armour clanged to the floor and he wept for the violation done to its spirit. First his breastplate was split apart, his gorget torn off and his shoulder guards broken in two before being ripped asunder.

'Not struggle,' warned the monster. 'You be fed to daemonculaba.'

'Get your damn, dirty hands off me, daemon spawn!' shouted Uriel.

The irritated beast slammed a heavy fist against Uriel's head and blood streamed down his forehead, bright flashes of pain bursting before his eyes. The robed creature carried him further around the tier of battery cages, blood dripping into his eyes as he was turned around to find himself looking through the mesh floor.

Below him, he saw a great rumbling machine with a blood-smeared conveyor laden with bullet-riddled bodies or corpses with limbs missing. Great rollers and crushers awaited the bodies of the fallen Iron Warriors and each was ground to a thick paste within the machine before being carried along pulsing pipes to the cages of the daemonculaba.

Together with the gene-seed Honsou had taken from Hydra Cordatus, Uriel saw that this must be how the traitors managed to reharvest their gene-seed for rebirth. This blasphemy against such a sacred and precious symbol of the Space Marines was almost too much to bear and he swore he would kill Honsou with his bare hands.

At last he was turned upright once more, seeing a number of other black-robed morticians working on convulsing daemonculaba. These sorry specimens had their bellies cut open and spread wide, pale pink folds of fatty flesh held open with clamps as the deformed mutants placed the panicked bodies of adolescent children within the opened wombs.

Where the genetic material fed to the daemonculaba would pass to the implanted children within...

The children screamed at the monsters, begging for their lives or their mothers, but the black-robed monsters paid them no heed and continued their macabre procedures.

Uriel twisted in his captor's grip, fighting desperately as he saw the opened belly of a daemonculaba before him.

'No!' he roared. 'Don't!'

Another of the Savage Morticians assisted its fellow surgeon with the ovariotomy procedure and Uriel bellowed in anger as he felt a blunt needle punch through the ossified bone shield that protected the organs within his chest cavity.

His struggles grew weaker as the powerful soporific sped around his body and overcame his fearsomely resistant metabolism. He felt rough hands laying him within the soft, wet embrace of the daemonculaba's womb and warmth enfolded him as he felt his limbs sutured into its bloody interior.

He felt pulsing organs around him and the rapid tattoo of a heart beating too fast above his head.

'You die now,' said the Savage Mortician. 'Too old to become Iron Warrior. Gene-seed will foster new growths to rupture your flesh. Mutant growths and unknown results ensue. You will be in pieces soon. In jars.'

'No...' slurred Uriel, struggling feebly against the incapacitating drug. 'Kill you...'

But the swathes of the daemonculaba's blubbery flesh were already being folded over his supine body to leave him trapped in darkness. Moist, blood-rich flesh smothered his face and he fought to free his hands, but a warm numbness suffused his body.

The last thing Uriel heard before he slipped into unconsciousness was the sound of the daemon womb's thick, leathery skin being stitched shut above him.

ʊ
FOURTEEN

ARDARIC VAANES FOUGHT the Savage Mortician all the way, though it did little good. It had a firm a grip of him in its bronze claws, his limbs held immobile and only his head able to move. The monstrous surgeon loped through the screaming chamber on long, stilt-like legs, its stride smooth and long, despite the unevenness of the ground. It towered over the abominable hybrid creations that toiled at blood-slick experimentation tables, making its way towards some hideous destination of its own.

'Pasanius!' he shouted. 'Can you hear me?'

The Ultramarines sergeant nodded dumbly, his head rolling slackly on numbed muscles, and Vaanes knew there would be no help from him until the drug he had been given wore off. With the exception of Ventris, he could see that the black-robed monsters were taking all of them to the same place, a procession of the grotesque creatures bearing them towards their doom. Pasanius was near as damn unconscious behind him, closely followed by Seraphys, the Blood Raven and the two Guardsmen. The remaining nine members of their warrior band were there as well.

Not for the first time since they'd begun the journey to Khalan-Ghol, Vaanes cursed Ventris for deluding them into believing they could pull this suicide mission off. But more than that, he cursed himself for falling for his fine words of courage. Vaanes was under no illusions as to his lack of honour, and should have known better than to believe the same tired old lie.

Honsou had been right when he talked of where honour got you. Vaanes had given up believing in such things long ago and all it had earned him were decades of wandering the stars as a rootless mercenary until he had ended up on this miserable hellhole of a world.

He had dared to believe that Ventris represented his final opportunity for redemption, that by taking this one, last chance, he would be redeemed and renewed in the sight of the Emperor. Now he knew better, as that promise turned to bitter ashes.

He shut out the cries and moans of those poor unfortunates who suffered in the Savage Morticians' lust for knowledge, their piteous cries unable to penetrate his bitter heart of stone. They were weak, allowing themselves to feel. To feel pain, remorse, anguish and pity. Vaanes had long ago shut himself off to those emotions and knew that it made him stronger.

'The strong are strongest alone,' he whispered, remembering those words when he first heard them from the mouth of one of his former paymasters.

At last their hellish journey came to an end as they entered a wide, circular arena with a dozen, rusted steel mortuary tables around its circumference, deep blood gutters running down the length of each one. An arrangement of iron poles, like the framework for some great gazebo, encompassed the anatomist's theatre, supporting a heavy block and tackle arrangement of meat hooks above each table. Large tubs and barrels for blood and waste trimmings were placed at convenient intervals, together with a long trough of dark water. A soiled workbench sat in the centre of the theatre, strewn with an assortment of short and long-bladed knives, cleavers, hatchets and hacksaws.

Swiftly, the Savage Morticians deposited each of the warrior band on one of the tables, securing their limbs with thick bands of iron and heavy bolts. Vaanes kicked out as the beast carrying him hacked off his jump pack with one blow and slammed him down on the table. A bronze claw slashed out, and Vaanes blinked away blood as the blade laid his face open to the bone.

The creature's dead features leaned in close to his own, hissing its crackling, unintelligible language in anger, and he spat blood in its eye. Its claw drew back to strike him again, but another of the Savage Morticians angrily hissed something and the blow never landed. Instead, it secured him to the table, ensuring that his hands were bound such that he could not unsheathe his lightning claws.

Vaanes watched as a robed monster on spiked tracks carried their weapons to an examination table and a pair of the Morticians began cataloguing them with studied interest. He tugged at the bindings on the table, looking to free himself and kill his enemies.

He didn't expect to escape alive, but perhaps he could take a few of these bastards with him before he died. Pasanius was bolted onto another table; his silver arm bound above the junction of metal and flesh, his forearm dangling over the sharp-edged sides. Their charges secured, most of the Savage Morticians departed, each of them eager to be about their own particular macabre experimentation.

Only two remained and Vaanes knew that if there was ever going to be a time to try and escape, this was it. The mutant creature their daemonic captor had called Sabatier limped into the theatre, nodding in satisfaction as he saw that the Space Marines were securely restrained.

'Not so defiant now,' it said to Vaanes, its malformed head still resting on its shoulder.

'When I get loose, I'm going to tear that head clean off and see if you still get back up, you damn freak!' shouted Vaanes.

Sabatier laughed his gurgling laugh. 'No. I going to watch you hoisted up on hooks and butchered. You and all your fellows.'

'Damn, you. I'll kill you!' screamed Vaanes, thrashing ineffectually at his bonds.

Sabatier leaned closer, its snapped neck causing its head to lurch and sway. 'I will enjoy watching you die. Watch you weep and soil yourself as they open you up and your innards spill out in front of you.'

Vaanes heard Leonid's familiar hacking cough, and twisted his head, his frustrations spilling out in an exclamation of rage. 'Will you shut up!' he yelled. 'Shut up or just die and stop making such a pathetic noise!'

But Leonid's cough was soon obscured as he heard the sharp whine of a sawblade powering up. Vaanes twisted his head to watch as the Savage Morticians bent over Pasanius, one extending steel clamps to hold his arm firm, while the other lowered a shrieking saw towards the flesh just above the sergeant's elbow.

Horrified, but morbidly fascinated, Vaanes watched as the saw bit into the meat of Pasanius's arm, sending arcing sprays of blood across the mortuary theatre. Pasanius yelled as the Savage Mortician worked the blade deep into his convulsing arm, the pain cutting through the fog of the sedative. The pitch of the slicing saw changed and Vaanes smelled the burning tang of seared bone as the blade cut into the humerus.

Blood flooded from the wound onto the floor, draining through a partially clogged sinkhole in the centre of the theatre with a horrid gurgling. Vaanes heard the two Guardsmen weep in terror at what was happening, but pushed them from his mind as he continued to watch the grisly amputation.

Within moments, the gruesome procedure was complete and the Savage Mortician who held the limb clamped tight lifted it clear of its former owner. Pasanius, the pain clearing his senses, rolled his head to see the horrific damage done to him and, though the light in this dreadful place was dim, Vaanes swore he could see the ghost of a smile crease the sergeant's features.

A gleaming cryo-chest was brought forth, wisps of condensing air gusting from within as it was opened, and the severed limb was placed carefully within.

The Savage Morticians straightened from their labours and moved around the theatre to the next body laid out before them: Seraphys.

'You will watch your men die one by one,' rasped Sabatier. 'Then you will join them.'

HE FELT NO pain and that was good.

The air was balmy, and condensation fell in a pleasantly warm drizzle from the cavern roof high above him. Uriel knew he should be working to gather in the long, gently waving sheaves of the harvest, but his limbs felt as though warm syrup flowed through his veins and he could not summon the effort to move.

A sense of peaceful contentment filled him and he opened his eyes, watching the stalks above him and knowing that he would be in for a hiding from his father if he didn't fill enough baskets, but, strangely, not caring. The sweet smell of moist crop sap filled his nostrils and he took a deep breath of the familiar aroma.

Eventually, he sat up, massaging the back of his neck where it had stiffened while he had been dozing, rolling his head back and forth on his shoulders. His muscles burned from his earlier exertion and he knew that he would need to stretch properly if he was to avoid painful cramps later. Pastor Cantilus's evening callisthenics at the end of the day should be enough to stave off such cramps though.

The soft, wet rain felt good on his clammy skin and he gave thanks to the Emperor for blessing him with such a peaceful life. Calth might not be the most exciting of worlds to grow up on, but with the entry trials for Agiselus Barracks coming up soon, he knew he would soon get the chance to show that he was ready for great things.

Perhaps if he did well he might...

Trials...

What?

He looked down at his limbs, seeing the powerfully muscled arms of a Space Marine and not the wiry arms of the six year old boy he had been when he had dreamed of entering the martial academy where Roboute Guilliman himself had trained. He pushed himself to his feet, standing head and shoulders above the harvest crop that had seemed so tall to him back then.

The people of his collective farm filled the underground fields, dressed in simple chitons of a pale blue as they worked hard, but contentedly, to gather the harvest. The field filled the cavern, stretching away in a gentle curve and following the line of the rocky walls of the underground haven. Silver irrigation machinery hummed and sprayed periodic bursts of a fine spray across the crop and Uriel smiled as he remembered many happy days spent industriously in this very cavern as a child.

But this had been before…

Before he had travelled to Macragge and begun his journey towards becoming a warrior of the Adeptus Astartes. That had been a lifetime ago and he was surprised at how vividly this scene, which he had long thought vanished from his memory, was etched upon his consciousness.

How then was he here, standing within a memory of a time long passed?

Uriel set off along the line of crops towards a series of simple white buildings arranged in an elegant, symmetrical pattern. His home had been situated in this collective farm, and the thought of venturing there once again filled him with a number of emotions he thought long-suppressed.

The air darkened as he walked and Uriel shivered as an unnatural chill travelled up his spine.

'I wouldn't go down there,' said a voice behind him. 'You'll accept that this is real if you do, and you might never come back.'

Uriel turned to see a fellow Space Marine, clad in the same pale blue chiton as the workers in the field, and his face split apart in a smile of recognition.

'Captain Idaeus,' he said joyfully. 'You are alive!'

Idaeus shook his scarred and hairless head. 'No, I'm not. I died on Thracia, remember?'

'Yes, I remember,' nodded Uriel sadly. 'You destroyed the bridge across the gorge.'

'That's right, I did. I died fulfilling our mission,' said Idaeus pointedly.

'Then why are you here? Though I am not even sure I know where here is.'

'Of course you do, it's Calth, the week before you took the first steps on the road that has ultimately led you back here,' said Idaeus, strolling leisurely along the path that led away from the farm towards one of the silver irrigation machines.

Uriel trotted after his former captain. 'But why am I here? Why are *you* here? And why shouldn't I go down to the farm?'

Idaeus shrugged. 'As full of questions as ever you were,' he chuckled. 'I can't say for sure why we're here, it's your mind after all. It was you that dredged up this memory and brought me here.'

'But why here?'

'Perhaps because it's a safe place to retreat to,' suggested Idaeus, lifting a wineskin slung at his waist and taking a long drink. He handed the skin to Uriel, who also drank, enjoying the taste of genuine Calth vintage.

'Retreat to?' he said, handing the wineskin back. 'I don't understand. Retreat from what?'

'The pain.'

'What pain? I don't feel any pain,' said Uriel.

'You don't?' snapped Idaeus. 'You can't feel the pain? The pain of failure?'

'No,' said Uriel, glancing up as the dark shadows of clouds began to gather in the topmost reaches of the cave and evil thoughts began intruding on this pastoral scene.

Dead skies, the taste of iron. Horrors unnamed and abominations too terrible to bear...

A distant rumble of thunder sent a tremor through the clouds and Uriel looked up in confusion. This wasn't part of his memory. The underground caverns of Calth did not suffer such storms. More clouds began forming above him and he felt a suffocating fear rise up within him as they gathered with greater speed and ferocity.

Idaeus stepped in close to Uriel and said, 'You're dying Uriel. They're stealing the very things that make you who you are... can't you feel it?'

'I can't feel anything.'

'Try!' urged Idaeus. 'You have to go back to the pain.'

'No,' cried Uriel, as a heavy, dark rain began to fall, hard and thick droplets sending up tall spumes of mud.

Suffocating, cloying, questing hands within his flesh, a horrific sense of violation...

'I do not want to go back!' shouted Uriel.

'You have to, it's the only way you can save yourself.'

'I don't understand!'

'Think! Did my death teach you nothing?' said Idaeus as the rain beat down harder, melting the skin on his bones. 'A Space Marine never accepts defeat, never stops fighting and he never turns his back on his battle-brothers.'

The rain pounded the fields flat, the workers running in fear towards the farm. Uriel felt an almost uncontrollable desire to join them, but Idaeus placed a palm on his chest and struggled to speak in the face of his dissolution. 'No. The warrior I passed my sword to would not retreat. He would turn and face the pain.'

Uriel looked down, feeling the weight of a perfectly balanced sword settle in his hand, the blade a gleaming silver and its golden hilt shining like the sun. Its weight felt good, natural, and he closed his eyes as he fondly remembered forging its blade in the balmy heat of the Macragge night.

'What awaits me if I go back?' he asked.

'Suffering and death,' admitted Idaeus. 'Pain and anguish.'

Uriel nodded. 'I cannot abandon my friends...'

'That's my boy,' smiled Idaeus, his voice fading and his form almost totally washed away by the hard rain. 'But before you go... I have one last gift for you.'

'What?' said Uriel, feeling his grip on this fantasy slipping and his perceptions growing dimmer. As the vision of his captain diminished, Uriel thought he heard him say one last thing, a whispered warning that vanished like morning mist… beware your black… sun? But the words faded before he could hold onto the sense of them.

Uriel opened his eyes, feeling the sting of amniotic fluids on his skin and hearing the heartbeat of the daemonculaba above him as reality rushed in once again. He roared in anger, feeling questing, umbilical tendrils invading his flesh. They burrowed in through the sockets cored into his body where the monitoring systems of his armour interfaced directly with his internal organs.

Suckling, feeding parasites wormed inside him, feeding and sampling his flesh.

CHAINS CLANKED AS a pair of dangling hooks connected by a horizontal iron bar were lowered from the framework that encompassed the anatomist's arena. Connected to sturdy block and tackle, the heavy hooks were dragged onto the metal gurney upon which Seraphys lay. As one Savage Mortician prepared the hooks, the other cut his armour from his body with practiced ease. Lastly, it removed the helmet from the Space Marine and produced a heavy iron mallet from the whirring mechanisms of its arm.

Before Seraphys could do more than shout a denial, it smashed the mallet repeatedly against his skull.

Seraphys grunted in pain, but after the sixth blow, his eyes glazed over and his head rolled slack. The Mortician nodded to its compatriot, who lifted the unconscious Space Marine's legs and sliced a heavy blade across his Achilles tendons then thrust a hook into each ankle for hanging support. Seraphys's legs were spread so that his feet hung outside the shoulders, and, satisfied his body was secure, the Savage Mortician hauled on the rattling pulley and dragged the body into the air.

'What are you doing?' shouted Vaanes. 'For the love of the Emperor just kill him and be done with it!'

'No,' hissed Sabatier. 'Not kill him. Not when he has such succulent meat on him. See how they keep arms parallel to legs? This provides access to the pelvis, and keeps his arms out of the way in a position for easy removal.'

Sabatier chuckled as it continued its gruesome narration. 'Observing anatomy and skeleton, you can see that you humans not built or bred for meat. Your large central pelvis and broad shoulder blades interfere with achieving perfect cuts too much. You are too lean as well, no fat. You see, some fat, though not too much, is desirable as "marbling" to add a juicy, flavourful quality to meat.'

'Damn you,' cursed Vaanes as he watched the Savage Mortician bend to the insensible Blood Raven. Red streams caked his face where it ran from the portions caved-in by the iron mallet. A long-bladed knife cut a deep, ear-to-ear slice through the hanging Space Marine's neck and larynx, severing his internal and external carotid arteries.

Blood sprayed from the cut before Seraphys's enhanced metabolism began clotting the flow. But Sabatier limped over and prevented the wound from closing completely by jamming the fused meat of his fists in the cut and allowing the bright, arterial blood to splash into a stained iron barrel.

Unable to bear the sight of the savage glee his captors took from his comrade being butchered like an animal, Vaanes turned his head away from the sickening surgery as a Savage Mortician prepared to remove his victim's head.

Vaanes heard the grotesque sound of muscle and ligaments being sliced and the ripping of tendon and skin as the Savage Mortician gripped Seraphys's head on either side and twisted it off where the spinal cord met the skull.

He squeezed his eyes tightly shut, straining at the thick fetters that held him immobile on the table. His face purpled and veins bulged taut against his skin as he fought.

'No use fighting, so do not,' called Sabatier, seeing his struggles. 'Just make meat tougher. Damage skin too, but no one cares about that, we get enough of that from flesh camps in mountains, despite what you destroy and burn.'

Despite the horror, Vaanes felt a sudden rush of interest. 'What do you need the skins for anyway?'

'To clothe the newborns!' said Sabatier proudly. 'The brood of the daemonculaba are expelled from the womb as mewling, skinless things. Those that survive have new skin to bind their flesh and make them whole, ready to become one of the iron masters!'

Vaanes felt his own skin crawl at this latest vileness. That the camps in the mountains were used to produce masses of skin to flesh newborn soldiers of the Iron Warriors was an abomination too far. He opened his eyes in time to see Pasanius rolling his eyes at him, desperately indicating that Vaanes should continue talking. For a second he was at a loss as to why, then saw that, without the length of his forearm, Pasanius had almost worked his cauterised stump from the iron clamp securing the limb to the table.

He forced himself to return his gaze to the horrific gutting. 'You said that the ones who survive have the skin bound to their flesh. What happens to the ones who don't survive?'

Sabatier rasped in laughter, fixing its attention squarely on Vaanes. 'Newborns too badly deformed or mutated are flushed away with rest of filth of Khalan-Ghol into mountains. Your bones and torn skin will join them soon.'

'The Unfleshed...' said Vaanes, recognising the terrible, red monsters that roamed the mountains from Sabatier's brief description. 'They are the failed births...'

'Yes,' hissed Sabatier. 'Most die in minutes, but some survive.'

'You will pay for this,' promised Vaanes, seeing Pasanius finally slide his arm from the restraint as the Savage Morticians continued their noisy work on the hanging carcass.

URIEL TRIED TO scream, but stinging birth fluids filled his mouth and his body spasmed as his weakened respiratory system fought to sift as much oxygen as it could from the liquid that filled his lung. He floated in the loathsome amniotic jelly of the daemonculaba's womb, his skin burning from leaking gastric fluids and the virulence of the flesh magicks used to warp and mutate the woman's body.

He struggled against the sutures that held him fast, feeling his strength grow with each one he felt rip from the blubbery flesh. His determination to free himself burned with a white heat in his breast and he thrashed like a mindless beast, tearing his bindings loose and leaving him floating and unbound in the womb.

Uriel clawed and bit at rippling folds of flesh, tasting blood and fatty tissue in his mouth as he tore his way upward, each breath a spike of fire in his lung. His vision was greying and his heartbeats sounded like thunder in his ears, thudding booms that echoed strangely, as though it was more than just his own heart he was hearing within this prison of flesh.

He twisted and kicked, always pushing up and stabbing forward with his hands.

Suddenly, his right hand burst into dryness, tearing through the drum-taut skin of the daemonculaba's belly. Galvanised by the prospect of near freedom, Uriel doubled his efforts, pressing his other hand into the tear and pulling it wider. The skin tore along the line of the stitches and frothing fluids drained from the beast's belly as it poured out onto the grilled walkway. Uriel pushed his head clear of the daemonculaba, vomiting up the foul birth juices and gasping in a great lungful of air. Stagnant and blood-soaked though the atmosphere in the chamber was, it still felt like the clearest mountain air of Macragge compared to the inside of the womb.

Twisting and turning, Uriel extricated his wide shoulders, using the additional leverage that granted to pull his bruised torso from the daemonculaba. And in a stinking wash of birth fluids, blood and viscera, Uriel fell from the creature's belly to the iron floor.

He lay coughing and gasping for breath, hearing cries of alarm nearby and looked up to see a pair of the hunched mutants in black rubber bodysuits racing towards him. They carried long halberds with curved blades and Uriel's fury surged around his body at the sight of them.

He pushed himself wearily to his feet as they came at him, stabbing their weapons towards his belly. Uriel dodged the first blade, swaying aside as the second jabbed for his groin.

Uriel gripped the haft of the first mutant's halberd, slamming his fist into its glass faceplate and pulverising its skull. He quickly reversed the weapon, easily blocking a clumsy swipe at his head, and stabbed his own blade through the second mutant's midriff, driving the haft clean through its body. The mutant shrieked in agony and Uriel kicked it from the weapon without pity.

He dropped to his knees beside the mutants, weeping and howling in blind rage, curling into a ball as anger and horror threatened to overwhelm him. He spat a mouthful of greasy fluid from his mouth, hearing a cursing, shouting voice.

Uriel forced himself to take a tight hold on the emotions surging within him as he recognised the voice as belonging to Ardaric Vaanes. He couldn't make out the renegade's words, but he could easily read the bitterness and fury in his tone.

His heart hardened with righteous anger, Uriel pulled himself unsteadily to his feet with the aid of the long halberd and set off in the direction of the shouting.

FIFTEEN

'EMPEROR DAMN YOU all to the depths of hell!' shouted Vaanes as Seraphys's dismembered corpse was taken down from the hooks on the block and tackle. Those hunks of meat not harvested for consumption were disposed of in the same barrels that overflowed with blood, and the clattering assembly was moved around the circumference of the theatre to the next Space Marine.

The Savage Morticians ignored his ravings and Sabatier just laughed, but their attention was fixed either on him or their next victim. And that was all that mattered.

He risked a glance towards Pasanius, and fought to keep a vengeful smile from his face as he watched the sergeant lean across the mortuary table. Using the ragged stump, he pushed the bolt from the restraint holding his other arm and the clanking of chains, Vaanes's shouting and the great booming of the Heart of Blood easily swallowed the squeal of rusty metal as the bolt slid through the clamp.

With his good arm free, he easily loosed the bolts holding his midsection and legs.

Vaanes shouted, 'Sabatier! The Unfleshed, what becomes of them?'

Sabatier looked up from dragging away the remains of Seraphys, his drooling features twisted in irritation. 'You ask too many questions! Cut out your tongue first!'

Vaanes saw Pasanius climb to his feet on the mortuary table and he shouted, 'Come here and do it then, Chaos filth!' as he saw the disgusting mutant corpse finally realise that Pasanius was free. It screeched a warning to the Savage Morticians, who spun to face him, surprisingly agile for such ungainly looking creatures. They shrieked in apoplectic fury, sounding more outraged than anything else.

Sabatier cowered behind the barrel of blood, but the Savage Morticians sped across the arena, bladed arms and pistoning legs carrying them with fearsome speed.

'Pasanius, watch out!' shouted Vaanes, but the sergeant had no intention of avoiding the incoming monsters. Instead, he leapt, feet first towards the nearest, and Vaanes heard metal and bone snap beneath his bootheels. It flailed for Pasanius, whirring drills and slashing blades cutting its own dead flesh as it struck at him.

Vaanes struggled uselessly once more as he watched the unequal battle, Pasanius gripping the black robes of the Savage Mortician with one hand as it tried to prise him from its body. The sergeant transferred his grip to the mesh scaffolding that supported its skull and slammed his forehead into its face. Even over the screaming Morticians, Vaanes heard the crunch of bone.

The Savage Mortician collapsed, its spider-like legs folding under it as it reeled from the impact. As it dropped, Pasanius released his grip on its body and dropped lightly to his feet beside it. The second creature tried to snap at him, but Pasanius kept the stunned creature between him and its slashing blades.

It backed away, unfolding longer, more deadly blades from the sheaths of its arms and Pasanius took the opportunity to step in and deliver a thunderous punch to the creature before him as it struggled to push itself to its feet. It howled in pain and Pasanius took hold of its quivering, beweaponed armature, alive with shrieking cutting implements, and rammed it into the monster's face.

Dead fluids and long-decayed skin flew as its own fist ripped its head to rotten shards. Desiccated flesh and bone sprayed, and its howls were silenced as it slumped forward with a long death rasp.

'Pasanius!' shouted Vaanes. 'Release me! Hurry!'

Pasanius looked as though he were about to take on the second Mortician alone, but nodded, backing away towards Vaanes as it leapt forwards on its long legs. He dodged the first slash of its blades, ducking below a high sweep of a second. Its leg hammered out and slammed into his stomach, doubling him up with a whooshing intake of breath.

Pasanius rolled aside as its blades stabbed the bloody ground and Vaanes saw that the sergeant would not be able to avoid its attacks for much longer. Sabatier ran from the dissection theatre as fast as his mutated gait allowed him. It screamed for aid and Vaanes knew that unless Pasanius could free him quickly, they were as good as dead.

Pasanius surged to his feet, leaping for the restraints holding Vaanes to the mortuary table. He lunged for the bolt at Vaanes's arm, his fingers connecting with the bolt and closing on the metal as another thumping blow sent him flying through the air. Pasanius landed with a steel crash on the table of saws, scalpels and their weapons, scattering bolters and Uriel's golden-hilted sword to the floor.

But Vaanes saw that the sergeant's effort had been enough. The bolt had been hauled clear as Pasanius had been kicked away and, with a feral roar of hate, Vaanes ripped his arm free and unsheathed his crackling lightning claws. With a few quick blows, the remainder of his restraints were hacked clear and he dropped from the mortuary table, bellowing a challenge to the Savage Mortician as it towered over Pasanius's battered form.

But before he could do more than take a single step towards the looming monster, a bloody, reeking figure vaulted onto an empty mortuary table and leapt for its terrible form. The figure held a long halberd above its head, with the wickedly hooked blade aimed towards the Savage Mortician's torso. He landed on the creature's back, driving the halberd deep into the monster's spine, the blade erupting in a flood of stinking, yellow fluids and gasses from its chest.

As terrible a wound as it was, the creature made no sound, but twisted on some internal axis to dislodge its gore-smeared attacker, while leaving the halberd embedded in its body.

'Uriel!' shouted Pasanius, hurling the golden-bladed sword towards him, and Vaanes was shocked to see that this wild, animalistic figure was none other than the former Ultramarines captain.

Ventris caught the sword on its downward arc, the blade flaring to life as he thumbed the activation rune. Without words, Uriel and Vaanes moved left and right, the Savage Mortician ripping the halberd from its body and tossing it aside, a blaring shriek of warning blasting from the vox-units on its throat.

'We have to finish this thing!' shouted Vaanes.

Ventris did not reply, darting in to slash at the Mortician's legs. It dodged back, stabbing for him with a roaring saw blade, longer than the largest eviscerator. Ventris rolled beneath its screaming arc and hacked his sword upwards through the arm, severing it in a wash of blue sparks.

Vaanes also leapt to attack, jumping onto the creature's arched back as it reared away from Uriel's blow. He hammered one clawed fist through its neck and held on with the other as the thrashing monster attempted to dislodge him. Hooks hanging from the structure surrounding the arena slammed into him, but he grimly held on, stabbing his claws through the Savage Mortician's body again and again.

The Savage Mortician shrieked in pain and he tumbled from the beast's back as Ventris chopped its convulsing legs from under it. Vaanes rolled away from its monstrous body as it thrashed and jerked on the ground, dying in agony as Ventris stabbed and stabbed and stabbed at its loathsome corpse.

'Ventris!' he called. 'It's dead. Come on, let's get the hell out of here!'

The Ultramarine stabbed the creature's chest one last time, taking huge, rasping breaths and looking more like one of the followers of the Blood God as he revelled in the slaughter he had just perpetrated.

'Uriel, come on!' urged Pasanius. 'We have to go now. There's bound to be more of these things coming!'

Ventris nodded, joining Vaanes and Pasanius and gathering up their weapons from where the Savage Morticians had dumped them. The bloody Space Marine sheathed his sword and hefted his bolter when Leonid shouted, 'Wait! Don't go, don't leave us!'

'Why?' asked Vaanes.

'What?' snapped Ellard, amazed that such a question had even been asked. 'We'll die otherwise!'

'What's the use in freeing you? You're going to die anyway,' said Vaanes, turning away and gathering up his own guns.

'Uriel!' cried Leonid. 'You can't mean to leave us here? Please!'

Ventris said nothing for long seconds, his chest still heaving with the thrill and adrenaline of combat. Vaanes moved past him, but Ventris gripped his arm and locked eyes with him, slowly shaking his head.

'We leave no one behind,' he said firmly.

'We don't have time for this!' snapped Vaanes. 'They won't make it, but we might!'

'I think I was wrong about you, Vaanes,' said Uriel sadly. 'I thought you still had courage and honour, but your heart is dead inside. This place has destroyed your soul.'

'If we don't go now, we'll all die, Ventris, cut to bloody rags by more of those things!'

'Everyone who serves the Emperor dies bloody, Vaanes,' said Uriel. 'All we get to do is choose how and where. Every warrior deserves that, and I'm not leaving without them.'

Ventris turned and ran back into the arena, and with Pasanius's help, began freeing the pitiful remainder of their once-proud warrior band.

'If they don't kill you, follow my tracks!' called Vaanes. 'Sabatier said something about all the filth of Khalan-Ghol being flushed out into the mountains, so there's got to be a way out of here!'

Ventris nodded, too busy to answer, as the shrieks of approaching enemies drew nearer.

Cursing the Ultramarine for a fool, Vaanes set off into the depths of the cavern.

URIEL FREED LEONID and Ellard, the coughing Guardsmen nodding their thanks as they clambered free and gathered up their own weapons. Soon they had freed the surviving members of the warrior band and set off into the macabre wilderness of the chamber, the great heartbeat and the screams of both victims and pursuers echoing weirdly from the rocky walls of the cavern.

Vaanes's trail was not hard to follow; the cloven bodies of mutants and overturned surgical tables clearly marking his passage through the cavern. The sounds of pursuit drew ever closer, their ragtag band weary to the point of collapse through a combination of sheer physical exhaustion and terror.

The sound of rushing fluids came from ahead and Uriel staggered into a vast, open sluice chamber filled with a multitude of filth-encrusted chutes and aqueducts that either pierced the walls of the cavern, rose up from below the ground or sluiced down from the upper tiers of the daemonculaba. The roaring noise of tonnes of excrement, waste matter and dead flesh rivalled the thudding of the Heart of Blood. Everything washed into a pool of stinking effluent that in turn poured through a colossal pipeway in the cavern wall.

A waterfall of filth, body parts, corpses and decomposing foetal matter poured from the cavern and away from the fortress. A way out…

Dead mutants littered the chamber, hacked in two by Vaanes's mad dash for freedom, and Uriel saw that there was only one way they would get out of this damnable place.

'We cannot fight them here! Into the tunnel!' he shouted and set off through the pool, wading thigh-deep in the bobbing detritus of surgical waste matter. He had no idea where the wide tunnel led or even if their situation would be improved by jumping in, but it had to be better than this.

The going was slow, but as he looked back over his shoulder to see a dozen or more of the Savage Morticians emerge into the sluice chamber, he pushed forward through the sludge with renewed vigour, sheathing his sword as he went.

The warrior band reached the churning, roaring waterfall of the tunnel and, one by one, leapt into its stinking darkness. Uriel heard the splash of thick, mechanical limbs entering the water behind him, and without a backwards glance, leapt in after his warriors.

Rushing filth enfolded him, its repulsive contents buffeting him as he tumbled downwards. Darkness and half-light warred with one another, and as he slipped beneath the surface of the scummy fluid, he was grateful for the shadows that hid the dead horrors flushed from the Halls of the Savage Morticians.

The roar of the tunnel was deafening, its slope too precipitous and the waters too deep to gain any handholds. He fought to the surface, gasping for breath and swallowing mouthfuls of foetid, frothing matter. The thunder of great pumps and the whining of enormous filters echoed from the encrusted walls and Uriel felt his skin burning with the pollutants and toxic discharge.

He slammed into the tunnel wall as it bent to one side, losing his grip on his bolter and watching as it spun off into the water. His fingers scrabbled for purchase, but he was being carried along too fast to find any kind of grip. Huge blades churned the water, hurling severed body parts and disembowelled carcasses into the air and Uriel desperately kicked out to avoid them. A rusted spar of sharpened metal slashed the water next to him and stinging water blinded him as he was carried along by the torrent, spinning him beneath the water.

As his head broke the surface, Uriel saw a huge foaming mass of spuming effluent ahead and heard the thunderous crash of water falling hundreds of metres. Jagged archipelagos of ruined flesh and foetal islands had agglomerated into decaying masses at the edge of a waterfall, and Uriel fought against the immense flow of the river of waste to direct his frenetic course towards one.

The roar of the waterfall and the stench of rotten flesh and organic waste matter filled his senses, threatening to overwhelm him. As the current hurled him onwards, he gave one last desperate kick and thrust his hands out to grip the mass of body parts before him. His hands closed on the clammy, greasy flesh, his fingers breaking the surface and spilling a mass of rotted innards into the water. Dead eyes and glassy features stared at him from the lifeless mounds as the sodden flesh disintegrated beneath his grip. He tumbled away, spinning around and cried out as he was swept over the edge of the waterfall.

Suddenly Uriel was in freefall, hurtling downwards through the air and tumbling end over end into the unknown depths. His limbs flailed uselessly as he fell and he roared in defiance at the darkness below. Was this how it was to end? Dying, broken to pieces within the refuse of the Iron Warriors?

He caught a glimmer of light on the fractured glass surface of water below and straightened his body to reduce the coming impact. His body knifed into the water, the filthy murk closing over him as he plunged into its inky black depths. Drowned corpses swirled in the cold darkness with him, rotted arms wrapping around him and eyeless skulls mocking him with their sightless gazes.

Uriel kicked for the surface, the breath hot in his supernumerary lung, fighting against the dead of the Savage Morticians who were dragging him down to lie with them forever.

His head broke the surface and he heaved a great breath of air, the dank stench of the rushing, water-filled tunnel welcome after the stinking depths. Swirling filth foamed around him and, as he shook his head clear, he heard and saw giant, churning blades chopping the water ahead of him, smashing the water and debris ahead to a fleshy morass.

Uriel fought against the current, spitting effluent from his mouth as he struggled against the worsening flow of water. The great fan blades spun too fast to dodge, but as he was carried ever closer, he saw that the leading edges of the fan did not quite reach the roof of the cavern...

Was it possible they didn't reach the bottom of the tunnel also?

Knowing he had only once chance of survival, Uriel took a deep breath and dived beneath the surface of the corpse-filled water, feeling the pressure waves of the huge blades buffet him from side to side as they foamed with water stained red with flesh and blood. The pounding pressure wave of the fan blades was a fierce force dragging him onwards, but with powerful strokes and kicks, Uriel swam downwards towards the bottom of the tunnel.

His lung burned with fire and his vision greyed, but through the murk of the water, he saw the soiled rockcrete base of the tunnel. Ahead, a thrashing mass of bubbles obscured the lethal edges of the fan blades, and he couldn't tell whether there was enough room for him to pass beneath. With no other choice before him, he pulled himself along the bottom of the tunnel, feeling the enormous beat of the blades.

He cried out, a breath of bubbles bursting from his mouth as he felt a searing slash across his back. Instinctively he pulled himself down and forward, letting what little air remained in his lungs pull him towards the surface as he cleared the blades. Uriel's struggles and kicks grew weaker and weaker, his limbs leaden as oxygen starvation took its toll on his already weakened physique.

And then his head broke the surface once more and he vomited up polluted matter, retching in a reeking lungful of air. The current beyond the fan blades was still strong, but he found that he could keep his head above the water with a little effort.

Amazed that he still lived, he circled in the water, searching for other members of the warrior band.

'Pasanius!' he yelled. 'Vaanes!'

His voice echoed from the dripping walls of the tunnel, but there was no response to his call and he despaired at seeing any survivors. Had they all been chopped to unrecognisable hunks of meat by the filtering blades of the tunnel?

Now that his immediate danger had passed, Uriel wondered where this tunnel eventually led. He had no way of knowing for sure, but felt that he must have travelled for many kilometres through these hellish passages. Where then did it empty?

Even as he formed the thought, he felt the speed of the water increase and saw a bright dot of white light up ahead. Once more, he heard the roaring crash of a waterfall, but this time there were no potentially life-saving archipelagos to cling to and Uriel was carried towards the tunnel mouth at greater and greater speed.

The white sky through the opening before him grew rapidly in size, until he was finally swept through into the open air.

Mountains soared above him and the dead sky spread its hateful whiteness above the dark rocks of Medrengard as Uriel was spat out of Khalan-Ghol hundreds of metres above the ground.

He tumbled downwards through the air towards a repulsive, scum-frothed pool, catching a glimpse of armoured warriors crawling from the water as he fell. The breath was driven from him by the impact as he slammed into the surface of the pool and he swallowed great mouthfuls of rank water.

Uriel spun through the murky liquid, kicking out, though he had no idea of which direction was up and which was down. He felt hands upon him and surrendered to their grip, feeling himself hauled upwards and dragged from the water. He retched, spewing huge mouthfuls of foamed, oily water and rolled onto his side as hands slapped him on the back.

He looked up to see the filthy, streaked face of Ardaric Vaanes, bleeding and battered.

'You made it out then?'

'Only just,' coughed Uriel, feeling as though he had done a dozen sparring sessions with Captain Agemman, leader of the Ultramarines veterans company. He sat up, feeling a measure of his strength returning with each stale breath he took. He took a moment to survey his surroundings, seeing that the deep pool sat in a high-sided basin of rock at the base of a tall peak of glistening rock, the water bubbling and swirling with treacherous currents. One side of the basin was a sheer face of smooth rockcrete, a vertical slab of stone with the pouring outflow they had fallen from hundreds of metres above them.

He looked around to see who else had survived the horror of Khalan-Ghol, feeling a cold hate suffuse him as he saw that the escape from the dungeons of the Iron Warriors had cost them dear. Ardaric Vaanes had survived, as had two other Space Marines, a Wolf Brother named Svoljard and a White Consul, whose name Uriel did not know. He let out a great sigh of relief as he saw Pasanius sitting on the wet rocks at the side of the pool. Such was his joy that it took him a moment to realise that his sergeant's arm ended just above the elbow, that his forearm had been removed. A crusted mass of knotted scar tissue graced the stump of his arm, and though the wound must surely have been painful, Pasanius gave no sign of it.

'What happened to you?' he asked.

'Those monsters cut it off,' said Pasanius. 'Hurt like a bastard.'

Despite himself, Uriel laughed at such masterful understatement.

Leonid and Ellard were also amongst the living, but Uriel could see that Sergeant Ellard was grievously wounded, a terrible gash running across his stomach. Uriel was no Apothecary, but even he could see the wound would soon be mortal.

'You are a survivor, colonel.'

'I would be dead were it not for Pasanius,' said Leonid, cradling Ellard's head and staring at his friend's terrible wound. 'But I don't think...'

Uriel nodded in understanding and said, 'No... but I am glad you are alive.'

Putting the wounded sergeant from his mind for now, Uriel turned to face Ardaric Vaanes. 'Where are we? Do you know this place?'

'Aye,' said Vaanes, 'and we should be away quickly.'

'Why?'

'Because this is the hunting ground of the Unfleshed,' said Vaanes, looking to the ridges surrounding the pool.

Uriel felt a thrill of fear as he remembered the malformed, red-skinned monsters that had devoured the wretched inhabitants of the Iron Warriors' flesh camp.

'You're right,' he said, pushing himself unsteadily to his feet and gripping the filmy hilt of his golden sword. 'We need to get out of here.'

'Too late,' said Leonid, pointing towards the ridge that ran along the circumference of the basin. 'They're already here...'

Uriel followed Leonid's pointing finger to the top of the ridge and the breath caught in his throat as he saw the silhouetted forms of perhaps a hundred of the Unfleshed surrounding them.

℧
SIXTEEN

URIEL WATCHED THE silhouetted shapes resolve into clarity as they descended the high slopes of the ridge above. They came quickly, scrambling their way over the jagged rocks with great speed despite their horrifically malformed limbs. Great intakes of breath heaved from wide chests as they scented their prey on the air and drooling jaws parted to reveal huge, yellowed fangs. Blackened claws slid from meaty fingers.

As hideously deformed as the beasts they had seen attack the flesh camp, these monsters were a similar horror of insane anatomies. Limbs turned inside out, pulsing organs grown and mutated through warped external skeletons, heads and chests fused with metastasised bone sinews, siamese twins wrapped together with fleshy streamers and some with grossly swollen bellies that resembled the daemonic mothers that had brought them into being.

'From one death sentence to another,' observed Ardaric Vaanes sourly, unsheathing his lightning claws.

'Shut up, Vaanes!' snapped Uriel as he drew his sword and the blade leapt to fiery life. The members of the warrior band who had retained hold of their weapons drew them and readied themselves for battle. It would be an uneven fight, but it was a fight they would make nonetheless. Leonid left the wounded Ellard and picked up a jagged rock.

The Unfleshed closed the noose about them, grotesquely muscled and swollen limbs propelling them rapidly across the rocky floor of the basin, hungry for the taste of warm, bloody meat in their mouths. The nearest beast splashed into the foetid water of the pool, the noise of the waterfall from the outflow not enough to cover its bestial grunts of monstrous appetite. Its muscled forelimbs formed powerful fists as it prepared to attack. Uriel and the others formed a circle as the creatures loped forwards, ready to die on their feet, facing their deaths like warriors.

'You meat...' hissed the Unfleshed as it waded through the water towards them.

Uriel started in surprise, amazed the creature could speak. Vaanes had told him that these beasts were the by-blows of the Iron Warriors and until now he had believed them to be nothing more than failed experiments carried out by the Savage Morticians, similar to the creature, Sabatier.

But seeing them up close and having been fed to the wombs of the daemonculaba himself, he now knew better. He pictured the children being sutured into the daemon wombs alongside him and knew that such an imperfect method of hot-housing Chaos Space Marines must result in more failures than successes...

'Emperor's blood,' whispered Uriel as the realisation of his shared kinship with the Unfleshed sank in. He glanced up at the outflow pipe high on the rockface above them, understanding how these beasts came to be in the mountains.

He returned his attention to the Unfleshed as the beast reared up to its full height and bellowed its challenge. Uriel felt a burst of adrenaline dump into his system at the size of the thing. Its barrel chest was crisscrossed with imperfectly grafted folds of skin, pinned to its muscular frame by shards of bone and its head was a vast, hydrocephalic nightmare with multiple, yellowed eyes and a distended jaw filled with blunt fangs. Perfect for grinding his bones to digestible mush.

'Blood,' said the monster, nodding its elephantine head and licking its lips.

The remaining creatures held back as the lead beast approached, and Uriel sensed a tribal, pack mentality at work.

Uriel stepped towards the beast and held his sword, two-handed, before him.

'What are you doing?' said Pasanius.

'I think this is the alpha male of the group,' said Uriel. 'Perhaps if I can kill it, the others won't attack.'

'Or they'll tear us to pieces all the quicker,' said Leonid.

'True,' allowed Uriel, 'but I don't think we have much choice.'

'Give it your best shot,' said Vaanes, sheathing his claws.

The beast watched Uriel approach, flexing the huge muscles of its upper body. He tried to read its expression, but its blunted features gave him no clue as to its thoughts.

'Come on then. Come and get me if you want to eat me!' he roared.

The monster sprang forward and Uriel barely avoided a swinging blow that would have taken his head off had it connected. He ducked beneath the punch and dodged around the side of the Unfleshed, swinging his sword for its back. The blade sliced barely a centimetre into its flesh and Uriel felt the shock of the blow up his arms, horrified that the lethal energies of his weapon had failed to cut the monster in two. Before he recovered from his surprise, the beast was upon him, its meaty fists clubbing him down. Uriel collapsed into the water, rolling from a thunderous stamp that sent up a geyser of brackish water.

'Uriel!' shouted Pasanius, stepping forward to help.

'No!' shouted Uriel, scrambling away from the monster on his backside and into the downpour of rushing water driving down from the Halls of the Savage Morticians. 'If you help me, they will all attack!'

Uriel pushed himself clear of the foaming torrent and lunged forward, stabbing for the monster's groin. The tip of the blade barely penetrated the Unfleshed's hide before sliding clear without further injury. It roared and picked him up in one fist, snapping its jaws shut on his side. Uriel shouted in pain and twisted in its grip, saving himself from being disembowelled and stabbed his sword for the monster's head.

The blade scraped across its eyeballs, drawing a howl of pain from the monster. Its claws spasmed and Uriel fell from its hand. He landed before the Unfleshed and thrust his sword straight forward with a roar of anger, putting his entire strength behind the blow.

He yelled in triumph as the point of the blade punched through a weaker section of the monster's flesh and he drove the blade clean through its body. A heavy fist smashed into his shoulder and Uriel was driven to his knees in the water. He felt his collarbone crack and released his grip on the sword hilt. He looked up into the Unfleshed's weeping-blood eyes and knew that he could not defeat it. Despite a crackling blade impaling its belly, the monster gave no indication that it even felt the wound.

Uriel had stood before the might of a star god, had destroyed the heart of a tyranid hive ship, had faced the unimaginable power of a rogue psyker and now he was to die at the hands of this monster that was kin to him at a genetic level. Its clawed hands reached for him, but before they closed on his head and crushed his skull to splinters, a bellowing roar echoed from the sides of the basin and, as one, the Unfleshed that surrounded them drew back in fearful respect.

A stillness fell, a sudden peace, and Uriel watched as a terrible beast, larger than the others, descended slowly into the water-filled depression. The Unfleshed Uriel had just fought was a gargantuan, swollen monstrosity, but this beast was an order of magnitude greater than that. Its physique was colossal and rippled with abnormal growths of fierce muscle, a powerhouse of primal, destructive energy. Red and raw, its body was a glistening mass of wet, exposed musculature, sinews bulging and contracting as it moved. If there was an alpha male of the Unfleshed, then surely this must be it. Uriel recognised the thing as the creature that had led the attack against the huddled slaves at the flesh camp.

Its head was lodged low between its shoulders, a red skull face with burning yellowed eyes set within a prosaic arrangement of gory features. Without the guise of flesh, its features were dead and expressionless, its mouth lipless, its nose a torn gash in the centre of its face. Unlike many of its brethren, it retained a measure of its humanity in its form, though massively built beyond even what the ancient legends told of the primarchs.

But worst of all, Uriel could see a gleam of intelligence lurking within its calculating gaze. Where the others of its kind might be spared the awful knowledge of their fate and the horror of their existence, Uriel knew that this terrible creature knew full well how the fates had damned it.

It descended into the valley with a guttural series of grunts and roars, the Unfleshed that surrounded them backing away from what must surely be their lord... the Lord of the Unfleshed. Uriel shivered as he conjured the phrase, grimacing at its appropriateness.

It stomped and splashed through the pool towards him and pushed the creature with Uriel's sword still lodged in its belly aside. It crouched in the water, its head still metres above Uriel and hauled him to his feet, dragging him close to its horrific features.

Uriel struggled against it, but its strength was beyond even that of a dreadnought and he was held firm. He was lifted from the water and held close to the Lord of the Unfleshed's face, the ragged flaps of skin around its nasal cavity fluttering as it smelled him.

A thick tongue slid from its mouth and Uriel gagged at the monster's corpse-breath as the leathery appendage licked the skin of his face. Before he could do more than retch, the Lord of the Unfleshed dropped him back into the water, and he grunted in pain as the splintered ends of his collarbone ground together.

The massive creature turned to the Unfleshed around the pool.

'Not meat yet! Maybe they Unwanted like us. Smell and taste flesh mother meat on him,' it said, its words twisted and guttural.

The Unfleshed threw back their heads and gave voice to a plaintive howling that echoed from the high peaks of the mountains, and Uriel could not decide whether the ululating cry was a gesture of welcome or a desperate cry of pity.

THE HALLS OF the Savage Morticians still echoed to the pounding beat of the Heart of Blood, the air still stank of desperation and the psychic deadness still draped the soul. But for all that it remained the same, there was a subtle shift in the dynamic of the chamber. Honsou had not noticed it at first, but as he followed the bronze-legged Savage Mortician through the paths of the dying, he noticed it in the downcast skull-faces of each of the black-robed monsters...

'Have you noticed...' whispered Obax Zakayo, reading his master's features.

'Aye,' replied Honsou. 'They are afraid, and that doesn't happen often.'

They had good reason to be afraid, though, thought Honsou. Prisoners entrusted to their destruction by the master of Khalan-Ghol had killed two of their number and escaped. Obviously dark memories of the fortress's last master still burned in the minds of the Savage Morticians and Honsou found himself relishing their apprehension as he reached the mortuary circle where the Space Marines who followed Ventris had been shackled.

In the centre of the circle were the mangled, dismembered remains of two Morticians; their flesh hacked to carven, grey chunks. Honsou knelt beside the nearest, pulling the dead arm bearing a vicious drill from the ruin of its head.

'I fear I may have underestimated this Ventris and his band,' he said.

'You think he might be more than one of Toramino's mercenaries?'

Honsou nodded. 'I'm beginning to think that he might not have anything to do with Toramino at all, that he might be here for reasons of his own.'

'What reasons?'

Honsou did not answer at first, but snapped his fingers and indicated that one of the hissing, dark surgeons approach. A tall beast with wide, bladed legs and clicking hydraulic claws for arms stooped to face him, its gleaming jaws centimetres from Honsou.

'You put Ventris in the daemonculaba?' he asked.

'Yes. Stitched him in. Into the womb with the others. He should not be alive.'

'No,' agreed Honsou. 'He very definitely should not. Show me.'

'Show master of Khalan-Ghol what?' hissed the Savage Mortician.

'Show me where you implanted him,' ordered Honsou. 'Now.'

The creature nodded and reared up to its full height, stalking off between the barrels of viscera and blood towards the nearest ramp that led to the gantries of the daemonculaba. Honsou and Obax Zakayo followed, noting with interest some of the more cruel and unusual experiments in pain that were being carried out in the quest for deathly knowledge.

'With all due respect, my lord,' began Obax Zakayo. 'Is it wise to concern yourself with a fate of a few renegades? The armies of Lord Berossus are at the gates of Khalan-Ghol.'

'And?'

'And they are within days at most of breaching the walls...'

'Berossus will not get in, I have plans for him.'

'Any you want to share?'

'Not with you, no,' said Honsou as they reached the top of the ramp. 'Understand this, Obax Zakayo, you are my servant, a mere functionary, and nothing more. You served a master who had forgotten why we fight the Long War, a master who had allowed the bitter fires of the False Emperor's treachery to smoulder instead of burning brightly in his breast.

Have you forgotten how our Legion was almost destroyed piece by piece by his uncaring, unthinking betrayals? Have you forgotten how he allowed us to stagnate and become little more than gaolers? The False Emperor drove us to this fate, condemning us to suffer an eternity of torment in the Eye, and while Forrix forgot that, I did not.'

'I only meant–' began Obax Zakayo.

'I know what you meant,' snapped Honsou, making his way along the gantry past the heaving masses of flesh that rippled in agony with new life. 'You think I don't know of your entreaties to Toramino and Berossus? You have betrayed me, Obax Zakayo. I know everything.'

Obax Zakayo opened his mouth to protest, but Honsou turned and shook his head. 'You can say nothing. I don't blame you. You saw an opportunity and you took it. But to think that someone like you could outwit me... please!'

The servo claws hunched at Obax Zakayo's shoulders reared up, snapping like the jaws of evil, mechanical snakes, and the giant Iron Warrior gripped his toothed axe tightly.

Honsou smiled and again shook his head as a pair of Savage Morticians loomed behind Obax Zakayo. The axe was snatched from his hands and broken like a twig as bronze claws snapped shut on his limbs and crackling, piston driven pincers cut the mechanised arms from his back.

'No!' shouted Obax Zakayo as he was lifted from his feet. 'I know things you need to know!'

'I don't think so,' said Honsou. 'Toramino is not so stupid as to trust you with anything of importance.'

Honsou nodded to the Savage Mortician and said, 'Do with him as you will.'

He turned away as Obax Zakayo screamed curses upon his name and was carried away by the Savage Morticians to his no doubt bloody fate. Honsou had not been surprised by Obax Zakayo's treachery; indeed it had proven to be extremely useful. Soon Berossus and Toramino would learn the price for trusting such a poor traitor.

Putting Obax Zakayo from his mind he walked along the grilled gantry to where a wheezing mass of blubbery, torn flesh was being prodded and cut further by the creature that had led him here. The pain-filled features of the daemonculaba stared at him in mute horror, its glassy eyes rolling in unspeakable pain. Honsou ignored its suffering and leant down to examine its torn belly, where recently sutured flesh had been rudely torn open.

'From the inside...' noted Honsou. 'He climbed out himself.'

The Savage Mortician bobbed its head, though Honsou could clearly see its confusion at such a thing.

'How could Ventris have done this?' asked Honsou.

'Not knowing. Daemonculaba tasted him, fed him soporifics. Should not have happened,' rasped the Mortician.

'And yet it did,' mused Honsou, pulling back the greasy folds of flesh from the daemonculaba's ruptured belly. The slippery innards of the great beast heaved and shuddered at his touch and Honsou drew back as the creature went into a violent seizure, its entire frame shuddering. Though it had no voice to call its own, a high, keening wail ripped from its ruined throat and a flood of gore gushed from the open wound.

'What's happening to it?' demanded Honsou.

'Womb ready to expel its issue,' explained the moribund surgeon.

More blood and amniotic fluids poured from the daemonculaba's belly and the Savage Mortician reached in to hack at its internal structure with long, sword-like limbs. Hissing, gurgling tubes carried away dead fluids and Honsou heard the crack of bone and the sharp twang of severed sinews from within the daemonculaba's body.

The Mortician cut the wound wider and with a final splash of blood and blue and purple viscera, the daemonculaba's offspring spilled out onto the floor.

He landed with a wet, meaty thump; powerfully muscled and hothoused far beyond the callow youth he had been when implanted. Honsou knelt beside the quivering newborn, the skinless body shivering with the violence of its delivery. Even wrapped in a mutated length of glistening umbilical cord, Honsou could see that this birth was perfect – no need to flush him into the pipes with the rest of the discards.

Filmy, acidic residue coated his muscles and he began weeping in pain as the Savage Mortician lifted him from the ground.

'Wait,' said Honsou, stepping forward and wiping handfuls of bloody, matter-flecked slime from the newborn's gleaming red skull and clearing the birth fluids from his skinless features.

The newborn lifted his head at Honsou's touch, looking into his face with a fierce earnestness. Honsou held the newly born Chaos Space Marine towards its dark, clawed midwife.

'Clean him and then clothe him in fresh skin,' he ordered. 'Give him Obax Zakayo's armour and bring him to me when he becomes ready.'

The Savage Mortician nodded and dragged away the mewling newborn.

And the master of Khalan-Ghol laughed, realising that the Gods of Chaos could sometimes have a sense of humour after all.

WHETHER THE MANUFACTORY facility had fallen into disuse and then been colonised by the Unfleshed or whether they had taken it by force was unknowable, but judging by the state of disrepair and wreckage strewn around, either explanation was possible. Uriel had been shocked at the hideousness of the Unfleshed he had seen on the surface of Medrengard, but they were nothing compared to the horrors of those who remained below in the darkness. How such things could live baffled Uriel, but even as he felt revulsion at their terrible forms, he felt a great pity for them. For they too were victims of the Iron Warriors' malice.

Uriel had no way of measuring, but reckoned on the passing of perhaps ten or twelve hours since they had escaped the dungeons of Khalan-Ghol. Led by the Lord of the Unfleshed on a gruelling march into the high peaks of mountains, they had set off to an unknown destiny, though it had been impossible to tell whether they had been taken as brothers-in-arms or prisoners. Uriel and Pasanius had bound Ellard's wound and carried him with them, despite Vaanes's protestations that the man was as good as dead and should be left behind.

Upon leaving the pool at the base of the cliffs where their lunatic flight from the depths of Khalan-Ghol through the sewage pipes had carried them, Uriel had seen that they were indeed many kilometres from the fortress. After covering many more, the warrior band had eventually been led to a great crack in the mountainside where noxious clouds of vapour gusted and spoil heaps of refuse and bones were gathered.

Descending into the stygian darkness of the mountainside, the rock passageway had eventually opened into a wide chamber where perhaps some underground earthquake had ripped an underground manufactory apart. Buckled, iron columns supported a bowing ceiling on vast, riveted girders, and beams of murky light speared down through shattered coolant towers that pierced the roof and illuminated the echoing space. Twisting bridges of knotted rope connected the forests of columns and a great pit had been dug or drilled in the centre of the manufactory floor where something unseen glittered and twisted in the dim light.

Piles of shattered machinery lay rusting in pools of moisture and groups of the Unfleshed, hundreds of them, gathered around them, their red bodies wet and glistening. These Unfleshed were the true monsters, so mutated and deformed as to be unable to hunt, or – in some cases – even move. Piles of altered flesh, twisted limbs without number and warped symbiotes of fused flesh that gibbered and howled in constant pain.

'So many of them...' said Uriel.

Further comment had been prevented as they were herded down into the depths of the manufactory and the Lord of the Unfleshed indicated that they should sit in the lee of a great pressing machine, with hammers the size of a battle tank.

'You. Not move.'

'Wait,' said Uriel. 'What do you want with us?'

'Tribe needs talk. Decide if you Unwanted like us or just meat. Probably we kill you all,' admitted the Lord of the Unfleshed. 'Good meat on your bones and fresh skin to wear.'

'Kill us?' snapped Vaanes. 'If you're just going to kill us, then why the hell did you bother to bring us here, you damn freak?'

'Weak of Tribe need meat,' rasped the monster, staring at Ellard with undisguised appetite. The sergeant had surprised them all by surviving the journey, though Uriel saw that he surely could not live much longer. Blood soaked the makeshift bandage of his tattered uniform jacket and his face was deathly pale. 'They cannot hunt, so we bring meat to them.'

'You had to ask,' growled Pasanius.

Vaanes shrugged and slumped to the ground with his back to the Ultramarines.

The Lord of the Unfleshed had then departed, making his way down to the floor of the manufactory to rejoin his tribe, leaving them in the company of a dozen gigantic monsters, each larger than a dreadnought and equipped with a fearsome array of gnashing fangs and long, dripping talons.

Since then, they had waited for hours in the stinking twilight as their captors – or brethren – debated whether to kill them or not. The creature Uriel had fought in the outflow pool was one of their guards, though it still appeared not to care about the weapon lodged in its flesh.

'Damn it, but I wish I knew what they were doing,' said Uriel, turning from the creatures that surrounded them.

'Do you?' said Pasanius. 'I'm not so sure.'

'We can't stay here. We have to get back to that fortress.'

'Back to the fortress?' laughed Ardaric Vaanes. 'Are you serious?'

'Deadly serious,' nodded Uriel. 'We have a death oath to fulfil, to destroy the daemonculaba or die in the attempt.'

'You'll die then,' promised Vaanes.

'Then we die,' said Uriel. 'Have you heard nothing I have said to you, Vaanes?'

'Don't you dare lecture me about honour and duty, Ventris,' warned Vaanes. 'I have seen enough of what your honour has to offer. Most of us are already dead, and for what?'

'No warrior ever died in vain who died for honour in the service of the Emperor.'

'Spare me your borrowed wisdom, Ventris,' sneered Vaanes. 'I have had my fill of it. If we survive this, there's no way I'm going anywhere near that fortress again. I am done with your heroics and will leave you to die.'

'Then I was wrong about you, Vaanes,' said Uriel. 'I thought you had honour left within you, but I see now that you do not.'

Vaanes ignored Uriel and stared sullenly at the lumpen, misshapen beasts that watched over them.

Uriel turned to Pasanius and said, 'Then we are on our own, my friend.'

'So it would seem,' agreed Pasanius, slowly, and Uriel could see that his friend was struggling to speak – burdened by the terrible weight of guilt.

An awkward silence fell between the two friends, neither knowing the right way to break it or how to begin to say what needed to be said.

'Why didn't you tell me?' said Uriel at last.

'How could I?' sobbed Pasanius. 'I was tainted. Touched by evil and corrupted!'

'How? When?' asked Uriel.

'On Pavonis, I think,' said Pasanius, the words, now undammed, pouring from him in a rush of confession. 'You remember that I hated the augmetic arm the moment the artificers of the Shonai cartel grafted it to me?'

'Aye,' nodded Uriel, remembering how Pasanius had complained that the arm could never be as good as one grown strong through a lifetime of war.

'I didn't know the half of it,' continued Pasanius. 'After a while I got used to it, even began to appreciate the strength in the arm, but it was when we fought the orks on the *Death of Virtue* that I first realised something was wrong.'

Uriel well remembered the desperate fighting to destroy the ork and tyranid infested space hulk that had drifted into the Tarsis Ultra system and heralded the great battle against a splinter fleet of bio-ships from Hive Fleet Leviathan.

'What happened?'

'We were fighting the orks, just before you killed their leader, you remember? One of the greenskins got behind me, nearly took my damn head off with his chainsaw.'

'Yes, you took the blow on your arm.'

'Aye, I did, and you saw the size of that blade. My arm should have been hacked in two, but it wasn't. It wasn't even scratched.'

'But that is impossible,' said Uriel.

'That's what I thought, but by the time we got away and were back at the Thunderhawk, it was as good as new, not a scratch on it.'

'I remember...' whispered Uriel, picturing Pasanius's arm reaching down to haul him to safety when their demolition charges had begun to tear the space hulk apart. 'It shone like silver.'

'I know,' agreed Pasanius, 'but it didn't register on me until we were back aboard the *Vae Victus* that my arm should have been pulverised. I thought maybe I'd imagined how hard I'd been hit, but now I know I didn't.'

'How is it possible? Do you think the adepts of Pavonis had access to some form of xeno tech?'

'No,' said Pasanius, shaking his head. 'The silver-skinned devils we fought beneath Pavonis, the servants of the Bringer of Darkness, they could do the same thing. No matter how hard you cut, stabbed or shot them, they could get back up again, their bodies putting themselves back together right before your eyes.'

'The necrontyr,' spat Uriel.

Pasanius nodded. 'Aye, necrontyr. I think maybe part of the Bringer of Darkness went into me when it cut off my arm, something corrupt that waited and then found a home in the metal of my new arm.'

'Why did you say nothing?' said Uriel. 'It was your duty to report such a thing.'

'I know,' said Pasanius, dejectedly. 'But I was ashamed. You know me, it's always been my way to deal with things myself. I've been that way since I was a boy on Calth.'

'I know, but you should still have reported it to Clausel. I will have to report it when we get back to Macragge.'

'You mean *if* we get back,' reminded Pasanius.

'No,' said Uriel, emphatically. 'When.'

Uriel turned as he heard footfalls approaching. Colonel Leonid, his face gaunt and worn stood behind him and said, 'Sergeant Ellard is dead.'

Uriel looked over to where the big man lay, and stood, placing his hand on Leonid's shoulder. 'I am sorry, my friend. He was a fine man and a good soldier.'

'He shouldn't have had to die like this, alone in the darkness.'

'He wasn't alone,' said Uriel. 'You were with him at the end.'

'It's not right though,' whispered Leonid. 'To have survived so much and then to die like this.'

'A man seldom has the choice in the manner of his death,' said Uriel. 'It is the manner in which he lives that is the mark of a warrior. I did not know Ellard well, but I believe he will find a place at the Emperor's side.'

'I hope so,' agreed Leonid. 'Oh, and you're wrong, by the way.'

'About what?'

'About having to get back into Khalan-Ghol on your own. I will come with you.'

Uriel felt his admiration for Leonid soar and said, 'You are an exceptional man, colonel, and I accept your pledge of courage. Though you should know that Vaanes is almost certainly right, this will, in all likelihood, be the death of us.'

Leonid shrugged. 'I don't care any more. I have been living on borrowed time ever since the 383rd was ordered to Hydra Cordatus, so I plan to spit in death's eye before he takes me.'

A slow clapping sounded and Uriel's anger flared as he saw Vaanes sneering at them. The renegade Raven Guard shook his head.

'You are all fools,' he said. 'I will say a prayer for you if we don't get killed by these monsters.'

'Be silent!' hissed Uriel. 'I will not have any prayers from the likes of you, Vaanes. You are not a Space Marine any more, you are not even a man. You are a coward and a traitor!'

Vaanes surged to his feet, hate flaring in his violet eyes and his lightning claws snapped from his gauntlet. 'I told you that people never called me that twice!'

Before blood could be spilled, a great shadow fell across the company and the mighty form of the Lord of the Unfleshed blotted out the light. A coterie of hideously deformed creatures accompanied him, and a hunchbacked monster with its head fused into its spine limped towards Ellard's corpse.

It dipped a long talon into the sergeant's torn belly and raised its bloody digit to its slit of a mouth.

'Deadflesh,' it said. 'Still warm.'

The Lord of the Unfleshed nodded its thick head. 'Take it. Meat for Tribe.'

'No!' shouted Leonid, as the hunchback effortlessly lifted the sergeant's body.

Pasanius reached out with his remaining arm and held Leonid back, hissing, 'No, don't. That's not your friend any more, it's just the flesh he wore. He's with the Emperor and there's nothing these monsters can do to him now. You will only get yourself killed needlessly.'

'But they are going to eat him!'

'I know,' said Uriel, standing before the struggling man. 'But you have pledged yourself to our death oath and if you break it, you break it for all of us.'

'What?' spluttered Leonid.

'Aye,' nodded Uriel. 'We are all bound to this quest now. Pasanius, me and now you.'

Leonid looked set to argue, but Uriel could see that the fight had gone out of the man as he realised the pact he had made with the Ultramarines. He nodded numbly and his struggles ceased as the Lord of the Unfleshed loomed above them.

'You come now,' said the monster.

'Where?' said Uriel.

'To the Emperor. He decide whether you die or not.'

℧
SEVENTEEN

THE EMPEROR'S ARMOUR was filthy, stained with the residue of uncounted millennia of industry, the eagle on his breastplate a series of rusted bronze strips. Beaten metal shoulder guards hung from his mighty shoulders and a pair of beatific wings of stained metal flared from his back. Over twenty metres tall and suspended by thick, iron chains within the great pit at the centre of the manufactory, it was a creation of supreme devotion.

Uriel felt like a child against its immensity, remembering the first time he had seen a statue of the Emperor in the Basilica Konor on Calth. Though the statue there had been masterfully carved from beautifully veined marble quarried from the deep wells of Calth, this one – for all its crudity – was no less impressive.

The Unfleshed's Emperor hung over the blackness of the pit, its armour and limbs fashioned from whatever scrap and machinery had been left behind when the manufactory had been abandoned.

Whereas some zealous preachers of the Ministorum might find it blasphemous that such hideous creatures had created such a crude idol of the Emperor, Uriel found it curiously touching that they had done so.

'May the Emperor preserve us!' hissed Pasanius as he laid eyes upon the suspended statue.

'Well we're about to find out,' replied Uriel as he realised his first impression had been correct when he had felt like a child before this idol.

Who knew how long the Unfleshed had lived beneath the surface of Medrengard or what their memories were of the time before their abduction and implantation within the horror of the daemonculaba?

But one thing was clear: of the innocent children who had been transformed into the Unfleshed, one memory had survived – constant and enduring: the immortal and beneficent Emperor of Mankind.

Through all the vileness that had befallen the Unfleshed, they still remembered the love of the Emperor and Uriel felt an immense sadness at their fate. No matter that they had been horrifically altered to become monsters, they still remembered the Emperor and fashioned his image to watch over them.

Uriel and the others were pushed roughly to the edge of the great pit as the Unfleshed painfully drew near. Uriel saw that there were hundreds of them – many unable to walk on their mutated legs, corkscrewed bones or fleshy masses that had once been limbs, and so were helped by their brethren.

'God-Emperor, look at them!' said Vaanes. 'How can such things be allowed to live?'

'Shut up, Vaanes,' said Uriel sadly. 'They are kin to you and I, do not forget that. The flesh of the Emperor is within them.'

'You can't be serious,' said Vaanes. 'Look at them. They're evil.'

'Are they? I'm not so sure.'

A ripple of hunger and self-loathing went round the pit as the Lord of the Unfleshed turned and drew himself up to his full height. He reached back and pulled Uriel forwards, lifting him easily from the ground. Powerless to resist, Uriel felt the ground beneath him fall away as he was dangled over the bottomless pit.

'Smelled mother's meat on you,' roared the Lord of the Unfleshed. 'You washed out from mountain of iron men, fell from the Wall. But you not look like us. Why you have skin?'

Uriel's mind raced as he tried to guess what response would not see him cast into the pit. The yellowed eyes of the monster bored into his and Uriel saw a desperate longing within them, a childlike need for... for what?

'Yes!' he yelled. 'We came from the mountain of the Iron Warriors, but we are their enemies.'

'You are Unwanted too? Not friends with iron men?'

'No!' cried Uriel, shouting so that the Unfleshed around the pit could hear him. 'We hate the iron men, came to destroy them!'

'Saw you before,' snarled the Lord of the Unfleshed. 'Saw you kill iron men in mountains. We took much meat then.'

'I know. I saw.'

'You kill iron men?'

'Yes!'

'Mother's meat on you, yes?'

Uriel nodded as the creature spoke again. 'Iron men's flesh mothers made us ugly like this, but Emperor not hate us like iron men, he still love us. Iron men try to kill us. But we strong and not die, though dying be good thing for us. Pain stop, Emperor make pain go away and make us whole again.'

'No,' said Uriel, finally understanding a measure of this creature that, for all its massive strength and colossal size, was but a child within its monstrously swollen skull. It spoke with a child's simplicity and clarity of the Emperor's love, and as Uriel looked into its eyes, he saw its deathly craving to atone for its hideousness.

'The Emperor loves you,' he said. 'He loves all his children.'

'Emperor speaks to you?' said the Lord of the Unfleshed.

'He does,' agreed Uriel, hating himself for such deception, but understanding its necessity. 'The Emperor sent us here to destroy the iron men and the dae... the flesh mothers that made you like this. He sent us to you so that you might help us.'

The creature pulled him close and Uriel could sense its suspicion and hunger warring with a deep-seated desire to take revenge on its creators, those that had made it into this warped form.

It smelled him once more and Uriel just hoped that the stench of the daemonculaba that had stayed its hand at the outflow pool was still strong on him.

But the Lord of the Unfleshed roared in anguish, drawing back his arm, and Uriel cried out as he was hurled out across the pit.

URIEL SAILED THROUGH the air, his vision spiralling in a kaleidoscope of images: warped beasts that had once been children, a rusted iron chain, silvered panels of beaten metal and the black, depthless void of the pit. He slammed into the hanging effigy of the Emperor and the breath was knocked from him by the impact.

He snatched at the metal, scrabbling for a handhold, feeling his ragged fingernails break off on rivets as he slid down the rough iron. The black hole of the pit yawned before him, promising death, but his fingers closed on a panel of beaten iron, not quite flush with the giant statue's body. Portions of its edges were sharp and he felt the tip of his middle finger slice off on the jagged metal. The panel bent and screeched, peeling away from the statue's body, but it slowed his descent enough for him to be able to secure a handhold on the bronze eagle on the Emperor's breastplate.

Uriel hung over the great depths of the pit, holding on for dear life with one hand, swinging above the darkness of the pit as the Unfleshed roared and – those that were able – stamped their feet, shouting, 'Tribe! Tribe! Tribe!'

Now that he had a better grip on the statue, Uriel pulled himself up the strips of metal that formed the eagle and swung himself onto the Emperor's shoulder guards, his breath coming in great gasps.

The Lord of the Unfleshed stood immobile at the edge of the pit, and Uriel had no idea what to do next. He watched as the Unfleshed took hold of the remains of the warrior band, dragging Pasanius, Vaanes, Leonid and the other Space Marines to the edge of the pit.

'No!' he shouted, risking standing upright and leaning on the swaying statue's giant helm. 'No!'

Then the miracle happened.

Whether it was some long-dormant mechanism within the battered machine forming the statue's helmet – given a brief resurgence of life by Uriel's movement – or the power of the Emperor himself, Uriel would never know, but at that moment, a radiant light burst from the crudely-formed visor.

A bass hum, like a charging generator, built from beneath the helmet and the Unfleshed drew back in terror from the great effigy as the glow intensified. Uriel felt the metal of the helmet grow hot to the touch and though he had no idea as to what was happening, was not about to let such a chance go by.

He shouted over to the Lord of the Unfleshed. 'See! The Emperor wants you to help us! Together we can destroy the flesh mothers and the iron men!'

The great beast dropped to its knees, its wide jaws open in rapture as a terrible moaning and wailing built from the throats of the Unfleshed gathered around the pit.

Hot sparks leapt from the metal of the helmet and Uriel realised he was going to have get off the statue soon or risk being electrocuted by whatever was doing this. He edged along the Emperor's shoulder guards, begging the Master of Mankind's forgiveness for such base treatment of his image as he worked his way over to the nearest of the supporting chains.

No sooner had he clambered onto the chain, lying across its thick links and pulling himself away from the helmet – which now shone with a fierce, blinding glow – when a great thunderclap boomed and it exploded in an arcing shower of blue lightning.

The Unfleshed wailed in fear as the statue of the Emperor plummeted into the darkness of the pit, the chains supporting it flopping with a great clang against its sheer sides. Uriel swung on the chain, bracing his legs for impact against the side of the pit and feeling the ceramite plates of his armour buckle with the force of it.

Uriel spun crazily above the depthless chasm, knuckles white as he held onto the flaking links of the chain. He hung there until he had got his breath back and carefully began the long climb to the top.

As he climbed he suddenly felt the chain being pulled from above. Able to do nothing else, Uriel awaited whatever fate had in store for him. He looked up in time to see the massive, raw hand of the Lord of the Unfleshed reach down and lift him from the chain.

He was lifted up and deposited roughly on the earthen ground beside Pasanius and Ardaric Vaanes, both of whom looked at him with expressions of fearful awe. Uriel shrugged, too breathless to speak.

The Lord of the Unfleshed knelt beside him and said, 'Emperor loves you.'

'I think that maybe he does...' gasped Uriel.

The Lord of the Unfleshed nodded and pointed to the pit. 'Yes. You still alive.'

'Yes,' gasped Uriel. 'You are right, the Emperor does love me. Just as he loves you.'

The creature nodded slowly. 'Will help you kill iron men. Flesh mothers too. Should not be more of us.'

'Thank you...' hissed Uriel.

'Emperor loves us, but we hate us,' said the Lord of the Unfleshed, painfully. 'We did nothing, did not deserve this. Want to kill iron men, but not know how to get into mountain. Cannot fight over high walls!'

Uriel pulled himself breathlessly to his feet and, despite his brush with death, smiled at the Lord of the Unfleshed as a portion of their journey into Khalan-Ghol returned to him with a clarity that was surely more than mere memory.

'That doesn't matter,' said Uriel. 'I know another way in.'

KHALAN-GHOL SHOOK with the fury of the renewed bombardment, shells exploding like fiery tempests against its ancient walls. Armies of heavy tanks and entire corps of soldiers mustered at the base of the gigantic ramp that led to the mountainous plateau which was all that remained of the fortress's outer defences and the spire of the inner keep.

Temporary, yet incredibly robust, revetments and redoubts had protected the workers and machinery constructing the ramp and now that it was complete, Berossus began his final assault.

A marvel of engineering, it climbed thousands of metres up the side of the mountain, beginning many kilometres back from the rocky uplands of its base. Paved with segmented sheets of iron, rumbling tanks climbed in the wake of a pair of monstrous Titans, their armour stained red with the blood of uncounted thousands of sacrifices, the thick plates still dripping and wet. Equipped with massive siege hammers, pneumatic piston drills and mighty cannon, these colossal land battleships also carried the very best warriors from Berossus's grand company. These warriors would lead the assault through the walls of the fortress and tear it down, stone by stone.

A gargantuan-mouthed tunnel led into the bedrock of the ramp, huge rails disappearing into the darkness and running to the very base of the mountain itself. Great mining machines had travelled through the tunnel and even now prepared to breach the underside of the fortress, burrowing into the very heart of Honsou's lair. Tens of thousands of soldiers waited in the sweating darkness of the tunnel to invade the fortress from below. The traitor, Obax Zakayo, had provided precise information regarding the best place to break into Khalan-Ghol and together with the frontal assault, Honsou's life could now be measured in hours.

Confident that this was to be the last battle, Berossus himself led the attack at the head of a pack of nearly a hundred blood-maddened dreadnoughts.

The final battle for Khalan-Ghol was about to begin.

'WE CANNOT STOP this attack,' said Onyx, watching as the Titans of Berossus began their inexorable advance up the ramp to the fortress. Though still many kilometres away from the top, the scale of their daemonic majesty was magnificent. 'Berossus will sweep us away in a storm of iron and blood.'

Honsou said nothing, the ghost of a smile twitching at the corner of his mouth. He too watched the huge force coming to destroy them. Hundreds of screeching daemonic warriors spun and looped in the sky above phalanxes of weapon-morphing monsters whose flesh seethed and bubbled with mecha-organic circuitry. Scores of howling, spider-limbed daemon engines clanked and churned their way up the ramp, jetting noxious exhaust fumes, the hellish entities bound to their iron bodies eager for slaughter now that they were free of their cages.

Clad in his dented and battered power armour, with a reckless look of battle-hunger creasing his pale features, and sporting a gleaming silver bionic arm in place of the one his former master had gifted him with, Honsou seemed unfazed by their approaching doom.

Onyx was puzzled by this, but had long since realised that the inner workings of Khalan-Ghol's newest master were a mystery to him – the half-breed did not resemble or behave like any of the warsmiths he had served in his aeons of servitude to the masters of this fortress.

'You do not seem overly concerned,' continued Onyx.

'I'm not,' replied Honsou, turning from the cracked ramparts of the topmost bastions of the spire. A hot wind was blowing, tasting of ash and metal. Honsou took a deep breath, at last turning to face his champion.

'Berossus hasn't let me down this far,' said Honsou, staring out at the great tunnel that led into the ramp and, no doubt, beneath his fortress. 'And I hope he won't now. Not at the last.'

'I don't understand.'

'Don't worry, Onyx, I know your concern is for your own essence, not my life, but you don't need to understand. All you need to do is obey me.'

'I am yours to command.'

'Then trust me on this,' grinned Honsou, and looked down to the level below, where smoke and crackling lightning conspired to obscure his own Titans and the masterful works he had prepared for Berossus. He stared up into the featureless white sky and the sun that burned like a black hole above him. 'I have fought the Long War almost as long as Berossus and Toramino and have stratagems of my own.'

'For your sake, I hope so,' said Onyx. 'Even if we manage to stop this attack, there is still the matter of Lord Toramino. His army is yet to be blooded.'

Honsou glanced to the glow of fires and forges beyond those of Berossus's encampments, where Toramino waited, unseen and unknown. Here, at last, Onyx caught a flash of unease.

'He waits for Berossus to grind us and his own warriors to dust before marching in to take Khalan-Ghol and become lord of its ruins.'

'And how will we stop him?'

Honsou laughed. 'One problem at a time, Onyx, one problem at a time.'

THE HATEFUL SOUND of massed artillery fire was muted and distant, though Uriel knew it must be perilously close to be heard this far beneath the mountains. Dust drifted in lazy clouds from the tunnel roof, and fine pebbles skittered and danced upon the floor. The darkness was absolute, even his enhanced vision had difficulty piercing the gloom.

Heat filled the tunnel along with the hot, foetid stink of animals, though these were no animals. They were, or at least had once been, human.

Hundreds of the Unfleshed filed along the fearful passages beneath the mountains, their winding route taking them through echoing crystal chambers, disused manufactorum and up dizzyingly steep stone channels hacked into the rock. Their massive bodies filled the passageways as they led Uriel and the others back towards Khalan-Ghol.

They travelled through dark and secret ways under the mountains, forgotten by all save them, the hidden, abandoned culverts and the lost, forgotten passageways that led towards their fate.

Behind Uriel, Pasanius grunted with effort, his journey made all the harder by virtue of his limb's amputation, but wherever he had encountered difficulty, the Lord of the Unfleshed reached back and lifted him onwards.

The giant creature led the way through the darkness, his huge form easily filling the width of the passage, and were it not for his hunched shoulders and stooped head, he would surely have dashed his skull open on drooping stalactites.

The Lord of the Unfleshed marched with newfound purpose, his long, loping stride setting a fearsome pace through the secret mountain paths. Uriel winced with every step, his breath painful in his single functioning lung and the pain of his cracked collarbone and ribs stabbing into him without the balms of his armour's dispensers to dull them.

Further back, a twisted creature with a withered twin fused to its back carried Leonid, the stunted sibling clutching the grimacing colonel tightly in its embrace. And further back yet came Ardaric Vaanes and his two surviving Space Marine renegades.

When the rapture of the Emperor's coming to life before the Unfleshed had died down, the creatures had embraced Uriel's cause with all the zeal and fervour of a crusade, mustering those who could hunt and fight to join them. It had made Uriel want to weep at the holy joy that infused every one of them and made his deception of them even harder to bear.

As he had gained his feet before the Lord of the Unfleshed, it had beckoned to one of its tribe, and another of the beasts loped towards him. Uriel saw that it was the creature he had fought in the outflow pool, his sword still jammed in its belly.

'Take blade,' said the Lord of the Unfleshed and Uriel nodded, gingerly gripping the hilt of the weapon. He had pulled, muscles straining as he fought the suction of flesh, bracing his feet on the floor of the manufactorum to gain better purchase. The sword was wedged tightly in the beast's body, and he was forced to twist the blade to allow it to move. At last, it slid grudgingly from its sheath of flesh, the creature remaining stolidly silent throughout. As it came free, the giant beast moved to join the remainder of its awed brethren.

'Thank you,' said Uriel.

The Unfleshed nodded respectfully and Uriel had felt a glowing ember of hope fan to life in his heart.

But his initial relief and elation at such a turn of events had soon turned sour when he had been reunited with his comrades and Ardaric Vaanes spoke to him.

'They will kill you when they discover you have lied to them,' said the renegade as the Unfleshed had girt themselves for war, gathering crude iron cudgels. Most needed no weapons however, their horrific mutations equipping them for killing without the need for such things.

'Have I?' Uriel had said, guardedly. 'I do the Emperor's work, and so now do they.'

'The Unfleshed?' said Vaanes, aghast. 'You think the Emperor would work through such beasts? Look at them, they're monsters. How can you think that such creatures are capable of being instruments of His will? They are evil!'

'They carry the flesh of the Emperor within them,' snapped Uriel. 'The blood of ancient heroes flows in their veins and I will not fail them.'

'Don't think you can fool me, Ventris,' sneered Vaanes. 'You are no messenger of the Emperor, and I can see in your eyes that you know you're not either.'

'It does not matter what I believe any more,' said Uriel. 'What do *you* believe?'

'I believe that I was right about you.'

'What does that mean?'

'That I knew you were trouble the moment I saw you,' shrugged Vaanes. 'It doesn't matter anyway. As soon as we get to the surface, myself and the others will leave you and your motley band.'

'You are really going to turn your back on us? After all that has happened, all the blood spilt, the death and the pain? Can you really do that?'

'I can and I will,' snarled Vaanes. 'And who would blame me? Look around you, look at these monsters. They are all going to be dead soon, and their blood will be on your hands. Think about it, you're going to try and storm a besieged fortress with a tribe of cannibalistic mutants, a dying Guard colonel and a sergeant with one arm. I am a warrior, Ventris, plain and simple, and there is nothing left to me except survival. To go back to Khalan-Ghol is madness, and attacking that fortress isn't my idea of courage, it's more like suicide.'

Vaanes gripped Uriel's shoulder and said, 'You don't have to die here. Why don't you and Pasanius come with me. You're pretty handy in a fight and I could use a warrior like you.'

Uriel shrugged off the renegade's arm and said, 'You are a fine warrior, Ardaric Vaanes, but I was wrong to have thought you might regain your honour. You have courage, but I am glad that I do not go into battle with you again.'

Hatred flared in the renegade's eyes and his expression became hard as stone.

Without another word, Vaanes stalked away.

Uriel put the renegade from his mind as he saw a patch of bright light coming from ahead and realised that the noise of battle was swelling in volume as well. With renewed vigour, he climbed after the Lord of the Unfleshed and emerged, blinking into the harsh while light of Medren-gard.

The noise of the battles raging around Honsou's fortress was tremendous, and Uriel saw that the secret paths of the Unfleshed had brought them out into the rocky uplands near the base of Khalan-Ghol itself, the plains before the fortress hundreds of metres below them.

High above, the ramparts of the fortress were wreathed in the fires of battle, and Uriel saw that they were going to have to ascend into the very heart of the maelstrom raging above them.

MANY KILOMETRES AWAY, the clang of picks and shovels echoed in the hot, lamp-lit confines of the mineworks beneath the great ramp. A wide gallery had been excavated, some nine hundred metres wide and with a gently sloping floor. A warrior in stained iron armour watched as hundreds of slaves and overseers hauled vast flatbed wagons bearing drums of explosives and fuel to be packed into the length of the excavations.

The long gallery was almost full, packed with enough explosives to level the mountain itself, knew Corias Keagh, Master of Ordnance to Lord Berossus himself. The tunnels to reach the underside of Khalan-Ghol would be his masterwork. It had been hard, slow work and cost the lives of thousands, but he had succeeded in getting the complex web of tunnels to exactly the right spot. It was almost a shame to blow such a perfect example of siege mining apart.

Thirty metres above him – if his calculations were correct, and he had no reason to doubt them, for Obax Zakayo had been very precise in his treachery – were the catacombs of the fortress, where the revenants of previous masters of Khalan-Ghol were said to haunt its depths. Keagh knew that such tales were probably nonsense, but in the Eye of Terror it never paid to scoff at such things too openly.

But word of these tales had filtered back to the thousands of human soldiers who had spent the last few months billeted in the garrison tunnels he had constructed within the body of the great ramp, and he had heard ill-favoured mutterings concerning this attack. He had ritually flayed these doomsayers, but a pervasive sense of dread had already taken hold.

Despite this, all the soldiers were armed and ready to begin the assault upon the opening of Khalan-Ghol's belly, and Keagh was eager to finally get to grips with the foe.

His armour thrummed in the heat, its internal systems struggling to keep his body temperature even.

The heat in the tunnels was fearsome – more than Keagh would have expected at such a depth – but he paid it no mind, too intent on the spectacle of destruction he was about to unleash.

THE BATTLEMENTS WERE aflame, gunfire and steel scything through men and stone in devastating fusillades of heavy calibre shells. Mobile howitzers moving in the midst of the armoured column approaching the top of the ramp rained high explosive shells within the last line of bastions, filling the air with spinning fragments of red-hot metal.

Men died in their hundreds, ripped apart in the devastating volleys or flamed from the wall by incendiary shells fired from the upper bastions of the approaching Titans.

But Berossus was not going to take Khalan-Ghol without a fight and Honsou's Titans and revetted artillery positions had laid-in targeting information and punished the approaching column terribly. Tanks exploded as armour-penetrating shells slashed down from above and tore through their lighter upper armour. Such casualties were bulldozed aside without mercy, tumbling down the steep sides of the ramp to smash to pieces on the rocks below. But no matter how many Honsou's gunners killed, the column continued its relentless advance.

Honsou gripped onto a splintered corbel of rock and watched the approaching army with a mixture of exhilaration and dread.

Logistically Berossus had the upper hand, and he was using it to strangle the life from the defenders of his fortress – or what was left of them. Onyx was right, they could not defeat this army conventionally.

But Honsou did not intend to fight conventionally.

'Come on, damn you!' he shouted into the deafening crescendo of noise. He struggled to penetrate the gunsmoke, but could see nothing through the acrid fog.

Onyx looked at Honsou in confusion, but said nothing as more shells landed nearby. Whizzing shrapnel ricocheted from the walls and Onyx leapt before Honsou, allowing several plate-sized blades of metal to hammer into his daemonic flesh rather than shred his master.

'Onyx!' called Honsou, dragging the daemonic symbiote to its feet. 'Look towards Berossus's army and tell me what you see!'

Onyx staggered over to the edge of the wall and shifted his vision patterns until he could see clearly across the entirety of the battle. Streamers of fire and starbursts of explosions flickered like distant galaxies, but his eyes pierced the chaos and confusion of the battle with ease.

The lead elements of Berossus's army had smashed their way onto the spire's plateau and were less than a hundred metres from the last wall that stood between them and final victory. Dreadnoughts howled in battle fury and the Titans strode behind them like avatars of the gods of battle, weapons roaring with prayers to their dark masters.

'Berossus is at the wall!' shouted Onyx. 'He will be upon us in moments!'

'No! The ramp!' returned Honsou. 'What's happening at the end of the ramp!'

'I see tanks, hundreds of tanks,' yelled the daemonic symbiote, barely audible over the concussive booms of artillery fire. 'They are gathered beside the entrance to the mineworkings at the base of the ramp and are simply awaiting their turn to begin the climb.'

'Excellent,' laughed Honsou. 'Oh, Berossus, you are even more of a fool than I took you for!'

SATISFIED THAT THERE was just the right amount of explosives, shaped and arranged to explode upwards into the fortress, Corias Keagh retreated swiftly from the gallery beneath Khalan-Ghol, unwinding a long length of insulated cable from the servo-rig on his back. Darting pincer arms mounted on the rig kept the cable from fouling and ensured that it remained straight and level.

'Here should do it,' he said to no one in particular as he turned into the armoured bunker he had constructed for just this moment.

The pincer arms cut the cable and craned over his shoulder to hand him the brushed copper end of its length. Synchronous timers had been calibrated from his armour's own power unit and he hooked the end of the cable into a power port on the chest of his breastplate. A winking red light on his helmet's visor turned to gold and he felt a physical stirring as the charges he had set armed.

He opened a channel to his lord and master and said, 'Lord Berossus, the charges beneath the fortress are set and ready to be detonated.'

'Then detonate them now,' came the familiar growling rasp of his master's voice. 'We are almost at the head of the ramp.'

Pausing to savour this moment of his greatest triumph, Keagh allowed the dim silence of the tunnel to enfold him before sending a pulse of energy along the length of the cable.

THE MOUNTAIN ITSELF shook with the force of the blast far below, thousands of tonnes of ordnance and fuel exploding in one simultaneous blast that instantly atomised a whole swathe of the bedrock of Medrengard. Honsou staggered and fell to his knees as the shockwave rippled throughout the fortress. Tall towers that had stood for millennia crashed down to ruin and every fighting man was knocked from his feet.

Tanks, and even one of Berossus's Titans, tumbled from the ramp as the shockwave fanned upwards from below. Cracks split the stonework of the battlements and hundreds died as they fell to their deaths upon shattered ramparts. The main wall crumbled, torn like paper and breached in a dozen places by the shear forces twisting the mountain.

Aftershocks continued to rumble, shaking Khalan-Ghol to its foundations and Honsou heard a deep, answering roar, as though the fortress itself cried out in rage at this violation.

His fortress had been breached, but Honsou felt nothing but elation as the growling tremors that gripped his fastness began to fade.

'Now I have you, Berossus!' he snarled. 'Iron Warriors, ready yourselves!'

PHASE IV – THE ENEMY OF MY ENEMY

EIGHTEEN

CORIAS KEAGH FELT the thunderous roar of the explosion force its way down his tunnels like the bellow of an angry god. He braced himself against the wall of his underground bunker, confident that his works would survive this violence he had unleashed. He heard the metal of his tunnel supports groan in protest at the power of the shockwave, but Keagh had been digging mines and bringing ruin to fortresses from below for thousands of years and knew his craft well.

Only when the temperature readout on his visor leapt upwards did he realise that something was amiss.

He heard it first as a whooshing rush of superheated air, forced through the tunnels ahead of something unimaginably hot. He rushed out into the tunnels as a terrible fear suddenly seized him.

Leaping from tunnel to tunnel, a flashing cloud of incandescent vapours foamed along the length of his workings. Behind it came a roaring, seething orange glow of molten metal and Keagh heard the screams of the soldiers as the lethally hot steam boiled the flesh from their bones.

He knew then that every one of the thousands of men in the tunnels beneath the ramp was going to die. His tunnels had not breached the sepulchres of Khalan-Ghol, but somewhere else entirely.

But how could that be, when the location of Keagh's breaching gallery had come straight from Obax Zakayo…?

In the split second Keagh had left of life, he realised that that they had been horribly deceived – that all they had striven for was ruined.

He turned to run, but even one as enhanced as an Iron Warrior could not outrun millions of tonnes of roaring molten metal as it spilled from the forges of Khalan-Ghol, destroying everything before it and liquefying the earth of the ramp as it went.

Keagh was engulfed in the rushing torrent of fire and had the exquisite horror of a last few seconds of life before his armour was melted away and his flesh vaporised.

URIEL FELT THE immense power of the subterranean explosion spread through the landscape and stumbled, gripping the sharp rocks of Khalan-Ghol's peak tightly as the tremors shook the foundations of the world itself. Plumes of glowing, orange steam geysered from the foot of the mountain and, as he watched, more and more began bursting from channels cut into the monstrous ramp.

'What in the Emperor's name?' breathed Uriel as he looked up and saw the top of the ramp sag and collapse upon itself as though the weight of earth supporting it was being steadily removed.

'A countermine?' shouted Pasanius.

'It would need to have been colossal to cause such damage,' said Uriel, shaking his head.

'Emperor angry at iron men,' roared the Lord of the Unfleshed. 'Strikes them from heaven!'

'He does indeed,' nodded Uriel, risking a glance at the gory features of the creature and feeling immense relief that Vaanes was not here to see the expression on his own face.

The renegades had turned their backs on them, spitting on this last chance for redemption and had marched away without a single word as soon as they had reached the surface. Uriel had watched them go, his heart heavy at their betrayal of what it meant to be a Space Marine, but relieved that he himself had been tested and not been found wanting.

Truth be told, there was some merit in what Vaanes had said. Perhaps this was a suicide mission and would see them all dead. And perhaps as well there was merit in survival, for where was the glory or honour to be had from their deaths?

But Uriel knew that for a true warrior of the Emperor there was no terror of death, only the fear that he might die with his works unfulfilled.

The death oath placed upon them by Marneus Calgar remained to be honoured and even should they fail in their quest, their deaths would respect the chance their Chapter Master had given them, so long ago it seemed, on Macragge.

As he watched Vaanes and the renegades depart, Uriel knew that though he was probably going to his death, his was the better choice.

'We fight iron men now?' asked the Lord of the Unfleshed. 'Show us way in!'

The primal ferocity in the Lord of the Unfleshed's face reminded Uriel just how precarious their situation was. There was no guarantee that his plan would succeed and he did not want to think of the consequences should the Unfleshed decide that he no longer spoke with the Emperor's voice.

'Soon,' said Uriel, resuming his climb of the rocks that led to the fighting above.

HONSOU TOOK THE steps from the high spire that led to the main wall quickly, thinking that the swelling roars of hate he could hear were a fine hymn upon which to wage war. He and Onyx and a coterie of his finest warriors emerged onto a cracked series of barbican ramparts, arranged in a saw-toothed pattern, freshly constructed behind the main walls.

Smoke wreathed the breaches and the Khalan-Ghol's main gate hung in splinters, a pack of frenzied dreadnoughts smashing through it. At their head, Honsou saw Lord Berossus, his mechanised arms hurling warriors before him in sprays of blood. A wild, orgiastic howling screeched from his vox-amp and Honsou grinned ferally as he knew that he would not allow Berossus to survive this battle.

Billowing clouds of scalding steam and the crack of splintering stone from beyond the ruined walls told him that the top of the great ramp was no more, the stone and earth running molten and collapsing under the strain of supporting Berossus's armoured column.

Virtually everything metal within the fortress had been smelted down and the forges had burned constantly to ensure that when Berossus's engineers breached the fortress from below – as Honsou had known they would – they would be tunnelling into a great reservoir of molten metal and not the catacombs they expected.

Honsou knew that a warsmith as gullible as Berossus did not deserve to live; his very existence weakened the Iron Warriors. To have believed that Honsou would not have known of Obax Zakayo's treachery and use him against his paymasters was ludicrous, but had proven to be his salvation.

Gunfire and explosions filled the interior space of the barbican as the vanguard of Berossus's army swarmed through the gate, though Honsou realised that it was no longer the vanguard, but its entirety. Now the odds were evened and Berossus would learn what it was to fight Honsou of the Iron Warriors.

Dreadnoughts charged towards the sandbagged gun pits, shrugging off weapon impacts and ripping men apart with wild bursts of weapons' fire. But behind the gun pits, disciplined teams of Iron Warriors picked off the armoured fighting machines with calm efficiency, their smoking hulks soon outnumbering those that still fought.

A dark shadow loomed above the fortress walls as the surviving Titan gripped the ruined battlements and began ripping them down with great sweeps of its piston-driven hammer arms. Blocks of stone the size of buildings crashed down amongst the warriors of both armies, killing a dozen men or more each time.

Huge assault ramps smashed down on the massive piles of rubble and debris, and Iron Warriors bearing the black and gold banner of Berossus charged from the shoulder bastions of the Titan.

'Iron Warriors!' shouted Honsou. 'Now is your time to show these bastards who is the master of Khalan-Ghol!'

His warriors roared in adulation, following their master down into the heat of the battle. The Iron Warriors of Berossus fought their way down the rubble of the breach, firing as they went and Honsou saw that they were warriors of courage and iron as volley after volley of lethally effective weapons' fire took a horrific toll on their numbers, but they did not falter.

The space between the smashed wall and the bunkers and saw-tooth walls Honsou had constructed was a killing ground: nothing could cross it and live. But with no way back, the Iron Warriors of Berossus had no choice but to advance into the teeth of Honsou's guns, and the carnage was awe-inspiring in its savagery.

More rubble fell from the main wall as the Titan smashed its way inside now that its cargo of warriors had disembarked. A shoulder-mounted cannon blasted a great crater in the centre of Honsou's defences and the warriors of Berossus cheered as they fought their way forwards once more.

Before it could fire again, a huge explosion ripped the cannon from the Titan's shoulder and a line of white fire stitched itself across its bloody carapace. From the smoke either side of the attacking Titan came a pair of similarly massive forms, Titans bearing the dread banners of the Legio Mortis. No longer required to guard the inner sanctum of Khalan-Ghol, the two terrifying daemon engines stalked from the rubble and smoke of the fortress's interior to do battle.

Berossus's last Titan roared at such worthy adversaries and turned its guns upon its new foes, leaving the Iron Warriors it had carried to look to their own battles. The ground shuddered at the tread of these mighty daemon machines, and whole sections of the walls were pulverised as they grappled with white-hot blades and screaming chainfists.

All subtleties and stratagems were meaningless now; the outcome of this storming would be decided at the end of a smoking bolter or upon the roaring blade of a chainsword. Iron Warriors charged one another, the battle degenerating into a close-range firefight and swirling melee of savage killers.

A fierce exhilaration pounded through Honsou's veins at the visceral thrill of such slaughter. He hacked his axe through the arm of an Iron Warrior, spinning on his heel to behead him before leaping the smoking corpse of a dreadnought to find more foes. Onyx followed him, killing any who dared come near the master of the fortress with casual swipes of his bladed fists.

Honsou saw the awesomely powerful form of Berossus through the swirling smoke and shouted, 'Onyx! To me!'

URIEL KNEW THEY did not have much time. The battle above was seething with the ferocity of a tempest, the screams of men in battle echoing from the high peaks. He climbed with all the speed he could muster, but their destination seemed always tantalisingly out of reach.

He did not want to get caught up in the fighting, but knew they had to reach the site of the battle before too much time had passed.

'Come on!' he shouted. 'We have to hurry!'

The Lord of the Unfleshed roared, 'You slow! Not fast like me!'

'I know!' shouted Uriel. 'But we cannot climb any faster!'

'We go faster!' said the Lord of the Unfleshed and reached out to grab Uriel's wrist, swinging him around and onto his shoulders so that he was being carried in much the same fashion as Colonel Leonid.

The ground swung dizzyingly below Uriel and he gripped onto the clammy, glistening flesh of the creature as it scaled the rocky flanks of Khalan-Ghol with terrifying speed.

He turned his head to see Pasanius scooped up in the same manner, and the speed of their ascent doubled.

'Go faster now!' promised the Lord of the Unfleshed. 'Tribe! On!'

Hundreds of the red, skinless creatures followed the Lord of the Unfleshed and Uriel was suddenly seized by a wild sense of abandonment.

They might be heading to their deaths, but what an end they would make for themselves!

He returned his gaze to the smoke-wreathed peak of the fortress, amazed at how different it now looked. When he had first laid eyes upon it, it had seemed utterly impregnable, fashioned from dark madness and impossibly hewn stone, and placed upon the highest peak. Now little of its lower reaches remained, save as blasted, dusty boneyards and its upper spire looked in danger of falling at any moment.

But having seen what happened to the huge ramp, Uriel knew that Honsou was not going to let his fortress fall without a damn hard fight.

He did not know exactly what had happened to the ramp, but watched in wonder as entire sections of its upper reaches cracked, and the tanks and men who climbed towards the fortress were swallowed whole.

Streaming lines of smoking, orange liquid boiled from cracks in the side of the ramp, pouring down its sides like lava spilling from the crater of an erupting volcano. A vast, oozing lake of molten metal poured from the mouth of the tunnel at the base of the ramp, growing larger with every passing moment.

Hundreds of vehicles had mustered here and were caught in the flash flood of killing liquid. Uriel watched tanks burn and explode as their fuel and ammunition cooked in the awful heat.

Madly revving tanks barged into one another, crashing together in their desperation to escape, but succeeding only in forming an impenetrable logjam. Soon an army of fighting vehicles was reduced to molten slag without so much as a shot being fired.

'No,' whispered Uriel, as Honsou's fortress drew ever closer. 'You are certainly not going without a fight.'

CHUNKS OF STONE and flesh were thrown skyward as wreckage and debris from the Titans' battle smashed into the ground. Another bunker was flattened and Honsou knew that, one way or another, this battle would soon be over. An Iron Warrior slashed a huge, crackling fist towards his head and he rolled beneath it, swinging his axe in a backhand sweep that cut the legs from beneath his opponent.

The warrior screamed and collapsed, clutching the stumps of his thighs as Onyx removed his head in the wake of his master, but Honsou carried on towards Berossus as the warsmith finally saw him coming.

'Half-breed!' roared the dreadnought, raising his arms in challenge. Though he was no longer a warrior of flesh and blood, Berossus had lost none of the ferocity he had displayed in life, his bronze-skulled sarcophagus blazing with diabolical energy.

The giant dreadnought braced its legs and lowered its monstrous drill ringed with heavy calibre cannons. Onyx leapt forwards as the cannons spooled up to firing speed, slashing his claws through the barrels in a shower of bright sparks.

For such a massive machine, Berossus was still inhumanly quick and his mighty, piston-driven siege hammer smashed into the daemonic symbiote and sent him spinning through the air.

'Now you die, half-breed!' screamed the dreadnought, bringing the monstrous hammer back for another blow and taking a crashing step towards him. Honsou struck out at Berossus's sarcophagus, but the thick, mechanical arms that sprouted from his armoured shell snatched out and deflected the blow, a screaming breacher drill stabbing for his chest.

Honsou spun around, the tip of the drill scoring across his breastplate and drawing blood before hammering his axe into the dreadnought's thick leg. The axe clanged from the limb, ricocheting from its thick armour and sending ringing shockwaves up Honsou's arms.

Another explosion rocked the ground and Honsou was pitched from his feet by the blast. The giant dreadnought barely shook and a great, clawed foot slammed down, centimetres from his head. Honsou rolled between the armoured legs as the battle raged around them, Iron Warriors cutting each other down with furious savagery.

Berossus spun on the axis of his waist and a pair of his augmetic limbs slashed the ground. Honsou rolled backwards, the tip of Berossus's clawed arm catching the edge of his armour and spinning him off balance.

He felt a stinging blow to his leg and roared in pain as Berossus's breacher arm stabbed through his thigh. The drill ripped a great wad of bloody flesh from his leg and Honsou dropped to one knee. The dreadnought stepped close and its clawed arm closed on Honsou's shoulder guard, lifting the struggling warrior high into the air.

'You have cost me dear, mongrel, but it ends now,' snarled Berossus. 'Your fortress is mine, no matter what happens.'

'Never!' shouted Honsou, fighting to free himself from his captor's grip, but Berossus had him firm and wasn't about to let go.

The dreadnought stabbed his breacher drill towards Honsou's face.

The master of Khalan-Ghol hurled his arm in front of the blow, the screeching of tearing metal and white-hot shavings spraying the air as the drill pierced the silver metal of Honsou's arm.

But instead of shearing straight through the arm and skewering Honsou's skull, the metal ran like liquid, reknitting itself as quickly as Berossus's arm attempted to destroy it. The dreadnought watched amazed as the drill stuttered and jammed within Honsou's arm. Even as Berossus paused, a black-armoured blur streaked through the air, twisting to land upon the upper mantlet of the dreadnought's carapace.

Onyx landed gracefully on one knee and powered both bronze claws down into the armoured shell of the dreadnought. The terrible machine roared in pain, its arms spasming and dropping Honsou to the cratered ground.

Honsou rolled away from the thrashing dreadnought as he heard a thunderous crashing behind him and the headless form of Berossus's Titan crashed through the last remaining portion of the main wall, hurling stone and blazing streamers of plasma through the air. One of his own Titans fell with it, shorn practically in half, and the impact to the two armoured leviathans sent shockwaves through the earth that were almost the equal of the blast beneath the ramp.

A great cry of dismay went up and Honsou knew that he could end this now. Berossus fought to dislodge Onyx, his clawed arms slashing and stabbing the daemonic symbiote repeatedly. Honsou gripped his axe and sprang to his feet, not about to waste the chance his champion had gained him.

With a roar of hate, he charged forwards while the dreadnought's attention was fixated on Onyx and hammered his axe with all his strength into the now-unguarded portion of the dreadnought's leg where the armour was weakest.

Screaming, warp-forged steel met ancient metal crafted by forgotten technologies in a blazing corona of flaring energy. Berossus roared and smashed to the ground, slamming down on his back as Onyx leapt gracefully clear of the toppled machine.

'Call me half-breed now, you bastard!' screamed Honsou, stepping in and hammering his axe against the dreadnought's sarcophagus. The ancient metal split and Berossus wailed in agony as the daemon weapon tore into his iron body.

'Still think you're better than me?' yelled Honsou as he hacked at the dying dreadnought's body. Metal and sparks flew as the master of Khalan-Ghol butchered his iron foe. Berossus fought to right himself, but Honsou and Onyx gave him no chance, darting away from his clumsy blows and hacking his uselessly flailing limbs from his body.

'You're nothing, Berossus, nothing! Do you hear me?'

A grainy wash of static-laced, incoherence blared from Berossus's vox-amp, and Honsou vaulted onto the dreadnought's sarcophagus yelling, 'Perhaps you can't hear me through all that iron.'

He raised himself triumphant on the warsmith of the attacking army and brought his axe down again and again on the grinning skull-faced sarcophagus, finally splitting it apart with his fifth blow.

The sounds of battle faded and, for the first time in months, the fighting stopped as the battling Iron Warriors paused to watch the unfolding drama being played out before them.

Honsou knelt atop Berossus's sarcophagus and punched his pristine silver arm into the dreadnought. With a grunt and wrench, he ripped something clear in a welter of black blood and amniotic fluids.

He held up his arm and shouted, 'Your warsmith is dead!'

In his hand he held a monstrously swollen skull and dripping spinal column, fused wires like veins dangling from the last mortal remains of Warsmith Berossus.

The tension was palpable and Honsou knew he had to cow the scores of enemy warriors or risk this slaughter becoming a battle of mutually assured destruction. With a roar of hate, he swung the spinal column like a club and smashed Berossus's skull to splinters of bone against the ruptured iron shell that had once housed it.

'Your warsmith is dead!' he repeated, hurling away the remains. 'But you do not need to die! Berossus is gone and by right of conquest I offer any warrior who wants it a place in my army. You have proved yourselves warriors of courage, and I have need of such men.'

No one moved, and for the briefest second Honsou thought he had made a grave error.

But then a warrior in heavily tooled armour of burnished iron and sporting a burnt and tattered back banner of gold and black stepped forwards. The warrior's armour was bloody and scored from the hard fighting. He removed his cracked helmet, revealing scarred and pitted features topped with a close-cropped mohawk.

'Why should we join you, half-breed?' he shouted. 'You may have defeated Berossus, but Toramino will wipe you and your fortress from the face of Medrengard.'

'What is your name, warrior?' said Honsou, jumping from the broken carcass of the dreadnought and marching purposefully towards the Iron Warrior.

'I am Cadaras Grendel, Captain of Arms of Lord Berossus.'

Honsou stood before the bloody warrior, seeing the defiance in his eyes.

'Aye,' agreed Honsou, raising his voice so that all the warriors gathered in the ruins of his fortress could hear him. 'You may be right, Cadaras Grendel. Toramino has the strength of arms to destroy me, I cannot argue with that. But ask yourself this... why has he not blooded his warriors yet?'

Honsou turned to address the rest of the assembled warriors, raising his arms and punctuating his words by punching the air with his axe. 'Where was Toramino while you all fought and bled to get here? You know who built this place and you know that only the bravest of warriors could take it. Where was Toramino while you were dying in your hundreds to storm this fortress?'

He could see his words were having the desired effect. Honsou felt a hot rush of adrenaline race around his body as he saw that he had correctly anticipated the rancour these brave Iron Warriors must have felt at the bloody work they did while Toramino's warriors watched them die.

'Toramino hung you out to dry and laughed while he did it. Even if you had succeeded here, do you think the spoils of Khalan-Ghol would be yours to plunder? Toramino has betrayed you, just as the Emperor betrayed the Iron Warriors in the ancient days. Will you be used like that or are you men of iron?'

'We are men of iron!' shouted Cadaras Grendel, the shout taken up by his surviving warriors.

'Then join me!' bellowed Honsou, gripping Grendel's shoulder guards. 'Join me and avenge this betrayal!'

Months of bitterness at the deaths of his men rose to the surface on Grendel's face and he nodded. 'Aye. Toramino will pay for this. My warriors and I are yours to command!'

Honsou turned and with Cadaras Grendel beside him roared, 'Iron within!'

'Iron without!' came the answering bellow from every Iron Warrior, shouted over and over again.

And Honsou knew he had them.

URIEL WATCHED THE two Titans collapse and, amazingly, heard the sounds of battle fade away. Had Khalan-Ghol fallen or had Honsou defeated the escalade? It was impossible to tell, and they would only know when they reached the top.

Their ascent up the cliff-face had been heart-poundingly fraught, as the Unfleshed had carried them swiftly up slopes Uriel would have sworn were unclimbable. Their strength was prodigious and their endurance phenomenal.

In the sudden silence, Uriel could hear the crackling flames from the burning vehicles at the foot of the mountain and the occasional explosion from a shell as it detonated in the heat. The infrastructure of Berossus's army burned and as the quietness stretched on, Uriel guessed that the attack had failed to take the fortress. Warriors who had fought their way through a breach were so fuelled on adrenaline and rage that looting and slaughter usually followed in the wake of a successful storming.

But silence... that was new to Uriel.

The Lord of the Unfleshed clambered over an overhanging splinter of rock, swinging his massive body up and over the lip of the plateau and Uriel had his first look at the bloody ruin of the final assault.

'Emperor preserve us!' breathed Pasanius as he joined Uriel.

'Even the storm of the citadel was nothing compared to this...' added Leonid as the fused twins deposited him next to the Space Marines.

The wreckage of a destroyed army lay strewn before the shattered remains of the spire's defensive wall, itself no more than jagged stumps of black stone jutting from the ground like rotten teeth in a diseased gum. Blazing tanks and bodies were strewn about the plateau; some crushed flat, others hollowed out by explosions. Pyres of ammunition sparked and blew, and the remains of the Titans burned with a bright glare of plasma.

Gun barrels the size of cooling towers lay cracked and useless amid the debris and even had anyone been keeping watch on the battlefield, the smoke and flames would conceal them from detection.

'Who won?' asked Leonid.

'I'm not sure...' said Pasanius, following Uriel through the corpse-choked rubble.

He bent to retrieve a fallen bolter with his remaining hand and checked its load before saying, 'Find yourself a weapon, colonel, and scavenge as much ammunition as you can carry.'

Leonid nodded and scooped up a battered, but serviceable lasgun, some charged clips and a bandolier of grenades. As he did so, his chest hiked in pain and he was bent double by a coughing fit. He wiped his hand across his mouth, seeing brackish, matter-flecked blood coat his palm before wiping it clear on what remained of his dusty, sky-blue uniform jacket.

The Unfleshed capered across the battlefield, stooping to feed amid the cadavers, tearing limbs from bodies and devouring the still-warm meat straight from the bone. The Lord of the Unfleshed lifted the limbless corpse of an Iron Warrior and tore off its breastplate, biting into the chest and tearing off a great mouthful of flesh.

Even though it was the body of an enemy, Uriel was appalled and said, 'No, do not eat this meat.'

The Lord of the Unfleshed turned, his face alight with horrid appetite and savage glee at this chance to feast on an Iron Warrior. 'Is meat. Fresh.'

'No!' said Uriel, more forcefully.

'No?' replied the Lord of the Unfleshed. 'Why?'

'It is corrupt.'

Seeing the creature's incomprehension, he said, 'It is bad.'

'No… is good,' said the Lord of the Unfleshed, holding out the opened corpse of the Iron Warrior. The ribcage had been bitten through and the warrior's internal organs were laid bare.

Uriel shook his head. 'If you love the Emperor, you will not eat this meat.'

'Love the Emperor!' bellowed the Lord of the Unfleshed and Uriel winced, thinking that the creature's voice could be heard even through the fury of a battle.

'Many iron men dead,' growled the Lord of the Unfleshed, angrily. 'Much meat.'

'Yes, but we are not here for meat,' said Uriel. 'We are here to kill iron men and flesh mothers, yes?'

The Lord of the Unfleshed looked set to argue the point, but with an angry snarl dropped the half-eaten body and said, 'Kill iron men now?'

'Yes, kill iron men,' said Uriel as he heard the sound of approaching engines from within the fortress. 'But we need to get to the heart of the fortress first.'

Uriel turned as Pasanius and Leonid approached, bearing guns, ammunition and grenades. Pasanius unslung a bolter from his shoulder and handed it to Uriel together with several magazines of shells.

'It galls me that we must use the weapons of the Enemy,' said Uriel as he slammed a magazine home in the bolter.

'I suppose there's a certain poetic justice in using their own guns against them,' said Pasanius as he awkwardly loaded and cocked the weapon.

'What's that noise?' asked Leonid as he finally heard the rumbling engine sound drawing yet closer.

'It is our way in,' said Uriel, gesturing to the bodies surrounding them. 'I want you to conceal yourself amongst the dead Iron Warriors. We will lie close to one another, but must make sure we're amongst the dead.'

Uriel turned to face the Lord of the Unfleshed and hurriedly said, 'Have the tribe lie down with the dead iron men. You understand? Lie with the dead.'

'Lie down with meat?'

'Yes,' confirmed Uriel. 'Lie down with the iron men, and when we get up we will be where we need to be.'

The Lord of the Unfleshed nodded slowly and made his way through the tribe, grunting and pointing to piles of corpses.

As the Unfleshed began lying down amongst the dead Chaos Space Marines, Pasanius said, 'You know they'll feed on the bodies.'

'I know,' said Uriel, 'but there is little we can do about it.'

'Truly the Emperor does work in mysterious ways,' added Leonid.

Uriel tried to put aside the thought of the Unfleshed's cannibalistic tendencies as they located a group of shredded Iron Warriors arranged on the edges of a shell crater, and secreted themselves amongst their corpses.

Even as he dragged an Iron Warrior's body over his own he saw their way into the fortress emerge from the rolling banks of smoke that hugged the ground.

Huge bulldozers, red and hateful, with tall banner poles hung with eight-pointed stars and iron tenders hitched behind them came from the Halls of the Savage Morticians.

They came to gather up the dead for crushing and feeding to the daemonculaba.

ʊ
NINETEEN

DEAD EYES IN a skull with the top blown off stared at him, sightless and fixed in an expression of surprise. No matter where Uriel turned in the blood-filled container, he could not escape the staring eyes of the dead. Scooped up with the rest of the corpses by the daemonic bulldozers, he had been unceremoniously dumped in the tender by the growling machine as it performed its automated and graceless coroner's task.

Bodies piled upon bodies, blood and entrails spilling to the sloshing floor and Uriel fought to claw his way to the surface, lest he drown in the stagnant blood of the fallen. He coughed red as he pushed his way clear of the bodies, keeping his head below the level of the tender's railings for fear of discovery.

The hot stink of blood filled his nostrils and slippery bodies jostled him as the trailer bumped over the uneven ground. He rolled onto his back, craning his neck left and right to see as much as he could without raising his head too far. He saw the shattered remains of a high wall pass, its fabric riddled with shell impacts and looking as though it had been struck by an orbital bombardment. Smoke curled, fat and black, from pyres and Uriel could hear chanting voices shouting from afar.

They had penetrated the walls of Khalan-Ghol and now just had to stay concealed until these bulldozers took them back to the nightmare Halls of the Savage Morticians and the daemonculaba.

A cadaver bobbed from beneath the blood and Uriel made to push it away when it blinked at him.

'Imperator! I thought you were a corpse!' exclaimed Uriel when he saw it was Pasanius.

'Not yet,' grinned Pasanius, spitting blood.

'Where is Leonid?'

'Here,' said a voice from the other side of the tender. 'By the High Lord's balls, this is almost worse than being flushed from the chambers below.'

Uriel raised an eyebrow and Leonid shrugged. 'Well, maybe not.'

'If I'm right, these will take us right where we want to go,' said Uriel. 'We just have to bear it for a little longer.'

'How long do you think it'll take to get there?' asked Leonid, almost afraid of the answer.

Uriel shook his head. 'I do not know for sure, but I do not believe these machines will be confounded by the magicks protecting this place, so not long would be my guess.'

Leonid nodded resignedly and shut his eyes, trying to block out the dreadful smell of the dead bodies.

As it transpired, the bulldozers' journey through the twisting interior of Khalan-Ghol took perhaps another hour, travelling along grisly thorough-fares of sacrificial altars, winding between dark-armoured bunkers and through the maze of manufactorum that the warrior band had become so lost in.

The vast shadow of the gate of the tower of iron at the centre of the fortress passed over them, and once again they were deep in the heart of Honsou's lair. Distant hammer blows and the grinding clanking of nearby machines filled the gloom, and Uriel heard the clicking footsteps of unseen creatures as they filed past the growling bulldozers. Sickly yellow light came and went as they passed along wide, rockcrete tunnels lit by flickering lumo-strips.

Eventually, Uriel heard the thudding beat of a monstrous heart growing louder and shared an uneasy glance with his companions. The booming bass note was all too familiar.

'The Heart of Blood,' said Pasanius.

Uriel nodded, his muscles tensing as he heard clicking and wheezing mechanical footsteps approaching. The bulldozer ground to a halt with a juddering lurch. A tall silhouette loomed over the edge of the tender and Uriel snapped his eyes shut, recognising the dead skin features of one of the Savage Morticians.

He remained utterly immobile as he felt metal pincers jab into the tender. Hissing claws turned bodies within the pooled and now sticky blood. Corpses rolled and flopped in the tender as the Savage Mortician inspected the dead for some unknown purpose.

He fought back a gasp of revulsion as he felt a claw close on his leg and turn him over, fighting to remain still as his flesh was jabbed and probed.

The Savage Mortician clicked and whistled in its incomprehensible lan-guage, presumably to another of its fell, surgical kin, before releasing his limb and clanking off on some other errand. Uriel kept his eyes shut and his breathing shallow until the bulldozer set off once again and they had put some distance between them and the hellish surgeons.

'Holy Throne,' he whispered, sickened by the Savage Mortician's touch.

Their nightmarish journey continued into the chamber of screams, the terrible beat of the daemonic Heart of Blood dulling his senses once more. Even over the heavy thuds of the Heart of Blood, Uriel heard the rumbling whine of heavy machinery as well as the grinding crack of bones and wet squelch of pulverised flesh.

'Be ready!' he hissed. 'I think we have arrived!'

Pasanius and Leonid nodded as Uriel slid himself over the carpet of bodies and raised his head slowly over the edge of the tender.

Sure enough, they were close to the great crushing machine that ground up the dead Chaos Space Marines and transformed them into genetic matter for the daemonculaba to feast upon.

But as before, his gaze was drawn upwards to the centre of the chamber, to the massive form of the Heart of Blood, the daemonic creature that hung suspended above the lake of blood on a trio of great chains.

He tore his eyes from the imprisoned daemon and saw that they were part of a great, curving procession of red bulldozers parked next to the iron ramp that led up to the gantry of the great, daemonic wombs. Their hellish conveyance was but one of perhaps a dozen or more of the bulldozers, lurching in fits and starts towards the blood-smeared conveyor that led to the sticky crushers and rollers. A pulsing forest of pipes pumped a pinkish, gristly matter from the machine to the cages of the daemonculaba and Uriel felt his gorge rise at such a blasphemy against what had once been the sacred flesh of the Emperor's body.

Vacuum-suited servitor mutants on a raised platform stabbed wide hooks attached to lengths of chain into the dead flesh in the tenders then wound the chains through heavy pulley mechanisms. They worked quickly and efficiently, loading the corpses onto the conveyor in a manner that spoke of many years of repetition.

Beside the conveyor, Uriel saw a cruciform frame holding what looked like a rack of meat, positioned close enough to be spattered by blood spraying from the grinding rollers. Uriel paid it no mind as he searched for any of the dark-robed monsters that were macabre lords of this place.

Seeing none, he eased his body up and over the edge of the tender, dropping lightly to the wet, churned ground.

He tapped the tender and said, 'Come on.'

Pasanius clambered to join him, cleaning blood from the action of his weapon and wedging the bolter between his knees to rack the slide. Leonid followed suit, wiping blood from his eyes and scouring the vent-breech of his lasgun.

The three warriors crouched in the shadow of the tender, breathing heavily and clearing their bodies of as much coagulated blood as they could.

'Well, we're in,' said Leonid. 'Now what?'

Uriel glanced around the edge of the tender. 'First we destroy that machine. If the Iron Warriors cannot feed the daemonculaba genetic material...'

'Honsou will not be able to create more Iron Warriors!' finished Leonid.

'And there will be no more of the Unfleshed,' added Pasanius.

Uriel nodded. 'And after that, well, we make for the ramp behind us and slay as many of the daemonculaba as we can before the Savage Morticians kill us.'

His companions were silent until eventually Leonid said, 'Good plan.'

Uriel grinned and said, 'Glad you approve.'

Pasanius put down his bolter and offered his left hand to Uriel, saying, 'No matter what happens, I regret nothing that has led us here, captain.'

Uriel took his friend's hand and shook it, touched by the simple affection of the sentiment, and said, 'Nor I, my friend. No matter what, we will have done some good here.'

'For what it's worth,' said Leonid. 'I wish I'd never even heard of this damn place, let alone been dragged here. But I am here, and that's the end of it, so what are we waiting for? Let's do this.'

Uriel racked the slide on his own bolter and nodded.

But before he could do anything more, he heard a great, bestial howl that was answered by a demented chorus of roars and bellows that echoed from the chamber's ceiling.

He rushed to the edge of the tender in time to see the Lord of the Unfleshed rear from hiding in a fountain of blood and limbs, and tear one of the mutant butchers in two with his bare hands.

THE UNFLESHED ERUPTED from the blood-filled tenders in a thrashing mass of knotted, deformed limbs, ripping into the mutants feeding the crushing machine with the frenzy of predators who had held their anger and hunger in check for far too long.

Uriel watched as the Lord of the Unfleshed's massive jaws snapped shut on a screaming mutant, biting him in two at the waist and silencing his screams forever. The beast Uriel had fought at the outflow pulled the arms from another foe before hurling its victim into the crushers of the grinding machine. The Unfleshed slaughtered a score of the servants of the Savage Morticians in the blink of an eye, and Uriel was horrified and grateful at the same time for their savagery.

'Damn it,' cursed Uriel. 'There goes the element of surprise!'

'Now what?' asked Pasanius.

'It will only be a matter of time until the Savage Morticians come to investigate, so come on. We don't have long.'

Uriel and the others broke from cover, running over to the roaring machine that had a potent aura of malice and hunger to it, its dark purpose imbuing it with a loathsome evil. The sooner it was destroyed the better, knew Uriel, as he drew near and a clawing sickness built in his gut.

Leonid staggered as he approached and coughed a flood of gristly vomit, the daemon machine's vile presence too much for his cancer-ridden body to bear.

'Uriel!' he shouted, holding out the bandolier of grenades he had taken from the ruin of Berossus's army on the mountainside.

Uriel snatched the grenades and ran towards the machine, passing the cruciform frame that held the dripping rack of meat, sparing it but a glance as he did so.

He pulled up short and turned to face it as he realised that it was not a rack of meat at all.

It was Obax Zakayo.

URIEL FELT NOTHING but revulsion at the sight of Obax Zakayo's ruined, mutilated body, but part of him wondered at the cruelty of creatures that could do this to another living soul. The Iron Warrior – or what was left of him – was pinned to the frame and drooled thick ropes of saliva from the corner of his twisted lips. Trailing clear tubes pumped life-sustaining chemicals into his ravaged frame.

'Guilliman's oath,' whispered Uriel as the Iron Warrior raised his beaten and bruised face towards him.

'Ventris...' he gasped, sudden hope filling his watering eyes. 'Kill me, I beg of you.'

Uriel ignored Obax Zakayo as Pasanius attempted to form the Unfleshed into some kind of defensive perimeter, and snapped grenade after grenade from the bandolier. The machine roared as he approached, filthy blue oilsmoke venting from corroded grilles and an angry bellow growling from its depths.

The gnawing sensation in his gut increased, but Uriel suppressed it and began attaching the grenades to the machine at power couplings, axle joints and even climbing on top of the machine to place one at the base of the forest of gurgling feed tubes. He worked swiftly, but methodically, ensuring that the machine would be comprehensively wrecked upon the grenades' detonation.

Uriel climbed down from the machine in time to see Leonid standing before Obax Zakayo, his lasgun shouldered and aimed squarely between the Iron Warrior's eyes.

'Do it!' wept the broken Obax Zakayo. 'Do it! Please! They feed me piece by piece to the machine and make me watch...'

Leonid's finger tightened on the trigger, but he released a shuddering breath and lowered the weapon.

'No,' he said. 'Why should you get off easy after you tortured so many of my soldiers to death? I think I like the idea of you suffering like this!'

'Please,' begged Obax Zakayo. 'I... I can help you defeat the half-breed!'

'The half-breed?' said Uriel.

'Honsou, I mean Honsou,' wheezed Obax Zakayo. 'I can tell you how you can see him dead.'

'How?' asked Leonid, stepping in and slamming the butt of his lasgun against the Iron Warrior's chin. 'Tell us!'

'Only if you promise that you will kill me,' leered Obax Zakayo, spitting teeth.

'Uriel!' shouted Pasanius from the barricades of the tenders. 'I think they're coming!'

'We don't have time for this, traitor,' snapped Uriel. 'Tell us what you know!'

'Swear, Ultramarine. Give me your oath.'

'Very well,' nodded Uriel. 'I swear I will see you dead, now speak!'

'The Heart of Blood,' began Obax Zakayo. 'It is a daemon of the Lord of Skulls and the half-breed's former master imprisoned it beneath Khalan-Ghol and fattened its essence with the blood of sorcerers.'

'What has this to do with Honsou?' demanded Uriel.

'Know you nothing of your enemies?' mocked Obax Zakayo. 'The Lord of Skulls is the bane of psykers and the Heart of Blood was driven mad by such polluted blood. The warsmith's sorcerers channelled their most potent null-magicks through the imprisoned creature, using its immaterial energies to cast a great psychic barrier around the fortress that no sorcerer has been able to breach in nearly ten thousand years!'

Obax Zakayo coughed and said, 'I have your oath that you will end my suffering?'

'Yes,' said Uriel. 'Keep talking.'

The Iron Warrior nodded and said, 'Lord Toramino has some of the most powerful sorcerers in the Eye of Terror to command and, though they have great power, they cannot breach the ancient barrier of the Heart of Blood. Destroy it and they will raze this place to the ground!'

Uriel looked into Obax Zakayo's eyes for any sign of a lie, but the Iron Warrior was beyond such deception, too immersed in his own misery and need for death. He felt the guiding hand of providence in the traitor's presence now, for here was a chance to fulfil his death oath and deny the Omphalos Daemonium its prize.

'Very well,' pressed Uriel. 'How do we destroy it?'

'The awls,' said Obax Zakayo. 'The silver awls that pierce its daemonic flesh and hold it fast above the lake of blood...'

'What of them?'

'They are hateful artefacts, stolen from your most sacred reclusiam or taken from those whose inquisitions delved too deep into the mysteries of Chaos. They are more than just physical anchors; they bind it to this place. Remove or destroy them and its dissolution will be complete.'

Uriel took a step back from Obax Zakayo and looked up into the darkness of the chamber above the hissing lake of blood where the huge daemon hung suspended in its writhing madness. He saw three gleaming silver pinpricks of light impaled through its scaled flesh, each attached to a chain that was anchored in the bedrock of the chamber's walls.

His eyes followed the line of the chains from the daemon and squinted as he sought where the nearest was embedded. Uriel turned back to Obax Zakayo and raised his bolter, saying, 'I will kill you now.'

'No!' said Leonid grimly. 'Let me do it. I owe this bastard a death.'

Uriel saw the thirst for vengeance in Leonid's eyes and nodded. 'So be it. Once he is dead, set the timers on the grenades and get clear. The Savage Morticians are coming, so stay close to the Unfleshed. They will try to protect you if you are near them, but you have to hold the enemy at bay for as long as you can.'

'I understand,' said Leonid. 'Now go.'

Uriel nodded and ran towards Pasanius.

Leonid watched as Uriel hurriedly outlined his plan to Pasanius and the two Ultramarines set off up the iron ramps that led towards the daemonculaba.

'Now, slave,' hissed Obax Zakayo. 'Ventris told you to kill me.'

Leonid raised his lasgun and shot Obax Zakayo in the gut. He smelled burned flesh and nodded to himself, satisfied that the Iron Warrior was in pain, but still alive.

Obax Zakayo raised his head and roared, 'Shoot me again, I'm not dead yet!'

Leonid stepped close and spat into Obax Zakayo's face.

'No,' he said calmly.

'An oath was given!' screamed the Iron Warrior. 'Ventris swore he would see me dead!'

'Uriel gave his word, but I didn't,' snarled Leonid. 'I want you to live in agony then die in pain when this place is brought down!'

Obax Zakayo wept and cursed him, but Leonid ignored his pleadings as he removed the grenade attached to the crushing machine that was nearest the Iron Warrior and slipped it into his uniform jacket's breast pocket.

'Don't want you dying by accident, now do we?' he said.

Without another word, Leonid turned and walked away.

URIEL POUNDED UP the ramp and ran past the heaving bodies of the daemonculaba, wishing he could stop to end each one's suffering. He knew that they had a better chance to end their torment if they could enable Honsou's enemies to do the job for them. He and Pasanius ran around the circumference of the chamber to reach one of the three awl-chains that pierced the Heart of Blood's body and kept it bound to Khalan-Ghol.

If they could pull even one of the awls from the terrible daemon, then it would be something...

'Great Emperor of Mankind, grant me the strength of your will to do this for you,' he prayed as he ran, his eyes tracing the line of the chain that ran from the daemon's body.

He saw it was higher than this level of daemonic womb-creatures, and as they reached the point on the gantry directly below the chain, he heard the explosive destruction of the crushing machine and the bestial roars of the Unfleshed echoing through the chamber. This was quickly followed by the bark of lasfire and the screech of the Savage Morticians.

'We'll need to climb,' said Pasanius.

Uriel nodded and turned to watch the battle below, seeing bodies flying through the air and leaping arcs of blue lightning as the denizens of this awful place fought against the Unfleshed.

'Emperor watch over you,' whispered Uriel as he gripped the iron bars of one of the daemonculaba cages and began to climb. The thick chain was some ten metres above them, and even in the dim light he could see it was firmly embedded in the chamber's wall with a rockcrete plug.

'I'll need a hand,' said Pasanius as Uriel reached the top of the cage, sounding thoroughly ashamed to be asking for help.

Uriel turned back, mortified that it hadn't occurred to him that Pasanius might have difficulty in reaching the chain with only one arm until this moment. He reached down and helped his sergeant climb to join him.

Rusted struts and long-abandoned scaffolding pierced the rock below the plug, presumably left behind by those who had put it there in the first place.

He heard a piteous, mewling cry of anguish from below him and looked down through the mesh of the cage roof into the weeping face of the dae-monculaba.

Uriel knelt as close as he could to the tormented creature. 'I will see your suffering ended,' he promised. Her eyes closed slowly and Uriel thought he detected an almost imperceptible nod of her bloated head.

'There is not enough suffering in the galaxy to make the Iron Warriors pay for what they have done here,' said Pasanius, his voice choked with emotion.

'No,' agreed Uriel, 'there is not, but we will make them suffer anyway.'

'Aye,' agreed Pasanius as they climbed onto the roof of the cage and made their way further up the sides of the shadowed chamber, their goal nearing with every heave upwards.

The sounds of battle continued to rage from below as they clambered over the protruding scaffolding spars wedged into cracks in the rock and pulled themselves level with the chain.

As thick as Pasanius's forearm, it stretched off towards the centre of the chamber and the Heart of Blood.

'Ready?' asked Uriel.

'Ready,' nodded Pasanius, spitting on his palm.

Taking a firm grip on the flaking, rusted chain, the two Space Marines pulled with all their strength to wrench the awl-chain from the Heart of Blood's body.

LEONID SPRAYED A burst of full auto lasfire towards the skulking, vacuum-suited mutants taking cover behind a row of blood-filled barrels. His bolts punctured the containers, spilling crimson arcs from their sides. He knew he hadn't killed any of them, but it kept their heads down. He'd seen the mutant creature, Sabatier with the armed slaves of the Savage Morticians and dearly desired to put a bolt through that monster's head.

Damn, but it felt good to fire a weapon in anger again! The chaos of the bloody struggle swirled and raged around him, the Unfleshed battling with a primal ferocity against their creators and their slaves to give the Ultramarines more time to bring down the Heart of Blood.

The Lord of the Unfleshed bellowed as he slew, his powerful fists bringing death to his enemies with every blow. A black-robed monster reared up on great pneumatic legs equipped with shrieking blades, but another of the Unfleshed, a gibbering horror of limbs and mouths, landed upon it and tore its legs off with savage jerks.

Leonid rolled into the cover of the smoking remains of the crushing machine to reload as the Savage Mortician collapsed and its killer leapt for another victim. The limbless form of Obax Zakayo screamed, 'Kill me!' from his cruciform rack, but Leonid ignored him, too intent on the battle around him.

As ferocious as the Unfleshed were, the Savage Morticians had been practitioners of the art of death for uncounted millennia, and if there was one thing they knew, it was the weaknesses of flesh. Even when it was as resilient as that of the Unfleshed.

Flying razor discs lopped off thick limbs and heavy darts coated with poisons that could only exist in the Eye of Terror stabbed into pounding veins to slay their victims before they were even aware they were hit.

Creatures were dying and even the relentless fire of the Savage Morticians' servants was taking its toll, volley after volley cutting down the Unfleshed where they fought.

Leonid rose from cover and saw a Savage Mortician with massive chainblades for fists scuttle behind the Lord of the Unfleshed as he tore the torso from the mechanised track-unit of yet another foe. Leonid swung the barrel around and squeezed off a burst of bright lasbolts.

His aim was true and the Savage Mortician's head exploded, its twitching form slumping to the ground behind the Lord of the Unfleshed. The massive creature spun as he heard it fall, his confusion at its death turning to savage joy as he saw who had saved him. He beat his fists on his chest and roared, 'Now you Tribe!'

Even as Leonid ducked back into cover, he heard the thump of booted feet behind him. He spun, bringing the barrel of his lasgun up, seeing half a dozen mutant slave warriors armed with cudgels and billhooks bearing down upon him. An iron-tipped club slashed for his head and he hurled himself backwards, too slow, the tip of the weapon thudding against his temple.

He dropped his lasgun, hands flying to his head as the world spun crazily and bright starbursts exploded before his eyes. The ground rushed up to meet him and he slammed into the hard rockcrete, closing his eyes as he waited for the killing blow to land.

The shadow of something hot and heavy fell across him and warm blood splashed him.

He opened his eyes and shook his head, regretting it the moment he felt hammerblows of concussion reverberate inside his skull. The Lord of the Unfleshed towered above him, his thickly-muscled body pierced by a score of long blades and burned by innumerable lasburns. The creature reached down to lift him to his feet, and Leonid saw the bodies of those who had been about to kill him.

They looked like an explosion in an anatomist's collection, a mass of severed limbs and burst-open bodies.

'Thank you,' managed Leonid, wiping blood from the side of his head and bending to retrieve his fallen weapon.

'You Tribe,' replied the Lord of the Unfleshed as though no other explanation was needed. Without another word, the creature hurled itself back into the fray. Scores of the Unfleshed were dead, but the remainder fought on, unrelenting in their savagery. More and more of their foes were pouring into the chamber and Leonid knew it would not be long until they were overwhelmed.

He looked up towards the gantries surrounding the chamber, willing Uriel and Pasanius to hurry.

THE VEINS ON Uriel's arms stood out like steel hawsers as he pulled on the chain. Bracing themselves against the raised edge of the scaffolding before him, they hauled with all their might on the chain.

Uriel's booted feet slipped and he spread his stance to gain better leverage. The grinding pain in his chest and neck from his cracked bones tore into him as he pulled, but he focussed his mind, using all the discipline he had been taught at Agiselus and in the Temple of Hera to shut it out.

'Come on, damn you!' he yelled at the chain, hearing the ferocious sounds of battle and knowing that the Unfleshed were dying for him.

He could not let them down, and redoubled his efforts.

Pasanius strained at the chain also, sweat popping from his brow as he hauled on the chain. The sergeant was much stronger than Uriel, but had only one arm with which to heave at the chain.

Together, they put every ounce of their hatred for the Iron Warriors into their efforts.

Uriel roared in pain and frustration as he kept on pulling.

And suddenly he felt give…

Yelling in triumph, the two Ultramarines pulled even harder, feeling tendons tear in their shoulders and arms, but pushing their bodies to the limits of power.

Without warning, the awl-chain tore loose and Uriel saw a flaring spurt of white fire as the silver spike ripped free of the ancient daemon's flesh.

The red-scaled creature dropped, silver-white flashes exploding against its body where its falling weight tore the other two silver awls from its body.

It landed in the lake of blood with an enormous splash, sending a tidal wave of crimson spilling throughout the chamber. It vanished beneath the churning surface of the lake and Uriel felt a prescient sense of inevitability seize him as he watched the hissing red pool.

'We did it!' shouted Pasanius.

'Yes,' agreed Uriel, watching as the surface of the lake parted and the massive daemon reared up to its full height, arc lightning playing about its lustrous, scarlet flesh, 'but I am beginning to wonder if we should have.'

HIGH UP IN the tower of iron, Onyx cried out as though struck and dropped to his knees, clutching his head as his soulless silver eyes blazed with sudden awareness. Honsou saw the movement and looked up, irritated at having his battle-planning with Cadaras Grendel interrupted.

Then he saw the look of alarm on Onyx's face.

'What is it?' he demanded.

'The Heart of Blood!' hissed the daemonic symbiote.

'What about it?'

'It's free…' said Onyx.

♉

TWENTY

THE HEART OF Blood threw back its horned skull and roared in lunatic pain, its bellow of rage and madness filling the chamber at a pitch that pierced the soul and drew screams of primal fear from almost every living thing within it. The lake of blood boiled where it stood and its eyes burned with white fire that blazed with ancient malice.

Its shaggy, horned head twisted as it surveyed its surroundings, as though seeing them for the first time, and its bloated body threw off great bolts of dark lightning that exploded with red fire.

The Heart of Blood's flesh was scaled and thick tufts of shaggy, matted hair ran down the length of its spine. The great wounds on its back, where the Savage Morticians had removed its wings, smoked with a liquid, red bloom, like a cloud of ink released underwater.

Its chest heaved violently, the thudding echoes of its heartbeat filling the chamber as it ripped away the pulsing red tube that pierced its chest and fed it the tainted blood of psykers. The flood of vital fluid gushed into the lake.

'Guilliman preserve us!' breathed Pasanius as the daemon stepped forwards, striding purposefully to the shore, the spark of its hoofed feet on the lakebed throwing up gouts of flaming blood.

'A daemon,' said Uriel. 'One of the fell princes of Chaos…'

'What do we do?' said Pasanius.

Uriel drew his sword as the huge daemon reached the edge of the lake of blood and reared up to its full height.

'We ready our souls for the end,' he said simply.

* * *

HONSOU WATCHED THE sky around his fortress burn with an actinic blue light. Hundreds of pillars of pellucid blue flame surrounded Khalan-Ghol, spearing kilometres upwards from the plain below, like oil-wells gushing with precious fuel. The azure fire seethed and Honsou could see living nightmares swirling within the flames, the dreadful power and malice of the warp contained within them.

'What's happening?' he demanded.

'The towers!' said Onyx.

'Towers? What towers?'

'The ones we saw when we made that sortie into Berossus's camp,' said Onyx. 'Tall, baroque towers of iron that were saturated with psychic energy. You remember?'

Honsou nodded, recalling the unsettling sight of their arcane geometries and the chanting groups of gold-robed figures who danced around them, anointing them with the blood of sacrifices. He had put them from his mind after the raid, confident that the power of the Heart of Blood could resist their magicks.

He rounded on Onyx, raising his axe and saying, 'You told me that no sorcerous powers could defeat the Heart of Blood!'

'And none can, but it is free now and not bound to Khalan-Ghol any more.'

'We are defenceless?' asked Cadaras Grendel.

Onyx shook his head. 'No. The fortress's own sorcerers can maintain the barrier for a while, but without the power of the Heart of Blood, it is only a matter of time until Toramino's magicks break through and destroy us.'

'Blood of Chaos!' swore Honsou, heading for the great doors that led from his inner sanctum and waving his chosen warriors to follow him. 'How could the daemon get free?'

'The warsmith bound the Heart of Blood with three defiled awls, and it could only be freed if someone were to remove them.'

'But who would dare risk such a thing?'

Honsou pulled up short as Onyx said, 'Ventris and his warrior band?'

'Of course!' snapped Honsou. 'I should have known Toramino would never have stooped so low as to employ renegades just to fight for him. He and Ventris must have planned this whole thing! Free the Heart of Blood and then destroy us with sorcery. I'll have those bastards' entrails fed a piece at a time to the Exuviae.'

'Then Toramino never intended to blood his army here!' snarled Cadaras Grendel.

'No,' agreed Onyx. 'It would seem not.'

'How long do we have before the barrier falls?' demanded Honsou, setting off into the darkness of the tower of iron and towards the Halls of the Savage Morticians.

His warriors followed him, bolters and swords at the ready.

'I do not know for sure,' admitted Onyx, 'but it will not be long.'

'Then we'd better hurry!' said Honsou. 'I want to kill Ventris before Toramino brings Khalan-Ghol to ruin!'

URIEL DROPPED TO the gantry that ran the circumference of the chamber, thumbing the activation rune on his sword's hilt and slashing its bright blade through the air. Pasanius landed beside him and together they hurriedly made their way to the chamber's floor as the Heart of Blood stepped from the lake, red liquid running from its crimson body in grisly runnels.

It towered above them, fully four or five metres tall, its powerfully muscled physique running with hot streamers of light that snaked beneath its flesh like fiery veins. It looked down on the bloody ground before it – at the corpses of the Unfleshed, the Savage Morticians and their servants – and a bloody leer split its bestial face. The surviving mutants fled before its terrifying power and even those Savage Morticians the Unfleshed had not killed backed away from this diabolical presence in their midst.

Only the Unfleshed stood their ground, too ignorant of the horrifying power of a daemon prince to fear it. Though they felt its abominable power, they had no concept of the threat it represented.

The Lord of the Unfleshed stood before the mighty daemon, his chest puffed out in challenge, and it regarded him with as much interest as a man might notice an ant. The Lord of the Unfleshed roared and charged the daemon, but before he could so much as land a blow, the Heart of Blood swatted him aside with a casual flick of its scaled arm.

The monstrous leader of the Unfleshed smashed into the side of the cavern with a bone-crunching thud and Uriel knew that the force of the impact must have shattered every bone in his body.

Seeing their leader so easily defeated, the Unfleshed howled and scattered before the horrendous daemon, seeking shelter in the dark nooks and crannies of the deathly cavern.

Uriel and Pasanius watched as the Heart of Blood turned from the fleeing Unfleshed, the tremendous booming of its vital organ diminishing now that sorcerous magicks were no longer pouring into it. Uriel felt his senses becoming sharper, the smothering numbness lifted now that the daemon was free.

Leonid hurried over to where they stood and shouted, 'I thought it was supposed to be destroyed when the awls came out!'

'So did I,' replied Uriel as the Heart of Blood threw back its head and gave vent to a terrible roaring that overwhelmed the senses, not through its volume, but by the sheer sense of loss and fury that it contained. Its hunger pierced the wall of the dimensions and echoed across the vast gulf that separated universes.

Uriel and every living thing in the chamber fell to the ground, shaken to the very core of their being by the daemon's cry.

'What's it doing?' yelled Leonid.

'Emperor alone knows!' cried Pasanius.

Uriel picked himself up, his hands clamped to the side of his head in an effort to shut out the monstrous noise of the daemon's howl. Something in the tone of the long, ululating cry spoke to Uriel of things lost and things to be called back. He realised what it was as he saw a twisting blob of dark light appear in the air before the daemon.

'It is a cry of summoning...' he said.

Pasanius and Leonid looked strangely at him as the daemon's roar ceased and the fragile veil of reality pulled apart with a dreadful ripping sound, as of tearing meat. A black gouge in the walls separating realities opened, filling the air with sickening static, as though a million noxious flies had flown through from some vile, plague dimension.

Awful knowledge flooded Uriel as he stared into the portal opened in the fabric of the universe. He saw galaxies of billions upon billions of souls harvested and fed to the Lord of Skulls, the Blood God.

'Emperor's mercy,' wept Uriel as he felt each of these deaths lodge like a splinter in his heart. New life and new purpose had once filled these galaxies, but now all was death, slaughtered to sate the hunger of the Blood God... whose fell name was a dark presence staining the coppery wind that blew from the portal, a stench of deepest, darkest red, whose purpose was embodied in but a single rune and a legend of simple devotion: Blood for the Blood God... *Khorne... Khorne... Khorne...*

A single shriek of dark and bloody kinship, a pact of hate and death. It echoed from the portal and grew to shake the dust from the ceiling. And there was an answering roar of bloody welcome, torn from the Heart of Blood's brazen throat.

Light blazed from the portal as an armoured giant, clad in burnished iron plates of ancient power armour stamped down into the chamber, the portal sealing shut behind it as it marched to stand before the Heart of Blood.

Taller than a Space Marine, its vile presence was unmistakable, its malice incalculable. White light, impure and corrupt, spilled like droplets of spoiled milk from beneath its horned helmet and its shoulder guards bore stained chevrons that marked the figure as an Iron Warrior.

The daemonic warrior carried a great, saw-toothed blade and a gold-chased pistol, both weapons redolent with the slaughter they had inflicted. Powerful and darkly magnificent, Uriel knew that this... thing was the most consummate killer imaginable.

Uriel caught a glimpse of a shambling shape limping towards the passageway that led from the cavern, recognising it as the vile creature, Sabatier. Barely had he registered its presence when the iron-armoured warrior snapped up its pistol and fired.

The bolt caught Sabatier high in the back, exploding through its chest and blasting a great crater in its body. Sabatier grunted and toppled over and Uriel felt sorry that it hadn't suffered more before it died.

'We can't fight both of them,' said Pasanius.

'No,' agreed Uriel, 'but maybe we will not have to. Look!'

The armoured figure dropped to its knees before the Heart of Blood, but Uriel could see that it was no simple a gesture of abasement. The daemonic Iron Warrior dropped its weapons and raised its arms, a blood-red glow spilling from every joint of its armour and bathing the Heart of Blood in its light.

'I return to you!' shouted a high voice from beneath the armoured warrior's helmet.

The Heart of Blood raised its arms, mimicking the warrior's pose and, piece-by-piece, the iron armour detached from the kneeling figure and floated through the air towards the massive daemon.

'Now what the hell's it doing?' said Leonid, barely keeping the terror from his voice.

'Oh no…' whispered Uriel as he remembered a tale he had been told not so long ago by Seraphys of the Blood Ravens in the mountains. A tale of how the Heart of Blood had forged for itself a suit of armour into which it had poured all of its malice, all of its hate and all of its cunning, a suit of armour so full of fury that even the blows of its enemies would strike them down.

Truly it was the avatar of Khorne, the Blood God's most favoured disciple of death.

Iron armour floated from the figure who now diminished as each piece deserted it. Though the Heart of Blood was larger by far than the armoured warrior, each piece somehow moulded itself to the daemon's form, darkening from the colour of iron to a dark and loathsome brass. Its greaves and breastplate clanged into place and, unbidden, the warrior's weapons leapt from the ground, writhing in midair to change from a pistol and sword to a moaning axe and snaking whip of rippling, studded leather.

Lastly, the iron helm was snatched by invisible hands from the warrior's head and placed upon the Heart of Blood's great, horned skull.

Where once had knelt a fearsome, armoured giant, there was now only a waif-like figure of a woman in a filthy and tattered sky-blue uniform of the Imperial Guard.

'383rd!' exclaimed Leonid.

'What?'

'That jacket,' pointed Leonid. 'It's the uniform of my regiment!'

'It can't be,' said Uriel. 'Here?'

'I know my own regiment, damn it,' snapped Leonid. 'I'm going to get her!'

'Don't be a fool,' said Pasanius, gripping Leonid's jacket.

'No!' protested Leonid, struggling in the sergeant's grip. 'Don't you understand? Along with me, she's probably the last survivor of the 383rd! I have to go!'

'You'll die,' said Uriel.

'So? I'm dying anyway,' shouted Leonid. 'And if I have to end my days here, I want it to be with a fellow Jouran. Remember your words, Uriel! We all die bloody, all we get to do is choose where and when!'

Uriel nodded, now understanding Leonid's desperation, and said, 'Let him go.'

Pasanius released his grip on Leonid, and they watched as he ran towards the swaying woman, gathering her up in his arms as another set of thick, curling, bronze-tipped horns ripped through the metal of the daemon's helmet. The Heart of Blood's eyes shone with renewed purpose and awareness as it lifted its head and sniffed the air, grinning with terrible appetite.

'Psykers...' it roared, turning towards the upright iron sarcophagi that surrounded the lake of blood.

THE IRON-MESHED cage sped downwards into the depths of Khalan-Ghol, ancient mechanisms and sorcerous artifice combining to make the journey as quick as possible, oily sheets of beaten iron slicing past at tremendous speed. But Honsou knew it was still not fast enough. The mystical barrier protecting his fortress was still holding firm against Toramino's sorcerers, but it wouldn't last much longer unless they could somehow re-imprison the Heart of Blood.

He and his chosen warriors, deadly killers loyal only to him, journeyed into the depths of the fortress, ready to kill whatever they encountered. Onyx stood backed into the corner of the speeding elevator cage, his silver eyes and veins dulled and sluggish in his features.

'What's the matter with you?' snapped Honsou as the daemonic symbiote moaned.

'The Heart of Blood is powerful...' hissed Onyx.

'And?'

'It could snuff out my essence in the blink of an eye,' snarled Onyx, his dead eyes shining with murderous lustre. 'And if it commanded me, I could not resist its imperatives.'

'You mean it could turn you against me?' asked Honsou.

'Yes,' nodded Onyx. 'It knows my true name.'

Honsou turned to Cadaras Grendel and said, 'If this creature so much as makes a move towards me, kill it.'

'Understood,' said the mohawked Iron Warrior, his scarred features alight with relish at the thought. 'I never killed one that's possessed before.'

Honsou looked down through the grilled floor of the cage, seeing only a dimly glowing shaft roaring upwards. Its end was lost to perspective, but as he watched, the dark square of the tunnel's base rushed up to meet them.

With a gut-wrenching sensation of nausea, the iron cage slowed and ground to a halt with a shriek of ancient metal. The grilled door squealed open, but before Honsou could step through, he was knocked from his feet by a tremendous impact and felt the crash of falling masonry from far away, accompanied by the distant boom of massed artillery.

'What the hell?' he roared, climbing to his knees as he heard the clang of metal on stone, and an approaching, crashing din.

Onyx dropped to his knees, screaming in pain and clutching his head with his dead-fleshed hands.

'The barrier is down!' he yelled. 'Gods of Chaos, the barrier is down!'

Honsou pulled himself to his feet and looked up as he pinpointed the source of the approaching noise.

'Out of the elevator!' he shouted, diving and rolling into the tunnel as he saw thousands of tonnes of rubble plummeting down the shaft. His warriors moved quickly, but some not quickly enough, as a torrent of massive chunks of stone and rockcrete hammered into the base of the shaft and crushed the elevator cage flat. Roiling banks of choking dust and smoke billowed from the wreckage.

The impact and deafening noise disoriented Honsou, but he quickly gained his feet, seeing that nearly half his warriors were missing, crushed beneath the deadly rain of debris.

Onyx stood unsteadily before him, the threatening form of Cadaras Grendel close by.

'If the barrier is down–' began Grendel

'Then that means Toramino is attacking!' finished Honsou.

Just saying the words gave Honsou a curious sense of reckless abandonment as he realised that this was probably the end. There was no way Khalan-Ghol could stand against Toramino's army and he had no more stratagems left to employ.

There was nothing left but vengeance for hate's sake and malice for the sake of spite.

If that was all he had left, then so be it.

It would be enough.

URIEL PULLED LEONID into the scant cover offered by one of the corpse bulldozers and helped him get the muttering woman he had dragged to safety into a seated position. Tears of joy streaked the colonel's face and he kept repeating the name of his regiment over and over again.

'Come on, hurry,' urged Uriel, desperate to keep Leonid out of the way of the Heart of Blood's murderous rampage. The mighty, armoured daemon was making sport in the centre of the lake of blood, ripping gold-robed sorcerers from their exsanguination coffins, toying with them in numerous terrible ways before slaughtering them with its axe or powerful, fanged maw.

It waded through the blood, letting the terrified magickers tear themselves to pieces as they desperately fought to free themselves from their coffins. Not one amongst them survived the daemon's predatory malice and it inhaled their deaths like a fine wine.

'Psykers!' it bellowed. 'The food of the gods!'

Uriel returned his attention to the wan, lean-faced woman Leonid had rescued from the clutches of the daemonic armour. Her hair was long, lank and falling out in patches, while her features spoke of horrors endured and a mind on the very brink of sanity.

'All dead, all dead, all dead, all dead...' she repeated, over and over.

'Who is she?' asked Pasanius.

Leonid fished out rusted dogtags from beneath her uniform jacket and turned them over to examine them in the chamber's dim light.

'Her name is Lieutenant Larana Utorian of the 383rd Jouran Dragoons,' he said proudly.

'Do you know her?'

Leonid shook his head. 'No, I don't. Her tags say she was part of Tedeski's lot in Battalion A and he didn't like other officers mingling with his soldiers. He was old school you see.'

'How in the Emperor's name did she end up here?'

'I don't know,' wept Leonid, holding her in a tight embrace. 'Perhaps the God-Emperor didn't want me to die alone without someone from the old homeworld next to me.'

Uriel nodded and locked eyes with Pasanius as he gripped his sword hilt tightly. 'Aye, perhaps you're right, my friend. If a man has to die, it should be with his friends.'

THE DEAD, WHITE sky burned with magickal energies, whipping plumes of blue fire shooting up into the heavens from the geomantic towers Toramino's sorcerers had constructed around Khalan-Ghol. Monstrously powerful energies had been unleashed, and now that the eternal barrier that had kept Honsou's fortress safe from the fell powers of the warp was no more, it suffered terribly under the immaterial assault.

Black lightning speared from the cloudless sky, blasting colossal slabs of rock from the mountain and fearsome red storms of bruised, weeping clouds hammered the few remaining towers and bastions with mutating rains that dissolved fortifications which had stood invincible for ten thousand years.

Great, ravening beasts of the warp swooped and dived around the high reaches of the fortress, tearing apart the flying creatures that circled the topmost towers, and a fog of magickal energies enveloped the redoubts and bunkers that Honsou had only recently rebuilt in the wake of his victory over Lord Berossus.

Nor was the fortress attacked only by sorcerous powers, for Toramino's grand artillery batteries were finally unleashed to bring explosive ruin upon the mountain of their master's enemy. Thousands of tonnes of ordnance rained down on Khalan-Ghol, smashing apart the very mountain itself.

Huge columns of soldiers and an entire grand company of Iron Warriors, led by Toramino himself, marched upon Khalan-Ghol, a host of thousands that would destroy whatever of the half-breed's force might survive the furious assault now wracking the mountain.

Khalan-Ghol's final doom was upon it.

URIEL FELT A familiar churning sensation in his stomach, hearing a chiming, splintering sound of glass breaking, and a terrible sensation of powerlessness gripped him. He experienced sickening vibrations deep in his bones as a restlessness rippled through the ground. A powerful vision of jagged stumps of bone jutting through the ground gripped him, and a mad howling built from the air, piercing and vile, with an unimaginable thirst for revenge.

He blinked as a fiercely painful sensation built within his skull, as though hot needles were being pushed out through his eyeballs.

'Oh, no...' he whispered, as he realised what was happening, and looked up into the face of Leonid, whose gaze betrayed the same knowledge that had just come to Uriel.

'God-Emperor, no,' wept Leonid. 'Not again, please no, not again!'

'What is it?' said Pasanius.

Before Uriel could answer, they heard the Heart of Blood roar in sudden awareness, sounding like a cry of unexpected pleasure.

'My old nemesis...' it rasped as the very air in the chamber became saturated with an electric tang of ozone and sulphur. Uriel felt his stomach heave and gripped onto the side of the bulldozer as the Hall of the Savage Morticians seemed to... *shift*...

The ground now felt soft and loamy underfoot, a weeping red fluid seeping upwards where his weight had forced it from the dark earth. Uriel looked up, already knowing what he would see.

Above him, a lacerated crimson sky, flecked with cancerous, melanoma clouds boiled, wheeling carrion creatures circling and awaiting their chance to feed. A familiar mad screaming, like the wails of the damned, echoed painfully, but it was nothing compared to the misery he had already seen in this place, and he pushed it aside.

Fleshless, bony hands reached up through the dark earth and Leonid kept his eyes shut tightly, holding onto Larana Utorian. Rippling spirals of reflective light coiled from the walls of the chamber, twisting the image of the rock behind like a warped lens. The walls seemed to stretch, as though being sucked into an unseen vortex behind, until there was nothing left but a rippling veil of impenetrable darkness, a tunnel into madness ringed with screaming faces.

Brazen rail tracks coated in crusted blood ran from the previously impermeable walls of the chamber, streamers of multi-coloured matter oozing from the cracked rock.

With no eternal barrier to stop it from reaching its hated rival, the Omphalos Daemonium manifested within the walls of Khalan-Ghol.

♈ TWENTY-ONE

ROARING FROM THE mouth of the tunnel like a dark force of nature, the Omphalos Daemonium thundered into the Halls of the Savage Morticians. The armoured leviathan's mad structure was doubly hateful to Uriel now that a suspicion that had been nagging at the back of his head was horribly confirmed.

'It knew...' he snarled.

'Knew what?' said Pasanius, shouting to be heard over the howling roar of the Omphalos Daemonium's arrival. Uriel ducked back as the swirling red tendrils of smoke that were the hallmarks of the Sarcomata slashed past, carried onwards by the passing of the colossal daemon engine. It came to a halt before a newly-raised platform of bloodstained rockcrete with the sound of squealing iron and brazen roars, hissing souls escaping from its billowing stacks in shrieking waves of pain.

'It knew we would try to defy it,' said Uriel, sick with the realisation that they had been used. 'It knew we would try and destroy the Heart of Blood.'

'Then why did it send us here?'

'Because now that the psychic barrier Obax Zakayo spoke of is down, it can manifest within Khalan-Ghol. Remember the tale Seraphys told us? These daemons are ancient enemies and now the Omphalos Daemonium will wreak its vengeance upon the Heart of Blood for trapping it within that daemon engine.'

Pasanius turned as the Heart of Blood stepped from the crimson lake, its slaughter of Honsou's psykers complete and the promise of battle with its ancestral foe drawing it towards the seething engine. The brazen machine heaved with power and red mist writhed around its thick plates as the heavy door to the interior heaved open and the Slaughterman stepped onto the platform, the thick, clanking iron plates of his armour dripping with a black, oily residue.

The daemonic Iron Warrior was as huge as Uriel remembered it, its bulk made all the more massive by the extra plates of armour welded and bound to its fabric over the millennia. It still wore its charred and blackened apron, stiffened with ancient blood and reeking of cooked flesh and blood.

A crown of dark horns sprouted from its battered helmet and Uriel was not surprised to see that it still carried its murderous, iron-hafted bill-hook, the blade broad and crusted with aeons of bloodshed.

The Heart of Blood roared with mirth as the Slaughterman stepped into the Hall of the Savage Morticians.

'Is this what you are reduced to?' it bellowed. 'To wear the flesh of your gaoler?'

'Only liveflesh left to me,' barked the Slaughterman. 'Enough words. I rip your warpself apart!'

The Heart of Blood broadened its stance and raised its enormous axe, cracking its whip and roaring its bloody challenge to the Slaughterman. Thick red tendrils of smoke coalesced around the gigantic Iron Warrior, becoming solid things of dead flesh and immaterial energies.

'Sarcomata!' snarled Uriel, seeing the featureless daemon creatures that had carried them aboard the Omphalos Daemonium's horrific daemon engine. Eight of them attended their daemonic master, each wearing a grey, featureless boiler-suit and knee high boots with rusted greaves protecting their shins. They carried knives, hooks and saws and, from the loathsome snapping of their jaws, looked eager to use them.

Their disgusting faces were red and raw, like the Unfleshed, but where the Unfleshed still possessed qualities that were human, even if they were only rudimentary, the Sarcomata were utterly flensed of the mask of humanity. Their eyeless faces were crisscrossed with crude stitches above their fanged mouths, and their narrow, questing tongues licked the air.

Uriel expected some form of retort from the Heart of Blood, but words were not part of the equation when it came to daemons of the Blood God. The Heart of Blood cracked its whip again, the barbed tip scoring across the Slaughterman's chest in a slash of sparks. The iron-armoured daemon roared and hurled itself from the platform and the Heart of Blood leapt to meet it, the two mighty creatures hammering together in a blazing corona of fiery warp energy.

Machinery was crushed and great, iron pillars were smashed aside as the two powerful daemons tore at one another with a hate that had burned for uncounted aeons. Deafening shrieks of diabolical weapons echoed as the cavern shook with the violence of their battle.

Uriel hunkered down against the bulldozer, realising that more than just the daemonic battle was destroying this place. He felt a bass thump, thump of impacts against the rock and smiled to himself as he knew what was happening.

'Honsou's fortress is under yet another bombardment,' he shouted.

Pasanius looked doubtful. 'The shelling must be incredible to be felt this deep.'

'Indeed,' agreed Uriel. 'Toramino must be attacking with everything he has.'

Rock and machinery flew, hurled aside as the two daemons fell back into the lake of blood. Geysers of flaming blood and flesh were thrown into the air and a foul red rain began to fall as the daemons tore at one another.

'Come on!' yelled Uriel over the din. 'We should get out of here. Toramino's army will destroy this place soon and I do not want to be any-where near these two creatures while they fight!'

'Where do we go?' asked Pasanius as chunks of rubble fell from the walls of the chamber, smashing to the ground and throwing up huge clouds of debris and smoke.

'Anywhere but here,' said Uriel, nodding to the long passageway that led to the elevator cage that had brought them here from Honsou's chambers. 'If that elevator is still working, we can get back to where that silver-eyed daemon thing brought us into the fortress.'

He knelt beside Leonid and said, 'We are going now, colonel. Come on.'

Leonid looked up through his tears and Uriel saw that the colonel was at the end of his endurance. The colonel shook his head. 'No. You go. I will stay here with Larana Utorian.'

Uriel shook his head. 'We will not leave you here. A Space Marine never leaves a battle-brother behind.'

'I am not your battle-brother, Uriel,' coughed Leonid sadly. 'Even if she and I get out of this place we will not survive more than a few days. The cancers the Mechanicus infected us with are growing stronger every day. It is over for us.'

Uriel placed his hand on Leonid's shoulder, knowing the man was right, but hating the feeling of betrayal that settled on him as he accepted Leonid's decision.

'The Emperor be with you,' said Uriel.

Leonid looked down into the face of Larana Utorian and smiled. 'I think He is.'

Uriel nodded and turned from Leonid as Pasanius said, 'Die well, Leonid. If we survive, I will light a candle for your soul to find its way home.'

Leonid said nothing, cradling Larana Utorian's wasted frame and rock-ing back and forth.

Knowing there was nothing more for them to say, the Ultramarines turned and ran towards the entrance to the cavern as more of the Savage Morticians' domain was brought down by the battling daemons.

Behind them, Colonel Mikhail Leonid and Lieutenant Larana Utorian of the 383rd Jouran Dragoons held each other tight and waited for death.

PASANIUS FLINCHED AS a huge cascade of rocks crashed down beside him, hurling him off balance and wreathing him in powdery dust. He coughed and shouted for Uriel as everything became obscured in banks of smoke.

'Here!' shouted Uriel, and Pasanius made his way towards the source of the shout.

He tripped on something on the ground and rolled, putting his arm down to push himself back to his feet and falling flat as he remembered that there was no arm to take his weight. He cursed himself for a fool, then saw what he had tripped over.

The gurgling form of Sabatier painfully pulled itself towards safety, its twisted, deformed body, dusty and covered in contusions. A great crater had been gouged in its back where the creature that had stepped through the portal had shot it, but Pasanius was not surprised to see that Sabatier still lived. After all, it had survived Vaanes snapping its neck like a dry branch.

Bone still protruded at its neck from that wound and Pasanius flipped the repulsive creature onto its back as it mewled in pain and fear.

'Not so proud now, are you?' said Pasanius.

'Leave Sabatier! He never did any harm!'

'No,' snarled Pasanius. 'He just gloated while my friends were butchered like animals!'

The huge sergeant knelt on Sabatier's chest, his weight alone cracking the hideous creature's ribs. A horrid gurgling burst from Sabatier's throat, but Pasanius felt no remorse for its suffering. It had stood and laughed as Space Marines were killed and for that Pasanius knew it had to die.

Keeping it pinned with his knee, he gripped Sabatier by the neck with his remaining hand and heaved.

The mutant's neck stretched and Pasanius heard the crack of splitting tendons before he wrenched Sabatier's head clean off. Sabatier's mouth still flapped, but no sound came out.

Pasanius had no idea whether he had killed Sabatier, but didn't care. To have struck back at it was enough. He stood and spat on the twitching body, stamping repeatedly on its altered limbs to crush the bones to powder before turning and hurling the mutant's head back towards the lake of blood.

If Sabatier could live through this, it would have nothing left of its body to return to.

'What was that?' said Uriel, emerging from the cloud of dust and beckoning him onwards towards the entrance to the tunnel.

'Nothing,' said Pasanius. 'Just some rubbish.'

LEONID STROKED LARANA Utorian's cheek, tears spilling down his face as the burning pain that had been his constant companion since he had been taken from Hydra Cordatus sent another spasm of hot fire into his belly. He knew that he did not have much time left – the cancers had devoured most of him already – and, looking at Larana Utorian, she did not have much time left to her either.

They were the last of the 383rd and the fact that they would die together gave him great comfort. He thought back to the men and women of his regiment and the last time he had fought beside them at the fall of the citadel. They had been magnificent.

Castellan Vauban, a courageous and honourable warrior. Piet Anders, Gunnar Tedeski and Morgan Kristan; his brother officers. And not forgetting Guardsman Hawke, the worst soldier in the regiment, whose unexpected depths of courage had very nearly saved them all.

They were all dead, and soon he and Larana Utorian would be with them again.

Colonel Leonid looked up, hearing a sibilant hissing, and drew a sharp intake of breath as he saw the two daemons stagger from the lake of blood. Both were ravaged and battered, their armours torn and rent by the mighty blows they laid upon one another. The violence of their struggle had devastated much of the cavern and portions of it continued to rain down in avalanches of rocks and rubble.

The Heart of Blood reeled from a terrible blow done to it by the Omphalos Daemonium... the Slaughterman... Leonid was not even sure he understood the distinction between these two beings, or that he wanted to even if there was one.

The daemonic Iron Warrior hammered its long billhook against the Heart of Blood's unguarded flank and hurled it backwards into a giant pile of mortuary tables and swinging cadavers. Bodies and debris clattered down amid the ongoing destruction and Leonid saw the Slaughterman turn and cast its gaze around the chamber.

No, Ultramarines, you do not escape my vengeance so easily...

Leonid cried out as he heard its filthy, loathsome voice in his head.

The Sarcomata shall feast on your souls for all eternity!

Leonid saw the eight daemons that were the servants of the Slaughterman dissolve once more into their smoky aspects, swirling in the air for a moment before speeding after Uriel and Pasanius.

'No!' shouted Leonid in rage. 'You will not have them!'

The Sarcomata ignored him, too intent on their prey, until he remembered their hunger for corruption. Leonid pulled the frayed collar of his uniform jacket away from his skin, slashing the rusted edge of Larana Utorian's dogtags across a swollen, cancerous melanoma growing on the pulsing artery of his neck.

Polluted, dirty blood spilled down his skin, pooling in his collarbone and soaking his uniform jacket. He smelled its coppery, unclean stink and shouted, 'Over here, you daemon spawn! This is what you want, isn't it?'

Almost as soon as his polluted blood sprayed out, the smoky comets of the Sarcomata twisted in the air and sped towards him, scenting the malignancies devouring his body as the choicest sweetmeats.

Colonel Leonid slumped to his haunches and pulled Larana Utorian tight, reaching into his breast pocket and removing something round and flat.

'All dead, all dead, all dead, all dead...' whispered Larana Utorian.

'Yes,' agreed Leonid. 'We are.'

Red mist enfolded them, sickening and moist, then vanished in an instant, leaving the two Jourans surrounded by the cancer-hungry Sarcomata, their writhing-maggot touch stroking their swollen sicknesses.

The daemons bit and tore at their flesh and he cried out in pain.

For the briefest instant, his eyes met those of Larana Utorian, and he saw the last fragment of her mind reach out to him.

She smiled at him and nodded.

Leonid pressed the detonation stud of the grenade he had taken from the crushing machine next to Obax Zakayo, obliterating them and the Sarcomata in the white heat of a melta blast.

'NO WAY OUT this way, Ventris,' said Honsou, gripping his axe and widening his stance ready for combat. The master of Khalan-Ghol and a score of Iron Warriors had emerged from the passageway just as the Ultramarines had reached it, and Uriel saw that there was no way past them. The silver-eyed daemon-thing that had called itself Onyx stood apart from the Iron Warriors, its movements tentative.

An Iron Warrior with the brutal face of a killer and a mohawk stood next to it, a huge gun that resembled a bolter with an underslung melta pointed at the daemonic symbiote.

The cavern continued to rumble as the two daemons fought at its heart, but a stillness held sway here, as though the universe held its breath and awaited the outcome of this particular drama.

'It is over, Honsou,' said Uriel. 'Your fortress has fallen.'

'I can build another,' shrugged Honsou. 'This one wasn't really mine anyway.'

'True, but it's Toramino's now,' shouted Pasanius.

'Yes, or at least whatever his sorcerers and artillery leave of it once they have pounded it to rubble,' said Honsou.

The Iron Warrior pointed towards the ugly red skies overhead. 'Tell me though, is this your doing as well, or another of your master's sorceries?'

'My master?'

'Come on, Ventris!' laughed Honsou. 'The time for games is long past. Toramino!'

'We have no master save Lord Calgar and the Emperor,' said Uriel.

'Even now you play your games,' sighed Honsou. 'Well, no matter, it ends now.'

'Aye,' agreed Uriel, raising his sword before him. 'It ends with your death, traitor.'

'Perhaps, but you'll follow me into hell a heartbeat later.'

Uriel shook his head. 'You think that matters, amid all this? I will fight you and I will kill you. That will be enough for me.'

'Fight me?' said Honsou, spreading his arms to encompass his warriors. 'You think we're going to fight a duel? My warriors and I outnumber you ten to one! What makes you think I'd give you a chance to trade blows with me?'

The Iron Warriors aimed their weapons at them, knowing that blood was soon to be spilled here, but waiting for their master's command before unleashing death.

Pasanius leaned close to Uriel and said, 'You take the ten on the right and I'll take the ten on the left.'

Despite himself, Uriel chuckled and stood back to back with his oldest comrade.

'Courage and honour, my friend,' said Uriel.

'Courage and honour,' repeated Pasanius.

The two Ultramarines prepared to charge as the Iron Warriors cocked their bolters.

THE HEART OF Blood fell to its knees, the Omphalos Daemonium's bill-hook tearing into its warp-spawned flesh and opening a great gash in its body. Dark ichor spilled down its armour and its strength was fading; too long imprisoned within the depths of Khalan-Ghol had robbed it of much of its diabolical vigour and power. Another blow smashed into its chest, sending it hurling across the width of the chamber.

'Eternity awaits you!' roared the Omphalos Daemonium. 'An age trapped in fire will be nothing to torments you will suffer!'

Smoke and rubble fell in a constant rain from the walls, crushing anything exposed on the cavern floor.

'You cannot destroy me. I am the Heart of Blood!'

The Omphalos Daemonium ran towards it, fierce, vengeful hunger burning in its eyes. The Heart of Blood sprang to its feet and lashed out with its whip. The blow struck its foe's head, drawing a bellow of pain and a spray of dark blood as it severed one of its gnarled antlers.

The Heart of Blood staggered away in the respite its lucky blow had gained, wading back into the lake of blood, feeling the invigorating fluid enter its immaterial flesh and new strength seep into its essence. But this was poor, stagnant blood, polluted with the taint of psychic energies and devoid of the hot, urgent nourishment it needed to defeat its foe.

As the Omphalos Daemonium came after it, memories thrashed and screamed in the Heart of Blood's skull, though it had not the faculties left to recall them. The lunacy that had consumed it during its incarceration had robbed it of any clarity of thought save that it needed blood, desired blood... craved blood!

A powerful vision of a great fortress swam across the fluid landscape of its memory – no, not its memory, the blood-soaked memories of the Avatar of Khorne, the creature the armour had become in its absence...

A battle alongside the Iron Warriors, a sorcerous foe in yellow armour – one of the corpse-god's followers – and a howling gale of gore that thundered like a hurricane and fed its spirit with unimaginable power.

Something in this memory was the key it needed to defeat its rival and drive the Omphalos Daemonium back to the fiery prison the Heart of Blood had confined it to for an age.

A single word penetrated the Heart of Blood's fug of amnesia and lunacy. *Bloodstorm...*

THE FIRST BOLT took Uriel low in the gut as he charged, tearing through the knotted mass of scar tissue that covered the wound dealt to him by the tyranid Norn Queen. He was too close and the bolt was moving too quickly for it to detonate within him, but it exploded a fraction of a second after punching out through his lower back and peppered his flesh with searing fragments.

The second shattered on one of the few remaining portions of his armour, the hot shrapnel scoring upwards across his cheek, and the third blasted a chunk of his side to red ruin.

He staggered, but kept going, hacking his fiery-bladed sword through the neck of the Iron Warrior that had shot him. Pasanius was hit four times, his armour deflecting the majority of the impacts, but unable to save him completely.

The sergeant fell, dragging down the Iron Warrior before him and breaking his neck with a loud cracking noise.

Another round hit Uriel and he fell to the hard ground.

Bolter rounds filled the air. Uriel heard a cry of pain and surprise.

Yelling voices and more shots.

He tried to push himself to his feet, feeling sharp pain flare as he moved, and wondered why he was not dead.

Bellowing roars of hatred echoed from all around them, howls of furious anger and anguish. Even over the stench of blood and death that filled this place, Uriel could make out the stink of wet, raw flesh and realised what was happening.

Blood sprayed from a ragged stump of an Iron Warrior's neck and Uriel shouted in triumph as he saw the battered but unbowed form of the Lord of the Unfleshed hurl the grisly trophy to one side before leaping onto another Iron Warrior who fired wildly into the attacking monsters.

'Iron men die!' he roared as the surviving creatures of the Unfleshed fell upon Honsou's warriors.

The mohawked warrior shot down the fused twins, the white-hot blast of his gun obliterating the creature with a hiss of superheated air. Onyx nimbly dodged the brutal, clubbing blows of a pair of the Unfleshed, spinning around them and hamstringing them as he danced aside from their attacks.

Uriel saw Honsou retreat from the attack of the Unfleshed, and rolled onto his side, dragging his bolter around.

He realised how much he missed the ministrations of his armour as the pain from the burning fragments of the bolter shell stabbed into his back. Pasanius lay atop a dead Iron Warrior, two large exit wounds blasted through his back.

'Pasanius!' called Uriel.

His sergeant turned his head, and Uriel saw his face was deathly pale, his cheeks ashen and sunken.

'Don't you dare die on me, sergeant!' shouted Uriel, putting down his sword and bringing his bolter to a firing position.

'Aye, captain,' said Pasanius, weakly.

Smoke and the thrashing combatants conspired to obscure Uriel's aim, but eventually he was able to draw a bead on Honsou.

'Now you die, traitor!' whispered Uriel as he squeezed the trigger and a crash of rubble and smoke exploded beside him.

But in the instant before he lost sight of Honsou, he had seen the master of Khalan-Ghol pitched backwards, his helmet spraying ceramite fragments and an arc of crimson.

BLOODSTORM...

The two daemons faced each other in the depths of the lake of blood, their shared hatred a physical thing between them. Swirling eddies of power gusted around them, the energies both had expended in their battle having drained them almost to the point of extinction.

There were no more words to be said. What could two beings that had been enemies since the dawn of time have to say to each other at this moment?

Words were now only for mortals and those with a future to remember them.

The Omphalos Daemonium had prepared for this moment ever since it had been freed by the random actions of two mortals, and its strength was by far the greater.

But the Heart of Blood and the Avatar of Khorne were once again the same creature, and the blasted armour had feasted on the death of an entire galaxy of souls. Both daemons were evenly matched, but none could yet see the other destroyed.

Bloodstorm…

The Heart of Blood spread wide its arms and gave vent to a shout of hatred that parted the vital fluid of the lake and sent a tidal wave of blood spilling outwards from its centre. A rippling whirlwind of raw, red hunger swept from the Heart of Blood's armour, spreading throughout the chamber like the pressure wave of an explosion.

A lashing storm of hate-fuelled energy roared around the ruined domain of the Savage Morticians, lashing like a blind, insensate monster and driving the Omphalos Daemonium back from the Heart of Blood with its unstoppable power.

The bloodstorm enfolded the few, cowering mutants that had hidden beneath the shattered machines and rubble of the chamber. It scythed through their flesh and blew them apart.

The bloodstorm tore into the mutilated ruin of Obax Zakayo, finally ending his suffering in an explosion of red bone.

The bloodstorm streaked past the fleshy wombs of the daemonculaba and, one by one, they exploded like great fleshy balloons filled with blood.

The bloodstorm hurtled around the circumference of the chamber, an ocean of blood swept up in the etheric whirlwind as it howled back to the Heart of Blood at its epicentre.

The mighty daemon swelled to monstrous proportions, its armour and weapons blazing with barely-contained power as it sought to master the energies ripped from the ocean of ripe blood it had just feasted upon.

Now it was ready.

Now all things would end.

ʊ
TWENTY-TWO

HOWLING RED WINDS swept through the Halls of the Savage Morticians, the harsh metallic reek of blood catching in the back of Uriel's throat. He rolled onto his side and scooped up his sword as the fury of the hurricane scouring the air swirled around them, tearing at their flesh with harsh lashes.

The Iron Warriors dived for cover as the etheric whirlwind tore through the cavern and the Unfleshed were hurled from their feet by its power. The desperate battle broke apart as the combatants found shelter or held onto giant boulders to prevent themselves from being swept away.

Uriel gasped as the very life was leeched from him, feeling as powerless as one of the weakling newborns left to die on the mountains of Macragge. But at the edge of the cavern the power of the bloodstorm was at its weakest and they were spared the horrors of those closer to the Heart of Blood.

Pasanius grunted in pain and Uriel watched as the clotted blood on his back liquefied and was snatched into the air by the vampiric storm. His own wounds ran freely as they fed the terrible daemon at the heart of the chamber.

'Not like this...' he hissed. 'Not like this!'

Then, it was gone – the sudden silence unnerving after the tempestuous violence of the diabolical storm. Uriel pushed himself to his knees, grimacing in pain as those around him began to recover from the hellish experience.

The Unfleshed howled in pain. Without the protection of skin to save them from the worst effects of the bloodstorm, their bodies looked wasted and gaunt, pale and anaemic.

Uriel used a fallen surgical table to pull himself to his feet, the pain from his gunshot wounds and cracked bones sharp and biting. His enhanced metabolism had clotted the blood and already formed scar tissue over the wounds, but he was still terribly injured.

'Come on,' he urged Pasanius. 'There's no way out here. We have to find another way.'

'I don't know that I can,' said Pasanius, but Uriel did not give him a chance to argue further, pulling the sergeant upright over his groans of pain. Eventually, Pasanius nodded slowly and said, 'All right, all right, you're worse than Apothecary Selenus.'

Painfully, Pasanius sat himself against a pile of rubble, freshly-clotted blood gummed on his chest from multiple bolter wounds.

THE SOUNDS OF the battle raging in the centre of the chamber continued to echo, but there was a renewed fury to the roars and clash of weapons. As the bloodstorm abated, Uriel heard savage laughter, brazen and malicious, and felt a sick sensation in his bones as his soul recoiled from its evil.

Through the swirling dust and cascades of rock, Uriel saw the furious climax of the two daemons' battle, the sight of such incredible power taking his breath away. The Heart of Blood towered above the Omphalos Daemonium now, swollen to three times its size, and its sheer physicality was like nothing he had ever seen before.

Even the Bringer of Darkness had not awed him as much with its dark majesty. Its nightmarish presence had filled his thoughts with tormented visions of his own darkness, but this...

This was something else entirely.

Where the Heart of Blood walked, death followed. A red mist came in its wake, a bloody veil that glistened with wetness, and its weapons clove the air with every stroke, leaving dark trails that split the very world open. The daemonic Iron Warrior fell back before it, battered and broken, the armour torn from its body and its wounds spewing ichor from every cut.

Each mighty blow of the Heart of Blood forced it to retreat, its parries growing more clumsy with each backwards step it took. It desperately fell back towards the hissing daemon engine that had brought it here, its screaming stacks billowing shrill screams of anguish.

But the Heart of Blood was not to be cheated of victory and its whip lashed out, snapping around the armoured daemon's arm and tearing it off in a fountain of black blood. The Omphalos Daemonium fell to its knees and bellowed in angry defiance, but it was in vain as the Heart of Blood stepped close and hammered its axe down against its shoulder, cleaving its head from its body with one mighty blow.

The armoured daemon collapsed, a flood of gore spilling from the mortal wound and the Heart of Blood raised its weapons to the heavens with an ear-splitting roar of triumph to the Blood God that shook the very walls of the chamber.

Dark energies swirled from the destroyed daemon and the Heart of Blood convulsed as it drank of the essence of its ancient foe, its limbs shuddering with the inherited power.

Even as it savoured the spoils of its victory, the red sky that had come into being at the arrival of the Omphalos Daemonium began to fade and the screaming souls trapped in the damned metal of its engine howled with renewed vigour.

Hissing bone-pistons ground upwards as the monstrous daemon engine built power to escape its dying master and the collapsing cavern.

Then, as though the battle and sheer power its victory had unleashed were too much for the terrible creature, it dropped to its knees, sated and overwhelmed with dark energies. The axe and whip fell from the Heart of Blood's clawed hands as it toppled onto its side, the lustre of its red flesh deepening to a hot vermilion that smoked and hissed like that of an electrocution victim.

With the collapse of the two abominations, the discordant shriek of clashing daemon weapons was silenced, replaced by the omnipresent thunder of artillery from outside. The battle within Khalan-Ghol might be over for now, but the violence unleashed by Toramino was still very much ongoing.

Uriel held his breath, afraid that even the slightest motion would bring the daemon surging to their feet again. But nothing of the sort happened and he let out a great, shuddering breath as the Lord of the Unfleshed limped over to him and leaned down so that its head was level with his.

'We kill iron men!' he said.

'Yes,' said Uriel, wearily. 'We did.'

'Emperor happy?'

Uriel looked around the ruins of the Halls of the Savage Morticians, seeing that there was nothing recognisable left of it, everything had been destroyed in the cataclysmic battle of the two daemons. The surgical horrors enacted here were gone, the suffering victims of the bizarre experimentations finally granted the Emperor's peace. The lake of blood was now nothing more than a dusty crater, the gantries where the daemonculaba had been housed reduced to twisted masses of mangled iron.

Of the daemonculaba themselves, there was nothing but sad piles of ruined flesh and Uriel felt a great weight lift from his shoulders as he saw that their death oath had been fulfilled. The creatures Tigurius had seen in his vision and Marneus Calgar had charged them to destroy were no more.

'Oh, yes,' said Uriel. 'The Emperor is happy. You made the Emperor very happy.'

The Lord of the Unfleshed reared up to his full height and beat his chest with his massive fists. The few of his surviving brethren did likewise and howled their joy to the fading red skies.

'Tribe! Tribe! Tribe!' they shouted, over and over.

Uriel nodded and copied the enormous creature, hammering his fists on his chest and yelling, 'Tribe! Tribe! Tribe!' at the top of his voice. Pasanius looked oddly at him, but Uriel was too caught up in the primal exultation of the Unfleshed to care.

As the chant faded, the Lord of the Unfleshed returned his attention to the few surviving Iron Warriors who began picking themselves up now that the fury of the bloodstorm had abated.

The Lord of the Unfleshed twisted his hungry head towards Uriel and asked, 'Meat?'

Uriel's heart hardened as he slowly nodded.

'Meat,' he agreed.

These Iron Warriors had been the mightiest of Honsou's grand company, but even they could not stand before the fully-unleashed savagery of the Unfleshed. The ground was littered with the dead, both Iron Warriors and their monstrous by-blows, but it was only a taster of the slaughter that followed.

Armour was broken open and limbs were torn from their sockets as the Unfleshed feasted on the still-living bodies of their hated creators.

Uriel helped Pasanius to his feet as he saw the daemon-thing, Onyx, surrounded by a pack of the Unfleshed. The dark-armoured warrior cut and stabbed with furious speed, but the Unfleshed fought on, uncaring of wounds that would have slain a lesser opponent thrice over.

Uriel felt no pity for Onyx, it was a thing of the warp, an abomination and, as it was borne to the ground beneath a roaring mass of the Unfleshed, he turned away.

'So WHAT DO we do now?' asked Pasanius, leaning against a shattered pile of rockcrete slabs and wiping dust and blood from his face.

'I am not sure,' answered Uriel honestly. 'We did what we set out to do. We fulfilled our death oath.'

Despite his obvious pain, Pasanius smiled, and the sullen weight his friend had carried since the last days on Tarsis Ultra seemed to slide from his face.

'It is good to see you smile again, my friend,' said Uriel.

'Aye, it's been a while since I've felt like it.'

'Our honour is restored,' said Uriel.

'You know,' said Pasanius. 'I don't think we ever really lost it.'

'Perhaps not,' agreed Uriel. 'If only there was some way we could tell them that on Macragge.'

'I don't suppose they'll ever hear of what happened here.'

'No, I do not suppose they will,' said Uriel. 'But that does not matter. We know, and that is enough.'

'Aye, I think you're right, captain.'

'I told you before, you do not need to call me that.'

'Not before,' pointed out Pasanius, 'but we've honoured our death oath, and you are my captain again.'

Uriel nodded. 'I suppose I am at that.'

The two warriors shook hands, pleased to be alive and enjoying the sensation of having achieved what they set out to do. No matter that they were still trapped on a nightmarish daemon world, thousands of light years from home. Their success felt good by the simple virtue of its accomplishment.

No matter what happened now, they were done. It was over.

The Lord of the Unfleshed approached, thick ropes of clotted blood dangling from his jutting, fanged jaws.

'We go now?' he said. 'Leave now?'

'Leave?' said Uriel. 'How? There is nowhere to go. The passage to the elevator cage is impassable and hundreds of tonnes of rock have shut off the outflow pipe. There is no way out.'

The Lord of the Unfleshed gave him a lopsided look, as though he couldn't believe that Uriel was being so dense. He pointed over Uriel's shoulder and said, 'Big iron man's machine leaves!'

For a second, Uriel was mystified until he followed the Lord of the Unfleshed's pointing finger and saw the dark shape of the armoured leviathan that had carried the Slaughterman here. It ground towards one of the skull-wreathed tunnels it had created to manifest within the cavern. The red-lit door to its interior was still open and though the masterless machine was slowly building speed, there was still time get aboard.

'Brought big iron man here,' said the Lord of the Unfleshed. 'Take us away too!'

Uriel shared a look with Pasanius.

'What do you think?' said Uriel, a ghost of a smile playing at the corners of his mouth.

'I think that wherever the thing takes us, it's got to better than here, captain,' said Pasanius, pushing off the rocks and clutching his wounds.

'I hope you're right.'

'Well, it's either that or we stay and get flattened by Toramino's artillery.'

'Good point,' agreed Uriel, turning to the Lord of the Unfleshed. 'Gather the Tribe. We are leaving.'

The Lord of the Unfleshed nodded, its massive shoulders heaving with the motion. It threw back its head and let out a rising howl.

Within seconds, the Unfleshed broke off from their grisly feasting and joined their leader. Less than a dozen of them still lived, and Uriel was shocked at how few had survived the mission to Khalan-Ghol. Ardaric Vaanes had been right when he said that most, if not all, of them would die here.

Uriel nodded. 'All right, let's get the hell out of here.'

FOR A MOMENT Honsou thought he was dead.

Once he realised he wasn't, he thought he was blind.

All he could feel was pain and all he could hear were heavy thumps of artillery impacting somewhere above him. He sat up, feeling a stinging in his eyes and reached up to the vacuum seals on his armour's gorget. They were cracked and useless, so he wrenched his helmet off, realising that he wasn't blind after all, but simply had clotted lumps of blood in his eyes.

Honsou scooped the clumps of sticky matter from his face and spat out a mouthful of dirt.

He wiped his face again, angry that he still couldn't see out of one eye. As he probed further he realised there a was good reason for this. Part of his head had been pulverised by the impact of the bolt round, and the left side of his face was a burned and bloody ruin, his eye a glutinous, fused mess.

Dizziness and nausea swamped him, but he put his silver arm out to steady himself, giving a short bark of laughter as he saw that it was smooth and unblemished despite the fury of the battles he had fought since it had been grafted to him.

'Damn you, Ventris, that's twice you've blinded me with my own blood.'

Honsou clambered to his knees, trying to piece the last few moments of the battle together. He remembered facing Ventris, and the Ultramarines' desperate charge that had ended in a hail of bolter fire.

Or, at least, it should have ended that way. The luck of the damned was with them and they had survived long enough to kill a pair of his warriors. As foolishly heroic as their charge had been, it had bought them moments at best.

But then the monsters had attacked.

Honsou still felt a shiver of revulsion as he thought back to their unimaginable hideousness. Their corpses were strewn all around him and as he pulled himself free of the rubble that buried his legs and swayed unsteadily to his feet, he was amazed that such incredibly abhorrent creatures could live.

He had heard of the Unfleshed, but had never dreamed they could have been so fearsome as to almost be his undoing.

The last thing he remembered was catching a snapshot of Ventris aiming a bolter for his head and twisting to get out of the way. Honsou remembered seeing the muzzle flash, a sensation of bright, burning pain in his face, then... then nothing until this moment.

'Iron within!' he shouted.

There was no answer and he knew that all the warriors who had accompanied him to the Halls of the Savage Morticians were dead. He put them from his mind and admiringly surveyed the destruction around him.

Nothing remained of the chamber, its entire structure laid waste by the daemonic battle and the continuous bombardment from Toramino's grand batteries.

A flash of movement caught his eye and he picked up his axe before making his way unsteadily towards its source. An Iron Warrior, trapped beneath the half-devoured corpse of another, moaned in pain.

Honsou lifted the body from the buried Iron Warrior and saw that it was his newest lieutenant, Cadaras Grendel. The armour of the warrior's legs had been torn away and great bites had ripped away a chunk of his quadriceps muscle.

'Still alive, Cadaras Grendel?' said Honsou.

'Aye,' replied the warrior. 'I don't die easily. Help me up.'

Honsou reached down and pulled Cadaras Grendel to his feet. The grim-faced killer retrieved his weapon from the ground and checked its action before saying,' It's over then?'

Honsou shrugged. 'Maybe. I don't know. It looks like it, though.'

Cadaras Grendel nodded. 'What about Toramino?'

'What about him?'

'I still want to kill him.'

'Don't we all?' said Honsou, looking through a great rent torn in the side of the mountain. Blue fire still hammered his fortress from the sorcerous towers that surrounded it. Toramino's artillery captains were thorough, thought Honsou, to have broken open a mountain.

He turned towards a gleaming pile of twitching metal lying beside the entrance to the passageway that had led to the elevator cage. Recognising a discarded set of bronze claws that lay beside the pile, he strode over towards the jumble of metal.

As he drew closer he saw that it was no simple debris, but the still-living remains of his champion. Onyx lay twitching on the ground, his black armour cracked and shorn from his body, his daemonic flesh ripped from the metal of his skeleton by the monsters.

The daemonic symbiote's immaterial flesh had housed a scion of the warp and without a body, it had been cast from its shell. All that remained of Honsou's champion was a collection of loosely connected, silvered limbs, brass pistons and a bronze skull with a slowly dulling silver light weeping from the eye-sockets.

'Are you in there, Onyx?' asked Honsou.

'For now,' answered Onyx, his voice little more than a rasping whisper.

'What happened to you?'

'The monsters…' hissed the creature, only just holding off its dissolution. 'They unfleshed me, gave the daemon in me nowhere to hide. It fled and left me like this…'

Cadaras Grendel joined Honsou and said, 'This the daemon thing you wanted me to watch out for?'

'Aye,' nodded Honsou.

'Don't look like much now.'

'No, he doesn't, does he?' said Honsou, turning away and limping towards the centre of the chamber.

'What you want me to do with it?' shouted Cadaras Grendel after his retreating back.

'Get rid of it,' said Honsou with a dismissive wave.

He clambered painfully over the many piles of rubble and bodies that littered the cavern, hearing the hot flash of Cadaras Grendel's melta gun and knowing that Onyx was no more.

The centre of the cavern looked like the epicentre of some great orbital bombardment, the ground torn up and gouged with the fury of the battle that had taken place. Bodies and wreckage filled the place, so smashed and unrecognisable as to give no clue as to what they had been in life.

A shorn suit of power armour, gigantic in its proportions, lay at the edge of a deep crater and before it lay the Heart of Blood. The massive daemon's body was a dull, smouldering red, the colour of threatening embers that can leap to life in an instant. Its chest heaved with sated lust and as Honsou watched, the fiery streaks of its veins pulsed with renewed life.

The axe lying next to the daemon was twice as tall as Honsou and though he knew it was unfeasible, he felt an undeniable urge to try and lift it. His own axe growled in his hand and he knew that it was the daemonic presence within the Heart of Blood's weapon that was calling to him.

Honsou marched over to the Heart of Blood's recumbent body and delivered a thunderous boot to its horned skull.

'Come on!' he yelled. 'You are free now, and there are sorcerers to kill! Up!'

The daemon's lava-hot veins flared and its eyes flickered open, a soulless white fire, like dying suns, burning from its skull. Shaking off the satiety of its victorious engorgement, the Heart of Blood raised itself to its full height, its gargantuan axe and whip leaping to its great, taloned hands.

'That's better,' snarled Honsou as the daemon towered above him.

'Who dares rouse me from my blood-reverie?' bellowed the daemon.

'I am Honsou. Half-breed. Master of Khalan-Ghol.'

The colossal daemon loomed over Honsou, but he stood his ground, determined that he would show no fear before this creature.

'You are touched by the warp,' said the Heart of Blood. 'You have been flesh for one of my kind.'

Honsou nodded. 'Yes, I was once briefly blessed with the touch of a daemon of Chaos.'

'I still smell sorcery upon this place,' growled the daemon.

'You do,' said Honsou. 'My enemies wield powerful magicks against me and seek to destroy my fortress.'

'You are the master of this place?'

'For the moment, yes,' confirmed Honsou.

'Where are these enemies that stoop to the use of foul sorcery?' demanded the daemon.

Honsou looked out through the great breach torn in the side of the mountain and pointed to the crackling blue fires beyond.

'Out there,' he said. 'The warlord who commands the host that attacks my fortress is a sorcerer and has many magickers attending him.'

'I will kill him and rend his soul for all eternity!' promised the Heart of Blood, turning and smashing its way through the tear in the mountain of Khalan-Ghol before disappearing from sight.

Honsou clambered over to the crack torn in the rock and looked out over the smoke-wreathed mountainside, watching with undisguised amusement as the unstoppable daemon smashed into the front line of Toramino's army.

'Yes,' he laughed. 'You go do that...'

ʊ
EPILOGUE

THE SANCTUARY ECHOED with the ghosts of the dead, its empty blockhouses and bunkers deserted and abandoned. It had been that way when they had first found the place of course, but now it felt truly empty, as though the warrior band's brief occupancy had been nothing more than its last gasp of purpose.

Ardaric Vaanes knew they could not stay here now.

This place was forever tainted in his memory.

It had been here that Ventris had foisted his lie upon him and his men.

The lie of honour. The same lie that had seen him cast from his Chapter in the first place. The same lie that had almost seen him dead on this bleak, miserable shithole of a world.

Honour... What was the use of such a thing when all it got you was death and suffering? Thirty warriors had lived and fought from this place, fighting their enemies and surviving... always surviving.

Until Ventris came.

They had not had much of a life here, but it had at least been life.

'You killed them all, you bastard,' hissed Vaanes, his hatred for the Ultramarines captain burning like a slow fire in his heart as he traced spirals in the dust with his lightning claw.

Svoljard, tall and wild in his grey Wolf Brothers armour and Jeffar San, the proud and haughty White Consul, were all that was left of his warrior band, and Ardaric Vaanes knew that they would be lucky to live through the next few days.

After leaving Ventris and his ragtag band of monsters and misfits, the three of them had made their way through the mountains to the sanctuary, watching the great battles around the fortress from afar.

The spectacle had been magnificent, and during the incredible attack up the great ramp, Vaanes had unaccountably found himself hoping against hope that Honsou would see off his enemies.

When the ramp had collapsed and the army of Berossus had been all but destroyed, he had wanted to cheer.

But as spectacularly destructive as that had been it was as nothing compared to the chaos and slaughter that followed it.

The streaming pillars of blue fire that had surrounded the fortress for days now hammered it mercilessly, tearing the mountain apart piece by piece. Storms of magickal energy bludgeoned the rock with unimaginable force, smashing impregnable towers and bastions to dust in the blink of an eye. Vaanes had never seen anything like it and though the destruction was awe-inspiring to watch, he felt a flicker of regret that Honsou had not managed to pull off one last trick to defeat Toramino.

Then the Heart of Blood came, and everything changed.

It had come from the depths of the mountain like a red whirlwind of death, killing and destroying everything before it in an orgy of destruction that was staggering in its violence. Nothing could stand before this avatar of destruction – not men, not Iron Warriors, not tanks, not even Toramino's daemon engines.

Everything that came near the colossal daemon died, butchered by its screaming axe or crushed beneath its monstrous bulk. The slaughter had gone on for days, but in the end, Toramino's army had broken before the Blood God's favoured avatar, the shattered remnants quitting the field of battle while they still could and abandoning the smouldering wreck of Khalan-Ghol to the half-breed.

Honsou was still the master of Khalan-Ghol and though Vaanes had been pleased that the arrogant Toramino had been brought low, he felt an icy shiver of apprehension.

He knew that the half-breed would surely wreak a terrible vengeance on those who had attacked him. Vaanes knew that that was exactly what he would do and, from what little he knew of Honsou, he suspected that they were not so different in that respect.

That had been a week ago, and with nothing left to them, he, Svoljard and Jeffar San had remained at the sanctuary as they tried to come to terms with their new circumstances.

What were they to do? Where should they go?

Find some way to leave Medrengard and ply their trade as mercenaries once more?

Perhaps, but Vaanes had lost his taste for desperate causes and did not relish the thought of wandering the galaxy and fighting for petty tyrants once more.

He was shaken from his bitter reverie by the sound of footfalls behind him. He scuffed out the spiral he had been tracing in the dust and turned, seeing Svoljard at the door, a grim look of inevitability etched on his lupine features.

'What is it?' asked Vaanes.

'Trouble,' said the Wolf Brother.

JEFFAR SAN STOOD at the entrance to the blockhouse, his bolter carried loosely over his shoulder and his long, dirty blond hair pulled in a tight scalp-lock. The white of his armour was all but obscured by the dirt and filth of their adventure into Khalan-Ghol, but he still carried himself with an arrogant air of faded grandeur.

'What's going on?' snapped Vaanes as he and Svoljard emerged into the bright, perpetual daylight.

'Over there,' said Jeffar San, pointing to where a single vehicle sat at the end of the shadowed valley. Vaanes recognised it as a monstrously powerful Land Raider battle tank, its hard, iron sides chevroned with yellow and black stripes and its upper armour plates fringed with spikes. A disembowelled body was bound, spread-eagled, upon the tank's upper glacis, its limbs bloody and loops of its entrails wound around the tank's spikes.

Massive guns housed in armoured sponsons were aimed at the blockhouse. The power of those weapons was enormous, knew Vaanes, easily capable of demolishing the blockhouse with one shot.

So why didn't they fire? Honsou – for no other would seek them out in this place – would have no reason to come here other than to kill them.

'Why doesn't it shoot?' hissed Svoljard, thinking the same thing.

'I think we're about to find out,' said Vaanes, nodding towards the massive tank as its frontal assault ramp lowered with a great clang on the rocks.

Three warriors emerged, all liveried in the armour of the Iron Warriors and carrying their weapons before them.

'What the hell?' said Vaanes as the Iron Warriors marched from the security and strength of their vehicle and came towards them, crossing the ruined trenches and skirting the jagged remains of tank traps.

As the Iron Warriors neared, Vaanes whispered, 'Be ready to fight when I give the word.'

The other two nodded, but he could see that they had no taste for this last stand.

The lead warrior removed his helmet and Vaanes was not surprised to see the battered features of the half-breed. One side of his face was a ruined mess, a knot of augmetics covering half his skull and a glowing blue gem replacing his missing eye. The second warrior had the face of a killer, his eyes hard and cold, with a jagged mohawk running over the centre of his skull. Vaanes couldn't see the third figure; his powerfully armoured form was obscured by Honsou's body.

'You've come a long way to just to kill us, Honsou,' said Vaanes.

The half-breed laughed. 'If I'd come here to kill you, you'd already be dead.'

'Then why are you here?'

'I'll get to that soon enough,' promised Honsou. 'You fought alongside Ventris, yes?'

'Aye,' spat Vaanes. 'For all the good it did me.'

'That's what I thought.'

'What are you talking about?'

'You carry great bitterness within you, warrior, but you are a fighter, a survivor.'

'And?'

'And I need men like you now. Most of my own grand company are dead, and those of Berossus's that swore loyalty to me are few in number. I offered Ventris the chance to join me, but he spat it back at me. I now offer you the same chance, but I do not think you will do the same.'

'You want us to fight for you?'

'Yes,' said Honsou.

'For what purpose?'

'For conquest, for war and blood. And to take revenge on our enemies.'

'Ventris...' hissed Ardaric Vaanes.

'Aye,' nodded Honsou, waving forward the Iron Warrior who had been standing behind him, and who now reached up to release the clamps holding his helmet in place.

'My champion is dead,' said Honsou, 'and I need someone like you to train his newborn replacement in the art of death.'

The warrior removed his helmet and Vaanes gasped in shock as he saw the face that was revealed.

The newborn's skin was ashen and ill-fitting, raw suture wounds ringing his neck and jaw line, but there was no mistaking the patrician cast of his features nor the stormcloud grey of his eyes.

It was Uriel Ventris.

ABOUT THE AUTHOR

Hailing from Scotland, Graham narrowly escaped a career in surveying to join Games Workshop's Games Development team, which, let's face it, sounds much more exciting. He's worked on many Codexes, written eight novels and a host of short stories for *Inferno!* magazine.